DRAGONS OF DENAY

RAGE OF LIONS BOOK EIGHT

MATT BARRON

BLADE OF TRUTH PUBLISHING COMPANY

BRIDGETOWN
In the years of the Usurper's war
Norgate
Loncastel
Murr River
Bell's Hummock
Salthatch
Oldbridge
White Lions Camp
Piers
Murr River
Greenmarsh
Follybridge
N
Sougate
The Vec

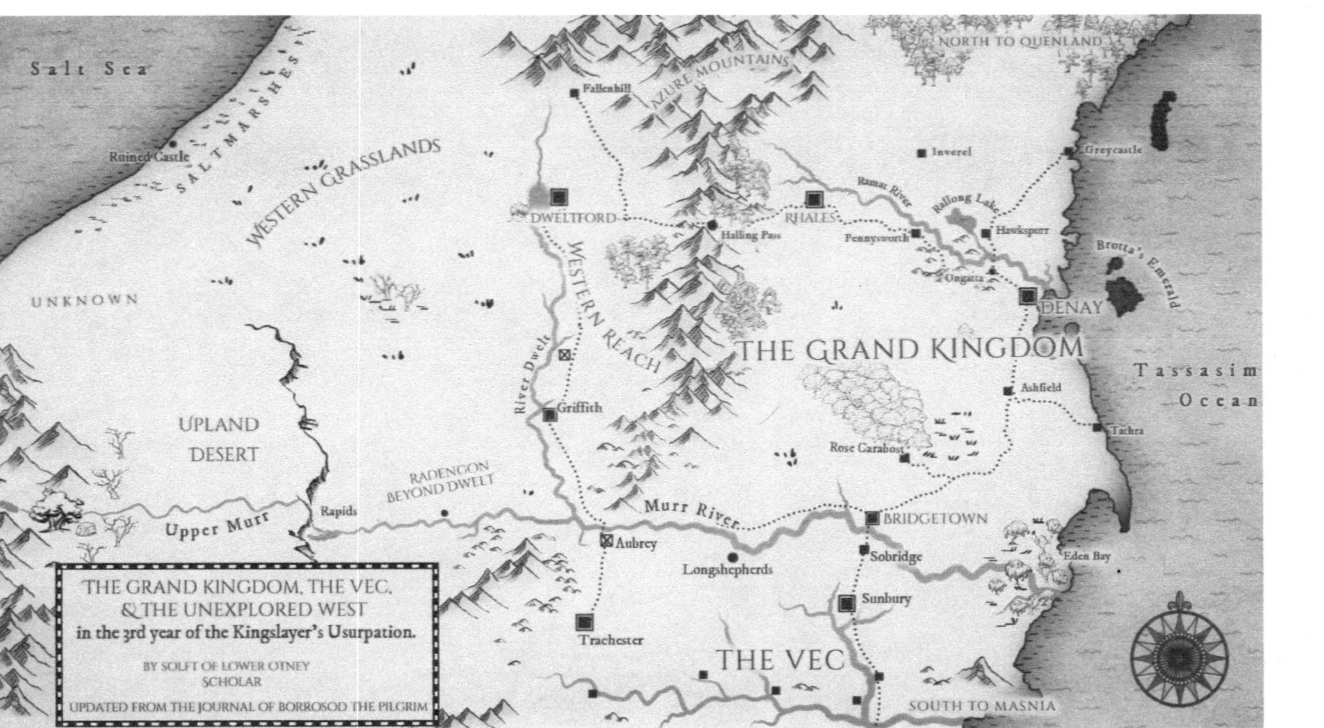

Salt Sea
SALTMARSHES
Ruined Castle
WESTERN GRASSLANDS
UNKNOWN
UPLAND DESERT
Upper Murr
Rapids
RADENGON BEYOND DWELT
Fallenhill
AZURE MOUNTAINS
NORTH TO QUENLAND
DWELTFORD
WESTERN REACH
Halling Pass
River Dwelt
Griffith
RHALES
Ramat River
Rallong Lake
Pennysworth
Hawksparr
Ongatta
Inverel
Greycastle
Brotta's Emerald
DENAY
THE GRAND KINGDOM
Ashfield
Tachra
Tassasim Ocean
Rose Carabost
Murr River
BRIDGETOWN
Aubrey
Longshepherds
Sobridge
Eden Bay
Sunbury
Trachester
THE VEC
SOUTH TO MASNIA
THE GRAND KINGDOM, THE VEC,
& THE UNEXPLORED WEST
in the 3rd year of the Kingslayer's Usurpation.
BY SOLFT OF LOWER OTNEY
SCHOLAR
UPDATED FROM THE JOURNAL OF BORROSOD THE PILGRIM

PROLOGUE

The girl had disappeared? How was that possible?

Like so many of Bridgetown's streets in the predawn hour, this thoroughfare, hemmed in on each side by tenements rising two and three stories high, was a path of ruin. The running battles of the night were passing, and in the meager light, ghost-like figures were emerging timidly from their homes to see what might be salvaged of their lives and their town. Amongst the yeomen townsfolk who were clearing the bodies of the slain from their gutters and wondering if they could find food in the coming day, the many-faced being known to those who did know it only as a lyrebird, affected the same shock as the Bridgetown natives—shuffling and seemingly bewildered. Inwardly, its ever-alert mind cursed the loss of the prey.

Chaos; disorder, it thought contemptuously as it passed a woman searching amongst the corpses for a lost relative. A woman, but after a swift, surreptitious survey, the lyrebird confirmed it was not the target maid. How could the girl have disappeared so easily?

The Usurper's army had arrived from the north, and like a leviathan sea monster that had swum all the way upriver from the deeps of the far oceans, the fleet had fallen upon the town. Men-at-arms, allied raiders, and piratical mercenaries, all sought to come ashore, slaughtering and pillaging wherever they could find a foothold. The lyrebird had known they were coming, as had its supposed superior, the minstrel spy Bluebird. Nonetheless, both scions of the Silent Hand had been shocked by the raging conflict the invasion birthed upon the islands and bridges.

A sound of shouts echoed from the end of the street where the narrow lane intersected with the Great Bridge Road, followed by running footfalls and the metallic rattle of armored harness. The entire street froze, folk poised like hunted rabbits who sensed the possibility of the predator's approach. A clutch of Aucks pirates, distinctive in their feather-collared cloaks, rushed past the intersection with their long, hooked boarding pikes in hand. They were soon followed by a half-cohort of White Lions, moving swiftly and pausing only for their Roarsmen to fire matchlock shots after the raiders. The denizens of the street watched, tense like taut boat lines and ready to flee into homes and alleys until the affray moved on.

The lyrebird froze with them, unafraid, but using the moment to fully study the various ones around it for the prey it had been following. Then, the cleaning up, the looting, and the search for lost friends and family members continued. It would be days before many of these folk knew fully what damage this first night of the Usurper's wrath had wrought. Even once they had made that tallying, they would still be faced with the true power of Daven Marcus and the Denay throne upon which he sat—not the least part of which were the Bronze Dragons, now coming ashore on the north bank of the river while Bridgetown's defenders were occupied with these ultimately pointless melees.

In the meantime, the lyrebird's hunt went on. When the first of the Usurper's boats had arrived, heralded by the cannon fire from Sougate Bastion the previous afternoon, the lyrebirds under the Bluebird—he had two of the rare agents at his command—had recognized the opportunity the invasion represented. Disorder was never to be desired, but it still afforded certain possibilities. Each agent of the Inquisition had moved swiftly in the service of their masters in the Vault Above the Pit. This lyre's first task had been the kidnap of a single trader who had been brought from elsewhere in the Grand Kingdom earlier in the year. The middle-aged man had served his purpose, and from now on his identity would be adopted by the lyrebird; the shape-changing scion was wearing the doomed man's visage even now. It was the common practice to kill those whose faces were stolen, even though it was not necessary to the magick. A lyre could copy a living visage well enough. It was simply neater if they were dead—disorder was never to be desired. The merchant whose identity the lyre now wore had come to Bridgetown with his aged father, and while both still had some usefulness to Bluebird's plans, neither needed to be free in the town any longer. Neat removal of both during this chaos was too convenient to pass up. After that first task, which had been completed even before midnight, the lyre had moved to more significant priorities—finding ways to infiltrate the witch from the west's forces and household.

The accursed "Lioness," the lyrebird sneered inwardly. The woman's continued life and power were an affront to the Silent Hand, who had collectively expended vast resources to curtail her. *Fruitlessly expended.*

The woman Amelia, who called herself the Lioness, was supposed to be declawed and dead by now. Instead, she and her household proved singularly defiant. The lyrebirds had been watching her all through the preceding autumn, and it had become clear that the cadre of anonymous handmaids the woman gathered about her, either wearing wimples or lace masks, was designed to be difficult to copy or infiltrate. The dullard allies Bluebird had recruited for brute work—jackanapes smugglers or would-be knights—had imagined they could simply put on nun's costumes and pass for loyal bodyguards. Fools. On first sight, the lyrebirds had known that there must be more to the woman's inner chamber and their odd costumes. The point of such obvious anonymity was that it must only work one way. Even as no one from outside the Reacherwoman's entourage could tell them apart easily, those inside the coterie must have secret signals of some kind—hand gestures, passwords or tiny tells in their uniforms, something.

So, once the merchant's identity had been adopted, the lyrebird had stalked across the islands to the vile woman's apartments, the Paramour's Chambers, to watch for an opportunity to snatch another identity from the world, one much closer to the Inquisition's ultimate target. Of course, the apartments had their garrison of guards, and no amount of stealth would be enough to simply sneak in, but there was always a chance that someone would have to leave, taking key messages somewhere in the beleaguered town. The Western Reach's obligations to Bridgetown were broad, and their significant forces were inevitably spread thin. It was by no means a guaranteed chance, but the hunters, Cerulean and lyrebirds both, all thought it was a possibility worth waiting for. The so-called "neophytes" regularly made trips abroad in the town without full escorts. They knew the value of subterfuge, even if they were still, in the eyes of the scions of the Silent Hand, mere amateurs. If they made the mistake of sending out one or two of the anonymous servant girls this night, that would be the perfect time for that girl to disappear without giving away that the Inquisition's agents had been involved. The maid could be snatched, interrogated for her passwords, and disposed of in the endless chaos to be discovered half-eaten by river fish many days from now, all marks of her last moments alive decayed beyond recognition.

Disorder was never to be desired, but it did provide opportunities.

Thus it was that the lyrebird, wearing the merchant's face and clothes, had sat most of the night in a niche it had created amidst detritus in an alley that let it watch the gate of the Paramour's Chambers surreptitiously. Then, the unlikely but valuable opportunity had arisen just before the larks had begun to herald the coming dawn, when a small flock of wimpled targets flew the coop. Like a hunting raven in service of the eagle of Denay, the lyrebird had picked its preferred target and taken wing.

And the little bitch had somehow slipped her hunter's gaze.

Surveying every figure it passed on the street, the lyrebird knew it had missed its opportunity. The fine-boned neophyte had somehow vanished, and the Inquisition agent was coming to accept that as a fact. Just from body shape and motion, none of the women haunting the post-battle roadway were one of the witch of the west's servants. That meant that the little figure had been able to sneak into one of the nearby houses or alleys in the blink of an eye. An annoying outcome. As a hunter, the lyrebird understood how patience and skill could still return fruitless from a promising night. As a loyal servant of the Silent Hand, the agent also knew that excuses were unacceptable.

Chaos, it thought spitefully yet again, shaking its head and pretending sorrow for the loss of life around it as it moved hunch-shouldered and doleful towards Great Bridge Road. Mournful grief was always a good cover for hateful annoyance. It would search for a short while yet, hoping to reacquire the prey's trail, but if that failed, it would take up another useful task and purloin key tools from the fallen militiamen in the streets. No matter how loyal the living were to the dead, the lyrebird knew it would be able to find a slain White Lion of the Western Reach to snatch away his uniform, his weapons and armor to build another useful disguise upon. It had missed the opportunity earlier in the year when the Young Hopefuls had vented their pride on hunting individual militiamen—another plot of the Bluebird's that had yielded mixed results.

This is a better opportunity at any rate, the lyrebird told itself. A uniform, armor, and weapons that went astray this night would not be missed at all. Simply counting all the dead would likely be beyond the witch and her wretched, unkillable heretic servitor.

The lyrebird shook its head, chastising itself inwardly. Not unkillable, merely not yet killed. Now that the Usurper had arrived from the north, Bridgetown's fate was sealed. No fortification, however ancient, however well built, could withstand the Bronze Dragons for long. The White Lions might say they could roar, but the voices of the ancient cannons were louder, fierier, and more terrible. The Dragons would serve the eagle as they had for a millennium, and the ravens, who took the forms of all the other birds of the air, would assist the eagle in his conquest. The disorder of the civil war would soon be over, and scions of the Silent Hand like Bluebird and the lyres, would be able to return to their God-given duty of governing the Grand Kingdom quietly with a silent hand, as it was meant to be.

CHAPTER 1

"This way, down the alley!" Prentice shouted, his hoarse voice hurting his throat. "They are heading for the dockside once more!"

And I do not want them getting away so easily, he thought but did not add. After pointing the way for the men with him, he followed them at a slow jog, weary limbs unable even to keep pace after the long night's battles. Looking up between the close-built houses and tenements, he could see the sky lightening to purple ahead of the coming dawn. Yesterday afternoon he had felt barely strong enough to ride to and from Sougate Bastion just to check upon the defenses. Then the Usurper's fleet had arrived, and he had now spent a whole winter's night—long, dark and cold—directing the defense of Bridgetown. Thankfully, he had not had to fight any of the invaders directly, but his body was exhausted regardless, and he could feel his thoughts moving slowly, as if wading through muddy waters.

"The horses will not fit this one," Prentice told his fey squire Dahyoor as he entered the alley. "Bring them around by one of the ancient bridges. Unless I miss my guess, this will open out onto the docks directly."

More than once the circumstances of the night's battle had forced Prentice out of the saddle, turning the care of his horse Boots over to Dahyoor. The fey man himself had not once dismounted his own mountain pony, though his bow had sung in the dark and in the fires' light, his arrows landing with typical fey lethality. Without a word, the squire now took both horses away to find a path on the broader roads. Prentice turned in the opposite direction and began to push through the narrow, wood-floored passage between two buildings. The still-dim light barely penetrated the shadows, and he tripped more than once, following his men and hoping to head off a crew of raiders who had been pushed back down a street farther east.

They are surely looking to reach their boats, Prentice thought. For much of the night it had seemed that the enemy had been hoping to capture the great ancient bridges at the core of Bridgetown's channels. Made from a kind of workable stone—a secret that had let the ancients of the Bright Age build enormous walls and pillars as if fashioning them like potters working with clay—it was those bridges that carried the town's central Great Bridge Road. If the invaders had landed and captured one or more of them, their forces would have been able to rush from there to any part of the town, and the invasion would have been all but complete in a single move. That was why Prentice had stationed the main of his forces on those very bridges and then sent cohorts out in lesser contingents to face individual crews and companies of raiders.

The height of the ancient bridges over the water had also given him two extra advantages worth maintaining. The first was that they made excellent firing positions, allowing his Roar matchlocks to shoot down into the channels and docklands with relative ease. It was part of why the initial assault on Sougate had been so swiftly turned away. The boats coming up the southern channel between the island of Greenmarsh and the Vec riverbank had come under a withering hail of Roarshot that had turned their decks crimson before they reached the bridge. Not a single man-at-arms from that assault had even come ashore.

The parts of the enemy fleet that had tried the other channels had encountered the second advantage. The ancient bridges were so strong that over the years the populace of Bridgetown had appended a vast, jury-rigged network of lesser jetties and walkways from them. The complex structure of haphazard docks stretched across the waterways like the mad web of some impossible giant spider that spun with wooden planks and jute ropes rather than silken threads. The structures impeded the invaders' boats, since the ocean-going vessels were simply too large to row or sail around or under the structures. Even some of the larger riverboats and barges could not fit into all the gaps. Forced to come ashore wherever they could, the enemy flotilla had disgorged their pillaging crews to spread fear and death along the dockside and fight their way inland wherever possible. Every time a crew made the attempt, Prentice sent Lions and Gryphons to make them pay for their efforts, plugging the ends of the narrow streets and alleys and doing their best to trap the invaders on the riverside.

Even with all those disadvantages, the Usurper's assaulters had proved horrifyingly determined, spreading fire and destruction across the eastern islands—Loncastel, Oldbridge and Greenmarsh. If they had not already faced the equally brutal Redlanders in their own western homeland, Prentice suspected his militiamen might have been overwhelmed by the savagery, especially in some of the bigger melees, despite their advantages in numbers and circumstances. Some of these raiders must have been legendary Aucks pirates, infamous on all the Tassassim coastlands for their bloodlust and cruelty.

Exactly the kind of mercenaries Daven Marcus would favor, Prentice thought as he emerged onto the south side of Oldbridge Island, looking down on the dock from the top of a short flight of rickety wooden steps. Already, the militiamen he had sent ahead of him were moving to control the section of the dockside that the steps let down onto. Making his way as swiftly as he dared on the slick wood, Prentice looked to either side of the water's edge to orient himself. To his right some distance away was the massive ancient bridge, built up with houses and jetties, ladders and steps hanging in every available gap so that the enormous grey footings were actually hidden out of sight. In every space and gap those wooden structures allowed, he saw a Roarsman, watching the docks through the smoke of their long-matches and ready to shoot at any enemy who appeared. On his left, Prentice was twenty paces from the mouth of the broader road where the retreating raiders were now emerging, hounded by a reduced cohort of militiamen.

"My Lord," a voice called from the direction of the main bridge, and Prentice looked back from the fray to see Knight Sergeant Gennet approaching with an escort of two lines of militiamen. "We had word they were being pushed back to the dockside again. Your work, I take it."

"Hardly mine alone," Prentice said, pausing a moment to draw a heavy breath. Now that he knew Gennet was here, he felt better able to relax a little. The next moment's battle would not depend solely on his fatigue-diminished leadership. "The Gryphons have done well holding them back, but they have decided to break for their boats of their own accord. They may have come ashore like Redlanders, but they are not suicidally devout like them. These are Tassassim pirates, not Blood Sect cultists."

"Just as brutal but not as fearless," Gennet summed up, and Prentice nodded. Gennet could always be relied upon to understand things simply.

"They will be aiming for their boats," the knight commander explained. "If we can keep the pressure on them, they will never be able to launch them safely. I want prisoners if we can take them."

"I'll pass the word, My Lord," Gennet said with a salute, and then spoke to a militiaman at his shoulder. Gennet's escort merged with the militia Prentice had brought with him, and the combined force pressed down the docks to where the fleeing raiders were fighting in the street, holding their pursuers at bay with long, hooked boarding pikes, doubtless seeking to make a space that they could use to flee to their boats. As Prentice's strengthened forces struck them from the flank, the pirates were forced farther eastward, retreating along the dockside, and the pursuing force of Reach militia also merged with Prentice's troop. Suddenly, the twenty or so desperate invaders trying to retreat were being harried by over a full cohort of White Lions—more than a hundred men-at-arms. Any moment now, they would be forced to surrender or else be slain. Escape would be all but impossible.

"Knight Sergeant, Knight Commander," the arriving cohort's leader greeted Prentice and Gennet with a jaunty salute. A corporal of the Claws, the man was brown-haired, with a neatly trimmed goatee and moustache, bright eyes, and a ready smile. "A pleasant night's hunting, is it not?"

"Hunting?" Gennet repeated.

"Indeed," the corporal said, turning to look at his command's ongoing fray. "This is our third encounter of the night, and each one has been as conclusive as this one will be. I am Corporal Denholm, Denholm Aquensfarthing."

Prentice was not listening all that closely, but in the back of his nearly exhausted mind he recognized that the corporal pronounced the "q" in his name as a hard sound, as in quay rather than as in queen. "*Akhens*-farthing."

"Aquensfarthing?" he repeated absentmindedly. Now that he felt the situation in front of him was nearly resolved, Prentice could feel his weakened body relaxing almost involuntarily. He would collapse soon if he was not careful. "You hail from the Quenland border?"

The corporal brightened even more, clearly pleased to be recognized and acknowledged by his commander. Even with the fight not yet fully resolved, continuing in a front across the docks not ten paces east of the three officers, Denholm Aquensfarthing removed his kettle helmet and bowed formally.

"My mother is a patrician manor-holder there," he explained readily as he straightened up. "I'm the third son, fifth if you count her first marriage. Left home at twelve, page to a squire who got his spurs and then chucked me off like a broken stirrup strap. After kicking around a few different camps and what-have-you, I came west as a hired guard for some rich refugees who managed to get their wealth out of their town 'fore it was put to the torch. Signed on with the Lions come the spring, since none of the merchants could pay. That drought gutted the Reach's banks, from what I hear."

"We're fighting here, Corporal," Gennet remonstrated with the man. "Leave off your pleasantnesses until after the battle."

Corporal Denholm stopped speaking, blinking in surprise, and then looked to Prentice, as if waiting for the knight commander to intervene in the interaction.

"Leave peaceable matters for moments of peace," Prentice said simply, backing his sergeant's rebuke but recognizing how weary his voice sounded as he did it. He blinked his eyes against fatigue and looked over the various piers and jetties around them, more as a matter of habit rather than searching for anything in particular. In several places, the damage of the night's conflict was becoming more obvious as the dawn spread across the sky. Planks and posts were smashed, and fishers' huts, nets, and drying racks were wrecked or burned. Here and there an enemy boat was entangled amongst the piers, abandoned by their crews when they came ashore.

"Surely the matter is don—" Corporal Denholm was saying when two loud bangs sounded amidst the melee, and hot air and powder smoke washed against the officers like a desert wind, accompanied by a swift buzzing like angry hornets flying past.

"A Roarsman's powder cooked off," Gennet suggested tersely, having bent down reflexively against the danger. Prentice had a different notion—the hornets had been the clue.

"Clamshell bombs," he muttered and scoured the scene for the source of the madman with the suicidal iron weapons. Little more than a small cache powder with a fuse encased in a metal sphere, clamshell bombs—sometimes called grenades—were supposed to be thrown at the enemy to be detonated by a burning wick. Their iron skins were made to split apart in the explosion, shooting out deadly, jagged pieces, but they also made the metal balls heavy and difficult to throw. That meant only the strongest men could use them safely. The explosive typically had the power to cast its rain of steel fragments farther than an ordinary man could throw, so it was a weapon potentially as dangerous to its user as it was to its enemy. Prentice had never even considered giving any of the mad tools to his militia, so those explosions had to come from the invaders.

"That surely seems to have dulled their ardor," Denholm said, rubbing at his ear, likely injured by the noise since he had had his helmet off when the explosions occurred. His observation was sound, however. The dockside battle had simply stopped dead as the smoke of the clamshells cleared and both sides assessed exactly what damage had been done. Being armored and helmeted almost to a man, the White Lions seemed to have come off better. At least half of the raiders were bloodied, either slain or fallen with wounds. The moment of quiet now that the clash of arms had paused was suddenly filled with the low moans of the injured.

"We'll wrap them up quick enough now," the corporal observed. "Looks like they've only done themselves a disservice." He spoke with a raised voice, doubtless because his hearing was damaged.

"Seems so," Gennet agreed, but Prentice had his eyes out over the farther piers.

"Brutal, not fearless. Keep a watchful out, Sergeant," he quoted back to his officer, adding a yeoman's saying to warn both officers to be alert. Whoever had set off those two bombs had not been amongst the ones fighting. Those men had been fleeing, not making a suicidal final stand. Somewhere else nearby was a grenadier—or more than one—and if they had two clamshells they could well have more. "Someone's throwing fireworks at us."

Gennet nodded immediately, and while Prentice searched the river and the riverside for signs of the bomb throwers, the knight sergeant took charge of the stilled conflict.

"Stop muckin' about, you lot! This fracas is over. Either put down your steel or die by the Lions. To the business, men of the Reach."

Prompted by his driving words, the more numerous White Lions suddenly swarmed the remaining enemy and quickly put them on their knees.

"So, since we're done now, My Lord," Denholm said, his manner nonchalant but his voice still over-loud, "perhaps now we might return to introductions."

"Shut up!" Prentice insisted tersely, struggling to concentrate on his search. He tracked windows and rooftops, boats and lean-tos on the dockside, anywhere an enemy with a store of explosives might be lurking. At the other side of the concluding fight, three raiders exploited a moment of confusion to sprint away down the waterfront, and Prentice watched them a moment to see if they might be running toward their man.

"They'll want a boat..." he muttered to himself.

"What?" Denholm demanded loudly.

Prentice did his best to ignore him. He looked for enemy craft, seeking the higher prows of sea-going vessels to distinguish from the myriad moored or damaged local boats. His eyes shot from one to the next until he saw one that seemed to be giving off smoke. Perhaps it had caught fire earlier and now smoldered, or perhaps...

"Sergeant Gennet, that boat has a lit brazier!" Prentice bellowed suddenly, in motion almost before he realized what he was doing. A small iron stove was perfect for sailors to keep themselves warm at night or to light the fuse of a bomb one meant to throw. "Two lines to that boat, quick smart. Any fool puts his head over the gunwales, feed him Roarshot!"

Not waiting to see if Gennet understood his commands, Prentice dashed down one of the jetties that poked out into the river, feet skidding on the slick boards. He had no chance of quickly getting around the mess of fighters in his direct path to the boat, so instead he did his best to plot a route over the bridges, jetties, and riverboats, thinking to leap and hop his way there like the rivermen who normally populated this area.

After all, you have seen the boat crews do it as easily as frogs and grasshoppers, he told himself mockingly. *How hard can it be?*

The answer came sooner than he expected as his first step off onto an abandoned lighter's deck caused him to slip and almost fall overboard. Prentice scrabbled back from the water as if it was a dangerous animal. He knew he could swim and in most circumstances would see a tip into the water as no more than a minor embarrassment. This morning, however, he was deeply fatigued and wearing a quilted buffcoat gambeson. In the water, the layered cloth would surely soak and weigh him down like a coat of plates. More than that, in the chaos of damaged docklands and so many boats, there would be a good chance that a fall would send him somewhere he might not be able to surface or else entangle him in wreckage. Even a skilled swimmer might drown in this predawn nightmare.

Getting back to his feet, Prentice saw that Gennet had already sent the men he had wanted into the mess, leaping and jumping as Prentice was trying to. The three escaping raiders were moving with the confidence and skill of experienced sailors, which let them stay ahead of the pursuing militia, but as they fanned out, finding what paths they could, the White Lions were slowly hemming the escapees in. Then Roarshot echoed over the water. Prentice looked at the target vessel in time to see someone duck back behind the raised prow.

"With care!" someone shouted from the docks. "I'll skin any fool as puts a shot in one of ours!"

It was a wise command, and almost as soon as the shooting had begun, it ceased. There were simply too many Lions in the way to allow the risk. Prentice took a more careful step off the riverboat deck, trying to keep watch on his footing and the enemy craft at the same time. The hiding foe poked his head out and swiftly cast a black object into the air, which arced overhead trailing fizzing sparks.

"Look out!" Prentice cried, and several others called warnings as well. Not knowing what else to do, he threw himself down in the stern of a rowboat. He heard a dull thud as the little bomb struck something on the river and then a whump and gout of water.

The throw had been rushed and landed short of the dockside. Encouraged, Prentice sprang to his feet and immediately swayed from the combination of exhaustion and the uncertain deck beneath him. Using what little energy he had left, he urged his militiamen on.

"Keep the pressure up," he shouted hoarsely. "Do not let them get a good throw off."

Barely balancing, he watched as fresher men followed his command, closing in on the dangerous foe. At least one of the fleeing enemies found himself cut off and suddenly went down on his knees on a rickety piece of walkway, hands on his head. The surrender was welcome, and two Lions turned aside to capture him. The remaining two runners neared their boat, calling in a foreign tongue to their comrade there. The raider stood suddenly, his whole waist above the gunwale, an iron fruit with a burning wick in each hand. It was clear what he planned, aiming to place them both in amongst the pursuing Lions to give his men their chance to escape. He was too bold, however, and before the first throw had been fully made, Roarshot struck him in the chest like the talons of an invisible predator. Falling backward, his dying motion made his first throw go over his head to land amongst the boats behind him. It plopped into the water, but to Prentice's surprise, it still detonated. He had heard legends of alchemical fires—automatic fire, some called it—that burned even when wet or under the water. Such a thing seemed fantastical to his weary mind, even though this was clear evidence. He had just enough time to wonder where the second grenade bomb landed when the enemy boat simply erupted in a series of popping bursts that seemed to grow ever louder until the force of the explosion threw Prentice from the barge he was standing in, striking his helmeted head on something hard before toppling him into the water.

CHAPTER 2

T he embracing dark closed around him, confusing and icily cold. His limbs felt heavy, as if weighted down, and it seemed he was sinking swiftly. It reminded him of the day he had fallen into the water with the rusted mask of the mantis men in his arms, but this was worse because now the weight that was sending him to the bottom was not something he could choose to relinquish.

We set off his arsenal, Prentice thought, a part of his mind feeling strangely calm about the deadly situation. From the force he had felt, he could only imagine how many more little bombs the sailor had had in his boat, and perhaps he had spare powder as well. The second grenade had doubtless dropped back into the craft and exploded there, detonating the lot.

Even as he was contemplating the situation, he did his best to fight his way back to the surface. Swimming in armor was not a new skill to him, having trained in it at Ashfield, but with the long night behind him and the lingering weakness of Cassian's poison in his limbs, this was harder than he had ever imagined. All his swimming practice had been in steel, with lighter quilting underneath. His thicker buffcoat was astonishing in the way it clung to him with its entangling heaviness. Every attempt to swim for the surface only felt like fruitless thrashing.

How many others are knocked into the water? he wondered. He twisted about, looking for the light on the surface, hoping for enough to see by. With so many boats and walkways over the river, it was possible that it would all just be shadows, and his hope to find the way up would be fruitless. One thrashing arm became entangled in something and he was about to try to free it when whatever it was locked around him, and Prentice remembered the other occasion he had nearly drowned. Hoping it was someone come to his rescue, he stopped fighting and soon enough found himself being pulled in a direction that did indeed seem like it was brighter and thus closer to the dawn light.

No transports in visions this time, at least, he thought, and a moment later his head broke the surface. Gasping for air, Prentice let himself be held up by the militiaman who had come to his aid.

"Good thing I'm an excellent swimmer, Knight Commander," Corporal Denholm shouted through Prentice's helmet. "Not many would have the strength to bring two armored bodies to the surface like this."

Prentice tried to thank the man, but only managed to cough filthy water from his lungs. Seeing the boards of a low-built jetty not far away, he reached out and clung to them, doing his best to take his own weight and relieve Denholm. The corporal released him to take a spot on the boards next to him. They shared a look of relief and the joy that a brush with death can sometimes bring. Denholm pulled himself out of the water and Prentice tried to follow suit, but he was too tired, slipping back into the water to catch himself just before sinking away again. He was so weary.

A moment later, rushing feet shook the boards, and the eager hands of a half dozen militiamen began to pull the knight commander to safety. Just as he was halfway clear, his body became entrapped somehow, and there was a moment of surprise before someone realized it was the hilt of Prentice's sword, caught on the boards. A moment's adjusting fixed the problem and then he was laid out on the jetty, water lapping at his drenched form.

"Sword was half out of its scabbard, My Lord," one of the militiamen told him. "Managed to save it, though."

"Oh, good. Mustn't lose my magick sword," Prentice joked wryly. Legends of arcane power swirled around the blade, but he trusted that his own men knew better than to believe them. In some ways he would like nothing better than for the beautiful artifact of war to be lost at the bottom the River Murr. He hated the nonsense talk of its magick. "How many men have we lost?"

The militiaman shook his head and held out his hand as Prentice reached out for help to get up. Feeling like a bent-backed old man, he slowly regained his feet and looked about, surveying the wreckage. The enemy boat was gone and there was a hole in the midst of the piers where it had been moored. Lions were clambering gingerly over twisted structures and the edges of half-submerged river craft. Even as he watched, one of the rescuers toppled into the water when whatever he was standing on shifted and sank further.

"Have care!" Sergeant Gennet commanded, and then he was at Prentice's side. "How do you fare, My Lord?"

"Better than dead," Prentice croaked. "What is our count of losses?"

"Men in armor sink swiftly when insensible..." Gennet began, recognizing the grim prospects for survivors, but his words were cut short by a cry that sounded over the water.

"Fire and iron, that is our fate!" the cracking voice called, and Prentice looked to see a militiaman some distance away over the boards. His uniform looked torn as if by weapon strikes, and there was blood smeared upon his face. He was not wearing a helmet.

"Who is that?" Prentice asked.

"I don't know, My Lord."

"Fire and iron, shackled and condemned to hell!" the wounded militiaman continued to scream. "Following a witch and her servitor! Better we all drown now than suffer what is to come. Nothing can deliver us from the righteous justice of King Daven Marcus!"

"Someone shut that fool up," Prentice said without thinking, and then immediately realized what his words implied. He looked to Gennet. "He is wounded, and his nerve is gone, Sergeant. We need to get him to his rest."

"Not a permanent rest?" Denholm asked, and Prentice could not tell if the man was serious or joking.

Prentice scowled and nodded to Gennet. The knight sergeant turned to pass the order, at the same time searching for a remnant safe path through the dock ruins, since otherwise, he would have to send someone all the way back to the old bridge and up and over to the other side of the channel. As it turned out, the militiaman pronouncing despair resolved the issue for them.

"I recant!" he screamed like a penny-prophet. "I repent my swearing to the witch from Dweltford and all her lies of lions. Lord God, forgive me! Death can be my only recompense. Let the water wash me clean of my sin against king and God."

With that the fellow threw himself into the river. Gennet and others started, crying out against the self-destructive act, but immediately they held themselves back. There was no point, the distance was too great. Even if someone felt themselves strong enough to dive in after him, as Corporal Denholm had for Prentice, they would be unlikely to reach him in time or to find him in the dark water that dawn had still not yet fully lit. Prentice bowed his head a long moment, then shrugged off his helmet.

"I guess not every man has the right courage for battle," Denholm said dismissively, but Prentice ignored him. He looked to Gennet.

"I am going to my bed, Knight Sergeant. Secure our prisoners and any wounded. Find the names of the lost and see that they are reported to the seneschal. Their widows will receive their pensions."

"As you command."

Prentice turned toward the riverside end of the narrow jetty he was standing on, and men moved aside for him to pass. He forced himself to walk upright, refusing to let his exhaustion rule his limbs, but he still knew his movements were stiff and weak.

"A last word if I may, My Lord?" Denholm called after him, and Prentice paused so the corporal could catch him up. The junior officer leaned in to speak confidentially. "I am new to the Gryphon

Banner, Knight Commander, arrived with the fresh recruits in the summer, marched from Fallenhill. Like all the newcomers, I cannot help but note that veterans receive certain marks of service—dragonflies and such."

Denholm gestured toward Knight Sergeant Gennet. On his left pauldron, the one embossed with the snarling mouth of a biting lion, there were two small medallions—one bronze with its own embossed dragon and another of polished steel with the mark of a dragonfly. They were campaign signifiers, indicators of specific, heroic service to the Western Reach and the White Lions. All the original Gryphon bannermen, those who had marched into the far west, had the dragonfly, but that was only one man in ten of the Banner Company, and one in twenty of all the White Lions as a whole. Fewer than fifty militiamen total had the bronze dragon, and as far as Prentice knew, Gennet was the only one to have both. It was part of his story as a *knighted* sergeant of the Western Reach.

"What of it?" Prentice asked with a croak that put him in mind of the merchant Welburne's weakened voice.

"Well, I was wondering what you thought the mark might be to commemorate this night's victory?" Denholm said, and Prentice felt his tired eyes go wide in disbelief. He looked over the smoking ruins, his men fishing bodies from the water where they could be reached, dousing the small fires set by the bombs, and tying the prisoners' hands for transport to somewhere more secure. He scoffed derisively.

"Death is the only recompense," he muttered, repeating the self-destructive militiaman's words for reasons he could not have explained, even if he had thought to justify himself to his subordinate. Leaving the puzzled corporal behind, he went in search of Dahyoor and his horse. It was not a far distance to travel to the bed he shared with his wife in the lesser apartments of the Paramour's Chambers, but he doubted he would be able to walk even that distance. When he found his mount waiting for him near the foot of the great bridge, he had to pause before trying to climb into the saddle, taking a moment to cough more disgusting water from his chest.

Brother Whilte will need to use yet more of his healing powers, he thought as he wrenched his body upward. As awkward as his fatigued mounting was, Dahyoor never moved a muscle to help him. A fey who could not climb into his own saddle was less than a full person. No doubt the same standard would apply to the *kreff enkreffra*, non-fey who had earned some place in fey society. That harsh cultural standard sat heavily on Prentice's thoughts and mingled with the dying man's pronouncement.

Is death the only recompense a failed man can make?

Inside himself, he knew that the answer was surely "no," but somehow his tired thoughts could not fight the notion off.

CHAPTER 3

"Open to me or find your historic doors forced. I will accept either outcome!"

Amelia, Archduchess of the Western Reach and guest of Bridgetown's ruler, glared at the two houseguards cowering in the shadows of Earlsbastion's gate. Her journey here from her own apartments had been short, but even that had been filled with the wreckage of the invaders' assault and the figures of the shocked populace, wandering the streets like ghosts amidst the smoke and blood. More than once in the night now-passed, fighting had come so near to the Paramour's Chambers that Amelia had heard it in the streets beneath her windows. That had felt frightening enough to her, even behind her garrison of loyal guards. She could only imagine the horror and terror that had ruled the hearts of ordinary Bridgetowners in the dark hours, hiding in their homes or else fighting the fires the invaders set and praying not to be slain in the attempt. When word came that her militia had endured the assault and thrown the enemies back into the river with the dawn, Amelia had gathered her courage and resolved to survey the injuries to Bridgetown, the houses, and the folk who dwelt within them.

And she was determined not to do it alone.

Which was why she was here at the gate of Bridgetown's castle, the seat of its ruling noble Lady Penelope, Baroness-elect, or possibly archduchess-elect, depending on what pathways still remained for the young noblewoman's ambitions to flourish.

She can rule as queen and angel of heaven come down for all I care, Amelia thought. *But she must* rule, *and her first duty of rulership is to her people.*

Amelia stared icily at the two guardsmen. By the quality of their dress and armor, they were unlikely to be mere militia themselves, which did not surprise her. Of late, the petty and bloodthirsty members of Bridgetown's traditional guards had been scarce indeed. By the initial reports, not a single man had turned out to support the White Lions in the defense of their town.

"Shirkers of duty one and all," Amelia's husband Farringdon had declared when he presented his report with the dawn that morning. After their recent shames, being involved in murders and even a massacre at the prompting of the now disgraced Young Hopefuls, the hereditary militiamen of Bridgetown had gone to ground.

But at least the girl had guards to protect her own home, Amelia thought, trying not to be too contemptuous. After all, she had spent the night behind a garrison herself.

"Well, gentles? What is your answer?" she demanded again of the two men-at-arms.

"You can't just force the gate," one said, more with a tone of disbelief than opposition. His wild eyes looked past her.

"Can I not?" Amelia asked, following his gaze to look over her shoulder. Behind her, besides the two Lace Fangs who were her current bodyguards—in this case Ladies Spindle and Daisy—the archduchess was also accompanied by a cohort of White Lions in two columns of fifty stern-faced men. If she gave the order, Amelia had no doubt these men would assault the castle of her ally without a moment's hesitation. The two gate guards might believe this number insufficient to make the breach, but they would not live to see for sure if they chose to offer any resistance. It was clear from the Bridgetowners' expressions that they knew it too.

"My Lady...," one of them began, his combative bearing becoming plaintive.

"Her Grace!" Spindle corrected sternly over Amelia's shoulder, her tone so sharp that the man reflexively tugged his forelock.

"So…sorry! Her…You…Your Grace," he stammered. "We have orders. Nothing we can do about that."

"You will not yield?" Amelia pressed.

"We can't. Please don't kill us, but we can't."

Despite her cold attitude to these servants of a failing ruler, Amelia could not fault men for loyalty or obedience, but that did not mean she had no other options. She turned to her escort, and Daisy, who was holding a large, waxed-cloth umbrella over her liege's head, moved aside for her.

"Corporal, take these two men into our custody," Amelia commanded the leader of the cohort. "Gently, if they do not fight. Disarm them and see if they keep a key to that wicket door. If they do, bring it to me."

She nodded toward the smaller pedestrian door built into the castle gate, designed to allow egress without having to fully open the main. Then she looked at the sentries once more.

"Will you accept capture, gentles, or must you die for your orders?"

The two militiamen lowered their heads glumly and readily yielded their spears to the White Lions, who took them prisoner. One of them did, in fact, have a key for the wicket, and soon enough a ten-man line had passed inside to open both full doors for the archduchess. Amelia entered Earlsbastion with ninety guards, ten militiamen remaining behind to hold the gatehouse and the two prisoners. As the armed column led by three noble ladies crossed the bailey with its white marble flagstones dulled nearly to grey in the dim light, stewards and other guards stopped to stare at them.

"Did they really only have two men to guard the gate?" Daisy wondered in a whisper. "What were they going to do if one of them raider crews made it this far up here? The knight commander's word was of pirates hired out as mercenaries. Even one boatload of such fellows would have made their way in here lickety-split!"

Spindle shushed her junior companion, but Amelia thought Daisy's point was well made. If a hundred militiamen had been enough for her to force her way in without a fight, she had no doubt Daven Marcus's hired savages could have done the same. She wondered just how near the raiders had come in the night and tried to remember whether any of the houses on the street up to Earlsbastion had showed much damage.

How close did you come to losing your home last night, baroness-elect? she wondered. If they had only known how vulnerable she was, the Usurper's initial assault could have captured the leader of Bridgetown this first night past. It was not a comforting thought. *Having forced my way thus far, should I wait for an escort, or simply push the rest of the way?*

Amelia paused at the entry to the castle's main manor-house building. It was so civilized and refined that it could hardly be called a keep any longer. It occurred to her that, in fact, she had no idea where Lady Penelope might be within. Amelia had only ever been to the main hall during her previous visits. Should she go searching, sending her men throughout the corridors like a force of pillagers, seeking for serfs to capture and drag away? Or should she wait in dignity and reserve, trusting that her presence with so many armed men would force a response from the household?

I have done enough waiting for this fluff-headed girl, the archduchess told herself. Bridgetown's folk had suffered through the night. The least their liege could do would be to come out of her hidey hole and look them in the eyes.

"Corporal, knock upon that door and tell whoever answers it that I require a steward or herald to bring me into their mistress' presence," she commanded her escort's leader. The man saluted and headed towards the manor's main doors. Before he could reach them, a fellow in a Bridgetown livery tabard emerged and walked toward Amelia, skirting around the corporal as if the militiaman was a dangerous animal on a leash. He stopped a short distance from the archduchess and gave a curt bow.

"I am bid by my lady to ask your purpose here, Archduchess Amelia of Dweltford," he said formally. Amelia cocked a quizzical eyebrow.

"I have come to escort your liege-mistress on a tour of her town to inspect the damage and console the aggrieved," Amelia told the man.

"I will pass that along," he said simply, already turning as if he thought to simply go and close the door in her face.

"I will make the invitation myself," she told him, eyes blinking in surprise at the man's impoliteness, "when you take me to her."

"I am bid only to take your message," the man replied swiftly, and Amelia found her patience was at an end.

"Are you in the habit of saying 'no' to peers of the realm, man?" she demanded. The fellow blinked and cocked his head, clearly surprised by the question. "I only ask, because with the town invaded and all manner of death and affray abroad, today might not be the day to so boldly forget your place in the grand scheme of things. Wouldn't you agree?"

As if the armed cohort behind her had only just appeared in the man's vision, his eyes went wide in alarm.

What is going on in this castle? Amelia thought as she watched the disquiet grow on the fellow's face. Had he *truly* only just now recognized the danger he was in by being so disrespectful to her? Bridgetown was called the Gatehouse of the Grand Kingdom. It had never been captured in all the centuries of its existence on the Murr River border, giving it something of a legend of impregnability. Did these castle retainers think that invincibility extended to their own persons? Had they not learned yet what it took to keep the town from being snatched out of their mistress's weakening grip?

"Go and tell this message to your liege," Amelia told the man before he could say anything else to annoy her. "Let her know that I will await her in the great hall. She may receive me there with some haste. I will not need an escort to show me the way; I have been there before. I trust *she* will not get lost on the way there either."

The servant likely recognized from Amelia's tone that he had been dismissed, but it seemed to have come to him in a fashion he had not anticipated, oddly enough, for he stood dumbfounded for a long moment. When he did not move to take the message, Amelia simply forced the issue once again and nodded for her escort to accompany her as she led the way into the manor buildings and through the corridors to the great hall. The hobnails of militia boots scratched and tramped on the polished floorboards. It was a brash act, more akin to the arrogance of Daven Marcus and his ilk, but Amelia felt herself left with no other options.

No more games, she thought. *If you would rule, then take up your duty, would-be Archduchess Penelope.*

CHAPTER 4

With her escort standing at attention, Amelia waited for what felt like at least half an hour of the candle before Lady Penelope finally entered the great hall from the side door near the main dais. The young noblewoman was dressed once again in her polished white-steel breastplate, carrying the longsword that had been taken from the Veckander Prince of Town Sobridge. Her long dark hair was not covered with any kind of veil or coif, only held back by a thin gold diadem that closely resembled a coronet. It was an adornment not normally seen except on royalty.

At least she looks *like a conquering queen,* Amelia thought sourly. *Halfway there.*

Lady Penelope moved with stiff dignity to the single throne on the dais and seated herself without making eye contact. She was accompanied by two young men similar to her in age—her cousins, the squires Cyprian and Wilforn. Both were in their own full plate harness, save for helmets, as if about to go to battle. They followed their liege lady and stood at either side of her throne, cold expressions on their youthful faces.

"My Lady," Amelia said, she and her Lace Fangs curtseying politely.

"Lady Amelia, have you come to explain your failure?" Lady Penelope demanded rudely, as if she were a lawyer in a courtly trial.

Failure? What on earth? Amelia thought, sure that her confusion must be obvious on her face.

"I have come to invite you to tour your own demesne, My Lady, after the night's battles," Amelia replied, trying to keep her surprise from her voice. "What is this talk of...?"

"Tour the battles?" Wilforn interrupted her, his voice dripping with disdain. "Having allowed enemies to assault all quarters of the town, you now think to lure our liege into the chaos? Do you think she doesn't see through your ploy?"

"Ploy?" Amelia repeated, astonished at the sudden strange direction of the conversation. Had she not forced this meeting? How was it she was being treated like the criminal before the magistrate?

"Her grace has survived this night only by remaining here in safety," Cyprian said, nodding to Penelope beside him. Amidst the confusion of Penelope's actual noble status, it was clear this cousin, at least, was prepared to treat her as an archduchess. "If she leaves the safety of Earlsbastion in your company, no doubt your overwhelmed forces will meet with an unfortunate occurrence."

"Are you saying...?" Amelia asked, but again the young men-at-arms did not wait for her to express her thought fully.

"A tragic outcome where somehow you escape unharmed, but my cousin perishes at an assassin's hands," Wilforn snapped. He sneered down on Amelia from the dais, reminding her of Daven Marcus on his father's throne as the nobles of the Denay court had been forced to swear allegiance or else be put to the sword. The two men were nothing alike in appearance, but in demeanor it was as if Wilforn was an actor playing at being the kingslayer, and playing the role reasonably well, the archduchess had to admit.

"You think I wish to lure you to an assassination?" Amelia asked Penelope, not bothering to conceal the disbelief in her tone. "Why?"

"Because Her Grace has survived your night of chaos," Cyprian declared, as if it were obvious. "The fires and blades have not reached her in the safety of our castle, so you must bring her to them."

She looked from squire to squire and thence to Lady Penelope, trying to read their thoughts by their expressions.

What paranoia is this? she wondered. How could even these proud and naïve young nobles believe something so patently upside down? She fixed her eyes on Penelope's, the contempt there as cold as the waters of the Murr. *So much for the girl who embraced me as a sister not half a year ago.*

"Lady Penelope, what possesses you to believe this story?" she asked, trying not to sound plaintive but seeking to speak as gently as she could. "Why would I do such a thing?"

"To take the town for yourself, obviously," Penelope replied, and despite her cold expression, Amelia thought she could read fear in the girl's eyes.

For all that it was a misplaced emotion, it was understandable. In the past year this young woman had lost her doting father, her loving uncles, and almost the entire of her array of courtiers. On top of that, a monster had attempted to kill her, her town's cathedral had been defiled in the process, and then one of her few remaining relatives had declared a duel, only to die of the poison on his own blade. In one sense, it was a miracle the young liege's mind had not come completely adrift from the world. All the same, understandable or not, this paranoia would only hurt the defense of Bridgetown, something both Amelia and Penelope were still firm allies and partners in.

"My Lady, I fear you are jumping at shadows," Amelia said, keeping her voice as level as she could make it. The disdain she felt for the accusations against her did not help. "The Reach is a loyal friend to Bridgetown, not its enemy. Not *your* enemy! Have we not served you faithfully since we came here?"

"Faithfully?" Cyprian asked coldly. "Have you not undermined her grace at every turn? She welcomed you like a lost relative, and since then, what have you done? Tried to interfere in our victory over the prince of Town Sobridge; allowed some kind of horrific beast to kill our uncles and nearly kill our liege; your favored convict man scuttled Bridgetown's acceptance into the Forberest Compact, the only chance the Grand Kingdom has of peace; and now, in spite of all your promises to protect her town, you have allowed the Usurper to land thousands of murderous pirates on our islands, undoubtedly in the hope that one of them might be accursedly lucky and reach her grace with a dagger. Perhaps envenomed. Since your arrival, poison has become a strange feature of conflicts here. It may be that is not a coincidence."

Amelia stood listening to Cyprian's twisted tale, and like a seamstress thinking to pick apart an impossibly knotted thread, she scarcely knew where to start. Worse, it was such a back-to-front tapestry of cobwebs that it should not hold up to the slightest tug on even one of its threads. Yet somehow it had ensnared these three.

Surely, she can see that, Amelia thought as she met Penelope's nervously imperious gaze. *It's a ridiculous tale...a Bluebird's song.*

The archduchess remembered the power of the curse or spell—whatever the right word was—that had been placed upon her by an Inquisition representative in Aubrey during the summer past. It had so clouded her mind that she had been unable to tell friend from foe. As she thought about the story Penelope's entourage was telling, Amelia became convinced that they, and likely the girl herself, were under such a spell. It was surely the only way this twisted tale could be made to seem straight.

But knowing that, how do I untangle the knot? she thought. Her own deliverance from the curse had required a prophetic dream and the intervention of an angel of God. Amelia had no idea if her words would be enough to achieve the same result in this case, and even if they were, how long might that take? The town was beset. There was no time for rational debate and the unweaving of lies from truth.

"Is your silence a mark of admission, woman from the west? Are you ready to confess, now that your schemes are unmasked?" Wilforn demanded.

It was strange to hear him speak so. In a sense, he was old enough to act so high-handedly if he wished. Amelia had been so treated by men of his age and station before, and that was what made the behavior so silly in her eyes. He might be of an age to do it, but he had nothing like the necessary power. She had faced down the murderer who currently sat upon the throne. In comparison to Daven Marcus's power and cruelty, Wilforn was a buffoon. And even if that were not the case, there was the cohort of armed men at her back. Involuntarily, she glanced over her shoulder, as if to comfort herself with their presence. The confidence they gave her made her smirk when she looked back, and as soon as she saw the faces of the young Bridgetown nobles, she knew both glance and smile had been a mistake. All three took the gesture as a challenge.

"Why not admit it?" Cyprian demanded. "You have come to conquer. It was your plan from the first."

"Look about on the streets outside, squire!" Amelia retorted, waving her hands around her as if to show the town through the great hall's walls. "Or in this vaunted hall itself. The only colors on the men-at-arms defending your islands and bridges are Reacher blue and cream. The Lion flies over Norgate and the Gryphon over Sougate. If I wanted Bridgetown, it is already mine! I have invited you to witness the suffering of your people, suffering you have done nothing yet to alleviate, would-be archduchess! You hold your throne, such as it is, by my effort and the effort of my sworn and loyal men."

Amelia forced herself to add that last observation. She could feel her temper slipping in frustration with her ally. Pausing to remember that the night's victories had been won by the blood and sweat of her militia helped her to keep perspective. She was not a tyrant, and the best way she knew to hold back from tyranny was to keep in the forefront of her mind the duty and loyalty she owed to those who were loyal to her. If only she could persuade Penelope to think the same way.

"So, you do admit it, faithless witch!" Wilforn shouted, pointing his finger like an accusing scribe at law. "You seek to take our town from us! It has been your plot all along."

"Why would I need to plot? Even Earlsbastion's door couldn't bar me," Amelia said simply, working to calm herself as best she could but finding that the repeated accusations were wearing her patience thin. She was starting to think it might be better to leave this meeting here before she or Penelope said something yet more damaging to their flailing alliance. "I am here in the castle right now with a hundred men-at-arms in my own heraldic colors. What need would I have for subterfuge if my plan was murder?"

The pure reality of that observation should have been enough to put paid to any conspiracy theory.

"And now you admit you have come to seize the castle?" Wilforn almost shouted, and it was all Amelia could do not to laugh, rolling her eyes at him contemptuously.

Like cats playing dice, she remembered her seneschal Lady Dalflitch's assessment—unable to roll properly and not knowing the rules to tell if they are winning or losing in any case. Prentice said the young nobility of Bridgetown were akin to children at play, and right now that was how they seemed to the archduchess. *And I had once thought Liam and Daven Marcus to be petty and childish.*

She decided there was nothing to be gained by continuing this conference. Watching the proud trio for one last quiet moment, Amelia felt a flash of pity for them. Not so long ago, the baroness-elect's father had sat in that chair and a hall full of loyal courtiers had paid him homage. That dais must have been overflowing with sound advisors—relatives and close friends. Now, in such a short time, that cadre was reduced to only these three cousins. The old earl's glory was a rapidly diminishing memory, and the power of his rule was almost all drained away. It was little wonder these cousins were armoring their hearts in pride and suspicion, just as they clothed their limbs in steel. What else was there for them other than the armors they were wearing and the belief that they could only trust each other? As foolishly as she might be acting, Amelia had to concede that the baroness-elect was not without some justification.

I had Prentice when it was all falling down around me, Amelia reminded herself. *He showed me how to pick true friends from false. This poor filly has these fool cousins.*

If only there was a way to protect the "child" from her cousins' foolishness and have her fulfil the adult role for whom there was no one else. Amelia knew she needed to speak with Penelope privately, but the young baroness-elect's expression made it clear that they would not have any such opportunity this morning. Odds were good they might never do so again, at this rate.

Time to stop throwing good coin after bad, she told herself, using an expression her merchant father had taught her years ago and which she had only come to understand properly in the recent years of her rule. She curtseyed formally and met Lady Penelope's cold glare.

"If you choose not to walk amidst your people and comfort them from the night's wounds, I will not try to force you, My Lady," she said, keeping her voice level. "Please believe that the folk of Bridgetown would value your presence—a chance for you to show them your love and for them to show you theirs in return. Even if you should choose not to do this, I urge you to at least come to Norgate and see the army arriving from Denay to besiege us. The foreign boatmen on your streets were only the vanguard. The Usurper's true power has yet to fall upon us. You should know the full extent of what you face, My Lady. In the meantime, if you need me, you may seek me out. We are done sending notes for now, I think."

Throughout their time in Bridgetown, the baroness-elect had used written communication to hold her ally at arm's length. Amelia had had enough of that as well and meant what she said. If Penelope wanted anything more from her, the young noblewoman could come cap in hand for once. All the baroness-elect had left was her unjustified pride, so that would be the currency she would have to spend to buy Amelia's attention. Turning away, the archduchess pointedly did not wait to be excused, even though as ruler in this hall it was Penelope's right to give or withhold that permission. The girl sat her "throne" by right, but she ruled only by the strength of her allies. It was time she began to realize the distinction.

"We know where to look for you, western slattern," Wilforn called after her, sounding so much like a sullen boy. "Who knew how well my cousin chose when she housed you in the whore's apartments!"

Having only just turned, Amelia could see the offense on her retainers' faces. She was thankful her militiamen were so well trained that not one so much as muttered, but all ninety, in two columns, held their positions and awaited her lead. So focused was she on their discipline that it surprised her when she heard another voice speak from beside her.

"Are you so eager for your lady to lose another cousin over a matter of honor?" Lady Spindle asked in a clear, clipped voice that would have done any veteran courtier proud. "Here stand men-at-arms ready for any cause of honor that might be called. Are you so sure you could defeat them all, one after another? For do not doubt—defame our liege too many more times and you may find you enjoy ninety challenges to such a duel."

Amelia froze. Spindle had not precisely spoken out of turn, and the archduchess appreciated her lady-in-waiting speaking in her defense, but the whole point of leaving had been to end this fruitless conversation before it did further damage, and challenging the two young fools on the dais to duel the entire cohort did not serve that goal at all.

"Hired militia too fearful to muck in when it comes time for true battle?" Cyprian mocked, cocking an eyebrow. "I might fancy my chances if you can promise they will not cheat, and each wait their turn."

"Your brother thought the same thing in this very hall against only one of her grace's men-at-arms," Spindle retorted without missing a beat. "And he was the one who cheated into the bargain. How is he, by the by? How fares his arm?"

Cyprian's brother Cassian was known to have killed himself, throwing himself into the river after his duel with Prentice. He had used a secret poison on his blade. When he cut himself with it the wound had sickened, and his sword arm had had to be amputated to save his life. It was a loss he had been unable to endure, and he chose suicide over life as a cripple. The whole matter had occurred only weeks ago, and it was certain that Cyprian's grief would still be raw.

"We will not win her back this way," Amelia muttered, scowling side-glance at Spindle. "I'm not her mother. She's not going to let me nag her or browbeat her into submission, even if I'm in the right."

The lace-masked lady-in-waiting nodded and turned her back, as did Lady Daisy, and before anything further could be said, they began to leave the hall. Perhaps one or more of the trio threw more words after them, but the escort had begun to march in place until they might follow their liege through the doors, and the clashing of ninety armed men beating their feet on the boards drowned out any other sounds.

CHAPTER 5

"All I'm sayin' is that Young Hopeful twit would have had ninety-*two* duels to face, if her grace was to let us off the leash. Not just ninety," said Lady Daisy, her voice echoing belligerently around the main room of the Paramour's Chambers as the archduchess and her entourage returned. "I mean, wouldn't you have thrown down for her honor, My Lady? Wouldn't you have wanted to, at the least?"

"Surely," Spindle replied, "but as I have said, it was not only her grace's honor that was challenged. The baroness-elect's cousins were also disdaining the might and skill of the Lions, and that meant the right of answer for the slur should have been theirs first. Besides, if we had suggested that we two in our skirts and bodices were another threat for those cocksure lads to face, that might have been a nose tweak too far for them."

"*Now* you're worried about tweaking their noses too much?" the archduchess asked, and at last the reality of her arrival penetrated Prentice's consciousness. Shortly after dawn he had come to the Paramour's Chambers, thinking to give his liege a report of the night's actions. When he had discovered that she was not here, he had sat down in one of the upholstered chairs by the fire, planning to await her return, and promptly fallen asleep. Blinking to clear the haze from his eyes and thoughts, he pushed his weary body up from the seat.

"Your Grace, welcome back," he said, and even to his sleepy mind his voice sounded weak.

"Baron Ash?" the archduchess answered, and the concern in her tone was clear. "What happened to you?"

Prentice looked down at himself and realized that in his exhaustion he had not thought to take off his wet clothes, save for the heavy buffcoat, which now hung on a peg in his own rooms on the next floor down. The damp cloth still on his body was warm now from having been near the fireplace, but he had dripped a puddle on the floor around his chair, and he was enwreathed in a dim cloud of steam as the heat evaporated the wetness. Smirking, he looked back at the archduchess.

"I took a morning dip in the Murr, Your Grace," he told her, and she tipped her head to one side with a look of affectionate puzzlement.

"You found the time to take a swim but not to remove your clothes first?" she asked. Despite the humor, her expression showed genuine worry.

"The activity was forced upon me, Your Grace," Prentice said, and then he began to unfold the tale of the grenadier and the forlorn militiaman.

"After that, I sent word to Marquis-Consort Farringdon and came here to await both you and he that we might consult on tactics," he said as he finished his story. "I fear I fell asleep in the warmth, if you will forgive me."

"Of course, Baron," the archduchess answered him. "Since the knight captain is not here yet, would you like a moment to change your clothes? I doubt Chaplain Whilte would be happy to learn that you undid all his good healing work by catching a chill within a day of leaving your sick bed."

As if on cue, Prentice coughed and felt the ache in his bones. He had almost certainly become ill from the night's exertions, though he did not imagine it would become too much of a burden. He did not think he was frail enough yet to be felled by a mere cold.

Says the man whose vital fluids were only recently envenomed against him by an arcane poison made from brakkis effar blood, he mocked himself inwardly. After almost dying from toxin, he would be a fool to think he was so recovered that a winter chill would not turn to the pneumonia on him if he was not careful.

"With your permission, Your Grace, I *will* change my clothes and then return," he said with a thankful bow.

"Do that, Baron," the archduchess replied, and Prentice withdrew from the chamber.

As he left, he heard Lady Spindle commanding two of the neophytes to clean up the wetness he left behind and was surprised when the instruction was accompanied by a rebuke to all the handmaids in the chamber for not offering him a dry, warm blanket. It occurred to him that, in fact, not one of the neophytes had even looked askance at him, barring the one who stood like a doorman, examining him as he entered.

What "tells" of my true nature did she see? he wondered idly as he made his way downstairs. By the time he had removed his wet clothes, he was shivering as if with fever, and although he did his best not to disturb her, he awakened his wife who had had a disturbed night of her own, soothing their twins through the sounds of the invasion chaos.

"Sorry, my love," he said with a smile as she sat up in their bed.

"Sorry for what, old man?" Baroness Righteous demanded of her husband. "Sorry for waking me or sorry for spending the whole night out and about in the cold when you ain't full well yet? And are you soaked from head to toe? What'd you do, go dancing in a thunderstorm?"

Prentice shook his head and tried to control the trembling in his limbs. He clasped his arms around his chest and his wife pushed herself onto her knees in the bed, snatching up the blanket to wrap around him. As it settled on his shoulders, she encircled him with her arms from behind while he sat on the edge of the bed.

"I know riskin' your life is what you do best, husband," she whispered in his ear, "and I ain't got no fear of you bein' weak or sickly. But even you have limits. You know that, don't you?"

"I know, my love," he replied, enjoying her embrace for a moment. Then he reached up to pat her bare arm gently. "Now I must dress and return to her grace."

Righteous recoiled from his touch as if it hurt her.

"Good lord, Prentice, your fingers are like ice!"

She reached up and touched her hand to his forehead.

"And you're on fire in your head," she added. "Get you into this bed and I'll tell her grace that you are too unwell."

"I have a duty," he began to object, gently fending away her hands as she sought to put him to rest.

His wife was having none of it. "You have many duties, old man, including to them two and to me." She pointed to their twins asleep in their cribs and then put her thumb to her own chest. His eyes followed the gesture and then lingered on that part of her.

"You know you look quite fetching in nothing but a sleeping shift, beloved wife."

He reached idly toward her linen-covered breast, but she fended him away, more easily than he had her, and gave him a stern look.

"You're too tired for her grace and much too tired for that!"

He nodded as he found himself slipping down to the pillow and the sleep that he knew, in truth, he desperately needed. As he settled down and his wife arranged the blanket on him, he smiled like a drunkard.

"When you speak to her, tell Amelia that I have divided the Gryphons into cohort patrols," he muttered, feeling sleep rising to claim him but determined to see that his liege had his report. "They know which parts of the islands to keep the watches on and they have the bridges buttoned up tight."

"Amelia?" he heard his wife ask him as he shivered against the mattress that was still warm from her body. "Am I to be so familiar with her grace now?"

"Of course not," he replied, not even sure he knew anymore what they were talking about. Or who. "I will take an hour's nap and then Farringdon and I can talk about how to respond to the invasion. Guillam's on top of Sougate with orders to fetch me if the Veckanders decide to exploit Daven Marcus' arrival. I got the feeling he was actually hoping they would try something. He is looking forward to shooting down from those walls."

"You think an hour will be enough?" Righteous asked him archly. "I'm kenning on you bein' here until I send for Whilte again. You're turnin' to be his favorite patient by the looks of it."

"Just an hour," Prentice insisted weakly. "No need to send for the chaplain."

Then he was asleep. He did not wake an hour later nor in the hours after that when Brother Whilte came to lay healing hands on his sleeping form.

CHAPTER 6

"The girl's going to burn her whole demesne down around her own ears before Daven Marcus even gets the chance," Knight Captain Marquis-Consort Farringdon declared, harking back to his wife's account of the morning's audience with Lady Penelope. They had spoken when he returned midmorning, but he left before the middle of the day. Now, as the afternoon wore on, he had come again to meet with her.

"She has lost her father, uncles, and at least one cousin all in the space of a year, husband," Amelia said, reminding herself as much as Farringdon of the young noblewoman's trials. If she did not, she was sure her own sense of frustration would have her spitting curses on the foolish ruler. "And all that while the Usurper's army seeks to conquer her family's hereditary title and lands. With only inexperienced fellows her own age to counsel her, it is little wonder she is making foolish decisions. Many are the trials that beset the Lady of Bridgetown."

"Then the silly brat should learn to tell friend from foe," Lady Dalflitch said with her typical imperiousness. "Pride is for the strong and mighty. Holding to it when one is weak and vulnerable is a recipe for disaster."

"You speak that word with such authority, My Lady," Farringdon said, giving the lady seneschal a respectful nod.

"I speak from experience, My Lord," Dalflitch responded, "as her grace well knows."

True enough, Amelia thought, remembering how it was this woman who had once considered her a rival had come to be one of her most trusted confidantes. Their eyes met in the candlelit dimness of the overcast afternoon.

There had been no more storms through the day, but the sky was yet crowded in with heavy clouds that veiled the sun and chilled the air. Through the ceiling there came a roll of thumps and thuds, interspersed with restrained feminine cries of discomfort.

"Neophytes at training?" Farringdon asked, casting a curious eye upward.

"Lady Spindle insisted that the little light the day provided should not be wasted," Dalflitch explained, as if women sparring in an attic was the most natural thing in all the world. "After her grace's audience with Lady Penelope, I fear the deadly Spindle returned with an abundance of distemper, which she hopes to exorcise through fighting lessons."

That is one way to put it, Amelia thought as another bump was heard from above. Fit to be tied was the better description of Spindle's mood, as far as the archduchess had been able to tell. When she had heard the report for herself, after delivering the news that her own husband had taken to his bed, Baroness Righteous had declared herself "ropable," and expressed regret that she had not given the Lady of Bridgetown a proper scar "to learn her by" when she had had the chance. After that, the two knife mistresses of the Lace Fangs had marched the neophyte students up to their attic training room, and the sparring had continued apace since then. As much as she felt some sympathy for her handmaids in this moment, the archduchess also realized how useful a lesson like this was for anyone who thought to live by their own steel. Better they face fury like this now, unpleasant as it would be, than to be first confronted by it in the eyes of an enemy who meant to see them dead. As her military leaders had often counseled her, every true fight had the potential to be the last. Better to be over-prepared by stern masters than dead at the hands of an enemy who had been.

The door to the main chamber opened and Baron Prentice entered, wearing a woolen winter cloak around his shoulders and accompanied by Brother Whilte, the Lions' peglegged healer, as well as Master Solft, the timid-seeming, hangdog scholar who nonetheless pursued knowledge and ancient secrets with the fearlessness of a pit bull ratter killing rodents in a ring. All three paused in turn just inside the entry to be received by a veiled neophyte who was serving as the "doorman." The three men submitted to her scrutiny without complaint, and Amelia found herself also scanning these trusted fellows for signs that they were not themselves—any indication, any "tell," that one or more of them might be a skin-thief agent of the Inquisition in disguise. They certainly seemed like her true retainers, but Amelia waited for the neophyte to do her duty without saying anything. The archduchess was developing the art of reading true folk from false just because it was what every woman in her chambers did. The neophytes were acquiring the skill as a matter of professional diligence.

The process also raised another unpleasant notion in Amelia's mind. Although her audience with Lady Penelope had been hostile, it had also been more than a little mad. Arrogant and naïve though the lady and her cousins were, it was pure insanity for them to disdain their ally as they had. Even children should be able to curb their tongues better than those three. It made the archduchess all but certain that one of Bluebird's agents, or the minstrel himself, had whispered a spell song in their ears, twisting their minds as her own had once been, making them turn on their loyal allies.

And how long ago was the spell cast? she thought. When she arrived with her militia in Bridgetown it had been as a savior, but in swift steps, her standing with the Lady Penelope had degraded inexorably. *A spell would explain that, although she could equally just be as much of a brat as my lady describes.*

The three men passed the door servant's assessment and walked the short distance to the main table, there to present themselves to their liege. Around them, every other handmaid and lady-in-waiting watched surreptitiously as well. If these were false, someone should notice something.

At least that is the hope, Amelia thought, not for the first time in recent days.

"Welcome, gentles," she addressed them as they all bowed. She waved at the chairs down the sides of the table and the men took their places. Prentice sat next to Farringdon and opposite Dalflitch, as Whilte and Solft then took the places farther down. The scholar placed his scribe's satchel on the tabletop and began to fish out both parchment and sticks of pressed charcoal. When he had them on the table, he looked to Baron Ash for some kind of permission. Prentice nodded, and Solft proceeded to roll out a larger piece of blank vellum. Without any more acknowledgement of those around him, he fished out a small bound folio and began to sketch from the book to the large page.

"What is this, Baron?" Amelia asked.

"Master Solft arrived a short while ago, Your Grace, and he thinks his research may have borne some fruit," Prentice explained, his voice rasping from his throat in a manner that was painful even to hear. Amelia could only imagine how it felt for him. "When he came past, I asked if he had any maps of Bridgetown and its surrounds that we might use to discuss the military situation with you. He has one, as it happens, but it is too small for our purposes—a common problem with maps of the frontiers of the Grand Kingdom of late"

Prentice and Whilte shared a knowing look, and Solft smirked without glancing up from his vellum while his hands moved with swift confidence, transferring the map of Bridgetown swiftly, if roughly, from the quarto manuscript in front of him.

"Master Solft is quite adept at this work, as you know, Your Grace," Prentice concluded. "It should not take him too long, with your permission."

"A map will be useful," Farringdon averred, and he watched the scholar's adept motions with fascination and probably a degree of professional envy. A learned man himself, as indeed every man at the table was to some degree, Farringdon had a talented hand for drawing and diagrams as well, but it was clear he appreciated the skill of a master.

"Now that the chaplain has had a chance to examine you, Baron Ash, what is the word of your health?" Amelia asked, turning to Whilte. He nodded his head politely. "How badly have you set your recovery back in my service this night past?"

Prentice consulted the chaplain wordlessly across the table, and Whilte took permission to answer on his patient's behalf.

"He has no feet in the grave just yet, Your Grace," the chaplain said. "Nevertheless, he needs rest, and if you will lend me your authority, I will command him to his bed for at least two more days."

Amelia looked to Prentice.

"What do you say to that, Baron?" she asked.

"That I would rather have my fingernails pulled than sleep through the next few days of this siege, Your Grace," Prentice growled out with a rueful expression. "But Inxyphos' wound to my chest still pains me, my limbs ache as I recover from Cassian's poison, and as you can hear, the cold of the night has perched itself in my throat and lungs. If needs must, I will take up my blade for you now and sell my life, but if I do not recover some strength, my next battle in your name will almost certainly be my last. I appear to have found my limit."

"Then take your rest and recover what vitality you may," Amelia told him, feeling earnest compassion for his list of harms. All those terrible things he had suffered in the last season had come upon him after a long summer's march farther west than any Kingdom folk were known to have ever traveled, save for those out of legend perhaps.

"I have done as you asked, My Lord," Master Solft declared suddenly, looking up from his work as if he had not heard one word spoken at the table around him. All eyes turned upon him. "At least I believe so. Would you check my work to confirm for yourself?"

"I trust your hand, Master," Prentice said, pausing to cough behind his own before reaching for the vellum and spreading it on the table in front of Amelia. Whilte and Farringdon moved candlesticks to make space. Looking down on the pale sheet, Amelia easily read the diagram in front of her. The River Murr was drawn as a channel down the middle of the page, with the islands of Bridgetown and the bridges themselves in the middle. The two halves of the Great Bridge Road, north and south, were shown, along with a rough position of the Vec prince Everard's army, hired by the Golden Heron Bank, on the south shore. Although it had been sketched swiftly, the map was excellent to Amelia's thinking, and she could see the reason for her husband's envy.

"Shall we begin with a description of the past day and night's events?" Prentice asked, and he began to outline everything that had happened since the Usurper's fleet had first emerged from the rains and mist the previous afternoon, pointing to the relevant portions of the map so that everyone present could see exactly what was being described. Beginning with the rebuffed attempt to capture the Sougate bastion and bridge, he told them of the raiders' frustrated attacks on the main bridges through the inner channels of the islands and their tactics of pillaging and burning wherever they did manage to come ashore.

"You call these fights 'running battles,' Baron?" Dalflitch said at one juncture after Prentice had noted the key points of the town where fighting had been fiercest through the night. "What does that mean for those of us who are not trained men-at-arms."

"Continuous melees with no line of battle, My Lady," Prentice said readily.

When his voice started to fail him, however, he nodded to Farringdon to take up the explanation. Amelia was surprised when it was Baroness Righteous who spoke from just back from the table. She had entered quietly with a baby in her arms, rocking the sleeping child back and forth.

"It's cobble-runner tactics," she said simply. "If you aren't about takin' their territory, then smack 'em and run. Let 'em chase you down one street while you sneak up a side alley and smack 'em again from another side. Keep the foe guessin' and wishin' he'd never got out of bed that mornin'." She leaned close to Prentice and whispered in his ear, though her words were audible to the whole table all the same. "Which is where you should be, husband, by-the-by."

He reached up and took one of her hands to kiss it gently.

"Not now, wife," was all he said, and the matter was at rest between them, it seemed. He turned his attention back to the map. "It is clear now that the fleet's prime purpose was not to take any ground but to run us ragged around the streets all night."

"I thought you said they were aiming to take the old bridges?" Dalflitch objected.

"If they could, My Lady," Farringdon answered her. "Those were likely considered useful subsidiary prizes, should they be captured, but the main purpose was the distraction while the rest of the fleet could come ashore on the north bank."

"Which is why you should tell us what was happening at our front door while we were chasing rats in the house, My Lord," Prentice said, and while his explanation made sense, Amelia suspected her exhausted knight commander was also glad for legitimate reasons to rest his voice.

As if his own health were not reason enough, she thought, wondering at the sacrifices her loyal retainers made for the good of her lands.

CHAPTER 7

Knight Captain Farringdon reached past Prentice with an apologetic smile and took up one of Solft's charcoal sticks that had rolled up the table somewhat. He used it to quickly sketch some extra details onto the map.

"While his mercenary pirates have been making affray about the town, our kingslayer king has been landing the main of his forces here," he explained, marking in some straight lines at a point that would be perhaps a league or so downriver from the northern-most island of Bridgetown, the one named Loncastel. "There is a significant pier here that locals call Lazy Farmers Jetty."

"Lazy Farmers?" the archduchess repeated, clearly hoping for an explanation of the name, but her husband only shrugged.

"We know there's a lot of soft mire and reed-banks on both sides of the Murr where average boats might put men ashore," he continued. "But Daven Marcus has brought his bronze monsters with him, and if he tried to unload their heavily laden barges straight onto the bank, he would risk losing them in the mire. Even bringing a typical lighter up on shore would be next to impossible with that heavy a cargo. Their keels would bite the mud before they ever reached the riverbank. A stone pier is their only hope to get the Dragons ashore, and Lazy Farmers is the only one nearby on the north bank to serve the task. Even as it is, the unloading will be a slow and complex process."

"Which explains why he sent his mercenaries on their suicide missions," Whilte added.

"To keep us distracted while he offloaded his precious toys?" Dalflitch asked, and the men-at-arms around the table all nodded.

Amelia had had the same thought and was glad she was right. "A pity we could not destroy that pier," she mused and looked surprised at her husband's enthusiastic reaction.

"There is no reason yet that we cannot, but I think we have other options," he declared. "So far, the men ahorse that Daven Marcus has landed are not enough to rule the fields unchallenged. I have had lancers riding patrols out on the north bank to watch their progress. They say that he has been as eager to set his impressive tents and pavilions as he has been to bring the cannons ashore. At least three heavily laden barges lie anchored in the river beyond the range of Norgate's own guns, sadly, but waiting to offload their Dragons. In the meantime, his own tents are being set here."

Farringdon quickly sketched a little tent encampment a short distance north of the Lazy Farmers pier.

"There are small woods there and solid ground," he explained. "My guess is he will set the Bronze Dragons in that location and fire on Norgate eventually. But even with the rush and distraction, his fleet has landed only two cannons so far. At this rate, he will not have the entire contingent ashore for days yet. We could assault the pier and destroy it, delaying their arrival for some time as he took them back downstream looking for another landing site. Or, we could wait until some—say half their number—had come ashore and then capture or destroy them, along with the pier, in a single raid."

"Is such a thing possible?" the archduchess asked, clearly taken by the audacity of the plan.

For his part, Prentice felt himself struggling to concentrate. His head was aching, along with all the other pains that were clamoring for attention in his flesh, and he felt his thoughts moving slowly—much slower than he liked. He needed his rest even more than he wanted to admit, it seemed.

"Baron?" the archduchess asked after a moment, and Prentice realized that she actually wanted an answer.

He thought about it for a painful moment. "Every hour we wait for another Bronze Dragon to be put ashore, they will also be unloading men-at-arms, their horses, squires, and all their bagatelle," he said at last. "Each prize we add to the purse will come with more guards. At some point, they will have a force ashore strong enough to hold any raid at bay. If we wait too long, we will capture nothing and lose any chance to destroy the pier into the bargain."

"So, you think the better plan would be to raid the pier and forsake the hope of capturing the cannons, Baron?" the archduchess asked.

He nodded. "With respect to your knight captain, yes," he said, acknowledging Farringdon. "If we could watch and gauge the timing closely, perhaps it might be worth the risk, but in this weather and with his forces growing in strength as we speak, better for us to raid now, even in the next hours, and smash that pier. We have powder enough to do the job. It would delay the siege by days, if not weeks, and we could still destroy or capture the two Dragons currently ashore. I know it would not be the decisive victory that Lord Farringdon hopes for, but it would be significant. Better a bad plan now than a perfect plan too late." Prentice turned to the knight captain and nodded to him apologetically. "I mean no disrespect, My Lord," Prentice told him. "Your plan is not a poor one, only too difficult to time in these conditions."

Farringdon nodded, and then a cunning smile lit his lips. "What if we could tip the odds a little?" he asked. "Force the Usurper to dance to our tune?"

"How would we do that?" the archduchess wondered aloud.

"We could force him to rush his cannons ahead of their guards," the knight captain explained. "At present, they are on their big barges anchored in the middle of the river, waiting for their chance to come ashore. They are safe there from capture, but as last night showed, just being in the water is not the same as being immune to danger."

"I don't understand," the archduchess said, but Prentice thought he did.

"Raiders of our own, or fire ships?" he asked, wincing as his head gave him a moment's extra discomfort. Even from behind him, his wife noticed, and he felt a soothing hand on his shoulder.

"Fire ships," Farringdon confirmed with an enthusiastic smile.

"It could work," Prentice said, nodding gingerly.

A moment's silence ruled the table, broken ultimately by an impatient tut from Lady Dalflitch.

"Again, for those of us not born to warfare, could you explain what a 'fire ship' is?"

"We take a barge, load it with some fuel—oil, powder, things of that nature. Then we set it alight and float it in amongst Daven Marcus' anchored fleet," Farringdon explained with the same eager smile he had whenever discussing the use of clever devices to solve problems. When he did so while discussing dangerous or deadly things like this, it gave him an unintentionally ghoulish cast.

"Who would crew such a death vessel?" the archduchess asked, clearly horrified by the prospect.

"No one," Farringdon answered.

"No one?"

"There is no need for a crew, Your Grace," Whilte explained. "Set the boat alight and let the river current take it toward the enemy. No need for a tillerman."

"What if it runs aground before it reaches Daven Marcus' fleet?" Dalflitch asked.

"Then it's wasted, but no harm done," Righteous chimed in. Eyes turned towards her, and though Prentice did not join them for the pain in his head, he could hear his wife's shrug by the tone of her voice alone. "I mean, I guess. What difference would it make if you missed? It's not like every Roarshot or cannonball lands true, nor arrows or crossbow bolts. Not even when the fey shoots 'em. Right?"

Prentice nodded gently and put his hand up to hers where it still rested on his shoulder, squeezing approvingly.

"Fire ships are usually only used to attack vessels in port or at anchor," he explained. "They are floated in on a rising tide. We have the advantage here because the river flow is with us. We can send them downstream whenever we like, but the enemy cannot make them float upstream at us."

Prentice thought back to the damage one grenadier with a death wish had done to the docks between Oldbridge and Greenmarsh. A proper fire ship loaded with oil and powder could have turned the wooden cobweb into an inferno in a quarter of the candle. The entire of the two islands could have been threatened, potentially.

"Won't the enemy simply move their boats aside?" Dalflitch asked, peering at the map and then the knight captain.

"They are at anchor," Farringdon said triumphantly. "It will take them some time to get moving—hopefully too long to prevent at least some damage. More importantly, while a burning boat is an enemy to every other craft on the water, fire is the devil itself to gunners and cannons like the Bronze Dragons. If I was Daven Marcus, I would have at least some powder and shot with every Dragon so the weapon could come ashore and be ready to fire in short order, at least long enough for the rest of the ammunition to be landed. Those crews on the Dragons' barges will be in a frenzy to get ashore the moment the first fire ship is sighted, lest their cargoes be detonated. He's kept his camp and his fleet out of range of our cannons, so let's send him some other fire."

Farringdon ceased his enthusiastic explanation, and another moment's quiet rested upon the table.

"Can it be done, Knight Commander?" the archduchess asked, and Prentice forced his pained mind to concentrate, to come up with a truthful answer.

"Yes," he began. "But again, timing will be key, which only makes it much like any other fight. After picking our moment and then acting with as much force as we can muster, I think this could be decisive, Your Grace."

"You would send both banner companies at once?" she asked, clearly surprised.

Prentice shook his head. "Not with the Golden Heron's mob on our southern doorstep. But the whole of the Lion Banner, with some of the Gryphon in support, would be a reasonable risk."

"Ten cohorts as a reserve?" Farringdon asked.

"I was thinking ten, yes, My Lord," Prentice agreed.

"Then if you would lend me them, Knight Commander, I would be indebted."

"I will send a word to Gennet before I take to my bed," Prentice told him, smirking self-deprecatingly at the notion. He had never imagined a day when any White Lions would march into battle while he was snug in bed somewhere else entirely.

Of course, I often never imagined I would live this long either, he told himself, so he accepted this strange turn of events with some equanimity.

"Very well, husband," the archduchess declared. "If you and the knight commander are of one mind on this, then I say go to. Let us see if you cannot use these 'fire ships' to beard the wolf...the eagle—well, the dragon, I suppose—in his lair before we are made to suffer his fiery breath in turn."

Prentice felt himself sigh inwardly, despite his many aches. If Farringdon's plan was a success, the second siege of Norgate by Daven Marcus's forces could end up being lifted as swiftly and easily as the first had been. He felt his attention fading and was surprised at how readily he wanted to return to his bed for rest. His liege's next words summoned him back.

"Master Solft? What now of your researches? Do you have good news to share with us?"

CHAPTER 8

"I do have good news, Your Grace," Solft answered Amelia's question, "though it might not be as significant as Lord Farringdon's plan. Likely not as decisive, certainly."

"Well, share it and let us judge for ourselves," Amelia told him.

Solft bowed his head. "Your Grace, I have told you of the scriptorium here in the town," he began after lifting his face once more. "It is owned by a man whose ancestors were from the Masnian coast of the Tassassim. A fellow with some far-reaching connections indeed. By dint of his efforts—which I fear have not been inexpensive—I have been reading a codex of forgotten knowledge written nearly five centuries past, if you can believe it."

He reached into the bag on the table and fished out a little ribbon-tied folio of parchments, which apparently contained his notations from reading this encyclopedia. He passed the sheaf up to the archduchess via Prentice's hand.

"I purchased the whole work from the scriptorium but left it in their care for now," he continued to explain as he sat back into his seat. "It is by far the oldest original text I have ever held in my hands, and with the rain, not to mention the conflict overnight, I did not wish to risk the fragile pages. The slightest mildew could destroy it within weeks, I have no doubt. My hands are still covered in scriveners' chalk from keeping them dry to handle the pages." He held them up to show their parched, white condition. Smudges of charcoal from drawing the map made it look as if his fingers were sickly and badly bruised—black against the ghostly pale.

"Songs of the Steeple Aviary?" the archduchess asked, reading from the notes. "Folk songs, Master?"

Amelia wondered at the usefulness of such low knowledge. Surely the magick secrets of the Inquisition were not contained within. Folklore was seldom committed to writing as it was, and she understood that trained scholars typically held the notions of the common folk in virtual contempt. The thoughts and deeds of the great and the good, these were the highest callings of a chronicler, so it was said, or at least Amelia thought she remembered one of her instructors telling her so during her days under Baroness Switch's tutelage. It seemed so long ago now.

"As I mentioned, the codex they come from was titled as an encyclopedia of lost knowledge," Solft explained readily, his usual near-groveling attitude replaced by the air of a competent teacher. It was an odd transformation but seemed to happen entirely without thought on his part. When in his element, he simply lacked no confidence. He continued, as if lecturing pupils in a classroom somewhere. "By the compositor's foreword, it is a tome of forgotten pieces of lore from the earliest years of the Grand Kingdom."

When Solft had been set upon his quest for the Inquisition's secrets, one of the things they had told him to watch out for was what he could *not* find—those gaps in the annals of the Grand Kingdom where the forest of knowledge had been laid waste in order to hide exactly which trees the Silent Hand of the Church had marked as forbidden fruit. Suddenly, the scholar's focus on "low knowledge" made sense to Amelia. A compendium of lost things, even low things, promised important clues if nothing else. Perhaps the Inquisition had been as dismissive of what the yeomanry knew as the average scholar, ideally to their own detriment.

"What secrets do these songs unfold?" Prentice asked as the archduchess handed him the sheaf of notes to examine for himself.

"Well, the title itself is telling. I venture to call myself well read, and yet I know of no institution of Mother Church, extant or lapsed, called the Steeple Aviary," Solft told them. "As I read it, I was reminded of things you yourself have shared with us of helpful visions, Your Grace."

Prentice was nodding almost immediately as he scanned the pages, his eyes narrowed in concentration. It looked as if even examining the pages was causing him further pain, and Amelia was about to send him to bed when he started to read aloud some of the titles of the poems in this codex.

"The Ancient Pride of the Eagle, Your Grace," he read, holding up the second page. Then he flipped to the third. "Trust Not the Raven's Song?"

Amelia sucked in a shocked breath and her eyes went from Prentice to Farringdon. Over the years, both she and Prentice had received visions in which the Silent Hand was represented by different kinds of birds, not to mention the royal house of Denay always being figured by its eagle heraldry. Here, in verses five hundred years old, preserved from centuries earlier than that, were those very same images, it seemed. Everyone around this table knew some of that—Solft himself had known enough to recognize the significance—but only her husband and Prentice's wife, after Amelia and Prentice themselves, knew all of it. Though a part of her mind counseled caution, something told the archduchess this text truly was significant. They should look for clues here, and she longed to read through the verses, hoping for swift revelation. She reached out and took the notes from Prentice's hand.

"Can we trust this text, Master?" Prentice asked. "How much risk do we face that this is a false trail, another of the lies the Inquisition did not fear enough to burn?"

Amelia smiled, only half-listening to his words. Prentice had already given voice to her main concern as she read the poems on the pages before her.

"This text, Your Grace, was never published in the Grand Kingdom," Solft said with a cunning smile, as of a person revealing a clever secret. "The original is in precursor Masnian—an old dialect. It has consumed my hours translating from my old friend Pawley's notes of Meerenmachter's works. The great scribe wrote his treatises in the precursors of Masnian and Kastrian both. He was a truly rare intellect in history."

Amelia let the explanation of scholarly disciplines wash over her as she tracked through the rough poetry, realizing that the rhymes and rhythms were now for another language altogether. She let out a nervous hiss as she found one verse too revelatory.

"Your Grace?" her husband asked, concerned.

Amelia looked to her husband, then handed the notes back to Prentice, pointing to the line that unnerved her.

"The lullaby of the fairy wren puts all men to sleep," the knight commander read from the text, shaking his head slowly with a furious scowl.

Farringdon was clearly unfamiliar with the species. "Fairy wren?"

"A bird of the forest, solitary and elusive, with vibrant azure plumage, My Lord," the knight commander explained.

"A bluebird?" Dalflitch asked softly as everyone around the table recognized the significance.

"Indeed. And several of us here have heard its lullaby," Prentice told her.

The power of the minstrel Bluebird's song to dull the mind, even to unconsciousness, was well known amongst the retainers of Amelia's inner court.

"Read of the lyrebird, My Lord, third stanza," Solft urged.

Prentice went to the passage and read swiftly. "The raven lies, but the lyrebird lies with many voices, and when it does, all believe its lies, though their own eyes rebel for truth."

"Skin thieves?" Amelia asked rhetorically.

Chapter 9

"I suppose we should be encouraged and thankful that someone took the effort to record these secrets for us, and that the Lord Almighty has not allowed time to claim them from us utterly," Amelia said, finding it little comfort at this moment. She felt like a child on the first day of their apprenticeship—excited to learn their new craft and only just now discovering the enormous journey between their knowledge and the skills of a true master. Her hand rested absently on her growing belly a moment, and it prompted another insight.

And I still have motherhood ahead of me, she thought, concern for her unborn's future rising in her mind, along with an appreciation of all the work she had already done to learn the art of rulership. *Just how many apprenticeships must I embark upon in this life?*

"For now, I wish to know what tactics, if any, this ancient scholar has recorded for us for fighting these wretched bird flocks of the Silent Hand and Denay," Prentice said coldly, eyes turning to Master Solft once more.

Seeing Prentice's face in profile, Amelia was struck by how drawn and pale he was. In the past, he had worked himself into sickness and been wounded many times on her behalf, but she had a sudden rush of fear that this time he might not fully recover.

Even diminished, he is a truer retainer and wiser than any others, save perhaps Dalflitch, she told herself, pushing her fears aside.

Just his focus on the immediate practical needs of the scholar's research reminded her of that.

"Believe in the sword that is sharpest," Solft said, and from his tone it was clear he was quoting from the notes in Prentice's hands. "The sharpest, two-edged sword will cut the lies, even from the air."

Amelia waited for the master to go on, but his expression indicated he had nothing further to say on the subject.

"What does that mean?" she asked. "Prentice, do you understand it? You know more of weapons than anyone else I have ever heard of. Is there such a blade, so sharp that it can cut words out of the air?"

Her eyes flicked to his champion blade, which he had unhooked from his belt as he sat and was now leaning in its scabbard against the table edge. Prentice saw her curiosity and shook his head, grimacing in discomfort.

"Aside from not being two-edged, Your Grace, my sword is most certainly not *that* sharp," he said with an uncomfortable smile. "I do not believe a mere physical weapon could ever possibly be."

Amelia raised an eyebrow as she looked meaningfully again at the sword.

"Not even an 'enchanted' one," he said with a low chuckle. Amelia was well familiar with the rumors of the weapon's magickal properties and how nonsensical her knight commander considered the notion. She laughed gently with him.

"With respect, Your Grace, I suspect it is a code of sorts, or a metaphor," Solft offered.

"And can you decipher it?" Amelia asked.

The man shook his head sorrowfully. "Not yet, Your Grace," he told her. "There is a note at the last page of the codex that claims to be from the author's apprentice. It says that a second volume was planned, but his master died suddenly even before this first volume was published. The apprentice wrote that he took the master's notes and completed the encyclopedia after returning to his homeland in Masnia, but the text's Kastrian annotations show that that was the preferred language of the compositor, I believe."

"Masnia was not his homeland—is that what you're saying?" Amelia wondered at the significance of that. Then, it became clear immediately. "His master was killed during the composition of the work, and the apprentice fled as far as he could, feigning returning to his birthplace as an excuse?"

"I think so, Your Grace."

"Thanks be to the Almighty that the man survived to put these words into print. I think you should continue your research down this path, Master. Would you agree, Baron Ash?"

Prentice did not answer at first, instead staring at the tabletop as if he had not even heard her speak his name. When he looked up, he seemed far more distracted than was ever the norm. He was plainly on the verge of complete exhaustion.

"The word," he muttered, not looking to Amelia but fixing his eyes on Whilte.

The chaplain met his gaze solemnly. "Sharper than any two-edged sword," the brother recited, nodding. "That was my thought, too."

"What is that?" Amelia insisted.

"It is scripture speaking of itself," Whilte explained to her. "The word—the scripture—is sharper than any two-edged sword, piercing even to between bone and sinew."

"It is the power that comes from the mouth of the returning messiah also," Prentice added. "He speaks, and from his mouth comes a sword. I had always supposed that to be a metaphor of some sort...but in light of this?"

"We are to 'speak' a sword against the power of the Inquisition's magicks? It seems this night has no end of things I do not comprehend," Dalflitch said, her voice and expression both showing how bewildering she found the notion. "How is that done, exactly?"

"We must speak the word," Whilte answered her simply. "The word of the Lord."

"Scripture quotes?" Amelia asked, not feeling quite as disdainful as her lady seneschal sounded but sharing her mixture of confusion and disbelief. The scriptures were the province of Mother Church, were they not? Did the Inquisition's magicks not spring from the same fountain, as it were? How could scripture be used against such a power?

"You are skeptical, Your Grace?" Whilte asked, suddenly seeming like a stern but faithful member of the clergy, and Amelia almost felt in his manner a shade of the other dire clerics who made themselves her enemy, a touch of Faldmoor's ilk in his displeasure.

"Perhaps skepticism is the right response," Prentice said, defending his liege even before she fully knew the need. "The truth never fears to be questioned. The mountain stands, whether folk believe in its height or not. Men might rage at the mountain, but the mountain is unmoved."

Whilte nodded, humbly accepting Prentice's comment, and the coldness Amelia feared seemed to fade from the chaplain's expression.

"I think Brother Whilte would agree, Your Grace, that simply reciting a catechism will likely not be enough," Prentice added, addressing Amelia directly. "Note the injunction to believe—*believe* in the sword that is sharpest. I think that will certainly be key. Whatever power the words have, it is not in them alone. This is not sorcery or the reciting of magick phrases hidden in scripture. Prayer is not the casting of spells. This is an articulation of trust, I think. We cannot expect the power of the Almighty to save us if we do not believe that power can, in fact, save us. If you do not believe there *is* a sword to draw, how can you wield it, two-edged or not?"

"That makes a kind of sense, I suppose," Amelia said, puzzling over the deceptively simple piece of wisdom. As she felt her own brows furrow, she noticed again the fading will in Prentice's expression. It was beginning to look as if even sitting here was a torment for his recovering body. She turned to Whilte, hoping to move to a swift resolution. "What of you, Chaplain? Do you concur with the baron's notions?"

Whilte held out his hand politely for Solft's notes and read them over, frowning but nodding slowly.

"Baron Ash's thought does seem to marry with these words," Whilte said at last. "Beyond that, I do not know what to say. I would need to pray and meditate upon this further before I was comfortable to form a strong opinion."

"Our enemies are many and our time too short for a hermit's seclusion and contemplation, Brother," Amelia told him tautly, feeling the many pressures of which Prentice's pain was only one, insistent though it was.

"I do appreciate that, Your Grace," Whilte answered uncomfortably. "Still, I am fearful of letting any sign of enthusiasm give you a false sense of hope."

"Do you not believe in the power of God to overcome dark magicks?" Amelia pressed, surprised to hear her uncertainty reflected in the chaplain's tone. He had always seemed such a devout man in the time she had known him. "Surely the miracle of healing that is done through your hands, through so many gifted folk, men and women across the many lands of our world, are a testimony of God's power. Your other miracles..."

"They are not *my* miracles," Whilte snapped and Amelia almost flinched. The atmosphere in the chamber, which had already been grave, grew even more fearfully still, as if the air had suddenly transformed to solid glass. For a long moment no one moved or spoke, as all no doubt wondered if the chaplain had gone too far, even for the usually forgiving Amelia of the Western Reach. A single glance made it clear that Whilte himself recognized that he had overstepped his bounds. Careful of the candles on the table, he bowed himself slowly until his forehead actually touched the tabletop—an exaggerated gesture of submission even for the oldest traditions of Grand Kingdom society.

"Forgive me, Your Grace," the chaplain said earnestly, head still down. "You know my history, the vain and self-willed man I have been in my life. Believe me when I tell you I have no holiness within myself that I might summon God to manifest his power at my command. Any miracles the Almighty chooses to do at my request happen because God is merciful. I always seek to discourage anyone from thinking those works he does through me make me special or worthy of unusual consideration. Please forgive my presumption speaking so to you, but this is a modesty I owe to a higher authority than any earthly power."

The stillness continued a moment longer, and everyone in the room waited upon their liege's judgement. Archduchess Amelia softly released a breath that was audible for all its gentleness. She hadn't realized how shocked she was herself.

"I think you are a humbler man than you give yourself credit for, Chaplain," she said, "and I accept why you were discomfited by my words. I ask you to forgive me also."

Whilte sat back and nodded his head solemnly.

"So, with consideration for the specifics of pride, humility, and the exactness of revelation, what does this all do for us, gentles?" Amelia asked, hoping to dispel the tension in the room with a soft smile. "If it takes a kind of belief that is not common and cannot be guaranteed, how do we make use of that?"

"Faith is surely still the answer, Your Grace," Prentice offered, eyes blinking as if he was surprised at himself giving that response. It was indeed a strange situation, a condemned heretic counseling others towards simple trust in God Almighty—not merely in his existence, but in his faithful power to aid mere mortals. What would the younger Prentice who had been banished over the mountains more than a decade ago have made of this turn of fate? "Without pressing unwanted glory on Brother Whilte, Your Grace," Prentice went on, "I have seen him draw this miraculous 'sharpest sword' of the word. We all have, in a sense. How else should we describe the manner by which we stopped Inxyphos in the cathedral square?"

It was true, Amelia realized. The *brakkis effar* that Inxyphos had become—the bear man—had been sent to assassinate Lady Penelope on her accession day and had been staggered by an obscure prophecy about drunkenness, hardly a typical subject of the usual catechisms. The power of this "sword of the word," if it could be called a power, was clearly not one of simple learning. Pure intellect or memorization would not attain it.

"I must concede that Baron Ash is probably correct that far, Your Grace," Whilte added while Prentice lapsed back into wearied silence. "I spoke only what came to my mind at that time, though I did trust in God to be true."

"All well and good, but we do not all have your seminarian educations to draw upon," Dalflitch said, sounding as sour as ever. "You both were pumped full of scripture at Ashfield for years. What of those of us who know less of holy writ than we do even of foreign lands?"

A fair objection, Amelia thought. How much of scripture could she quote if the need arose? And what could she do to apply it to a specific situation? The question sat in Amelia's mind for a long moment, croaking at her like a crow's mocking call. As soon as she saw her thoughts in that light, though, like the song of an unwanted bird—a bluebird, a lyrebird, raven or whatever other the Inquisition's vile flock attracted—Amelia shook herself and resolved to do almost anything rather than to let those thoughts continue, even if she hardly knew what could be done.

What was it Prentice said? Better a bad plan now than a perfect plan too late?

"This is some of the best news on this matter we have had in too long, Master Solft," she told the scholar, who seemed to have shrunken back into his timid form. He was surely no skin thief, but nonetheless his shifts in emotion were almost as mystical in their extremity. Amelia looked to Brother Whilte.

"In the meantime, Chaplain, humble or proud, you are our man most familiar with the workings of these miracles. It seems to me that Baron Ash is correct. You have seen the faithful application of scripture turn waters aside and stun a devilish beast in its tracks. Whether by your will or by your speech, Brother, the light of heaven has shone through you too many times for false modesty. You must seek out the fullness of this and turn it from experience into wisdom—wisdom you can share with others." As she said this, Amelia felt her "bad plan" forming. "Our militia will need more than one healer in coming days," she went on. "And when we face magicks, either Redlander or Inquisitorial, we will need more who can speak the word with faith as you do. You must find us more clergy like yourself, ideally healers and theologians both."

Whilte's eyes went wide, as if in fear, but he nodded slowly, accepting her word. Amelia turned to Prentice, his expression even grimmer than the chaplain's, though that was likely from his pain, not fear.

"I am sure the chaplain will do what he can to find such folk, Your Grace," Prentice told her sternly, through gritted teeth. "Healers cannot be bound, but they can pledge themselves. I believe that Brother Whilte may persuade some to make that commitment. Even amongst the mercurial community of the healers, surely some will recognize the need, see that Daven Marcus' rebellion requires a new approach, else the whole Grand Kingdom will drown in fire and blood."

Amelia agreed with her knight commander, but he was not thinking the right way for her. "You are a heretic, Baron," she said and smirked at his scowl, trusting him to realize she meant no insult. Time and his exhaustion brooked no delays for pride; it seemed that was the lesson for them all in this moment. She looked back to the chaplain, talking at once to both men and ultimately to the whole table. "Cast off by men of supposedly superior theology to yours, and yet, in the wasteland west, far beyond the supposedly ordained lands of our Grand Kingdom, God and revelation came to you. By dreams and visions, as well as your own sweat and blood, you have taken the most worthless of men and made of them an army unrivaled and faithful to its own pledges. We have taken riverfolk maidens and gentle ladies-in-waiting and made of them lionesses, with huntress's eyes and sharp claws of their own. I do not need theologians, gentles—*we* do not need such. What we need is to do in chaplaincy what Baron Ash has done in warfare—pray God for the vision to turn dross to gold, broken and worthless into vital and powerful. Brother Whilte insists that the power is not his, that the miracles will come by faith, not by the man...or woman. Then let us petition the Almighty to put that faith in other hands as well. Surely, we can do that, would you not say?"

The stillness of the dark afternoon only seemed to intensify as Amelia stopped speaking and let them all absorb her meaning.

A bad plan now? she wondered, sharing their uncertainty but unable to think what else to do. They had gone looking for the secrets the Inquisition had sought to hide, and this was what they had found. What else could they do but trust that they were on the right path? It was what she had been doing, one way or another, since the day her river barge had been ambushed by Redlanders on the banks of the Dwelt.

Trust—just another word for faith.

CHAPTER 10

Dahyoor, Prentice thought as he lay his aching head upon the pillow. *Before Farringdon sends the Lion Banner out, we should have Dahyoor scout for us. Even if only for an hour.*

While they were not perfect or invincible, Prentice had the utmost respect for the fey, especially their stealth and insights of the land around them—both invaluable talents for scouting. His faith in Dahyoor or other fey allies was not unquestioning, but he was confident that anything his squire could not sniff out, no mere mortal scout would likely discover either. The knight commander just wished he had hundreds of them to depend upon. At present, his horse archer allies were wintering in the mountains. They had promised to return after the rains.

Lord, hasten the spring, was his final thought before feverish sleep claimed him. At some point, his wife returned and offered him a cup of something that tasted bitter, which he assumed was a laud of some sort. It warmed his lips and throat as he sipped it, half awake, and he thought to tell Righteous what he wanted to do with Dahyoor before the raid on Lazy Farmers. The words would not form properly in his mouth, sounding even to his ears like a drunken slurring. Then he was asleep once more, warmer and more restful for a long time.

The dawn lark's song began to penetrate his rest. He rolled over with a groan, wondering if one of the little feathered heralds of the morning was perched on a nearby window, its song was so loud. His shoulder ached and the air on his face felt bitterly cold. Even so, the lark sang, and as its song penetrated deeper into his mind, Prentice thought it sounded like more than one bird—many more. Their voices rose and rose until it felt as if his small bedchamber was awash with the cacophony. Forcing himself to sit up, he half expected to discover a flock of the little tormentors resting on every possible perch. Instead, he found that he was not in bed at all. He was lying on the floorboards of a strangely shaped room—octagonal with walls made of weathered boards through which cracks of watery winter light penetrated. High above, the walls soared and came together into a point as a peaked roof, so tall that it was almost lost in shadows out of sight. Thick crossbeams supported the walls as they became the roof, successive networks of reinforcing interlocking all the way up, and on every beam, flocks of birds roosted and sang.

The Steeple Aviary, Prentice thought, remembering the term from Solft's research and knowing immediately that that was what he was seeing.

A dream then, he thought with an inward shrug. Some part of him felt it was an inappropriate reaction to a prophetic vision, but this was hardly the first time he had been touched by messages from the spiritual realms. That being said, most of his dreams and visions had been disconcerting experiences, to say the least. On top of that was the fact that his last memory was of being given an apothecary's concoction to drink. *So, a dream then, but one of vision or drug? Or just the fever?*

Realizing that he was using feigned cynicism to steel himself for whatever shocks this dream might bring, Prentice pushed his aching body up from the icy floorboards beneath him. As soon as he was upright, it seemed as if those very boards fell away, and he saw himself balancing on a beam like those above, though there were no birds roosting beside him. Where the floor had been, now there was a deep pit, and just looking down slapped him in the face with a powerful vertigo. He staggered back to lean upon the wooden wall. It stabilized him, but his hand went through it, or more truly, his hand pushed a part of it away, for he had found a shutter to a window. Looking out, he saw that he was very high up in the midst of a vast city. In the manner of dreams and visions, he saw out of the window from inside and looked on the window as if he were outside looking in both at the same time. From the inside, he was looking on the city. From the outside, he saw that he was indeed standing in the steepled roof of an impossibly tall tower. Twisted, as if built by masons who had had no plan to begin with, the tower looked like it might fall at any moment and in any one of a dozen directions.

The cacophony within the steeple continued, but on the outside not a single bird was heard. As he noticed that fact, Prentice realized that it was true of all birds. Not only could he hear nothing of the inside songs, but across the whole city there were no other birds trilling or calling. The air above the roofs was silent. Then, some distance away, far beyond the walls of the city, a single raven was heard to make its croaking cry. Instantly, a flock of hunters arose, flying out from the steeple's other windows and shooting across the sky like a flight of arrows, hunting that one sable-feathered singer. Ravens blacker than their prey, the hunters had beaks of iron, and smoke came from their mouths as if a kind of silent cry of its own. They fell upon the lone bird and ripped it to pieces, scattering the feathers and bringing back flesh and bones in their jagged metal beaks.

"The Silent Hand," Prentice whispered, as if fearful these dream creatures would hear him and rip him apart as well. He had seen the agents of the Inquisition as birds in visions before, and he had seen them as ravens, especially. What did it mean that they had hunted one like one of their own? The returning predators circled the steeple, which Prentice now saw stood in the midst of a citadel. Inside the walls of the citadel, the bailey and yards were filled with blood, as if the whole fortification were a dire cauldron, brewing horror. In a long stream across the sky, the flight of ravens moved back and forth, each one bearing a freshly torn strip of dripping flesh in its beak. They dropped the pieces into the fortress draught. Following them across the sky, Prentice looked up to see that the steeple itself was topped not with the cross of a church—for the steeple's cross had been broken away at some point—and instead, a vast golden eagle perched there, a statue of a heraldic creature. The sight of it reminded Prentice of the dragonfly that had perched at the far western end of the Murr, ancient and mystical. But where the dragonfly had rested on an obelisk of mighty stone, this eagle seemed barely supported by this twisted wooden edifice. It was as if the weight of the gold was crushing the steeple, twisting it slowly until it must surely collapse.

"This is Denay," he said to himself, recognizing the city by the eagle and realizing the meaning of the symbolism. "But what is this pit beneath it?"

He looked back into the steeple, and suddenly the vast shaft beneath him seemed shallow and not so frightening. It was now a mere vault, more walls than space, and the walls crowded in. It was stacked with piles of gold and silver that were all stained with blood and corroded, even though true gold could never corrode.

"This is not the real pit beneath the eagle," a voice echoed from somewhere far off. "That one is not here."

"Then where is it?" Prentice asked, knowing it was the question he was supposed to ask without understanding why. Quite suddenly, his vision flew across the sky to a place he knew was south of the city. The knowing made him almost smirk—dreams and visions were often like that, it seemed. Any wry amusement he might have felt was shorn away, however, like the clipped wings of a bird as his vision suddenly dove terrifyingly downward into a true pit so vast and deep that for a moment he imagined it might pierce the earth to the very depth of hell itself. Indeed, as he fell, he saw that this was a prison like unto hell, for on all its descending walls were men and women, chained in place, their naked bodies torn and bleeding.

The ravens flew down beside him as he fell and pecked at the prisoners, tearing off strips to fly away with and feed the eagle standard's cauldron. The deeper the pit went, the older the prisoners were, until the ones near the bottom were ancient—wizened, and white-haired. They begged the ravens for food or drink but were given nothing. Many of them wept. At the very bottom of the pit were two men—one chained to the wall, his white hair shaggy around him like a regal lion's mane, not completely dissimilar to the flowing mane of the lion angel that Prentice so often saw in visions. It was patchy, though, with pieces torn out and stained by marks of bloody torture. This spray of hair was nothing so glorious as the angel's, for all that it was like a mane.

The other man at the bottom of the pit was naked as well, drenched in blood, and he read from a stack of tomes, each one bound in human skin. The fellow sat upon a rock with another book on his bare knees, where he wrote fresh words with a quill dipped in the blood upon his body.

"Dear God, who is this?" Prentice whispered, but no angel's voice brought any word. He waited, watching as some of the ravens dipped their wings to circle down and land upon the bloody scribe's shoulders. They whispered in the man's ears, and he directed them to which martyrs they should feed upon. When he spoke, it was with many voices at once, all of them sounding the same even as they were different.

"He is Sanguine," the maned man chained to the wall said, his voice strong but echoing, as if from an impossible distance. "He is the last of a line that has been bloody from the first, all different and all him. Jailer though he is, his will alone has not forged this prison. He has never forsaken its purposes and only ever made it deeper and stronger. I am not the first prophet he betrayed, nor the last, but I am the last to look him in the eye as he plunged the dagger."

At that, the man Sanguine stood from his rock, carrying his book in one hand, quill in the other. Suddenly the quill's nib had swollen in size and changed until it was the shape of the bone knives the serpent witches of the Redlanders used for their sacrifices in the far west. He stabbed the chained prisoner and wrote some more with the blood he drew. Prentice looked over the vile scribe's shoulder and realized that the book he was writing into was the scripture itself.

The merciless preachers of mercy, he thought, remembering the fey name for the militant churchmen who taught the gospel of Christ but picked and chose which of its teachings they obeyed. He remembered also the many times he himself had received similar treatment at the hands of sacrists and ecclesiarches. This was the blood that had dripped from the eagle's wings at the feast in the Bridgetown great hall the night Prentice had been poisoned in the duel. This was the blood that poisoned the whole Grand Kingdom, filling the symbolic cauldron-citadel in the middle of Denay, the revered and ancient capital. This was blood as the Redlanders knew it—brutally shed and used for power.

"He thinks he can overwrite the words of the Almighty and force God to do what *he* wants," the ancient prisoner said. "The prophets can read the words beneath the blood, so he feeds them to the ravens first and they, in turn, feed the eagle."

"He must be stopped," Prentice said, and cold fell upon him like the still air of a pure night frost. It swirled from within his memories and the core of his heart. It was akin to the fury he knew in battle, but there was no storm in it, not yet. It had to be stirred up somehow.

"Would you stop it?" the prisoner asked, and as he did, a raven came and pecked at his eye. Trapped in his chains, he had no choice but to endure the assault. Prentice wanted to beat the bird off, but the vision would not allow him. What was happening to this man had happened too long ago.

"This *must* end," Prentice breathed, shivering with cold and frustration. Suddenly Sanguine looked up from his book straight at him but apparently not seeing him. Pointing with his bloody quill, Sanguine directed a raven toward Prentice, but though the bird circled him, it could not find him, pecking only at the air nearby. At its frustrated cawing, a bluebird fluttered down and landed on Prentice's head, singing loudly. The raven tried to follow the song and others came to help, but still Prentice was beyond their assaults.

"He seeks you out, but he cannot find you because he is looking for my scion—a lion of my blood—and you are not and never were," the prisoner said. "The lioness has confused him. She is not the lord of the pride he has feared to hear roaring in the night, and so he thinks himself safe. He is patient with his ravens, but they are running out of time. If you had been of my line, he would have known you, and the ravens would long ago have brought the pride here in chains. But he is fooled. They all have been, thinking the words they write are truth and not the veil they have pulled over all eyes to blind the world—blinded leaders leading the willfully blind."

Kreff, Prentice thought, remembering how significant sight was to the fey as well. The Wind Rising folk of the mountains sought to stay hidden from all, and it seemed that was something the Inquisition wanted as well. Would it serve Prentice now that he was *kreff enkreffra*—the blind man who was permitted to see?

The prisoner in chains drew a sighing breath, as if the exertion of speaking was almost too much for him. Prentice could well believe it.

"Because he does not understand you, he cannot quite find you, though he knows where you are. You are the gryphon, the impossible lion that was made, not born. You have the claws of a lion, but you have a beak like theirs for you were almost one of them, and they cannot fathom it. You know the taste of blood as they do but never have longed for it, and they cannot forget their thirst. You have given the lioness her roar, but your cry is the cry of the hunting hawk, the voice heard in the eyries too high for mortal men, thin and icy. You see and speak with the rising wind, and your wrath falls from heaven, cold and unyielding. None of these secrets are understood by Sanguine, even though his books hold them all. He is too fixated on overwriting them. He has not even read them for many of his lifetimes."

The writings destroyed by the Inquisition, Prentice thought. *The secrets they have hidden. How do we recover them?*

He had a sudden hope the vision would reveal something more of what had been lost.

CHAPTER 11

The prisoner stopped speaking and hung his head. His shoulders began to heave, and Prentice wondered if he was weeping. Soon, though, he shrugged and, as if it were a cloak or shawl, the mane came away from his head and shoulders, falling to the ground. His scalp underneath was roughly shorn and broken, and his limbs twisted and swelled with the memory of brutalities inflicted. He was like a figure of the Biblical hero Samson, but with no power to topple the temple, not by those broken limbs. That was a burden he was forced to bequeath to the future. The prisoner looked at Sanguine, whose head was bent as he began to scribble again. Prentice watched, and the murderous scribe tore out a page and screwed it up hatefully, as if it were something his scribbling could not blot out. Prentice longed to know what was written on that crumpled piece of paper, but it burned to ash as soon as it struck the ground.

"I told him just before he plunged the final knife that if he did not relent of his course, the mercies of this prison would come upon him, overthrow him and all his works with him," the chained man croaked, his voice rasping from his throat. "He boasted that he was the master of the cells, master of the prison, of the vault one step above the pit. The keys of hell were in his hand, he said, and he thought to open the gate to throw me in. I told him that one who had known his hospitality, a lion like unto myself, would come, and when he did, this prison would collapse upon Sanguine and all his ilk. That is why none who are brought to him here are ever allowed to escape alive, so that none may return and fulfill my words. It has become his strongest law, and as each of him has followed, they have only reinforced it. All who come to this ancient vault suffer, and all who do so die here. Only the birds fly free, for a time, and even they die here eventually. He has even spread lesser pits across the land to feed this first one, and by that hubris he is to be undone."

The prisoner paused and sighed, his chest and limbs shuddering with the effort. After a moment, he continued.

"You have been where I am now—not here but hanging from these chains all the same. You have hung, the bite of fire and iron in your flesh. You have felt the mercy of the merciless and lived. Sanguine has not relented, not once in all the years of all his lifetimes, and while he goes into hell himself with his head held high, expecting nothing but the Almighty's reward, in this pit they have added fresh sin to old, heaped it upon itself until the cry for justice echoes out of the mouth of the earth all the way to Heaven—over the mountains, the rivers, the seas, and the forests and plains."

The shorn and chained man stopped speaking and then there was nothing remotely regal about him, not anymore. He looked as any other who had been tortured to the brink of death might, all mortal pretense of greatness or glory stripped away. Just another man in agony and praying for relief, like Christ upon the cross. Prentice knew it on sight and had a sudden affinity he hadn't expected. If this was a man, or the visionary remnant of a man, speaking to him from a place in the past where he was suffering the same kind of tortures that Prentice had suffered—the same mercies of the merciless—then Prentice felt an overwhelming fraternity with him.

Who else in all the world could understand me like this man? he thought, and the tortured figure smiled at him, nodding as if the strange prophet could hear the words. Prentice was seized with a sudden desire to end his suffering, to somehow free all the prisoners and abolish this prison pit. He looked upward and saw far above the inside of the steeple where his vision had begun. Now as he looked, he could see a central pillar that ran from the very floor of this pit all the way up to the top of the spire. Just as the steeple itself was twisted under the golden eagle, so the pillar was likewise bent and corkscrewed in places, shored up with boards and off-cuts. Looking at it, Prentice thought he might be able to make it topple with one strong push, and so he was seized with a sudden desire to do just that. He put both of his hands on the base of the pillar, but before he could exert any force, the ancient prisoner spoke once more.

"Would you be like Samson, bringing the temple down on their heads?"

"Isn't that why I am here, to tear this foul place down?" Prentice asked over his shoulder. He thought of his lost health and strength, the weakness that had driven him to be in bed to dream like this in the first place. "Am I not shackled with weakness?"

"Are you? Is your life so bereft that you would spend the rest of it to push the pillar? Are there no other duties before you yet?"

Prentice snapped his head around, and an angry groan sounded from deep in his chest.

How much more duty would you lay upon me? he wanted to demand, but the bitter reality of the broken man's condition stopped the words in his mouth. How did one argue against such certitude, against a man or woman who could hold to their righteous purpose in the face of such treatment. He remembered his own interrogation, hanging from a chain in the ceiling of a dark cell, fire and knife and other tortures ravaging his flesh. At first, he had resisted, even thinking to trick his tormentors with clever lies to make them look foolish. Then the Inquisitor had come with his healer nun who had not one dram of mercy in her cold blood, and they had tortured him until he wept and begged, soiling himself and praying just for some water to wet his cracked lips. His mouth was the only thing they left mostly unabused, for how can a man confess his heresy if he cannot speak? They had broken him, and only the call of a crusade had stopped Prentice from affirming any lies or truths they wanted of him just to end the agony.

Then my blood would have been added to all the rest that Sanguine uses to write his lies, he thought.

"It's alright," the prisoner said comfortingly. "As you would not want my life, so I do not envy you yours. Judge the man by the burden, not by the burden his neighbor carries, for none of us could carry the true burden. That is already borne for us all."

Prentice looked down, ashamed that he had thought to vent his resentment on this man of preternatural calm. As he did, his eyes fell upon the discarded mane where it had landed and he saw that it glowed a fresh white, as if dropping it had somehow cleaned it, made it like new.

"*That* is why you are here," the prisoner said, fixing Prentice with his one good eye. "You must take that up for the Lioness and carry it to her. If you leave it here, she will never escape this pit. Only when you bring it to her can the temple be torn down."

Looking down on the fallen mane, Prentice felt a sudden longing to preserve it, both for this man lost in ancient years and for his liege somewhere back in the mundane world where he hoped his body was still sleeping and regaining its strength. He looked up and felt his longing to break the pillar again, then bent to fetch the regal shock of white.

"Be warned," the prophet said to him immediately, nodding at the scribbling Sanguine. "When you take it, he will know, and he will send his ravens to hound your every step until you come here bearing my mane, now the mane of the Lioness. He will begin to realize his mistake. If you can be stopped, he will stop you. He will take love, life, and hope from you, slash you and burn you afresh until only ashes remain. You must be ready to be the last, to be the Ashen Man unto the end, for it may *be* your end. There is nothing he will not destroy to fulfil his promise to hold the eagle aloft over all others."

Prentice looked at the scribe of gore and hate once more, and he felt his teeth clench in resolution.

"Only once you have broken the power of Sanguine will you be able to turn your attention to the eagle and his golden standard. His banner pole is the pillar, and the pillar is rotted by the blood at its base, but you will have to swim that blood to reach it. If the ravens, all the birds, are yet roosting in this vault, they will stir up their cauldron of crimson, redder than the far land I never even knew, and you will be drowned. Return to their cells and then to this pit. Put their roost to the torch. Only then will the golden eagle fall. Only then will he drown, choking on the blood."

Prentice nodded, accepting the warning even though he hardly began to understand it, and reached for the mane regardless. He had suffered too much already in his life to balk at the final call to duty.

"You are so willing to be Samson, but learn from his failures," the chained prophet warned him. "You need not make his mistake."

Samson's mistake? Prentice wondered, trying to remember what he had been taught of the ancient scriptural hero. Realizing he actually knew little of the figure, he nonetheless still put his hand upon the mane. He would puzzle out the warning when he awoke. Come warning or wounding, he knew he had to take this mantle out of here for his liege's sake. He owed her at least that much. Immediately that Prentice's fingers grasped the thick, glorious skein of hair, Sanguine's head snapped up and he began summoning birds—bluebird, ravens, and others, including a heron, weighed down with chains of gold. Prentice wondered if they were about to attack him when from above, he heard a forlorn gasp. Looking up, he saw a thin figure in a dark robe standing on one of the crossbeams, swaying and nearly falling into the pit. Before he could decide who it was or what they might represent, the figure fled, and the bluebird lifted up from Prentice's scalp, chasing the fugitive.

"That pitiful fellow," the prophet said sadly. "He glimpsed the inside of the pit once and fled in terror. They have hounded him ever since."

The chained prophet's expression became a calm smile, as of one who has accomplished a great work and looks forward to resting.

"Now you have heard all the remaining words of the first and last prophet king to sit the throne in Denay," he said. "My mantle is in your hands until the end. Make yourself ready, for as they hunted and hated me, as they did the one who came before us all, so they will hate you and you will know no more rest until the race is run. They will try to confuse with their cries and to steal my mane, my crown, from your hands. But that is not the end; it is only the starting trumpet. They will try to break you, to kill you, and they will use blood to do it. Remember that the only blood that ever was worthy has already been shed. Trust to that and fear no other."

Then the prophet sighed and hung his head. Mane in hand, Prentice reached out for the pillar with the other, determined not to lose this chance. Perhaps it was rotten enough that he could do the task with one hand. He strained to reach it, one hand out, the other entangled. Then suddenly, the air around him was chill again and he was straining toward the bedroom wall, half out of his bed. Behind him, his other hand was knotted in the bedsheets. He stopped straining, drew in a cold breath, and noticed that it was not painful. It seemed so long since he had been able to do that. Realizing he was awake, he snatched the bed covers from the mattress and wrapped them around his shoulders. He would not risk another chill upon his chest now.

I have a race to run and an ancient temple to tear down, he thought. *And a lesson to learn.*

The sheer complexity of the vision threatened to overwhelm him for a moment. He tried to remember each little detail, scrutinizing his memories the way the neophytes above him scrutinized all faces, looking for the tiny clues that told true from false.

"Make ready to run the race?" he wondered out loud, and immediately he looked down on his arms and chest under the blanket. Not since his days as a convict had he been so lean, and his lost strength reminded him of how unready he was to walk, let alone run.

Too bad, he thought. *This is the fight. This is the race. Gather your strength and put one foot after the other until the finish. What else is there?*

He nodded at his own harsh, unspoken admonition. What was his next step then? Surely it would be to untangle the mysteries of his vision. Where was this pit? Was it a real place or only figurative? Was Sanguine a real person or a spiritual figure, like the multi-headed serpent or the birds? Was there some revelation in his dream about how to spy out skin-thieves? And what of Daven Marcus—the golden eagle? Where were his Dragons of Denay in the vision? Their absence surprised Prentice suddenly. Perhaps they were irrelevant.

I must find Whilte and discuss all this with him, he thought, and stood from the bed. *Solft too. Between us we should be able to puzzle out the symbols and the meanings. At the very least, Whilte should be able to tell me what Samson's mistake was, so I don't make it myself.*

CHAPTER 12

"**I**n bed three days?"

"Almost," Lady Dalflitch confirmed as Prentice sat at the main table, eating fish soup with a hunk of dark sourdough. He had indeed been in his bed for three days, and he wondered how much of that time had been in his dream.

"Where is her grace?" he asked after another spoonful of the nourishing meal. There was a salty smokiness to the fish that enriched the flavor wonderfully.

"Archduchess Amelia is at Norgate Bastion," the seneschal told him, speaking formally but with a softer tone than normal, as if to an old friend. Prentice scraped his spoon across the bottom of his bowl and then dipped the last of his bread in, soaking up the dregs.

"You could have more, if you wished, Knight Commander," Dalflitch said calmly without looking up from her documents. "We have plenty. A fishmock sold one of the neophytes an especially fine batch of smoked trout. We've all been enjoying it these last two days. You missed the fillets, but personally I find the soup made from the bones to be the better flavor. It brings the full smoke out..."

Prentice nodded, only half paying attention to the lady seneschal's comments, his mind still sifting through the imagery of his dream and enjoying the simple pleasure of breaking his fast.

"Trout is a river fish," he muttered, almost without realizing he was doing it. River fish, smoke, and salt—the three notions interacted in his mind like the tumblers of a combination lock. "Inxyphos did not have to come from the sea."

He paused, staring at his empty bowl.

"I'm sorry, My Lord, I didn't quite hear you," Dalflitch said politely.

"You have your ear to the dockside gossip, My Lady," Prentice told her, letting his thoughts form themselves for a moment, trusting that the astute Dalflitch would catch any profitable meaning in them. "What word of the smokers? What was it you said they were called—fishmocks?"

"That's the local name for them," Dalflitch agreed. "You find their little salt-and-smokehouse dens all over the docks. Of course, after the kingslayer's visitors, the ones on the east side are all smashed, along with everything else the pirates could get their vicious hands on. But the ones on the west side of the great bridges remain—Bell's Hummock, Piers, and Salthatch, especially. That's the island where they are most thickly congregated, as the name likely tells you. They're doing a runaway trade I would expect."

Prentice nodded. "Bluebird would have known the Usurper was bringing his fleet upriver and would want a spot that could survive against invasion. He would want to be west of the great bridges where they would be smoking *trout* and other river fish."

Dalflitch set aside her quill and looked at him directly.

"What is this word of Bluebird, Baron?"

"Inxyphos...when he attacked in the cathedral square...his burlap cloak smelled of salt and smoke. I assumed he must have come from the ocean," Prentice explained, a grim smile coming slowly to his lips. "But trout is a river fish."

"What have trout to do with the bear man?" Dalflitch pressed. Prentice merely gave her a patient stare, as of a teacher waiting for a student to work out the question for themselves.

Suddenly, her dark eyes went wide. "They hid him in a smokehouse," she all but shouted before regathering her aplomb. "Right on the docks, straight from boat to lair unseen by prying eyes. It makes perfect sense. Oh, curse me for a fool, I should have puzzled that much out. I have been so confident of my informers on the river that I let my suspicions sleep when they should have been watchful."

"You need not chastise yourself, My Lady," Prentice told her. "After all, I am the one who smelled the smoke and salt, not you." Prentice was more than happy to accept the blame, but Dalflitch waved him away with a dismissive tut.

"Fie on that," she responded sternly. "It is my responsibility. Would you let our militia be ambushed in the field and excuse yourself for the lapse, Knight Commander?"

Prentice did not bother to answer the question, only giving a wry smile and shaking his head.

"We will have a new trail for the neophytes to hunt in the coming days," Dalflitch went on. "My thanks, Baron. I was becoming most frustrated, sitting like a black widow in my web and finding no flies coming to be trapped and devoured."

"Such a pleasant image," Prentice told her, and she bowed her head as if receiving a compliment. "I appreciate your thanks also, My Lady, but you may find that whatever lair by the water our enemy has had, it is destroyed now in the invasion, or else abandoned."

The Bluebird is surely that cunning, at least, he thought but did not add.

"True, but unless the Inquisition's agents are all invisible and silent as the grave, they will have left some sense of their passing, and our girls from the riverside will find the footprints, I promise you." Dalflitch leaned in closely to whisper. "We are stern with our underling retainers, you and I both, Knight Commander. But in truth, these ladies of her grace's chamber are canny little minxes one and all. We have put knives in the hands of maids and turned dormice into vixens—cunning indeed."

She sat back again.

"Now that the Lions have taken the battle to the Usurper, it is the responsibility of the Lace Fangs to see that the town is secure behind them."

Dalflitch's resolution comforted Prentice more than he would have credited. He had so many problems to watch for that any one he could surrender to another set of competent hands was a blessing.

"The fireships will be sent out?" Prentice asked, turning his mind to the strategic situation and immediately getting a sense of misgiving. The point of the fireships had been to rush the cannons ashore. Leaving it for the three days while he had been abed would have been anything other than a rush.

"They were sent the past two nights and yesterday as well, though there was some rain the last morning that suppressed them," Dalflitch explained. "*This* morning, they are making their raid. The Lion Banner marches out even now."

"Now?" Prentice repeated and chewed his lip a moment as he considered what he was hearing. "Why the delay? The fireships were to rush the Usurper's cannons ashore. Three days is hardly a rush."

"The ships worked their confusion too well," Dalflitch explained. "Yesterday morning, before dawn, the third boat—Marquis Farringdon tried five in all—was sent down the river, and by fluke it landed exactly up against Lazy Farmers Pier itself. Of course, the stones had nothing to fear from flames, but it meant that any unloading was forced to stop. So, far from hastening the Bronze Dragons ashore, that fireship delayed the whole process. Then the rain came for the main of the day and nothing more could be done until last night."

Prentice did not like that report. The whole point of the fireships had been to force the landing into a haste-filled rush. Three days was not haste. He stood from the table.

"If you will, My Lady, I will go watch the assault with the archduchess."

Lady Dalflitch gave a polite nod, but Prentice had already turned away, leaving the room to fetch a winter cloak and make for Norgate.

Chapter 13

T he wind on the roof of Norgate Bastion snatched the door out of Prentice's hand and slammed it against the stone wall as he emerged onto the battlements. Militiamen standing watch started and looked ready for danger but relaxed upon seeing their knight commander. Archduchess Amelia smiled as her eyes met his.

It is good to see you out of bed, Prentice, she thought, pleased to note he was in a warm cloak that swirled around him as he strode toward her and bowed. Wearing their own warm, hooded cloaks to protect against the fine sprays of misting rain that blew across the rooftop from time to time, the three women—Amelia and two bodyguards—returned his respects with gestures of their own. The grey sky had pressed down all morning, threatening another winter storm, and Amelia had no intention of being caught unprepared should it burst upon them.

"I am glad you could join me, Knight Commander," she said. "I had hoped Lady Penelope would be here, too, but she has spurned my invitation it seems."

"Yet again, Your Grace?" Prentice asked with a rhetorical tone, and the archduchess gave a dismissive sniff.

"Yet again, My Lord," she agreed and looked back out over the rampart at the battle unfolding. "Are you well after your sleep?"

"Mostly, I think, Your Grace. Thank you for your concern."

Amelia nodded politely and turned her attention eastward. Presuming upon his rank, Prentice stepped up beside her and together they looked down on half the Western Reach's army, arrayed in the field and marching towards Lazy Farmers and the Usurper's growing encampment.

"After what feels like too many years, we are finally facing the kingslayer on the field of battle," Amelia said with determination but also an undernote of concern, which she was sure Prentice would detect. Daven Marcus, the Usurper—the monster who had haunted their dreams for so long—was now within their reach. Or they were within his. In Amelia's mind it was hard not to imagine him as a monster, welcoming every battle, devouring children and slaughtering yeomen-folk for his own pleasure.

"You feel some nervousness, Your Grace?" Prentice asked quietly.

Amelia shook her head, then paused and looked down at her own feet. When she looked up again, she felt her smile broaden.

"Yes, Prentice," she admitted simply. "It embarrasses me to say but, indeed, I am nervous. I stood on the wagons at Aubrey while Markas held the shield over my head and the crossbow bolts fell like iron rain. Here I am as safe as ever I have been on a battlefield, and yet still I feel nervous. Am I so timid a creature, or is it pregnancy? Fear for my unborn?"

Prentice looked her in the eye and returned her smile.

"I have seen you frightened to your core, Your Grace," he said. "I have seen you half-starved and brutalized. Never in all the years we have known each other have I seen you as timid, if you will permit me to say. Your nervousness is natural—every battle brings its fears. Also, Your Grace, your beloved husband marches into the fight. It is enough to undermine any spouse's confidence, I would think."

Amelia let his encouragement enter her for a moment to console her thoughts. And it was true—the main of her nervousness was, in fact, for Farringdon. She had great confidence in the Lions, but even in victory a skilled man-at-arms could be injured or killed. Battle was ever that way, and she had more than enough experience of such things to know it.

"Thank you, Prentice," she said at last, and reaching out, touched his arm in a gesture of appreciation. Then she straightened herself, adjusting her stance for the presence of her growing belly and turned her attention once more to the battlefield. "Counsel me, Knight Commander. Tell me what you see as our forces march to war."

Her eyes flicked back to her bodyguards for a moment.

"Lady Elizabeth? Lady Agatha? Join us," she said. "The baron ever encourages many voices in counsels such as this. It will be good experience for you."

The two ladies with their lace half masks stepped up as instructed. Each curtseyed to Prentice, and he returned the courtesy with a nod.

"We see an army marching to battle. Tell us, My Lord, what do you see?"

Prentice's professional gaze swept the field below.

"Lord Farringdon has divided the Lion Banner into columns, five cohorts each," he began. "See, they are sweeping out in a wide arc and will merge soon to form a line north to south, facing the east. He has his lancers in the center because he plans for them to ride straight for the enemy cannons to take them from the battle before they can do too much damage."

Prentice pointed from the Lions to the enemy camp, still little more than a clutch of tents pressed up against the woodland a league or so distant. To one side of the encampment were the three Bronze Dragons that would be the knight captain's prime target.

"Did we send some Dragons to the bottom of the river with our burning boats, Your Grace?" Prentice asked Amelia, eyes still on the enemy.

"Not that we heard, My Lord," Amelia told him. It had been something of a disappointment for Farringdon that his plan had not resulted in any sunken cannon boats, for all that the burning craft had set the fleet in the river to chaos. Even now, looking downriver, the once mighty collection of vessels remained diminished and scattered. "It would have been good to set some aflame, but Farringdon said it had been an optimistic hope at best. He decided that we had achieved whatever we could with fireships and that this morning's break in the rain was the best moment to deliver a harsh blow to Daven Marcus' army."

Prentice nodded, momentarily scratching at his beard.

"My Lord, if I may?" Lady Elizabeth asked, pausing first to look to Amelia for permission to speak. The archduchess nodded and the lady-in-waiting continued with her question. "I see the Lions' war wagons down in front of Norgate, but they are lagging behind. Will they not miss the battle this way?

Prentice took a moment to look to his left to see for himself. In front of Norgate was a series of ditches and raised embankments, not to mention rows of sharpened spikes. The bastion's garrison had spent weeks digging those extra defenses, and two of the White Lions' cannons were emplaced in earthen bulwarks there. Just past those additional defenses, four battle wagons were now rolling slowly in a line along the edge of the road that turned right toward the east, accompanied by a column of five cohorts—half the reserves Farringdon had "borrowed" from the Gryphon Banner Company. The other five cohorts were waiting across the bridge on Loncastel Island behind them. Farringdon had prepared himself a strong force. The knight captain planned to deliver a "harsh" blow to the Usurper, indeed. Prentice nodded as he watched the force on the road for a moment and then turned back with a smile.

"My Lady, those wagons and the militiamen with them will not be joining the battle proper," he told Agatha. "They are a part of Marquis Knight Captain Farringdon's thoroughness. They are Gryphons and are being set to watch the path back to Norgate in case the battle turns against him."

CHAPTER 14

"Does the knight captain not think we can win?" Amelia asked, shocked by the notion that Farringdon might lack basic confidence in his plan. He had shared no such uncertainty with her.

Prentice shook his head. "This is not a battle to the death, Your Grace," he explained readily. "This is a raid, although I will concede the knight captain is 'raiding' in force. All the same, unless the outcome is overwhelmingly successful, say if Daven Marcus is captured and his army put to full flight, then the Lion Banner will be returning to Norgate. The knight captain has set wagons and a rearguard to make certain his return path is secure."

"How is a raid different to any other battle?" Lady Agatha asked.

"A raid is to seize or destroy something in particular, in this case those Bronze Dragons and the pier," Prentice explained. "When that is done, they will retreat to safety, although as I look at it, I wonder why we bother. The Lion Banner Company alone outnumbers the force the Usurper has in the field..." Prentice's voice trailed off as his eyes searched from the wagons below, up the Great Bridge Road northward, then back to the tents of Daven Marcus's camp.

"You see that the knight captain has left his cannons behind in front of the bastion here," he said slowly, as if his thoughts were already on something other than his words. "They would move too slowly and would be unable to retreat...three days? No...there is no possible way that is three days' disembarking."

"My Lord?" Agatha asked, clearly thinking that she was supposed to be following the knight commander's disjointed explanation.

"What is it, Prentice?" Amelia pressed, recognizing his thoughtful tone. He had seen something, a flaw in the plan. Her nervousness flared higher. What was it? "What's wrong?"

"What have our scouts told us of the fields straight north of us, Your Grace?" Prentice replied.

Amelia blinked in surprise and looked to the empty ground directly ahead of them, thick with winter grass and weeds. No crops had been planted there for more than a year thanks to the sieges. Even so, the green sward was deep, some of the grasses almost the height of a man. Threading the middle of that lush carpet, Great North Road snaked away to the horizon, disappearing eventually into the sweeping fields. A small ridge of knolls was the only other feature she could see off to her left, perhaps a league to the northwest. It was crested by low scrub that likely once had been a good source of firewood for the poorer folk of Bridgetown.

"I don't know that we scouted any of the north ground, Prentice," Amelia told him nervously, scanning the seemingly empty vastness. "Not since Duke Robant's force was driven off. It's just open ground, uninhabited."

"And trodden down," he said flatly, pointing up the road to the spot Robant's army had had their camp—the siege the White Lions had broken in the late summer. "We should have camped two or three cohorts on that rise from the day we arrived!"

Trodden down? Amelia wondered, and she looked northward again. Sure enough, she could make out a line through the grasses that came from the Great North Road, and just at the edge of her vision swept a curve all the way behind that row of knolls—a long trail of half-crushed growth. Amelia realized that she had been accustomed to seeing the wreckage of the old enemy camp whenever she had looked that direction from Norgate—broken ground picked clean of any booty but otherwise full of smashed tent poles, churned earth, and other detritus. So used to the sight of the destruction was she that the new path had merged into the damaged ground unnoticed.

"What is the danger, Prentice?" she asked. "Surely that little portion of raised ground is not enough to hide an army."

"It does not have to be, Your Grace. It is defilade enough," he responded tersely, not bothering to explain more fully than that. Turning away and calling over his shoulder, his words were punctuated by the sound of the first cannon shot echoing through the air. "The Usurper does not have to hide an entire army, only the rest of the Dragons in defilade—out of sight of our own guns. But if he has managed to bring the Dragons that close, what else has been hidden from our eyes?"

Amelia was barely absorbing Prentice's words when she realized that the cannon blast had not come from the east where the lancers were now charging toward the three Bronze Dragons and the tiny force that had arrayed to protect them.

The north? she thought, looking toward the scrub-topped rise and seeing a column of smoke rising in the air from behind it. Even as she looked, a second shot boomed and more smoke arose. It occurred to her to wonder what their target was, but almost immediately she knew. A crash of wood and stone echoed up from below, and Amelia looked to see that one of the battle wagons had been turned to matchwood by a direct hit. A third shot rang out, and while she watched, the enormous stone ball skipped slightly over the grass and smashed like the hammer of God himself into the earthworks in front of Norgate. Mud fountained into the air, followed by shouts of alarm and confusion.

Even before Prentice had reached the stairs, two more shots had fired from behind the hills, one flying very wide to the west, while the other clipped the back of a war wagon, sending it tumbling over the field like the thrown toy of a giant infant. Men were scattered from the mobile fortification, bodies flying or diving for cover. Many fell to the ground to move no more.

"What is happening, Your Grace?" Elizabeth asked, her tone reflecting Amelia's own unnerved state.

"The enemy has ambushed us, My Lady," Amelia told her through gritted teeth. "Knight Commander Ash is going to rally the reserve and counterattack."

"You are so sure?" the Lace Fang asked, apparently surprised at her liege's battle sense.

"There are Bronze Dragons on the other side of that little ridge," Amelia explained. "Somehow Daven Marcus has fooled us and brought his monsters closer than we ever suspected possible."

"Are we in danger?"

"Very much so," Amelia said with certainty. She gripped herself inwardly as memories arose of the last time she had stood on a battlefield while the cannons of Denay rained shot upon her army. Despite her best efforts, she felt her fingers begin to tremble and quickly hid them in her sleeves so that no one would see. The Lioness must not seem afraid.

"Should we go, Your Grace?" Lady Elizabeth asked.

Amelia shot her a suspicious glance but was comforted to see not fear but resolve in the Lace Fang's eyes. She was not asking to flee. She was looking to her liege's safety. "Not just yet, My Lady," Amelia forced herself to say, resisting the demands of her own terrors. She remembered the way in which the Bronze Dragons had been captured during their retreat from Aubrey after the Red Sky when Lord Ironworth had ambushed them with shots from a hill in a similar fashion. Once the battle was joined, it had not been too difficult, comparatively, for a force to capture the cannons and remove them from the battle.

"As we just learned, Knight Captain Farringdon has left forces behind to protect against precisely this kind of action," Amelia told her ladies. "Those reserves will enter the fight, and with so many, even against the fire of the Dragons of Denay, they will take the bronze monsters out of the battle soon enough."

Amelia was pleased she could keep her voice steady as she spoke. However much her confidence was real or just for show, she knew that the next hour or so would be bloody until the reserves captured those cannons. At least that seemed likely, though in fact, as she looked on the changing situation in front of Norgate, Amelia found her confidence in victory deepening. They had captured the cannons under Ironworth's command years ago, and they were sure to do the same with these. In that previous battle, the Knight Marshal of Denay had sought to protect his guns with knights ahorse, and the archduchess now wondered why Daven Marcus had not done the same this day. As she had said to Prentice, there was no way that an army could be hiding behind the ridge. It simply was not large enough. Moreover, they would have revealed themselves by their tracks. The cannons' passage had gone unnoticed, but a large force of knights would have left an unmistakable trail behind them.

"I will wait here awhile," she told her attendants. "It would not be seemly to flee if a victory is imminent."

Looking back to the east, Amelia could see Farringdon's large force was already pressing up to the woods, and any moment the three Dragons there would be captured. Then the whole raiding force would be able to turn back to finish off the guns behind the ridge "in defilade," as the knight commander described it. The battle was almost over already. Two more stone balls flew through the air, one ramming itself into the earthworks, gouging a long trough through the dirt, stopping just short of a Lions' cannon. The other struck a patch of harder ground and skipped like a rock across a pond, bouncing up and past Norgate to splash into the Murr behind them.

"We are not fully safe just yet, though," she told her ladies, affecting a casual smile she did not feel. "Perhaps we will withdraw to Loncastel's bridge keep for safety."

The Lace Fangs nodded, and the trio were turning toward the stairs when a long horn blast echoed on the wind. Knowing that her own forces did not use horns for signaling, Amelia turned back to the battlefield, expecting something more from Daven Marcus.

"Horsemen, I think, Your Grace," Agatha said, and she pointed up the road to the horizon. A large smudge in the distance was rapidly growing, approaching down the Great Bridge Road.

"His knights," Amelia muttered, and she shook her head. Surely, they were coming from too far away. In the time that it took them to arrive, the reserve cohorts in front of Norgate would have crossed the distance to the Dragons hiding behind their ridge. For all that the cannons had wreaked destruction on the war wagons, the men-at-arms were already rallying and beginning to march toward that fire. Knowing what her husband had told her about cannons and matchlocks, the way their shots arced through the air like arrows when fired over a long distance, Amelia was even comforted to see her militia on the march. They would be able to get "under" the shots of the Bronze Dragons, the cannons unable to tip back enough to shorten their looping fire. For all the risk to herself, Amelia still felt confident that her two commanders had the better of Daven Marcus's plans. Prentice was already running to summon the rest of the reserve across the bridge, she was sure of that. Word would be being sent to Farringdon, even if he had not seen the coming men ahorse. Amelia felt herself smile, and then the monster Usurper performed a magick trick and her stomach fell.

"Where did they bloody come from?" Lady Elizabeth demanded, all pretense of formal manners falling away in her shock.

Down in the long grasses, the untrodden ground between Norgate and the low ridge that Prentice had called a defilade, a mass of several hundred figures had simply appeared. In truth, they had been hiding in the long growth and had just now stood up.

"Are they bear men?" Agatha asked, her voice full of horror.

For a moment it seemed to Amelia that they must be, but as she looked closer, she realized that the force that had simply arrived on the battlefield appeared to be made up of mortals, each one wearing a heavy coat and a large hat that looked to be of some dark fur. Nevertheless, their human faces were clear. Far from rampaging with inhuman claws or fangs, these new men-at-arms were carrying weapons. The advancing Gryphon militiamen paused a moment in their march, no doubt shocked by the sudden appearance of this new enemy force. Then the front rank of foes ran through the long grass a short distance, hefting something in each of their hands, throwing them through the air. Looking like children playing pitch and toss at an extreme distance, a flock of black globes arced forward, and the throwers dropped back under the grass, disappearing as swiftly as they had arrived.

Behind them, the rest of their force was arrayed in ranks, with what looked like two weapons to hand. Even in the moment's glance she was afforded, Amelia recognized what she was looking at—long guns and poles to brace them on. The lines of men in fur hats stood and lowered their weapons to aim at the paused Gryphon militia. The air crackled and rippled with smoke as one hundred long guns fired a volley into the White Lions' unready front at a range of fifty paces. No sooner had the volley struck than the thrown balls began to pop like fireworks, tearing the ground apart right in front of the Reacher militia.

Even before the smoke cleared, the next hundred gunners marched ahead of the of the first line and, planting their poles, aimed and fired. Then a third line. It was precisely the kind of disciplined shooting that the Roar practiced and, unprepared for it, Amelia watched in horror as at least one cohort withered and died right there in front of her, gone like the smoke drifting away on the breeze. In the north, the approaching knights were drawing ever closer, and behind their sheltering ridge, the Bronze Dragons continued to fire.

"Curse you, Daven Marcus," was all Amelia could think to say as her two bodyguards ushered her down the steps.

CHAPTER 15

He's a monster, not a fool, Prentice thought as he rushed down the steps. Even through the Norgate's stone walls he could still hear the dull thud of the Bronze Dragons' shots. *We should have anticipated something like this.*

You were too busy sleeping, a harsh inner voice chastised him, and he nodded to himself, even though he knew it to be an unjust criticism. He had been poisoned and then fought through a night's battle. How much strength was he supposed to have?

He reached the bottom of the stairs at a run and turned himself, about to head back over the bridge to Loncastel. On the way out the bastion's bridge door, he paused to clip a drummer across the shoulder.

"Beat-call the reserves! Do it!" he shouted at the lad who stared at him wide-eyed for a moment before taking up his sticks and beginning the signal rhythm. Prentice did not wait, though. The extra forces had to be on the battlefield now before Daven Marcus could spring more of whatever trap he had planned. The archduchess had been correct when she said that the ridge could not hide the Usurper's army, or even a large portion of it, but that only made Prentice more certain they had not yet seen everything. The Bronze Dragons were more precious to the kingslayer than almost anything in the world. He would not have deployed them on the field without a protective escort. More than that, there was no point in just shooting at Norgate. The target was Bridgetown, and the bastion was just the doorway to the town. Capturing that doorway would always have been the enemy's main plan, all of which meant that Daven Marcus must have another force nearby, something not yet seen. Pelting over the bridge to fetch the rest of the reserve, Prentice tried to think what that force would be or where they would come from.

On more boats? he wondered, looking frantically up and down the river for any invading craft but seeing only the ones far downstream in the enemy fleet. *Not the river, then. The north road?*

Without thinking, he paused to look back at Norgate, as if he could see the Great Bridge Road through its stones. Behind him he heard the sound of hoofbeats and Dahyoor rode up, leading Prentice's mount Boots. When the fey squire reined in, Prentice clambered awkwardly into the saddle and then tried to use the extra height to see more of the river and its bank.

Still nothing, he thought grimly. The calling beat was continuing from the drummer in the gatehouse, and it was joined now by the tromp of marching feet as Knight Sergeant Gennet led the other five Gryphon cohorts to the battlefield. As they approached, Prentice wracked his mind to divine the enemy's strategy. The camp near Lazy Farmers was backed up against a woodland that could easily conceal an ambushing force. But it would be child's play for the Lions to simply pull back from that. Farringdon had secured his rearguard to protect just such a withdrawal.

So, Daven Marcus has set the Dragons to blast away at the path of retreat, Prentice thought, but that seemed an incomplete notion to him as well. What was to stop the Lion Banner from simply turning part of its force back to drive off the cannons or even capturing them? Farringdon had over four thousand militiamen in the field. Indeed, the knight captain could easily set the men-at-arms afoot to fight whatever emerged from the small forest and then ride back against the cannons with his lancers alone.

"They have something coming down the north road," Prentice called to Gennet as the knight sergeant closed the gap and saluted.

Prentice turned Boots to walk beside him rather than slow the advancing cohorts crossing the bridge. "I do not know what they are yet, but there can be no doubt. We need to get out there and be ready to hold until the Lion Banner comes back to us."

Gennet accepted that word with another salute, but Prentice was already turning to his squire.

"Ride for the knight captain," he told Dahyoor. "Swift like an arrow. Find him and tell him I say to withdraw, no matter what the battle looks like from his end."

Dahyoor said nothing but geed his horse at Norgate, and his swift pony was already at a near gallop before the fey man ducked under the bridge-side door. No sooner was he out of sight than a new set of sounds, akin to fireworks popping off, were heard from the other side of the bridge gatehouse.

"What the hell...?" Gennet wondered out loud.

"The Usurper's other surprise," Prentice muttered, sure that that was what it must be. He looked over his shoulder at the marching cohorts. "Double time! Swift of foot and out in columns!"

He geed Boots to a trot, which was as swift as his limited horsemanship let him dare, and a moment later he was ducking down to pass through the gatehouse. Unlike Dahyoor's smooth transition, Prentice felt like he was about to fall from the saddle for a long moment, and he had to rein Boots in so that he could right himself.

"Do we shut the gates, My Lord?" a sentry called fearfully.

"We have thousands out there, man," Prentice bellowed back at him. The sound of cannon fire was now mixed with the crackle of matchlocks, filling the air with noise, along with the shouts of battle, commands bellowed and drummed, and the cries of the wounded and dying. Slowing Boots to a walk through the outer door, Prentice was confronted with chaos. The earthworks were mainly intact, but the gouges and craters already in their embankments made him think they would not last much more than an hour of this bombardment. The gunners of the two emplaced cannons were looking about, bewildered, unable to find a target.

Of course not, Prentice thought. *The Dragons are breathing their fire from hiding.* That was the whole point of a defilade—to conceal them on the far side of the ridge, out of sight.

"Look to the road!" he shouted at the nearest gunner when he managed to get the man's attention. A foreigner—a Masnian from the lands of the far south—Prentice wasn't even sure his instructions were fully understood, but he gave them all the same. "Anyone coming down the road from the north, let them eat iron shot!"

Behind him he heard marching feet as Gennet led his militiamen out of Norgate. Prentice turned to ride beside the knight sergeant once more, but even before he could set Boots into motion, the whole company ground to a halt. Ahead of them, the path through the earthworks was blocked by a stream of Gryphon militia fleeing in disorder, bloodied and panicked. Many never even bothered to use the path but clambered over the pickets, rushing through trenches and damaged embankments. They were in the way of the Norgate cannons and the approaching reserve equally. This was something Prentice had never faced before—a body of White Lions in rout. Near their front was a man carrying a tall pole with a pennant of Reach blue flying from it. As he approached, he was waving the retreaters towards Norgate while pushing past them himself.

"Corporal Denholm?" Prentice called as he recognized the man with the banner.

Chapter 16

"Hold, you curs!" Gennet cursed at the fleeing militiamen. The command was all but unnecessary—the reserves marching out through the Norgate blocked any chance of further retreat so that the fleeing men-at-arms found themselves pressing into whatever space they could find in front of the bastion. Many crouched behind any little cover there was, while others cringed from the sounds of cannon fire and the nearer gunshots.

"What the hell are you doing, Denholm?" Prentice demanded. He looked at the flag in the man's hands. "What is this?"

"It is a rally pole, Knight Commander," Denholm answered. The man's face showed a clear nervousness, but there was another emotion mixed in that Prentice could not quite fathom. Happiness? Pride? Whatever the corporal was feeling, it did not stop him from making his report, shouting confidently.

"Knight Captain Marquis-Consort Farringdon gave me this duty, to mark a rally point if a retreat was necessary. I take the honor seriously and have led the withdrawal in order to save our lives."

He flinched as one stone-shot from a Bronze Dragon slammed full force into Norgate, gouging out one corner in an explosion of dust and debris. Men hunched and groaned in fear. Even some of Gennet's waiting reserves looked unnerved by that shot, though the one hit did little real damage to the bastion. It would take many to truly weaken it. But that did not mean that every man in the midst of this anarchy was not in already deadly danger. Before all those lives, though, Prentice knew he had higher duties.

"Knight Sergeant," he shouted at Gennet over the cacophony. "Send a runner to her grace with my compliments. She must withdraw—at least to Loncastel and ideally farther than that. Your fastest lad!"

Gennet did not even pause to salute, giving the command to a boy of no more than ten who turned and dashed through the legs of the massed militia, using his size to his advantage.

"May I suggest we do the same, My Lord Knight Commander," Corporal Denholm shouted up at Prentice, affecting an insouciance, but as Prentice looked the man in the face, he could see the fellow's growing panic in his expression. He was the leader of this rout, and though he tried to affect a devil-may-care attitude, it was his fear that was undermining the Gryphon Banner reserves right at the moment when they needed to be most resolute. Fury snapped in Prentice like the crack of a banner in a high wind, and almost before he knew he was doing it, he leaped from Boots's saddle to the ground, shoving Denholm in rage. The surprised corporal staggered, and Prentice snatched the rally pole from his grip as he did.

"You are the anchor, you damnable coward! You are the bulwark that holds for others to retreat to! This flag does not lead a rout—it stops one! You and this flag stay the field to the death!"

He shook it one-handed in Denholm's face, and combined with being assaulted and called a coward, it cracked the corporal's feigned nerve. His false smile fell away.

"That field is death, you fool!" Denholm retorted. "There are beast-men out there—hundreds of them! And they have matchlocks and clamshell bombs."

Another Dragon shot flew by, landing with an oddly wet thump in amongst the muddy reeds of the river. Despite its unimpressive end, Denholm seemed to think its arrival punctuated his argument perfectly.

"And then there are the Dragon cannons hidden somewhere! It's not cowardice; it's common sense. If we stay this side of the Murr, we'll all die!"

Prentice wasn't sure how many of the panicking men around them heard Denholm's words, but he had no doubt the effect such statements from a leader would have. Any moment now, the routers would break from all discipline, and then they would set upon the orderly reserves, fighting their own comrades just for the chance to flee. A sudden memory of the Reach militia facing off against the bloodthirsty Bridgetown forces during the battle outside Sougate earlier in the year flashed into Prentice's mind. That confrontation had been a knife edge from disaster, but even that had not been this dire.

"Beast-men and bombs," Denholm persisted. "And this time, no river water to dive into and hide! Anything out there will die!"

Prentice blinked and stared at the corporal as if the entire battlefield around them had ceased to exist.

Water to hide? he thought. Denholm thought Prentice had deliberately dived into the water on the docks? To hide?

"Redlanders do not use black powder," he said, working to sound confident and praying inwardly that he was not wrong.

"Then what is that sound?" Denholm demanded with a sneer, as if talking to an argumentative fool. He cocked his head, and it was clear there was a sound of matchlock shots coming from not too far away. Prentice scowled at him.

"That is the sound of shots being exchanged, Corporal," he said, and suddenly all the shaking, confusion, and genuine terror for his own life stilled within him. "You may have fled like a coward, but someone is fighting yet, holding the gate open for Knight Captain Farringdon's force to return—something you should be doing!"

Denholm opened his mouth to argue again, but Prentice shoved him backward before he could. The knight commander had wanted to punch the man, but Denholm still had his helmet on, and Prentice was not wearing gauntlets or, indeed, any armor.

He had not intended to be on the field today, just to watch from Norgate. Daven Marcus's cunning had put paid to that plan.

Faced beast-men with a stick and wearing rags before today, he told himself as he stepped back up into the saddle, enjoying a moment of clarity as his next course became clear in his mind. *In comparison, a warm cloak and an arming doublet is quite the luxury.*

It was difficult to remount with the rally pole in his hand, but Prentice was determined not to relinquish it. It was going back out onto the field where it belonged, and he was going to take it there. As he reached his saddle, he looked down to see that Denholm was glaring back, his hand on his sword in its sheath. Now Prentice sneered. Even if the man was fool enough to skin his steel for the sake of his wounded pride, the militiamen around him would not allow him to strike. Even as Prentice settled himself to his saddle, he could feel eyes upon him. He forced himself to sit as straight as his poor horse skill allowed, hoping he did a better job of not looking frightened than Denholm had.

"Corporal Denholm, you are stripped of rank in the White Lions of the Reach," Prentice shouted, and the normally placid Boots shifted under him. If he did not give the horse a better command than to stand still, it would doubtless bolt soon, infected by the panic and danger around it. "If I were you, I would pray that none of us sees the end of this day alive because our next conversation will be less pleasant even than this."

Prentice turned from him, and as he did, his eyes caught those of some of the men around him. Amidst their terror, some seemed to have noted the sting of dishonor, and Prentice hoped that would penetrate their panic. It was almost all he had.

"Knight Sergeant, bring this rabble to order. Beat to ranks—every drummer until his arms fall off!"

Gennet saluted, and Prentice could see in his knight sergeant's expression that he recognized the desperation of their position. A cannon shot ripped through a crowd of militiamen somewhere to their right, and fresh screams arose while clods of mud fell like rain. Their only hope in this battle was to counterattack. Farringdon's company was far from the gate, and a large force was riding down from the north to stop that army from returning to safety. In the fields ahead and on their left were some fresh men-at-arms with guns of their own, as well as clamshells, and behind them the Bronze Dragons, safely hidden from sight and return fire. If the Gryphon reserves did not hold the retreat path for the Lions, Farringdon would be trapped outside the town, and even if his forces had the measure of the arriving knights, the Dragons would have free rein to slaughter too many Reachermen before victory was won. The kingslayer had planned this ambush to perfection, and either the jaws of the trap were held open, or they would snap shut and half the Reach's strength would be swallowed whole.

"Drummers beat to ranks!" Gennet bellowed.

"When you have them back in order, send them to me," Prentice told him.

"Where will you be, My Lord?"

"Out with this rally pole, where *it* should be!"

Prentice was about to put his heels to Boots's sides when Gennet suddenly snatched at the reins.

"My Lord, shouldn't we fetch you some armor?" the knight sergeant asked, explaining his presumptuous action. "We can get you a buffcoat at least, since your brigandine..."

Prentice's personal torso armor had been torn apart by the claw of a mighty *brakkis effar* beast man not long ago, and since then he had been using borrowed armor. Of course, he was missing even that now. Prentice looked from Gennet to the other men around, many watching despite the danger and the moves to reestablish military order. It surprised him to see that many looked genuinely concerned for his safety, even as they feared for their own.

There is no time for that, he thought as he shook his head. He gave his knight sergeant a wry smile.

"At least let us fetch you a halberd or something," Gennet urged.

A polearm would allow Prentice keep an enemy at a distance in a fight, or it would give him the chance, at least. That would mean fighting from foot, though, and his current plan was to hold the flag aloft from the saddle. It would make him a target, but it would also be a sign men could look for on the field, and right now that was the best weapon Prentice could wield on his militiamen's behalf. Panic was their worst enemy at this point, even if there were beast-men with guns out in front of Norgate.

Lord let them not be.

Prentice shook his sword in its sheath with his free hand.

"If I need more than this out there, Knight Sergeant, then we have more problems than a buffcoat's worth," he declared as loudly as he could, hoping to sound heroic and feeling like a fool doing it. Then he snatched the reins back and geed Boots forward. Men stepped back reflexively, including the now irrelevant Denholm, and Boots charged up through a gap in the spikes on an embankment that had been gouged by a previous cannon shot.

"Corporals and line firsts," Gennet shouted behind him, "form lines and cohorts, and once you do, follow the knight commander. He rides for the Gryphons and the Western Reach."

There was a scattered cheer behind him, surely not much more than ten or twenty men amidst the confused hundreds, but enough to quell the panic another fraction, Prentice hoped. He gave Boots what guidance he could, but mostly that was just to keep the animal in motion and roughly pointed away from Norgate. Beyond that he had no control of what path Boots took through the tumbledown earthworks and crowd of gradually reforming militia.

One-handed and holding up a banner pole, Prentice thought as he bounced along, recognizing that what for any knight would have been a mundane activity was for him a challenge at the very limit of his skills.

"Dear God, just don't let me fall off, not after that display," he muttered, enjoying worrying about his pride for a moment as he charged his faithful mount into a maelstrom of smoke, fire, iron and blood.

CHAPTER 17

The distance from Norgate to the space where matchlocks were still exchanging fire was not more than two hundred paces, at most. The ride took mere moments, and Prentice gritted his teeth as he realized that whoever had ambushed Denholm's force with bombs and shot were so close that whenever they wanted, they could turn their fire on the gatehouse itself. Noise and smoke made it easy for him to decide where he was headed, but he circled Boots about as best he could to make certain he came up on his own forces, not the enemy's. Now that he was clear of the shouting men and the Dragon shots were flying overhead, he was convinced that there was someone still out here making a fight of it. Denholm had not drawn everyone away in his rout. Through the acrid clouds of powder smoke, Prentice made out a small clutch of Reacher blue figures and geed Boots toward them.

"Keep watch. They'll be firin' again once they clear with their axes," a throaty female voice shouted as Prentice rode up to what was perhaps a half a cohort's worth. From what he could see, there were maybe a dozen Claws with their halberds, one with a pike, and perhaps two Fangs with swords and shield. The rest of the rump unit were Roarsmen, close to thirty, it seemed, arranged in the center and protected by their melee comrades. The diminished body of men-at-arms was following the directions of a stout line first, a woman whose helmet was gone and whose hair was hanging half disheveled over her left shoulder.

"Lost your helmet, Line First?" Prentice asked as he rode up, and the woman looked at him as if he were a ghost emerging from the smoke. Suddenly, the cloudy air ahead of them burned with crackling flame and the air buzzed with the sound of shot whipping past. The powder smoke was so thick that Prentice thought he could see the trails through the air that one or two of the little iron balls left as they passed. One of the Roar gunners went down with a cry, but his fellows only ignored him.

"Give it 'em back!" the woman officer shouted. "They're slower'n us—show 'em how much."

The Roarsmen returned the shots, but it was clear they were fewer in number than the enemy. Prentice waited for the next attacking volley, wondering how long it would be until the opposing gunners noticed him and his banner and he became their prime target. He was surprised when the next volley fired came from the White Lions.

"They're good shots but well slower than us," the line first told him proudly. "We get two to their one, sometimes more—mostly when they decide they want to use their axes."

"Axes?" Prentice asked, and the woman pointed to some dead bodies in the grass nearby. Many were Gryphon militia, but a number were enemies, dressed in fur-lined coats of mottled colors. More than one had a long axe to hand or nearby—not quite as long-handled as a Claws' halberd, but the blade was taller and sat away from the pole in an odd way. Despite its minor differences, the weapon was clearly to be used in much the same way as the Reachermen's polearm.

"They use them axes like support poles for their guns," the line first explained. "Sit it in the notch there where the blade leaves the shaft. Clever, but means they have to choose between shootin' and fightin'. We can outshoot 'em, but they're savages once they come to it. Smashed our pikes apart right at the start."

Another volley of enemy fire whipped through the air like a flight of hornets, and it seemed to Prentice that the enemy must surely be firing blind into the smoke. The entire company of

Gryphons crouched, and the shots flew over their heads. Despite his exposed position, none of the shots seemed to draw close to Prentice himself.

"We heard they were beast-men," Prentice said as the Roarsmen stood again to fire.

"Not that I seen," was the reply. "I mean, they're doughty buggers, make no mistake, and those bally hats make 'em look ten feet tall when they rush at you out of the smoke, but they're just men, far as I can tell."

There was a sound of running from Prentice's right and two Reachermen—Fangs by their uniforms and swords—rushed up, carrying armfuls of leather pouches with powder horns slung over their shoulders.

"This is what we could find!" one declared to the woman officer.

"Well, don't just stand there. Hand 'em out!"

The two rushed to the lines of Roarsmen while their officer turned to Prentice once more.

"Out shootin' 'em means we're chewin' through our powder and shot right fast!" she explained. "I sent them out to fetch from the fallen."

"Good work," Prentice said with a small smile. This was what Denholm should have been doing from the first. He was about to ask the line first her name when several of the Claws in front of him looked up.

"Hear that?" one shouted. "That's rally on the standard."

"And here's the standard," Prentice shouted back. Men who had been watching the enemy the whole time looked back in astonishment to see their commander holding up the rally flag on his horse. "Knight Sergeant Gennet is bringing up the reserve. Not long now—"

"Here they come again!" another militiaman shouted, and dark figures emerged out of the smoke. Their bulky coats over mail and fur hats did indeed make them look enormous, and Prentice could see how someone filled with panic might have confused them for beast-men. They advanced in lines, axes forward, marching with grim resolution. It was all but impossible to judge accurately in the poor visibility, but it was clear they were many times the number of the remaining Gryphons. Around him, Prentice was impressed that not one Reacherman routed, even though there were not enough of them left to fight as they had been trained. The Roar continued to stand their ground and fire into the advancing enemy while the halberds kept out of the way to the side, waiting for the last moment when it would come to blows. Some gunners reloaded after their shots, but others dropped their matchlocks to take up a sword or halberd of their own, no doubt looted from fallen comrades. At least one gunner hefted his firearm like a club, thinking to batter the enemy with the stock.

"Hold this for me a moment," Prentice told the line first, and he handed off the rally flag before dropping from the saddle. He did not fight from horseback. He was simply not horseman enough for that and given that the militia he was with were not withdrawing, he certainly would not ride off. Drawing his sword, he was about to take the rally pole back, but a shouted order rang out over the enemy and the advancing men halted no more than forty or fifty paces away. There was a moment's calm, and around him Prentice could hear men hissing whispered prayers or groaning in pain from their wounds.

"They'll be bringing up more of their thrown bombs, you watch," the line first whispered, and for the first time her voice showed more fear than resolution. Prentice could not blame her. He had felt the force of clamshells himself, and around him were any number of Gryphon militia bodies torn apart by the kiss of iron shrapnel. He tried to listen out for the marching beat of Gennet's approaching reinforcements, but if it was there, it was lost behind the hammer of his own heartbeat, thundering in his chest. Then he noticed there was movement behind the enemy's first line, more than would be needed to fetch up throwing bombs. A large proportion of the rear ranks were moving away to the right, it seemed, and for a moment he thought they meant to encircle this tiny remnant who refused to yield. If that happened, these Gryphons would be annihilated in moments. The race between ambushers and reserves was in its home straight already. Then a signal trumpet sounded from farther away to the northeast, which meant that Daven Marcus's knights had reached the battlefield and were engaging with Farringdon's force. The axe and gun men in their coats and hats were splitting into two groups, sending half or more off to join the main of their army while they left a smaller contingent to finish off this last piece of the White Lions' rearguard.

"Cocky mongrels!" Prentice cursed as he realized. A sudden indignance arose within him. It was one thing for his militiamen to be overwhelmed by a more powerful foe, but for the enemy to show them so little respect...? A moment ago, he had been preparing himself to die beside these resolute men and women. He remembered Sir Gant's salute across the broken bridge and how the knight had dived into the battle, determined to sell his life dearly. Prentice realized that that was how he felt now. How dare this foe not show him and the Gryphon Banner the respect of their full strength? Suddenly Prentice knew he had to punish them for their arrogance.

"Keep up your fire, Line First," he told the woman beside him. "Whatever happens next, do not fear for us. Just keep firing."

"Us, My Lord?" the junior officer asked, but Prentice was already in motion away from her. He trusted she would understand him in a moment. This fight had barely gone on for half an hour of the candle, and yet the woman had divined the enemy's tactics and could predict their actions when they came on. She had an excellent head for strategy, there could be no mistaking that. A moment later and he was at the front of the crowd of militiamen, still moving forward.

"Claws and Fangs to me!" he shouted and paused only long enough to see if they were answering his call. Some hesitated, obviously confused by his sudden appearance amongst them, but others responded, and their fellows accompanied them. A moment later, a clutch of ten men gathered behind him and he began to walk slowly.

"Do you men know me?" he asked.

Some nodded, others looked to their mates.

"You're Baron Ash," one of them said, and pointed at Prentice's weapon in hand. "I know you by your magick sword."

Inwardly, Prentice cringed. Much as he hated the fool reputation of a "magick sword," he hated what he was about to do with that reputation even more. He lifted his blade high in the air.

"Do you know how I was named Ash?" he asked, still moving forward. The little crowd of halberdiers and sword-and-shield men was perhaps forty paces from the enemy. Prentice could see the foreign faces of the men in front of him, round and sallow, with dark, focused eyes. Wherever in the world these warriors came from, it was a hard land that bred hardy folk, that much was obvious. Just like the line first had predicted, clamshell bombs were being brought up behind the enemy's front rank. As the White Lions roared before they charged, so these men only charged after they had cast iron and fire amongst their foes.

"They call you Ash 'cause you're always there in the fire, even after the fire," the fellow who had named him declared. "You lived through the Brook, when the angel felled the enemy with flame, and you took the Horned Man's head alone with just a dagger in your hand."

Prentice smirked and had to resist shaking his head. A typically abbreviated tale that was more hero worship than history, but it was exactly what these men needed. They had to fight to the death, or the gatehouse would be closed, Farringdon's army encircled, and the Dragons left to feast on too many Reachermen's bones. Hero worship was the best inspiration Prentice had to offer right now.

"Alright lads," he declared, and he pointed back at the Roarsmen who were watching now, confused by the strange, quiet turn of the conflict. "Those are our angels behind us there, bringing fire to our beastly enemy. This is our brook—no water, just smoldering grass and smoke."

He swept his sword around as if to point out the smoke in the air and the scorched grass where previous clamshells had detonated, or matchlock fire had cast burning wadding. In many ways, this patch of open ground was every bit as fiery and smoke-filled as the field of the Brook had been, for all that there was no angel lion here. There could be no better place for a man named Ash to fight. He lifted his sword once more, holding it for all of them to see, mimicking all the fool speech-giving knights and princes he had ever known, hating himself as he did it. They were barely thirty paces from the enemy now, and the fizzing of fuses was audible. Ten against perhaps a hundred—suicidal odds even for the best trained knights.

To hell with odds; the gate must *be held open.*

"Those are our beast-men. Let us go and show them how I took the Horned Man's head and what it means to face Gryphons, Reachermen, Lions of the Reach!"

Not waiting for them to agree or cheer or indeed to do anything, Prentice burst into a run, searching the smoky gloom for any enemy holding a clamshell bomb. His body was still not truly restored to its previous strength, but he did not care. If he paused, if he considered, he knew he would collapse in fear and exhaustion. His heart was hammering, and his limbs wanted to tremble. Only driving them to some extreme action could keep him from breaking like a coward now.

You are a damnable fool, the rational part of his mind told him. *No armor, no helm? Not even gauntlets. One straight shot and your nonsense hero's charge ends with a hole punched through your heart.*

As if summoned by his thoughts, he heard a shot whizz through the air nearby, not to mention trumpet blasts, drumbeats, cannon shots, and the crackle of flames. Behind, his tiny escort force was yelling, releasing their fears at the enemy as they ran to keep up. Yet it all seemed quiet, distant, and the only thing that was loud in his ears was his own breathing and the hammering of his blood through his veins. Ahead of him, he could see the looks of disbelief on the faces of the ambushers. In mere moments, the final gap between them was closing, and while many of the axe-wielding men were calm, some in the line were clearly unnerved by this suicidal moment.

Not enough, Prentice thought, certain that at any moment a shot was going to end him. Instead, two of the axmen stepped into his path, the pointed ends of their blades held forward to receive his charge like spears. Two to one, with the advantage of reach? He would be hacked apart before a bullet could get him, it seemed. Suddenly, from Prentice's left, the shaft of the last pikeman plunged into view, driving at the charge into one of the enemy axmen. Catching the foe with his weapon out of position for defense, the pike point struck him in the chest, driving him backward. His mate, who had seen the elongated spear coming, turned from Prentice's advance to hack at that pike while other axes came forward to the fight as well. It was a sound tactic and one the ambushers had doubtless used all morning to smash the points of Claw pikes out of the way. But it was a tactic made to wreck a fighting formation, not a headlong charge into the teeth of hell.

Sparing the man hacking at the pike shaft no more than a fruitless smack with his blade that barely landed, Prentice plunged through the little gap created in the enemy line and aimed straight at a grenadier. The heavy-coated enemy seemed enormous, and Prentice felt a fresh snap of terror as he barreled towards him, though a part of his mind sneered inwardly. Tall and burly this foe might be, but this was no Horned Man. In the foe's hand, the black sphere of a bomb was ready, the fuse fizzing. It was a deadly weapon, but useless in close quarters like this. The fellow had depended on his comrades to protect him while he prepared to throw, and they had failed him. The ambusher tried to get away, to get distance to throw the device that was now as much a threat to himself as Prentice's sword, magick or not. However, no man could move backwards as fast as a charging man could run forwards, and Prentice drove a slashing cut to the head that knocked away the big fur hat and opened the enemy's face in a bloody spray. The grenadier staggered and the clamshell dropped from his hand, barely rolling even a pace in the trampled grass.

Hardly pausing to think, Prentice dropped his shoulder and caught the dazed and bleeding man in a clinch. Using his full weight and momentum, he pushed the falling enemy down on the dropped explosive and then threw himself on top of his body, holding man and bomb to the ground. There was a moment that seemed to drag on impossibly long, and then Prentice felt himself thrown off his opponent while his ears were hammered by a deep-sounding whomp. His vision swam as he tumbled over and over again until he collapsed against fallen corpses, though of whose side he did not know.

CHAPTER 18

I n the air around him Prentice heard the shouts and cries of battle, along with the distant thud of cannon shots and the crack of matchlock fire. He lay on his back a long moment, head half turned to the sky, though mostly he saw the grey of smoke, not the clouds above. His eyes stung as he blinked them, and when he tried to move, his body resisted, held down by pain and fatigue. He struggled against himself and managed to roll over just as hands reached down to grab him. Panic and renewed battle fury lent him fresh strength, and he fought for a moment against the grappling until they had him half upright and he realized they were the helping hands of allies. They released him even as he stopped fighting, and for a moment he staggered, his head ringing with pain before he finally managed to get his legs steady and take stock.

Gennet's reserves, he thought as he looked the fresh militiamen over. Around him, Gryphons were driving off the rest of the ambushers or else taking prisoners. Blinking against the sting of smoke and sweat, Prentice took a moment to realize someone was speaking to him. His ears were still ringing.

"Say that again," he demanded and realized that he was shouting. His breath felt like it was rasping into his chest. Someone approached and something was thrust into his hand. It was his sword. Doubtless, the force of the explosion had thrown it aside, but some loyal militiaman had made sure the Ashen Man did not lose his "magickal" weapon.

"I was asking if you are badly wounded, My Lord," a voice penetrated through the confusion in Prentice's hearing.

Badly wounded? Prentice wondered. How could he tell? Looking down, he could see blood and tears in his trousers and doublet, though many fewer than an explosion like that would have caused him if he had not had an enemy body to shield behind. Were any of them serious? Even one of them could sicken, and that would be the end of him in the long run, but were any bad enough to take him from the field right now?

Before he could think of answers, the crowd of blue and cream around him parted and Knight Sergeant Gennet was there, accompanied by the woman line first. Prentice was glad to see she had survived this far.

"That was the bravest thing I think I ever see'd," she said, and when Prentice managed to puzzle out her words through the noise, he wanted to scoff. She had held her command together through the worst ambush any White Lions had ever faced. That was the kind of bravery he wanted in the militia, not his fool headlong rush.

"What is the word, Knight Sergeant?" he asked Gennet, spitting the taste of soot and blood from his mouth. "Are the rest of these fur hats headed off to support the Usurper's attack on Knight Captain Farringdon?"

"That's about the look of it, My Lord," Gennet reported. "You've seen off the fraction they left to finish up, so we've got the left of the field for ourselves again, save for the Dragons over that ridge, of course."

Prentice nodded and his head swam for a moment. He tried to get a grip of himself, but before he could, the nausea overwhelmed him, and he bent over to throw up.

Some hero, he thought as he finally retched out the last of his breakfast and managed to get himself upright again. Around him his officers waited dutifully. Hoofbeats thumped and Dahyoor rode up, leading Boots by his reins. Prentice blinked in surprise, and the line first looked down shamefacedly.

"I lost him. Sorry, My Lord," she said, speaking of Prentice's mount. "A bomb spooked him, and he bolted. It's my fault."

"Dahyoor had just come back from the knight captain's company, and he said he could fetch your horse better than anyone else," Gennet added.

Sitting his own pony as calmly as if he were riding in a spring meadow, Dahyoor looked down on them all without expression.

"Speak," Prentice told him.

"The *keshkirae* of the Lion flag has seen the enemy trap," the squire reported, describing Farringdon as if he were a fey war leader—a *keshkirae* commanding a sworn warband, a *keshiyaa*. "He has heard your word and moves to obey. The Lion returns to the settlement in the waters."

Good, Prentice thought, and he nodded. Farringdon was withdrawing, though he would certainly have to fight the main of Daven Marcus's forces from the north to do it. The Gryphons had rallied from the ambush and would be able to hold the left corner of the battlefield, keeping the "gate" open. There was another rumble from the north and another stone cannonball flew overhead, tearing up the earthworks some more. Several of the stakes from the embankments flew like giant skittles to rattle against Norgate. From this distance, it looked like the Dragons had managed to land at least one more direct hit on the famous gatehouse that had never fallen. It would not last too much longer at this rate—a day at the most. Prentice looked northward and then to the northwest. For just this moment, he held this corner of the field and had a direct path to the Bronze Dragons. A quarter of the candle and he could march his cohorts up and over that ridge, into the defilade, to smash the damnable engines and their crews into pieces. But if he did that, he would leave the "gate" undefended. Worse, there was no chance Daven Marcus would not see them marching to attack his precious cannons. He would likely detach some knights ahorse to protect the Dragons or just to tie Prentice's detachment in place while the rest of his army encircled Farringdon's Lion Banner Company. Just as had happened the day the Gryphon Company had arrived in Bridgetown, Prentice felt forced to choose the wise option over the prize opportunity.

"We need to hold this ground and as much of the field east of us as we can," he told Gennet. "Set us up forward of the bastion, hopefully inside the arc of their cannon shot, and get ready to hurt any Usurper's men who try to cut off the Lion Company's retreat."

Gennet saluted, but before the knight sergeant could turn to pass the orders, Prentice held up his hand and turned to the line first.

"What's your name?" he asked her, and she stood to attention. Her expression was sober, even through the swelling from the blow that had knocked her helmet away, and Prentice realized that she was expecting a dressing down. His own stern manner probably wasn't doing anything to disabuse her of that notion.

"Kathrine, My Lord," she said swallowing. "Most call me Kate—Sootface Kate actually."

Sootface—the perfect nickname for a gunner. All Roarsmen had dark smudges on their faces from powder and smoke firing in the pans so close to their heads when they shot. Prentice nodded and then turned back to Gennet.

"Sootface Kate is taking Denholm's command," he told his knight sergeant. "See that word is passed so the line firsts under her all know and are ready to respond. This day's battle is not finished yet."

"My Lord?" the woman asked, eyes wide and voice so breathless with shock that Prentice only just heard her. "That's a corporal's command. You know I'm just a line first?"

"Not anymore, Kate," Prentice told her. "I need a corporal, one who won't run at the first sign of danger. That is you. I have seen it."

Hells bells, now I'm playing at hero and *fey warrior—Prentice Ash, Knight Commander and keshkirae both?* Prentice sneered at himself. If Gennet or the newly raised Kate shared his sense of disgust, they did not show it. Orders were passed, cohorts were redeployed, and the Gryphons stood at last to fulfill their duty, securing the rally point for the retreating Lions. Prentice climbed back into the saddle, groaning in discomfort as he did. Dahyoor watched him with wordless contempt, and Prentice glared at the fey man, daring him to comment about his master's poor horse skills. The fey squire said nothing.

CHAPTER 19

"They call it a bardiche," Benlow Sent-Fane, the Masnian weapon maker and commander of the White Lions' cannons explained to the officers gathered in the lamplight of Dog's Leg tavern taproom. "Those men who attacked you are from a wild highland in Masnia. They are the Rangers of the Jerwahl Mountains, and this is their favored weapon."

He held up one of the enemy's axes in front of him. During the retreat, a number had been captured, along with some of their guns and even some undetonated clamshell bombs. When it had been realized that these newcomers were foreign mercenaries from the south, Master Sent-Fane had been summoned to share his knowledge of the mysterious men clothed in bearskin and stealth. The weapon's haft was five or so feet in length and the blade on top had an extra sweep upward so that the edge turned into a point, making the weapon useful for both chopping and thrusting, just as the Lions' halberds were wielded, even though it was a good foot shorter. More intriguing was the way in which the blade was made to come away from the haft so that there was a notch just behind the upward sweep. It was in that notch that these Jerwahl men fitted the barrels of their firearms, and so the stout weapon also made an excellent stand from which to fire. Prentice stared at the bardiche, studying it with professional focus. It wasn't until water dripped on him that he realized Marquis Knight Captain Farringdon had arrived at the table, winter cloak sodden with rain.

"It's coming down a deluge out there," the knight captain said apologetically as he pulled the wet garment from his shoulders and laid it at his own feet, dropping into a spot at the long table's simple wooden bench. The taproom was crowded to the rafters with militiamen, all damp from the rain so that the drinking house stank like a wet dog, and the warmth of the two fireplaces made the air steamy and thick. It would be hours before anyone here was fully dry, if they managed it at all, but there would be few who resented the rain. Holding the left flank, Prentice's Gryphons had prevented the Lion Banner Company from being encircled, but that did not mean it had been an easy withdrawal, and the fighting had been fierce for a long hour. Worse, the Bronze Dragons, unchallenged in their secret firing position, had hammered whatever part of the battlefield they wished, only avoiding risk to their own men-at-arms. The White Lions had been faced with a grim choice—press into the melee against Daven Marcus's knights or try to stand back and be vulnerable to the Usurper's massive guns.

Then the cloudburst had opened up, and the battle had changed almost completely. Slowed as the ground churned to mire, the enemy horsemen lost their ability to easily outmaneuver the Lions' men afoot. Even better, the Dragons had been forced to cease their fire. Having moved into place swiftly and secretly, their cannoneers had yet to create shelters to shoot from beneath when the weather was inclement. As Farringdon settled into his seat and accepted a cup of stout that was poured for him, a fresh rattle of that saving rain beat on the tavern's slate roof, so heavy that it was audible even over the conversation.

Saved us and stopped us at the same time, Prentice thought of the downpour, pausing from examining the enemy weapon. The rain that had stilled the Dragons' voices had also silenced the Roar. When the battle had shifted under the wet weather, Prentice's first instinct had been to send his contingent up and over the ridge to punish the Denay guns, perhaps even destroy them outright. Yet it had been too hard to see what the enemy was doing in the grey. The rain cut visibility back to next to nothing as it washed over the fields in wind-driven waves. Every man was drenched in it, shivering and exhausted from the cold. Another opportunity was left to go begging, but it had been the better strategy for the Reach to quit the field, taking shelter in Bridgetown once more. The frustration of that wisdom made Prentice scowl.

One day we will have to take the risk, he thought, *or those fire breathers will hound us to our graves.*

"How goes the evacuation?" he asked, and Farringdon's already unhappy expression turned further sour.

"Norgate Bastion is empty. We've managed to save one of the guns, but the other is a wreck," he said. "The barrel itself is dented like an old copper pot. Took a direct hit from one of those stones, I'd say."

While the Dragons had roared all over the battlefield, Norgate and its earthwork defenses had been their most desired target. Ironically, by rallying the retreating cohorts, Prentice had taken his militiamen away from the most dangerous part of the battle. Only once the rain interrupted the cannon fire and the Western Reach forces had been able to disengage and withdraw across the bridge had they also seen just how much damage the mighty guns had done, tearing up the earthworks, smashing against the ancient stones, crumbling at least one half of the battlements on the roof and destroying one of the defensive cannons outright. Another day or so of such hammering and the legendary Norgate would be battered down to the foundations.

The minute the Dragons began firing, that was inevitable, Prentice reminded himself, but it was a truth that brought little relief. Prentice saw his sour thoughts reflected in Farringdon's expression as the marquis-consort stared into his cup a moment. Around the table, other officers showed by their faces that they shared their leaders' discontent. Compared to the disaster the battle might have been, their defeat was actually no great tragedy, but Prentice did not expect anyone here to take much comfort in that notion, so he turned his attention back to Master Sent-Fane's briefing on the captured weapons.

"What of their matchlocks, Master?" he asked, looking down at the captured firearm laying on the table before them. It was made of a dark hardwood and there was an elegant gold filigree embossed in the stock. Much of its mechanism seemed made of brass, highly polished and clearly well maintained.

"Do you see any match?" the weaponsmith retorted as if Prentice was a fool. "This is a wheellock."

Prentice ignored the man's superior attitude—arrogance and competence seemed to go hand-in-hand with Masnian weapon makers, at least from the knight commander's experience. Also, Sent-Fane's comment was demonstrably correct. The captured firearm did indeed have a wheellock trigger mechanism such as the lancers used for their pistols rather than the simpler, burning long-match that the Roar gunners used. The contained nature of the device surely made it ideal for men-at-arms who hid in the land, as these Jerwahl Rangers appeared to, where they might have to lay in puddles or mud. A wheellock meant less risk of water getting into their powder once the gun was loaded to fire.

"Are all the Rangers' guns wheellocks?" he asked, and Sent-Fane nodded.

"They live in high fastnesses, hunting and warring in stealth amongst their own clans," he told them, "Only sometimes coming abroad to hire on as mercenaries. The first payment each man demands is a wheellock, which they love because it does not smoke before firing, revealing their hiding places. They always fight from hiding. Past emperors have campaigned to suppress them, bring them to heel, but none has been permanently successful."

"I can believe it," Sootface Kate muttered, taking a swig of one of two small pewter tankards. She had the two cups on the table in front of her, drinking through the swelling on the side of her face from the injury she took during the fight. Apparently, one tankard contained an unpleasant-smelling concoction from an apothecary to ward off infection, and the other was a spirits cup with the taphouse's signature gin. Peculiar to the Dog's Leg, the drink had a distinctive bitter juniper aroma, and locals apparently gave it an uncharitable nickname. Grimacing with the taste of each cup in turn, the wounded woman corporal moved back and forth between the two drinks, as if needing the flavor of one to remove the taste of the other. "Them big hats on their heads and they still were hid in that grass like they were invisible. We seen nothin' and then they were there, popped up and chucking these at us. Solid metal and they were pitchin' 'em like boys havin' a late harvest apple fight!"

She poked the iron "apple" sitting on the table, another souvenired weapon that Prentice had insisted all the officers examine and understand. Its wick had been pulled and its black powder tipped out, but it still looked grim and deadly in the candlelight.

"Hmm," Benlow Sent-Fane muttered, nodding sagely. "Only their most mighty and skilled are ever permitted by their elders to leave the mountains to fight as mercenaries. Each of those men had first to kill a bear with his own axe to prove his valor and then skin the beast himself. The hat and coat are his mark as a great man of his clan, and they prefer mail to wear under the fur."

God be thanked for that, Prentice thought. The man he had used to shield himself from the dropped grenade had been wearing a coat of mail under his bearskin, and the knight commander was convinced that was the only reason the both of them had not been ripped apart by the explosion. As it was, the iron fragments had torn into the man's belly through the mail. When his body was found nearby to where Prentice fell, the foreign mercenary's organs had been torn to bloody ribbons by iron shrapnel and fractured links of his own armor.

Sent-Fane concluded his explanations. "They are near-legend, and the few times they have chosen a side in Imperial conflicts they have been much feared. They have many other names, most of them dishonorable, but in the main we know them as the Jerwahl

Rangers. Besides their strength, they are also greatly skilled men of the wilds, as you saw this day."

Prentice was persuaded of every word. These Rangers had remained hidden mere hundreds of paces away over seemingly open ground. If he had not known the mystical stealth of the fey already, he would have credited these men with magickal powers.

Men in bearskins come to skin the Bear of Bridgetown, he thought, wondering if such poetry had occurred to anyone else. If the notion had come to the Usurper, Prentice could well imagine the arrogant Daven Marcus giggling to himself at the lyrical nature of his ambush.

"Thank you, Master Sent-Fane. Go now and look to your own remaining guns," he told the Masnian cannoneer. "You have a duel coming with the cannons from Denay."

The man stood from the table and accepted Prentice's dismissal with a deep bow, his long, dark plait falling over his shoulder. When he straightened once more, he swept it back with a dramatic flourish and moved off through the crowded tavern. Prentice looked over those still sitting at the table. Apart from Farringdon and the newly raised Corporal Kate, he had Knight Sergeant Gennet, the senior Gryphon Banner officer in the day's battle, as well as Nunel and Sedgewick, two of the three Lion Banner seniors. Only Knight Sergeant Markas was absent from the Lions, while Guillam and Porth were missing from the Gryphons. Guillam still held his post on Sougate, but both Markas and Porth were injured. Markas had taken a blow during the day's fighting that he insisted would only need rest and a clean bandage. Porth was yet in camp, recovering from the amputation of his arm some weeks before. Even if the two men were fully hale, both banner companies were still short one senior sergeant. The Lions needed a Roarsman so Nunel could go back to the Lancers, and the Gryphons still needed a banner sergeant, someone to carry the standard when the company took the field in full.

Someone who will not run at the first sign of trouble, Prentice thought, and he paused to consider Denholm and the disaster the near rout might have been. *Her grace needs more chaplains, more healers, and more officers. Better officers.*

He cast a glance down at the somber Kate where she looked to have settled in to drink away her pains for the night. He wondered what motivated a woman to want to march with a banner company and shoot a matchlock, then realized that he did not care.

"That will be your last cup tonight, Kate," he told her, and the whole table looked at the poor woman who stared back, stricken, plainly wondering what she had done to offend him.

"My Lord...I wasn't...I..." she struggled to defend herself, mouth working but words not coming.

"In a short while I will send you back to camp with Knight Sergeant Gennet," Prentice told her, and Gennet, as if sensing what was coming, gently reached out and removed the two cups from in front of her, one after the other. "He will show you your new duties and introduce you around to the corporals that will be under your command."

"Under my...My Lord?"

"I am appointing you the new Gryphon's Sergeant of the Roar," Prentice told her, and the woman stared back at him.

"But I'm just a line first," she protested. "I mean, you only done made me a corporal some hours ago. I figured you for sending me back to the ranks any breath now."

"Well, you have that wrong." Prentice looked the whole table over again. "Daven Marcus laid out a trap for us this day, and we stuck our foot squarely into it. If not for your nerve and fighting sense, Kate, holding the trap open for us, we would be one foot short now. No one here doubts that."

"Here, here," Farringdon said, and though he was trying to be encouraging to the newly promoted woman, it seemed to Prentice there was a tinge of moroseness in the marquis-consort's expression. It would not have been surprising, since it was Farringdon's plan that Daven Marcus had outwitted. Defeats tended to breed moroseness and self-pity, and Prentice knew it was his duty to see the two notions did not take root in the wake of this particular defeat.

"We took a hiding today, make no mistake," he told them levelly. "So be it. Let us set ourselves to learn from it and be ready for the next time, for if there is something I can assure you it is that there will be a next time. The Usurper and his Dragons have only just begun with us."

CHAPTER 20

Prentice stood, ready to leave them to their final drinks, and as he did so, a runner came wending his way across the taproom, pushing around or through the crowd, holding a folded packet up in his hand whenever someone got in his way.

"Knight Commander, this come to the camp for you. I was told to run it straight here," the lad said breathlessly when he found Prentice, saluting and then flicking his damp hair out of his eyes. He handed over a small, folded bundle of oilskin which Prentice undid to find an unsealed note on paper inside.

"Not too wet are you, lad?" he asked, giving the messenger a quick smile.

"Just damp, My Lord," the boy of about thirteen answered readily. "Think the rain's been slackening the last hour or so."

"Well, get yourself something to warm you before you go back to camp." Prentice looked at Kate. "You are finishing your drinking for the night, Sergeant Sootface. Why don't you stand the lad a stoup?"

The messenger looked at Kate as she stood, her expression about as awestruck as the lad's. Then the pair went to the bar where the taverner was likely to run dry soon with so many in the taproom all wanting as much as they could drink to soften the taste of defeat.

"Is it from her grace?" Farringdon asked as Prentice read the note by the light of the table's one candle. The knight commander shook his head.

"No—from my brother."

"Your brother, but I thought he…"

"My older brother, Xavoer," Prentice explained, knowing that Farringdon was likely thinking of Pallas, his younger brother, the disgraced Church knight.

"Oh, didn't he leave with the rest of the Forberest folk?" the marquis-consort asked.

The last time Prentice had seen or spoken to his older brother had been the night of his duel with Squire Cassian, the night the Forberest Compact representatives had tried to persuade Lady Penelope into their alliance, and she in turn had hoped to woo the Compact's leader into a different kind of pledge. As with the marquis knight captain, Prentice had assumed his brother was a part of the Compact's entourage and had left town with them.

"Apparently not," was all he could think to say. The note in his hand was simple, in a plain-seeming script, and contained a message he had never once imagined he might receive. *Come swiftly. Father is dying.*

Beneath that line were others, including the name of a rooming house on the island of Bell's Hummock, where Prentice was supposed to find his father and brother both. He blinked as he read the missive, feeling suddenly as near drunk as Sergeant Kate seemed.

Why is father here in Bridgetown? he wondered, *And how?*

Almost unthinkingly, Prentice turned away from the table, heading on self-willed feet toward the taproom's door. He barely even noticed himself putting his cloak around his shoulders before he stepped outside, but as his hand touched the latch, Farringdon came up beside him.

"My Lord? Your brother sends dire news, I take it?" the marquis-consort asked, and Prentice looked at him a moment, feeling as if his eyes would not focus properly. Then the door opened in front of them and two Lion corporals stumbled to a halt just inside the entrance. Recognizing the senior men in front of them, both officers saluted reflexively, and Prentice and

Farringdon returned it. It was the burst of cold air from outside that helped Prentice, though, and he blinked as if his sight was clearing.

"Family matters, My Lord," he told the knight captain. "Something I should attend to."

"Something urgent, I assume, if you are attending to it now," Farringdon said, no doubt having noticed the distracted way Prentice had been leaving.

"Urgent?" Prentice repeated, stepping outside. *Come swiftly.* "I do not know."

Father is dying.

"Well, if you will permit me, I can walk with you some of the way or all the way, if your brother's business leads you close by the Paramour's Chambers."

"Bell's Hummock," Prentice began to explain, surprised to realize that he had indeed been intending to go directly to this rooming house. He tried to think why. When was the last time he had spoken to his father? Fifteen years ago? More? And his father's last words to him had been to disown him at the insistence of an Inquisitor. What did all that mean, now that he was apparently dying? What debt of urgency did Prentice owe the man?

"We can at least walk some of the way together," Farringdon agreed, and they headed down the Great Bridge Road, still busy with militiamen, even at this late hour. They had gone not a half dozen paces when a voice called to Prentice from the corner of the Dog's Leg in the entrance to a narrow alley.

"Knight Commander?"

Prentice and Farringdon both looked to see Corporal Denholm, bedraggled and cold, water dripping from the brim of his hat. It seemed the discredited officer had been waiting outside the tavern for some while. Despite his forlorn appearance, he stepped forward with some confidence and bowed.

"My Lord, I have come to plead my cause with you," he said with an exaggerated sense of formality.

"Your cause?" Prentice repeated, surprised by the man's sudden appearance. He looked to Farringdon a moment, but in the poor light on the street, the marquis-consort's expression was unreadable.

"Yes, I feel it only right," Denholm continued. "We both spoke rash and angry words this day, but it would not be justice to let those stand between us. I come willing to humble myself and make the first step toward reconciliation."

"To humble yourself?" Farringdon asked quietly.

The corporal acknowledged the marquis's words with a lordly nod, and Prentice found himself struggling to put his thoughts in order again. His mind had been mostly occupied with memories of his father's rejection overlaid on the strategic questions the day had left to him. Now Denholm had stepped from the shadows, acting like an old friend or comrade estranged by an embarrassing misunderstanding. A part of Prentice's mind wanted to almost laugh at the man's boldness, while another could not forget the nightmare of only half a day past—the Gryphons in full flight, running from the battlefield.

"If you want to humble yourself, then go to your duties, militiaman, and cease intruding on my night," the knight commander snapped, thinking that ending the conversation was the best answer to his confusion. Denholm was determined, however.

"I was following the orders I was given," he insisted and gave Farringdon a meaningful look, clearly inviting the knight captain to speak on his behalf. Prentice did not give Marquis Farringdon the chance.

"Are you saying Knight Captain Farringdon ordered you to flee the field?" he demanded.

"I was given the rally flag to mark the safe withdrawal," Denholm answered with a cold expression. "The wagons were destroyed, and men were dying. There was no safety there. We needed to withdraw to a less harmful location."

"Less harmful?" Prentice repeated. "Have you seen what the ground before Norgate looks like now? You drove your cohorts like a rabble into a killing ground. The Dragons would have made carrion of them, a feast for the crows."

His own mention of crows reminded Prentice of the Inquisition, their symbolism, and the many confused emotions he was feeling began to beat at him like the flock of ravens the figure Sanguine had summoned to attack him in his dream. Memories of his own treatment at the hands of the Inquisitors mixed with his father speaking the words of disownment and then again with the terrors of the battlefield, charging a man with a clamshell bomb in hand and feeling the detonation shuddering through him. More and more emotions swarmed in Prentice's mind until he hardly knew what he felt or wanted to say.

"Am I a seer? How could I know what would happen next?" Denholm demanded, still defending his actions.

"It was not yours to see or know," Farringdon answered him quietly, and Denholm turned on him, spitting accusation.

"No, it was yours. Did you see the Dragons or those fur coat gunners? Did you know what was going to happen?"

"No...I didn't," Farringdon admitted and there was a clear note of regret in his voice.

"I did what had to be done..." Denholm persisted, but Prentice had had enough.

"What you did was lead the first rout of any White Lion company," he declared, his voice rising in the night so that it echoed off the walls and wet stones of the street. "While the archduchess watched from Norgate's walls, you led the Gryphons into disgrace. You disgraced us before the Lioness herself!"

"Better that than dying a pointless death under a cannon's mercies," Denholm shouted back. "How many of those loyal fools the woman called Sootface kept on the field lived to worry about your shame and disgrace?"

That was the last brick of the dam for Prentice, and the confusion of his thoughts and emotions poured out in a torrent.

"Do you not see what you have done to us?" he challenged the excuse-making corporal, and the quiet inner part of his soul remembered his father making the same demand of him the day he had been disowned. For a moment it felt to Prentice as if his memory was repeating, only this time he was his father and Denholm was the one being cast away. He struggled to bring himself back out of his memories, if only because he hated the thought that he would ever treat someone the way he had been treated. He tried to remind himself that the two situations were not the same.

"If you had kept your mouth shut, I might have let you wash away the shame with service," he declared, his loud voice causing his head to ache and his stomach to churn. "But this sneering shadow-play of an apology? For this I have no mercy. Get you gone, Denholm. You are no longer a White Lion of any stripe. Surrender your sword and armor and let me never set eyes on you again."

From nearby, a squad of militiamen approached, drawn by the noise, it seemed. The one at their head was carrying a short, brass-bound rod, marking him out as a provost—a junior officer given authority and responsibility for the night to keep order.

"If that's your word, then I claim the blood debt between us," Denholm insisted, having stepped back a pace. His hand had gone to the hilt of his sword when Prentice mentioned it.

"Blood debt?" Farringdon asked, and Prentice shared the marquis's confusion. Talk of a blood debt made no sense in the chaos of his thoughts, but as he tried to puzzle it out, the effort of concentration made his head throb with more pain.

"If not for me, you'd be dead, drowned at the bottom of the Murr twixt Oldbridge and Greenmarsh," Denholm answered. "You owe me your life, and I claim it back in this. Restore my command and put all these matters to rest."

"Are you a fool as well as a coward?" Prentice ground out through the agonized grip that constricted his mind. He put his own hand to his sword, and for the first time Denholm's sense of confidence showed a crack of uncertainty. Prentice wondered if the man was about to turn his demand of an honor debt into a challenge. He was ready to skin his steel if the need arose, fool notion as he might have found it in a quieter moment. He took a half step forward and Denholm appeared to set himself into a fighting stance. Before anything more could happen though, the pain in Prentice's head overwhelmed his stomach and he bent at the waist with a groan. Suddenly he felt himself retching into the gutter, and he realized he had not eaten anything since the smoky fish soup that morning.

"What is this matter?" a fresh voice demanded, and it seemed the provost had thought to intervene at last. Prentice wanted to stand and explain to the officer, but his empty stomach was still seeking to vomit out contents it did not have, making him heave and spit.

"Provost, take this militiaman into custody," Farringdon said in a clear voice, and Prentice noticed the swirl of the marquis's cloak out of the corner of his eye. Farringdon had revealed his armor to confirm his identity.

"You can't do this!" Denholm shouted, but there was a dull thump, and he gave a pained cry. One of the provost's patrol had hit him with the butt end of a halberd and others moved to seize him.

"Take him back to Runners Field," Farringdon went on. "Strip him of his armor and take back all that he has from the hand of the archduchess. See that nothing that is his is kept from him, then put him out of the camp. He retains no rank and no pension."

"As you command, My Lord," the provost said, and the patrol escorted the groaning Denholm away. Gradually, Prentice forced himself upright. He tried to spit the taste from his mouth and realized the moment of weakness had at least calmed his crazed mind. He yawned suddenly.

"I sound like he does," he observed to Farringdon, nodding in the direction Denholm had been dragged away.

"Perhaps, but he will be the worse off of you two come the morning," the knight captain joked. Prentice smiled and nodded gently.

"Ugly business," he said.

"He forced it on us," Farringdon added, and Prentice did not argue. "Are you still going to Bell's Hummock?"

Prentice thought about it a moment. The urgency had gone from his mind now. *Come swiftly*, the note had said, but he no longer felt the need to accept its direction. So many men had died this day; did it matter that his father was one of them?

Am I even certain I care? he wondered as he and Farringdon quietly crossed over to Oldbridge Island and headed toward the Paramour's Chambers.

Chapter 21

"Are you quite well, Your Grace?"

Amelia barely heard the question from one of the merchants and guildsmen standing close to her. The work of the nearby gun crew filled the chamber with sounds enough that it would have been difficult to converse as it was, but the pain in her back made the whole effort even more of a challenge. Yet, it was not these things that kept her thoughts from the discussion—it was the sight of Norgate. Amelia, her entourage, including Lady Dalflitch, in this instance, and the gaggle of dark-coated Conclave worthies were all standing in a large chamber in the Loncastel keep, across the first bridge from the north bank of the river. A galleried series of windows with diamond glass panes looked out northward, and several of those windows were thrown wide as the gun crew prepared their weapon to fire through the opening. A thin drizzle sometimes blew in through the open windows, but otherwise the cannon would be well protected from the rain and able to fire come any weather. Through the floorboards, hammering and heavy thuds could be heard as a carpentry crew reinforced the chamber floor from below. Since the siege had paused three days under winter's hand, Amelia had decided it was safe enough for her to tour the defenses as they were being shored up across Loncastel Island. She had another four cannon emplacements to see after this one.

Assuming my back can endure the journey, she thought. For the most part, her pregnancy had been no great distraction to her, not once her stomach had finally ceased from morning sickness. She certainly felt no need to go into seclusion as some mothers of the peerage did in the late stages of gestation. Nevertheless, this morning's climb up the stairs to the keep's gallery room had given her a back pain she had not been prepared for. Even now it took more of her will than she liked to admit merely to stand with dignity in front of these patrician men of the town. It had not been her intention to conduct any counsels of business during her inspection, but she had been pinned down by this delegation of merchants, and now it seemed she had no choice but to face them and her back pain at the same time.

"I'm sorry, Good Master, what was that you said?" she asked, turning to the six dark-clad guildsmen who clustered near her like a flock of plaintive courtiers.

"I enquired after your health, Your Grace," said the merchant with the polished, golden guild master's pin on his cloak, declaring him as a leader of the influential Carders Guild, traders and crafters in all things woolen. "With this inclement weather and your...condition...I only wondered if perhaps there might be a better place for you to meet with us."

Better for me or for you, Master? Amelia thought, knowing it was uncharitable. *I am on my feet despite my difficulties. Can you not make a similar effort?*

Her eyes went to the cannon crew as they stacked iron shot and sighted the gun. The team's leader had four of them working with long iron bars that they used to lever the mighty weapon back and forth, practicing the efforts they would have to make in order to aim it in a battle. There were ten men in all in the gun crew, and it seemed to Amelia that it was barely enough. She looked from their sweating industry to the six richly appointed men who seemed to think standing for this meeting would be too great an imposition. No wonder the yeoman folk so often despised the patricians.

Yet their work is no less necessary to me than the gunners', she reminded herself. Of the six merchants, four were sworn quartermasters—traders who had committed their entire business to supplying the White Lions with their many needs. In a real sense, these men were as much loyal servants of the Western Reach as the militiamen themselves, though no doubt still with one eye out for their own profits.

The other two in the crowd of bejeweled sable wore Bridgetown Conclave guild pins—one the master carder, whom Amelia remembered now was named Herrimans, while the other had the hand and wheel pin of the Potters' Brotherhood. Potters was a low guild typically, of little prestige in most towns, but in Bridgetown they were nonetheless eager to be good friends to the Archduchess of the Reach, at least according to Lady Dalfitch's previous assessments. This meeting seemed to augur otherwise.

"Gentles," Amelia addressed them all with a benign nod, "I must be here because of the needs of my realm. *You* asked to meet with me, so it is here we must meet."

She gave Lady Dalflitch a signal to have her take up the conversation, then turned to look northward once more at the now all but abandoned Norgate. In less than a day's firing, the Bronze Dragons had sheared away perhaps a quarter of the gatehouse, as well as smashing its mighty gate with a single extremely lucky shot that had killed nine men and reduced the portal to kindling. To Amelia's mind the historic bastion looked like a broken tooth, freshly cracked and soon to rot.

The moment this rain lets up, Daven Marcus will see the rest of the tooth is properly pulled, she thought. *And then he will set about beating in the rest of the town's face.* Somewhere ahead past the damaged fortification were the Bronze Dragons, hiding in the rain and waiting to roar again. *While we gather our strength, so do they.*

Farringdon had removed his garrison from the failing strongpoint, though there were still some out digging in the rain to restore the earthworks beyond the gate. He insisted that the next part of the siege would fall mostly upon the mighty guns, but they still had to maintain the gate defenses or else Daven Marcus might snatch the bridge from them while they weren't looking, as it were.

"If I may, Your Grace," the carder Herrimans was saying, and Amelia realized that again she had not been listening, "we first want to be clear that what is happening is not our desire. We are all thankful—carders, spinners and weavers, one and all—thankful for everything you have already done for our town."

Amelia felt herself stiffen inwardly. Any meeting which contained such effusive praise from a nervous man promised bad news.

The more they love you at the start the more they'll gouge you in the end, Amelia remembered her father saying once. She knew, of course, that it was not a trustworthy saying and that there were many reasons Master Herrimans might choose to say what he was, not the least of which was that the wool trades, concentrated as they were on Greenmarsh, did indeed owe her and her militia a great debt. Even so, the archduchess found herself steeling for the inevitable apology and almost cringed when it came.

"It is because of all you do and have done that we are asking this price at all," the Conclave guildsman said, literally wringing his soft hands as he spoke. He kept ducking his head in exaggerated respect.

"What price, Master?" Amelia asked him, realizing that she was even farther behind in the conversation than she had thought. She glanced at Dalflitch, who had an expression of stern displeasure.

"Master Herrimans and Master Jetty have come as 'friends' to tell us they wish to renegotiate our contracts with them," the lady seneschal explained, her voice colder than the rain. "They will no longer accept the agreed-upon exchange of eight guilders for each Masnian we pay with."

Master Jetty, Amelia thought, recognizing the potter's name now as well.

"Eight?" she asked. "I thought we agreed for ten."

"That was even before..." Master Jetty began to explain, but a look from Dalflitch stilled his voice in his throat. He was a burlier man than Master Herrimans, with thickly callused fingers that were likely natural to his trade, not to mention a bull-like neck. Even so, he seemed just as shamefaced as the carders' representative, if less groveling.

"Our initial round of contracts traded at ten to the piece of gold," Dalflitch explained. "But after a while it was told to me that there was a growing...what was the word you gentlemen used? A glut?"

"A glut, yes, My Lady—tis the word," Herrimans said and bowed his head several more times.

"A glut of gold in the town," Dalflitch continued, "and so the worth of each Masnian is diminished. We would then receive only eight in exchange value, I was told."

As a former merchant's daughter, Amelia felt she understood well enough the notion of a glut. When something became more common, its value went down. It was usually cheaper to buy food or animals just after harvest or at the spring birthings than at other times of the seasons. The idea that such a thing could happen to the coins themselves seemed almost fantastical, though. Could the town really have so much gold in it?

"What, then, am *I* being offered now?" she asked, hoping to make clear to the men in front of her that it was she personally they were reneging on contracts to, and it was her personal displeasure they were risking as they did.

"On some contracts, six, Your Grace," Dalflitch said, tapping a folio which she held in one hand. It contained the documents being discussed. "On the rest, five."

Five guilders to the Masnian gold? Amelia thought, astonished but keeping her expression as neutral as she could. *Spindle and Caius had thought it extortion at eight!*

"And this...pauper's rate...is the exchange we will receive from now on?"

The two masters looked at each other, clearly fearful to answer the disapproving noblewoman and hoping the other would do it instead. At last, it was Herrimans who took the bit between his teeth—another "privilege" of being wealthier and more important.

"No, your Grace," he said, his hands visibly shaking, like a man facing a death sentence from a magistrate and hoping to plead for leniency. "This is what we can offer on the contracts we have. There will be no future contracts—not for Masnian gold. Mayhaps, if you have your reserves melted down, we could trade for ingots..."

The begging explanation began to rush forth, and Dalflitch stilled the man with a cough and a hand gesture.

"What is this?" Amelia asked, uncertain what the carder could possibly mean. Surely these guilds were not refusing to trade with her outright? The potters would be no great loss to the Reach, but wool was one of the west's great riches. A break with the Carders Guild was unthinkable.

"The Bridgetown Conclave Council has met in full assembly—every master of every guild—and determined that no members can trade in Masnian currency, coming as it does through the...what was the expression...the 'shameful roads of the south'?" Dalflitch explained, and by her tone it was clear she was ready to tear strips off these men, so deep was her fury.

"Shameful roads?" Amelia repeated, trying to decipher the phrase. Her eyes widened in astonishment as she realized. "Through the Vec?" She sighed with disgust and waved a hand in the air dismissively. Disbelief turned her lips in a sneer. "Bridgetown has grown fat for centuries on trade between the Grand Kingdom and the south, and now, of a sudden, the Conclave has discovered its ancient piety and not only cannot accept truck with the heretic, rebel princedoms but cannot even accept monies that have traveled through those lands?"

She knew her tone now mirrored the anger in Lady Dalflitch's voice, perhaps with a greater shade of disbelief. No wonder these two masters stood before her like men awaiting the gibbet.

"Words like these were said in your defense during the assembly of the Conclave, I assure you, Your Grace," Herrimans moaned. "In the end, we kept loyal to you, I swear, but the rest? They voted this course. They felt compelled to."

"Compelled?" Amelia asked, and she turned in place to face them fully, her back spiking suddenly in pain. She let forth an agonized hiss, a lapse in dignity that only hardened her mood. "What precisely compelled you? The leanness of your purses in the winter season?"

As soon as she asked the question, Amelia was certain that was not the cause for a moment. These men were not gouging her, not any longer. They were refusing to trade. As one, the entire mercantile community of Bridgetown was rejecting her commerce. It was an embargo, and given her wealth, it was destined to cost them even more dearly than it would cost her, potentially. They would have to have been compelled to do this, but what hope, or fear could drive the Conclave to such extreme action. And why target her...?

"You think Daven Marcus will win?" she demanded as soon as the obscene notion occurred to her. "You all want to distance yourselves from me for fear of the Usurper's reprisals when he finally captures Bridgetown!"

From the look on Master Herrimans's face, it was clear she was right. She took a step back in disgust. Her militia had died, and were dying, to keep Bridgetown out of Daven Marcus's hands, and these...men...wanted to be ready to welcome him through the broken gates?

"It's not all of us, Your Grace, I swear," the carder insisted plaintively. "I voted against, I promise you, as did Master Jetty here. But even as we did, senior journeymen of our fraternities with speak-right argued over us."

"Am I so hated or simply disrespected?"

Will my sex or birth forever be counted against me? she wondered.

"You are neither, I swear utterly," Herrimans maintained, and his face was becoming florid with his efforts. "But the cost to us is not small, Your Grace. We are sorry, but we are doing what we can. The rest of the Conclave tried to insist that we even break our contracts unfulfilled. It is only out of loyalty that we came here to try to renegotiate our existing obligations and tell you of the embargo in person. The others are livid we have gone this far. It is costing us more than you might think, even as it costs you, Your Grace."

"Costs me?" Amelia repeated, her mind already sifting through the numerous needs of her army—most especially victuals. Would Dalflitch even be able to buy food for them if the Conclave refused to trade? How much did they already have stored? What point would there be in resisting the Dragons' breaths if her militia starved while they did so?

"If it costs you so much, then why do it?" she murmured, more to herself than to the men presented in front of her.

"Because it's better to sacrifice coin and debt than hands," the potter said, his own voice harsh for the first time, so belligerent that it made Amelia look up sharply.

"And what does that mean?" she demanded.

The man reached under his long coat and drew forth a black velvet bag from within which he produced a folded letter. In her role as seneschal, Lady Dalflitch took it from his hand. Master Jetty was not of a rank to hand something to the archduchess directly. She read the note aloud.

"So ends the hands of all who touch Masnian gold or any shameful gilt of the Western Reach."

When Amelia's expression showed confusion, Dalflitch explained further.

"Gilt as in gilding, Your Grace, not as in guiltiness."

Amelia nodded slowly. It was such an awkward phrase. She turned back to the two guildsmasters in front of her.

"How *they* end? What end?" she asked.

Herrimans hung his head and Jetty held out the bag. Dalflitch took it and pulled at the strings to open it fully. Reaching in, her hand recoiled and she put it to her mouth in horror.

"What is it?"

"A hand, Your Grace," Dalflitch said, letting Amelia take the bag from her. "A severed hand."

Amelia looked into the dark container, and the putrid aroma of rot assailed her, hot-seeming against the cold atmosphere blowing in through the open window. It took her aback, and she let the bloody-ended part stay in the cloth without further investigation, thankful her stomach did not betray her into the bargain.

"That was my nephew's right hand," Jetty said, and there was a crack in his voice. "Fellow had the makings of a true master. Best glazier I ever knew. Had the feel for it like nobody's business. And now…apothecary says the pain will pass eventual like, but ain't no way to heal back his hand nor his soul."

There were tears in the man's eyes and Amelia felt her heart clench for him. She was about to offer his nephew a pension, some way to help, but immediately caught the words before she spoke them. If handling her money had done this to the man already, what might he fear from accepting an ongoing payment?

"He was the worst, but not the only one, Your Grace," Herrimans explained. "Footpads that steal nothing but make sure to give their victims a proper beating. Apprentices with their teeth knocked in as they are shutting up workshops for the night. Even one member of the council, a master, was set upon and belayed unholy. The healers have set his fingers in splints and told him to pray for no infection or else amputation will be necessary."

Amelia gave Dalflitch another glance, and it was clear that the seneschal was only learning this part herself now. For a long moment a grim silence reigned between them, with only the sounds of the wind and rain and the gun crew working at their weapon. Amelia looked past the pleading guild leaders to address her loyal quartermasters.

"I take it, gentles, that you have been told something similar by the Conclave? Or have you been threatened directly?"

"No threats, Your Grace," said one, "but we can buy nothing with Masnians, and there are mutters that our guilders will soon be worthless too, seeing as they are from a 'counterfeit' mint and must surely be no better than 'hacksilver.' Adulterated is the word that's being thrown about most often."

Amelia nodded sorrowfully, glad that at least her own people were safe.

Because the Lions guard them, she thought. *I cannot set the banner companies to watch every street and business in all of Bridgetown. Even if we did not need them on the gates and bridges, they are militia, not bailiffs. This is work the Conclave themselves should be seeing to.*

Perhaps they were. And perhaps the bailiffs had been as intimidated as the Council itself was. Amelia had no doubt who must be responsible, and giving the bag one last look before pulling the tie and offering it back to Master Jetty, she had to acknowledge her enemies were not being gentle or subtle, for all they were still being stealthy. At last, she drew in a deep breath that the lingering scent of rot made unrefreshing.

"I want to thank you, masters, both of you, for taking the risk to come to me like this," she forced herself to say, not feeling the least bit thankful. "I also offer you gratitude for at least planning to honor the contracts we already have drafted. I will not accept less than the agreed upon eight guilders exchange, and please tell your members that if they renege, the entire Reach will be closed to them for the rest of their lives. Any Reacherman caught trading with them will have his own goods and chattels forfeited to the throne in Dweltford, along with the traded goods and the boats, wagons, or pack animals used to carry them."

The two men looked aghast, but Amelia's sympathy for them had run its course. They were being pressured to abandon her, to seem neutral in the conflict in case the Usurper won, but that was their problem and their burden, not hers. The trouble with seeking a neutral course in all conflicts was that one could not claim the rewards of loyalty. She would be understanding of the Conclave's actions but not all-forgiving.

"You may go, gentles," she said, indicating by a nod of her head that she meant the entire group. They tugged their forelocks and shuffled away morosely.

Enemies without and within, Amelia thought and looked back out the window at Norgate. Did the fools really think Daven Marcus would leave them unmolested if he took the town? Did they imagine the kingslayer might deal fairly with them if they simply proclaimed themselves neutral? The ill-taste of the meeting swirled in her thoughts for a long while as she stared into the north. Despite the rain, workmen could be seen moving about like ants on a mound, setting the Usurper's camp more fully for a long siege. Earthworks, those to close the town in, were being dug across the swarded fields in front of the ridge that had hidden the Bronze Dragons during the battle, likely by forced levies, drafted from the nearby villages. How many of them would sicken and die this winter as they labored under Daven Marcus's lash?

"Aye up, here comes trouble," Amelia heard Lady Elizabeth whisper beside her. She was about to chastise the Lace Fang for such common speech when she saw where the lady-in-waiting was looking and noticed that Lady Penelope had arrived in the gallery chamber with her cousins in tow. All three wore damp cloaks with the hoods still pulled up.

Another meeting with fools? the archduchess wondered, rolling her eyes and this time not bothering to conceal her feelings. She gave the approaching liege of Bridgetown a sidelong glance but pointedly did not turn to greet her. *My back hurts too much to waste effort on pleasantries that will be disdained in any case.*

CHAPTER 22

Flanked by Cyprian and Wilforn, Lady Penelope walked straight to Amelia and stood staring at her. The archduchess kept her eyes on the northern bank of the river and the fields beyond, studying the growing enemy camp. Silence in the chamber grew to become a palpable thing, seeming to flatten out the other sounds, even the metallic clanks of the gun crew's iron poles.

From the corner of her eye, Amelia noticed that a pair of armed men in Reach colors had come through the room's main door, just behind the three Bridgetown nobles. They stood like sentries flanking the portal. A moment later another pair came in and took up positions with their fellows. Word of recent hostilities between the two allies and their retainers had likely circulated amongst the whole militia company by now, especially since her last audience with Lady Penelope, and it seemed these militiamen had come upstairs just to keep watch for possible conflict. Amelia appreciated the show of loyalty.

The quiet of the tense moment continued until...

"Will you not even face me, Amelia?" Lady Penelope demanded suddenly, rainwater from her journey spitting from her lips.

"She disdains you openly," Cyprian insisted.

"I thought disdain had become the character of our meetings of late, My Lady," Amelia answered calmly. "You do not hesitate to disdain my title, after all. If you wish to return to our previous warm affection, you have only to show it by your own words and actions."

Penelope was clearly taken aback by the quiet rebuke, and for a moment her eyes narrowed to mere slits.

"You invited me to tour the defenses," Penelope said in a forced tone.

"And as we arrive, the first we find is this vandalism," Wilforn chimed in, waving his hand at the gun and its crew. "When my father was castellan of this keep, this was his own chambers. Now you do this to them?"

"Your father was castellan here?" Amelia asked. "I wasn't told."

"There was a bed here and some other furnishings, Your Grace," Dalflitch confirmed. "They were removed even before the gun was brought up. The cannon was swung in through the window, but I fear the bed was demolished to make it easier to remove. I can only imagine in this season of death and woe how important a soft bed would be to you, good Squire."

"You mock me?" Wilforn demanded, and Amelia was almost surprised the proud young man had wit enough to realize.

"Heavens forfend," Dalflitch protested without the least fraction of remorse in her tone.

"What happened there?" Cyprian demanded in a loud, shocked voice. He was looking out the galleried window and had seen the damage to Norgate. Everyone else turned at his question, and Penelope's hand went to her mouth.

"Good God," the liege of Bridgetown muttered, her brown eyes full of horror as she looked upon the destruction.

"What did you do?" Wilforn demanded, looking at the White Lions' cannon crew, as if it were the gun in this room that he suspected had damaged the ancient fortification.

"What did *we* do?" Amelia asked, feeling her own emotions rising at the accusation and her self-control slipping as the pain in her back only grew worse. "*We* held off the Usurper while he tried to put your town to the torch, you petty..."

She managed to choke off any insult before she spoke it, but it was not easy. The provocative little twit was determined to work Amelia's every last nerve, it seemed. She had a sudden notion that perhaps Wilforn was a skin-thief, the true noble cousin now long dead somewhere and replaced by an agent of the Inquisition, seeking to provoke conflict between the two noblewomen at every turn. Almost immediately, Amelia dismissed the notion. For all that Wilforn always sought to be an instigator, he was nowhere near subtle enough to be a servant of the Silent Hand. Cyprian was the more likely skin-thief, if either squire was.

I hadn't thought of that, Amelia realized, suddenly troubled by the possibility. If one of Penelope's closest confidantes had been replaced by a sorcerous enemy, it was little wonder the girl was so inconstant in her thoughts and loyalties. If a skin thief was at her side, whispering in her ear continually, she would likely never pierce the veil of lies around her. Of course, all the poison between Amelia and her allies could just as easily be the product of their youthful pride. Conspiracy was not necessary to explain it. Worse, the one did not preclude the other. Both could be equally true—pride and conspiracy. Whatever the truth, perhaps one or more of the neophytes should be set to watch comings and goings around Earlsbastion or to look out for sightings of the last two Young Hopefuls if they go about the town. They might inadvertently lead to Bluebird. Any trail to the fiend's nest.

"Are you saying Daven Marcus did that to Norgate?" Penelope asked, and for the first time in a long time the girl seemed to Amelia to be experiencing an honest emotion, not tinged by her pride or dreams. "His forces have barely been ashore a week."

"The Bronze Dragons did that in a single morning, My Lady," Dalflitch said matter-of-factly, and all three of the Bridgetown nobles looked at her agape. They were silent for a long moment, Penelope looking back and forth from the Lions' cannon to the damaged gatehouse.

"You lie," Wilforn said breathlessly at last.

Dalflitch showed not the slightest offense. "Why would I bother?" she asked off-handedly. "The next time there is a break in the rain, you can come here and see for yourself. Better yet, go you to Norgate and witness firsthand."

"But Norgate has stood for centuries," Penelope objected and once again Amelia felt a twinge of pity for her.

The river is rising, and she refuses to let us pull her to safety, the archduchess thought. *How long until she realizes this is a torrent she cannot swim alone?*

"What have you been doing while the Denay king has been vandalizing our history?" Cyprian demanded.

"It is by dint of her grace's efforts that your precious history has not been erased entirely, young Squire," Dalflitch answered him with a swift, harsh tone.

Amelia was happy to let her lady seneschal carry the conversation at this point. Her own attentions were focused entirely on Lady Penelope. The archduchess was now convinced that the Bridgetown liege had been affected by an Inquisition spell. Having been through the experience herself, she felt she could recognize the signs.

At least as well as I might pick a skin thief from a true mortal, she thought.

As she watched, Amelia was sure she could see a moment of clarity in Penelope's expression. The damage to Norgate—the sight of something she relied upon so naturally, smashed so easily—seemed to have pierced the veil of deception around the noblewoman's thoughts. Amelia had no idea how long that might last, but it was an opportunity she was loath to waste. If the light was shining through the fog for a moment, how might she add to that and perhaps blow the obscuring clouds from Penelope's vision completely?

Master Solft says scripture, Amelia thought, and she wracked her memory for a piece of holy writ that might apply, that might abolish the lies in the girl's head. Were there any scriptural verses referenced in the poems he had copied for them? The Steeple Aviary songs?

"What should we do?" Penelope asked, her eyes on no one in particular.

"Pray," Amelia said reflexively, and Penelope looked at her, her expression showing that the answer only increased her confusion. Amelia knew how weak that word would sound to ears that did not know what she knew of their enemy. She wanted to explain her comment, but her tongue was slowed by trying to think of a piece of scripture that fit the moment. In the delay, Cyprian and Wilforn both scoffed loudly.

"Is that all you have?" Cyprian asked, his sharp gaze more filled with eagerness than shock, as if he was glad to see Amelia look so weak in the face of Daven Marcus's demonstrated power. Given how bitter he must feel over his brother's recent death, Amelia could understand why, even though it was such folly.

If I am weak, then you are doomed, fool, she thought, but a part of her suspected that Cyprian was the sort who would accept his own doom if it meant he could get revenge on his enemies. *It is my land's strength that holds your enemies at bay. How can you children not see that?*

"Prayer?" Wilforn repeated derisively. "What of your mighty army? What of your much vaunted militia, Amelia of Dweltford? Nothing but a rabble of rogues foot, as I have always said." He waved his hand dismissively at Amelia and her ladies. "Knights and true men-at-arms are banished, leaving your land ruled by wenches and guarded by convicts and slatterns with daggers up their skirts!"

Amelia felt herself stiffen at Wilforn's insult, more because she feared how the militiamen in the room might react than for the sake of her own pride.

"Have a care whom you insult, Squire," Dalflitch said coldly. "Your own land is ruled by a woman."

It was a true retort and reasonable in the face of the squires' contempt, but Amelia's heart sank as she saw the earnestness on

Penelope's face start to harden into pride once again. Cyprian's next comment closed the veil over her eyes completely.

"It may be our liege is a woman, but she at least was born to the peerage and understands the value of her knights," he said, and he reached out his arm to put a supportive hand on hers. It was an odd gesture, not only because of the awkwardness of the steel plates on their gauntleted fingers but also because of its level of public familiarity.

"What knights?" Dalflitch demanded archly. "The entire of Bridgetown's peerage is in this room, and there's not a knight amongst us!"

That was the last straw for Lady Penelope, it seemed. She snatched her hand from Cyprian's grasp and laid it upon the sunburst pommel of her longsword. She straightened her shoulders and looked down her nose at Amelia and her entourage.

"I see I have made a mistake," she declared, and Amelia felt her heart sink. Whatever hope she might have had to pierce the lies around Penelope's mind was surely lost now. "I should never have invited you here. I opened my hand in friendship, and you have bitten it like a bitch cur in the street."

The heaviness in Amelia's heart meant she felt no sting from Penelope's insult. She only shook her head sadly.

"You have tasted Daven Marcus' 'friendship' already," she said with a soft voice. "You did not like that any better."

"I am not so sure now," Penelope retorted, and then she turned on her heel and headed to the door. Cyprian followed immediately, but Wilforn paused to give Amelia one last condescending look before he went with them. The sentries left the room to follow them out.

"That's all got to be mad talk, don't it?" Elizabeth asked quietly once the three Bridgetowners were gone. "I mean, with your permission, Your Grace, but she's got nothin' of her own holdin' this town in her hands, does she? It's all the Reach, isn't it?"

"She has grim days on her hands and fell voices in her ears," Amelia said.

"You were hoping to cut the lies from her ears with the sharpest sword, Your Grace?" Dalflitch asked, and Amelia could not tell if the seneschal's tone was sad or skeptical. She nodded solemnly.

"When the lady saw Norgate, it was as if she was looking into an abyss," Amelia explained. "It seemed as if her confidence was deeply shaken a moment, and I hoped that might undo some of the knots of folly around her thoughts, but I was not quick enough, I think."

"Would any of us be?" asked the seneschal.

They were quiet another moment.

"I'd bet that cousin of hers is sweet on her," Lady Agatha, the other Lace Fang present, suggested softly. Amelia felt the notion send her thoughts on a different path for a moment.

"The hand holding?" she asked, wondering if the simple gesture had indicated as much as the lady-in-waiting was suggesting.

"And his eyes," Agatha added. "Not kindly, exactly, but watching for her nods and smiles—leastwise tis how it seemed to me."

"Quite familiar," Dalfitch agreed.

"But cousins?" Amelia asked rhetorically, not protesting exactly, but struggling to accept the possibility.

"Hardly unknown amongst the high peerage, Your Grace," said the seneschal. "But I think his ambitions might still be unknown to the lady herself. Unless I miss my guess, the Lady of Bridgetown will still have eyes for the handsome Count Lark-Stross."

Ugh, what a mess, Amelia thought. Bridgetown's ruling house was an almost empty basket. The few eggs it did hold were all nearly rotten, and the whole thing was a mass of entangling webs into the bargain. The thought conjured images of a disgusting muddle of mold and filth in Amelia's mind, which prompted a different consideration. *If it disgusts me, how must it feel for the young woman forced to live in it?*

She was seized with a sudden desire to help Lady Penelope, a care for the floundering noblewoman that she had not felt for months. Before, Amelia had imagined that defending the town was what the girl mainly needed. Now the archduchess realized that Penelope was as much a victim of the Silent Hand as she herself.

"We must clear away the webs for her and give her some chance to deal with the rotten eggs," she muttered, and Dalflitch cocked an eyebrow. Amelia smiled at her friend and closest female advisor. "Our hostess is even more ensnared in the Bluebird's plots than we are, My Lady," she explained. "That gives us double the cause to hunt him out and end his songs. It will not make worthy retainers out of those venal squires, but hopefully it will clear her mind enough to make some wiser judgements for herself."

"And if she is still a silly filly after all?" asked Dalflitch.

It was Lady Elizabeth who answered. "I reckon I'd want to know if my follies were from my own foolishness than from some conjurer's trickeries, no matter whether I loved 'em or hated 'em. Better we know, too, even if it changes nothin' else for us." She paused, and it was clear from her expression she was unsure if she had spoken out of turn or not. Then she shrugged. "I'm only saying, is all," she added, and Amelia shared a knowing, amused glance with Lady Dalflitch.

"It has the ring of wisdom about it, Your Grace," the seneschal joked. "As to finding the Bluebird's roost, we ladies of your chamber have some new notions to pursue, and we are following after them with all vigor."

"I have no doubt," Amelia said, feeling encouraged by Dalflitch's confidence. Her smile was choked away as a new lance of pain shot up her back, and with only her closest entourage near her, she took the moment to rub at the aching spot. Her eyes went to the gun crew, still fixed on their preparations, though she was sure they had a degree of surreptitious curiosity about their noble guests.

"We will leave now, ladies," the archduchess announced, removing her comforting hand and doing her best to hide a wince as she forced her aching back straight.

"On to the next cannon emplacement, Your Grace?" Dalflitch inquired. "Marquis Knight Captain Farringdon explained that the easiest way to reach that one is via an alley a little east of the Dog's Leg." The lady seneschal's lip curled at the tavern's name, as if even having to speak of something so base was unsettling to her. It was an affectation, of course. There was little in all the world that could actually disgust the Lady Dalflitch. It was just another performance for their martial audience, a character she never failed to portray in public.

"No, My Lady," Amelia told her, raising her voice a little to be better heard across the room. "If the other guns are even half as well bestowed as this one, our defenses are well in hand. Let us return to those other matters."

She smirked as she led them from the chamber, Wilforn's father's former bedroom, and down the stairs.

The defenses are well in hand, indeed, she thought as they came out onto Great Bridge Road. *Let us see if we cannot get our hands on some of our feathered "friends" now as well.*

CHAPTER 23

For several days, Prentice tried to ignore the note from his brother, leaving it folded away in his belt pouch. Initially, the aftermath of the battle kept him so busy that he was almost able to forget the stark invitation. With all the wounded being cared for, many of whom survived the battle only to die of their wounds in the next day or two, it was easy to think of his father's passing as just one more death amongst many. By the end of the second day, however, the note became more of a presence in Prentice's thoughts. The night of their defeat, while the knight commander had been promoting Sootface Kate and demobbing Corporal Denholm, Dahyoor had gone ashore alone to scout the perimeter of Daven Marcus's growing encampment and the lands to the north. Knowing it would likely be days before the fey man returned, Prentice put him into the back of his thoughts as well and looked for other duties to occupy his mind.

What I most want is to ask Whilte about my dream, he thought more than once as he traipsed his way back to Runners Field to check on the wounded who were being cared for mainly in two large infirmary tents. Of all his past dreams and visions, this one was the worst for raising at least as many questions as it offered answers. *What did the chained prophet's mane represent, and when will I have taken it up? What was Samson's mistake that I must avoid? And who was that fellow who had seen into the pit and fled? What part does he play?*

If there was a man, a real mortal man, who had seen into the inner workings of the Inquisition and escaped alive, that was someone Prentice earnestly wanted to meet, assuming that man could be found. For all the knight commander knew, the fellow could be alive and well, living in hiding on the other side of Aucks or Masnia, as far beyond reach as the home of the Redlanders across the salt sea.

Any hope of speaking with the chaplain about visions and symbology was scotched when Prentice saw Whilte at work in the infirmary tent. There were rows of men, each at least with his own blanket, though few had a cot or some other way to rest off the ground. Most were on nothing more than sod beds, but many of these at least had oiled canvas under their bedclothes to keep their resting places from soaking through. Whilte stood from ministering to one fellow, ready to move to the next when Prentice intercepted him. The hollows under the healer's eyes made it clear he must not have slept since the battle, or near enough. The chaplain's homespun cassock was spattered with bloodstains, old and fresh, some crimson, some faded to rust on the undyed fabric

Never mind talk of dreams and visions, Prentice thought. *We need to find him other healers to share the load. As like as not, this will not be the only time we have this many wounded in coming days.*

At the Battle of the Red Sky and its aftermath years before, Prentice had been forced to leave wounded behind after a battle, thinking that they would have been safe because chivalry demanded the injured be given parole as a matter of course. Instead of mercy, Daven Marcus's men had slaughtered the entire contingent in a fit of indignation. Since that day, Prentice had resolved never to leave the wounded ill-served or unprotected. The Lioness's pride guarded the injured—that was the rule now.

"What do you need? What can I get for you?" he asked the exhausted chaplain, putting his own priorities aside.

"Fire, stoves, *something* to heat these pavilions," Whilte said with a weary wave of his hand over the vast space of the tent. "We have unction enough to wash wounds and I've sent barrel carts as far west as they can go to fetch fresh water rather than the filth that flows past Runners' shore. But it's like a mountain fastness in here of a night. I'll lose as many as I save to the chill if we don't do something for the cold. You know what it's like."

"I will see to it today," Prentice agreed, and he nodded solemnly. He did indeed know what a simple "chill" could do to a wounded man. Whilte hobbled away to the next patient to pray for healing. Prentice looked around himself and considered what else he might do to assist. He wandered up and down the rows as he contemplated his militiamen's needs. After a short search, taking time to return every salute he received from the wounded who noticed him passing, Prentice found Sergeant Porth, the loyal Claw officer still healing from the brutal ambush the Young Hopefuls had sprung upon him. As a senior man, he at least had a cot, and he sat up awkwardly when he saw Prentice approach, obviously struggling with his changed balance. The bandaged stump of his amputated right arm waved in the air a moment and he almost fell back before he got himself upright. Prentice waved at him to keep his seat.

"Can't salute you now, neither, Knight Commander," Porth said, shaking his head in bitter resignation.

"You have done more than your share of saluting, Sergeant," Prentice replied sincerely. "I will take your future ones as already given."

Porth nodded a sorrowful thanks, but his frown spoke of his true emotions.

"Not a sergeant anymore, though, am I?"

"No? You planning on going wayward? Thinking to desert your comrades?"

"Never!" Porth answered without thinking, and then his expression changed to one of confusion. "But, I mean, look at me, My Lord. I ain't goin' to march no more, am I? Can't hold me pike like this, nor a sword, nor even a dagger. What place can I have in the Gryphons now?"

Prentice knew that kind of thinking. How much damage had Cassian's poison and his sickness since done to his own vitality. It was not the loss of an arm, but he knew that such inner infirmities could cripple a man or woman as completely as a missing limb. Then he thought of Whilte, working himself to exhaustion with a missing leg, bringing healing to others.

I yet have two arms, two legs and a heart beating in my chest, he thought. *If that is not enough strength, then I had best find some more from somewhere. I still have a race to run—apparently.*

Remembering the injunction from his dream that he must prepare for a race of some kind helped to put some notions together in Prentice's head. Crippling was an inward thing as much as outward it seemed—as much of the spirit and heart as of the body.

"It may seem that there are no marches ahead of you, Sergeant," Prentice told Porth, "but I am afraid the archduchess cannot release you from service for something as trivial as a missing arm."

"Beggin' your pardon, but what's 'trivial,' My Lord?" Porth asked, and Prentice smirked. Years amongst common folk and living even lowlier than that, and still he spoke like the most educated scholar.

"Small; easy; cast off; simple," he explained. "Like taking a leak in the morning."

"Yea, well that used to be easy, too," Porth muttered, looking down at his body on the cot, and while he said it with a kind of grin, his bitterness was unmistakable.

"The Gryphons need a permanent Banner Sergeant, and since you do not think you will be marching with the Claws anymore, I am minded to give you the role, Sergeant Porth."

Now the crippled man did rise from his bed, his face full of shock.

"You know I'm missin' me arm, My Lord?" he said, waving at the stump with his other hand. He misjudged and his finger caught the bandaged end, making him wince and hiss. "See! I never knew how much I used my right hand for just about everything, but I'm havin' to relearn every damnable thing, from eating and drinking to wiping m'self at the other end. Can't even wave me hand about safely!"

"You will learn," Prentice replied firmly, as if he were a parent with a frustrated child finding a new chore too difficult. Porth did not seem so easily consoled, however. Even so, for all that making him banner sergeant was a spontaneous notion, the idea was swiftly taking full form in Prentice's mind.

"And carryin' a banner?" the one-armed sergeant persisted. "I'm a Claw and no small man, but neither me nor you nor even your mate the castellan knight is big enough to carry a proper banner one-handed."

"We will have a harness made for you," Prentice told him. "You will be able to carry it one-handed with a strap across your other shoulder, once it is comfortable enough. In the meantime, I will give you some other Gryphons to share the duty with you."

Porth shook his head in wonder.

"Why?"

"Because I will not give the mongrels the satisfaction of thinking they have us beaten, Sergeant," Prentice told him honestly. It was part of the resolve that had kept him getting up in the morning every day as a convict. "You became sergeant of the Claws because you were more than a big body that could thrust a pike over other men's shoulders. You lead, and you are good at it. They may have taken your arm, but they have not taken the rest, and I will not let you throw it away so easily as this. Gryphons are not so effortless to defeat."

The wounded sergeant stared at the ground beneath his feet, as if shocked to discover he was standing up. He raised his head once more and his eyes ranged about in wonder. It was as if the whole world must be changing around him, and he seemed to find it a delight. Still, he had some thread of fear that dimmed his burgeoning smile.

"What if I can't do it? What if I'm not strong enough or good enough?"

"Then I will replace you and you will be given other duties, Sergeant. Same as it has always been," Prentice said as if this was as matter of fact as any other command. "The Gryphons need a banner sergeant and you are my best choice by far, two arms or not. I have a new sergeant I plan to give the Roar over to, and I will send Guillam over to take the Claws in hand for you."

"He won't like that none, My Lord," Porth said with a chuckle.

"And like you, the archduchess expects him to do his duty and fulfil his orders. As for you, even as things stand right now, I do have duties you can perform while your arm...while your stump...heals. Do not overdo it. Husband your returning strength, but I want you to start organizing teams of men to cut sedge, as much of the winter growth as they can find, and also to dig the earth around the infirmary tents."

"Dig the earth, My Lord?"

"We have not the time nor men to build full walls, but we need to do something to keep the winter winds out. A mud-and-grass wall is something we can stretch to, I think," Prentice explained. "Do you know the technique?"

Porth nodded uncertainly. "I seen it done once or twice," he said.

"Ask about, I am sure there are some in the ranks who know the method. I will leave this duty to you while I see if we cannot scare up some iron stoves from the merchants in town—get some proper warmth into this place."

"I'll...I'll sure and do my best, My Lord," Porth said, his personal discomfort seeming dispelled by a renewed sense of purpose. "I'd best get to it, with your permission."

Porth left his cot and headed to the tent entrance, where he consulted with a line first who looked surprised initially, then headed out with the injured sergeant. The knight commander smiled to himself.

"Well might you smile," said Brother Whilte's wearied voice from behind Prentice. "I pray daily for the healing of men's bodies, but that was a miracle of the soul, My Lord."

Prentice turned to the chaplain who stood nearby, leaning on his "prophet's" staff with its broken spearpoint head. Even as talk of a miracle was still in his ears, Prentice was assaulted by memories of all those he had known who had suffered as Porth had suffered. How many had walked at his side and lost a hand or foot? Been crippled, lamed or tortured? Or simply died because he ordered them to? He remembered his protest to the chained figure in his dream, that he was shorn like Samson, but he thought how foolish that sounded now. How could he think of his own woes in the face of all these who suffered and died around him? A word from his childhood, a chastisement of one of his training masters, came back suddenly to his thoughts.

Are you yet breathing? the stern man had demanded after young Prentice, in tears, had insisted that he could face no more training and demanded to know why he could not simply hear some praise for his efforts. *If your heart still beats and your chest takes in breath, then you can do more. The grave and a good epitaph—these are the only rest and the only praise a true knight craves.*

The sudden harshness of that memory hardened Prentice's emotions and he felt a momentary flash of anger at Whilte. Why would the chaplain bat at him with talk of miracles like this? *He* knew the effrontery of false praise.

"I like talk of miracles by my hand no better than you do, Chaplain," Prentice said sharply, shying from the implied praise as an animal shies from fire, as if a good report might burn him. "Such speech has ever been more burden than praise. You have said so yourself more than once. I will go now and see what I can find you by way of stoves to heat the tent."

He left the infirmary, intending to simply go about the town seeking the necessary items, but still he found himself rushing out of the camp as if fleeing from it.

CHAPTER 24

Although he ostensibly kept his eye out for ironmongers where he might purchase stoves to heat the infirmary tents, and he did stop to speak with each group of militia sentries or patrols he passed, Prentice found himself moving persistently westward across Bridgetown almost without realizing he was doing it. Weaving his way along a busy thoroughfare on the island called Salthatch, he passed a foundry that seemed to manufacture all manner of ironware and fixtures for riverboats. The workshop's brick furnace served no fewer than four anvils, with four mouths breathing flames and roaring in time to the heavy bellows pumped by sweating apprentices at the sides. With a shed opposite the sheltered anvils that seemed to contain a large stockpile of already manufactured pots, cauldrons, and other ironwork, the foundry seemed the ideal place to purchase stoves. Even if they had none amidst their stores, the place could surely build a half dozen in mere days. Thinking to have some guilders ready to make a downpayment, Prentice reached into his belt pouch and instead of his purse, drew forth his brother's note. He held the folded paper up, and despite the spitting rain, he unfolded it. He stared, bewildered, as the water droplets threatened to make the ink run.

"You lookin' to buy sumtin', good fellow?" one of the foundry's other workers asked, a wiry individual with bare feet.

"What?" Prentice asked him, struggling to understand the man's question for some reason.

"Do you want to buy?"

"No," Prentice said, shaking his head and turning away to the west. Behind him, he heard the fellow mutter disgustedly.

"Drunk at this hour? Pfft!"

Looking along the busy street over the heads of the crowd, Prentice could see through to the final bridge westward, the one that led to Bell's Hummock. With note in hand, he continued through the press, not rushing but with slow determination. As he stepped onto the bridge itself, the crowd stayed busy, but the typical houses that clung to the edges of other bridges around the town fell away. Suddenly fully exposed to the river and the open air, Prentice was caught by a gust of wind and misting rain, but he barely noticed. A moment later he was on the dockside of the smallest of Bridgetown's settled islands.

As its name suggested, it was likely originally shaped like the hump of an unknown water creature—perhaps a turtle, though it would have been a turtle larger than the largest castle. Despite its lesser size and the openness of the bridge that crossed to it, the little landmass itself teemed with buildings, pressed up against one another like an encircling wall and crowded almost to the river's edge. The dockside, such as it was, was no more than paces across from buildings to water. The ground floor of every structure was a warehouse of some sort, and above those were rooms and apartments maintained by wealthy families—patricians and Conclave folk one and all. As in other towns where the wealthy and well-born lodged upwind so as not to suffer the smoke and smells of their lessers' lives, so in Bridgetown the patricians lodged upriver, so that the water they drank every day was the cleanest and least odorous—the opposite of the murk flowing past Runners Field where the White Lions were now encamped at the other end of town. Somewhere nearby would be the place where Whilte's barrel teams fetched their clean drinking water for the injured.

Pausing only to ask a dockworker for final directions, Prentice headed around the waterside to a point where a narrow set of stairs between two buildings led to the Hummock's tiny inland space. Mounting the stone steps, he came to a wrought iron gate. Through the bars he could see a park of some sort. Amidst the encirclement of three- and four-story buildings, the residents of Bell's Hummock maintained a tiny green sward with two ancient willows that were waving gently in the grey rain. The rare open space in the crowded town was clearly jealously guarded, appearing to be accessible only from the residents' own buildings or by this lone stairway. Prentice was peering through the bars, looking for a bell or similar, when he discovered just how much the denizens of Bell's Hummock worked to keep the riffraff out of their park. On the other side of the gate appeared a towering giant of a man in polished mail, wielding a heavy-looking cudgel bound in brightly gilded brass. With a full beard and broad shoulders, the fellow looked as if he could beat even Turley in a wrestling match.

Malden would have found this one cause for hesitation, Prentice thought, though he did not feel intimidated personally. He had been invited, after all.

"What you want?" the guard demanded from behind the tall iron bars of the gate.

"I am looking for Master Xavoer, a trader," Prentice answered him. "He lodges in a place called Vespers, so I am told."

"Vespers Remembered," the guard said, knowingly. "Sure'n the merchant Xavoer has rooms there, but not for the likes of you."

"The likes of me? I have an invitation." Prentice held up his brother's note, damper and more crumpled from being carried in the rain, and he wondered if it was harder to read now. Not that he expected this fellow to know how to read.

"Invite?" the man said, peering at the note and then at Prentice's face. He stood back and turned a key in the gate's lock, swung it wide and stared, narrow-eyed, at Prentice some more. "You a leader bloke from them jump-up'd militia bods?"

"I am Knight Commander of the White Lions, yes," Prentice told him.

"I heard to watch for you and to let you in," the guard said, but he did not move aside for a long moment. "You were s'posed to be here two nights back."

"Well, I am here now."

The guard looked Prentice up and down one more time, his gaze lingering on the champion sword in its sheath. Prentice wondered if the man knew some of the rumors or if he was just mentally comparing his own armament, assessing the risk Prentice might pose to the residents the sentry was paid to guard.

A diligent man, this one, he thought. *Diligent or proud.* Prentice decided it made the most sense to assume both.

"I have come at an invitation, not to make trouble," he reassured the man who shrugged and sucked at his teeth.

"None of my business, I s'pose," he said, turning around suddenly and leading the way into the inner garden of Bell's Hummock.

Prentice followed him, wondering how many of the common folk of Bridgetown had ever seen this patch of cultivated greenery. The sentry's behavior was one of the odd phenomena of the Grand Kingdom's stratified society—the pride a low-born man might take in serving his betters, lording his share of their reflected glory over his fellow yeomen. As soon as he thought about it, Prentice remembered Turley's diligence in protecting the archduchess's dignity, and in his mind, the guard's condescending attitude took on a new light.

Is that why I am not so annoyed by him? Prentice wondered as the man led the way around a path of crushed sandstone to one of the many doors that opened onto the garden.

"Knowin' as how you're one of them hoity toity bods from upriver—strut around the streets and markets, think you own the bloody place—well you can see how I might ken you for hasslin'," the sentry explained over his shoulder with a surly twist to his lip. He pushed open a heavy wooden door that had no lock.

"The White Lions are protecting Bridgetown from two sieges at the moment, or had you not noticed?" Prentice asked him, feeling his annoyance growing after all.

The guard whirled on him in the doorway and gave him another suspicious glare, as if changing his mind about Prentice causing trouble for the folk he protected.

"That's all fine and good for the downwash sloppers, but the gentles of Bell's Hummock can and do protect themselves. They don't need some jump-up trial day charms to watch over their goods and chattels. We know pilferin' and thievin's all got worse since your rogues got to town."

Rogues? Trial day charms? Prentice thought. It was a long time since he had heard that particular epithet. Since convicts were all on a chain, they were said to be like a charm bracelet writ large, put together by magistrates on trial days—hence the term. "Devil's prayer beads" was a similar slang name for the convicted but more used around Rhales, as far as Prentice understood. The guard stared down at him, as if he was waiting for the knight commander to bite back at the accusation. Prentice only held the man's gaze. Eventually, the guard shrugged once more and led the way into the ground floor of the building. Prentice followed silently.

I am too tired to waste effort with this fool's ignorance, he told himself. Tired, not yet fully recovered from poison, illness, and near drowning. No point spending what little vitality he did have on arguments like this. *I have more important matters to concern myself with, like stoves for my men.*

That notion caused him to pause in his steps. What was he doing here when he had come into the town for a completely different purpose? He was about to leave when the guard struck flint on a quick match and, blowing upon the smoldering length of twine, used it to light a lantern from an alcove in the wall beside the door. As soon as the light began to glow, Prentice found his attention drawn to the odd space where he stood.

The ground floor of the building was almost a single open chamber, akin to a hall, with brick pillars incorporated into the walls and rising to vault the ceiling. The entire room was an otherwise empty oblong, but at the far end away from the door, there was something painted onto the wall—an illuminated scene of some sort, like those that were muraled onto the walls of monasteries, convents, and churches. Like the ones that had been on many of the walls at Ashfield, Prentice recalled. Most of the picture had faded away, but the image in the center of the mural was still brightly colored. It was a bear, rampant, painted in marigold orange, the heraldic bear of Bridgetown. Prentice found himself drawn toward it.

"That's the oldest heraldry in the whole town," the guard said proudly as he walked up behind, holding the lantern high so that the entire mighty animal glowed in the light. While most of the wall was faded and peeling away, the bear still seemed fresh, and there looked to be new torch sconces built into the masonry. "The good folk of the Hummock keep the bear in fine condition as a matter of pride. Tis older even than anythin' in Earlsbastion."

"Have you ever been in the earl's castle?" Prentice asked absently, knowing that almost certainly the man never had.

"Don't need to go there to know it's there!" the guard retorted in a surly tone. "Like Denay or Rhales. Bridgetown's as ancient as any place in the world."

Prentice smiled at the man's parochialism, still studying the image on the wall. It was an especially fine work.

If only Bluebird had had access to this to inspire Inxyphos' transformation, he thought, remembering the crude version of the earldom's bear heraldry they had found on the slain bear-man's corpse. Solft the scholar suspected that that image had been used to guide the *brakkis effar* transformation in the right direction—a picture of a bear to remind the ensorcelled man what form his flesh was expected to take. Prentice reached out a hand to touch the picture on the wall in front of him but stopped himself, feeling a sudden fear that his touch might ruin the proud monument. He looked around again at the large but dim and empty chamber.

"Why is this here?" he asked. "What is this place?"

"Tis in the name," the guard insisted. "Vespers Remembered. Used to be this was an abbey. The mother of nuns was the one drew the first bear for the first earl, so they say. The nuns repainted her drawing here on the wall and prayed every day for the prosperity of the town. That was, until they all caught the plague and died. Some folk say you can hear their plaintive prayers still at night sometimes. You ain't afeared of ghosts none, is you?"

Prentice smirked at the folktale, shaking his head. He had seen too much in his time to fear anything that might simply go bump in the night.

"Where are my brother's rooms?" he asked, turning away from the mural. He was supposed to be buying stoves, not playing historian of folklore. That was Solft's task. The guard pointed with the lantern, and as the light played over the walls, Prentice noticed an iron ring embedded in one of the chamber's pillars. Having noticed the one, his eyes swiftly searched the gloom and found three other such rings, each in a pillar, so that they were at the corners of a square. From what he could see, they looked newly installed as well.

"I thought you did not suffer to have convicts on Bell's Hummock," he said to the guard, feeling a sudden rush of fury. The rings were exactly the kind that were used to chain convicts in place of a night, and this chamber was precisely the sort of barn-like space overseers liked to use to do it—somewhere where they could stand in one place and see every chained prisoner at once.

"What you talkin' of?" the guard demanded, his pride clearly pricked at the accusatory question.

Prentice met the man's gaze in the lamplight for a long moment and then wondered why. If this room had been used to house convicts, even recently, what difference did that make? He shook his head.

"Just show me to my brother's rooms."

CHAPTER 25

T he guard showed him along a corridor and led Prentice into
   a simple room with grime-stained walls and floorboards.
A window opposite the entrance was glassless, with locked
wooden shutters, and the little light in the room came in through
the cracks. From outside, the sound of riverfolk loading and
unloading boats wafted in as a rattle of rain beat upon the shutters.
The dim room was cold, but there was a chimneyless grate to one
side where a small fire might be built. A table and a threadbare
cushioned armchair sat next to the grate. A second door on the
right led to an inner chamber, it seemed, and the entire space
resembled servants' lodgings, with nothing personal to reveal the
nature or character of the occupants. While it was no poorer than
many places Prentice had stayed himself in life, he was astonished
to think this was where his brother was living in Bridgetown.
Compared with their family's home and holdings when Prentice
was growing up, this was poverty incarnate.

"How long has he been here?" Prentice wondered aloud, but
the guard took it as a direct question.

"Week or two," he explained. "Not much, is it? Still, better than
them tents you lot huddle in."

Only two weeks? Prentice wondered. Perhaps Xavoer *had* left
with the Forberest nobles and then returned shortly after to take
these rooms. It made him wonder what kind of business his
brother might have that would cause him to leave and return in
such a fashion. That thought was crowded out, though, by the

guard's comment about huddling in tents. How many militiamen in the infirmary tents would delight in a closed room like this, fire in the grate, door and shutters to block out the draft, if only a little. Prentice, Righteous, and their children shared rooms no larger than this in the Paramour's Chambers, and suddenly the servants' quarters seemed like such luxury compared to his men-at-arms' conditions on Runners Field. He felt a mild sting of shame.

And our rooms are nothing like so cold as this, he noted. *Is Xavoer fallen on such hard times that he keeps no fire, or is he just a skinflint?*

"Is my brother in there?" Prentice asked, nodding at the other door.

"Nay, not less he's become a ghost to come and go without my gate," the man answered, smirking at his own comment, apparently thinking it some kind of great jest. Prentice looked at him with a furrowed brow and the fellow shrugged. "He's out, is what he is, like most of the days. Rarely ever here, truth to tell. The old fellow's in that room."

"Old fellow?"

Prentice felt his gaze fix upon the other door as if nailed to it. He could not have looked away even if he wanted to.

"Aye, old bod, near to death if you ask me," the guard continued as Prentice walked unthinking across the tiny room. "Master Xavoer brung him in day after he rented the room, saw him into his bed, and then left. I get paid to bring him food twice a day and to take his pot away of a mornin'."

"Is that all?" Prentice asked, only just managing to pause long enough to do so before his hand was on the latch of the inner door. An old man was in the next room, and like a child lured into the forest by the whispers of nixies in a fey tale, Prentice knew he had to open that portal and go inside.

"That's all I'm paid for," the guard said. "Bring him food and, when you showed up, to...*usher*...you in."

Prentice's inner thoughts vaguely registered the man's strange emphasis on that one word, but he gave it no real consideration.

Instead, he opened the door and moved inside. The inner room was barely more than a cell, with whitewashed walls that were as grime-streaked as the wood of the outer room. Rain rattled against a second shuttered window here, and there was another small grate. This one held the banked remains of a fire, which gave the room at least a whisper of warmth. A single bed was the room's entire furnishing, and its richly brocaded blankets were the only part of the whole apartment that resembled his family's old wealth and status. Under the covers, a wizened, sleeping figure clutched the warm blanket up to his neck with cadaverous fingers. Wheezing snores wafted through the air.

Father? Prentice thought and hesitated. His father was more a figure of myth than a man in his memories, a force that towered over his childhood and defined all its parameters and boundaries. What would meeting him now mean? The last time they had set eyes on one another the man on that bed had disowned him at the prompting of the Inquisition. What would it mean to face each other now?

"What does he sicken from?" he asked, and when he received no answer, he turned to realize that the guard had left them. The sudden thought that he was alone with his father gave Prentice an unexpected thrill of fear. Like a crack from an overseer's lash, it awakened him from his reverie, at least enough to gird his heart.

Father or no, he is an old man on his sickbed, Prentice told himself. *Fear is unnecessary.*

Prentice stepped to the bedside and crouched down, touching his father's shoulder. The sleeping man stirred weakly and blinked, peering through rheumy eyes.

"Xavoer?" he asked, his voice more like a frog's croak than a man's.

"No, Father, your other son," Prentice told him, surprised at the gentleness in his voice. For all their past, he realized that he did not want this potentially final meeting to be hateful or acrimonious. What good would that serve? His father still did not recognize him, though.

"Pallas?" he muttered, apparently thinking Prentice was his own younger brother, the youngest of the four sons, the one forced to shoulder Prentice's obligations to the family after Prentice was convicted and excommunicated. "They said we would not speak again. They told me they could spare you no more from your duties."

Knowing the shame that Pallas must have brought on himself and his family when he murdered Baron Ironworth, Prentice could only imagine the tales the old man must have been told to preserve his image of the golden child, the son who had succeeded in becoming a Church knight.

"No father, not Pallas. Prentice," he said quietly and hesitantly laid his hand on his father's bony fingers.

"Prentice?" his father asked, peering at him as if through a fog, his brow knotted in disbelief. If the man's remaining memories told him that Pallas's presence was unlikely, then surely Prentice's must have counted as an impossibility.

"Yes, Father, it is I," Prentice forced himself to say, hating how weak his voice sounded. He had heard it could happen between a man and his parents, but to become a timid child once more in the presence of such a weak and sickly figure galled him. His father blinked, and as if a curtain had been removed between the two of them, and the man looked on his estranged son with a shocked expression. Then his pallid features took on a hard but weary cast.

"Oh, you? Come to look upon your works, boy? Or are you hoping to repent for what you did to us?"

Repent? Prentice thought, almost swaying backward with the disbelief he felt. Repent for what? Before he could ask, his father spewed forth words in a venomous stream.

"Come, kneel at my feet if you want. Grovel. Beg forgiveness for your vile sins, for your betrayals. You know the pits of hell that await traitors and heretics. Perhaps, if you can persuade me, I will forgive the debts you owe the family before God, lighten the burden of your punishments in the world to come a little. Don't take too long though, I am not long for this world. If I die before you can persuade me, I take your hope of deliverance with me. I might just take it anyway, so you'd better make it quick and make it good."

Prentice recoiled, snatching his hand away and nearly stumbling as he pushed back from the hatred. He stared at the bedridden man as if he were a cackling demon of hell itself. How could anyone hate his own son so? Suddenly, it was as if they were back in that cell under Ashfield, Prentice hanging from chains in the ceiling while his father and brother spat on him with disgust. Redlanders had feared him as the Ashen Man, Liam had given his whole life to the raging need to kill the jumped-up convict, and Inxyphos and Cassian had despised him, yet in all his bloody and violent experiences Prentice could never remember being as hated as he felt in the eyes of this man who was supposed to be his loving father.

He pushed himself to his feet, and almost without thinking he felt his hands grip the hilt of his sword under his cloak, but as soon as he realized they were there, he absolutely froze any impetus to draw the blade to stillness in his heart, and it was a true battle for his soul. On the one side was the desire to respond to this old man's hate with hatred of his own, to vent his own inner wounds and injustices on this embittered, dying elder. That part of him wanted nothing more than to scream curses in the wizened face as he swung the curved sword down, hacking through the fine blankets at the aged body, slaughtering before disease could finish its work to exact one final moment of fury and rejection for all the rejection this man had heaped upon him. Against all this was the icy rage of steel will within him—the flat refusal to let his enemies make him into the thing they said he was. Born of the cold in the night-dark fields, sleeping in chains, hungry and alone amongst enemies, it was the will that had invited more strikes from the overseer's whips rather than submit. The unyielding fury that had held the Serpent Witch by her chained collar and let the flood wash over them.

Hate me if you want, I will not be what you say! Prentice swore inwardly, and his hands shook on the hilt of his sword. As if hatred were giving his father renewed strength, the invalid pushed himself up from the mattress, weak limbs trembling with the effort or from the emotion he was now venting.

"You were supposed to be my prize," he choked, throaty speech spitting phlegm.

"I was your *plan*," Prentice retorted. "The prize was a noble title for your line; I was merely the horse you planned to ride to win it. I did everything you told me and still it was not enough for you!"

"Every son owes obedience to his father," the elder declared, and his voice was becoming strong now. It resonated with the memory of the powerful man he had been in Prentice's youth—the tyrant who loomed large over every one of his earliest memories. "You should be thankful after all we sacrificed for you!"

"*You* sacrificed...?" Prentice repeated, forming the words slowly. Bitterness burned hot within him, different from the icy rage of the battlefield. It cried out for revenge, demanding he draw his blade and end this fool. Still, his hands shook upon the hilt. The pressure that had been building from the moment Xavoer's note had been handed to him outside the Dog's Leg was now like a fountainhead, forcing its way through his soul to the surface. He suddenly knew that if he did not leave soon, any moment he would be unable to stop himself. He had not quite imagined that there would be a tearful reconciliation here, father and son reunited as in a morality play, to beg each other's forgiveness on the deathbed. Nevertheless, he had not realized how much he had hoped for something of the like, nor how readily that hope might transform itself into vengeful spite.

"So much was doted upon you," his father continued the bitter tirade. "All the time I would say it to them, 'Prentice needs tutors. He must learn and learning costs money.' Always, new books or a new instructor—etiquette and swordplay, theology and laws, writing and reading. All the things for you, did you never wonder what they cost or how that cost was paid? What would you be without our tireless efforts?"

What would I be? The question thundered in Prentice's thoughts like the drums calling the White Lions to the march. It summoned up the hot anger, the resentment he had thought put to death by his success, by his victories in his liege's name. Was rising to the rank of baron not enough to heal this rejection? *What would I be, old man? Loved? Accepted? Would I not at least have a few less scars?*

"You handed me over," he ground out, knowing that every moment he prolonged this encounter he grew closer to patricide and damnation. "You saw what they had done to me, and you still sided with *them*. You believed their lies without question and spat on me for good measure. What do you imagine I could yet owe you? You took everything from me, old man!"

His father coughed and wheezed, as if in a kind of mockery of laughter, and his head fell back to the pillow once more. Even so, he continued to mutter his denunciations.

"If I took everything from you, why am I the one in destitution while you are a warlord prince in a rebel land? Where do you think your skill at war and death comes from, heretic? By whose efforts do you have the strength to rise and slay?"

Prentice felt the hatred inside him burning up like a sacrificial pyre, like the Redlander magicks summoning the Red Sky, and its heat scoured him from within until there were only two forces in his being—the blazing desire to avenge himself on this bitter scarecrow and the deep winter resolve to hold himself back.

"Take your forgiveness with you to your grave, for I will never ask it of you!" he told his father, forcing himself to take another step away from the bed. "You disowned me, remember? Whatever was between us is done. I have nothing for you and want nothing from you."

He turned on his heel and left the room. Behind him it sounded like his father might have tried to say yet more, but the bloodless man's voice collapsed into another phlegmy cough.

You are a fool, Xavoer, Prentice derided his absent brother in his thoughts as he walked back through the tight corridor and down the stairs to the open chamber at the bottom of Vespers Remembered. *How could you have asked me to meet with him like that? Did you want him to curse me one last time?*

He wondered if that had, in fact, been his brother's intent, if Xavoer had been hoping to vent some final venom as well himself. The last time he had seen his brother, the middle-aged merchant had been in the company of the Primarch Faldmoor and fallen Earl Sebastian, both of whom wanted Prentice dead and had helped the young squire Cassian to issue the challenge to their fatal duel. Prentice felt suddenly naïve to have imagined that he might find reconciliation with either his brother or his father, and the embarrassment of that realization became another goad, driving him either to murder or escape. It was a relief, like being dragged above the surface of drowning waters once more, when he exited the building and paused in the open air, looking up and letting the rain cool the heat in his face. He sucked in gasping breaths of the outside air, reveling in the smell of the grass and nearby greenery.

"Is he still alive?" asked the Bell's Hummock guard, and Prentice looked to his right, surprised to see the mail-clad man standing there with three other fellows, similarly dressed and armed. Likely they together comprised the entire of the little island's cadre of private watchmen. They were standing in a cluster, out of the rain under the eaves of the next building across, and they regarded Prentice with wary expressions. They looked like bailiffs sent to arrest someone they expected to be trouble. Prentice looked down and realized that he still had his hands on his sword.

"Of course he is still alive," he told them, water flicking from his lips as he still stood in the rain. In moments, even his cloak would begin to soak through. "Though he does not look long for this world, so if there is aught you would say, do not tarry." Prentice scowled at them, though his anger was still for his father, not these brute keepers of order. "For myself, I have spoken all I will with the man."

The group continued to stare at him a long moment.

"No blood on him," said one, as if he had expected to see Prentice sprayed with his father's crimson.

"And that sword's still in its sheath," said another.

Prentice blinked and felt a fresh wariness settle into him, an anticipation of danger that flattened down his other emotions, like throwing water on a fire. If he had met a random group of men in the street who looked and spoke to him like this, he would have assumed they meant to bushwack him. As it was, he thought it likely their leader had fetched them because he had assumed Prentice's encounter with his own father would end in violence. Except that it had come so near to exactly that, Prentice would have been insulted by the man's presumptuousness.

Another petty authority playing king of his own tiny domain, he thought and forced himself to turn away. If his anger was insufficient reason to strike at his own father, it was even less of a justification to engage in an affray with a pack of hired bailiffs.

"Can I open the gate myself, or do I need you to do it for me?" he called over his shoulder as he headed towards the garden's exit. With a huff loud enough to be heard at a distance, the burly main guard trotted out into the rain, splashing footsteps in the puddles as he caught up with Prentice and then went ahead to unlock the gate. As Prentice passed through, the fellow gave a nearly apologetic shrug.

"You were supposed to be here the other night," he said quietly and closed the gate behind him.

Prentice had no idea what the man meant by it, but he was at the bottom of the stairs and stepping onto the docks proper before he recovered enough self-control to release his grip on his sword. A short while later he was walking amongst the crowd crossing back over the bridge to Salthatch when he was intercepted by two militiamen with a request that he come immediately to the Sougate Bastion.

CHAPTER 26

"One of your drudges must have done this," Benlow Sent-Fane decried loudly, his voice echoing off the moist stone walls. "I told you it must be kept dry. Dry! Do you northern barbarians even understand the word?"

"He's been like this since this morning, My Lord," Sergeant Guillam muttered, looking away from the enraged cannoneer gunsmith at a blank section of wall as if it were the most fascinating thing in all Bridgetown.

"I can imagine," Prentice said in a sour tone.

The three of them were standing just out of knee-deep water while the men around them, wearing no metal of any kind, labored to move as much of their powder stores out of the poorly lit chamber as they could. When the Gryphon Banner Company had captured the Masnian cannons and ammunition in the autumn, it had seemed a Godsend—more powder and shot than the White Lions could use in five battles. Benlow Sent-Fane had insisted *his* cannon crews be given charge of the stores, and those men had placed much of it here, secure in this basement in the foundations of Sougate. It had seemed a sound notion, far from the winter rains or enemy attack—except what no one had known was that in a dark corner, unseen at the back of the room, was a riverside gate for shipping in supplies when the river was low, such as it had been the previous two summers. Once the winter rains began to feed the Murr River, the level had risen, and either the gate had not been properly secured, or its seals had failed.

Two men who'd been sent to explore the dark waters had only just been able to even find the portal, built half below the level of the floor as it was. So now the powder store was flooded and the powder was leaching, being ruined beyond recovery. Prentice did not know much of the alchemy of the black powder's creation, but he knew enough to know that even if they managed to dry it out once more, it would never fire properly. So it was, this team of half-dressed, shivering men rushed to fetch out the dry parts of the stores that were stacked on others and so not yet soaked to uselessness.

We never even thought to look for a summer gate, Prentice thought bitterly. If he or one of his men had just realized, they might have found it and fixed whatever was amiss. It might have been as simple as pulling a watertight door closed and properly latched. *Always assuming this was not someone's deliberate sabotage.*

Prentice knew it was unlikely that Bluebird or an agent of his could have snuck into Sougate and opened the aperture, but it was difficult to dismiss the paranoid notion from his thoughts. It was possible, though even less likely, that the portal might have been opened from the outside. Most probable was that the entrance was all but forgotten to even the most established Bridgetowners, a remnant of the town's ancient sieges against the Vec. Prentice stepped aside as two Roarsmen struggled past, hefting small but heavy barrels on their shoulders. As much as this was a loss, and as much as Benlow Sent-Fane was making it sound like the fall of the Bright Age and the collapse of civilizations all over again, in fact, it looked like they would still be able to salvage a good deal of their arsenal. It helped that a large portion of the Lions' total powder store had already been redeployed for use on the north side of the town.

"Send a messenger to Norgate, Sergeant," Prentice commanded, recognizing the potential for more disasters like this. The winter rains would not abate anytime soon. "Tell the knight captain of our situation and warn him of the risk of repeating our mistake."

Guillam saluted, but even as he left, the livid Master Sent-Fane took fresh umbrage.

"*Our* mistake?" he said, his accent making his words seem too shrill in the sloshing, echoing chamber. "You think to blame my gunners for this, do you?"

"I said *our* mistake, Master, not yours," Prentice told the prickly man, suppressing a sigh. Were all Masnians so proud and defensive or only their weaponsmiths? "*You* insisted on taking full charge of the powder and its storage, but *I* command the Sougate. The responsibility falls on my shoulders."

Ultimately, I could not give a tinker's cuss who is to blame, Prentice thought. Assuming this was not enemy action, and paranoia notwithstanding, he had no reason to believe it was, then apportioning blame now was only a wasted effort.

"Once we have saved what we can, please find a new space suitable for the salvaged powder, Master," he said, thinking to go to the battlements and assess the status of the southern siege while he was here.

Foes upon all sides, threats from without and within, he thought, acutely aware of the fact that it was ever the enemy they never knew to look for, the vulnerability they never imagined, that would do the most damage. *Like the Jerwahl Rangers. Like this shambles.*

Before Prentice could leave, however, Benlow Sent-Fane had not finished his complaints.

"It is all so damp in here now that even what we save will be diminished," the Masnian cannon master declared. "It will surely burn no better than your northern muck. I will find another place, as you say, but you must send me the drudges—proper diligent ones—to check that there are no other gates or doors or other ways my powder might be ravaged again."

That demand was a step too far for Prentice. He remembered the contempt the Bell's Hummock guard had shown for the

White Lions—the sneering about trial day charms—and the discovery that the supposedly sacred Vespers' chamber had once been used to house convicts. Some of the hot anger moved in him again, and the knight commander halted on the stairs, turning back to face the grousing man in the poor light.

"It is not *your* powder, Master Sent-Fane," he said, holding his voice steady by sheer will, his face only finger widths from the cannoneer leader. "It is the archduchess' powder, and as her hired retainer you will do everything within *your* capacity to secure it and its safety. Understand?"

The master visibly worked to maintain his calm and dignity in the face of Prentice's stern rebuke, but it was clear even in the dimness that he was not finding it easy. He swallowed and blinked, but Prentice was not finished.

"Further to that, these men around you are not 'drudges.' Nor are they serfs, nor peons, nor any other such term, and they are most especially not rogues. I will thank you not to refer to them as such. They are the finest fighting men afoot in the known world. Valiant, diligent, and to be respected. Am. I. Clear?"

Sent-Fane nodded, and for the first time Prentice had ever seen, the man looked chastened and humble. Prentice was pleased to see it, but as he turned and mounted the steps to the bastion's main floor, he wondered at his sense of satisfaction. What difference did it make, truly? And who was he to think to put a foreign nobleman in his place? For most of his life he had been no more than a "drudge" himself, either laboring as a pupil or slaving as a convict. Whatever power or authority he enjoyed, Prentice knew it came from the hands of others—the archduchess in the main but also from God, if his dreams were true and not the delusions of a proud spirit.

Or from my father's plans, he thought, and that notion stopped him on the stairs halfway between the main floor and the gateworks level. His father's hateful words swirled again in his mind, encircling him and slashing like the wrapping strike of an overseer's lash, so that he physically recoiled, tossing his head as if he could avoid a thought. It wasn't true, was it? Did he owe his survival through all his years of convictry and exile to his father's harshness in his youth? Was he alive only because the bitter patriarch had been so demanding, like the heat from a forge or the blows of the smith's hammer?

Resisting the possibility froze Prentice in place upon the stairs, trapping him in his own thoughts for a moment, such that though he dimly heard the sound of trumpets echoing from outside, he hardly registered them. It was not until the echoes of rushing boots came down the stairs that Prentice was able to shake off his hesitation, coming to himself only a moment before a militiaman turned around the twisting staircase and almost barreled into him. They did not actually crash but only because the surprised man-at-arms halted and saluted his leader reflexively.

"My Lord, word from the battlements," he reported in a loud voice that echoed up and down the twisting stairwell. "The Veckanders are attacking."

"Has the rain stopped?" Prentice asked with a disbelieving frown.

"Some, My Lord, but not much. Sergeant Guillam told me to run to Knight Sergeant Gennet and get the reserves. It's a big force they're sending."

"Then go to, militiaman," Prentice said, and he stepped aside as best he could so the runner could get past.

A big force? he thought as he mounted the rest of the stairs. He could scarcely credit it. A siege was a grim affair to maintain in winter. If nothing else, his own experience at Fallenhill confirmed that ancient military truth. An assault on a fortification over muddy ground, in the rain? That was a recipe for disaster. What were the Golden Heron commanders thinking?

Passing by the closed door to the barracks level, he could hear the few Roarsmen stationed there already shooting through the archer's loops. Then there was an almighty blast that set the dust on the steps and walls jumping into the air. The cannons stationed in the room were firing as well. The rains would make the guns on the battlements more of a troubled proposition, but the two that Benlow Sent-Fane had set in the barracks would be able to fire all day, rain or shine.

Until our powder runs out, Prentice thought grimly, but he knew that was not going to happen in one day, even with their diminished stores. In truth, the real danger of the leached powder was that the Lions would have less for the inevitable duel that was coming with the Bronze Dragons on the north shore. Until that fight arrived and was settled, the knight commander knew he would never feel like he had enough ammunition for Roar and cannon alike. He wondered how long before the Fallenhill workshops sent replenishments down from the north. Keeping one hand on the wall as the other big gun thumped out a shot, Prentice headed on up to the top and the battlements.

Looks like I will get a very good look at the Veckander siege dispositions, rain or not, he thought. He had not been expecting another battle so soon. Was there no limit to the plans the archduchess's enemies had for Bridgetown and the White Lions?

CHAPTER 27

"For men of the craft they ain't much chop, are they?" Sergeant Guillam observed, still shouting, even though the guns had paused a moment in their firing. The "craft" to which he was referring was warfare, as if men-at-arms were merely members of yet another guild. Rainwater ran down his chin as he chewed and watched the enemy reforming in the muddy fields below them. Only last season, that ground had been the site of a vile massacre, with the Bridgetown militia slaughtering Vec peasant levies as they tried to surrender. Now there was another defeat being inflicted on the Veckanders, and while it was nothing like a massacre, it still felt murderous to Prentice as he watched it happen.

The mixed army of the Golden Heron mercenaries and Prince Everard of Sunbury's sworn men and levies had arrayed itself behind the remains of the earthworks that had been dug for when the Veckander army had had cannons of their own—cannons the Gryphon Banner Company had captured and now turned to the defense of Bridgetown. The muddy works themselves had been so washed away by the recent heavy rains that they were now little more than a low line of turned earth across the Great Bridge Road. If no one thought to repair it, it would be gone by the end of winter at this rate. Before the rains set in, the cannoneers in Sougate had been using the embankment as target practice, sighting and ranging their shots by it, so there were already large gaps in the lumpen ground. Because of that, the Veckander army could have no doubt of the deadly range of the cannons, and so the whole force was massing on foot, safely beyond the danger. As best as Prentice could make out in the grey haze, there was only a small number of men ahorse in the rear center of their formation, under a canopy of sorts, held aloft on pikes thrust into the muddy ground—the leaders of the southern army.

They turned out to watch, at least, the knight commander thought, noting that being at the rear, they clearly had no intention of leading the ongoing assault on Sougate. The rains had abated somewhat but were still enough to obscure half the standards and banners held by the varied array of units, being soaked and beaten down by the falling waters as they were. Even so, Prentice found it a simple matter to tell the true professionals in their suits of plates from the levies who were clearly just a collected mass of peasants—poorly armed and equipped in haphazard rows and lines that it would have been generous to call formations. It was the levies who had made two attempts to assault Sougate so far, and both had been easily repelled.

At the foot of the bastion, the bridge's main gate was only accessible via a long ramp, no wider than the road. That path's narrowness had been further complicated by the addition of sharpened stakes in offset rows, so that the way to the gate was now a tight switchback that would delay any approaches even more and make a battering ram a near impossible proposition. The Sougate garrison had also dug the sides of the gate ramp with trenches to protect the walls, but as with the other earthworks, the rain was washing them away, and they were already half their previous depth. The bottoms, though, were mirey and thick with mud, which was all to the good.

For two forays, the peasants had been sent forward toward Sougate, hauling long scaling ladders. Once they passed the washed away earthen battlement in the field, they came into the range of the cannons, but because the guns could not be made to fire straight downward, there was only an effective space of about one hundred paces, perhaps a hundred and fifty, that the Sougate guns could shoot upon. That meant if they were swift, the charging levies might be exposed to only a single shot from each cannon, two at the most. Prentice had arrived midway through their first assault, and so had missed the beginning of that attempt, but after seeing them repulsed and then attempting again, and now reforming for a third try, he found himself disgusted by what he was watching. The Veckander plan was clear—they hoped by continuous waves to simply overwhelm the defenders, but as the ground between the besiegers and the bastion was further churned into sucking mud by hundreds of feet rushing across it, persistence was only guaranteeing a more bitter Vec defeat.

"They are not giving us the courtesy of their professionals just yet, Sergeant," Prentice said in response to Guillam's comment.

"No? I was told they was mercenaries," the sergeant replied.

"Many are, but if I had to guess, I would say the Sunbury prince is using his levies to bring those scaling ladders up to the gate and then the mercenaries will make the crossing of our firing field. The professionals do not want to risk our cannons until they know the ladders are here and waiting for them. Hard enough to cross that ploughed mud in armor as it is without having to stand at our talus and wait to climb."

It was an ugly, cold-hearted arithmetic, but Prentice was sure that was how the Vec army leaders were thinking. Mercenaries cost more coin per man than peasant levies. Already at the foot of the walls, three scaling ladders had been dropped, one of which was broken in pieces.

"So, they're all proud not to have convicts in their armies, but they still use rogues of a sort?"

"Of a sort, Sergeant," Prentice agreed, watching the levies readying for the next desperate, stumbling run over the wretched ground, aiming for some point near Sougate's wall where they could lift a ladder and mount up to the battlements, or at least hold it in place so the mercenaries behind them could make the climb. In their previous attempts, the levies had managed to get a handful of the siege tools against the walls, but the Gryphons had pushed them off readily before the true men-at-arms even attempted a run. While that happened, the militiamen above punished the crowds at the footings, dropping stones through the machicolations and pouring boiling water from the cauldrons set for the purpose. In the mud, as broken and discarded as the fallen ladders, were the scalded remains of too many ordinary men. Prentice could not hear their moans or cries anymore, and he hoped that meant that the ones still living had managed to retreat, but he doubted it. He had given orders that no gunners or Roar were to target retreating men. It was a pittance of mercy, and it revolted him in its paucity.

A short distance from where Prentice stood, Knight Sergeant Gennet was at work supervising teams bringing fresh, dry wood to boil the next pot's worth of deadly wash, while farther back a line of Gryphons labored to haul buckets of water up from the river to refill the siege cauldrons.

"Well, it makes our job so much the easier," Guillam said, not unhappily but without enthusiasm. "Feel a bit bad for the poor saps as are being sent at us, but better them than us, eh? All in all, a comfortabler way to fight a battle, I'd say."

Prentice did not respond. The sergeant's assessment was self-evidently correct. This was about as fruitless a form of battle as he could imagine. It was surely as bad as the wretched attempt Liam had made in his last conflict, charging his knights repeatedly into Prentice's first true Lions' cohorts, refusing to see his age-old tactic was failing. At least Liam had the excuse of being unable to fathom the transilience he was confronting. The kind of folly the Veckanders were embarking on was as old as siege warfare itself, and every one of the professionals down there had to know it. That was surely why the hired men-at-arms waited and watched from safety. If attackers in a siege did nothing to suppress the defenders on the wall, assaults were almost always doomed. Archers, crossbows, or siege engines should all be brought to bear, hammering the battlements until the garrison was forced to hide or cower, unable to defend the wall, while other men-at-arms fetched up the scaling ladders. Of course, the Roar and the cannons made it all the harder for the Vec to bring such weapons close enough to attack the top, but that was why siege engineers were supposed to dig trenches and earthworks of their own, so they could get close more safely and then unleash their engines on the walls. There was a reason sieges were long, slow processes; it was the only way they could be successful instead of wasteful slaughters like this. A swift assault could take a fortification by surprise, Prentice himself had proved that more than once in his service to the archduchess but only if circumstances were especially favorable. Otherwise, patience was king.

This is nearly suicidal, Prentice thought as he watched the third attack begin. It gave him a vile feeling in his stomach, and he spat on the rain-slick merlon beside him. He had never wanted this kind of thing for the White Lions. Princes and professionals were supposed to look at fortifications like Sougate and know better. It was clear the mercenaries did, refusing to carry the ladders themselves, but still the assault came on. New teams of levies bore fresh, heavy climbing tools on their shoulders. Others were rushing empty-handed, and they would likely try to salvage the ladders fallen at the foot of the mighty gatehouse. The cannons and Roar in the barracks fired again, smashing the back half of one ladder team in the killing ground. Screams wafted through the rain-soaked distance as other men stepped over the fallen to take up the slack, but the whole group stopped when they realized the ladder itself was broken and ruined. The other cannon fired, missing them, but the entire team turned and ran for safety all the same. Prentice shook his head as he watched them go.

Not nearly. It is suicidal. What must the Golden Heron or Prince Everard be threatening these men with to drive them forward so?

On Sougate's ramparts, carpenters had been hard at work in recent days to build wooden hoardings amidst the crenelations for the Roar to shelter under to keep their powder safe from the rain, with archers' loops—gunners' loops, effectively—to fire through at the advancing enemy. Only two were completed at this stage, and Prentice stood just under one, safe from the wet, while beside him a line of Roarsmen began to fire down upon the enemy. The hoardings' other purpose was to protect the shooting men from enemy crossbows and missile weapons. The Veckanders had several companies of shooters in their force, skilled and effective by all accounts, but this rain made them unusable. If their bowstrings got too wet, they would rapidly stretch and become loose. Likewise, with no trenchworks and no shelters for new cannons or more traditional siege engines like catapults, there were no such weapons to suppress Sougate's defenders in any way. Rain would be an enemy to most catapult works for the same reason as crossbowmen or archers. Trebuchet workings were less vulnerable to rain, but they took a long time to build and needed even more protection during their construction, since they had to be built already within range of the walls. Though the Gryphon Banner's own cannons' effectiveness was diminished by the rain—the wet making it impossible to keep powder fully dry on the battlement even with precautions—this was still the easy battle Guillam had been looking forward to since he had first been given main command of the bastion. Despite his desire to keep every White Lion as safe as possible in every combat, Prentice felt none of the sergeant's satisfaction, however.

What is going on down there? he wondered. Was Prince Everard a monster, like Liam or Daven Marcus, heedless of his lowborn folks' sufferings? Or had the Golden Heron driven him to this point? What motivation would they have to do that? They were the world's largest bank. Surely, they did not fear losing money. If they did, all they needed to do was dismiss the mercenary companies until the summer. The levies and sworn men of the prince would be enough to maintain a blockade of the gate through winter. If Sunbury wanted to use his cheap, low-born footmen to do all the miserable duties, a winter camp was dour enough, surely. Why not hire the professionals back come the spring?

Unless...unless it is impossible for him to wait that long, Prentice thought, and his disgust at the slaughter suddenly deepened until it all but turned his stomach.

"Everard, you are a bloody fool," Prentice muttered as he came to a dire conclusion. Prince Everard must have seen Daven Marcus's vast horde on the north bank and decided that he was losing his main chance. If he did not capture Bridgetown before the Usurper, he never would.

If we cannot hold Bridgetown against you, Prince of Sunbury, what on earth makes you imagine you could hold it against Daven Marcus? Especially if it costs you this much to take it in the first place, Prentice wondered, his fists clenching in fury that ordinary Vec men were now being killed for their prince's greed. He nearly punched the merlon he had just spat on but managed to restrain himself. Even if Everard despised them as serfs, less than full men, how could he be fool enough to sacrifice so many of his own farmers and laborers for such a mad dream?

Bridgetown was the victor's gold ring, the highest prize in this tourney, but just by taking the province of Town Sobridge from its previous prince, Everard had won himself a massive enough prize, surely. Could his ambition not be satisfied with that? Prentice knew nothing of the man to judge by, but what he saw put him in mind of the worst of the Grand Kingdom's proudest peers. To send so many to die in hopes of capturing Bridgetown was a callous sacrifice to a false and bloodthirsty god who would give no rewards. It was as vile as the worst excesses of the Redlanders.

A fresh thought occurred to Prentice. Everard might be plotting only pillage, not occupation. Perhaps the Prince of Sunbury did, in fact, recognize that he had insufficient strength to hold on to Bridgetown even if he managed to capture it. Perhaps he only planned to play the burglar, to kick in the back door and loot the house while the defenders were distracted by the monsters out the front of it. By the time Daven Marcus battered his way through Norgate, Everard could be off back to the much more defensible Town Sobridge, leaving the treasuries empty behind him. That possibility cast this monstrous assault in a new light.

Just how desperate are you for Bridgetown's moneys, Your Highness? Prentice wondered. Was this greed or was this financial necessity? Were the bankers starting to mutter about calling in their loans, as they had threatened Archduchess Amelia? Ultimately, Prentice knew it did not matter to his militia nor to the levies being thrown like clods of mud to splash against the walls and footings of Sougate. The bastion was an altar to a pagan god of war, and Everard, Prince of Sunbury, was sacrificing his people upon it in dreams of a reward of untold riches. Worse, to Prentice's mind, was that he and his militiamen were being forced to plunge the sacrificial knife on Everard's behalf.

He sighed and spat again. He had seen visions and miracles and had faith enough to believe there truly was a God in heaven who watched over all mankind. Even so, he knew he still fell far short of the Lord's injunction to love his enemies. But admitting that, he could not imagine hating Veckanders enough to be comfortable with this much killing. In the heart of conflict, feeling merciful compassion for one's enemies was a dangerous pastime, something best left to saintlier men like Brother Whilte. Even so, Prentice almost wanted to order the guns to cease fire altogether to give the harried and dying levies a fighting chance.

Fool bloody thought! he chastised himself, but he felt it all the same. Surely almost anything would feel better than this.

This is what you made of my investment in you. You went west to the witch and became her pagan warlord, his father's voice sounded in his thoughts, so vivid that it was almost as if the old man was standing right there next to him. Prentice almost looked about to see if he were there. Could the man have died in the last hours and become a ghost to hate him from the beyond? He shook his head. He did not believe it, but even if it were true, what should he care of one more ghost amongst so many being sent to their judgement this day? If his father had passed and wanted to vent his eternal spleen, he could join the crowd.

"Could it be some kind of feint, My Lord?" Gennet asked as he came to Prentice's side now that the fires were blazing up again and the pots were on the way to boiling. Any who survived the fall of iron on the muddy field would be welcomed with a fresh, scalding baptism that would terrify the best of men. The prospect surely terrified Prentice, though it took him a moment to drag his thoughts away from the inward torment of his father's voice.

"A ploy?" he repeated rhetorically. He had considered it earlier, and there were sentries set on the flanking towers at the bastion's corners, watching the river to see if there was a force trying to sneak closer from the sides while they were distracted by the frontal assault. Nothing had been seen, and short of more of the Masnian Jerwahl mercenaries with their uncanny stealth, there was almost no chance this was a diversion.

Daven Marcus does not share his toys, Prentice thought, dismissing the notion that the Usurper might have loaned some of his mercenaries to the Prince of Sunbury. It would have been self-defeating into the bargain. Why would the kingslayer help Sunbury beat him to the gold ring? *It is a race between them, and no matter if Sunbury or the Golden Heron comes first, they will not win any prize they can keep. The Usurper will see to that.*

It had to be about pillage and plunder. There could be no other reasonable motivation.

Still the levies came on, less swiftly and with more hesitation. The third assault was the last, and when the rain began to grow heavy again in the mid-afternoon, the Veckander force finally quit the field. Prentice left the battlements at that point, telling Gennet and Guillam to rotate fresh cohorts up to relieve the defenders who had stood and lost not a single man the whole day. They needed to get somewhere dry and have something to eat. The knight commander was sure most of them would be as thoroughly sick of the day's conflict as he was.

CHAPTER 28

"It sounds such a horror," Amelia said softly as Prentice finished his account of the day's combat at Sougate. He and Farringdon sat with her at the main table while a short distance away Lady Dalflitch attended to a small wooden cage which contained a newly arrived batch of messenger birds from Dweltford. The little creatures' cooing floated softly through the air as their new handler determined how well they had survived the journey downriver in their containment. Amelia felt a kinship with the little birds. It had never been her intent to go into seclusion for her pregnancy, but as winter's dark closed in the days earlier and earlier, so she felt more and more confined to this one room. She wondered how long it would be until midwinter when the days would begin lengthening again toward spring. Soon after that, her baby would make its way into the world.

Is every war like this? she wondered, turning her mind back to Prentice's bitter report of victory. Where was the shining glory of the histories or legends? Were the days of noble heroes passed, or were the armies of old as brutal as this, with chroniclers glossing over the mud and blood, like the Inquisition purging the histories of unwanted details?

"Grim for Sunbury and the Golden Heron, Your Grace," Prentice agreed with her sentiment. "For us, the loss of the powder is the much worse cost."

"That I should count mere stores above the lives of men, even my enemy's," Amelia said and shook her head.

"It is the arithmetic of war, my love," Farringdon told her from his seat at her side, and he reached out to clasp her hand comfortingly. His eyes went to her large belly, and she took his meaning immediately—horror or not, he would much prefer men died at the foot of Sougate than broke into the town to threaten his wife and child. For all his dour mood, Amelia was sure Prentice must feel the exact same way.

"How dearly does this loss of powder cost us?" she asked, forcing her mind forward.

Prentice and Farringdon looked to one another.

"For now, not at all," the knight commander said.

"Although, watchers on Loncastel say that it can't be long until Daven Marcus will have his Dragons emplaced to commence firing," Farringdon added. "Once that day comes, every grain of good powder will be that much more precious to us."

"Well then, that tells me what the first message for my new friends to take back north for us is to be," Dalflitch said, hand gripped firmly but gently around one feathered messenger before she thrust the bird back into the cage, closing the latch swiftly lest any escape. "Then we will have only to fear breaks in the rain."

"Not so, My Lady," Farringdon countered her sentiment. "Daven Marcus is building shelters large enough that his beasts will not have to fear the rain at all. Moving powder will always be best achieved in fair weather, but as to firing, soon the Dragons will not care. Then we will duel cannons in earnest, I assure you."

"Can we win that duel?" Amelia asked.

Her husband frowned pensively and then shrugged. He looked at Prentice, and Amelia followed his glance.

The knight commander seemed equally as noncommittal. "Ask us again after the siege is broken, Your Grace," he said with a cold expression. "We will have a better answer for you then."

"And what if the siege does not break?" Dalflitch asked, coming now to the table and taking her seat demurely.

"Then you will not need to ask, My Lady," Prentice told her, grey-eyed gaze like steel. "You will already have the answer."

It was a grim pronouncement that seemed to suit the wintry afternoon light, and Amelia was not surprised to see Prentice muttering under his breath a moment, though she did not quite hear what he was saying. She sipped her tea, which had gone cold in its cup, and it chilled her fingers, making her shiver slightly. She wondered if she should order more wood put on the fire.

Or else take to wearing gloves in my own chamber, she thought.

"I say, My Lord, were you successful in your quest this morning before you made for Sougate?" Dalflitch asked Prentice, and the knight commander gave her a shocked glance. He had been staring at the table, lost in thought, it seemed. Dalflitch gave the tabletop in front of him a strange look and then shifted her gaze back to his face.

"What do you know of that?" he asked, and Amelia felt there was an almost belligerent or guilty tone to his question, as if he had something to hide. She had no idea what it might be.

"Only what I am told. I thought you might have had something to share," Dalflitch said simply, and it seemed to Amelia that her lady seneschal was also speaking in a guarded fashion, her words containing hidden meanings. Was there some secret between them that Dalflitch was moving to unfold? She went on. "I sent to the camp for you and my messenger was told you had gone into the town to buy stoves for the wounded. Were you successful? I only ask because our quartermasters are likely better connected to the town's ironmongers."

"No, My Lady," Prentice answered her. "I was not successful. If I had been wise enough to think of you and the quartermasters, I could have saved myself a wasted journey."

"Hardly a great foolishness, surely," Amelia countered, inserting herself into their discussion, brows furrowed. Perhaps she was overreacting, but she felt troubled by this interaction. It seemed to herald conflict.

But who am I protecting from whom? she wondered.

"No, indeed, Your Grace," Dalflitch agreed. "But I could have saved you the longer walk out to Bell's Hummock, Knight

Commander. I would gladly have told you there were no more metalworkers past Salthatch."

Prentice's expression grew even more stern, eyes narrowing. "How do you...?" he began to ask and then paused to look around the room. Amelia wondered if he feared to speak, then realized that he was watching the neophytes and Lace Fangs about their chores. His gaze went from one to the next, and Amelia could see that he was studying their faces.

He is trying to guess which one he did not notice on the street, she thought. *If one of them informed on him, which was it? But why does he care?*

At last Prentice let out a heavy sigh, and Amelia had a sudden notion that he was about to release a significant secret. It made her wonder what it could be, but when he spoke, she found her anticipation deflated.

"I went the whole way to Bell's on a matter of family business, My Lady," he said simply. "Although it would have been welcome, your advice would not have saved me the journey. I was meeting with my brother, Xavoer. And may I say, your eyes about the town are sharp indeed."

"Thank you, Baron," Dalflitch told him, accepting his word as a compliment. "I wondered if the report of you going to the westernmost island was entirely accurate. If it had not been, my little maids might have been seeing something far worse than a Reach nobleman on a misguided errand. There might have been a skin thief about the town, mimicking your form."

"Of course," Prentice agreed, and much of the tension seemed to have released from his expression. It made Amelia want to ask him about his meeting with his brother, but respect for his privacy leashed her tongue.

If it is aught I need to know, I can trust Prentice to share it with me, she told herself.

"Further to that end, has Brother Whilte any more word about scripture to oppose our foes?" Dalflitch continued.

"Not yet, My Lady," Prentice answered. "The chaplain has been all but overwhelmed just in treating the wounded from the battle."

Farringdon sucked in a breath and looked down at the tabletop, scowling and shaking his head. Now it was Amelia's turn to place a comforting hand upon his, encouraging him to cease blaming himself.

"Perhaps Master Solft has more word?" she offered, but Dalflitch, to whom the scholar was in the habit of reporting from day-to-day since arriving in Bridgetown, only shook her head.

"Also not yet, Your Grace," said the lady seneschal reported.

Amelia nodded and thought that perhaps she and the seneschal should take more time with the Steeple Aviary folk verse, looking for clues there. At that moment, she was distracted by her child kicking within her. It was not an unpleasant sensation, but after feeling it, she noticed that she also felt hungry and thought now to take her evening meal earlier than typical.

Would that count as a tell? she wondered, and while the notion seemed humorous, it was not as idle as she would have liked. She resolved to sit quietly until her usual mealtime, enduring the hunger. Perhaps she could nap for an hour in bed.

"Well, gentles, if the worst news the day brings is that the Golden Heron has diminished their strength some and our overflow of black powder now no longer quite overflows, then it has been far from the worst day we have known together. Go you now, each to your duties. I must attend to the needs of my unborn."

The senior counselors nodded and stood, although Farringdon waited a moment as Amelia called an attendant to prepare her bed. Then her husband helped her to stand, and they moved to her "bedchamber" behind the curtains at the other end of the room. Once they were there and the neophyte who had turned down the bed for her had withdrawn, Amelia took Farringdon's hand and asked him to stay with her while she napped. It pleased her when he agreed without hesitation, stripping off his arming doublet and boots almost immediately. For a moment she feared he might have misinterpreted her desires, thinking she hoped for an amorous moment, but that fear proved unfounded. When he was down to his undershirt and loincloth, he climbed in beside her and encircled her in his arms.

"Rest, my love," he whispered. "I will want to go back to the defenses in an hour or so, but if you sleep, I will do what I can to not wake you."

Amelia smiled and closed her eyes.

CHAPTER 29

Prentice stood in the entry to the building, surveying the mostly empty space in front of him with a sense of satisfaction. More of a size to be called a shed than a barn, it was a single-story wooden building on the north edge of Runners Field. In days gone by it had served to store saddle tack and feed for the horses that had used the tiltyard, but had now been converted to a corral for the Lion Banner lancers' mounts. There was a small haystack still in a corner away from the door, but otherwise the floor was clear, and there were empty hooks all around the walls that once would have held bridles, reins, and other riding equipment. The other side of the tiltyard had a larger stable with a hayloft, more suited to the lancers' requirements, and so this shed had lain empty since the White Lions' arrival. Prentice thought it would be perfect for his plans. Of course, it still had its limitations, not the least of which was the smell of old horse dung that had not yet been cleared out, but he thought that would be a good physical activity for his recovering flesh—a small task to begin rebuilding his strength upon.

Once the assault on Sougate had been repulsed, Prentice's mind had returned to ploughing and reploughing the ground of his confrontation with his father. Most especially, he kept coming back to the claim that whatever he had in life, even after being disowned, he owed to that scarecrow devil clinging to its last breaths by hate alone. It was as if with that one accusation his father had robbed him of all his strength, even more completely than Cassian's poison.

Every son owes obedience to his father, he heard his pater say in his memory of the encounter. But how did one obey a father who had consigned him to die? What did he truly owe to that man, and what right did the dying patriarch have to command it from him? Try as he might to keep his mind upon his duties, Prentice found that the questions dominated his thoughts.

"The tutors were his," he muttered to himself as he took up a pitchfork he had borrowed from the lancers' stable and marched to the haystack. "The tutors were his because he paid for them, paid for them because the plan was his. Make a knight of his little third-born lesser patrician's son."

Prentice thrust the fork into the stack and hefted out a bundle of moldy, foul-smelling straw. Carefully, he carried it out the door to the handcart he had waiting in the rain. Despite his best efforts, one part in three of the load dropped onto the ground on the way, leaving a noisome trail from stack to door. He was not worried; he had a broom for that.

"Then there was Ashfield," he told himself, walking back for the next forkful. "That was *his* as well."

Another load went out into the rain and another after that. Prentice worked, sweat rising despite the cold weather, limbs aching too soon for his liking. That was all a part of the problem and part of the solution he planned, of which this little barn was another important element.

I cannot owe what I am, or what strength I have, to him, Prentice told himself as he slaved at the mucky job. After the fourth load, he pulled off his arming doublet and put off his boots, despite the iciness of the ground under his feet. With only undershirt and trews, he felt again at least some of the discomfort of a laboring convict.

That, at least, is all mine.

Prentice had heard that many an adult man could be made to feel like a child again under a harsh father's hand. He had never imagined such might be his fate, but then he had long ago thought never to see his father again. However, with all his duties to his archduchess, his wife, and his children, he could not afford to have his strength robbed from him by mere family bitterness.

Never mind that I am meant to be preparing for some kind of "race," whatever that might be, he thought, remembering his dream and the monstrosities of the prison pit. If he needed the might of Samson to topple the temple, he could not depend on any strength an old man could snatch from him and take into the grave. The only solution Prentice could devise was to go back to the beginning and train himself over again, reclaiming for himself all the skills of war he had learned since his earliest childhood. By so doing, by following the path again, not for his father's failed purposes but for his own place in the world, he hoped to regain the strength the poison had drained from him. He would prepare himself for the prophesied race and put himself beyond the grasp of the bitter wraith his father had become. If the old man died this night, Prentice had little doubt he would hear the ghost's haunting moans before dawn.

He can wait his turn, the knight commander told himself as the filthy task made him look more like a convict laborer again with every load of rotten straw. Many were the fallen in Prentice's past who would have a claim on the right to haunt him.

The cold evening wore on, and Prentice lit a covered lantern to keep working by. Despite the bitterness of the task, he found the hardship comforting in a way, for it reminded him of a time when he had had no expectations on him other than to work to exhaustion and then drop. The troublesome thoughts quieted some as the fatigue in his limbs increased. A part of him noticed that any moment he paused to take a breath of rest, the hounding thoughts—guilt and rejection especially—came back, which was a worrying notion, but when he returned to the work, that concern was also dimmed under the pain of exhaustion. That night he fell asleep wrapped in his cloak on the cold ground, his wearied mind only occupied with the plans to turn this little shed into his new training hall where he would make his skills and strength his own once more.

CHAPTER 30

For the next week the rains continued, not constantly, but with enough persistence that the town and the two armies besieging it were never dry. It made the process of building the earth wall around the infirmary a near fool's errand, almost as much mud washing away with each bucketful. Nevertheless, Sergeant Porth refused to let the task overwhelm him or the men he took into his command. He sent teams to the old quarry to fetch bucketloads of any small stones they could find to add reinforcement to the wall, while others formed squads of cutters, sickles stripping the waterside of sedge. After seven days, a reasonable windbreak had risen around the tents, and talk had turned to making a more permanent roof. The stoves Prentice had promised were delivered after four days, courtesy of Lady Dalflitch's quartermasters.

It was on the eighth day that Lord Farringdon's prediction came to fruition and Daven Marcus proved he would not need any more breaks in the rain to set his Dragons upon the town. The first massive shots roared out soon after dawn, crashing into Norgate's remains. Stone balls shattered stone walls until, by noon, the historical gatehouse bastion was no more than a pile of broken rubble.

"At least it will still block easy access to the bridge," Farringdon observed as he and Prentice surveyed the damage from the rooftop of Loncastel Keep.

"It will also make any swift sallies on our part impossible as well," Prentice said.

Farringdon nodded grimly. "Is that his purpose, do you think?" he asked. "Or is he simply punishing us for daring to resist him?"

Prentice considered the question. "Most likely a measure of each," he said at last. "As well as the pure enjoyment of watching his war engines about their work."

"My wife tells stories of his use of the Dragons during his 'crusade' west," Farringdon added to Prentice's assessment, nodding as he accepted its wisdom. "Waiting a week for the chance to use them this time might have driven him to distraction, I suppose."

Prentice looked past the site of the destroyed bastion to the set of large shelters that now dotted the fields. From this distance, they could have been mistaken for hay stores or open-fronted stables, but each one protected a bronze cannon, the broad throat of the beast sometimes partly visible through the gaps in the earthworks built up to shelter them from counter fire.

They appear not so different from our infirmary, Prentice noted, though of course the Usurper's shelters protected no wounded. He wondered if Daven Marcus even made any provision for those who were injured in his service. He must surely do something, but how much or how little? Wherever that was, it was far from Prentice's sight.

"I haven't given the command to fire back," Farringdon told him. "Not yet. So far, they've only targeted Norgate, and given your warning about our powder situation, I thought it better to wait and let our gunners sight themselves as long as they like. Each crew is watching and ready for me to let them off the leash to hunt, like peregrines with their falconers."

Birds are the servants of the Inquisition, Prentice thought, glad he at least had the self-control to keep his tongue. Of late, the Silent Hand often dominated his thoughts anytime he paused like this, and he almost hated to stand still. His daily routine had become a morning tour of Sougate and all the town's key strongpoints, ending here at the northern bridge. Then he would report to her grace at Paramour's and lunch with his wife and children. After, he would return to the camp to supervise any matters there before another visit to Sougate and then training in his shed through the evening. In the last seven nights, he had slept there four times, exhausted on the bare ground. Sometimes he had thought of the new regimen as akin to his days as a convict laborer but each time reminded himself that he had never eaten so well on the chain as he did now, so he had no cause for self-pity.

"Good to conserve the powder," he forced himself to say, dragging his distracted thoughts back to the matter at hand. "Lady Dalflitch dispatched a bird north with a command to send more, but that resupply might be a month in coming."

"Surely not so long?" Farringdon objected, but Prentice only shook his head. In truth, a month was a pessimistic estimate, but given how things had gone for them since coming to Bridgetown, better pessimism than a nasty disappointment.

More self-pity? he chastised himself inwardly and felt a sudden urge to be on the move once more. He turned toward the stairs and an ache in his back caused him to roll his shoulder to release the tension there.

"Are you in pain, My Lord?" Farringdon asked, following along at his side.

"Bumps and bruises from exercise," Prentice told him.

"Exercise?" the knight captain pressed. "The rumor going about the Lion Banner is that you have issued an open challenge to any militiaman who thinks he can take you in a wrestling match. Your evenings are spent in continuous fist fights and grappling, so tis said."

"Not quite." Prentice shook his head, although it was not an unreasonable summary of his training. In his childhood, he had been sent as a student to masters of the infamously harsh Seven Rings Cross fighting school. The school's symbol, literally a cross drawn of seven interlinked rings, was also the basic format of its training method. Each circle of the cross stood for one of the system's key skills, and students were expected to master each before moving on to the next. It was a slow, unnecessarily complex method of training, which nonetheless produced exceptional fighters if a student could persevere into the later rings.

The first ring was physical conditioning, and in the traditional schools a pupil was expected to invest at least two seasons into this ring before being permitted to advance to the second, which was unarmed fighting—wrestling and striking. Prentice did not feel he had half a year to wait to recover his strength, so he had decided to incorporate the two first rings into one effort for himself. The first day he had asked Gennet to give him the names of any Gryphon Banner militiamen with a reputation for wrestling or pugilism, and the third night he had begun to ask them to come and fight him in the shed. The last night three men had shown up, and he had fought fisticuffs and grappling with each in turn, followed by inviting them to all assault him at once, another key part of Seven Rings Cross training. In order to advance from one ring to the next, a student must face seven opponents of their current level, at least half of those at once. Hoping himself ready to try three on one had led to him being tossed summarily on his backside.

That should teach you not to rush, he told himself and shook his head. His inner voice had echoes of others within it.

"No challenges, My Lord," he told Farringdon as they headed downward. "But if you know of any strong fellows under the Lion Banner that think they know a thing or two about unarmed fighting, please commend them to me. I need all the assistance I can get."

Farringdon nodded.

"Are you planning a second life as a prize-fighter, Prentice?" the knight captain asked as they exited the keep onto Great Bridge Road. "I only mention it because I would have imagined your duties as knight commander would keep you too busy for such an ambition."

Prentice turned on Farringdon so quickly that the rainwater sprayed from the swirl of his night-blue cloak. The marquis-consort was still safe from the rain at the edge of the keep's vault over the road. He had an odd smile on his face, which made Prentice think he was making a joke, but the knight commander did not share the humor.

"I am seeking to recover my strength, My Lord," Prentice said sternly. "Between poison and...other robberies...I feel...diminished. I need the exercise to build myself up again to..." He paused. It was not the first time he had tried to explain his intentions with the training, but in each instance, he found it difficult to articulate. He was not accustomed to being so at a loss for words.

"Build yourself up to...?" Farringdon asked, his smile receding into a concerned expression. "Up to what, exactly?"

"Up to..." Prentice had to force himself to speak to coral his rebellious thoughts. It should not be this hard to explain what he was about. "To my previous strength. To the strength that your lady wife needs of me."

There was a harshness to his tone that he had not meant, a note of accusation, but he had no way to stop himself. Every moment he was not in motion, not thinking upon the defense or the coming tasks, two forces rose up inside him to make their own war—the hot rage that wanted his father to pay, wanted to make him into a patricidal murderer, and the cold fury that refused to be reduced to the dog on a chain that men like that same father or Daven Marcus tried to make of him. At a moment like this, he could not even say for certain which of the two it was that made him speak so sharply to his friend.

"And what of your needs, Lord Knight Commander?" Farringdon asked quietly.

"My needs? My needs, My Lord, are simple enough—more powder and shot, Bluebird hanging from a gibbet by his neck, and fighters to train with to recover my lost strength. Lady Dalflitch is about the first two tasks, My Lord, and I ask you to help me with the third. If your own duties occupy you, please do not concern yourself. I am not yet so recovered that I have run through all the training partners I already have. Good day to you."

With that, Prentice turned away again to march down the road, thinking to make another tour of the guard posts around the town. Even lunch with his wife seemed like too much pause for him today. With luck, he might find a clue about Bluebird and his infiltrators—word of his smokehouse, if nothing else. Farringdon called after him.

"I could send word when I take the falconer's leash off. Would it not be good to see the Dragons eat some fire themselves for once?"

"You need not send word," Prentice said over his shoulder. "I will hear the shooting and come when I have time."

He was not a handful of paces farther gone, eager to return to his many duties that never ceased from piling up, when the echo of a trumpet call sounded faintly through the rain. Turning on the wet cobbles yet again, his eyes met Farringdon's and both men listened, ears tipped to the sky. Another blast rang from Daven Marcus's camp, and they each looked up the road through the keep's undercroft, out to the north bank and the rump of Norgate. Already, two cohorts on duty, garrisoning the Loncastel end of the bridge, were sending men forward in the rain to see what was coming. Without a word, Prentice and Farringdon turned to go with them. Every militiaman of the White Lions, from highest to lowest, knew that a trumpet augured no good for them on any battlefield.

CHAPTER 31

"He actually sent a herald?" Amelia asked again as she rode her horse Silvermane along Great Bridge Road with a full cohort escort ahead of her, pushing for way through the townsfolk while a second cohort marched behind. The cannon fire of the morning had driven many to hide in their homes, but now that it had ceased, word of new actions on the north bank drew them out.

"He sent three, in fact, Your Grace," Prentice told her. "In full livery, as you might expect. And without a knightly escort of any kind."

"Bold of him," Amelia said, trying to keep fully upright and dignified in her saddle in spite of her sore back and the strange feeling of supporting her pregnancy while riding. It was no challenge to her skill, but it felt uncomfortable, nonetheless.

My dress does not help, she thought. When a runner brought word from Norgate that Daven Marcus had called for a parley with Bridgetown's leaders, Amelia turned to her ladies-in-waiting to help her make ready, and it was discovered that her only overdress in Reach blue, made to replace the one ruined at Aubrey, no longer came close to fitting her. A swift adjustment was forced, and now the two halves of the dress's front hung wide to either side of her belly, which protruded, covered only in white linen.

"I look like a pregnant nun," she had told Lady Spindle, who apologized profusely. Several of the neophytes smirked at her comment, and Amelia had had to tell herself they were laughing at its humor and not her appearance.

"Perhaps a chain of silver," Lady Dalflitch had suggested, and a moment later the wide-hanging blue sides were pinned across her belly by a length of silver necklace that held the dress in place with at least a modicum of dignity. Now that she was in the saddle though, the chain simply rode up and her belly protruded once more.

Like the enormous white egg of some gigantic bird, Amelia thought bitterly. Beside her, Lady Dalflitch sat her own horse upright and glorious, wearing the dress with marigold sleeves that Spindle had made for her. The archduchess sighed inwardly and told herself that sitting beside the Grand Kingdom's most celebrated beauty would have made her feel like a bundle of old laundry no matter what she was wearing. She gave Prentice another glance as he rode Boots on her other side and had to suppress a smirk of her own. Even in the short look, she saw him shifting in his saddle, clearly uncomfortable and bouncing as much as riding.

And he lacks the excuse of a pregnancy, she thought. *What an odd trio we must present.* Her amusement choked away as she remembered who it was they were riding to meet. She schooled her face and manner to courtly reserve, reminding herself that dignity was ever more than appearance or dress. Poorly covered pregnant belly or not, she would be fully the Archduchess of the Western Reach in the sight of the kingslayer and his minions. She would allow herself nothing less. As their escort arrived at Loncastel Keep, Farringdon met them, already mounted on his own horse, with two lancers accompanying.

"Are we ready, My Lord?" Prentice asked, and Farringdon nodded with full politeness.

Amelia could see that both men were using their most formal manners with each other, putting themselves into their own courtly postures, just as she had.

"We are, Baron," Farringdon replied. "Four cohorts await on the road and bridge to secure the bridgehead—two of Gryphons, two of Lions as you wanted, as well as fifty lancers."

"I will command the foot, you will the men ahorse," the knight commander ordered, and Farringdon accepted the instruction without question.

Amelia was relieved as she watched their interaction. In the past few days, Prentice had seemed somewhat distracted, and she assumed it was because of his meeting with his ailing father. She could only imagine the impact such an encounter must have had—to face the man who had disowned him, now on the very doorstep of the next world. Lady Righteous had insisted that her husband could withstand any challenge his elder might lay upon his soul, but Amelia suspected she was being loyal rather than truthful. Prentice could be bleeding to death on the ground in front of her and Baroness Righteous would be hard pressed to admit it to herself.

In this matter though, his mind seems fully focused, the archduchess told herself, and that was reassuring.

"Well, how fares our guest's mood, husband?" she asked. "We've had him waiting an hour. I suspect he will be becoming impatient."

"Sadly, I believe he feels no frustration, Your Grace," Farringdon told her. "I would imagine he is admiring his war engine's destruction of the Norgate bastion. Our observers report that he picnics quite comfortably, despite the gloom."

I'll bet.

It had taken Amelia the better part of an hour to ready herself for this meeting, but that had been ultimately to their good. Prentice had proposed a number of plans he wanted in place before he would "permit" her to cross the Loncastel bridge to face Daven Marcus in a parley. And then there had been the matter of Bridgetown's liege. Prentice and Dalflitch had both had the same thought as Amelia on the matter of the young noblewoman.

"Relevant or not, to not invite her only feeds the Bluebird's rumor that you have seized the town from her grasp, keeping her virtual prisoner in her own domain," the lady seneschal had said. "The parley is called with the leaders of the town, and that still includes her, even if only in name."

"I've seized nothing from her," Amelia had replied to that, "save the duty to protect her lands. Send to her."

Now that the Reacherfolk were ready to meet with Denay's tyrant, the question of whether Bridgetown's rightful liege would actually attend the conference with them remained unresolved. Amelia was about to ask if they should wait any longer when the crowd began to grumble and shift on the road behind her. Three nobles ahorse approached with only a single liveried man in escort. The remaining Twin was leading his liege and her two cousins, as he always had.

It seems no traditions are safe from our war, Amelia thought, *no matter how charming or how banal.*

Somehow that lone herald, who had only ever been seen in the company of his partner up until now, embodied so much of the loss the Usurper's civil war had brought upon them all. Amelia felt a strange sting of grief for the loyal fellow and tried to remember again that no matter how foolishly or hatefully Bridgetown's remaining peers behaved, it was always because they were being driven to it by the monster waiting on the other side of the bridge. The trailing escort cohort made way for the small delegation, and in moments, Penelope was seated on her own horse beside Amelia, Prentice and Dalflitch politely making way.

"Greetings, My Lady," the archduchess told the younger woman.

"Greetings," Penelope replied, looking down her nose. "You seem very pregnant this day."

"I do," Amelia agreed, not wasting time or energy being offended. She smiled down at her pronounced belly, flicking her cloak aside to present it in all its awkward glory, then covering up again before looking at Penelope's own torso, clad as usual in steel and Bridgetown's chivalric colors. "You yourself seem as martial and noble as ever, Lady Penelope. I doubt either estate will make much difference to the Usurper, though. He is ever adept at finding fault." Amelia turned to face the bridge and took in a breath. "If you are ready, My Lady, shall we greet the man who seeks to wrest your father's earldom from his heir's grasp?"

Penelope blinked, then waved dismissively, her lips twisted in a sour grimace, and Amelia gave Prentice the slightest of nods. He passed the signal to his drummers and the beat was taken up. The combined leadership of the besieged earldom of Bridgetown rode out to face Daven Marcus, the Usurper King of Denay, Rhales, and the Grand Kingdom. A funereal march could not have been dourer.

CHAPTER 32

"This reminds me of that feast in the west years ago," Amelia whispered to Dalflitch as they rode up to Daven Marcus's "picnic."

"That will be deliberate, Your Grace, I assure you," the seneschal confided, and Amelia had no doubt she would know. Few in all the Grand Kingdom understood the Usurper as Dalflitch did, having shared his bed and once dreamed of being his queen.

During his failed winter crusade against the Redlanders in the west, Daven Marcus had come to a feast Amelia held to commemorate her first husband's passing. It had been raining lightly that night, as it was now. The then Prince of Rhales had upstaged her at her own feast and deliberately induced an argument that had led to a duel and the death of one of her loyal vassals. Apparently, he had considered it great sport and a personal triumph over her. Now, as he sat under a vast awning in the wet weather, its royal red brocade dripping heavy droplets from golden tassels, it was clear that Daven Marcus was mimicking that "victory"—surely the first of many snubs he planned to deliver to her this day. The awning was easily twenty paces across its front, and it looked as if the team of liveried men holding it aloft numbered ten at least. Beneath it, woven carpets were soaking water from the muddy ground while two large, black iron braziers blazed with logs, banishing much of the cold. Daven Marcus sat a grand throne with eagle-claw feet, chased in gold leaf, beside an ornate table laid with wine and goblets, as well as a small pile of papers, weighed down, it seemed, with a heavy statuette of a gold eagle, wings spread wide.

"I do not know if I ever fully apologized for my part in that evening, Your Grace," Dalflitch added, recalling the feast long ago. "But please know I regret every fraction of what I did to you and your people."

"Forgotten and forgiven, My Lady," Amelia reassured her honestly. Few, if any, who spent time in the orbit of Daven Marcus's flame were not lured into scorching themselves. He was like an unbroken house pet, seemingly well-groomed and well-bred but liable to bite at any moment. Thus, Amelia approached his polite-seeming gathering the way she would the den of a dangerous predator. Watching him as she drew near, she realized that the extra grandiosity of his picnic compared to her past feast was not the only difference. Daven Marcus himself had changed. The golden youth she had met years before was gone, and the Usurper was beginning to resemble his murdered father. He had grown a full beard, as bushy as his blonde curls, which were themselves darkening to a deeper brown-gold. He was stouter as well, and the filigreed steel of his breastplate clearly encircled a more barrel-chested man than he had once been. Despite the changes, the mocking gaze of his blue eyes and sneer of his lips were exactly as Amelia remembered.

"Ah, so the lazy wench finally approaches," he declared as if speaking to those around him but loudly enough to be heard dozens of paces away. Standing beside him in his own suit of plate was the Usurper's most loyal nobleman and general, Duke Robant. Also present were two men in the black robes of legal scholars and another fellow in armor—this time a coat of mail—whom Amelia did not recognize but knew to be a Church knight by the green and black crosses on his surcoat. It seemed like a spartan crop of attendants compared to the flock of sycophants Daven Marcus had traipsed around the Western Reach with years before.

Perhaps his 'loyal' retainers have all abandoned him, Amelia thought, though she dismissed the idle notion immediately. Hundreds of paces back, a vast array of knights ahorse sat waiting in the rain, their polished armor dulled by the grey misting, their banners limp. Nonetheless, their presence was a reminder of the Usurper's true power. For all Daven Marcus's affected leisure, no one offered parley from a position of weakness. *He has only a few retainers present because that is all he wants.*

"We hope you have come to pay your respects and congratulate us, Amelia," the Usurper went on grandly, using the royal plural to refer to himself. "We are recently, and happily, married. You can stop all that foolishness about being wayward now. We've put the matter to rest."

Despite herself, Amelia blinked in surprise and felt her expression harden in annoyance. Daven Marcus had accused *her* of being a wayward wife after first trying to force her into a marriage and thinking to rape her in front of a crowd of courtiers as a way to consummate the match. Yet here he was talking as if her waywardness was her own claim and that the matter between them was of her making. She felt her teeth grinding and she dared not release them, fearing that she might say something rash in response. Daven Marcus kept looking at her expectantly, inviting her to protest, to risk making herself look foolish. The moment continued and Amelia suddenly became aware of the gathering drops of the misting rain that were now dripping off the hood of her winter cloak. Before she broke and made a comment, Daven Marcus turned to Penelope.

"And who is this poppet in plate?" he asked, sounding suddenly like a kindly, if mocking, uncle. "Is this the famed daughter of the beset earldom? We had heard her slain at the hands of a bear. Most unbecoming of a daughter to fall to her father's own heraldry. Most embarrassing."

"I am yet alive," Penelope declared. "Your assassin beast failed in its purpose."

"*Our* beast?" Daven Marcus asked with an expression of nearly sincere shock. "You are misinformed, My Lady. We have never assassinated anyone in our entire life. Our enemies, and we hope you do not count yourself amongst them, have ever received the respect of being faced in open combat."

Amelia heard Dalflitch tsk quietly beside her and struggled not to scoff openly herself, though part of her wondered why she was bothering, precisely.

"But since we are newly known to each other, let us make you this pledge, young Penelope, so that you can test the character of the new Denay throne for yourself," Daven Marcus went on. "If you find us anyone, any witch or conjurer, who was a part of this plot of sorcerous murder against you, we will see them swiftly executed. They will be drawn and vivisected according to Kings Law. We will even provide you the executioner that it might happen in your own town square. Our man is a master of the craft."

It did not surprise Amelia to imagine that Daven Marcus had an expert torturer in his employ, nor shock her to hear it called a "craft," but it did surprise her to hear him offer the man's service so readily. Although it made perfect sense now that it was happening, she had not expected the Usurper to speak so gently to Penelope. She had expected demands that they grovel at his feet and beg for forgiveness, not words of comfort and largesse. Of course, it was only Penelope who was receiving the offers so far.

Demands that I grovel might yet be coming, she conceded to herself. As she thought about it, though, it was clear that Lady Penelope was equally caught wrong-footed by this moment of politeness and the offer of assistance rather than demands of surrender. While she was wondering, Amelia saw one of the black-robed scholars of law shuffle forward, stroking his neatly waxed beard.

"Your Majesty, please," he asked earnestly, like a pleading supplicant. "We must observe the forms."

He moved ahead of Daven Marcus's throne to confront the Reach and Bridgetown worthies.

"Lady Penelope of Bridgetown, Baroness-elect, heir to Earl John the Ninth," the scholar addressed them in a loud but croaking voice, "and Amelia of Dweltford, do you both in full honor and the righteous sight of God in Heaven pledge to obey all the laws of chivalry here now in this noble parley?"

Behind the scholar, Daven Marcus rolled his eyes theatrically, and for once Amelia felt herself in full agreement with the murderous tyrant. Would anyone here trust any oath of parley between them? Was any one of them so naïve?

Perhaps this aged one hopes to return us to more civilized times, she thought as the lawyer continued, reciting the full text of the old pledge from memory. Amelia had attended her fair share of battlefield conferences, and never once had the full pledge needed reciting. It seemed the lawyer did, indeed, hope to reassert the old ways to rebuild the old order.

You are destined for disappointment, old man, Amelia thought. *Not while Daven Marcus sits any throne, whether I agree or not.*

"Oh, enough, Itzac," Daven Marcus cut the lawyer short with at least a third of the old legal oaths unsaid and certainly before anyone had actually pledged to uphold them. The Usurper reached for his goblet and took a long swig while the interrupted man looked back with a perplexed expression, as if he did not understand the tyrant's interruption.

"Look at them," the Usurper continued. "They come armed for war and with that escort close to hand."

He waved his cup in the direction of the White Lions standing in two columns on either side of the access to the bridge, one lot facing west the other east. In the ground between them was the churned earthwork defenses and the cracked and toppled stones of Norgate. Just riding their horses through the wreckage had been a challenge for Amelia's entourage, but now they, followed by fifty fully armed lancers, had managed to wear down a route of sorts, though it was more like a winding forest path, rising and twisting over broken ground, than the road it replaced. Daven Marcus finished making his point.

"They will not trust us no matter what earnest protestations we make," he told the legal scribe, though it was clear he was speaking for Amelia and Penelope's benefits. "And in truth, we can only trust one of them. One is a loyal daughter, adrift in a stormy sea of betrayals and witchcraft. The other is a cuckoldress with a line of betrayed husbands behind her, of whom we are only the most prestigious and not the last."

"Cuckoldress?" Amelia blurted out before she could stop herself. "You lying little...!"

"Better you call *me* by that title, Highness," Lady Dalflitch announced, cutting Amelia off and saving her from embarrassing herself. The archduchess felt immediately grateful, even as her heart clenched for her lady-in-waiting, voluntarily humiliating herself to protect her liege's honor.

"After all," Dalflitch went on, "you yourself contributed so much effort to the infamy of at least one of my marriages."

CHAPTER 33

Daven Marcus peered at Lady Dalflitch on her saddle as if she were difficult to see. After a moment, he sniffed dismissively.

"Sorry," he said to her, "we don't think we've had the pleasure."

"I certainly had no pleasure," Dalflitch answered instantly, and Amelia smirked.

Daven Marcus's polite demeanor began to harden on his face like a mask. "Perhaps we do remember you a little," he said coldly. "Were you not a slattern that lurked at the fringes of our court during our young days in Rhales? We were told you had given up trying to lure good knights and nobles to your filthy sheets and taken up finally with a lame and leprous dog. A fitting fate, from what we hear."

"Neither lame nor leprous, Highness," Dalflitch answered readily, and Amelia noticed that she was still addressing Daven Marcus by the term for a prince, subtly refusing to acknowledge his kingship. "In fact, having sampled so many of the men-at-arms of Rhales, all the way to the highest bed there, I have finally found a true man with a worthy weapon and actually skilled in its use. I find no need to pretend any longer, and it is such a relief."

Amelia choked on a laugh at the lewd insult, and whether it was Dalflitch's words alone or her own amusement as well, it was clear Daven Marcus knew Dalflitch had scored the point in their exchange. She looked to her opposite side at Lady Penelope, however, and it was equally obvious the young noblewoman was not so amused.

"So, we neither trust each other, kingslayer," Amelia said quickly, realizing that even if she won all the "points" in this conference, she could still ride away a loser overall. For the sake of her army and her errant ally, she was obliged to entertain this nonsensical parley, but the sooner it was over, the better. Of course, there was still a slight chance Daven Marcus would have something to say worth hearing, but she doubted it.

"Hear what she calls us?" the Usurper asked, and the question was obviously addressed to Penelope. "She seeks to stain us with her own crimes, even as she lured us toward her own pox-ridden bed. Lord Robant, you were there the night our father was killed. Who was it that plunged the dagger?"

"Amelia, the Witch of Dweltford," Robant said like a magistrate pronouncing sentence. "I saw it with my own two eyes."

Amelia at last scoffed openly and was considering whether it was even worthwhile to try refuting the claim, but Daven Marcus went on before she could come up with any retort.

"You see, dear little Penelope, you and we are both victims of magicks and the foulest unrighteousness. We are the King in Denay, Sovereign Unchallenged over the entire of the Grand Kingdom, now cruelly fractured by the evil witch that keeps you prisoner in your own castle."

Keeps her prisoner? It's all I can do to get the girl to step out of her own bedchamber, Amelia thought.

"Now that our own beloved father has been taken from us, we have been forced to mount the dais to the throne and become a father to all," the Usurper went on, switching from the royal "we" and making his next words seem more intimate by doing so. "It is ever the king's burden that he be father to the nation, but like you, I recognize that we are now all orphans. Too many good fathers have been taken from us too soon."

"Lying filth," Amelia muttered under her breath before she could stop herself. She remembered all too vividly the bloody night he had slain his own father. To hear him speak like this sickened her so that she was sure her own unborn baby must be turning in disgust within her. On her right side, Lady Penelope was shifting uncomfortably in the saddle, and Amelia realized his smooth words might be proving persuasive to the young noblewoman.

"You must not believe him," she whispered to the liege of Bridgetown but suspected it might already be too late. Whatever her cousins and the Bluebird's secret voices had whispered to the girl had prepared the ground and Daven Marcus's masterful lies were taking root. Amelia could sense it, though it was little wonder. The Usurper spoke so earnestly one could almost think he believed it himself. If she had not been there that very night and knew herself to be innocent, Amelia might almost have believed him as well. He was that persuasive.

"We know you have great hopes for your father's legacy," Daven Marcus said, and Amelia looked at him, thinking that she must find a way to end the parley, but short of force she knew Penelope would not cooperate. "Like any good daughter, you have ambitions to build on his fine service to the throne. It sorrows us so that we have been forced to do such damage to your heritage, cracking its stones. We know that you have been driven to your rebellion, but rebels must be brought to heel. A goodly father disciplines unruly children, as your father and uncles no doubt did for you. Those of us born of noble fathers understand what true parenting is, so much more than merely rutting and spawning, as the lower orders do."

And there's the insult to my birth and heritage, Amelia thought, as if ticking off Daven Marcus's typical affronts on mental fingers.

"My Lady, we should not waste time with these pointless lies," she said as gently as she could make herself, reaching out to Penelope's arm.

The lady spurned her gesture. "You want me to ride away from a parley with the king?" she demanded. "My town is besieged, and you would spurn a chance for peace."

"He is no king and he offers no peace," Amelia retorted, more loudly than she intended.

"Are we not?" Daven Marcus asked, still affecting his kindly, avuncular tone. "Father" to the whole Grand Kingdom. "Judge us not only by the rod of discipline we are forced to wield. Judge us also for the rewards we offer for obedience. Every good father rewards obedience."

Amelia's mind raced, trying to think what he could be about to offer. Surely, he wouldn't quit the siege, just like that. What else was there? Her eyes searched back and forth from the Usurper to Penelope, willing the lady not to be persuaded. Another moment and Amelia knew she would have to force an end or lose her ally outright. Of course, that would change no military aspect of the siege. Penelope's support was purely symbolic at this point. Nevertheless, Amelia was resolved. She had not come to conquer Bridgetown but to save it, which she could not do if its liege decided to side with the kingslayer king.

"What rewards?" a voice asked from behind Penelope, and Amelia looked aghast as she realized it was Wilforn's. The brat was speaking out of turn once more. Her head whipped around to Daven Marcus, who scowled for a space, and Amelia felt a momentary relief. He was as offended by Wilforn's violation of manners as she was. It lasted only a breath, however.

"There is a new dukedom in the north," Daven Marcus said grandly, standing and sweeping his arm around in a clearly rehearsed gesture. "There is a heretic in Bridgetown and a rebel army on its southern doorstep. Perhaps the time has come for a new duchy here to defend the south, with a true and regal duchess on its seat."

Amelia heard Penelope suck in a breath and knew she had lost the girl for good. She wondered if there was anything she might say now to persuade the Lady of Bridgetown back to her side when a harsh, high-pitched whistle sailed through the sodden air. All eyes turned to see a high-arching signal arrow falling, the shrill tone coming from its specially carved head. It thudded into the muddy ground between the two factions, suddenly silent and standing straight upright.

"Red fletching," Prentice bellowed suddenly. "East side!"

Daven Marcus and Duke Robant recoiled, clearly wondering what was afoot, though the duke and the Church knight moved to interpose themselves between the Usurper and the Bridgetown delegation. They need not have bothered.

CHAPTER 34

As soon as the arrow struck the earth and Prentice had called
out his command, the entire White Lions escort was in
motion, enacting the plans their commanding officers had agreed
upon. Whatever Daven Marcus plotted for this parley meeting,
neither Prentice nor Farringdon doubted the kingslayer would
have an ambush of some sort planned as well. His main army was
too far back to snatch Archduchess Amelia and Lady Penelope
before their escort could see them safely across the bridge, and if
the Usurper had not left his army that far back, the Bridgetown
leadership would never have risked venturing forth to conference
in the first place. If he planned to capture Amelia or Penelope,
he had to dangle a bait—himself, obviously—and then he would
have to find a way to hold them in place while his army charged
the gap to complete their capture. Of course, the Usurper had
already shown that he had the perfect tool for such a mission—the
Jerwahl mercenaries—which was why Prentice and Farringdon
had primed the militiamen to watch for this signal.

Unseen in the rain, according to the mystic ways of his people,
Dahyoor had been riding as a scout up and down the banks of the
Murr on either side of the Loncastel Bridge. His instructions had
been simple—if he found signs of the Jerwahl Rangers amongst
the reeds and long grasses on the west side of the bridge, a signal
arrow with yellow fletching was to be shot. If on the east, red
fletching. If both, then two arrows. Having received the warning,
the entire escort sprang into action. The western militia column

moved to secure the bridgehead and the passage back through the ruins of Norgate. The eastern column formed up facing east, Claws and Fangs at the ready. Urging his pony to half swim, half climb through the river's edge to the open meadow, Dahyoor rode the uneven gait as if his mount were merely walking, all the time firing whistling arrows into a patch of the riverside. Commanding the east flank, Sergeant Gennet pointed at the same location.

"The weasels are nesting in there, lads," he bellowed. "Watch the mud and let's make a charge of it."

"What if they shoot at us?" someone called from the ranks. "They can, but the Roar can't in this rain."

"Then we take a volley," Gennet shouted back. "Now get in there and mow some grass. Don't let them get more than the one shot."

The White Lions marched forward on the beat, struggling almost immediately as they plunged into the boggy riverside. Their left flank, at least, was on solid ground and those lines advanced the faster. In a significant battle, the collapse of cohesion might have been disastrous, but this would not be a long enough fight to worry about that. The entire purpose of the charge was to keep the Rangers from capturing the bridgehead. In less than a quarter of the candle the full White Lions contingent was to be back across the river. To that end, the fifty lancers spurred their horses into motion, encircling the two noble lieges and their entourage's, using their armored bodies and horses to cover against any wheellock fire.

"You must go, Your Grace," Prentice said to his liege, and she nodded, wheeling about immediately, as did Dalflitch. Lady Penelope was too dumbfounded by the sudden shift around her, it seemed.

"You too, My Lady," Prentice told her, but she only glanced at him before looking to her cousin, Cyprian, apparently hoping he would explain what was happening.

With their hiding place revealed, the ambushers rose from amongst the reeds and as predicted, unleashed their wheellocks in a heavy volley. Their shot "mowed" good sections of the river grasses, and several Lions fell. Nevertheless, the militia continued to lumber forward, closing gaps in their ranks as best they could.

"The lancers, My Lord," Prentice said to Farringdon. The next part of their plan involved the Reach horsemen riding on the solid field of the riverside to flank the Jerwahl men-at-arms and fire into them with their own short wheellocks from the side. Pinning the mercenaries between men afoot and men ahorse should break them swiftly enough. Farringdon, however, was looking straight north.

"He's so close, Baron," he said to Prentice, and the knight commander glanced to the broken road and meadow where Daven Marcus was now retreating on foot, having to be dragged by Duke Robant, it seemed. The pavilion he had been under was collapsed now, the men holding it aloft also fleeing with the Usurper. Farther north, trumpets were sounding, and the waiting army was spurring itself to action, but they would be several moments away yet. It might have been enough time for fifty lancers to ride swiftly and capture a tyrant. At the very least, they would have a chance of killing him outright. When they had been making their plans, Prentice and Farringdon had discussed just such a possibility. The marquis-consort had been optimistic and ready to gamble. Prentice did not disagree but knew the available time would be knife-edged short. Fifty lancers could find themselves trapped on the field and slaughtered by an army of thousands at the charge.

"And if the Jerwahlers overpower us, we will lose your lady wife and all with her," he had told the knight captain.

Farringdon had reluctantly agreed, but having seen the main chance now, he was clearly having second thoughts.

"Do not let the bastard lure you into another bad mistake," Prentice told Farringdon, and the marquis-consort nodded grimly, clearly stung by the reminder of his defeat in the previous battle before turning to his part in their plan, leading both noble parties of the Bridgetown contingent back into safety. Since his wife and her attendant were already weaving through Norgate's ruins, Farringdon presumed to seize the reins of the shocked Penelope, and he led her horse the same direction. As arranged, many of the lancers closed in tight, bodily protecting them and effectively forcing the Lady of Bridgetown to go with them, like a leaf on a stream, made to go wherever the water flowed. The rest of the lancers rode to their duty, flanking the ambushers. Prentice watched and then cast one last glance north at the fleeing tyrant. Even more reluctant than Lady Penelope to move from the broken parley, Daven Marcus was struggling with his attendants to remain close to the combat. Prentice suspected he had wanted to watch the ambush and was too excited with the cleverness of his trap to realize it was failing. There was still a moment before a horse would be brought to him and he would be able to flee the field or else remain, flanked by a thousand men-at-arms. Prentice was suddenly struck with memories of the Israelite judge Samson once more and recalled that the mighty hero had once struck down a thousand enemies with no more than the jawbone of an ass.

Oh, for the jawbone of an ass, he thought, wondering for a moment if that was the lesson of Samson he was meant to learn, to think of himself as the mighty hero his enemies seemed to fear him as. He looked down at his sword, still sheathed at his belt, and nearly laughed out loud.

"You are an ass," he scoffed at himself quietly.

Trumpets continued to sound, and they were answered with cannon shot from the Loncastel keep guns. Three balls in the volley were well sighted, and the flying iron tore long, bloody gouges into the charging lines, men and horses falling. Nevertheless, the Denay army was coming on. Until they had secured Daven Marcus's safety, Prentice was confident the enemy would not unleash the Dragons to fire, but that was only a matter of time. The tyrant's presence was the reason he was confident that the Jerwahl Rangers would not throw their clamshell bombs either, but that was another danger only delayed. As soon as he heard the drumbeat announcing that the archduchess and baroness-elect were safe, Prentice ordered the full withdrawal. Lancers kept a flanking watch while Gennet's militiamen, who had clambered over the reeds and managed to bloody the Ranger's noses, now disengaged from their haphazard melees and turned straight north from the riverbank, the shortest distance out of the entangling ground. As soon as they were onto the firmer meadow, they switched westward and ran back toward the Great Bridge Road. Some of the Jerwahl force tried to follow or to reload their guns despite the drizzling rain, but several of the lancers had kept one of their own pistols in reserve and they dissuaded the enemy with shots of their own. Dahyoor also kept up his own shooting for as long as he could before the wet ruined his bowstring. On a dry day, Prentice imagined the fey man would have fancied his chances to take an enemy with every shot. When the last of the escort force reached Norgate, Prentice turned Boots around and joined Dahyoor so they were the final pair to ride back into Bridgetown.

Stationed at points along the bridge itself were pairs of militiamen with barrels on their shoulders. The Loncastel bridge was not like the mighty and ancient stone bridges in the middle of Bridgetown. Prentice doubted there was enough powder in all the White Lions' stores to even damage one of those edifices. Loncastel's span, however, was a typical wood-and-mortared-stone-pillar affair and all the more vulnerable for that. As he passed each pair of men, they broached the casks in their arms and began to pour slick alchemical oil onto the boards, running backwards as they did so. No wick or long-match could be trusted to stay alight in this weather, so the Lions had had no choice but to use this viscous mixture to bring flame to the casks of powder stacked at the north end of the bridge. As each pair of militiamen fled, so they joined fellows, until by the end, an entire line's worth of Lions were soaking the far half of the bridge. When their small barrels were empty, they cast them away and then fled as a blazing torch was brought to light the oil.

Having been splashed with the alchemical brew in their work, the barrel-bearers kept well away from lit fires. Farther back down Great Bridge Road, long past the keep, other militiamen waited with lambskins, and the oil bearers stripped off their dangerous clothing, rubbing themselves down with the flame-resistant, wool-covered hide. Until they were cleaned, the merest candle flame could set them alight, even in the rain, such was the liveliness of the fuel. While they shivered, naked in the wet, to make themselves safe, the torch was thrown and Loncastel bridge became a path of flame over the river. The blue and orange blaze rushed north where, even as he watched, Prentice could see some bold Rangers trying to take a position amongst Norgate's ruins, apparently readying their grenades to throw. Then the fire reached the powder and there was a sputtering cough followed by a mighty roar that cracked the bridge apart and threw a fountain of water from under the span. Broken boards collapsed into the river as a number of the bridge's stone pillars cracked and pieces toppled from them. Whatever other plans Daven Marcus hoped for his ambush, he would not cross Loncastel bridge into the town—not this day.

CHAPTER 35

"**B**astards! Mongrels!"

Prentice turned from the light of the flames and the breaking bridge to see Wilforn slipped from his own mount, spitting curses in every direction. His horse's rear leg staggered as it moved, unable to take any weight, and Prentice noticed blood trickling from its rump. It had taken a shot from the Rangers during the retreat.

"You just violated a parley!" he shouted, his voice echoing from the stones overhead. "Honorless dogs! Witch's bitch hounds!" He continued to rant, ignoring the lancers who watched him with cold eyes. "Peace with honor! You just cost us peace with honor! Our lady made a *duchess*, true and honest before the throne in Denay, not some bastardized Vec copy. We could have had it all, and you just put it to the torch. Was Norgate not enough? You must smash this keep and our bridge as well? Do you just want to hammer us to the river line, or is it your intent to drag us all into hell with you?"

"You speak out of turn, Squire!" Farringdon shouted over the young man's tirade, wrenching his helmet from his head to ensure he was heard properly.

"I heed no rebel Veckander's rebuke," Wilforn shouted back. "I am a true and honorable son of Bridgetown and the Grand Kingdom."

"But Daven Marcus is not," the archduchess interposed with a strong voice, not shouting but clearly heard in the echoing space.

"He is a regicidal and patricidal murderer. He slew his own father on the very throne he now thinks to sit for himself. He has no honor."

"He claims you did the deed," Cyprian said, adding his voice to the quarrel, and Prentice looked to see Lady Penelope's other cousin, still in his saddle, leaning across to take his liege-lady's reins out of Farringdon's hands and return them to her. Farringdon released them with a polite but wary nod, and Lady Penelope took them back.

"Why should we believe your version of events?" Cyprian continued, quieter than Wilforn but the more menacing for it.

"Because we were there and you were not," Farringdon told him, but it seemed even he realized it was a far from persuasive argument. In the shadows of the undercroft, Prentice mostly watched the archduchess and the baroness-elect. Her grace could end this fruitless confrontation at any moment with a word. For all the fury he was venting, Wilforn was a yapping dog, not a true threat to anyone present, physically or politically. Yet Archduchess Amelia was allowing this to go on—peers of the realm, such as they were, arguing like fishwives on the docks—while around them loyal members of the lower orders stood by, po-faced and pretending not to hear. All this was for the benefit of Lady Penelope, Prentice was sure—another morality play, another fruitless grasp for reconciliation, hoping that the young ruler would recognize the folly of blaming the Reach for the evils that beset them all.

This trio's resentments are too deep, Your Grace, he thought. *Wilforn could vent his spleen like this all day and never find the end of his bile. And even if he did, surely Cyprian has plans of his own that would scuttle any hope of resolving the widening gap between you.*

"Do you forget how your town suffered under Daven Marcus' hand when his men occupied you?" Amelia asked, looking straight at Penelope. "We came at your invitation, to aid you."

"Yes, after we turned him out! You stole upon us like thieves while we were celebrating our victories," Wilforn interrupted. "At every turn you have sought to rob us of our glory and honor. You trample our heritage, ruining everything you touch, from Norgate to Runners Field."

"It was not we who slew a sacrist on your cathedral steps," Farringdon retorted, and that seemed to shock Lady Penelope out of her uncertainty a moment. She stared at him with slitted eyes, but the knight captain had only begun to give his rebuke. "Nor was it we who slaughtered surrendering men in front of Sougate."

"Cowards," Wilforn sneered. "At Sougate you cringed while we won *another* great victory. See? My cousin carries the sword we took from the slain Vec prince."

"Then go do it again!" Prentice shouted, and all eyes turned on him, likely because of the unexpectedness of his words as much as their volume. He had not planned to do it. He had thought himself content to let his liege follow her hope for resolution. But the longer the pointless argument went on, the more Wilforn and Cyprian reminded him of the odd children from his vision the night of his duel with Cyprian's brother—mad infants, dancing and playing while blood rained from the sky, blood that dripped from a great eagle's wings. Prentice fixed his gaze on the querulous squire, letting the fullness of his contempt show through. "If you are so sure of yourself, go do it again. There is still another Vec prince at Sougate's doorstep. See if you can take *his* sword for your cousin as well. Or if Veckanders are not your fancy, chance your arm against the Usurper and his Bronze Dragons. They await across the river. We will not stop you."

The blunt challenge stole the wind from Wilforn's sails as Prentice hoped, and the squire's mouth hung agape a long moment. As if to punctuate Prentice's assertions, the cannons in the keep above them thundered again, their iron shot whistling northward through the air.

"We...we have...have no...no army of a size to fight either force," the squire stammered, looking to his cousins for support. Cyprian leaned close to whisper something in Penelope's ear. Prentice could only guess what it might be, but the baroness-elect seemed to accept his word, then looked away from Wilforn, as if in embarrassment. The angry squire seemed to recognize the gesture, and his resentful expression melted into a plaintive hopelessness.

"No?" Prentice asked rhetorically when he saw the shift. "Then perhaps cease yapping like a petulant housedog, young Wilforn. You only make yourself look a fool."

Withering like a flower in the drought sun, the squire fell completely silent and looked down at his feet, seeming suddenly even more like a child amongst adults, standing as he was amidst the mostly mounted escort company. Prentice looked to Lady Penelope and her other cousin, silently inviting them to comment or else quit the fruitless argument. Both met his gaze for a moment, and just when Prentice thought they were about to look away, Cyprian threw another jab—as always, calmer and better aimed than Wilforn's asinine ranting.

"We didn't destroy Loncastel bridge," he said simply, and Penelope looked to him suddenly, as if he had made a conclusive point, then back to Prentice, demanding an explanation by her expression and a tilt of her head alone. It was the most regal thing Prentice had ever seen the girl do, and at another moment it might have given him hope that she was finally growing properly into her role as baroness.

Too little, too late, he thought as he gave Cyprian his full attention.

"Yes, the bridge falls. Wooden bridges can be rebuilt. Dead baronesses do not come back to life. Dead fathers do not return to life and lost legacies are not reclaimed. If we had not broken your bridge for you, you would be dying here in this road under a keep that has not fought a war in centuries. Those Rangers would be tossing you iron apples, blasting you to bits. It is not we who stole your glory. It has been bleeding out of your town through generations of peace, running away through your ancestors' fingers. Now, at last, you realize that you are not your founders. You are not the chivalric heroes who forged your inheritance for you. You are mere children, *playing* at war."

Prentice could see both Penelope and Cyprian's expressions hardening under his stern rebuke, but he did not care. The time for polite entreaties was past. What did catch a corner of his attention was the archduchess, who had her eyes downcast and appeared to be muttering something. He hoped she was not signaling him in some quiet way, because he did not understand her meaning if she was. Nevertheless, he could hear the cannon crews at their thunderous duty and anticipated Daven Marcus would turn his Dragons loose on Loncastel at any moment. One lucky stone shot through the keep's undercroft roadway and his liege would be slain, and all this talk would become infinitely pointless in a breath. He resolved to finish his angry sermon and see the archduchess to proper safety.

"Your losses are many, My Lady," he said to the baroness-elect, moderating his harsh tone slightly. "But you are not the first or the worst victim of this war. Count your losses as you must but cease from imagining that tomorrow it will all be returned to you. Whatever is to come, it must be something new, because what *was* has led to this moment."

He paused and then looked Cyprian in the eye in turn.

"For all his faults, your brother at least knew this much, maddened with hate though he was," Prentice told the squire. "He used poison on his blade because victory was all he cared about. The same is true for the Usurper. Everything you value is burning and falling away like that bridge because you refuse to accept that against such loathing or ambition, no peace can be made. Even defeated, even with his arm cut from his body and his list of sins laid bare, Cassian would not yield and repent. He chose to die rather than find another way. The kingslayer across the river is a hundredfold the same. Will you repeat your brother's mistake? Will *you*, My Lady?"

There was a moment of quiet, and it seemed as if his words might be penetrating the young noblewoman's thinking. Cyprian was a different matter; it seemed his course was set.

"My brother should not have killed himself," he said in a low tone that almost sounded like an animal's growl. "Your duel was unresolved, and the matter was incomplete. No guilt of his was proven."

"He confessed the use of poison," Farringdon said in a scoffing tone. "How much more proof did you need? And what is this talk of no defeat?"

"Both men fell that night," Cyprian retorted, waving dismissively at Prentice. "Neither held his cause proved aright. Your lowborn baron only walks and rides now because your riches bought you the better healing."

Losing his arm was not enough for you? Prentice wondered at the squire's assertion. A quick glance told him that his own liege was still whispering, though her eyes were flicking back and forth over the conversation, watching with an expression of fading hope. He sucked in a breath and the smell of oily smoke made him want to cough, a sensation he did his best to suppress. A sudden splash of a stone ball striking the river behind them washed a vast amount of water over the bridge, momentarily dulling the flames, until the alchemical fuel stirred them up once more. The quartermaster merchants had assured Prentice that once the oil was lit, nothing short of a deluge mighty enough to wash away the whole town would extinguish the fires. They would still not be enough to do more than scorch the winter-drenched, mighty boards before the fuel finished burning, but they had done their main job. The close stone cannon shot was enough to jump the conversation to its conclusion, however.

"We must go, cousin," Cyprian said to Penelope, and she nodded in agreement. As they wheeled their horses toward the town, Cyprian gave Prentice one last glare.

"My brother's duel is not finished," he said calmly, looking down at Prentice's sword in its sheath. "The day you have no magick sword to cheat with, that will be the day it comes to its rightful end."

"Your brother had his own magicked blade. It poisoned him," Prentice retorted, not bothering to control his tongue for this moment either. He took hold of his sword's handle. "This one has no magick in it, I assure you, and I would just as soon spurn it as your brother did. Unfortunately, such is not my fate."

"Your fate...," the squire began, but stopped, as if he realized there was no rebuke worth making. He geed his horse to follow his baroness's. "Your fate be damned!"

"Wait," Wilforn called after the pair, being still on foot. He rushed back to his own horse, the steel soles of his sabatons clanging like poorly tuned bells on the cobblestones. He made to mount up, but the wounded beast shied from him and whickered in pain. There was no doubt the creature would have to be put down, and the most merciful thing would be to do it now. Whether he realized the grim truth or not, the squire made no effort to do the deed, instead leading the pitiful creature down the road, following after his cousins. As he passed the escort lancers, he gave them all hateful looks that only served to maintain his impression as a petulant child.

"Not like you to be so blunt with the peers of the realm, My Lord Knight Commander," Archduchess Amelia said quietly as she steered Silvermane closer to him. Dalflitch and Farringdon joined them. "You are normally much more circumspect."

"Until he is pushed past his limits, Your Grace," Lady Dalflitch observed, though from her tone, Prentice could not tell if she approved or not. In truth, it did not matter to him. His words to Lady Penelope were like the flames and powder on the bridge. The deed was done.

"I spoke as a peer to a peer, Your Grace," he said simply. "I am a baron and she a baroness-elect. I was within my rights."

"Indeed, you were, My Lord," Farringdon agreed encouragingly.

Prentice appreciated the support but recognized the archduchess's underlying concern for his behavior. He felt his lips twitch in an apologetic half-smile as he bowed his head to her. "Of course, I must ask your forgiveness since I think I might have put the final nail in the coffin of your alliance," he said.

The archduchess shook her head gently.

"I do not begrudge you your words, Prentice, for all they were direct," she said. "The entire time I was praying as you spoke, reciting whatever scriptures I could recall, in the hope that what besets Penelope's mind might be pierced with the truth we all can see. To no avail, it seems. I am coming to think I will need to go to her with Whilte at my side if this holy sword of words is to cut through the lies in her head."

"He would not thank you for that duty, Your Grace," Prentice told her, still speaking bluntly. This time he did not mean it the same and as the hard words left his mouth, and he ducked his head once more. "Of course, he would still obey your command all the same."

"I hope he can send us someone else to rely upon in his stead, then," Lady Dalflitch suggested, and the archduchess nodded with her.

"Is there progress in that cause yet, Prentice?" she asked. He was forced to shake his head, and in his mind he heard the whisper of his father's voice, reminding him that such was another failure. The "father" in his thoughts had eyes that saw all his mistakes, missteps, and defeats, never missing a one.

"I will ask the chaplain this evening, Your Grace," he promised. "I am soon to return to camp."

"I look forward to your report, then," the archduchess told him.

"Of course, all our hopes of dispelling the ensorcellment from her mind rest on one factor," Dalflitch added. "It might be that the filly needs no help from the Bluebird. She might like what she is told and hold to it willingly. After all, most folks need no magick to help them believe pretty lies."

"True words, My Lady," the archduchess agreed, and then she nodded away from the bridge. "We've given them enough time to get ahead of us, I think. Let us depart. I'm sure you would rather we were safely farther back from the Dragons' targets, Prentice."

"I would, Your Grace."

The archduchess led her entourage down the road and the lancer escort formed up around them at a nod from Knight Captain Farringdon.

"Oh, before I forget, Prentice," the archduchess added as a last comment, "thank you for your anticipation of that ambush. And do not fear for your blunt speaking. The thing about the last nail in a coffin is that by the time it is driven home, the body inside has been long since dead. It was never you who slew the alliance."

"As you say, Your Grace," Prentice agreed with a nod, not feeling any release from the blame he might place on himself. From beside his lady wife, Marquis-Consort Farringdon also nodded a thanks. Prentice hardly noticed it. In his mind, the driven knight commander was already plotting the next duties that lay before him and how he might not fail at them as he had so many other things in his father's eyes.

Will I never be free of him? he wondered, and he did his best not to hear the hateful voice within that whispered, "Never—never, never!"

CHAPTER 36

"You could stop cutting your hair," Whilte offered facetiously as he laid hands upon Prentice's shoulder, healing the injury there. The evening's wrestling training had been particularly taxing, but the knight commander had managed to win five straight bouts, including a two-to-one fight. Soon, he judged, he would be ready to step up to the next ring of the cross, introducing weapons back into his training. That, of course, raised a new question—which ones? The Seven Rings Cross school had its set of preferred weapons for its practitioners, one for each further ring, but some of those were of little use to Prentice now. He was a White Lion, so surely it would be better to concentrate on those of the militia. But was that shirking the task he had set for himself to recover the whole of his training, bringing it under his control and away from his father?

"That is your only advice?" Prentice challenged Whilte. He had been hoping for wisdom rather than humor when he outlined his dream. The chaplain cocked his head. He was standing to the side and rear while Prentice sat on an upturned bucket so he could more easily minister to the injured shoulder.

"Well, what else do you know of Samson?" Whilte asked in turn as he pressed his palm against the bruised flesh. Prentice felt the pain begin to recede almost immediately. While the chaplain was treating him, Prentice had taken this opportunity to discuss his dream, at least the parts he felt able to share. Brother Whilte had fixated mainly on the notion of Prentice learning the "lesson" of Samson, it seemed.

"He slew a thousand men with a bone," Prentice suggested, "and toppled a temple with his bare hands."

"Hmmm...he also married a foreign woman, forbidden to his people, and was lured into infidelity with another foreign prostitute," Whilte mused.

Prentice turned to look the chaplain in the eye, shrugging off the healing hands for a moment. "I hope you are not implying something about my wife," he said flatly.

Whilte stood back, shaking his head. "Not at all," the chaplain answered vehemently. "Forgive me, I spoke without thinking."

Prentice nodded and turned back to stare at the shed's far wall while Whilte returned to his work.

"So, the lesson of Samson? What is it, do you think? Or is it merely something a weary and fever-drenched mind fashioned out of its own imaginings?"

"Is that what you think it was, My Lord?" Whilte asked.

Prentice thought about that for a long moment. The night sounds of the camp could sometimes be heard dimly through the shed's door—men calling to one another around their campfires and a drummer practicing a beat quietly on the edge of his drum so that no one thought he was sharing an actual message or command.

"I do not know," Prentice told Whilte at last, knowing it was a lie. In truth, he was convinced the dream was a genuine one, but he *wanted* to doubt. He wanted to believe it was all the product of a fever dream, though he could not understand why, not precisely. In the main, he felt such a skepticism might silence the whispering voice in his thoughts, even though he recognized the flaw in that motivation.

A poor reason for believing or not believing anything, he told himself, but the truth of that thought, in turn, also lacked impact. Like an old piece of cloth that was fraying, all his thoughts seemed to be coming apart at the edges. The only thing he felt he could trust was the center of the cloth where the woven pattern was still visible—the core of his being. What was that? Hard training and obedience to his liege's needs? Those were things he understood, so that was what he turned to again and again, hoping to bury the whispers under cold-hearted effort.

Effort and injuries.

At last, Whilte ceased his healing work and stood back. Prentice pushed himself to his feet.

"How does that feel, Knight Commander?" the chaplain asked.

"As well as it did when I started the night," Prentice told him.

"After such days as you've had recently, I wonder that you had the strength for tonight's exercise at all."

"I need to recover my strength *and* my skill," Prentice told him, and while Whilte gave him a doubtful expression in the lamplight, he said no more on it. "And what of you, Brother? How go your healing duties?"

"Every day another few men recover enough to leave the infirmary, thanks be to God. The stoves you provided keep the tents warm, and Sergeant Porth's work to build a wall is beginning to do its task as well, cutting down the blowing through the sides of the tent."

"Lady Dalflitch and her quartermasters are to thank for the stoves," Prentice said reflexively. He moved over to a spot where a single training pole, like a long quarterstaff, was leaning. Taking it up, he stepped to the middle of the shed and looked to the back wall where he had used chalk to draw two circles interlinked near the base. As he remastered each ring, he would add another circle until the seven rings were there in a cross shape—five in a vertical row and one on each side near the top.

"Do you mean to train yet more tonight?" Whilte asked in a disbelieving tone.

"I am not ready for bed quite yet," Prentice told him and began to slowly move the pole through a tentative rendition of the Claws' halberd techniques.

"When you are ready, will you go to your bed or simply collapse on the floor here again?"

Whilte's question drew an unexpected ire from within Prentice. He realized, of course, that the physician was only trying to watch over his patient's recovery, but it annoyed him all the same. There was no time for him to lounge about in a warm bed. Whatever he had not yet recovered would have to return under the discipline of training.

If I was still injured, I would be in a cot in your infirmary, Brother, Prentice thought harshly, deliberately not looking at the chaplain.

"You let *me* look to where I lay my head! You have your own duties. Have you made any progress toward your other obligations?" he asked while practicing an upward stroke that rolled into another on his other side. It was a movement that required no small amount of strength in the upper body, and his recently treated shoulder grumbled as its stiff flesh was forced to exert itself so soon after recovery.

"Which one?" Whilte asked. "Learning scripture as a weapon or finding other healers to join our cause?"

"Either. Her grace awaits your wisdom on both subjects."

"No new revelation of the sword of the word, My Lord," the chaplain reported soberly. "I seek the Almighty in my prayers day and night, and I do not yet know more than I did. Please beg the archduchess' forgiveness for me. As to healers, I have put the word about in some quarters where I have acquaintances who might know others to help us."

"And in response they have said…?" Prentice asked, suspicious that there was more bad news coming.

"They have said that they would send me an answer soon. When they do, I will take their response directly to her grace, without delay, I swear to you."

Prentice frowned, but accepted Whilte's answer. What else could he do? He continued the movements of the practice pole until the whole of the Claws' training repertoire was complete.

He paused a moment, considering how he felt, and when the whispering voice started to creep in like mist at the edges of his thoughts, he reset himself and began the repertoire again.

"You're moving comparatively well," Whilte said after a long moment, and Prentice realized that the chaplain was studying him.

"If you have any corrections for my form, I will not shirk the advice," he told the brother. They had trained together at Ashfield, and Whilte would surely still remember the fundamentals of combat training enough to give good advice.

"I was observing more from the perspective of your health and healing," Whilte said, and it sounded like he chuckled a little as he did. Prentice was already facing away from him, continuing with the simple weapon drill. "You surely do not need my opinion of you as a man-at-arms, Knight Commander."

"You and I had the same teachers," Prentice countered. "You were taught what I was taught."

"Not entirely true," Whilte told him, "but even if it were, I was never the paragon of diligence you were."

If you had been, perhaps you would still have two legs, Prentice heard in his thoughts, but he had no idea whose voice it came from—his or the inward version of his father and the instructors from his youth, the unyieldingly stern teachers who were never satisfied and likely never could have been. He was only glad that he was able to think the words without speaking them. They would have been a shameful cruelty to inflict on his friend. By the time he managed put down the punishing thought and felt able to risk saying something different, Brother Whilte had already left the shed. Prentice smiled thinly to himself and continued with the repertoire. When he eventually felt weary enough to stop, the camp sentries had already marked the hour as after midnight and he decided to sleep here once more, wrapped in his cloak.

CHAPTER 37

For more than a week, the Bronze Dragons and the White Lions' own cannons fought the opening salvos of their duel, exchanging shots across the northern channel of the Murr. Only the heaviest of the winter storms halted the shooting. In all other weather the grim business went on. Already, the north shore of Loncastel was as much wreckage as town, with more and more patches of the dockside growing to resemble the battered-down Norgate. Once or twice, some of the Dragons fired on the fallen Loncastel Keep as well, which Prentice and Farringdon guessed was in the hope that the Denay army might still use the northern bridge to assault the town. Both leaders were confident that such a plan was more than overly optimistic. The powder explosion and fire had damaged enough of the bridge that it could surely only be safely repaired after the siege was lifted.

"Daven Marcus' only hope now is to cross in boats, Your Grace," had been the knight commander's assessment. "He will be sending word to the coast for more now to replace the ones we destroyed during the first night of the invasion. Until they arrive, he has nothing else but to batter the town to vent his own impatient fury."

Now it was Loncastel's turn to suffer as Greenmarsh had when the prince of Town Sobridge had turned his cannons on that island in the early autumn. As the Carders Guild that dominated the southern island had come to her then to plead for relief, so now a new delegation of Conclave members presented themselves at the Paramour's Chambers to beg for salvation for Loncastel.

"We are being smashed to pieces, our holdings and our livelihoods with us," one of the dark-robed men told her earnestly. "Something must be done or else the fate of Norgate will be all our fates."

"Something *is* being done," Lady Dalflitch told the delegation. "Have you not seen that our own cannons are returning their fire to them? By the knight captain's latest report last night, two of the Bronze Dragons have ceased their shooting, destroyed by our shot."

"Two? That is hardly enough," another of the guildsmen protested. "Daven Marcus has at least eight more, from what I am told."

"What you are *told*?" Amelia asked, scowling through a painful headache. "Have you not seen for yourself?"

"Well...no," the man replied with a frown of his own. "I've had to withdraw the whole of my business from the island. My warehouses are locked and empty, my boats now moved to other piers. I send a man around once a day to ensure no thieves or skips have taken to squatting in my properties and to check if they have been smashed by cannon shot. It is too dangerous otherwise."

"Yes, it is most perilous," Amelia agreed with the man, gazing at him sternly. "And yet every day, from dawn until after dusk, my own husband is on Loncastel, commanding our guns and risking his life. Not to mention the members of the Lions already slain in the exchange of iron and stone."

Since Daven Marcus's attempted ambush on the north bank, the Bronze Dragons had managed to damage or destroy three of the Lions' six cannons on the north side of the town, killing many gunners and other militiamen from the garrison force. At this very moment, Knight Captain Farringdon was taking time away from the north island to supervise the transfer of two of Sougate's cannons to Loncastel. Prentice had offered them willingly to replace the northern losses. He was convinced he would not need them to repel the wilting Golden Heron army. In the intervening time, there had been only one more half-hearted attempt to assault the southern bastion, and it had been repelled as easily as the previous ones. Peasants continued to die while professional men-at-arms waited for their safer chances.

"I did not mean to compare sacrifices, My Lad…Your Grace," the man pleaded, correcting his misstep in speech before Lady Dalflitch had to do it for him. Mostly, these men of the Conclave were senior enough to know the correct etiquette, but they still slipped up on occasion, and the senior lady-in-waiting was always ready to pounce. It was not the first time it had happened even in this day's conference. "I only mean to say that if the Bronze Dragons are not silenced, they will scour Loncastel down to the bedrock. We will have no north island left to us."

"Then I suggest you find another part of town to do your business from," Amelia answered the man tersely. "In the meantime, good patricians of Bridgetown, I also encourage you to remember that we are all here in this siege together and none of us escapes the costs upon us. In the meantime, protect yourselves as best you can. That is what we Reacherfolk are doing, as much as it costs us."

Reading Amelia's meaning from her tone, Lady Dalflitch stepped forward and gestured with an open palm towards the chamber's main door.

"Your petition has been heard, gentles," she told them. "You may now depart."

The merchants and guildsmen were clearly unhappy to be dismissed summarily but also knew there was nothing else they could do, so they turned with sad expressions and headed out the door past the sentry neophyte who watched them from behind her veil. When they had fully exited there was a moment of quiet and then Dalflitch sat at the table and rapped a coded knock on the wood surface. Around the chamber, the neophytes all turned back their veils, revealing their faces once more. Amelia put her fingers to her temples and gently massaged them for a moment, finding less relief from her headache than she hoped.

"Not a month ago, they refused to trade with me because they feared Daven Marcus so much," she said bitterly, eyes closed. "Now they come to complain that we do not do enough to defend them. They're alive, aren't they?"

"Their businesses do suffer, Your Grace," Dalflitch said quietly, and Amelia's eyes snapped open. When the lady-in-waiting saw her liege's expression, she nodded her head apologetically. "I make no excuse on their behalf, but when Greenmarsh was subject to less assault, the White Lions rode out and swatted away the Veckanders. The Bronze Dragons are exacting a higher toll by far and it seems that we will suffer their assaults for a long while yet."

"You know why that is, My Lady," Amelia said and closed her eyes once more. There were, in fact, several reasons the situation on Loncastel was different from Greenmarsh, and every one of the archduchess's senior advisors knew what they were. For a start, Greenmarsh was a fortress on the side that faced the Vec, its high-banked southern fortification designed like the talus of a castle wall. For centuries it had faced an enemy land, and it was built as such. Loncastel's north shore had only ever faced friendly land—vassal holdings of Bridgetown itself, in fact. It was in no way reinforced to endure the hammering that now fell upon it. More than that, the guns that Town Sobridge had aimed at Greenmarsh were half the power of the Bronze Dragons, so that every current hit had the potential to be that much more devastating. All those facts were secondary to the main limitation, however. The reason Daven Marcus could not easily invade the island was the same reason the White Lions could not sally forth like they did in the south. There was no bridge to cross. Other than trying to cross the river by boat, a miserable prospect that no one wanted, the duel of cannons was the only way the two armies *could* fight one another. In the light of that fact, it was actually a relief to Amelia that Daven Marcus set at least half his guns to hammer the island in indiscriminate petulance rather than focusing their fire on her cannons. She knew it was a horrid thing to think, and she understood how it frustrated the men who had just left her. It was only natural that they did not want their lives and livelihoods sacrificed, even if someone's must be.

The grim arithmetic of war, she reminded herself and tried to steel her heart away from too much sadness.

"Could we not arrange something more footpad-akin, Your Grace?" Lady Spindle asked from where she sat with another Lace Fang and two neophytes, sewing as happily as if they were in their own homes or a milliner's workshop somewhere. With her husband still ill, but resolutely clinging to life, Spindle was spending at least as much time with him as she was in Amelia's chamber. Nonetheless, whenever she was present, she was continuously at work. Amelia suspected that the former seamstress found the activity relaxing and a relief from worrying for her husband's health.

"Footpad, My Lady?" Amelia asked, not understanding the notion. Spindle looked up from the cloth in her hands and smiled.

"When we were all besieged in Fallenhill and the traitors were plotting our downfall, we were able to deal with them stealthily in the night. I was so green to fighting I hardly knew one end of a poniard from the other, but me, Prentice, and Right..." Spindle paused in her account, and she tilted her head back a little, adopting a more dignified expression. "Lord and Lady Ash and myself were able to dispatch the ambushers despite our relative inequality in arms. Perhaps the White Lions could send a small number in the night to do harm to the Bronze Dragons in some similar fashion."

Amelia smirked through her pain at Spindle's turn from the knife-fighting convict girl whose exploits she was remembering to the senior lady-in-waiting she now was. Despite her amusement, the archduchess also thought the idea itself was a sound one, but she suspected it was something that was already in Prentice and her husband's thoughts. If they were not preparing some kind of raid, there would be a reason for it, she knew.

"I will ask the knights commander and captain what they think of your suggestion, My Lady," Amelia said, sighing in discomfort. "But I would guess they are already ahead of you."

"Of course, Your Grace," Spindle said with a formal nod. "I would not think to teach them their craft."

"No, indeed," Dalflitch agreed. "We none of us should be so foolish, I think." She looked to Amelia with a note of concern in her face. "Would you like a draught of some kind, Your Grace? Something for the pain? We yet have some of the physick left from Baron Ash's treatments."

Amelia nodded gingerly.

"I will take that and then retire for a nap," she said. "If I can rest until dinner, that would be ideal."

Dalflitch nodded and signaled for a neophyte to prepare the drink. It would have to be warmed, so Amelia stood and began to make her way to her bed; she would drink it there. As she had told her visitors, Farringdon was unlikely to be back before sundown, so she might have several hours' peace if the draught did its work.

So much for not going into seclusion, she thought, appreciating the irony though it brought no smile to her lips. Her head hurt too much for that. As she passed the sewing women, she paused to look at their work and forced an encouraging expression for their sakes.

"I will be resting some while, My Lady," she told Spindle before she moved away. "If you wished to stay and dine here, you would be welcome, but you have my leave if you prefer to return to your husband."

"Thank you, Your Grace," Spindle replied. She looked over the work of the other women around her. "I think I can let them follow the paths they've set for themselves here. Perhaps I will return to Caius. He can barely lift himself from the mattress many days, yet if I am not there to remind him, he will miss a meal without even noticing. His attention is ever diligently upon his obligations."

"He is an industrious man, indeed, My Lady. A man to make a wife proud."

"Quite so, Your Grace. Thank you."

CHAPTER 38

A chill wind skittered down the narrow road in the late afternoon dimness. Winter's early night was closing in, making the overcast sky the color of slate. It would be the solstice any day now, though few if any in Bridgetown planned a celebration this year. Prentice rode Dusty as the horse walked through the middle of the lane, sitting at the height of the awnings and shades that protected the traders who persisted in their business even in the misery of war and winter—such was Bridgetown. Riding from his second daily visit to Sougate, where it seemed the Heron army languished in ever increasing misery, Prentice's mind was now set on his return to Runners Field. He plotted a warm meal and tried to decide if he felt himself worthy yet to bring dagger training into his nightly regimen. He felt he had to do it soon, and yet he could not fully silence the doubting critic within that told him he did not deserve to. He hadn't completed a challenge for hand fighting, nor for polearms and staff.

I completed them in my youth, he told himself, but that was a fruitless argument. Wasn't the point of this retraining to bring his first education fully under his own credit and power? How would he do that if he shirked the demands and disciplines of the old? How could he defeat his father's curses this way? How could he exceed the old croaking ghost's expectations if he could not even meet the old standards? He had embarked upon this path of retraining to bring his life and will into order, yet the more time that passed, the more disordered he felt within and without. Nevertheless, he woke every morning resolved to fulfill his duties and put none of them aside in any day.

I have gone without sleep before. I can again.

He was deep in thought when he heard a market girl call him out from beneath one of the dripping canopies at the corner of an alley.

"'Ere, mighty man!" the young woman's voice sounded out to him. "I reckon I know you! You one of them captain blokes, right?"

Prentice cast a sidelong glance in the girl's direction. She was shivering in a ragged skirt and bodice, a thin, open-weave shawl of undyed wool around her shoulders. Her hair was held back with a cawl that looked like it might once have had pearls or similar jewelry hanging from it, but those riches had now been pulled away, leaving only the wire fixings—another poor young wife or widow forced to sell her dowry to survive. She had a wicker basket hung on one arm from which protruded some faded floral colors.

"'Ow 'bout you spend some them easy silvers you westerfolk have and buy your lady wife some o' me last blooms?"

The girl stepped out towards Dusty and pulled the cover back to reveal dried spring flowers, their vibrant colors preserved but still dimmed in the wintry light.

"Not today, goody," Prentice said, meaning to be polite but firm. The young woman did not intend to take no for an answer, it seemed. She pushed herself right up against the stirrup, clutching his booted foot.

"Oh, but sure'n your wife's a righteous sort that might be cheered by a flower on solstice eve," she pleaded in an oddly loud and flirtatious manner. Prentice had a thought that she might be a tart hoping for some rich man's company, but that was quickly swamped as he recognized the woman's mention of a "righteous" wife. It was too much coincidence for him.

"What do you know about my wife?" he asked in a tight whisper, reaching down to seize the woman by her wrist. She flashed him the swiftest of cunning smiles.

"I know that Lady Dalflitch sends you word, My Lord," she whispered back, their faces only a finger span apart in the rain. "She says to say that Master Solft has been missing for days. Word to his scriptorium pals returns unanswered. Nuns and lace ain't turned nothin' up neither. In case we've been tumbled, she proposes that you might know where to seek him out to see that he's safe. You ain't been round the Paramour's much o' late, so she sent me out to find you once she was sure Solft ain't just turned himself after a doxy or some such. My lady's word is that she must hand this to you and the Lions or else go to the bailiffs." The girl shrugged. "Course we all know what they'd be worth."

Prentice stared her, not releasing his grip. Solft was missing?

"Tell Lady Dalflitch I will see to it at once," he whispered. "Get yourself out of this weather and take her the message. I will speak with her on the morrow of what I find."

He let her go, but she clutched him back before they could part.

"If I can hazard, My Lord," she added quietly. "Baroness Righteous misses you somethin' fierce. One meal a day with ye ain't to 'er liking."

"She told you this?"

The girl shook her head. "Lady Righteous? Not likely!" she replied as if it were a truth of the world that even a three-year-old knew in their bones. "But we all can see it."

Prentice wanted to rebuke the girl for daring to speak into his marriage, even in such a kindly way. He nearly snapped a cruel retort at her, but he realized it would only be a vent to his pride. The truth was that he was comforted to think his wife would miss him; he missed her, too, but he had to follow this course he was on. The town was beset, and his responsibilities were many.

"Thank you, neophyte," he whispered, "but you speak a word out of turn. I will look to my own marriage and family."

He paused and looked up and down the nearly empty street. It seemed as if no one would have even noticed this surreptitious meeting, but subterfuge was best built on consistency.

"You feign playing the doxy as your identity on the street, I take it?" he asked her.

"Don't take no offers, My Lord, but I have two fellas in the Lion Banner that I can call on to act the satisfied customers for me," she answered him. "I'm on Oldbridge most, and amongst them I'm a young widow with a taste for militiamen whose eking 'er way through winter."

Prentice nodded and then made himself scowl harshly.

"Then this is for the sake of your false character. Do not take it amiss. I will mention your diligent service to Lady Dalflitch. Get yourself somewhere warm."

Before the girl could ask what he was talking about, he forcefully shook her hand free, so violently that she stumbled onto the cobbles.

"Unhand me, wretched doxy!" Prentice all but shouted at her, looking down imperiously from the saddle. "Keep your flowers and your flirtations!"

He reached into his purse and fished out a pair of guilders which he threw at her so that they bounced from her skirt to skitter on the road in the wet.

"Take those and learn to beg, if you have no better craft! Rather that than sell what little charms remain to you!"

He turned Dusty away, leaving the neophyte spy to scrabble on the stones, retrieving the fallen coins the way a desperate woman might. It took all his will to keep his back straight and proud, face set away from her. His stomach turned at the vile act, bringing bile to his throat. He wanted to spit. Behind him, the neophyte played her role, hurling a resentful harlot's curses after him.

"Go to 'er then, jackanapes!" she called. "I should take these silver and throw 'em in the Murr, beg a river sprite to give you the droop. See 'ow much your proud lady wife likes you in 'er bed then!"

As disgusted as he was, Prentice found himself smirking. The girl's performance was pitch perfect and a pleasure to be a part of. Lady Dalflitch's former 'skips-turned-spies were exactly as they had been envisaged, it seemed. That, at least, was a comforting notion on a miserable dark afternoon.

And my wife misses me, he thought, though of course that was both a comfort and a criticism to his troubled mind. He resolved to spend more time with her when he next visited Paramour's, but that would have to be after he learned what might have happened to Solft.

Chapter 39

The scriptorium of Belknap and Corris was a narrow brick-and-plaster house wedged between a basket weaver and a chandler, all backed onto the northeastern riverside of Piers Island. It had a solid door, freshly painted rust red, and no windows on the street side. A noxious odor of rendering animal fat followed Prentice from the chandlers as he was ushered into the small business by a bent-backed fellow with a single wax candle in a silver holder.

"Good evening and welcome to our humble place of business," the scribe said while tugging his forelock, which made Prentice think that the man was a member of no guild and therefore not strictly one of the patrician class—a man between the cracks of society just as his home was between other businesses. "I am Master Belknap Junior. By what title may I address you?"

"Baron or My Lord is good enough," Prentice told him, feeling no desire to make a new friend. "I am not here to commission your work. I come from the Archduchess of the Western Reach, seeking her sworn man, the scholar Solft of Lower Otney."

"Yes, Master Solft, a frequent customer this winter," said Belknap, and the man gave an apologetic smile. "I have no fresh news of him, I am sorry to say."

"Fresh news?" Prentice repeated. "When did you last see him?"

"Not for days," was the reply, "as I told her grace's nun servant when she came for Master Solft's works."

"Her grace's nun?"

"Yes. A veiled woman with a wimple, one of the humble servants of her grace's household." Belknap paused and then leaned forward conspiratorially, as if their conversation here in the empty entry hall might be overheard by some invisible observer. "Is it true what they say, that the archduchess keeps nuns and masked women about her because she wants no competition to her beauty as age overtakes it? They say that in her youth she was a raven-haired creature of rare fineness."

Prentice looked at the eager rumormonger, inwardly amused at the mixed elements of his story, combining the ingredients of Archduchess Amelia's chambers—neophytes in wimples, the Lace Fangs, and Lady Dalflitch's appearance—into a recipe that produced not a whit of truth. It was exactly the kind of false confection that Lady Dalflitch hoped to foster, like the fraudulent harlot on the street. The less folk knew of the truth, the greater the advantage. Even so, Prentice found it another displeasing moment. He did not like the notion of his liege, or of his wife as one of his liege's ladies-in-waiting, being gossiped about in such fashion.

"You surely do not expect me to speak of the privacy of my liege's chamber," he said and narrowed his eyes ominously, looking down on the shorter man. The scribe immediately stepped backward.

"No, of course not, and quite right, too," he said primly. He flicked at his shoulders, as if the temptation to gossip was a kind of dust he might brush away.

"Master Solft has not been back since the nun in her grace's service asked after him this morning?" Prentice asked, returning to his reason for being here.

"Not for days, My Lord," Belknap told him, and now the scribe's brow furrowed in confusion. "But the nun did not come for him this morning. She was sent three days past to collect all of the master's workings here, as I said. No one came for him this morning...no wait, I misspeak. There was a girl here this morning, soon after dawn—river trollop stinking of smoked fish and rotten grasses. Insisted the master had paid her half for a load of dried trout. Refused to take no for an answer. My wife chastised her for her cheek and packed her off quite rightly. Men of good repute such as Master Solft, especially ones with secure incomes, they draw young things like flies to dung, hopeful to smile their way into a bed or a marriage."

"I can imagine," Prentice said drily. The girl this morning was surely Dalflitch's agent looking for Solft, so who had been the neophyte "sent" to collect the scholar's things days ago?

"Well, good folk of Bridgetown are no fools," Belknap added. "Eels born under bridges don't sleep under silk, as we say."

Tonight is not a good night to call women eels in my hearing, parchment-collector, Prentice thought, and he looked down the hall. There were two inner doors leading from it, one to the left and the other at the end. Both were closed.

"Where are your books and papers?" he asked. "I would see what the master was working upon."

"They are through there," the scribe answered, pointing to the door at the end of the corridor. "If you will await my return, I will fetch you a light."

The man went through the side door, and while it was open, Prentice caught a glimpse of a double bed and a table, making him think that the room beyond was the scribe and his wife's own apartment. The building was three stories high, and Prentice wondered at the amount of space that must be given over to writings and records if the proprietor only afforded himself such a humble dwelling on the ground floor. It reminded him of the Paper House that Solft had presided over in Dweltford until the Inquisition's agents burned it down. No wonder the renegade scholar had spent so much time here. It must have felt comfortably familiar. Belknap returned with a second candle fitted into a waxed-paper lantern.

"The master's gratuity is not fully consumed, so I can afford you two candles," he said, holding up a second, unlit candle. "If you need more time than they offer, I will have to ask for another token to cover the cost of more wax. I fear I cannot offer you rushlights or tallow. They are much too unreliable amongst so much paper."

Solft had already crossed this scribe's palm with a small fortune in silver. The notion that all that legitimately remained was the price of two candles was a nonsense to Prentice's mind. He said nothing of it, however, and allowed himself to be ushered into the scriptorium's archives.

CHAPTER 40

The room beyond the door seemed at first exactly as Prentice had imagined it would be—narrow, lined with shelves from floor to roof, and stocked with all manner of scrolls, codices, and folios. What surprised him, however, was how small the room was. It stopped no more than ten paces back, or at least its floor did. A low bookcase acted like a balcony railing looking out over a shaft at the back that rose upward for the three stories of the building. In one corner, a narrow spiral stair of wrought iron ascended into the darkness, and every wall of the narrow shaft was stacked with shelves as well. Shelves full of papers and documents covered the walls like a tapestry of learning, laws, and histories. Prentice leaned out into the open space, the lantern light not penetrating to the roof.

"The stairwell we use to keep local merchant records, in the main," Belknap explained proudly. "As well as copies of all the earldom's proclamations, going back over two centuries. There are some other local works on the above levels, as well as three lifetimes of literature, gathered since my grandfather founded us here in the time of Earl Nartens—Nartens the Third that is. On the top floor, we have a collection of architects' plans dating back almost to the founding. We even have the only folio of the plans for your liege lady's apartments. The Veckander prince who commissioned them took the main with him, but the architect made a copy, and my grandfather secured it on the scribe's death."

Prentice nodded, hardly listening. He put a foot on the stairs, and while the ironwork shook slightly, it did not groan or make him think it was unsafe.

"Master Solft was more concerned with documents from farther afield," he said to the scribe. "Which floor would I find them on?"

"A mix of both above, I would say, but he also spent a good deal of time below."

"Below?" Prentice asked, and he looked down to see that the document-lined stairwell also descended another floor.

That must be down to the waterline, virtually, he thought, wondering at the level of damp and mildew such a location would induce on any paper or parchment stored there.

"There is space down there to set a cot and a small stove, which we use to keep the air dry. It's not lit now, of course, since we would never let it burn unattended, but if you wish I can fetch some charcoal. For a small fee."

No doubt.

The man's mercenary attitude was making Prentice think that Belknap might simply have sold all of Solft's things and invented the story of a neophyte to cover his avarice, but he dismissed that as unlikely. Solft was a treasury that would surely have showed no signs of bankruptcy yet. Belknap looked the sort to wait a season at least before resigning his greedy heart to losing such a good customer.

"So, the master's things were down there and you simply gave them away?" Prentice asked, stepping back a moment.

"At his patron's request," Belknap protested. "One of her servants came for the chattels, as you recall."

"How did you know the woman was from her grace?"

"Because, apart from the Reacherwomen, the only other nuns in Bridgetown these days are the ghosts in the old cloister out on Bell's Hummock."

"Vespers Remembered?" Prentice said, and Belknap brightened.

"You know of it? I had not realized you men of the west took such interest in history and legendaria. There is talk of the ghosts being stirred up of late, moans in the night, that sort of thing. Doubtless the ancient holy women object to the foul murders of the earl's nobles, and I have an account of the nunnery and the sisters' fate, if you should like to purchase it. Old, but in excellent condition."

"Doubtless it has another rendering of the original golden bear," Prentice said, shaking his head as he came to the conclusion that this was going to be a fool's errand. It seemed that Solft must have been abducted and a fraudulent neophyte sent to collect all the "dangerous" research that might have helped them unpick the bonds of the Inquisition's magick webs.

"Golden bear?" the scribe asked, his perplexed expression showing that Prentice already seemed to know more of the legend of Vesper's Remembered than he did.

It may be a history in excellent condition, but you have not read it, have you? the knight commander thought. Mostly, though, his mind was occupied with a sense of his own failure. Solft was gone, most likely dead now, killed by Bluebird or a hired thug. Was it even worth searching through the scriptorium? If there was the slightest chance that something of Solft's had been left behind, he had no doubt the whole building would already have been put to the torch, just as happened to the Paper House. After years on the run, the adventurous scholar had met his fate at last, it seemed.

"However many nuns there are on the islands and bridges, you should not simply have handed his goods over to the first woman in a wimple to ask for them," Prentice said, his harsh tone venting the fury he felt at his own defeat. It was his duty to protect the archduchess's sworn retainers.

"I did not *simply* hand them over!" Belknap protested, drawing up his small form to its full height and huffing in offended pride. "She came with a note signed by the master himself. I can show it you if you wish!"

"I do," Prentice said, more from reflex than because he imagined the missive would yield anything useful. Belknap left him with only the lamplight for a long moment and he sighed as he looked over the shelves of documents, imagining the many more on the other three levels. He could search here for days or even weeks and never truly know what the scholar had last been working upon. Surely the encyclopedia that contained the Songs of the Steeple Aviary would be gone, of that much he had no doubt. The whole point of setting Solft to the search was that no one else could spare the time nor possessed the instincts for the research. Belknap returned with a small, folded paper that he handed over to Prentice and then held up the candle to make it easier to read.

"As you can see, signed by the master and in his hand," the scribe said, but Prentice ignored him, focusing on the contents of the message. It did indeed request that the neophyte be given all assistance in packaging the entire of Solft's research and leaving with it that day.

So, they abducted him and kept him alive, at least long enough to force him to write this, Prentice thought, wondering at how much suffering Soflt's last moments might have contained. Wherever they kept him, it was unlikely it was a smokehouse. Torture needed a place where a subject could make noise and not be heard. Could a hut on the riverside in the middle of the busy docks be used for that purpose? Dalflitch's maids looking for the fishmock's business were probably already another step behind.

"Did the girl say anything as you helped her?" he pressed, no longer hoping for important clues but going through the motions.

"I was not with her the whole time," Belknap answered. "My wife stood by to see no theft was done, but I went out to purchase the other wax-cloth to wrap the codices in against the damp. As you can see, his note asks for fresh ones. I assumed he lost the ones I had already provided. The nun made more than a little fuss about being forced to pay for new."

"I can imagine," Prentice said and headed back toward the corridor door. There was nothing here for him to learn that he could in the time available to him. They would have to trust to Brother Whilte's revelations against Inquisition magicks from now on, at least in the immediate term. "I will take this note with me to show her grace."

"That forms part of my own records," Belknap protested with the indignance of an archivist at losing a piece of his collection, however tiny. When Prentice scowled at him, he shrank back sheepishly. "Of course, since the master and you are both the archduchess' men, I suppose your claim on it is equally strong. I yield to you."

"Good of you," Prentice said, and he stuffed it into his belt pouch with the other paper. He paused a moment in the hallway while Belknap opened the outer door, then stepped out into the rainy night and waited on the doorstep, head down, as the door was closed behind him. He thought about going straight to the Paramour's Chamber with his news, but since he had nothing useful to report, he decided to head back to Runners Field. There, he would set some officers of both banner companies to ask through the night, especially amongst the provosts and watch leaders, to see if anyone in the militia had some other word of Solft or his disappearance. Come the morning they might have some better sense to take to the archduchess.

In the meantime, he could do his evening training and have the sergeants report any successes to him at the shed before he went to Paramour's in the morning. If there was one thing that was clear from Solft's disappearance, it was that there was no time for the Knight Commander of the Western Reach to rest.

CHAPTER 41

"Your Grace? Forgive me, Your Grace, but you must wake up."

Amelia rolled over uncomfortably to see an earnest neophyte leaning over her, tallow wick in hand. It was completely dark now, but Farringdon had not yet returned from Loncastel. Unless the battle of the cannons had taken a fresh turn, keeping him on the northern island, it must still have been reasonably early in the evening.

"I will go without dinner for now," the archduchess said, turning back to her pillow. "I am more needful of the rest than the food."

The neophyte reached out, daring to shake her mistress by the shoulder.

"With your pardon, Your Grace, but you mustn't go back to sleep."

Mustn't? Amelia's sleep-dulled thoughts repeated. It was a rare moment when a steward or handmaid of her chamber thought to be insistent with her these days. Matron Bettina would surely have been the last one to try it, and she not for years now. Clattering thumps resounded through the ceiling, and the archduchess felt a sudden annoyance that her ladies-in-waiting would be training at this hour, risking disturbance to their mistress's rest. The neophyte's candlelit expression became even more concerned as she looked upward after the sounds, and Amelia wondered if the girl feared being blamed for their commotion. Then, at last, the blanket of sleep finally slipped from her mind and Amelia realized something untoward was happening. She sat up, rubbing her eyes and forcing herself to wakefulness.

"What is it?" she asked quietly and noticed that on the other side of the bed from the neophyte with the candle, another girl had an over-robe ready for her to put on. She held her hand out for it and the second neophyte helped her arms into the sleeves.

"We don't know for sure, Your Grace," the girl with the candle explained, her voice little more than a whisper. "We heard dire noises from the roof and Lady Elizabeth took two neophytes up into the attic room to see if someone was breaking in. Lilly and me was told to wake you and take you outside, once we know for sure its safe down the stairs. Another's gone to fetch the guard cohort from the courtyard. You'll have a full escort in moments."

Amelia accepted their guidance, fitting her feet swiftly into the slippers set for her. In a moment the archduchess was being led into the main space of Paramour's, where the rest of her inner chamber were standing, knives and daggers in hand, watching the ceiling as the thumps came from above.

"I make it at least two, likely three," Lady Agatha said. Being the most astute of the new Lace Fangs—sharpest of eye and ear, it was said—Amelia had no hesitation accepting the young woman's assessment. The main of the rough noises stopped, although the boards still creaked, and infrequently there was a bump or thud still, with a ringing quality to them.

"Men in armor," Lady Daisy decided with stern confidence, and there was a grimness in her expression that spread across the shadowed faces around Amelia. Whatever came next was sure to be serious, and they all knew it. Amelia was suddenly struck by the youthfulness of her entourage at this moment. All of them were barely of an age for marriage. Surely none had seen twenty summers. Lady Spindle was clearly gone for the night, tending to her sick husband. Lady Righteous was with her children and their wetnurse, no doubt, and wherever Dalflitch was, it was not here.

Only the freshest were with Amelia in the Paramour's Chambers this night.

The unblooded, Amelia thought, using the sort of term Prentice or Righteous might have to describe this cadre's relative inexperience. The door opened and Amelia looked with the others, hopeful to see the cohort commander entering with a mass of White Lions to escort her to safety. Instead, it was Lady Elizabeth.

How long does it take men to come up from the yard? Amelia asked herself as the third of the new Lace Fangs consulted with her two equals in the room.

"There's no one up there," she said, her confusion evident even through her mask and whispered tone.

"Don't say that," Daisy retorted, quiet voice belying her unyielding tone. "We can *hear* the mongrels."

"I don't know what I can tell you...," Elizabeth began to explain, but was cut short by a desperate whisper.

"Look to the walls," one of the neophytes hissed, and it was immediately clear what she meant.

A light was shining between the seams of wood panels on the chamber wall. With the main of the room dark, save for a candle or two and the ruddy glow of the banked fire, the dim radiance through the fine gaps was readily noticeable. Amelia had always assumed that the area behind the decorative boards was simple brick, but as the light descended from the ceiling, moving down from one panel's seams to the next, it became abundantly clear what was happening. There was a concealed second staircase there, and someone with a lamp was now descending it. The unknown steps creaked softly through the thin "wall," and all knew it confirmed their fear. Whoever was coming down the secret stairs was weighted with armor.

Without any words, the three Lace Fangs moved swiftly to the wall, tracking the moving light and readying themselves to be beside whichever panel proved to be the door into the Chamber. Daisy gave silent, finger-gesture instructions to the neophytes until they were gathered into tiny squads, one of which dutifully formed up around Amelia. In the dimness, a hail of barely visible hand instructions was thrown and caught around her, and she understood nary a one. The archduchess had a sudden notion of what it must be like to be deaf in the midst of a social occasion or spirited debate.

"We don't know if the yard is safe yet, Your Grace," the neophyte Lilly whispered in her ear. "But we may be forced to take the risk. Please be ready to come with us if needs be. We will be rushing you down the stairs if the Fangs is overwhelmed."

It felt strange to Amelia to hear such a martial assessment of the situation come from so feminine a voice in the dark.

But is that not what the Lace Fangs have always been for? she told herself. With an unthinking hand protectively around her pregnant belly, Amelia readied herself to go wherever her bodyguards led.

The light stopped behind one particular panel, and Beth and Agatha were poised on either side. The lamp must have been doused or shuttered, as all sign of the glow vanished. Then, in the tense silence, a whispered male voice could be heard on the other side, and it was odd how distinctly it could be made out.

"Be ready. Once we jump out and put the fear into them, they'll start screaming. We'll have only a short while before those levies come running. Harrin, you'll bar the door to keep the bitches from escaping and any would-be heroes coming to the rescue from getting in. Remember, we're here for the witch, but if we have to slay a few slatterns to get her, no one will weep for their passing."

Amelia almost laughed, even amidst the horror of what was coming. It was so ridiculous to hear these clumsy assassins think themselves to be so in control of the situation. If it weren't for the unrestrained, murderous contempt in that voice, she might well have chuckled. It was almost a comedy. On the other side of that thin piece of graven wood, assassins were readying to spring forth and ambush a clutch of terrified women. On this side, trained—if inexperienced—dagger-fighters were waiting to spring an ambush of their own. Heard more than seen in the dimness, the hidden door unlatched and swung open a touch. Then it swept wide, and with the unmistakable clash of heavy armor first one and then two others burst into the room, shouting and growling like animals.

"Behold your doom, harlots!" their leader cried aloud, and Amelia recognized the voice. Of all those she had thought to fear at this moment—Daven Marcus, his favored lackey Duke Robant, another *brakkis effar*, perhaps—this was the least and also the least frightening to her. Now she almost did laugh and for a moment imagined that if Prentice or even her beloved Farringdon were here, they surely would have. The three assassins entered only a few steps into the room before stopping, doubtless trying to locate their victim and to see what the other occupants were about.

"Now," was Daisy's singular, quiet command, and the melee commenced. Wary and poised to dash for the door, Amelia saw even less of the fracas than the meager light normally would have allowed, but she knew what her ladies would be doing. Agatha and Elizabeth would each have picked one of the two following fellows, attacking their targets from behind. They would throw themselves bodily upon them, seeking holds with their free hand and legs and using their full bodyweight whenever they could to counter their enemies' advantages in strength while their knives sought whatever weaknesses they could find in the enemy's armor harness. Steel dagger points would hunt for the backs of knees, elbows, or armpits—all places where steel plate was nearly impossible to wear. If visors were down, then eye slits were valued, or throats, if the enemy was wearing no bevors or gorgets. Fighting against men-at-arms in suits of plates was an artform in itself, and while none of the neophytes or fresh Lace Fangs were mistresses of the art, they were apprentices and journeymen—journey-women—to some of the greatest living exponents of the skill.

Daisy took the leader herself, and each of the three Lace Fangs had neophytes in support, tackling and striking, looking to bring the intruders off their feet and make them more vulnerable.

Screams and shouts resounded, steel clashed, and even some sparks flashed in the darkness. It was as if an enraged flock of maddened animals was seeking to tear each other and the world around them apart. One of the room's chairs was heard to go tumbling over the floor, and what Amelia guessed were plates or cups shattered as they were sent flying. Then the door burst open and lit lanterns shone into the room as armored Lions tromped in, swords drawn.

"Cease and yield or be slain!" the command was bellowed, and for a moment it seemed that no one would obey. Then, as the beams of the bull's-eyes flashed over the mass of struggling opponents, the neophytes sprang apart, knowing that they had done their duties and now needed to clear the way for their liege lady's men-at-arms to finish the job. Their diligence and bravery were unquestionable, but against men in armor, other men in armor were the best opponents. The sudden calm revealed one intruder face down on the floorboards, unmoving, with another on his knees, Elizabeth's poniard at his throat while a neophyte was busy wrapping herself around his feet, using her full strength to keep him from getting any control of his legs back. As militiamen moved to point their own Fangs' swords at him, he ceased to struggle, and Lady Beth released him to them.

The third assailant was more intransigent. As the light fell on him and the corporal of the Lions demanded his surrender yet again, he kept his feet and clutched a gauntleted fist around a neophyte's throat as he grasped her to himself bodily, using her like a shield in a vicious embrace. Despite her vulnerability, the young woman kept struggling while the intruder pointed his sword at the militia, as if to keep up the fight.

"Let me pass, or I'll kill her," he growled, and the militiamen hesitated.

"Don't be a damned fool, Wilforn," Amelia said, half stepping from amidst her closest guardians. From that first moment of this inept assassination attempt, Amelia had recognized his voice, and the lamplight now confirmed the fact for her.

"Do you doubt me, witch?" the squire demanded. He laid his blade against the neophyte's belly. Amelia had no uncertainty that the edge would slash her shift to ribbons in an instant, and even if he did not use the weapon, her red face showed that his grip must surely be brutally painful around her throat. If his blade did not wound her, he would soon throttle all breath from her body.

"Release her or you will die, no matter her fate!" the leader of the militiamen declared.

"I don't take orders from convict scum like you!" Wilforn spat back, his expression twisted with contempt. "Now, you release my comrades and make way or watch this harlot suffer as you cannot imagine."

Amelia might have snorted with contempt at that threat if her handmaid's life were not in the balance. Wilforn had no idea what kind of suffering she had experienced or witnessed in her life, let alone what she could imagine.

Let me sit you down one evening with my closest retainers, fool boy, she thought. Between them she, Dalflitch, Righteous, Prentice, Turley, and Whilte would be able to turn the squire's hair white with their tales, she had no doubt.

The standoff continued for a breath of a moment, but then behind Wilforn one of the neophytes who was half hidden in the fractured shadows hefted the scattered chair with both hands, and spinning herself like a hammer thrower in a midsummer games, cast the furniture at Wilforn's back. It struck him in the legs, knocking him forward. His hostage sensed her opportunity and made to break free, though she cried out as she did so. The Lions saw their own chance and they fell on the squire.

"Don't kill him!" Amelia shouted, but she need not have feared. The Lions' leader showed the way, and he and another militiaman used their shields and the basket hilts of their swords to pummel Wilforn to the floor, taking him prisoner. After another moment's combat, completely one-sided, the battle was done. Looking over her chamber in the inconsistent lamplight, Amelia could see her ladies gathering themselves, bruises and cuts interspersed with damaged clothing. At least one girl was doing her best to keep her torn bodice from falling open, her hands clutching the fabric to her chest. One of the Lions removed his cloak and wrapped it around her without asking permission, but it was received with a thankful curtsey that seemed almost ridiculously formal in the wreckage of the moment.

"My thanks for your timely intervention, Corporal," Amelia began to praise the Lions' leader, but she was cut off by a cry of dismay.

"Verony!"

All eyes turned to where Wilforn's hostage lay unmoving on the boards. Blood was pooling under her form and two neophytes dashed to her assistance.

"A healer!" Amelia commanded. "Send to Whilte or whomever is closer!"

There came a sound like contemptuous scoffing, and Amelia looked to see Wilforn, his helmet removed and his scalp bleeding from one of the blows that subdued him. He was being held in the firm grip of two militiamen, sneering at Verony's fallen form.

"I warned you, bitch!" he said hatefully and spat bloody spittle from his swelling lips onto the floorboards. Amelia turned and stalked toward him and the other prisoners.

"Bind and shackle these fools!" she commanded. "We will hold them for trial by the magistrates under my peace."

"No magistrate would dare convict me," Wilforn declared, and Amelia noticed that it did not occur to him to be confident for his comrades. "And even if one was fool enough to try, my cousin will pardon me the same hour."

"That is probably true," Amelia said, drawing closer to him so that he would be able to see her expression clearly, regardless of the poor light. "But even if it is, I will see you hang. Your cousin sits alone in Earlsbastion. She is less even than a fae-tale princess in a tower. If you imagine for a moment that eight thousand or more Reacher men-at-arms will let you live, you are a greater fool than you make us all suspect."

"This one's dead, Your Grace," the Lions' corporal said matter-of-factly, looking over the third intruder's body, still face down. Amelia nodded to her man and then looked back to Wilforn.

"You will hang for this night's work, Squire Wilforn. And if my handmaid dies, you will wish for such a merciful fate as hanging before I am done with you. You will for certain envy your friend there and his swift entry into the afterlife."

She nodded to the guards restraining him to take him away.

"Peers don't hang!" he cried as he was dragged off.

And you will not die a peer after raising your blade in assassination, she thought but did not bother to say. In this age of rebellion upon rebellion, even that bit of basic King's Law had little power to it. Amelia also knew that she was unlikely to actually order Wilforn tortured, even if Verony died from her injury. The failing squire was like a village idiot—so inept and uncomprehending in everything he did that he was difficult to resent, even at his worst. If his folly did not come with such vile behavior, she might even have pitied him.

"We will set the chamber aright as soon as we can, Your Grace," Lady Daisy said earnestly, "If you wish to return to your bed, we are able to oversee this matter from now on."

Amelia was almost dumbfounded by the sudden return to calm. True to her reputation as a growing exponent of the short blade, Daisy seemed little more than ruffled by the combat, her mask slightly askew. All the same, a bruise was rising on her cheek.

"I will rest once Verony is seen by the healer, and we know for certain she will live, My Lady," Amelia said formally. "In the meantime, take the maid to my bed where she can be cared for. Have some of the Lions carry her—gently. See to clean water and cloths that may serve as bandages."

Daisy curtseyed, but before she could go, Amelia took her by the hand.

"My Lady, when the night is back in order, I want you to take a moment to express my thanks to each and every lady of my chamber," she said. "Do not mistake me or stint on the praise, Daisy. I am alive by your diligence, and every one of you has earned your names, your places, and my unending esteem. Make sure it is clear."

"As you say, Your Grace," Daisy answered carefully. She turned away, and as she was giving instructions to the neophytes and Verony was gently lifted to be carried to Amelia's bed, Lady Righteous appeared in the doorway.

"I heard the ruckus and just saw that twit cousin of the baroness being hauled off," she said, approaching Amelia, looking her liege up and down, clearly seeking injuries. "Are you hale, Your Grace?"

"I am, thanks to the guards you and Spindle have trained for me."

"Surely they didn't break in through the guards in the yard?" Righteous marveled. Amelia shook her head and then nodded toward the wall where the secret portal was still open. "A back door? Well, that's a bloody cheek!"

Amelia wasn't convinced that Righteous's indignation wasn't based in her jealously that she had not been involved in the fight itself.

"Many great houses and castles have secret passages and the like," Amelia said, "for wives and children to sneak out in an invasion and so forth. I suppose if the legends of the Paramour's Chambers are true, the prince who commissioned them wanted to come and go unseen to his mistress' lair. A gesture at discretion, at least."

Righteous nodded pensively. "Course, not so secret that Wilforn didn't know about it," she mused. "How many others have had the knowledge and not shared it with us? Lady Penelope, for example?"

Amelia nodded. Her own mind had been beginning to look to such questions, now that the rush of blood from the attempt on her life was receding. Whatever else came of this night, she would surely have yet more uncomfortable conversations with Bridgetown's floundering liege ahead of her. As ill-feeling and furious as the whole experience left her, Amelia thought she should probably eat something now. She would need her strength.

CHAPTER 42

The Paramour's Chamber had been put to right within the hour, but now as each member of Amelia's inner court arrived, summoned by news of the assassination attempt, the mood in the main room was, if anything, even more belligerent. Between them, Lady Spindle and Lady Righteous seemed ready to invade Earlsbastion to capture the strongpoint by themselves and put all they found within to the blade. They muttered about dragging Lady Penelope out by her hair and throwing her at Amelia's feet to beg for her cousin's life. Lady Dalflitch stood in utter silence, but her eyes flashed like shadowed fire whenever she looked around the room and, in her own way, seemed so much more dangerous for her quiet. Farringdon came in his armor, and while he made a comment about seeing Wilforn hang, he more quickly moved to Amelia and embraced her desperately. From that moment he remained diligently at her side, so that if she so much as twitched, he moved in response. Brother Whilte came looking like a man who had forgotten the meaning of sleep but went immediately to minister to the injured Verony. Prentice arrived last of all and seemed somewhat embarrassed to be so laggardly.

"Forgive me, Your Grace," he said with a bow as he arrived. "I was about...matters in the camp. It took runners a time to find me."

Amelia nodded to him from her chair where she sat, like a sovereign upon a throne, while nearby two neophytes were scrubbing blood from the floorboards in the candlelight. Nobody else was sitting. Every senior courtier was too tense to take a chair, that was clear. Prentice looked the room over, eyes lingering on the blood and the secret door in the wall that was not yet reclosed.

"We will have a carpenter come and seal that off by morning," he said flatly.

"Our quartermasters will know a man to trust," Dalflitch added. "With your permission, Your Grace, I will send to them now."

"A moment yet, if you will, My Lady," Amelia told her, holding up a hand. "There are matters I would discuss first. Now that the knight commander has arrived, I would hear your opinions on one matter over all others. Why? Why has Wilforn done this?"

"The mongrel hates you, Your Grace," Spindle said as if the answer was obvious. "He's made it clear enough afore now. He lost his best horse and was made to look a fool after the parley collapsed, so they say."

Everyone present nodded, but the lady-in-waiting's answer had missed the key point of Amelia's question. No doubt several of them realized that, but Dalflitch was the one to articulate it.

"I believe her grace's question was *why now*, My Lady," the seneschal said. "He has hated her grace almost from the day we arrived over the bridge. What has moved him at this moment?"

"We got 'im in chains. Let's go ask him," Righteous said, and she drew a long poniard that she was carrying by its scabbard, twisting the bared edge to catch the light. "I'll wager I can make him want to 'up the answers."

"In time, My Lady," Amelia said, sharing the same vengeful emotion. There was no sense of rebuke in her tone, and she suspected her own expression reflected the wolfish eagerness of the two most senior Lace Fangs. Likely the entire sisterhood of the masks would line up for their strip of flesh off the imprisoned squire's back if permitted. "Before I knock on that door, though, I would like to have a clearer sense of what I will find behind it."

She looked over her advisors and was surprised to see Prentice scowling at his wife. Surely this was one instance where he would not begrudge Lady Righteous her vengeful streak? Then Amelia remembered his past and how much more intimately than all of them he understood the realities of judicial torture, the pettiness of revenge that clothed itself in false holiness. She suddenly recalled her own experiences as Daven Marcus's prisoner and felt a flash of shame.

Let me never use my power for petty revenge, she thought but realized that resisting the temptation might sometimes be beyond her, especially in a moment like this.

"This was prompted by Bluebird," Prentice declared with a certainty that surprised Amelia. By their expressions, others in the room were equally impressed with his confidence.

"You are sure?"

Prentice met her eye a moment and then looked down at his feet. He scowled again and shook his head.

"Master Solft is abducted and likely slain, Your Grace," he said in a rueful tone.

"Is there no doubt, My Lord?" Dalflitch asked him, her own expression one of professional concern.

"*I* have no doubt. From the crumbs left behind, I would lay money he was not taken by mere cobble runners. Bluebird certainly targeted him somewhere on the streets between the scriptorium and here, then sent a fraudulent neophyte in your name to scavenge all of Solft's researches. His notes, the encyclopedia, every last scrap has been taken. They were very thorough, it seems."

"A neophyte did this?" Spindle demanded, sharing a furious glance with Lady Dalflitch. All around the room there was a moment of hesitant stillness. Silent and inconspicuous, every handmaid was listening and felt the implicit coming of a storm of accusation. The room itself seemed to palpably relax when Prentice allayed that fear.

"Fraudulent," he reiterated, "A girl in a wimple and veil, able to pose as one of the chamber to the uninitiated."

"Like the ones who tried to rob Caius' strongroom?" Spindle asked. Prentice shook his head.

"Smarter than they, I would say. This one came alone and was an actual maid this time, not a thug in a skirt."

Dalflitch looked to Spindle and Righteous.

"We must keep watchful," the lady seneschal insisted. "If they have a girl skilled in playacting as one of us, they will put her to every use they can."

"Let her try it to one of our faces," Righteous said, her meaning clear.

Others nodded eagerly.

"We all know our tells, My Lady," Daisy added from her place at the archduchess's left shoulder. "Ain't no false floosy gettin' to her grace past any one of us. I swear't!"

"No one doubts that, Daisy," Amelia said, raising her hand to still the conversation. She looked back at Prentice. "This is dire news, and I will hear what plans you have to find the taken Master Solft, but first I must ask you, Prentice: what has this to do with Wilforn's folly this night? That was the question at hand."

"When I was at the scriptorium, the owner-scribe boasted of his collection, including a copy of the architect's plan for your apartments, Your Grace," Prentice explained to her and sighed heavily, as if confessing a sin. "I thought nothing of it at the time. A man's pride in his heritage, that is all I took it for."

"Why would Solft want the plans for the Paramour's Chambers?" Farringdon asked. "What purpose could it serve him?"

Prentice shook his head.

"Likely he did not. The scribe offered the boast unbidden. He is something of a gossip, it seems, making connections and concocting tales of the high-born."

"Like every other merchant and guild journeyman I ever knew," Spindle offered. Mutters of ascent circled around Amelia's advisors. Telling tales was the pastime of every town community, from Quenland to the Murr. Gossip greased the wheels of commerce.

"Even if Solft wanted nothing to do with the plans, Your Grace, the scribe would likely have told Bluebird's girl of their existence as well, and she might have scooped them up out of diligence."

"Canny as well as false," Dalflitch said, clearly appreciating the quality of agent the Inquisition used. They were not all daft thugs and over-ambitious noblemen.

Amelia absorbed the conversation and found herself feeling ever grimmer over the night's events. Prentice's explanation made clear sense. In taking Solft and the Paramour's Chambers' plans, Bluebird would have learned of the secret passage and fed that information to Wilforn. There was the answer to the question: why now?

"And now we know the path the Bluebird's song has taken to Lady Penelope's ears," she said, concluding her thoughts out loud. "Do you think Wilforn only met the Inquisition's man in secret, or did he introduce him to his cousin directly?"

The others all considered the question.

"He would not need to meet her at all, not if he could have sent her one of those scribed spells," Farringdon said after a moment. "Why risk an encounter that might be noticed by enemies?"

"We do not know if a skilled voice is needed to make the spell leave the page," Dalflitch countered. "Her grace was only taken in when a Church knight read to her. It might be that just as our sword of scripture needs a faithful wielder, so it is with the spell papers as well."

"Well, whether in person or by document, we can at least rest a little now that we have Wilforn in our custody," Amelia said. "There will be no more songs into the Lady of Bridgetown's ears."

"Not so, Your Grace," Prentice told her bluntly. She looked at him, brow furrowed, and he cocked his head with a half shrug. "If a spider's web catches flies, it does not weave only the one."

Amelia looked at him a moment, then to her other advisers to see if they comprehended his meaning.

"If Bluebird could reach one of her closest companions, you think he might try for more than one?" Dalflitch mused. "You would guess at the squire Cyprian, I take it?"

"Perhaps," Prentice accepted with a pensive nod. "Or the remaining herald."

"The other Twin?" Amelia asked, surprised. Surely Cassian made more sense as a channel to Penelope's thoughts.

"They were only ever seen together, Your Grace. It is their most renowned characteristic," Prentice explained. "Then they were lured into danger together and one was slain while the other lives. Do you imagine if one was taken the other would flee for his life and not throw himself in loyalty after the partner he has stood beside every day for God alone knows how long?"

"Slay not one, but both, and then replace one with a skin thief?" Dalflitch wondered out loud, grudging respect growing even more in her sour expression.

"But what of the tells?" Lady Agatha asked, risking speaking out of turn, but now plainly growing in her confidence in this higher company. "How could it pass without being found out? Ain't the Lady Penelope known these Twins bods since she was a little girl?"

"It's a town in chaos, lass," Righteous explained to her readily. "No one's real sure what's the way it's supposed t'be no more. And the fellow's just lost his closest comrade. Sure he's like to be a little different in his manners for a time. Any mistake a skin thief made could just be down to his 'grief' over his mate, a good excuse for some while, I'd say. At least long enough until he got his act down to perfect."

"And the Lady of Bridgetown's household is nothing like as diligent as the maids of my chamber are, Agatha," Amelia added. "They do not even know to look out for such sorcery."

More than once, Amelia had wanted to explain the danger to Bridgetown's liege, but by the time she realized the need, their relationship was already so damaged that she expected Penelope to simply spurn her and dismiss the idea. How do you tell someone that the bad blood between you was because they were under the influence of magicks—magicks wielded by the ones most trusted to fight magick, no less? What rational Kingdom folk would believe you?

"We never noticed Flick when she was swapped," Lady Elizabeth observed, and all the Lace Fangs shook their heads remorsefully. Amelia only knew some of the story of the trainee who had been replaced by a skin thief in Fallenhill, but it was clear all the neophytes and ladies-in-masks had learned a dire lesson by the girl Felicity's murder.

"So, we have Lady Penelope's second last cousin in our grasp, with no just way to spare his life, or at the very least to save him from a shameful exile. After this night, we are down one scholar, and Bridgetown has lost itself another of its few remaining peers. But in all other ways, nothing more has changed?"

Amelia felt her hands clench to fists as Dalflitch coldly summarized their situation. The bitterness of it galled her, and she felt a fresh desire to see Wilforn punished brutally for his actions.

"Bluebird still sings, and we are still dancing to the tune," Prentice said quietly. "We need to get ahead of his plans, or we will only ever step where he directs us. More of us will die no matter what we do."

Such a dire prognostication, Amelia thought, watching her knight commander. Were they finally reaching the limit of Prentice's strengths? It was clear he was carrying the burdens of leadership more heavily these days. She wondered if perhaps she should reduce his responsibilities somehow.

"Sougate is yet secure, My Lord?" she asked, and many eyes turned to her at the sudden twist in the conversation.

"More than any other place between the banks of the Murr," Prentice replied. "The Heron is in too much of a hurry to let their army do its job properly."

"And if they change their tactics? Will they be able to turn the tide swiftly?"

"No, Your Grace. At least not unless they devise some new artifice of siegecraft that I have not seen. Such has always been the danger in this war."

"Is that likely, My Lord?" Dalflitch asked, and Prentice shook his head.

"Who could say? Until we see it, I cannot know what it might be. How could I?"

"So, we currently have no cause to fear on that account, at least," Amelia pressed. "Given that, Baron Ash, I would have you turn your command of the southern bastion over to the knight captain if you please, so that you might concentrate your efforts on your other duties."

"My love?" Farringdon asked her, brows raised and eyes wide. "You want me to command both gates—well, one gate and one riverbank?"

"Baron Prentice's reports are that he is only ever there for less than an hour morning and night each day," Amelia told her husband. "Surely that would not be an onerous addition to your duties."

"Well, no, my love, but why?" Farringdon asked, his surprise causing him to be familiar with her.

"Because as well as Lady Dalflitch and her agents have acquitted themselves in the search, Baron Ash is correct. Bluebird is still calling the tune. It is time we found his roost, or roosts, and silenced him for good. To that end I would give the duty wholly into your hands, Prentice."

He nodded, accepting her command wordlessly. Around the room, however, there was a brittleness to the quiet, as if others did not fully understand what was happening.

"This is because I value your insight in puzzling situations of this nature," she emphasized with Prentice, hoping to disarm the concerns of those around her. "Remember how well you served me hunting out Malden's conspiracy in Dweltford? You are my best for this task. I am not stripping you of rank or honor. You understand that, I trust, Prentice?"

"It would not matter if you were, Your Grace," he replied with his strictest formality, and she smiled. She could always rely on his loyalty and selflessness in her service.

Amelia looked to Lady Dalflitch. "And this is no criticism of your efforts, My Lady," she told the seneschal.

"I would not take it as such, Your Grace," Dalflitch said, matching Prentice's etiquette formality for formality. "It will be something of a relief in the next few days, in fact. My husband arrived this afternoon at the head of a small flotilla of barges from Dweltford. I was down at the dock overseeing their offloading this evening. A plethora of supplies have come to us and will need days to disperse."

"That is good news, at least," Amelia said and smiled gently. The Conclave boycott should be less of a problem from now on.

"And we put an end to another Dragon this afternoon," Farringdon offered, taking the lead from his wife's improving mood, it seemed.

"So not all our circumstances are dire," she said, hoping to comfort her courtiers, as well as herself. At that moment, Whilte emerged from the curtains, his hands ruddy to the elbows in the lamplight. He approached Amelia's chair through the standing crowd and bowed awkwardly on his wooden leg.

"I am sorry, Your Grace, but the girl has passed," he said grimly. "Her wound was too deep, and I could not save her."

And nothing now will save Wilforn, she thought as she accepted the news with a stern nod. Cousin to Penelope or not, she could not let the squire escape this outrage. He had drained every last drop of the privilege of rank. His fate was sealed.

"Brother, if you could see to her funerary rites, I would be very grateful," she told the chaplain, and he nodded. Around the room Amelia heard something that sounded like sniffles and imagined there would be more than a few tears shed this night. She would likely cry some herself, but only once she was back in her bed and in her husband's arms. Come the morning, the time for tears would be past.

"Send word to Earlsbastion that we have the murderer and will execute him. Lady Dalflitch, see that your account of this evening's events is clearly writ and explains without question the reasons he will hang."

"As you say, Your Grace."

Chapter 43

At dawn the next morning, Prentice explained the change in command duties to Sergeant Guillam on the battlements of Sougate. With each passing day, the building of hoardings and other reinforcements of the fortification progressed, and even though the siege continued, the bastion was stronger than ever. Atop the stone crenelations, an array of extra wooden protections grew and multiplied. Roarsmen could fire their matchlocks down on assaults now regardless of the weather or any falling missiles from the Heron army.

Precious little of those, Prentice thought, furious at his enemy for neglecting even such basic elements of siege warfare. It was too much like the cold contempt that Grand Kingdom knights had for rogues, wasting their lives seemingly without a second thought. But even Grand Kingdom knights hesitated to use free men for such a purpose. At least they made the pretense of only throwing men who "deserved" it into the fire. The pallid dawn lit a wretched, miry field below the garrison on the battlements with what looked like frost in some of the lowest-lying places—craters where multiple cannon shots had churned the earth during the previous attacks. The soft white would not even last past midmorning, though. Remembering the bitterness of the winter siege in Fallenhill, Prentice knew he was looking on an enemy that was losing strength as surely as if their blood was bleeding away from an open wound. Her grace was not wrong—Sougate had not needed his full attention for weeks. Even come spring, unless the bankers hired yet more mercenary reinforcements, the Golden Heron would scarcely be able to maintain the siege.

We will worry about spring when it comes, he told himself.

"So, the knight captain's in charge o' the Gryphons too now?" Guillam asked, his lip turned down on one side in a half frown. Scars on his chin ran a jagged split through the dark stubble on his jaw.

"No, I still command the Gryphons."

"We givin' up the gate to the Lions, then?"

"No Sergeant, the Gryphon Banner Company will still hold Sougate," Prentice explained. He had not expected this level of intransigence from his man. He should have known better.

"So, when they attack us again, who do I send to?" Guillam asked, apparently working through a series of questions from his thoughts, one after the other. For all his rough manner, the sergeant was no fool and had his rank for a reason. These were the questions an astute officer *should* be asking.

"You send word to Knight Captain Farringdon," Prentice told him. "He commands the bastion."

"And if they make a proper go of it and we need reinforcing?"

"Then send to Sergeant Gennet, same as always."

Prentice felt himself becoming annoyed but did his best to keep his calm. Guillam's questions were all practical and better addressed now than in the heat of battle. The next question, however, cut a little too close to the quick.

"And what will you be doin', My Lord?"

"I will be about the town at other matters for her grace, and that is all you need know," Prentice snapped.

Guillam saluted and nodded again.

"As you say, My Lord."

It was clear he was not happy about the arrangement, and it put Prentice in mind of another matter that likely displeased the sergeant. "How has the transfer of command been?" he asked. "Are you becoming happier as Sergeant of the Claws?"

Since Guillam was already in a poor mood, it would do little harm to follow up this issue as well. The sergeant sucked on his stained teeth.

"I tell you true, Knight Commander, if'n you'd handed my Roar over to anyone else, I'd have cursed you in me prayers every night. Lose my favorite place, and to a woman no less?" He paused and spat on the stones. "But you had the right of it. Every word I get back is that she's a total sow—that's correct word for a she-bear, ain't it, a sow? Sootface is a right sow, and she's got 'em drillin' hard and marching swift. Should hear her talk 'bout what it's like to march into the teeth o' them big fur-coated beggars. She's got the Gryphon Roar steppin' swifter and firin' straighter than even I could. First Lyrach and now Kate—you keep sendin' folk my way to show me up. I feel safer in the Claws now. At least Porth ain't comin' back to make me look bad with the pikemen."

Prentice smirked at Guillam's complaints, pleased to hear that Sootface Kate was fitting aright into the command structure. News that she was a demanding leader was exactly what he wanted. A sow she-bear was what the Gryphons' Roar needed. That was something he and Sergeant Guillam could agree on, at least.

What Bridgetown needs as well, he thought, but that was the archduchess's purview. He had other duties, and he turned his mind back to them. Leaving Guillam in charge of the bastion, he made his way down to the southern bridge and was half across it when he encountered Farringdon, accompanied by Knight Sergeant Nunel, riding their horses towards the gatehouse.

"Come to take command, My Lord?" Prentice asked, meaning it pleasantly, even as a joke of sorts. "I have already informed Sougate of the change of leadership."

"At her grace's insistence," Farringdon answered defensively. Prentice realized the marquis-consort had taken the attempt at humor amiss, but there was nothing that could be done about it without the risk of making it all worse. He looked to Nunel instead.

"Not a lot of need for lancers here, Knight Sergeant."

"Still in command of the Roar and lancers both, My Lord," Nunel answered. "Also, I'm more than a bit familiar with the big guns, too, after the last seasons. Thought I'd see how Sougate is disposed. I might learn something else new."

Prentice smirked and rubbed at his beard.

"Sergeant Guillam will love to give you a tour, no doubt," he said and saluted them both, meaning to move off before the odd situation of change of command made things uncomfortable again. The point of having two banner companies had been to avoid this kind of complexity. Nonetheless, the archduchess had asked it of him, and he would not refuse her. Such was his duty.

Farringdon was not of a mind to let him leave just yet, however. The knight captain dismounted to stand next to Prentice.

"Before you go, My Lord, I have something I would like to discuss with you."

"Is it urgent?" Prentice asked, hoping Farringdon was not about to try for some kind of reconciliation. There was no serious problem between them, not from Prentice's perspective at least, and any comment or overture the marquis consort might make only promised to be awkward. He did not have any hurt feelings to care for and needed no sop for his pride. He took whatever role his liege commanded.

"I suppose not truly urgent," Farringdon conceded. "But it also won't take too long."

Prentice forced himself to nod and inclined his head to listen as Farringdon spoke swiftly.

"I was wondering about the possibility of sallies. It's the true reason I asked Nunel to come with me this morning, so that we could discuss it."

Prentice looked back at Sougate.

"We did it in autumn well enough, My Lord," he said, considering the notion. It was not the worst idea in the world, thinking to break the Golden Heron more swiftly. It was simply unnecessary. The weather was doing that task for them. "The ground will not be ideal, though. We are not far enough south for full frost. The mud will not have hardened. Poor terrain for men ahorse."

"I was born a Veckander Prentice. Nunel, too," Farringdon retorted with a smirk of his own. "We do know what winters are like in our homeland."

Prentice blinked as he looked at the marquis's amused expression. He tried to remember the last time he had been put on the back foot by the knight captain like this and thought that it might never have happened, in fact. So much for any hand-wringing reconciliation. If anything, Farringdon might be as confident and independent as he ever was.

Not a bad thing, Prentice thought honestly, although his father's voice tried to tell him it made him more redundant to the needs of his liege. *Good, even. I will be able to retire and raise my family in Fallenhill at peace with the world.*

He did not believe any of it, of course, but the ongoing arguments and fights with his father's cursing that occupied so much of his daily thoughts sometimes had moments of ridiculousness like this when even his worst fears could not find purchase or bite.

"Actually, Prentice, I was thinking of Norgate—well, the north bridge, since there is no Norgate anymore," Farringdon continued.

"The north bridge is no more either, My Lord," Prentice replied.

"Not so, actually. I have been looking it over in the night when the danger is least. We only destroyed about two spans' worth and the riverbank footings. It's all fully reparable."

That was always the point, Prentice thought. Destroy only as much as we had to. Eventually the bridge will have to be rebuilt, when there is peace, and the siege is lifted.

"We are holding our own in this duel of cannons, Prentice," Farringdon continued, "but we haven't the depth or power that Daven Marcus has. Even if we took all the cannons off Sougate and brought them up to Loncastel, I would give us no more than an even chance to win out in the end. If the Usurper gains some more wits or decides to listen to wiser voices for once, he could concentrate his guns on one of ours, one at a time, each in turn, and leave us no more than bronze debris to take back to a smelter in a matter of days."

Prentice understood the knight captain's concern, but it felt as if Farringdon was being overly optimistic once more, thinking to ride out to destroy the Bronze Dragons. It was a tactic that had failed once already.

"The Denay army will see you making any repairs and attack before they are even close to completed enough for a sally," the knight commander said flatly. "That concentrated fire that you fear will all fall on the bridge and the laborers you set to make the works. Mortar won't harden in the rain, so you will have to make shelters or work only when the shooting will be the easiest—when the rain stops. And shelters on the river will be juicier targets than the bridge itself."

Farringdon nodded impatiently.

"I know all that, Prentice, but what if we could put two spans in place swiftly? The Redlanders crossed the whole Murr in the space of less than an hour."

"With magick we do not have on boats we do not know how to build," Prentice shot back, feeling his own mood sour further under Farringdon's determination. "Even if we could, do not forget that the Lions held the Redlanders at their bridgehead throughout that night. Daven Marcus is encamped close enough that he will be able to do the same in short order. Like his father, he will turn his Dragons on the bridge behind you, destroy it, and you will be cut off and left to die on the far bank, swamped by an overwhelming wave of enemies."

In Prentice's mind, he was seeing again the Night of the Red Sky, when King Chrostmer had severed the enemy bridge with cannon fire and left many White Lions militiamen to die at the hands of the enraged Redlanders, including his friend Sir Gant.

The memory hardened his sour mood to ice, but Farringdon's expression told of a similar darkness of sentiment.

"My wife bade me find a way to raid across the river last night as sleep eluded us both," the marquis consort said in a low voice through gritted teeth. "Would you have me refuse her? Would you?"

"No, My Lord," Prentice answered him, nodding somberly. He understood better now. Farringdon was under pressure to produce results, just as he was. As he thought about it, Prentice accepted that, in fact, some kind of raid would be a useful stratagem if it could be achieved. And Farringdon was innovative and expert in matters of construction. If anyone could do it, the marquis knight captain should be the one.

"The command of Norgate is yours, My Lord," Prentice told him, hoping he sounded as earnest as he meant to. "If it can be done, you will find a way."

"If you could lend me your fey man, perhaps he could help me devise something more cunning for the purpose," Farringdon said. "Or better yet, five hundred like him, like the company of fey you arrived with."

"They will not return before spring, My Lord," Prentice replied, frowning. There was nothing he could do about that fact, and Farringdon should know better. "I will send Dahyoor to you, though, as you request."

"Well, my thanks for that, at least."

With that, they saluted, and Farringdon remounted, even though the distance to Sougate was hardly enough to justify not walking his mount the rest of the way. Prentice let the two men ride on and was glad to aim away from the bastion that was no longer his responsibility.

You should have kept your fey allies on a tighter leash, he heard his father's inward voice chastise him, but again, it was a criticism too far. He scoffed at it, recognizing how mad it must be to argue with himself in such a fashion.

Oh, of course father, he thought. *And I should throw a rope around the moon, break it to my will, and ride it into battle like a horse. Perhaps I could ride it all the way to the end of the Rampart—see if the glowing band across the sky truly leads to heaven like some say.*

The inner voice seemed rebuked a moment, but it muttered a sour retort as it withdrew to the frayed edges of his thoughts.

You might as well. At least that would be a true achievement, an honor and prestige that might not be snatched from your weakling fingers.

Shaking his head at the depth of the poison in his soul, Prentice set himself to walk the town until he could devise a new way to track the Bluebird to his nest and make an end of him. That was the duty before him now, honor and prestige be damned.

CHAPTER 44

"You are not an easy man to find," Prentice heard someone say loudly from the shed door and he turned to see his friend, Sir Turley, standing there, accompanied by two men in Reach steward's livery, holding lanterns whose flames jumped and guttered in the cold evening's breeze. Midwinter might just have passed, but the nights would be cold for a long while yet.

"I have been here the past hour at least," he said, putting his practice pole aside against the wall and heading over to take his friend's hand.

"Why on earth for?" Turley demanded, turning his nose up at the shed's smell. "It's like a damned midden in here."

"You and I have been in many places worse than this," Prentice said, and he shook Turley's hand, forcing himself to smile. He was happy to see the knight castellan back in Bridgetown, but all his pleasures were a little covered with frost these days. Winter was freezing his mood, it seemed, and the warmth of happiness needed some help to push through to the surface most days. It was not an impossible effort to make, at least for Turley's sake.

"Well, sure, I slept in many a filthy place in my time," Turley agreed. "But that was because they chained me to it, not by choice. I'm set free now. I don't even go into stables to fetch my own horse no more. I give that to my squires to do. I'm a man of rank and privilege now."

Prentice looked round the little space. To him it smelled so much better than when he had first found it. It amused him to think his rough-and-tumble friend might turn his nose up at it.

"To answer your question, I am training my combat skills. A place like this is ideal for the purpose," he told Turley, heading back to this practice weapon. Soon he would be ready to move on from polearms, which meant he would have to ask halberdiers and pikemen in to spar against. Given the length of such weapons, perhaps this shed might not be so ideal, especially not if he wanted to fight them more than one at a time.

"What's the matter? All your Church knight war arts not enough anymore?" Turley asked with a cheeky smile.

"No," was all Prentice said in reply.

Turley thrust out his bottom lip and shrugged in surprise.

"Hmm? Well then, mayhaps this'll be a help to you," he said and turned back to the men standing behind him. He shooed the lantern bearers out of the doorway and waved men farther back to come forward. Three entered bearing heavy burdens wrapped in oilcloth.

"What's this?" Prentice asked him as Turley directed the bearers to put their burdens on the ground to one side.

"A gift. What do you reckon on it being?"

"A gift?" Prentice repeated. He moved to the first bundle and nudged it with his boot. It was heavy, that was for sure. A slightly firmer kick returned a metallic sound. Curious, he crouched and unwound the ties, pulling the cloth aside to reveal a pair of steel faulds—articulated steel plates designed to protect the hips and upper legs as part of a man-at-arms' full armor—attached to the bottom of a breastplate. It was hard to judge the quality of the steel in the poor light, but as he lifted the armor piece, the connected plates seemed to flop about too much for a typical set of faulds.

"I know what you're thinkin'!" Turley said, holding out an appeasing hand before Prentice could make any comment. "None of the fixin's are finished yet. That's why I brought this fellow with me." He reached into the crowd of retainers standing behind him and thrust one of them forward by the shoulder. Wearing a sleeveless leather tunic over his doublet and with his hair tied back in a tight single plait, the man was instantly recognizable as one of the Masnian smiths from Fallenhill.

"I brung Ganner here with me—Ganner Soort-Almin—to finish up the suit right for you," Turley explained. "Fella's a wizard with steel and no mistake. You should see the comfortable thing he's made for me. Look like a statue in it, I do—metal from head to toe."

Tourney armor, Prentice thought from his friend's description. If Ganner Soort-Almin was one of Yentow Sent's surviving journeymen, Prentice had no doubt the man was a skilled armorer. Sent had ever been an exacting taskmaster.

"I do not need armor that heavy or close-fitting," he said, putting the faulds back on top of their bundle. There were other pieces in that load, and looking to the other two bundles, knowing now what they were, Prentice could make out the shape of more elements of armor under the cloths.

"I know that," Turley said with a tut and roll of his eyes. "You ask 'em. I already said you wouldn't have nothin' to do with them silly, pointy steel shoes and what all. Trust me."

Prentice cocked an eyebrow at his friend's description of sabatons and smiled. The Masnian smith stepped forward and bowed in the foreign fashion, stiff from the waist.

"I will do best work for you," he said in a broken accent. "Lord Turley already tells his wife to rent good forge. One week, that's all it will take."

"How can you say no to that?" Turley asked with a smug expression of his own.

"*Lord* Turley?" Prentice asked him, enjoying his friend's company more than he would have credited. Perhaps that was all he needed—more time with good company.

"The fella knows quality in armor and in men, and knows how to treat both with due respect," Turley declared with mock pride, nodding at the Masnian and pulling at the sides of his cloak in a prim manner. Prentice snorted a quiet laugh.

"Pity your poor wife lacks the same judgement," he retorted.

"Only in my one case," Turley returned without hesitation. "She weren't never turned to you for a breath. She thinks she's seen through the dross, but since I look so good next to you, she's been fooled. Why do you think I don't let her back up north while you're down here?"

Prentice nodded at his friend's cheeky grin.

"You were ever the canny, charming one," he said.

"And you were ever the hard, grim bugger," his friend told him. Turley's eyes ranged over the shadows of the shed and his expression turned concerned for a moment. He looked back to Prentice. "What are you really doin'?"

Prentice shrugged and looked at the pole in his hand, another weapon he felt rushed to master and barely adequate to the task. And still there were only four chalk rings on the wall.

"Some days need a grimmer sort of man," was all he could think to say. He looked to the Masnian smith again. "A week you say?"

"The at most," Ganner Soort-Almin replied, muddling his Kingdom speech expressions. "I will take measures now and make the first finishes tomorrow starting."

He held forth a piece of rope just long enough to reach from his own hand to his elbow. As he moved a little closer, Prentice could see brightly colored rings of finer threads wrapped around the cord at regular intervals. It was a measuring tool that Soort-Almin would use to mark Prentice's exact dimensions so he would not have to stand for days in the forge workshop while the smith made all the final adjustments that would fit the plates correctly. As it was, the mere notion of having to stand still for the half a candle or so that it would take for all the measuring made Prentice's skin crawl. He had not been still for half a candle for weeks, except when exhaustion forced him to sleep.

"Must we do this now?" he asked Turley as Ganner Soort-Almin closed the final distance and politely took the practice pole from Prentice's hand, setting it aside.

"You got somethin' better to do?" Turley challenged him, and while much of him wanted to say yes just to return to his evening training regimen, Prentice only shook his head. He did need a replacement for his armor and there was no point in delaying such a small task. He stood as relaxed as he could, letting the smith manipulate his body and take his dimensions with the single piece of rope as a guide. Prentice had no idea how the man proposed to remember each measurement since the smith made no notations on paper, wax, or even clay—nothing Prentice could see. Nonetheless, he said nothing about it. One did not question a master craftsman at his work, especially not a Masnian, and if the final product was inferior, it could always be adjusted again or else simply not paid for.

"Brought you another present, by the by," Turley said as Prentice held his arms out wide, like a man on a cross, for Soort-Almin to measure his shoulders.

Grim image, he thought, shaking his head.

"What present?" he asked. "A doublet like the ones your wife makes you wear?"

"Don't be daft," his friend replied. "I want to keep you alive, not lookin' as good as me. Folk need to tell us apart somehow."

Prentice chuckled. In all the time he had known Turley, not a single person would have confused them. Other than both being tall, in manner, character, and appearance they were as chalk and cheese and always had been. Their loyalty to each other was possibly the only true thing they had in common, and Prentice knew he could rely upon it utterly.

Until you fail him as you did your family, his father's voice sounded in his mind, echoing with the tones of his teachers from the past. Nowadays, the enemy within his soul always spoke with a dozen critics' voices from among the Seven Rings Cross teachers and others from Ashfield. Sometimes he even thought he heard the Inquisitor's cold-blooded tones echoing out of the cell he was tortured in. But always at the fore was his father's voice, telling him how worthy he was of the hate he had suffered.

"So, what is your gift then?" Prentice asked, knowing his own voice now sounded like he was speaking through a mouthful of vinegar. Turley nodded to one of the bearers and the man ducked out of the shed, only to return with yet another bundle. It seemed they had a handcart or something similar outside and the steward fetched it from there. It was typical Turley to turn something so mundane as delivering a suit of armor into a mock ritual. The knight castellan accepted the new bundle and held it up to Prentice like a sacrist with a newly christened baby.

"Fresh wheellocks for the lancers," he said proudly and unwrapped the cloth to show Prentice one of two newly manufactured pistols. "Fallenhill blokes say they've got the secret of the triggers down pat now and can make replacements at will. Good, hmm? A pair for every saddle now."

"Yes indeed," Prentice agreed. Each morning after he had slept here in his training room, he was awakened by the sound of lancers, practicing their techniques and tactics on the only open part of Runners Field still left for the purpose. With just enough wheellocks for half their number, the drills had to be done in small groups. If Turley had brought sufficient to fully equip every rider, that would be a big step up in strength. Farringdon would likely be more eager than ever to take them out against Daven Marcus. Hopefully, he would not let his eagerness carry him into another trap this time.

Not your business, Prentice told himself sternly.

"You have more than just the one pair for each rider, I take it?" he asked Turley.

"Course," came the swift reply. "And I brought you a gun maker to keep 'em all in the best nick. Runnin' repairs and replacements from now 'til the war's over."

"Excellent," Prentice told his friend. "Then leave me that pair tonight, if you will. It is about time I understood properly how the little killing engines work."

Turley knotted his brows a little, plainly surprised by the instruction, but he shrugged and nodded, accepting it all the same.

I need to master the weapons of the Lions, Prentice thought, knowing that he did not want to have to explain himself to his friend. How could he? He hardly understood it himself. He only knew he had a duty to command the militia wisely, and that meant understanding fully the capability of each man-at-arms under him.

You'll be presuming to become a cannoneer next, the mocking voices sneered. Prentice shook his head at them as Ganner Soort-Almin measured the distance from his temple to the point where his neck met his shoulder. The smith thought Prentice was reacting to the rope and took a polite step back a moment. The knight commander smiled apologetically at him and waved him back to his task. He gritted his teeth and forced himself to remain still for the rest of the measuring.

Militiaman, gunner, cannoneer, convict—whatever my liege requires.

CHAPTER 45

The second morning after Wilforn's failed assassination dawned with rare brightness, cool winds blowing away the clouds for a time. Astute eyes about the town noticed the next wave of storms gathering upon the horizon, but the wet stones of the road and shingles on the roofs glittered with droplets that captured the cool sunlight. The town was almost beautiful for a moment, even though the rumble of cannons on the north bank never let Bridgetown's folk forget they were at war. The bright morning was not a chance Daven Marcus would pass up, and Farringdon meant to match him shot for shot if possible. Fresh supplies of powder and cannonballs had arrived with Sir Turley's barges, so there was no fear, at least, of running out of ammunition.

Now I only have to worry that a rare unfortunate shot might take my husband's head from his shoulders, Amelia thought as she looked out the open window that faced both east and a little north. Spindle and her seamstresses had adjusted Amelia's winter overdress for her pregnancy and she was warm under the Reach blue velvet, but the chill air on her face made her sniffle all the same. She dabbed at her nose with a lace handkerchief, happy to endure that discomfort for the pleasure of fresher air than the enclosed room with its constantly burning fireplaces offered. Of course, fresher was a relative term since the air outside her window was still that of the densely packed islands with their population crammed three and four stories high on any permitted square inch. Real fresh air would entail taking a ride out into some open fields or a forest somewhere—an activity that would also require no siege and a comfortable saddle.

Come spring, peace, and you my darling little one, she whispered inwardly to her child, rubbing her belly. *Is this how Lady Dalfitch's messenger birds feel, waiting in their cages? They always seem so eager to fly free when given their chance. When we drive off Daven Marcus, I will be the same. Dear Silvermane will be run to exhaustion before I'm satisfied, most likely.*

For what seemed like an hour, at least, Amelia sat at the window, enjoying the rare sunshine and dreams of spring rides. From the streets below came snatches of the typical noises of townsfolk, including the sound of children's laughter, rarer in winter and the more joyful for it. It made the archduchess all the more eager for her child's birth. Sometimes there were more serious cries to be heard—hawkers selling wares or, for a short while, a grocer cursing a farrier loudly. From what Amelia could overhear, the horse-shoer was not actually present. Judging by the man's loud complaints, it seemed the grocer's workhorse had thrown a new shoe and been badly injured in the process, so that as the man sought to remedy the situation that threatened not only his morning's trade but possibly his one good animal and cart, he declaimed the farrier's failings at length, seemingly to the street in general. As real as the grocer's indignation likely was, even his complaints brought a smile to Amelia's lips. The serious but mundane problems of a street trader were better to her mind than the bloodshed and destruction that every boom of "thunder" from Loncastel heralded. The broken livelihood of one man might be healed, but the north island might never fully recover from the hammering it was still receiving. Under her momentary pleasure, Amelia hoped and prayed Farringdon would indeed devise some tactic against the Dragons—something that would surprise Daven Marcus, for once.

The grocer had ceased his complaining and likely moved on through the maze-like streets beyond Amelia's sight when new sounds of curses and arguments began to arise. They were slightly farther distant, and after a moment, she realized they were coming from the front yard of her building. Exact words were difficult to make out, but it was clear they were angry and boded violence. Moments later, Lady Righteous entered the main chamber, mask in place and moving with martial purpose. Since the night attack on Paramour's, none of the Lace Fangs had seemed to relax fully but were even more vigilant and ready for a fight than usual.

"Trouble in the yard, Your Grace," Righteous said as she curtseyed before Amelia.

Not another attack? Amelia wondered but realized immediately that no real threat was likely to penetrate the guard she had now. Since Wilforn's attack, rooftop access to the secret passage had been nailed shut, and half the cohort's gunners now took turns patrolling the roof of the building so no other secret entries could be exploited that way. Any invaders would be shot from above. The war wagons closing off the gateway had been reinforced as well, and on the riverfront below, more militiamen stood watch over Paramour's footings so there was no unguarded access to Amelia's person from any possible direction.

"Even if they arrived on the wings of birds, our Roar marksmen would have them before they landed," Farringdon had reassured her.

"What trouble, My Lady?" she asked, and Righteous showed her a contemptuous smirk under her black lace half-mask.

"The usual—the filly's come to grouse at you some more. Only, from the look of it, she's riled even more than typical."

Penelope? Amelia thought and then shook her head. *At last, the girl leaves her castle uninvited. Pity it had to cost her her cousin.*

"I take it she has come to treat with me for the squire's life?" she asked her lady-in-waiting as she stood and took a deep breath. It should not require so much effort just to stand up. How had Righteous ever been training and fighting right up to the moment she went into labor?

"I guess she must've, Your Grace, but from the look of her, she might think to fight her way in and rescue him by force."

Amelia smirked at that as well until she realized just how angry Lady Penelope must be. At an earlier time, the archduchess might have prepared some kind of politic speech, hoping to soothe the noblewoman's ire, but that season had passed now, just as autumn had given way to full winter. She had Wilforn in chains in a side room of the apartments, and now that his liege cousin had arrived, Amelia would have the fool tried and executed. Even with the improved mood the morning's sun had given her, the archduchess doubted she would allow anything less. Penelope would have to make an unbelievably good case to even gain the young man permanent exile.

She had best not make mention of weregeld, Amelia thought as she fitted overshoes on her slippers and began to make her way down to the yard. The thought that the Lady of Bridgetown might try to use noble privilege to ransom her cousin out from under his sentence by the ancient tradition of weregeld threatened to tip Amelia into a rage of her own. She let Righteous open the outer door for her with Daisy and Beth at her back, and she stepped into the bright yard, blinking in the light.

"At last, you come," Penelope's voice assaulted her, and after a moment Amelia was able to sight the girl, standing just inside the yard gate in a gap created between the two war wagons. She was dressed as she always was, in house colors and armor. It made her seem almost as bright as the day Amelia first met her on the roof of the now-demolished Norgate. Nevertheless, the girl's face was ruddy and her eyes bloodshot. It was clear she had been crying, likely for some long while. Beside her was the remaining Twin, and next to him, Cyprian. Penelope had her longsword drawn and was waving it about as she spoke. Amelia had no fear for herself, however, as a formation of fifty White Lions formed a virtually impenetrable barricade between them

"Have I not suffered enough for you, woman? Is there some forgotten blood between your merchant forebears and the earls of Bridgetown that you would do these things to me?"

"I have done nothing to you but respond to your own follies," Amelia said directly, moving as close as she could behind her garrison, so she did not have to shout. The little yard was crowded like an overfull boat transporting livestock, save for the tiny gap between the three Bridgetown worthies and Amelia's men-at-arms.

"Follies? For follies you do this to me?" Penelope shouted, pointing the sword directly at Amelia. "If you were not a frail woman, I would call you out and we could settle your plots and lies once and for all."

"You'd have to go through me first, girl," Righteous retorted before Amelia could answer the odd challenge. "And you know right well what happens when you and me face each other for more than *points*."

Righteous's sneering emphasis on the final word made it plain to what she was referring—the two baroness's had had a "training" session that had ended with Righteous humiliating Penelope. Amelia reached out and gently touched her Lace Fang's shoulder. There was no need for this meeting to be more belligerent and bitter than it must. After all, the Reach was unassailable here.

When a man rants at the mountain, the mountain does not answer his foolishness.

"It was never meant to reach this pass, My Lady," she said earnestly to Lady Penelope. "But now that you are come, we can conclude the current matter."

Amelia turned to the corporal in command of her garrison.

"Send men to fetch the prisoners and I will judge them now," she told him quietly. He looked at her with an unmistakable confusion.

"Prisoners, Your Grace?" he asked.

"Yes, the squire Wilforn and his surviving accomplice," Amelia explained. "Bring them both from their cells and I will judge them here where the lady can witness that I am doing nothing from subterfuge."

"We don't have the prisoners no more, Your Grace," the corporal answered her, his confused expression deepening, as if he was being forced to explain something everyone already knew for certain.

"What do you mean, you don't have them? Where are they?"

"Wherever you sent them to, Your Grace." It was clear the corporal was becoming increasingly uncomfortable.

"What's this bally foolishness, militiaman?" Righteous demanded in a whisper. Amelia cast a glance at Lady Penelope and her two escorts, at least one of whom she realized was quite probably an agent of the Inquisition, either by proxy or an actual eldritch shapeshifter. She felt confident, at least, that if either was a skin thief, he would not be suicidal enough to try for her assassination right now in the face of such impossible odds.

"Her grace sent a note with another corporal and an extra militiaman yestereve," the corporal explained. The man looked like he was beginning to sweat despite the cold air. It was clear he was unnerved by this turn of events. "They took the pair away in shackles. I figured to some better cell than the room inside, away from her grace and her ladies."

"I never sent any such note or men," Amelia protested. "Why would I?"

That was a pointless question. In all likelihood, if his story was true, the corporal would never have thought to wonder about his liege's motives, only to fulfill her commands.

"Who was this corporal?" Righteous pressed.

"Don't know his name," the garrison leader told them. "He was from the Gryphon Banner. That was part of why I figured him for on the plumb and true. We all know that the Gryphon is the knight commander's banner, and he ain't commanding no defenses no more. If he's figured to do other business, then sure that must include bestowing or executing prisoners. Was I wrong?"

Not two days and everyone knows I've taken Prentice's command of Sougate away from him? Amelia thought, and she wondered if perhaps she had made a mistake. It had not occurred to her in the moment she did it how the militiamen under him might react to this change. *It is not punishment, and I meant him no dishonor.*

"What more lies are you concocting, Amelia?" Cyprian demanded loudly, and she looked up at him.

"None, arrogant squire," she retorted, raising her voice as well without meaning to. "Your cousin will not escape his punishment, and it will be done openly."

Once we determine who has spirited him away and have him back in our hands, she thought but did not say. The words she did say were enough to push Lady Penelope over the edge into hysteria, however.

"*Escape* his punishment?" the girl screamed, fresh tears streaming down her face. "How much more punishment could you plan for him? Is his current fate not enough?"

"What fate?" Righteous asked.

"*What fate?*" Penelope repeated in a wild, mocking tone. "What fate? The fate of being hung up like a hog and butchered for his meat."

Oh, dear God, Amelia thought suddenly and realized that things were far worse than she had even imagined. When the corporal had told his tale of a note in the evening, she had expected Wilforn must have been rescued by friends, or perhaps a distant relative. Although every effort had been made to give slain White Lions fitting burials, weapons and armor reclaimed by the banners, it would not have been impossible for someone to have looted a dead corporal's uniform and posed as an officer. Amelia had been thinking that she would have to send the neophytes and Prentice into the streets anew, looking for Wilforn, as well as Bluebird—perhaps the one might even lead to the other. This entire event might in the end have worked out to her good. It was not to be.

"Where is your cousin, My Lady?" she asked, fearful of the answer.

"Where? Where!" Penelope cried. She pointed over her shoulder with her sword, northward. "He's where your killers nailed him. He was like a younger brother to me, and you…"

She stopped speaking, her voice choked off with sobs. Cyprian came to her then, wrapping an armored arm around her shoulders so that the steel clashed on her own spaulders. She shrugged at his assistance but half-heartedly. He was not pushed off. The lady's attention was still on Amelia, however.

"You had him butchered, eviscerated, and splayed, hanging on the walls of your husband's favorite pub! Is there no evil you westerners will not sink to?"

"We did not do this! Her grace knows nothing of it!" Righteous insisted, but that only drew fresh ire from the Lady of Bridgetown.

"Shut up! Shut up! I know all about you now, the true you. You're nothing but a knife fighting whore who kills for titillation! I should have had you executed for your impertinence that day! I will do the deed now, God give me strength."

Lost to her grief and rage, Penelope struggled to rush forward, sword leading, as if she thought to fight through the entire garrison to strike Righteous down, or perhaps Amelia.

Both of us, most likely, the archduchess thought. She was pleased that first Cyprian and then the Twin worked to hold the noblewoman back, but Penelope still struggled against their arms, spitting yet more curses. In response to her uncontrolled demeanor, several of the militiamen closest to her lowered their halberds or put their hands to their swords, ready to defend against the possibility of a reckless assault. Lady Penelope hardly noticed, but the two men with her did. Cyprian moved to interpose himself between the noblewoman and the targets of her wrath. Amelia barely heard what he said to calm his cousin, but at least one phrase she thought he used was, "Not now." Yet more foreboding for their futures.

"You have just faced the liege of Bridgetown with drawn steel in array," the Twin declared over his shoulder as he helped the squire escort their baroness-elect back between the wagons. "Now there is no mistake between us. The Western Reach and Bridgetown are enemies."

If we are, it is because you made us so, Amelia wanted to respond, but she held her tongue. The mountain did not answer a man's foolishness.

"Corporal, I assume talk of Marquis-Consort Farringdon's favorite pub means the Dog's Leg on Loncastel," Amelia said to the garrison commander when the Bridgetown nobles were gone. "Send men there, or to wherever the dead boy is if not there and have him brought down. Even if she hates us, Lady Penelope must have her cousin's body back."

The garrison leader saluted.

"Your Grace, I'm so sorry like for all this..." he began to apologize earnestly, but Amelia had no need for his regrets.

"We are all victims of this calumny, Corporal," she said flatly. All the relieving joy of the bright morning was washed away now. She looked up at the sky and felt a sudden longing for the black clouds to close over her head once more.

"Shall we go back inside, Your Grace?" Righteous suggested politely, and Amelia lowered her face again, nodding. Before she returned to her chambers, she grabbed at the corporal with a fresh thought.

"Do not have the squire cut down yet," she told him. "Send word to Knight Commander Ash. Have this entire circumstance explained to him and say that I want the matter investigated to its utter end. Like the dragonfly at the head of the Murr, I want him to find who did this and drag them to me in chains. They will regret the day of their birth when I am finished with them."

The corporal saluted again and picked runners from his command to take her orders to Prentice. At last, Amelia went inside, and on the threshold, she felt her baby kick within her.

Poor thing, she thought as she slowly mounted the stairs. *What kind of birthing are you to have, growing through such a bitter season as this.*

From Righteous and Prentice's own rooms came the sound of one of their twins crying, and Amelia waved her Lace Fang to go to her child, even without being asked first. Hers was not the only heir who would imbibe the sorrowful milk of this war. By the time she reached the top of the stairs she realized that she had heard no cannon shots for a while, and soon after, the rains returned, turning the afternoon sky back to hoped-for darkness.

Chapter 46

"Well, that's a mongrel dog's leavings and no mistake," Turley said as he stood beside Prentice, with Dahyoor on his pony behind them. All three were looking up at Wilforn's body, hanging from two iron spikes driven into the wooden beams between the plaster of the Dog's Leg's second story. The white sections beneath the corpse had red streaks down them, but less than so much bodily damage should have produced. The body was exactly as they had been told to expect—the belly was cut open from beneath the navel to the neck, the ribcage and the flaps of skin splayed apart and pinned back like a macabre cape. Some of the internal organs had been removed already, but others hung down revoltingly.

"No point sending for a healer for him," Turley added by way of a joke.

Prentice did not laugh, but he knew his friend's sense of humor already and did not resent him using it to face this kind of ugliness.

"He was dead in the night," Dahyoor said, as if they did not realize. "Healing is not his need. Judgement or miracle are the only fates now."

Turley looked back over his shoulder at the mounted fey, giving him a raised eyebrow, and then to Prentice. He said nothing, but his expression made it clear he thought the humorless Dahyoor was trying to teach them how to suck eggs.

"No point dismounting for just this, I guess," he whispered, noting the fey-man's reluctance to leave the saddle.

"For a *mere* gruesome murder?" Prentice responded jokingly as if the notion was ridiculous. He studied the corpse in situ for a moment longer as the light rain soaked his cloak, then turned to a waiting line first and his ten-man squad. "Bring it down now."

With ladders and tools they had already brought for the task, the militiamen set about climbing up and freeing the body.

"'Bout bloody time, too!" the publican declared loudly from the doorway of the tavern. "What do you reckon that's done to my reputation? Folk'll ne'er want to drink here again!"

"You've got two dozen Lions in there right now, downing your swill and likely to drink your cellar dry 'fore the week's out!" Turley retorted.

The tavernkeeper harrumphed. "Siege ain't to last forever though, is it? What am I to do when you lot move on?"

"Change the place's name and charge extra for the tale of the vivisected squire's ghost," Turley told the man, stepping under the tavern's eaves and removing his hat to shake away the excess water. "Tell folks you're haunted, and travelers'll line up to boast they braved the ill luck for a glimpse of the ghoulie."

Prentice wasn't convinced Turley's plan would work as easily as his friend made it sound, superstition being what it could be, but the publican gave no more complaints. The man was about to go back to his business, but the knight commander had another line of questions for him.

"What time did you notice him up there?" he asked.

"This morning. Brewer's boy sent me word. Pale as a sheet he was. Be havin' nightmares for years, don't you doubt."

"And do you live here, or did you lock up for the night?"

Prentice watched the sour fellow closely as he probed for answers. Nailing a body on the wall of a public house was not an easy task to perform stealthily, not even for someone like Bluebird, who had access to God alone knew what kind of magick to aid in the fell activity.

"I left after I closed up, after the midnight bells," the publican confirmed. He met Prentice's probing stare with a belligerent expression. "He weren't up there then, I can assure you."

"Would you have noticed if he was, in the dark of the night as you walked away?" Prentice pressed.

"Your provosts enforce a strict chuckin' out time on me, Baron," was the answer. "Ain't not one of your fellows waking up on the floor of my taproom. They all head back to their tents like good lads. Each and every night. That's with the midnight bells, so sure even in the dark, someone of your fellows would've seen. So many on the street and the provosts with their lanterns."

That made a kind of sense to Prentice, so it gave him a marker of the time involved. Someone had taken Wilforn away from Paramour's soon after sundown and sometime after midnight nailed his body up here. That was enough time for the execution and mutilation itself, but wherever they had done the deed, they still had to escort him unseen through the streets to their hideout and then bring his body through the dark and put it up on the wall. He looked down the Great Bridge Road in the two directions. The Dog's Leg took its name from being placed at the corner of the street, like being in the crook of a dog's leg. He tried to imagine it as he knew it in the night. Even as well-lit as it might have been with the provosts and their lanterns, there were a myriad of alleyways, dark corners, and odd paths off to the riverside. Bringing Wilforn here unseen would not have been the challenge it might seem. Still, someone should have heard the nailing, at least. So far, questions up and down the street had yielded not a single witness, not even to the sound of one hammer strike.

"I am growing to hate this town," he muttered. Beside him, Turley nodded with no sense of irony. Prentice looked over his shoulder at Dahyoor.

"Could you track the path they took to bring him here?" he asked his squire. Dahyoor looked at the body being levered off the wall, then down at the ground in front of the tavern. He turned his head up and down the road.

"No," he said at last. Prentice was not surprised. Even the fey must have limits to their powers. "The other *kreff keshkirae* sent tortoises to summon me today," the fey rider continued, referring to Farringdon. "Is it your wish I do as he wants?"

"I have seen this," Prentice told him with a single nod, and without another word Dahyoor wheeled his horse about and rode in the direction of Loncastel keep.

"*I have seen this,*" Turley mocked Prentice when the fey squire was gone. "You kenned their speaking while you were off in the west, did yah?"

"Enough to give a few instructions."

"Useful skill, in some spots, I guess." Turley gave the notion a thoughtful frown.

"Be more useful if they got themselves together and came with a company or two to aid us," Prentice said absently, most of his attention on Wilforn and the murder.

"Springtime, you said?" Turley asked.

"That is what they told me."

"And they always keep their word?"

"So far." Prentice tasted the metallic tang of the blood in the air as the corpse was finally dropped to the cobbles. The men with the grim cleanup duty paused to let him look it over, but he felt no need to be too attentive, only giving it a swift examination for arcane words marked in the flesh or onto paper or cloth. When he was satisfied there were none, he told the line first to have the body wrapped and delivered to Earlsbastion.

"If they will not answer your knock, leave it on the doorstep."

"What now?" Turley asked as the body was hauled away.

"If he was not killed here, the deed was done elsewhere—but where?"

"Somewhere they had space and time to cut his gizzards out without folks hearin' too much, if I had to guess."

They certainly made him suffer before they let him pass over into the afterlife, Prentice thought. Wilforn's dead face was a twisted rictus of agony. The jaw was bruised and swollen, but Prentice would lay odds not from any blows of fist or weapon. The squire had clenched his jaw in pain for so long as he died that it had injured the very flesh of the muscles. Even in death his mouth was locked tight against his last screams. Prentice knew the feeling.

"Any idea where they could'a hidden him?" Turley prompted as Prentice moved slowly to the corner of the tavern to look down the alley at its side.

"None."

The alley was open enough that determined men could carry a body down it, even in the dark. There was no way they could have tortured him there, though. The hammering of spikes might have raised no witnesses but groans and screams surely would have.

"It's a real head scratcher, Baron Ash," Turley said. "What's all that fancy learnin' o' yours tellin' you?"

Prentice looked up and down the road one more time. At the northeast end was Loncastel keep with its garrison. The road turned south at the tavern, which was always full of militiamen at their rest between their garrison duties. Southward, the road crossed the first of the great bridges, with its own guards still in place since the first night of the invasion. It was all but impossible that Wilforn could have been brought up the road from either direction without being seen by someone of the banner companies. Prentice turned his face up to the rooftops. The Dog's Leg was apart from the buildings on either side, and the gap was not one that could be easily jumped—especially not with a dead body in tow.

"Unless they flew, they have to have brought the body here by the river, either down that alley or one of the others nearby along the street." He waved at the other openings and tiny passageways into the rabbit warren of paths off the main street. It was the same between every major Bridgetown thoroughfare and whatever waterside docklands were nearby.

"So, we go down to the river now, right?" Turley pressed. "Unless you're full well serious 'bout 'em flying."

He scanned the dark sky above as if he expected harpies or some similar monsters to descend at that very moment. Prentice chuckled.

"If the Bluebird or his ilk can actually fly, we have a whole new set of problems I do not want to even contemplate," he said, shaking his head. "And there is no point heading to the docks. They carried him in a boat on the waters of Bridgetown in the night. We would have as much chance picking one specific fly from a swarm over a midden as the one boat out of so many."

"Ergh, what a fine thought," Turley said, poking out his tongue as if the very idea left a bad taste in his mouth. Prentice nodded southward and they set off back into the main of the town, contemplating the horrific murder and its implications. He did not want to report yet another failure to his liege. Already the contemptuous crowd of voices were whispering at the misty edges of his thoughts.

"Look at all these folks' houses stacked in on one another like a pile of firewood," Turley said. "In on top o' one another. Hard to ken that not one heard anythin'."

More likely that any who did are scared to say, Prentice thought, knowing that willful deafness was more likely than simply not hearing. He had lived too many years as a convict to expect a frightened witness to speak up merely because they were asked.

"You know, one of the boat polers that brought our cargo in the other day told me a saying they have here," Turley continued his musing. "They say, 'What's whispered under one bridge is heard under them all.'" Just a pity this Wilforn fellow's murderers never said nothin', hmm?"

"A secret cannot be kept long amongst so many others; that is what it means," Prentice told him, stepping around a pile of wet dung in the street, complete with flies, as if left there to illustrate the knight commander's previous point. Now it was Prentice's turn to receive one of his friend's annoyed expressions.

"I'm not addlepated for all I'm important and noble now, you know," Turley protested. "All I'm saying is that since it's so hard with so many folks in close, maybe these sneaking bird fellows have special quietenin' magicks too. Could they do that, d'you say? Your fey friends from the mountains can ride about like ghosts in the night. What if the Inquisition know the trick as well?"

Prentice stopped in his tracks, and when Turley turned to face him, he gave the knight castellan a canny smile.

"I think I know where they took him," he said.

"You mean I was right 'bout silencing magick?" Turley asked, and Prentice cocked his head before shaking it outright with another smile.

"No. Not in the slightest."

He slapped Turley happily on his good arm and then headed off with a fresh spring in his step. In truth, he had no reason to know one way or another if Bluebird had supernatural stealth in his toolkit, but it did not matter if his current intuition was correct. Hiding and keeping silent would be too difficult and relying on intimidation to keep everyone willfully blind and deaf was a pointless quest in a place like Bridgetown. Even terrified gossips would struggle to resist the temptation eventually. But almost no stealth at all would be necessary if everyone who heard you about your business thought you were something else entirely.

"So where are we going?" Turley asked as he followed Prentice onto the impossibly sturdy stonework of the first great bridge.

"We are going to find ourselves some ghosts."

CHAPTER 47

Moanings and groanings had been heard in Vespers Remembered. The rumor was already well about the town. The long-dead, loyal nuns were said to have returned from the grave, stirred up by the horrible crimes committed against and by the earldom. A haunted place, surrounded by wealthy folk who locked their park up and kept the riffraff out. Not exactly ideal for torture, but in all likelihood the best place Bridgetown had to offer. After all, gossip or no, what patrician wanted to admit they were frightened of noises in the night?

"You figure this'll be the place they brought him?" Turley asked as he mounted the stairs to the Bell's Hummock park behind Prentice.

"It is what I can think of," the knight commander told his friend. The hope that they would be able to resolve the murder so swiftly had been helping keep the inner voices down, but he was now feeling uncertainty grow as he realized that going inside meant drawing close to his father once more. Was the man still living, or was he now one of the ghosts that groaned in the night? Prentice would not put it past the bitter old man to cling on beyond death, cursing in the night watches. He reached the barred iron gate and found it locked again.

"Gatekeep! Open up," he called out. From nearby, an elderly man in a faded tunic and winingas leg wraps entwined around his lower trews stepped into view, peering through the bars.

"What you want?" he demanded.

"If you have the gate duty today, open up for us, good man."

"I have the gate duty, and I open it to those as are permitted," the man argued. "That's folk I know to see. I don't know you. Go your way. This is a patrician's park, not the garden at the back of a taphouse where you can take a slash."

"We are not looking to use the garden at all," Prentice said. "I need to go to Vespers Remembered. My brother rooms there with my father."

"Ain't no Reachermen roomin' here!" the gate keeper declared. "Be off with you."

Prentice sighed in frustration. "Fetch the other gateman," he said, "and he will tell you who I am."

"What other gateman?"

Prentice was about to describe the burly watchman in mail he had met the previous time, but Turley pushed forward impatiently.

"Look old man, open this gate in the name of the Archduchess of the Western Reach or else we'll go straight back to the bridge garrison and fetch up some right nasty fellows. They'll come, break down this silly gate and drag you off in fetters. You'll end your days on a chain up in Dweltford, digging ditches and sleeping on straw in a filthy barn. You want that?"

The elderly man scowled at Turley a moment, then turned up his lip and shrugged. Pulling a key, he unlocked the gate and stepped back as if the pair of them were dangerous animals. Turley gave the man a smile and a benign nod as they passed. When he and Prentice's eyes met, the roguish ex-convict was all charm.

"What? You and me been spoken to like that enough times. Must be 'bout our turn to throw some weight around."

Prentice only shook his head. He led the way around to the Vespers' door. Once inside, he looked to the lamp niche on the wall but found it had only a tallow candle and some half-burnt rushlights.

"How we going to light these?" Turley asked.

"Go ask your friend. I will look about in the meantime."

Turley went searching for the gatekeeper, leaving Prentice to investigate the former cloister's ground floor hall by no more than the grey winter light coming in through the door. Even his careful footsteps echoed in the dark space, and when it blew by the door the outside wind took on a hollow, howling quality that might easily pass for ghostly moaning to a superstitious ear. Slowly he made his way toward the far wall with its golden bear. He heard rather than saw the wetness of the ancient flagstones under his footfalls, but his nose told him it was not water. The telltale smell of blood and the buzz of unseen flies revealed this was the place Wilforn had been brought to see to his demise.

Xavoer has our father rooming directly above Bluebird's nest? The coincidence was too fantastical to Prentice's mind. Were his brother and father still doing the Inquisition's bidding as they had the day they disowned him? Xavoer had come to Bridgetown originally in the company of Revered Master Faldmoor, who was supposedly an enemy of the Inquisition. Increasingly, Prentice was growing to doubt that as well. Whatever side he was on, Faldmoor was certainly an enemy of the archduchess. He had been instrumental in driving Cassian to his fatal duel with Prentice. It was also in keeping with the nature of the Inquisition that they might be manipulating all sides of the civil war equally, as if every man and woman of the Grand Kingdom was their secret servant.

Silent puppeteers? Prentice wondered and tried to imagine what cause could motivate them to create such conflict, or at least to keep it driving forward.

Turley arrived with the gatekeeper and a lit candle. Even in the limited glow, the congealed red on the floor was obvious—crimson thickening to rust and black. From the size of the spray and pooling, Prentice was willing to guess only one man died here, exactly as gruesomely as Wilforn looked on the wall of the Dog's Leg.

"A right charnel house, eh?" Turley muttered, tutting at the remnant evidence of the crime. "Looks like where he found his end alright."

"What in God's name is this?" the gatekeep breathed, plainly shocked by the sight.

"The work of your ghosts in the night," Prentice told him. "You did not truly think it was dead nuns making all the moans, did you?"

The old man shook his head, and his brow furrowed in confusion.

"They been stirred up an' all, but not to this," he muttered and bowed his head as if in prayer. "Saints preserve us, let the tormented sisters not turn harridans on us."

"Fear not—this was the work of the living," Prentice said.

"And they sure weren't no saints," Turley added.

By the location of the blood pools, the murder had been performed almost exactly in front of the ancient heraldry on the wall, and as the candlelight glimmered in the dark, Prentice caught the painting in the corner of his eye. He had expected it to come into sight, but it was not as it should be.

"This way," he commanded the gateman, pointing the short distance to the back wall. The elder watchman started forward and immediately stopped, eyes on the defiled floor. Still prayerfully nodding his head, he made a point of skirting a broad circle around the murder site.

"Got to keep your feet clean, I guess," Turley said and scoffed dismissively. More likely the fellow felt a superstitious fear of the blood. Prentice did not care, only impatient for the light. As the candle moved away and then drew near to the wall once more, it became clear that the ancient bear was almost gone. None of the bright gold remained, and even the image itself was faded almost into the plaster.

"What happened to this?" he asked the gatekeep.

"What mean you?" the man demanded in return. "What happened to what?"

"The heraldry. The ancient bear icon. What happened to it?" Prentice pointed to the wall and the faded, dirty mural.

"It got old. What do you think happened?"

"But it is kept fresh by the folk of Bell's Hummock. A point of heritage for the patricians."

"Who told you that?" the gatekeep asked, looking at Prentice as if he were mad.

"The other gatekeeper, the burly one in the bright mail," Prentice insisted. "And besides, I saw it with my own eyes."

"When?"

"Not half a season past. I came here to visit my brother and...and my father."

The older man stared up at Prentice a long moment and then looked to Turley. The taller man shrugged.

"Don't look at me," Turley told him. "He's doin' the talkin'!"

"But he ain't making sense." The gatekeep turned back to Prentice and tugged his forelock. "Truly beggin' your pardon, My Lord, but that's the God's honest right of it. Ain't no one maintained this picture in...well ever. Folk hardly e'en come in here. The sisters haunt the place. We hear 'em in the night."

Prentice listened to the man's earnest protests for only a moment before he lost patience.

"Enough," he commanded, holding up his hand. "If no one comes in here, then what are these?"

He led the way toward the nearest of the brick pillars where he knew the fresh iron rings had been installed. The candlelight followed him hesitantly. At the first pillar the metal fixing was gone, but there was a clear hole where it had been broken free, brick and mortar cracked to release it. Puzzled, Prentice moved on to the next pillar and there, at least, he found a ring. He half expected to see it rusted and ancient, as if his first visit to Vespers Remembered had somehow reached across into the past, but the iron there was freshly forged, still black and uncorroded.

"What about that?" he demanded of the gatekeep. The fellow scratched his head.

"Never noticed that before," he muttered.

"Because it's not been there long!" Prentice insisted. He grabbed the man by his shoulder and pointed at the iron fixture in the brick. "Not more than a year—less given there is no rust of any kind upon it."

"If you say so, My Lord," the man said plaintively.

"There was another back there, and there are, or were, two more on the far wall."

The increasingly confused yeoman shook his head at Prentice's words. He had no answers other than what he had given, or else that was what he wanted the knight commander to believe. Prentice could not tell which was which, and he felt a growing frustration at the insanity of the situation. Did the fellow really expect him to deny the truth of his own eyes and memory? Whatever had happened to the bear since his last visit, it had been there, just as he remembered. The rings were in place as well. What kind of game was Bluebird playing at and how far into it was this one? He turned the older man around in his grip and shook him, free hand on the hilt of his sword.

"Are you a skin thief?" he demanded of the terrified-looking yeoman. "Is that the game? Reveal yourself, viper. I will find you out!"

"I ain't!" the gatekeep protested in either genuine or perfectly feigned terror. He tugged at his forelock desperately. "I don't e'en know what that is! I truly don't!"

"Liar!" Prentice shouted, not at full volume but loud enough to echo around the ancient cloister hall. He switched his grip from the man's shoulder to his throat and drove him against the wall so that his head struck the brick, hard. Drawing his sword, Prentice held the edge near to the man's wrinkled throat. The gatekeep whimpered in terror, continually tugging his forelock in the universal gesture of peasant respect and apology. The yeomanry always knew the safest course was to apologize to an enraged nobleman, even if they had no idea what they were supposed to have done wrong.

"Prentice?" Turley asked from behind them. "Are we throwin' our weight around after all? Only this seems like a lot o' weight to throw, is all."

Prentice looked back at his friend and realized how he must appear, holding a drawn warblade on a frail old watchman who likely hadn't been in any kind of fight for a decade or more. He must look as if he had gone mad, but the reality around him no longer fit. He felt sure Turley would still back him, no matter what he did now, but it was clear from his friend's expression that he did not understand what Prentice was about.

"I have not taken leave of my senses, I promise," he told his oldest friend. "Come on, let's go upstairs and I will prove it!"

"What's upstairs?" Turley asked.

"We will go ask the residents." Keeping hold on the old man, Prentice started toward the door to the upper floors. "Our timeworn watchman here might have heard nothing, but what do you bet we cannot find one who will testify of the extra ghostly noises."

"There are no residents," the gatekeep said, his voice cracking in plain terror. "No one lives here. It's haunted. You said it yourself."

"Enough!" Prentice bellowed at the man. "My brother Xavoer keeps rooms here and my father has spent his final days abed here. I spoke with him when I came last time!"

With the single candle guttering from rough handling, Prentice dragged the gatekeep through the door and up the stairs. Turley came behind, saying nothing.

CHAPTER 48

"I said so," the gatekeep told them as they stood outside the door to the rooms where Prentice had met his dying father.

It was shut and, when Prentice demanded a key, the watchman protested that he had none. No one had, he insisted, and when the knight commander shook his head in disbelief, the elderly yeoman pointed out that even if did have, the door itself was nailed shut. Prentice shoved his weight against it and the portal moved not a whit.

"What is all this?" he muttered. The whisper of the hateful chorus of voices in his mind was a susurration under his confused thoughts. Like the flow of a stream, he could hear it, but it was faded into the background. Instead, a fresh anger was demanding to be vented.

He's a liar; a skin thief! Slay him and be done with his evil in the world.

The pressure was almost overwhelming, so much like the fury that had tried to drive him to slaughter his dying father the last time he was here, if his father had even been here. Staring at the sealed portal, Prentice was beginning to doubt even his own memories. He felt a tremor through his limbs and the whispers began to speak of doubting—doubting his self-control.

"Take him," he said, thrusting the old man into Turley's grip before the inward motivations drove him to a foul crime.

"I'm sorry, My Lord, I promise," the fellow continued to plead, clearly sounding like a man begging for his life in the face of a ruthless murderer.

A skin thief! Put an end to him before he harms the archduchess some new way.

"Please, it's clear you been here before. I was wrong to doubt you," the gatekeep continued to implore them both, looking up over his shoulder at Turley, who was holding him by both arms, then back at Prentice. "But it's all haunted, all the way to the top. Haunted and cursed. Master Foxman, the old merchant, used to use the attics at the top to store his cloth when I was a boy, but the roof fell in, and everythin' spoiled with mildew. And that was 'fore I e'en got married. I swear, honest and true, ain't no one lived in the Vespers since then. Folks want to knock it down, save no one wants to pay the cost, and they all argue over who would get to buy the land after it."

Prentice listened to the man's tale while the suspicious voices within him insisted it was all just a perfectly performed ruse. After all, what better actors in the world would there be than Inquisition skin thieves, whose entire lives were an act, one false identity after another? He looked over the trembling fellow's head to Turley, who continued to hold him prisoner, watching Prentice with an utterly po-faced expression. In any other person there would be nothing to see there, but when compared to Turley's usual happy-go-lucky demeanor, the stern countenance spoke volumes. The knight castellan and former convict was deeply uncomfortable with how close he knew they were coming to killing an old man.

Telling, Prentice thought, recognizing the uncomfortable and yet loyal support in his friend. Tells—the entire of Archduchess Amelia's court were seeking the tells that would reveal a skin thief amongst their friends. What tells could he find in a face he had never seen before?

Kill him! Do it now! Right or wrong, it is the safest course! He is old, too. If you are mistaken, you take not so much from him.

"The hell with that!" Prentice muttered in response to the utterly heartless reasoning that tried to drive him to the deed. Turley cocked an eyebrow and Prentice lowered his head, sighing heavily.

"Leave us the candle, gatekeep, and go. Go now!" he told the man, and a moment later he heard the rushed footfalls on the wooden stairs. Prentice hung his head for a long while and Turley said nothing, politely holding the candle for them both. Prentice had an idle thought that the thing might burn down and leave them in the dark if he stood there too much longer, and it made him snort in amused derision.

"Are you sure it was this one?" Turley asked, clearly trying to sound supportive. "Maybe it was another and you don't have the memory quite right. We could check on the other floors."

Prentice sighed again, raising his head and looking past his friend to the other door off this hallway, which they had passed to reach "Xavoer's rooms." He could not see in the poor light, but he had no doubt that it would be nailed shut as well. All the rooms would be, he was sure.

Did I even meet my father? he wondered. The whole incident could have been a moment of madness. *Except my brother did send me that note with this address. Farringdon was there when I received it. I did not imagine that much, at least.*

"There is nothing more here for us," he told Turley. "Let's just go now."

Turley accepted the instruction and led the way back down the stairs to the cloister hall. As they walked into the open space, Prentice paused to glance one last time at the muraled wall and the blood on the floor. He half expected the flagstones to have become clean and perfect in the time they had been upstairs, but the flat surfaces were still stained with their gore. It looked as if in his haste to leave, the gatekeeper had run straight through the center of the puddles and left a trail of bloody footprints to the distant exit.

I suppose a madman's drawn sword is a more imminent terror than the threat of a murdered ghost's curse, Prentice thought, sneering inwardly at his behavior. Threatening the elderly and low-born? What a true Grand Kingdom nobleman he was becoming.

There was a metal clank and Turley cursed as he tripped over something, nearly losing the candle in the process. The flame threatened to gutter again, but when it returned to its strength, he held it closer to the ground to see what had caught his toe. It was a length of chain, laid across the floor and trailing off into the shadows. A quick investigation showed that it was anchored to one of the other iron rings, still in place. The chain was as fresh forged as the ring.

"Well, we both know what this kind o' thing is for," Turley said, and Prentice nodded distractedly, hardly registering in the midst of his regret and confusion. "Obvious though. You'd think they'd have to chain him up to do what was done to him."

That was true enough. No one vivisected a living man as Wilforn had been without making sure the victim was securely fastened in place. Prentice remembered the times he had seen it done. The escaped convict during the Fallenhill siege and the fey victims of the Serpent Witch *imzuss* at the headwaters of the Murr came back most vividly in his thoughts.

"Odd they had him chained here though, if they killed him over there," Turley mused as he looked back and forth from the short length of chain to the blood stains.

"Perhaps they needed to hold him in place while they readied their tools," Prentice said, barely interested.

"Then how'd they hold him there? And why drag him that far if you already had him in place?"

Prentice recognized the sense of his friend's questions, but the pressure of his need to leave this mad place made it hard for him to sort any meaning from it in his thoughts.

"It's a bit of a mystery, ain't it?" Turley asked, sounding as if he was genuinely musing on the question.

"Perhaps," Prentice acknowledged, but he still turned to the door and headed out into the fading light of the winter's afternoon. He had found where Wilforn had been murdered and right quickly, but all that did was offer a new swathe of mysteries.

And I am thoroughly sick of mysteries, he thought. Outside, they found the gate left open, but the gatekeep was nowhere in sight. That, at least, was no mystery—Prentice was sure the poor old man was hiding lest he draw the fresh ire of the mad baron from the Western Reach. It wasn't until he was down on the dockside again that he realized he still had his drawn sword clutched tightly in his hand.

Just like last time, assuming I am remembering aright and am not as mad as I seem.

CHAPTER 49

Upon returning to camp in the late afternoon, the knight commander sent a short, written account of what he had found by messenger to Paramour's. He could have delivered the news in person, but it felt so pointless that he did not want to waste the effort, or his liege's time. Instead, he ate an early dinner of camp bread and stewed lamb with turnips and onions, then readied himself for another training session. He was of a mind to work himself hard this evening to purge the crazed thoughts from his head.

I would dearly love to see Righteous and the children a moment, he thought, *but I would not want* them *to see me like this. In the morning, when my mind is more settled.*

A quiet, rational part of his thoughts noted that they were seeing less and less of him of late, and Righteous was unlikely to be greatly overwhelmed by his emotions at any rate. She was hardly a stranger to his fury, after all.

If I would not let it fall on my father, then I must keep her and the babes all the safer from it, he told himself.

The evening watch beat was sounding through the camp, and Prentice was returning from washing out his plate and bowl like any other member of the banner companies. As he approached, he saw a young militiaman standing outside the training shed, and drawing closer, realized it was Solomon. It cheered him, and seeing the lad in his buffcoat and kettle helmet made Prentice feel a moment of pride. He was still a skinny youth, a good distance from his full manhood but so clearly on the path in that direction. After that pleasant moment, an almost equally strong displeasing notion whipped out of the tormented fringes of Prentice's thoughts—why was the lad here? Had he come to complain? To prevail upon his close relationship with the knight commander for some favor or another? In an instant, Prentice's image of Solomon threatened to transform into that of a venal child, like Wilforn or Cyprian, entitled and selfish. The knight commander shook his head, just hoping to shake the unjust image loose. If there was a more loyal man than Solomon in all the Lions, Prentice had never met him. He forced his frayed mind to remember that fact, at least.

"Militiaman?" Prentice addressed Solomon when he reached the shed door. The young man straightened himself and saluted.

"Knight Commander. May I speak with you, My Lord?"

Prentice nodded warily and then returned the salute.

"On what matter?" he asked. If Solomon was asking permission to speak, he was not here on White Lions' business, which meant he was asking for himself.

Please God, do not let him be seeking a favor, Prentice thought, sure that the anger inside himself that he was struggling to hold in check might burst forth on the lad if he did ask for some special treatment.

"If it please you, My Lord," Solomon began, and Prentice was struck by the young man's good manners. His one summer serving Lady Righteous and the archduchess's chamber had taught him no small amount of etiquette, it seemed. "I have heard that you have put the word about for men to wrestle and fight with in the evenings. A training discipline, they are saying."

"I have," Prentice told him.

"Can I...that is, is it alright, My Lord...if I put my hand up for the duty?"

Discipline? Duty? Prentice thought, considering Solomon's words—not the things privileged folk often desired. Still, his suspicious mind wondered if the lad was thinking past the initial burden to later reward. After all, knights suffered brutal levels of training for the promise of glory and power.

"I put the call out for skilled militiamen who could test me, Solomon," Prentice told him. "I am not giving lessons. And do not take this amiss, but you are not of a skill or size to put me to the test."

"I know that, My Lord. But I heard that you were moved on to pole and blade sparring as well, and I figured a short blade is something I know fair well competently. I kenned that I could spar you with dagger or even fang and shield. I'm not you or the baroness, but if you need opponents for a two-on-one or three-on-one, I could fill out the numbers. Even if you'd just let me watch, I'd full value the chance, I swear Knight Commander."

He begs and pleads, Prentice's father's voice sneered, but the response was ready in his thoughts. He might suffer his father's contempt for himself, but Prentice refused to let the old ghost's hate fall on this earnest and loyal youth. Whatever his father's disappointments, they were Prentice's burden to carry, not Solomon's.

He seeks the best place within the banner company that he can make for himself. It is no more or less than I did at his age, and he does a good sight better job of it than I did.

Seeing his youthful self reflected in Solomon's image for a moment, and then even better than himself, Prentice's pride swelled deeper and more powerfully than ever before. The rising water of it momentarily doused any fires of hate or bitterness that might have been arising from the edges of his thoughts. Like a fountain flooding out of a besieged castle, for a moment Prentice felt like his old self, the man who deserved to be called Knight Commander.

"Show me your poniard," he told Solomon, and without hesitation, the young militiaman drew it forth and offered it handle-first. The sun had all but sunk behind the grey clouds, but there was enough light from nearby cookfires for Prentice to see the dagger was being kept in fine order, no signs of corrosion, and his thumb across the edge showed that it was sharp without being over-sharpened. He returned the blade and Solomon resheathed it.

"Show me your helmet," Prentice told him next, and in a trice it was off the lad's head and being offered. Prentice took it and looked it over. It was properly polished, the steel shining. "You are looking after it."

Solomon took the statement as a question. "I use good, fine sand and vinegar when I can get it," he reported. "Polishes up sweet. Course, when I can't, I use the other, but I don't like that so much cause the smell can get in the cap."

Prentice did not need to see Solomon's sour grimace to know what the "other" was. Vinegar and sand were the preferred method to polish steel the world over, but when eight thousand men demanded the sour liquid, the whole of Bridgetown would not supply enough. So, as the squires of poor knights all learned the world over, the next best thing was their own urine. All but the wealthiest of peers knew what it was to have had the stench of their own water on their hands when they had done their stints as squires. Prentice turned the helmet over and looked inside.

"You have glued your arming cap in place?" he asked, poking at the quilted lining, which would normally be worn as a hood under the steel, cushioning the head as an arming doublet cushioned the body against mail or plates.

"My line first told me to do it, My Lord," Solomon replied without any sense of defensiveness—just a competent man speaking of the why of his actions. "The entire cohort does. Makes it easier to put our helmets on swift like. We aren't knights with squires to help us tie every piece in place. Militiamen need to be ready to hop to it."

Prentice nodded, liking the sound of that wisdom, and he poked at the quilting inside the helmet. With that in place, it was obvious why Solomon would not want to use his own urine to polish the steel—the stink would soak the cloth without a doubt.

Anywhere the glue was it should also act like a waterproof layer of lacquer at any rate, further protecting the metal.

"What does your line first say about you being here?" Prentice asked last of all as he returned the head protection. "Or have you not told him?"

"Asked him first afore anything else, My Lord," Solomon reported. "He's given me from dinner beat to the hour before midnight watch. I'm to make sure I eat first and be back to my bedroll for a full sleep, I have the dawn watch patrol."

"Why is that? Punishment duty?"

"No, My Lord! The line first has us out to march and drill early every day and I...he wants me to show them all what I learned from you and the baroness." Solomon paused, and for the first time his expression grew hesitant. "Thing is, I figure I need to come back and learn some more, or I'll run out of tricks to share."

"Tricks?" Prentice asked archly but managed to hold his tongue beyond that so one of the memory instructors did not rush from the fringes of his thoughts to give some pointless, harsh rebuke.

We do not do tricks, a voice he hardly remembered sounded from some cold place in his past. *The blade is an art, and every true technique is worthy of respect. Tricks are for tumblers and market day mummers. Try to do tricks on a true man-at-arms and you will awaken to see the Almighty laughing at your folly on Judgement Day.*

"How does your line first feel about you showing them tricks?" he asked instead. "Do any of the others object to being shown by the youngest in the line?"

"One did," Solomon said simply.

"And what happened when he did?"

"He ended up on his backside in the mud," Solomon replied matter-of-factly, no boasting or even much pride in his tone. "After he gave me a black eye, though."

"Did you make an enemy?" Prentice asked, now curious about the tale.

"Don't think so, My Lord. He's the one always asks first to be shown another trick nowadays. Bloke's name is Bradley. Comes from round Griffith, so he says. About my size but too used to doing it all with his arms alone. Doesn't move his feet enough. If I'm not careful, he'll be putting me on the ground soon, though. He still doesn't like that I'm so young, and I figure he's of a mind to pay me back, but I don't think he's bitter about it."

Prentice stared long at Solomon as the lad put his helmet back in place. A smile split the knight commander's lips, and he nodded.

"Well, militiaman, it seems to me that you have everything in its rightful place. Come inside and warm up with me while we wait for any others."

"Thank you, My Lord," Solomon said with another salute, and he stepped aside to wait for Prentice to lead him inside. No sooner had the knight commander put his hand on the latch however, than another voice called his name.

CHAPTER 50

"I have some healers for you, My Lord," Whilte said to Prentice as he followed the knight commander and Solomon into the shed. "But you must come with me to meet them now."

"Now?" Prentice asked.

"This very night, even right now."

"Why the rush?"

"Because they have only bribed the patrols for the first half of the night," Whilte told him earnestly. As if he read Prentice's confusion from his expression, the chaplain added, "I only received their word myself this hour."

"Why are they bribing our patrols?" Prentice asked, but even as he did so, he realized his mistake. The brother's answer only confirmed it for him.

"Not our patrols, Prentice. Patrols across the river."

"They are amongst the Usurper's army?" the knight commander demanded, incredulous that Whilte might be in contact with servants of the enemy. How had he even achieved it? For a town besieged, Bridgetown seemed to have more holes than a fishing net.

"They are not crossing from the north bank," Whilte explained, "but from the south."

"The south? They are coming from the Vec?" To Prentice's mind that was virtually as bad and just as vulnerable to treachery. "What have you been saying to these supposed healers from the

Vec? Surely you are not fool enough to trust our hopes to our enemy."

"Have I ever been disloyal since I repented?" Whilte demanded in a low voice, not angry exactly, but grim, nonetheless.

It is a ruse, a trap, Prentice's inner chorus all said, his father's sour contempt one voice with his instructors' iron-willed judgementalism. Even the remembered voices of his Academy instructors were there now. *He still hates you and wants revenge for his brother, after all.*

It was paranoid rubbish—Whilte had suffered too much and forfeited too many easier chances for revenge for this to be part of some long-planned conspiracy. And still Prentice could not fully quiet the whispers in his mind.

"And where would we meet our enemies for this conference?" he forced himself to ask. His eyes flicked to Solomon who was off to one side, examining the various weapons and practice tools that Prentice had hanging from the shed's old wall pegs. "Am I to go through the Sougate postern and meet them in the earthworks?"

It would be a bold ambush to try to spring if it was at the foot of the bastion, but in the dark of a winter's night, with even the Rampart hidden behind clouds, it might be possible. Whilte's answer surprised Prentice further, however.

"Sougate is too closely watched by the Golden Heron's guards. Our friends want to meet us on Follybridge."

"Follybridge?"

The tiny island of Follybridge lay off the eastern end of Greenmarsh. Little more than a rocky outcrop in the flow of the Murr, barren and uninhabited, the story Prentice had heard was that it took its name from a failed plan of a long past group of Conclave selectmen. They had conceived the notion to use it to build a second bridge from the town to the Veckander side of the river, hoping to open up another path for trade—a path for which they could charge their own tolls. So taken had they been with the notion, they had purchased much of the initial lumber and had it transported to the island before they even paused to consider how the then earl might react to the plan. Once the liege of Bridgetown was informed, the guildsmen's compact found themselves swiftly imprisoned for treason and the island declared forbidden for any Bridgetowner to even visit. The bridge was never built past the initial few pylons, and the lumber was left to rot. The Conclave member's naivety was commemorated in the island's new name—Follybridge.

"I understand your doubt, Knight Commander," Brother Whilte said earnestly, switching from Prentice's name to his title. "But you and the archduchess commanded me to find healers ready to help us, and the only ones hereabouts not in hiding or offering their service to the Denay army are in the Vec. I have spoken with them already and they are in earnest, but they must meet you first. They have to explain their terms."

Terms? Prentice thought, his mind running to catch up with all the new developments being revealed. What terms could men from the Vec have for him? *They are healers—of course they would have terms for a service like this.*

Prentice studied Whilte's face, hoping to search out anything not yet said. Tells and more tells. He looked down at the chaplain's wooden leg. Could a skin thief transform his foot to look like a prosthesis? Or would one be loyal enough to his masters to cut off his foot for the ruse? After his experience this afternoon in Vespers Remembered, almost nothing seemed too fantastical to Prentice's mind. He considered it all for a long moment, knowing that the safest decision would be to simply dismiss the entire notion. But safety was not what his liege required of him.

"What if I do not go alone?" he asked. "What if we set cohorts upon Follybridge and Roar on the shore of Greenmarsh for safety?"

"Then they will never cross the river," Whilte answered sourly. "They will see it all and abandon the whole plan. And I will have no hope of winning them or any other healers to her grace's cause. Not after I betray them like that."

Prentice nodded. That all made sense.

"So, I can bring no one with me?"

"No, My Lord. Just you and me. That is one of their stipulations."

Only one? Prentice thought and this time did nothing to keep himself from the bitterness. He did not like being dictated to, but the seller had the right to set the price, especially if the buyer was desperate, and right now Prentice was more than a little desperate. He, the archduchess, and the two banner companies—it was desperation that covered them all in its blanket. Just looking at Whilte, it was clear the chaplain healer was ragged with exhaustion, dark circles under his eyes, cheeks drawn and pinched beneath his beard. Never mind a reputation for miracles, just looking at the man it was a miracle he was still standing.

"I will not go unarmed," he said bluntly, and Whilte smiled wanly at that.

"They expected as much and agreed."

"I suppose you already have a boat for us?" Prentice asked, and Whilte nodded at that, too. The knight commander sighed heavily. Fighting off a night ambush on a wet rock in the river—that would be a more demanding training session than even his most severe inner teacher would have demanded. "Alright."

Whilte turned for the door immediately and Prentice suspected the cleric did not want to give him any time to change his mind. Not that he would. Whilte was correct. For the chance of providing the White Lions with more healers, he must take this risk. His liege required it of him.

"Can I help, My Lord?" Solomon asked, and Prentice smiled at the young man.

"You heard the chaplain, militiaman. Only I can go."

Solomon nodded, then looked to one of the pegs on the wall.

"I can load those pistols for you," he said.

"You know the knack?"

"Corporal Lyrach showed me."

"When?" Prentice asked.

"I get chances some days to practice riding, and Lyrach is there sometimes. He showed me the weapons and some things for the saddle. He says I'm becoming competent."

"With the matchlocks or horsemanship?"

"With the saddle," Solomon admitted sheepishly. "I could hardly hit the side of this shed when I'm riding past, shooting. I know how to load them right well, though."

Prentice was not surprised. He hadn't tried firing from the saddle yet and only rated himself a lackluster shot when standing dead still. He was able to hit a fang's round shield on the back wall of the shed from the door, but beyond that distance, he did not favor himself at all. Even so, the two pistols would be a useful addition to his options if this night trip to Follybridge did turn out to be some kind of snare.

It would not do the Veckanders much good if it is, he thought, taking the belt from the peg and handing first one pistol and then the other to Solomon. *Farringdon commands the defenses in the south and the north now. Taking me out of the way will change the siege not one whit.*

True to his claim, Solomon showed he knew how to load the pistols—powder and shot, wadding to hold it in, and the trigger charge into the wheel. He was nothing like as smooth or adept as a Roarsman with a matchlock, but that was no criticism. They weren't under fire here. Prentice received the pistols back and put them into their holsters. His pride swelled again for a moment, and unable to stop himself, he reached out a hand and put it on Solomon's shoulder, giving it a fatherly grip.

"My thanks, militiaman," he said. When he released his hold, Solomon saluted him again.

"And to you, My Lord."

CHAPTER 51

"This is the best you could find?" Prentice asked, looking down at the tiny coracle Whilte had led them to on one of the eastern docks of Greenmarsh. From where they stood, Prentice could see the fires of Runners Field, seeming so close. The journey had been a long one, however, around from Runners Field, through Oldbridge and the main town, across the great bridges, and ultimately down Greenmarsh to this eastern promontory with its wrecked piers, unrecovered from the first night of the invasion. Of course there was likely a shorter path across the piers and bridges of the channel between the two islands. Despite the Usurper's raiders and the mad bomb-thrower, much of the intricate and haphazard network remained or had been repaired. All the same, Prentice had no intention of risking his safety over that wood on a winter's night. He had endured enough near drownings in the Murr for this season.

"There's only two of us, Prentice, and the water between here and there is full of wreckage from the invaders' boats. Did you want to navigate something larger through those hazards in the dark? Are you that skilled a boatman, because I am not."

Prentice smirked at Whilte's belligerent humility and acknowledged the right of it with a nod. Seeming to almost fall off the dock as he lowered himself into the leather-skinned boat, Whilte grunted and huffed, proving his avowed lack of skill with every moment. His task was made all the more difficult by having to accommodate his prophet's staff, which he ultimately laid across his knees so that the ends poked out over the sides.

"Will you even be able to climb out again?" Prentice teased as he took his turn hopping down. Whilte scoffed, but his face was hidden in the darkness now. When Prentice was settled, they untied the tiny craft and pushed off.

"You know we have no lantern to find our way," the knight commander mused as he took his oar and began to paddle out into the dark water. "We could just as easily miss Follybridge in the night and find ourselves floating down into the remains of the Usurper's supply fleet."

That's his plot, the paranoia whispered. *You'll be in Daven Marcus's hands within the hour.*

Now it was Prentice's turn to scoff in the dark. He doubted the Usurper even knew his name. A plot like this to capture the archduchess? That he might believe. But him? Why bother? He was replaceable, and it was Marquis Farringdon and Archduchess Amelia that Daven Marcus needed to remove from Bridgetown. The irony of his sudden sense of unimportance amused him. His inward tormentors could not despise him as a worthless and discardable failure with one breath and then scare him with farfetched plots to have him captured and killed. If Daven Marcus or the Inquisition wanted Prentice dead, it would have already been accomplished. Whatever else Bluebird knew or wanted, he could surely have found a chance for an assassination by now.

As in my dream, he thought. The blood-covered figure of Sanguine that he remembered, whether it was a real man or a spiritual symbol, did not even know to look for him. The thought so captured Prentice's wearied mind that he almost missed Whilte explaining his plan for them to navigate the short journey across the dark water.

"The lights of the town give us a lot of reflections to see by," the chaplain explained. "And there's all manner of old pier footings, sunken raiders boats, and other such things to watch for. We can follow them like a trail downriver. Once they peter out, we should be able to make the rest by dead reckoning."

Prentice was not fully convinced, but if things went wrong and they missed the rocky outcrop, he was confident they could row for Runners Field. The camp there was visible enough to aim for. As it turned out, all his concerns were unfounded, and with the favorable flow of the river, Whilte brought them up against Follybridge's stones and failed footings in little more than a quarter of a candle. As he clambered out of the coracle, Prentice was reminded of the journey he and Turley had taken across the Murr the night of the Red Sky.

Let us hope this night is more auspicious, he thought and then snorted quietly as he realized that if something like that were to happen now, they would at least be able to see their way across the water.

"Something amuses you?" Whilte whispered, and Prentice shook his head until he realized there would be no way for the chaplain to see the gesture. That drew another derisive chuckle at his own follies, and he began to wonder if he were actually becoming a little mad.

"Where are your friends?" he asked as they tied the boat off to a piece of lumber.

"Around the east side. There's a cleft there that skips use to trade goods, apparently."

Prentice was not surprised to hear that, but he was glad when he realized that the entire southeast edge of Follybridge was actually a narrow, flat section, almost like a path, and easily negotiated even in the dark. He and Whilte were climbing over the only uneven section when they were challenged by a voice and a bared candle that shone behind some larger rocks.

"How come you this far south, man of the north?" was the question that was clearly a call for a password.

"Even the north bank of the Murr is too far south for most northerners," Whilte replied cryptically. From the shadows about the candle, four cloaked figures emerged, and drawn daggers caught glimmers of the flame. "This is the knight commander, as I promised."

Prentice tensed involuntarily and his hand went halfway to his sword hilt. If this was an ambush, that would be the signal. Nothing untoward happened, but for a long moment he watched like an animal that detects a predator, listening for treachery, all senses straining to pierce the darkness.

"Thank you for coming, Baron Knight Commander," one of the newly arrived folk said with a throaty voice. "I am Halleon Lyle, a healer from Barellat, west of Grey Hill. I will not introduce all my companions tonight, but we will name ourselves to you at another time if we settle on terms here. The one fellow with us I will name is Prett, here. He is a free man of Town Sobridge."

The speaker, Halleon Lyle was gesturing to one of the others, but their cloaks all merged in the dark, so Prentice had almost no idea which was the free man Prett. Their faces were masses of shadow, even with the candle.

"Well met, Halleon Lyle, Prett of Sobridge," he told the four shadows. "I am Prentice, called Ash in the Western Reach."

"Not Baron of Fallenhill?" asked Halleon Lyle. "Nor Knight Commander of the Western Reach?" There was a clear tone of surprise in his voice.

"I am those things as well," Prentice said, wondering why this purported healer might care.

"Baron Ash is not given to a love of titles or honors, good men," Whilte told them. "Which is all to our advantage, since if he were to begin to list all that was his to claim, we might well be here until dawn."

"Hmm," was Halleon Lyle's only response, and while it sounded doubtful to Prentice's ears, it was at least not any kind of scoff or dismissal. Was the healer pleased that Prentice had many titles and honors, or glad he did not bother to recite them?

"You the one that's in charge of the gate?" the figure Prentice took for Prett asked in a sour tone.

"I was."

"During the assaults? That was you then, weren't it? You and yours have killed or maimed a lot of my mates," Prett said coldly, as much a statement of fact as an accusation.

"And will again, if they come against the Sougate," Prentice said equally coldly. "Someone else commands, but our liege's instructions for the bastion remain the same."

The night became silent and even more tense for a moment. Prentice wondered why he was trying to antagonize these men. There was no sign this was to be an ambush. Was he so ready for a fight that he would turn it into one? Prett stared with shadowed eyes for a long while.

He hates you, his father's voice sounded in his thoughts, but Prentice had a ready retort.

So do you. So do so many others. More than ever loved me, I would say. Why would this Veckander from Town Sobridge be any different?

Even as he thought that, however, Prentice realized that his claim about those who loved him was possibly not true. In fact, he had to admit that he was making every effort to avoid those he trusted to love him in his life. Why was that?

"The knight commander was only doing what he must," Whilte protested on Prentice's behalf.

"There's a lot of that going around this season," Prett replied.

"Good men, this is not what we're here for," Halleon Lyle said earnestly, and Prentice felt the unseen man holding his hands up for peace.

"Perhaps we should explain to the knight commander why we are here," Whilte said.

"Indeed, what have you told him?"

"Only that there are healers in the Vec willing to sign on to assist the White Lions in the campaign against the Usurper," Prentice interjected, eager to get to the meat of this conference on a river rock in the middle of the night watches.

"That is true," Halleon Lyle agreed. "But did the brother explain our price and terms to you?"

"Not fully. He did make it clear that there would be terms and prices, and precious little negotiation."

"Damn right," said one of the unnamed fellows.

The healer from Barellat sighed heavily, shaking his head as if he doubted the possible success of this meeting as much as Prentice did.

Just how dire are these terms and prices? the knight commander wondered.

Chapter 52

"The men of the Vec are proud of their freedom," the healer began afresh. "They fought with their earls centuries ago to put away the tyranny of the northern thrones and they have never lost that impetus to rule themselves, even against each other."

Prentice recognized the wry aside in that last statement. The earls of the Vec who had become the first princes had acted in concert that one time and then almost never united again, save in exceptionally rare occasions. The princes' wars against each other were almost the defining feature of Vec politics. As a former Vec prince himself, Marquis Farringdon's tales were astonishing at times, even to those who had survived the vicious court politics of the Grand Kingdom.

"Reachermen are of a similar cloth," Prentice admitted, hoping there might be some sense of fraternity to be found between them. He thought he heard Prett snort derisively, but it was a soft sound, if it was really there and not in his imagination.

"From what we hear, your Western Reach is three fourths on the path to your own break from the tyrant's thrones," Halleon Lyle went on. "It encourages us."

"Archduchess Amelia is determined the Reach remain loyal to Denay, once the Usurper is dethroned," Prentice said warily. He had a sudden notion that this was some kind of prelude to trying to draw the Reach into the Vec's Grey Hill compact, and he was certain that his liege would never accept such a prospect, even if the entire Grand Kingdom united against her. The Reach would become its own kingdom—or queendom—long before it joined any more closely with the fractious Vec.

"Her decisions are her own, of course," Halleon Lyle said quickly. "I only note the nearness of our experiences so you might understand what is happening here, south of the Murrflow."

"Murrflow?" Prentice asked. It sounded to him like the noise a cat made.

"It is what Veckanders call the Murr," Whilte explained.

Prentice shook his head. That was something he had not known. "Alright, what is happening that you think we Reachermen would understand?" he asked, forcing his unruly mind to concentrate on the main matter. *You can play curious scholar later,* he chided himself.

"Until a hundred years ago, indenturing for life was unknown amongst the yeomen of the Vec," Halleon Lyle explained. "Then it was permitted in a few princedoms. It spread, and swiftly the freeborn were sold into debts they could not afford, becoming serfs in all but name."

"Extortionate taxes to finance pointless little wars leave all but the most prosperous farmers in endless poverty," Prett said, and Prentice was struck by how educated the man sounded. If he was one of those that threw themselves against Sougate, then this was a peasant levy of the Sunbury prince, yet he spoke like a patrician, and a learned one at that. "'Tis a trap from which we have almost no escape. Now, princes like unto Sunbury capture other city states and levy our folk without remorse. We are thrown at your walls to burn and scald and die, all to preserve the lives of mercenaries that strut about the streets of our towns, taking liberties with our women while we crouch in cold fields, sickening and dying. But for the name, how are we different from your Kingdom rogues?"

"The Reach has no rogues in its army!" Prentice declared reflexively, and he felt a resentment stir within himself. Even with the hardships described, the current state of the Vec levies was not what convicts endured in the Grand Kingdom. All of his sufferings and scars reared up in his mind like a petulant animal, ready to fight to defend his wounded status. It took all his will to force the unhelpful feelings back down. He was not here on his own behalf, and his own pains were irrelevant. Comparing scars and boasting of one's sufferings was for comrades sitting around warm fireplaces in comfortable taverns. It would serve the archduchess nothing to waste time with such things here.

"That we have heard," said the healer, again sounding conciliatory. "It also gives us hope."

"For what?" Prentice demanded bluntly. He could feel his emotions within him pushing him to disrupt this delicate conference, as if the fury and hatred did not know whom to vent itself on and simply demanded the first target close to hand.

And that is why I cannot see my wife and children as much as I might wish to, he reminded himself.

"The time of the princes must end," Prett declared, his voice almost rising above a whisper. The way he spoke the words, they sounded to Prentice like a slogan, a phrase this Veckander yeoman spoke frequently. Suddenly, Prentice realized who he was meeting with. Prett was an assemblist—an agitator pushing for princedoms to cease being hereditary, to become republics, with fully elected governments and officials. Such men envisaged lands ruled by conclave-like "assemblies" or some similar bodies, after the manner of charter towns, with no recourse to a peerage at all. The most extreme even wanted to see peerage abolished outright. No wonder Prentice's reluctance to use his titles had been noted.

"You are agitators," he said, not meaning to sound so accusatory but finding himself no less wary for all that he now better understood their motives. "Even the healers?"

"We are not given to matters of rulership...normally," Halleon Lyle said, and it was clear he felt less than comfortable with this truth. "We typically keep apart, as our gifting requires. But what point healing men who are used worse than dogs only to see them used so again the next day. We have men in the camp across that water whose bodies have been injured and healed so many times that while their limbs are hale, their minds are broken."

He paused, and from the way his cloak moved it was clear he was looking across the water at the dim lights of the Golden Heron's camp. Still facing southward, the healer continued his explanation.

"Like a mule so beaten that it no longer even shies from the goad, these fellows walk about like ghosts amongst the living, neither knowing themselves or others about them. I have knelt over the bodies of brutalized men, the power in my hands working and knowing..."

He paused, and something like a broken sob escaped his lips. He sucked in a steadying breath.

"I have healed them and known that it would have been more merciful to let their wounds take them into the next world."

"More than one of us has mixed a physic into the drink of a man we might have healed and let him go with peaceful sleep," said another of the unintroduced shadows.

"Brother Whilte has known that desperation, I am sure," Prentice told them.

"I have," the chaplain said with a surprised tone. "I wasn't certain you had noticed, My Lord."

"Brother, no man serves the Lions or the Reach with the diligence you do," Prentice said absolutely, his tone making it clear he meant this as a statement of fact, not flattery. "Except perhaps Sacrist Porlain, but he is not with us these days."

There were approving mutters amongst the shadows. Gold was the price of mercenaries, but respect was the currency of veterans. After a season facing unconquerable walls, levies like Prett had the right to call themselves veterans, and they were clearly pleased to see respect being paid here to a healer's work. Prentice could guess from his own experience what life in the Vec camp was like for these men pressed into military service to a conquering prince.

"What do you want from me?" he asked them, realizing that he knew enough now to cut the tale short and begin speaking terms.

"We want you to attack, to sally with a full army, like we saw you do on the north bank against your own tyrant false king," Prett said, apparently equally glad to be getting down to the tacks.

"You want us to forsake our impregnable walls so you may defeat us in the field? That was what the Usurper almost did," Prentice told them archly, not really thinking that was their purpose but trying to show why he would be reluctant to agree to such a thing.

"That's what we want Sunbury to think you're doing," Prett replied easily. "We want the tyrant to imagine you've taken leave of your senses and given him an easier victory."

"You think him fool enough to assume we are fools as well?" Prentice asked.

"Perhaps not," said Halleon, "but he is as venal as the legends of your current king. Excepting the moments when he orders men to their deaths, Everard Prince of Sunbury rests comfortable in a hall in the town. If you attack, he will not even be ready to defend against you."

That did not surprise Prentice either. Just because you made your army suffer in the fields was no reason for a prince to join them if he did not have to. He almost felt a moment of renewed respect for Daven Marcus on his crusade west years before. He, at least, had taken to a tent in the winter. Still legendarily venal in other ways, though, just as Halleon said.

"His mercenary contracts are costing him more than he can afford, not to mention his pledges to his own knights," Prett added. "He feasts them nightly to keep them loyal, pleading with the Heron to stretch more credit out for him, but both bankers and men-at-arms are growing to disbelieve him outright. He needs the plunder of a conquest soon or he's going to have a mutiny on his hands, feasts or no. He'll jump at a pitched battle when he gets word of your march, we swear."

"How does that help you or us?" Prentice asked, suspecting he knew the answer.

"When he arrays and you face him in battle, we'll give him his mutiny. We in the levies will defy him, and together you and we will sweep the despot and his hired men out of Town Sobridge for good."

Prentice stroked his beard. As a strategy it seemed sound, and it could be as decisive as the sudden appearance of the Jerwahl troops had almost been in the battle with Daven Marcus. Assuming the offer was legitimate, of course.

"So, we make ourselves vulnerable, suffer our own losses, all that you may win a battle and overthrow your ruler. Then what? I will have your pledge you will lift the siege at least, I take it? Or is some healers' service all you offer?"

"Actually, it won't be as simple as that," Halleon Lyle admitted, and Prentice could almost hear the man swallow nervously. What else could he be about to demand now for his healing?

It better not be too much, Prentice thought. *This is risk enough you want of us. I doubt her grace will agree even to this much. Add more to your invoice and she will refuse the sale out of hand.*

"I know you understand Vec politics at least well enough to know that toppling the Prince of Sunbury will be of little consequence in itself," the healer said. "The folk of Town Sobridge might defeat him, imprison, or even kill him, but another prince will simply see that as an open invitation. You must have heard that the Earl of Longshepherds is already covetous of his neighbor. His army, such as it is, will be knocking on the town's door the day after Sunbury's overthrow."

Even in the deep shadows Prentice could see the direction this faction of revolutionaries was heading, and the audacity of it was almost breathtaking. As he heard them speaking, he could see the other pieces they were hoping for slotting into place.

"You want us to drive off the Sunbury forces *and* the Golden Heron's mercenaries into the bargain," he said, summing up for them before Lyle or Prett could continue. "Not just from this siege, but all the way out of Sobridge's lands, town and all. Then you want the White Lions to hand power to you, or whatever electoral cabal you envisage, and to remain as your military arm while you consolidate power. For how long? And exactly what would be her grace's advantage in all of this? She already fights her own better judgement looking for reasons not to seize Bridgetown for herself and make it a part of the Reach's domain. Why would she not do it to your lands as well? She already claims Aubrey as her own."

"If she did that, she would prove what we always have suspected south of the Murrflow," Prett retorted. "That the Grand Kingdom is full of the worst tyrants, and even the evils of the princes of Grey Hill are more desirable than the rule of the slaves of Denay and Rhales...*and* Dweltford. We would live to throw her off as we threw off Sunbury."

"*You* won't have thrown off Sunbury," Prentice told him in turn. "We will have.

Despite his fidelity to his liege, Prentice found himself smiling in appreciation of this man Prett and the faction he represented. A large part of Prentice hoped the man truly was a member of a group as strong as he purported to be. He doubted it, though. Peasant rebellions were rarely as powerful as they thought themselves. Yet, how could he not love this earnest, would-be revolutionary. There was so little guile in him. If he was not successful in bringing about the Sunbury prince's overthrow, his own fury at the injustice his people suffered would surely get him into fatal trouble very soon. Prentice knew all too well what it was like to have to carry resentment like that, hiding it from the tyrannical powers that be. He couldn't help but like this fellow he could barely even see in the night.

"I cannot know for certain what her grace will say," he told them, ready now to end this meeting and return to the safety of Greenmarsh. "But she will surely require at least some concessions, not the least of which will be friendship between Town Sobridge and the Western Reach for years to come. Favorable trade and tariffs, space to garrison troops at ready rates, perhaps some other requirements I cannot yet foresee."

"If she will acknowledge our assembly of electors and allow us to govern ourselves freely, there is little we will not concede," Prett said readily, his voice making it sound like he was struggling to keep a leash on his own hope.

"Be warned that a garrison may need to stand for some time," Halleon Lyle interjected, clearly sounding nervous that things might be suddenly progressing too quickly. "Town Sobridge will have no knights or men-at-arms and little opportunity to raise funds to hire them."

"Mercenaries are a blight," Prentice said readily. "You will need your own troops as soon as they may be raised. The White Lions will train them for you."

"As you trained the Bridgetown militia?" one of the anonymous shadows demanded sullenly, and Prentice understood *that* emotion as well. The Bridgetowner militia had perpetrated a vile massacre on the first army of levies that Town Sobridge had fielded for this war, a shameful event that would likely never be forgotten in the Vec province's annals.

"We were brought to Bridgetown on a promise to train the militia here, that is true," Prentice allowed. "But the stiff-necked mongrels in orange and gold have submitted to us not one day for training. I do not even know if they still exist as a force, but ask your fellows who survived that day. It was the Gryphons that pulled them from the maelstrom when the bloodthirsty little beasts would not accept surrenders."

"That's true," Prett conceded. He turned to his resentful fellow and nodded, shown by his hood bobbing in the shadows.

"You should have seized their damned town right then and there, if you had the wherewithal," the anonymous conspirator insisted.

"I do not entirely disagree," Prentice told him. "But what is done, is done. What we are discussing now is what will yet be done."

"So will you help them defend themselves after they turn on Sunbury?" the healer Halleon Lyle pressed, sounding increasingly optimistic.

"And in return, your healers will march with her grace's army against the Usurper on the Denay throne." Prentice's tone made it clear he was not making a request.

"You can't command us," the second anonymous silhouette insisted. "Healers go where they will."

"Not after this night," Prentice countered. "At least not for this one bargain. You have involved yourselves already. You cannot now claim to stand apart when it suits you."

"You know what happens if you force us."

"I will force nothing," the knight commander retorted. "You will make the pledge, or you will go back to healing men with broken minds, wondering if it would be more merciful to give them poison. We have no part south of the 'Murrflow' save to protect Bridgetown's gatehouse. If you want us to pledge more than this to you, then offer your terms and commit yourselves to keep them. Or else Sougate awaits your walking corpses with stubborn walls and hot welcome."

"Or we could just kill you now," said the anonymous rebel, and Prentice fell into stance, his sword half drawn. It occurred to him to pull one of his loaded pistols as well, but he had no chance before the night suddenly blazed with pure light.

"No!" Whilte declared, his glowing broken spear staff held aloft. "You will not betray our trust."

Four Veckanders, two wearing only dun-colored homespun, one in a cassock as poor as Whilte's and a scholar in a quilted, wine-colored coat, all shrunk from the abrupt, impossible blaze. As soon as Whilte's words were spoken, the light faded, but the damage to their secrecy was surely done. There would be patrols on the south bank coming to investigate shortly. Prentice had no doubt any bribes paid would not have been enough to ignore this.

"The knight commander will take this word to her grace," the chaplain told the men in the returned shadows. "Watch from the bank of the Murr. If the archduchess agrees to your plan, you will see this glow on the shore of Greenmarsh in the night. That morning the Gryphon will ride forth and you will have to fulfill your part of the bargain."

"And take warning," Prentice added, annoyed that Whilte had seized control of the discussion but not unhappy with the outcome in any case. One man had spoken out of his resentment—hardly cause to scuttle the whole negotiation. "There is a chance that if Sunbury and the Heron's mob array against us we might be victorious without your help. If you are baiting a trap for us and we still win through, you best be running for Town Sobridge's far borders without looking back. The wrath of hell itself will be preferable to what will be riding after you in that case."

"We will not betray you if you do as you have pledged," the man Prett insisted, and then the sound of footsteps made it clear they were withdrawing to whatever craft they had used to reach Follybridge.

"We'd best be away now, too," Whilte said. "A patrol will be on the south bank with lanterns any moment, I expect. The boats in the Usurper's fleet are like to come looking as well."

"And whose fault is that?" Prentice asked, happy to tease the chaplain once more, even though the holy light was almost certainly exactly what the dangerous moment had needed. If Prentice had been left to resolve the incident his way, there would be spilled blood and dead bodies now to join the discarded timbers of Follybridge. It was a good chance he would have been one of them.

CHAPTER 53

"Rebellion, Prentice? You wish me to foster rebellion?" Amelia suspected she was overreacting to Prentice and Whilte's news of their mission in the night, but the incredible nature of their tale seemed to draw it out of her. She looked away for a moment, staring out the window, but that only showed the winter sky lit through with occasional flashes of lightning from a storm that must be raging somewhere far to the east.

Storms in the east, she thought. The perfect metaphor for the days of her nobility. *Except, of course, for the first and worst tempest which arose in the west and almost swept us away in a torrent of blood and sorcery. And now, rumblings in the south, and Prentice wants me to help the flood waters rise there as well!*

That thought made her shake her head at herself. What the knight commander and chaplain were proposing was far from so cut and dried. Every year, sacrists across the Grand Kingdom preached sermons about the great sin of pride that had led the Vec earldoms to rebel and declare themselves princes—heretical rulers defying the God-ordained thrones in Denay and Rhales. It was virtually an unwritten rule of the clergy that there must be an annual call for crusade against the Vec somewhere in the preacher's schedule of sermons. If she assisted free men in Town Sobridge to overthrow Sunbury—one of the "heretical" princes—would that not be the sort of thing Mother Church had been calling for?

No, because it would foster a different abuse to the divine order, Amelia told herself, knowing the answer automatically. The same Church that defended the rights of the throne in Denay against the Vec princes would also defend princedoms in general against peasant rebellion.

"Am I not rebel enough?" she mused, not exactly to her gathered courtiers. "They denounce me as such already." While everyone else seemed to understand the question was rhetorical, Amelia was surprised when Sir Turley gave her a straightforward answer.

"If they're already givin' you the guilty sentence, how bad can it be to do the crime as well?" he asked with a shrug.

"Demonstrating once again, husband, why you are neither a sacrist nor a scribe at laws," his wife Dalflitch said with an arched brow. If she meant to see him chastised by her tone, his smile put paid to that hope.

"He is not wrong, Your Grace," Prentice said quietly, and Amelia lifted her hand to still his words. She wasn't looking to be persuaded at this moment. She still wanted to know what her own thoughts on the matter were. Daven Marcus and his Dragons continued to hammer Loncastel, along with her gunners there, Bluebird was yet at large, and the best Prentice had found of him was the probable site of Penelope's cousin's murder. Beside all that, the Golden Heron army on the south of the river had been so well contained as a threat that Amelia had begun to forget about it, at least while she had other more dire questions in her mind. A large portion of her difficulty, she realized, was that this change moved what felt like one of the least of her priorities to the top of the list and brought with it the riskiest kind of plan imaginable.

"What do you say, husband?" she asked Farringdon.

"Well, assemblists, also known sometimes as vote-takers, are about as reviled in Vec courts as the princes themselves are hated in the Grand Kingdom," the marquis replied with a thoughtful frown. "My father tried two of them for treason in my lifetime. They died in prison, as far as I know, and that was only for publishing a small pamphlet—not much more than the nonsense Bluebird puts about against you, my love."

It was clear to Amelia that Farringdon was uncomfortable recounting this fact of his father's reign, and she appreciated his honesty. As an answer to her question, however, it missed the main point.

"What I want to know is what would this mean for us strategically?" she explained. Farringdon's expression showed he was not happy being asked that, in particular, and he shot a sidelong glance down the table at Prentice.

"The knight commander...," he began to say, but she cut him off.

"Is busy hunting down the men who murdered Master Solft and Lady Penelope's cousin," Amelia said more curtly than she intended. "You are in command of our defenses. I wish your opinion of this matter from the military perspective."

The archduchess recognized the cause of her husband's reluctance. He clearly did not want to embarrass Prentice since it had formerly been his place to be the first and last word on strategy. And in all likelihood, it would be again someday. For now, though, Amelia had given a different role to Prentice, and the longer Farringdon equivocated over the shift in responsibilities the longer he delayed everyone accepting the change as nothing to be worried about. Prentice had come to accept it, after all. She trusted in that because if he had had any objection, Amelia was sure he would have brought it to her privately.

Farringdon turned back to her and nodded thoughtfully.

"Truly? I would say that the plan has merit," he started carefully. "If what this healer named Lyle says is true, there is no reason the plan couldn't work, at least to overthrow Everard of Sunbury. I don't know what would happen come the summer when word that Town Sobridge has no prince becomes more common knowledge amongst the others of the Grey Hill Compact. The council could be called, and the princedom handed back to Sunbury, if he lives, or to the Earl of

Longshepherds. It's the sort of thing that has happened before. They might even send the earl a joint army, of sorts, to enforce his new claim. Or it might become a free-for-all, with prince after prince marching to try to oust the last. Like waves on the shore, they could wash away any garrison we leave in the town, even if no one of them was strong enough to do the job alone."

"And in the meantime, I become ever more the enemy of the peerage that Daven Marcus names me," Amelia muttered, adding her confident assessment of the political implications from the Grand Kingdom side. None of the nobility would favor her siding with an anti-noble faction, even across the Murr in the Vec. "What of our situation at Sougate if we do nothing but what we have been doing?"

Farringdon shrugged in his breastplate and pauldrons, the odd gesture making the steel pieces grate against one another. As uncomfortable as the armor seemed to make him look in his chair, its presence comforted Amelia in an odd way. It reinforced the difference in roles that she had assigned him and Prentice. After all, the baron was still going about without armor. Farringdon looked the part of a military commander at war.

"Sougate is as secure as ever it was, Your Grace," Farringdon reported, "from the day the knight commander set the defenses in place."

Amelia tutted and her lips turned downward in a sour frown. Her husband was intent on keeping the wound fresh and rubbed raw, it seemed. She would have to explain her desire more clearly to him the next time they had a private moment.

When will that be? she wondered. She was so tired most of the days, and Farringdon remained at the siegeworks so long into the evenings that by the time he returned to their bed, she was already long asleep. In the meantime, she had a decision to make.

"What is the true chance that this is a ruse?"

"Of Everard's? I suppose it could be," Farringdon conceded, but it was clear he did not think it was likely.

"With respect, Your Grace, it is almost impossible," Whilte said confidently from farther down the table. Amelia nodded for him to go on. "It is violation enough to the practices of healers for these men to intercede at all. Their consciences troubled them just taking a side to this degree. The idea that they would offer themselves as agents to lure us into a bloody trap is unthinkable."

That made sense to Amelia. She looked to her knight commander.

"Do you agree with the chaplain's assessment, Prentice?"

He regarded her solemnly as he answered, his expression, if anything, more inscrutable than normal. "His reasoning is sound, Your Grace, but we have seen many impossible things in this war and even in recent days. It would be utter folly to think this law is the only inviolable one."

"Healers go where they will, Prentice!" Whilte declared, his voice filled with shock and disgust. He clearly could not credit his brethren of the art with such vile motives. Prentice's experience told him something different, and Amelia knew immediately where his retort was coming from.

"Yes, Brother," he told the chaplain in an icy tone, "and some of them choose to go to the Inquisition, to stand beside torturers and extend the hours and days of suffering until they seem to have no end."

The two men regarded each other through slitted eyes, and Amelia was astonished to think that they might come to blows. It had never happened between the men of her inner court before.

"You think this is a ruse of the Inquisition?" Whilte demanded. "You think Lyle is in the service of Bluebird?"

"Can you be certain that he is not, Brother?" Amelia interjected, deliberately turning the hostile attention back to herself.

Whilte snapped to look at her and immediately recognized the difference. He stopped before speaking and lowered his head respectfully. In the sudden break, it seemed he took a moment to consider his answers more carefully as well. He shot a last swift glance at Prentice before responding to her question.

"No, Your Grace, in truth I cannot be certain. It galls me to the depth of my soul, but as Knight Commander Baron Ash makes so clear, I cannot say for sure that this is not another part of the endless shadow campaigns of the Silent Hand. If they have embraced sorcery, blood magicks, and murder as mere tools, as well as turning healing into a tool of torture, it seems right to say there might be nothing they cannot twist to evil, even something as earnest-seeming to me as this."

Amelia smiled at Whilte, thanking him for being so honest with her, even though it offended his sensibilities to do so. She considered all the elements before her.

"Well, my lords, although the offer is tempting and I do trust your judgement, Brother, it is not without significant risk, as all battle is." Ignoring the specific hazards of this odd plan, simply taking the field carried great danger, even for her mighty army. She did not want them to forget that fact. "Since we cannot be more certain and we are yet fighting two other battles here in Bridgetown and across the northern water, I will decline this offer. It will cost us little."

"Except the service of other healers, Your Grace," Whilte said quietly, and for the first time ever, she heard a tone of bitterness and resentment in the humble man's voice.

"Healers go where they will, Brother," she said, offering Whilte's words back to him. "Are you truly saying that in the coming days of this war all will disdain to heal White Lions' wounded because I refused this near-unthinkable conspiracy?"

She arched her eyebrow at the chaplain but was shocked when it was Prentice who answered her question.

"Likely they will not, Your Grace, but in the meanwhile more men will suffer and die needlessly at the foot of Sougate."

"Not Reachermen, Prentice," Amelia retorted.

"No, Your Grace," he conceded, his face as emotionless as ever and all the more judgmental for it. "But there was a time when you were not so easily comforted by that distinction."

Amelia's eyes went wide in shock, and she sucked in a short breath, but Prentice was not finished.

"I know for truth that the difference means less to men who have witnessed one slaughter on that field already and are now being asked to perpetrate another. Soon, all the winter rains in the world will not be enough to wash the blood from Sougate's stones nor from the hands of the men forced to stand guard on its battlements, whether they have the right of it or not."

The archduchess felt like she had just been slapped in the face, and she sat forward in her chair in a fury.

"You think to chastise me in front of the world, *Baron*?" she demanded, reminding him from where he received his title and space to speak at all in her presence. Were all nobles so recalcitrant? Was that what happened whenever a man took on a peerage? How could Prentice not see that she had a long list of those who depended on her for her care, ranging from the highest to the lowest. No, she was not heedless of the loss of life as Sougate was pointlessly assaulted, but those lives were lost on Everard of Sunbury's account, and they rated lower on her list than even the businesses of the Conclave still being pummeled by Daven Marcus on Loncastel. Certainly, she held her own men-at-arms' lives higher, not to mention Prentice himself and all the other people in this chamber and the surrounding rooms, including Prentice's own children. Highest of all, she had her husband and her unborn. As she opened her mouth to continue her rebuke, it was her child who protested first.

"Oooh, dear God in heaven," she gasped, putting a hand to her belly as she all but fell back in her chair.

"What is it, Your Grace?" Dalflitch asked, while Farringdon leaned close in concern, reaching for her hand. A new pain struck Amelia's belly, and she gasped again.

"No, it's too soon," she managed to hiss, her face screwed up against the intense discomfort. Around her, everyone's worried expressions told her that she need not explain what was happening.

"Send for a midwife," Farringdon commanded, and someone left the chamber at a run, though Amelia had no idea who.

"Daisy is closer," Dalflitch said, and a moment later Lady Daisy was at Amelia's side.

"Thank you, My Lady," Amelia managed to say to the midwife in a lace mask. After Righteous's testimony of Daisy's helpfulness in her own labor, the archduchess was more than willing to trust herself into the young woman's hands.

"No trouble to me, Your Grace, but let's wait and thank the true midwife when she comes, eh? I know some o' the craft, but we're only at the start o' the journey right now."

Her calm confidence comforted Amelia even in spite of the girl's humble protestations, and the archduchess did her best to smile through the next pain. It seemed they were coming on so quickly, not at all how she had been told they would progress when her time came. The realization frightened her somewhat, undoing Daisy's good work. The Lace Fang looked to Lady Dalflitch.

"Her Grace needs be moved to her bed."

"I...uh...," Dalflitch hesitated, and Amelia wondered why they were even pausing to talk about it. Then she realized it was likely for two reasons. First, Dalflitch had never had children of her own and probably had next to no idea how to respond to the situation. Second, and worse, everyone was uncertain who had the right to give orders if Amelia could not give them for herself. They had all just been in the midst of a confrontation between the two highest nobles of the Western Reach. Amelia had a sudden flash of memory of the confusion Daven Marcus had created during his crusade west, playing favorites and refusing to honor existing roles and lines of authority.

"I've been…been a fool," she gasped, her face feeling florid and hot.

"Maybe that's enough o' that, Your Grace," Daisy told her, taking charge as much as she likely dared. With a wave of her hand, she summoned two neophytes to come and assist her to help Amelia out of her chair. Amelia let herself be levered to her feet, and as she was, everyone else in the room stood. The three ladies-in-waiting led her toward her curtained bedchamber while the men simply withdrew without needing to be told. Before they could leave completely, Amelia reached out a pleading hand toward them.

"Farringdon, do not go, my love, please," she whispered as loudly as she could. It was nearly all she felt she had the strength for.

"Of course," he said readily, and he drew slightly nearer, though clearly making an effort to stand apart and not interfere with the ones who knew what they were doing in this matter. They were about to lead her off when she reached out again and met Prentice's gaze. He seemed less distant for a moment, but there was no closeness there, not like she remembered between them. Perhaps he had been more wounded by her changes to his duties than she imagined. But what could she say about it now? It would be more sensible to let it rest until after her labor. Surely a few hours would not make reconciliation impossible.

"Find him," she said instead, knowing he would know she meant Bluebird. The Inquisition's agent was the real cause of their conflict, and come what may, he had to be stopped. Once the Bluebird was ended, the deaths in front of Sougate could be looked to. "Find that damnable bird and finish him."

Her last words were constricted into gasping tears, and she surrendered herself to her ladies' ministrations as the pain made everything else irrelevant—everything except the fact that she should not be giving birth so soon.

CHAPTER 54

"False labor?"

Amelia had never heard of such a thing, and by Lady Dalflitch and Lady Righteous's expressions, neither had they. The pair stood by her bed as the archduchess sat up in just her shift, the blanket now pulled around herself.

"Tis common enough, so the midwife says," the lady seneschal explained. "Your body is practicing for the time itself, apparently."

"Did you go through it, My Lady?" Amelia asked Righteous, and the baroness shook her head.

"Not as I noticed, Your Grace, but as you know, it took my thick skull some while to even tell when the real thing was upon me, so mayhap I just never realized."

"Chance would be a fine thing," Amelia muttered, and both ladies-in-waiting smirked at her wry humor. "Will it happen again?"

"It might. The midwife has told Lady Daisy what to look for and some massage tricks she says will help. In the meantime, she encourages you to not take too much time away from your bed."

Amelia sighed heavily and leaned back against her pillows that were propped upon the bedhead. Confinement—exactly what she had been determined to avoid, and now it was to be forced upon her. She put her hands to her belly and looked down.

Do you plan on being this demanding when you arrive, little one? Just because you are to be my heir doesn't mean you get to act the brat.

Righteous and Dalflitch stood by politely, the very picture of ladies-in-waiting—dresses of fine cut and cloth, cauls, and lace hoods in place. Righteous had returned to wearing her mask almost always, and her body was rapidly recovering her former shape. Even with a wetnurse, hungry twins demanded much food from a woman's body. Her waif-like form seemed to be returning, although with one distinction—her cleavage much more resembled the famed beauty next to her these days. The observation made Amelia smirk, and she wondered idly what Prentice made of his wife's developments, but that thought turned her mind onto their last conversation. He never seemed happy these days, and whatever was weighing him down, it was clear that his wife's joyful motherhood was not enough to lift his mood.

Surely, he is not so wounded by one small demotion? she thought. It was hardly even a demotion, just a fresh division of duties. Prentice had never been one to care about matters of crass prestige in the past. She remembered her thought that perhaps nobility poisoned every man's heart to some degree, and while it was so at odds with the Prentice she had known for years, Amelia could not quite shake the fear that it was the cause.

"How fares your husband, My Lady?" she asked, thinking to take the question up with Righteous, but both seemed to think the inquiry was for them, and there was a moment of shuffling as they decided whom should answer first. Righteous deferred to Dalflitch, and Amelia nodded to her seneschal. "I had meant the baroness, My Lady, but by all means, you speak."

Another silent round of "you first; no, you" was played between the two courtiers, and while she knew it was silly at one level, at another, it delighted the archduchess to see it. These two had once loathed each other on sight and now they were like sisters, respecting one another's roles and places in the scheme of things, to each other's great advantage. Righteous had grown into her ladyhood after Dalflitch's example, and Dalflitch's own considerable astuteness benefited from the former street fighter's low cunning. Neither would usurp the other at anything now, and Amelia felt her own security deeply reinforced by the fact.

"Sir Turley is well and about your business, Your Grace," Dalflitch reported proudly. "We are all but done debarking the supplies from the boats, and he spends the main of his days taking new orders from the quartermasters. He will return with a full list to Dweltford just as soon as he chases down one of the craft."

"Chases down, My Lady?" Amelia asked.

"He contracted all of them for the return journey but left them free to take short jobs while he went about other matters here in Bridgetown. It seems that one of the larger merchantworkers has gone off and not returned yet. 'Slipped its moorings,' as the skips like to say."

"He thinks it's been purloined by smugglers?"

"That is what he believes, Your Grace," Dalflitch said with a nod. "As you know, my husband is quite intolerant of rats in your household. He means to find out where the boat has gone before he leaves for Dweltford. Our own people on the docklands will be helping him."

Amelia nodded with a smile. Although it was not a concern she cared much about, she was pleased to hear that the matter was being attended to and that her lady would have some more time with her husband before he returned northward. Although some sacrifices were clearly direr than others, the war put its demands on them all, including upon their marriages. Which turned her thoughts to Righteous once more.

"And you, Baroness?" she asked.

"Me? I reckon as you'd have to ask my husband yourself, Your Grace," Righteous replied sourly. "You have as much access to his thoughts as any of us these days."

Amelia wasn't sure if Righteous's tone was one of mere resentment or if it was tinged with something else, like jealousy.

"You do not know your husband's mind?" she asked, surprised by the notion. Who else would know Prentice as Righteous did?

"He has given away speaking with me to any depth of late," the baroness told her liege, and it was clear Righteous did not like having to admit that fact.

"Even when you are together in private?" Amelia pressed, risking being too forward. The answer caught her completely unprepared.

"When was that, Your Grace?" Righteous asked rhetorically, her polite expression now turned to a frown that would sour cream. "He ain't even come to our bed in more'n a week. I thought it was a nightmare to be without him while he was away in the west, but this is worse. When he was a month westward, I never thought to hope for him. Now that he's a quarter of a candle's walk away and still not beside me, stings like a sticker's stripe!"

"Sticker's stripe?" Amelia repeated, not recognizing the expression.

"Quick cut with an alley fighting blade, Your Grace."

Amelia nodded, realizing that the explanation of criminal vernacular was not actually what she cared about. Prentice was keeping away from his wife? Why would he do such a thing? The first and most obvious explanation occurred to her, and she would have dismissed it out of hand, but his behavior was becoming so unlike himself that she found it harder to discount the possibility. She wondered if the same thought troubled Lady Righteous.

"You surely do not think he goes to another in the night, My Lady?" she said, reflexively hoping to reassure them both.

"He better bally not!" Righteous said, her frown turning to a furious sneer. "I'd have the little slattern's guts for garters, whoever she was. Then I'd do something *really dire* to him."

There was no doubting the baroness's sincerity as she promised brutal death to whatever hypothetical maid might play the harlot with her husband, while beside her the ever-perfect Dalflitch nodded with serene support. The combination nearly made Amelia burst out laughing.

"Evisceration is not dire, My Lady?" she asked, feeling herself smirk.

"Not compared to how he'd end up—forcin' me to make a widow out of myself? There's no punishment good enough."

Amelia's sense of amusement melted as she realized how serious the situation might be.

"I cannot believe he would actually play you false, Righteous," she said, wishing she felt more certain herself. It was Dalflitch who provided the true reassurance, however.

"I can guarantee it," the seneschal said. "Word from the Runners Field camp is that the knight commander is continually at work all day, inquiring into the matter of Bluebird and the like, while in the evenings, he is in a shed he has turned to some kind of fighting school."

"Fighting school?" The notion surprised Amelia. Why would Prentice waste time teaching fighters? He had any number of skilled underlings in the Lions to undertake that duty. And what skills did they lack? She had always been reassured that her militiamen left Fallenhill with all the weapon-craft they could possibly need.

Isn't there a moment when the sword is sharp enough? she wondered, certain she had heard such a martial aphorism somewhere, or perhaps she had read it in one of the military manuals she had studied. It was some while since she had last looked through one of those books.

"Fighting school, training hall, something of the sort," Dalflitch explained. "Reports vary. What is certain is that any who go there are invited into a brutal experience, and none suffer more than Baron Ash himself. As near as I can ascertain, he sleeps there every night, often first drilling with weapons into the deep hours."

"To what purpose?" Amelia asked.

"No one knows for sure, Your Grace," Dalflitch conceded. "But the rumors are multifarious, as you might expect. Surviving a night in the commander's school of combat is becoming both a dread activity and a marker of pride amongst the banner companies. The gossip I choose to believe is that he has taken it upon himself to search out the best to form an elite guard of some kind."

Elite guard? But the point of the White Lions was to steer away from such pride and privilege, wasn't it? For all that it scotched any rumor of Prentice being unfaithful to his wife, this news only distressed Amelia all the more. Was he seeking out a personal coterie, an inner company sworn first to him as the knights like Sebastian and Liam had built for themselves? Where was her loyal general who always put his duty ahead of his ambitions? What had happened to him? Amelia swallowed heavily and pulled the reins on her runaway thoughts.

This is more of pregnancy than true feelings, she told herself, remembering that only hours passed she had been through a false labor. Now was not the time to jump to extreme conclusions.

"You miss your husband, My Lady?" she asked Righteous, deciding that whatever might be behind Prentice's unexpected behavior, the best course was to consult the source.

"You know that I do, Your Grace," Righteous answered.

"Then I release you this night to go to him," she said. "If he is not seeking you out, then seek him."

"You playing matchmaker, Your Grace? We are already matched and with children birthed 'tween us."

"Aye, My Lady, and now, like a goodly mother-in-law might, I give you my advice to keep that state," Amelia joked, but Righteous did not understand, it seemed. She let her smile drop and gave her lady-in-waiting a more direct look. "Go to him, ask what keeps him from you. Reassure yourself, and then in the morning you can tell me what he said—whatever is right to share, of course."

Righteous accepted the instruction with a solemn nod, and Amelia sat back, thinking to rest. Whatever was happening with Prentice, she felt sure Righteous would be able to ferret it out if they had a chance to speak, and she trusted the baroness to report truly on whatever she could.

If I trust her, why can I not trust her husband to not betray me as other barons and earls have in the past? she wondered but knew there were no easy answers in her mind for that question. Perhaps after she had had a rest. After all, she was to have a great deal of rest in the coming days. She might as well use it to refresh her mind, as well as her flesh and her growing heir.

CHAPTER 55

Prentice drilled alone in the shed. Having been reassured that the archduchess and her unborn were well and that her false labor was not cause for concern, he had spent the afternoon inspecting the new drainage works that Banner Sergeant Porth had begun for Runners Field. Winter camp sickness was almost inevitable—men with flu and fevers—but those were nothing compared to the possibilities of bloody flux and other illnesses a poorly drained settlement would cause. With a work crew already proven through the infirmary task, Porth had moved on to digging the drainage ditches deeper and lining them with stones so the muddy water would flow more naturally rather than simply silting the channels back up and forcing them to be continually re-dug. Canopies had been set up in one corner of the quarry rockface, and men hacked at the stone every day, rain or no.

"Don't need no mason's skill for that task, My Lord," Porth had reported that afternoon. "We ain't makin' marble fountains—just scree and large gravel for the ditches."

Prentice had looked over the works and been impressed. Porth was surely in no small amount of pain from his lost arm, but still he kept himself at his duties, improving the lot of every White Lion and Gryphon. The example had inspired Prentice to make even more effort to be worthy of the command of such men, even though it had been all but stripped from him. Inwardly he understood the archduchess's reasons for reducing his duty to no more than the hunt for one elusive enemy, but the chorus of derision within him also never ceased mocking and warning him to expect the final shame any day now.

She cannot trust you anymore, weakling, they told him. *You failed your father, then Mother Church, and now your liege.*

He wanted to ignore them, command them to shut up, battle them to silence, but how did a man make war upon his own thoughts? All he had was to tend to his duties in the day and drive himself to exhaustion in the night. If he let his thoughts wander even a step, the hate would rise like a miasma from filthy water. So, he pushed himself through the warm-up drill this evening while waiting for any who would come to fight with him and make him earn his rest this evening. When the shed door creaked open, he was surprised to see the figure of a single woman there and delighted when he realized it was his wife.

"So, this is where you've been keepin' yourself from me?" she asked as she walked in, wrinkling her nose at the smell, causing her lace half-mask to move on her face. "I could almost wish you *were* gone wayward on me. Better I lose out to some painted doxy than have you prefer *this* to me. It's an insult!"

"Who told you I prefer this to you?" he asked, approaching her and marveling at her attractiveness to his eyes. The ragged urchin he had first met was long gone, and while his wife might never be praised for her womanliness as Lady Dalflitch was, no one in all the world delighted him as Righteous did. Her fine dress and courtly poise only reinforced his desire for her, and he suddenly imagined releasing her strawberry blonde hair and kissing her. Looking her up and down, he noted another more recent change to her appearance.

"Motherhood suits you, my love," he said with a half-smile.

"Oh, you remember I'm a mother, do you?" she asked, and her eyebrow cocked beneath the lace. "I only ask because I can't recall the last time you laid eyes on your poor babes. Will you even know 'em the next time you see 'em?"

"Of course I will," Prentice retorted and scowled to have his compliment rebuffed. He turned away and moved to the wall where the practice weapons were. It pleased him to see his wife, but the training was too important for him to waste time on a pointless argument. Behind him, he heard Righteous walking into the middle of the shed by the swish of her skirt on the dirt floor.

"What's this?" she asked, and when he looked over his shoulder, he could see she meant the chalk rings on the wall.

"Training guide," he told her bluntly and then turned back, pretending to be picking a weapon to practice with.

"Five circles? I thought there were meant to be seven. And all straight up the wall in a line? Where's the cross-shape you bods is famous for?"

"So far, I only have five of the seven rings recovered. The cross will come when I have them all."

"Recovered?" she repeated, and there was a slight mocking tone to her voice. "Recovered from where? Someone thieve 'em from you? If you just need some chalk to draw 'em up there, I can get you some easy enough. We can put 'em up there inside the hour and then go back to our bed for the night. Your babes can learn your forgotten face again."

Her implicit ridicule was beginning to grate on him, and inwardly the hateful chorus joined her, ironically not saying anything specific but quietly laughing at the scouring of his soul.

"Each ring goes on the wall when I am confident that I have reacquired the skills," he said to her through gritted teeth.

Liar, the inner voices chanted. In truth he had not put himself through any of the proper tests for the stages of the Seven Rings Cross, not formally. Every time he thought to do it, some other duty had arisen or else one had been waiting for him on the next morning. He knew that he could not risk being injured if he was not fully up to the test. When a Seven Rings' student passed their next ring, they were often so strained by the exertion that they could take a week or more to recover and return to training. Prentice did not have the time to indulge that level of weakness. Bluebird was still at large. Of course, the hateful chorus only saw that as yet another excuse.

"Well, if that's the delay, show me what you're up to. Maybe I can help," Righteous challenged him.

Prentice heard the sound of his wife drawing a blade and looked at her again to see her favorite poniard in her hand. He wanted to scold her, to pack her off, but he remembered that she was an expert with a short blade and would be ideal to test his skill.

You won't beat her, of course, his father/instructors mocked. *She was never weakened by poison and failure. She drills her charges daily, and they do their duty excellently. Wilforn's fate proves that. She'll put you on your backside in front of all the others that come tonight. How will Solomon feel, seeing you humiliated by your wife in her skirts?*

"We can spar a little," he forced himself to say, pulling a wooden practice dagger from where it hung on a hook, "until the others come, at least. Usually, the evening begins with wrestling, for which you are not suitably dressed."

"Is that the only problem? You'd allow me to go wrestling with a clutch of filthy low-born militiamen if I was dressed for the game, would you?"

"Is that what you would want?" Prentice snapped back at her before he could stop himself. He hardly knew where the question came from but recognized the petty jealousy in the words easily enough. It was unjust. His wife had never given him any cause to believe she was unfaithful in thought, word, or deed. The poisonous chorus laughed at him, and he could see in her eyes the fury his stinging comment had caused.

She came on for the first pass, steel edge leading. Despite her anger, however, she did not move at her full speed, which he knew would be down to her more restrictive clothing and not being warmed up. He intercepted her attack with his free hand on her forearm and flicked his own dagger back at her, which she checked by blocking his elbow. Their exchange of attacks moved swiftly through a series that some called "knife fighter's catch," each attack seeming to lead to a counter, defensive hands blocking and deflecting—or "catching"—making openings for the next blade strike. Eventually, Prentice managed to get himself on the outer side of her weapon hand and, checking the whole arm, was able to lever her away using his greater mass. Her defensive reflex was to keep going, to escape the dagger to the ribs or back that would have come in a true fight. After three steps, she whirled about to face him. Her breath was a little deeper now and her face was somewhat flushed. Still, her mask and caul were yet perfectly in place, and she was as ladylike as the moment she had entered.

"You seem warmed up now," Prentice teased. "Shall we do it properly?" It was the kind of comment he often used to provoke her during sparring. She knew he would not mean it truly, but he also knew she liked to let herself feel affronted as a form of play. This time, however, it seemed the flirtation landed differently.

"What do you know about proper?" she demanded, looking him up and down as she circled him before the next pass. "Look at you—filthy in a filthy shed like a convict. All you lack is the fetters."

"You fell in love with a man who looked like this, as I recall."

"I fell in love with a man with a spine," she retorted. "A man on the path to becoming a baron, a peer of the realm. Not a ragamuffin who smelt like a pigsty and aspired to live in one."

With that she rushed him again, clearly seeking to reverse the advantage he had just demonstrated. Keeping all her strikes aimed at his lower body, she crouched as low as her skirt allowed, blade coming upward many times, forcing him to strike overhand more than he would normally want. Even so, their game of catch felt slower than it should, and that puzzled Prentice. It took him a handful of exchanges, but soon enough he found an opening that let him get his wooden blade over top of hers, trapping her weapon hand at the wrist. If he had been using a live blade, he would have been free to slash her tendons with a simple draw cut. As it was, he locked her arm and pulled his weapon back, disarming her adroitly. Her own sharp steel fell to the earth some distance away and he pushed her off, not bothering to mimic the finishing strike he would have used in a true combat.

"What are you doing?" he asked her as she recovered the lost poniard. She was faster than this. Why was she not showing him that speed?

"What does it look like I'm doing?" she demanded through gritted teeth.

Now she was much more disheveled, and she took a moment to remove the loosened pins in her headdress, casting the caul away and letting her hair fall as he had imagined only moments before. The firelight shining in through the doorway touched her strawberry blonde with orange highlights that made him think of a haloed angel in a stained glass. An avenging angel, as it happened, and for a third time she came at him, her expression one of ferocious resolve. It made him think that this time she would finally test him and cut him when he fell short.

Except that she did not.

Again, they played knife fighter's catch, and Prentice felt his hands find their places almost at will. He couldn't understand it. Why was his wife not giving it her all as she normally would? And then the thought struck him. She was going easy on him.

She doesn't think you can handle her, the hateful voices mocked instantly. *You've fallen so far beneath her that she pities you.*

The notion wrapped itself around his thoughts like the bite of an overseer's lash, and he snarled in fury at the pain of it. Almost without thinking, he switched up their patterns and caught her under the shoulder while one foot hooked behind her ankle. She tumbled toward the ground instantly, having no chance to resist a technique designed to put a knight in full armor off his feet. Despite his hurt and anger, Prentice had no desire to actually harm his wife, and he caught the main of her weight, so she did not fall hard on the packed earth. The motion drew him down with her and he ended up over top of her, pinning her in place. She stared up at him a moment, breathing more heavily from the fall.

"You're ruining my dress," she said breathlessly, and now there was the mocking flirtation in her eyes.

"You should have fought me harder then," Prentice told her, and the anger of his stung pride faded swiftly, melting into love and desire for the woman he was sworn to for life. He reached a hand up and pushed away her mask, looking deep into her eyes.

"I miss you," she told him, smiling, and he felt himself smile in return. It occurred to him that it might have been the first sincere smile he'd felt in days, if not weeks.

"I have missed you too, beloved one."

He was about to lean down to kiss her, her eyes already on his mouth, when there was an almost polite cough from the direction of the door.

Chapter 56

"I'm not interrupting anything important, am I?" Turley asked as he took a step into the shed.

"Of course you are," Righteous said, looking daggers at him. "Now rack off! And close the door behind you!"

Turley clutched his hand to his breast as if wounded.

"Oh, the cruelties of the peerage to those of us low-born folk, cast away with insults," he sighed loudly. "And me with so many earnest and generous gifts for his lordship, the baron." Silhouetted in the doorway behind Turley were a number of other figures who seemed to be waiting for their permission to enter the shed after him.

"We will we have to postpone this, my wife," Prentice told Righteous, pushing himself away from her and up onto his feet. "It seems my other training partners have arrived after all."

"That's not them," Righteous disagreed. "Not unless they rebelled 'gainst me. I told 'em to take the night for 'emselves."

"Why would you do that?" Prentice asked, feeling his earlier anger and resentment seeking to stir again.

"Cause I wanted a night with my husband, why do you think?" she spat out at him as she stood, brushing the dirt from her dress. "And now this lout's gone and spoiled that!"

She glared at Turley again. Prentice felt a sudden compassion for his wife. With the sharp-edged nature of some of their relating, it was easy for him to forget that his spouse actually wanted to be his wife. She had chosen him as much as he had chosen her—more, in fact, since she had known her mind on the subject before he had.

"Perhaps Sir Turley's matter will be a simple and swift one," he offered her. "When he is gone, we might return to 'training.'"

"Is that what folks is callin' it these days?" Turley asked cheekily, and Righteous rolled her eyes before bending to fetch her headpieces and mask. Prentice scowled at his friend, who shrugged with unconcern. "Sorry to say, old mate, that you're not like to want to stick around here once you've heard all my news."

"News? I thought you were bringing gifts."

"The one can be t'other, can't it?" Turley asked, and he looked back to usher some of the waiting figures inside. First was Ganner Soort-Almin, the Masnian armorer, and behind him came four men carrying pieces of armor and a cross-beamed stand for the panoply to hang upon. Turley directed them to the rear wall, and Soort-Almin oversaw the armor being set on the stand so that the full suit sat ready to be donned. When it was in place, the bearers were shooed away and the armor's crafter stood beside it to present it to its new owner.

Prentice approached and looked over the steel while one of the bearers held up a lantern for him. The work was remarkably fine, and he found himself marveling at each detail. The plate steel had been blued, a process that darkened the metal and made it resistant to corrosion. It was an unusual technique that all the Masnian smiths favored, and while the armor would still need to be polished somewhat, it would never shine "white" like the more typical Grand Kingdom panoplies. What astonished Prentice was that the burnishing of the steel had been accomplished in such a way as to leave a slightly lighter border around the edges of each piece, increasing its beauty and the complexity of its finishing. He had heard of such things, but Prentice had never seen an armor of this sort up close before.

"Sir Turley insists that you will not wear greaves or sabatons," Soort-Almin said, pointing to the space at the bottom of the stand where the lower leg protections would normally be placed.

"He says that you prefer only boots for greater mobility. For this reason, I have made none and kept the cuisses smaller and strapped differently to make running easier." His pointing finger moved up to the plates for protecting the thighs, showing how they connected to the faulds and strapped around the leg. Compared to the comprehensive and interlocked nature of the upper body protection, Prentice's new suit was much more spartan on the lower body, exactly as he preferred. He had run and marched through too much mud on too many battlefields to desire a full knight's panoply.

"You want to try it on?" his wife asked him as they looked the impressive suit over.

"You helped me into the last one," he told her. "Shouldn't it be you again this time?"

"Putting clothes *on* your mucky body had not been my main plan for the evening, but we can play it that way, if you want."

If any of the other men present heard Righteous's flirtatious comment, they studiously pretended not to.

"I will need my arming doublet," Prentice said, looking down at the tunic he was wearing. Of late, he had taken to wearing only a simple garment under his cloak rather than reminding those around him that he no longer had his militia uniform. Several pieces of a man-at-arms protection could be worn over virtually any garment, often just a thick buffcoat. But a full upper suit such as this required a special padded undertunic with ties to help keep every individual piece in its place, the weight more evenly distributed over limbs and torso.

"Well, you can take time to fetch one up, if you want," Turley said, "but once you hear what else I have to tell you, you won't want to wait, I promise you!"

Prentice looked to his friend and waited for him to continue. Turley returned his expectant gaze without saying anything. Eventually, the knight commander sighed in frustration.

"Well?" he demanded of his playful friend. "Bad enough you have interrupted my wife and I in a private moment. Must you drag it out and make it as annoying as possible?"

"No, not exacting like," his friend conceded, smiling in the enjoyment of being difficult. "It's just that I need a favor of you, and I'm weighin' if I should ask that first or after I give you the best part."

Prentice rolled his eyes, but Righteous had had enough of being frustrated for someone else's amusement.

"Just ask your dashed favor, give us your news, and then sod off, you difficult oaf!"

Turley feigned being hurt once again but smiled.

"Right, well the favor first it is, then," he said. "I been readyin' to go on back up the Dwelt to home, but one o' my hired boats is gone missin'."

As with his wife, Prentice noticed that Turley's affected manners seemed to slip whenever he spoke of common matters.

"I been searchin' the docklands and there ain't hide nor hair the whole length o' the bridges," the knight seneschal continued. "Some of our trusted skips hear that the thing went upriver on a short job, and I think someone up there is playin' silly beggars with me. I mean to find out where they've put it ashore and catch it on the way back—teach the boat master the folly of muckin' her grace's man about."

"Sounds like an effective plan," Prentice agreed. "You want me to send a cohort or two with you for the cutting out? Is that the favor?"

"Nah, God love you, old fellow," Turley said, waving Prentice away as if his offer was amusing. "I already got that sorted through my Dalflitch and the marquis knight captain. No, no, what I needs is a goodly set of eyes on the riverbank. You know what skips can be like, secret coves and hidden jetties and all. We might sail right past this boat and ne'er know it was there. I need your fey man's service, you know, like him and his mates did on the Dweltwater in summer."

Dahyoor? Prentice thought, annoyed that the idea had not occurred to him already. It seemed obvious now that he thought about it. He nodded.

"You know, Marquis Farringdon has Dahyoor at work scouting the Dragons. You should have asked him for the help when your wife arranged for the Lions for taking the boat back."

"What? And gazump you? He's your squire, ain't he? He might be doin' a task for the knight captain, but that don't make him free for me to play the overseer with." Turley seemed genuinely surprised by Prentice's suggestion.

He is respecting my place, the knight commander thought, and it pleased him, though the bitter voices snapped in with their immediate condemnation. *For now. For now. Soon enough that will leak through your pathetic fingers like water, too, and you'll have nothing.*

That was a mockery too far for Prentice, though he could not say precisely why. Perhaps the notion that his longest and truest friend might betray or reject him was beyond belief.

Enough, he shouted inwardly, as if the voices were rebellious militiamen on a training field. *I have what I have—the love of my friends and family, my duty, and whatever strength I can find to execute it.*

The sneering haters reminded him quietly that he had had all those things once before, and they had all been stripped from him to put him on a convict chain. See, he was living as a convict once again. It was his inevitable fate. He shook his head, which Turley took for a different signal.

"You can't lend me the fellow?" he asked, and Prentice realized he was not being clear with his friend.

The baron looked to his wife, who watched him closely as well, and forced himself to smile. "I will give Dahyoor the command when I next see him. You know the fey are swift riders, but unless he finds your lost boat near to town, it will be some days before you hear back. A week or more, most likely."

"That'll give you more time here with your lady wife," Righteous added. "She'll thank you for that. She misses your daft face when you're away, for some reason."

"No accountin' for taste, Baroness. Thankfully," Turley said, satisfied, and then looked to Prentice. "I'll hang about a clutch o' days, but I'll have to head out after that or it'll look suspicious. The boat takers might just put it to bed for the rest o' the winter. If they see me take to the river again, they should feel safer to put it about and we'll spot it. I'll leave word with a friendly skiff poleman to act as messenger and take my sweet time on the return journey. If your squire finds 'em out, Dalflitch'll see word sent to me on the water and we'll pounce. How's that for a plan?"

He folded his arms proudly and looked from Prentice to Righteous and back, as if inviting applause.

"Sounds as if you have the whole bag sewn up," Prentice told him, ignoring the petty thought that his old friend hardly needed him any longer. He sneered at the notion. Self-pity like that could wait for the night watches.

Cry on your pillow later, he told himself harshly. *For now, keep your hand to the plough.*

Turley stood in his smug success for a long moment, as if he had just won a significant debate over a long-held opponent. At last, Righteous tutted loudly and he nodded.

"Oh, right, my news," he said. His expression took on a conspiratorial cast. "I found us another ghost."

CHAPTER 57

The little, hutch-like building was tucked in behind some stairs that led up to one of the rises on the edge of Salthatch from a rotten old pier that mostly seemed to service poorer fishers and local small craft. Knowing that Salthatch Island had been a particular focus of Lady Dalfitch's agents' searches, it surprised Prentice at first that this had eluded discovery for so long. Now that he looked at the place from just down the dock, it felt more plausible. It really was hidden in a tiny cleft in the midst of Bridgetown's endless bustle. Ideal, in its way.

"When I started to put the wind up all our loyals on the docks, I got word of all sorts of odd news," Turley explained. "Daft stuff, most of it! But one little tidbit was talk of a haunted smokehouse. Seems that in just the autumn, the owner—pokey little fellow who kept putting his nose in other folks' matters—drank himself silly and fell in the river. Drowned, even though there was any number of strong swimmers standing around on their boats and piers. Then, later the same week, his long-lost cousin or some such sails into town and takes the place as his own."

Prentice saw instantly the implication of this tale—a smokehouse that had recently lost its owner and been claimed by an outsider, who could easily have been Bluebird. Of course, he could just as easily be a long-lost cousin as described. Turley continued his tale.

"This cousin fellow, he shakes all the hands and thanks all the locals for watchin' over the place for his dead relative. Then he's in the wind so far as anyone else knows. Course, they don't much blame him cause almost right away, the dead fellow's ghost is heard there in the night, weeping and moaning. They figure on the cousin just abandoning the place, and no one's seen none go in or out any time o' the day or night. Just like your old nunnery, Knight Commander."

Prentice nodded to his friend.

"When were you in a nunnery?" Righteous demanded from Prentice's other side.

"Old nunnery, My Lady," Turley reassured her. "Only nuns there were ghosts like, completely dead."

Righteous sniffed, apparently reluctantly mollified. Prentice was not paying attention at this point. His eyes were on the target. No one had been seen here, but the ghostly sounds indicated it had been put to some use. Almost certainly it was where Inxyphos had been hidden before he had been finally let loose on Lady Penlope's accession ceremony. Of course, now that he, Turley, and Righteous were here, along with two lines of the Gryphon Banner, all sticking out amongst the evening community like sore thumbs, anyone alert in the hutch would know they had been tumbled.

"How long have you known about this place?" he asked.

"Since this morning," Turley told him.

"And you waited this long to tell me?" Prentice demanded in a whispered hiss.

"We had a girl on the place like a swoopin' hawk, don't you worry," Turley retorted with a scowl. "My Dalflitch's ladies know their craft."

"Dalflitch's ladies?" Righteous asked sharply.

"Well, I s'pose they're her grace's ladies right first," Turley conceded, but when he looked at Righteous, it was clear she was still unhappy. "Oh, and yours, and Spindle's too, My Lady."

"Keep that straight," she chastised him, and Prentice smirked. He cast his eyes around the dockside where the locals were all already keeping a distance.

"So where is this girl?" he asked quietly.

"She'll show 'erself soon enough. Be patient."

Prentice shook his head but said no more. The pause gave him a moment to appreciate his new helmet, which was the only piece of his armor that he had bothered to don for this exercise. As he might have expected, it fitted him excellently well. The salet had been fashioned with an integral visor that could be lifted open smoothly and hooked out of the way. It offered no lower face protection, however—that was to be given by the bevor, which fitted to the breastplate that Prentice was not wearing currently. Interestingly, the armorer Soort-Almin had clearly heard about other Lions proclivities for helmets. He had glued in an integral padding for Prentice's head, and it all fit perfectly.

"'Ere, you louts is scarin' off the fish and the good folks!" a shrill voice echoed through the dark and lamplight. Heads turned to see a young fishwife with a half-repaired net slung over her shoulder, a shuttle in her hands. She was standing some way away between two drying racks, empty now that winter weather made outdoor drying impossible. "Why don't you pack off back upriver and leave Bridgetown in peace."

"What is your name, wench?" Righteous called to the woman.

"What's it to you, Lacey-face?" the fishwife demanded in turn, and Prentice heard his wife tut furiously.

She turned to the waiting militiamen. "Line first, bring that trollop here!"

"Trollop?" the offended riversider repeated, but her indignation was her undoing as it seemed to take her a moment to realize that the militiamen were coming for her. The line first and two others detached from the rest and moved to catch her. The fishwife made to flee but tangled herself in the net as she tried to put it off her shoulder. By the time she had freed herself, the two militiamen had her in their grip, and they frog marched her up the pier to present her to the offended baroness in the Lace Fang mask.

"This ain't right," the young woman protested, but as she was forced to her knees on the boards, her anger seemed to readily transform into fear.

"Are you in the habit of insulting peers of the realm to their faces? Even in masks?" Righteous asked as imperiously as Dalflitch at her most superior.

"You say...?" the woman asked, clearly becoming terrified by being face-to-face with this well-dressed lady who had companies of militiamen at her command.

"My Lady!" Righteous corrected loudly. "I am Baroness Righteous of Fallenhill, lady-in-waiting to Archduchess Amelia of the Western Reach. You will address me as My Lady, and you will apologize for your...words."

Hearing the pause, Prentice wondered if his wife had been trying to pick a better term. He was fascinated by the extent to which she had this noble persona ready to deploy now, like another blade in her considerable arsenal. It was so effective that her next words shocked him a little. It was hard to remember that she would never carry them through.

"Line first, fetch the trollop's net and cut some cords from it," she said. "We'll use them to give her a thrashing until she learns some manners."

"Not me net," the woman wailed, showing the true priorities of poor fisherfolk. A flogging would be cruel but easily enough survived. Damage to her net would be damage to her livelihood that might well see her going hungry until it was repaired.

"Maybe we'll just flog you with it whole then," Righteous said with a pitiless tone, leaning in so close that Prentice could no longer see the fishwife's face for a moment. "Unless, of course, you apologize."

"I'm sorry," the young woman said in a panic, her hands reaching up to tug her forelock. Her fingers shook with the fear that must be thrilling through her. "Please God, I'm sorry, Highness."

"My Lady!" Righteous snapped at her.

"My Lady! My Lady!" the woman repeated, and at last, Righteous stood back, staring imperiously down at the docksider now put in her place. It was an ugly display of a kind familiar to serfs and yeoman all over the Grand Kingdom. It brought a sour taste to Prentice's mouth as he watched, and a moment later his spouse dismissed the humiliated fishwife. The woman scampered across the dockside boards as if frightened to stand back up before she had escaped her tormenters. Prentice looked from Righteous to Turley, but both seemed equally unmoved by the pitiful sight. When she was gone into the shadows of the waterside community, Righteous turned to them both.

"Tilly says that no one's been in or out of the smokehouse since before noon," she told them quietly. The flickering fingers had been the incognito neophyte's way of giving her report to her superior. Prentice blinked a moment, comforted by the notion that his wife's display had been all an act but still troubled by it all the same.

"Did you have to play the bitch noblewoman quite so fully?" he asked her.

"That was for Tilly's sake," Turley answered for Righteous. "She's got herself in pretty deep with the locals on Salthatch. She says they's all sneak-cheats and shady folks, dealing out their front doors and back doors both. They hate patricians, bailiffs, and nobles, one and all. If Righteous had spoken even one word soft to her, the locals would've taken it amiss."

Like the flower seller you pushed into the gutter, Prentice told himself. He realized afresh that as much as he understood the need to play some dark roles in service of his liege, he would probably never be comfortable doing so. He wondered how his wife felt about it.

"So, no one has gone in, and no one has come out," he muttered. "And there is no sign of any back door. By now, word of our presence here will have crossed to the other islands, let alone all over Salthatch, so Bluebird will know soon that we have found this nest, if he does not already. That leaves nothing else for it—let us see what we have found."

Prentice realized that for all the legitimate reasons to hope upon this discovery, he in fact had little faith that anything truly useful waited for them inside—just like Vespers Remembered and the rooms his dying father had apparently never been in.

CHAPTER 58

It was a noisome little hovel of a place, filthy with fish oil and soot. A powdery soil, as much dropped grains of salt as dried mud, ground underfoot on the floorboards. Drying racks that had not been used in a month or more were pushed to one side of a rough table and two wooden stumps to serve as stools. Even Righteous was forced to bow her head under the low roof, and once she, Turley, and Prentice were inside, there was little space for anyone else.

"Seems they don't live well, these Inquisition men," Turley joked as he looked around in the light of the oil lamp in his hand.

"I imagine a zealot like Bluebird would endure conditions that would make convicts faint if his duty called for it," Prentice said. It was another reason he drove himself every night. If his enemy had the kind of zeal that made him uncaring about this level of discomfort, Prentice had to be ready to do the same. Victory too often belonged to the side that was prepared to do what their enemy considered unthinkable. It was a key part of the Redlanders' early triumphs, for certain. Knights could not imagine an enemy that would care nothing for glory and take no plunder. Prentice was convinced that the Inquisition was the same in that regard.

"Well good for him, then," Righteous said, and then she spat the foul taste of the air from her mouth in a truly unladylike manner. "I hope he hated it as much as we would have."

Prentice and Turley both nodded at that thought. A quick scan of the enclosed space confirmed Prentice's main fear—there seemed to be nothing of significance here. Whatever Bluebird had used the place for, that had passed. Except, the ghosts were sometimes still heard, so what did that mean? Prentice looked around again and his eyes fell upon the rudely fashioned furniture.

"Why all up against one wall?" he mused.

"They wanted the space?" Turley offered.

Prentice shook his head. "I do not think so."

The knight commander took the two steps to the furniture and picked up one of the stools. Then he moved it across to the opposite wall, head bent down the entire short distance. Once he had put it aside, he returned and grabbed the second one. He gave his friend a sharp glance.

"Are you just going to watch me, or are you going to pitch in and help?"

"What? A knight castellan such as me?" Turley asked in mock offense. "What am I, a mere steward that I would be set to moving furnishings like a convict?" He sniffed at the air theatrically and his sour face showed how that was its own punishment in the thick smells of the smokehouse.

"You did not used to be a knight castellan," Prentice retorted. "Not so long ago you *were* a steward, and before that a convict laborer with fetters on your feet and overseers above you." He put the second stool down and stepped back for the table.

"Yes, I *was* a steward," Turley agreed. "Now I am not so lowly a man, given to such lowly work."

"But you still remember how it is done, don't you?" said Prentice, and that drew a smirk from Turley.

"Someone has to hold the lantern," the former steward pointed out, lifting the light up a little higher.

From beside him, Righteous tutted loudly and seized the lantern from his hand.

"Give me that, you daft lout," she said impatiently, the light dancing crazily as she snatched it by its iron hook. "Now get you to the work that my husband, the baron, is too soft a nobleman to command you to, twit."

Turley feigned tugging his forelock and took the other side of the small table for Prentice so that they could remove it across the room as well.

"She's a high-prancin' filly, this new baroness o' yours," Turley told his old friend. "What happened to that rough and ready convict lass you used to kick around with? She was much less coin over kindness."

"She taught me how to stick a lazy fool for his laziness, is what happened to her...oh, hells bells!"

Righteous's sour but playful retort had been cut off by her oath, and Prentice and Turley whirled to see what had caused her such concern. Because of the shadows and the crazed motion of the lantern they had not noticed, but once they had moved the table away, the light revealed a patch of the wooden floor against the hidden wall that had an irregular circle of writing around it. Righteous and Prentice had seen enough Redlander magick to know it immediately, even in the limited light. All three of them stared at it, horrified.

"What if we'd put a foot on it while we were moving the table," Turley said, aghast at the narrowly avoided death.

Righteous nodded and moved back a pace toward the door involuntarily.

How did we not? Prentice wondered, suspicious that in the tiny space they had not been caught in the trap, if it were a trap.

"That's Redlander sorcery," Righteous whispered, and Prentice was sure she was remembering the horror of such enchantments, especially their experience in the defiled Ditch Prison in Aubrey where they had rescued Farringdon from a serpent witch. "We need to burn this place down."

"And the whole dock with it," Turley concurred.

Despite his companions' justified fears, Prentice was not about to put the lantern flame to the boards, if only because a fire like that could burn half the Salthatch dockside to the water before it was controlled, even in the winter. He crouched down to examine the writing. Was it Redlander sorcery or something else?

"Bring the light closer," he told his wife, and as the glow near the floor increased, he began to see differences in the sigils, or thought he did, at least. There was a refinement to the...penmanship? The lettering was clearer, more closely resembling actual written Kingdom speech or similar languages. It reminded him of Solft's examination of some of the graven symbols on the obelisks in the far west.

If only we still had the master with us, he thought, and then a second curse from his wife revealed something more. He looked up and saw on the now uncovered wall, no more than a foot up from the floor, a large iron nail driven through the palm of a severed human hand. The flesh had begun to rot, clearly, but it was also rimed with salt that had likely leached from the wall boards, so it was halfway to mummified as well. Looking at it in the lamplight, it was hard to judge what color or size the withered thing had had in life, but there were darker stains on the fingertips that told Prentice all he needed to know about its former owner.

"Now we know where they took Master Solft to kill him," he said coldly, infuriated by the discovery. The man's right hand severed—exactly the kind of punishment he could imagine the Inquisition inflicting on the poor scholar for the sin of seeking to transcribe the truth from ancient documents. *But why nail it to the wall?*

"Like a thrupenny thief," Righteous said, and by the shadow, Prentice could tell that she had put her free hand to her cheek, likely touching the scar under her mask—her brawler's brand. Grand Kingdom law was harsh in its treatment of habitual criminals. This was more than that, though, Prentice was sure.

"I can fetch Brother Whilte if you want, Prentice," Turley offered, all sense of playfulness gone from him in the light of the discovered arcana. "We should at least make certain we ain't walkin' in some kind o' curse."

"Good idea," Prentice told his friend, not looking away from the strange placement of evil magick—a circle on the floor, just large enough for a man to crouch in if he kept himself pressed against the wall, a nail on that wall, and the moaning in the night.

Inxyphos had stunk of smoke and salt before he transformed, he remembered. *They must have kept him here—inside that circle?*

The door opened and closed as Turley left.

"Should we go, too?" Righteous asked, her voice softer than usual as it so often was when they were alone together and being serious. Prentice did not think there was any tinge of fear in her tone, but he would not have blamed her if there were.

"In a moment," he told her and continued to work the pieces of the puzzle in his head. Inxyphos first, kept here and held back from a final transformation that like as not he was never supposed to recover from. That would probably have required the magick to accomplish, and Prentice wondered if the symbols on the floor were mirrored on the piece of paper they had taken from Inxyphos's bear-form corpse.

Then later they brought Solft here, he thought. *They could have used the sigils to imprison him.* Prentice imagined Solft cowering in the circle, fully aware of the power with which he was contained.

"Why nail it there, though, hidin' it and all?" Righteous asked.

"What do you mean?"

"Well, I ken they wanted to hurt Solft for all his uncovering their secrets, and cutting his writing hand off, ain't that just the way of a petty magistrate, but..."

"But, what?" Prentice asked his wife, looking back over his shoulder at her puzzled expression.

"But, like if you cut a traitor's head off or a thrupenny pilferer's hand, then you nail it up on display as a warnin' to other low folks like. You don't put it behind all the furniture."

They might have used it to refresh the magicks, Prentice thought as he nodded at his wife's astute observation. Then he realized that that was surely not the most likely explanation.

"They kept him here a time, and they wanted him to feel the despair of his fate," he said, recalling something her grace the archduchess had told him about assassins who had been sent to kill her by the Serpent Witch that had bound the Wind Rising fey to her service. Despair had a power or a purpose in magicks, it seemed, and now that he had realized it, Prentice was certain it must be true. Then he smirked as he made the obvious connection.

"Despair is the enemy of faith," he muttered, and the pleasure of that insight stilled his inner enemies for the first time in weeks. They faded like mist in the sunlight, and he enjoyed the near euphoria it produced.

"What's that?" Righteous asked.

"The sword of the word," he explained. "Whilte says it likely needs those who believe in it to wield it—belief, faith, trust. Three words for the same thing, and nothing undoes trust like despair."

Now that he had made the connection, he was still unsure why darkling magick wielders might need hopelessness in a time that no one remembered the counter power of scripture, but it could be a remembered habit from a time when the two powers were more plainly at odds. If folk of faith had forgotten the power of the sword, perhaps the wielders of sorcery had forgotten why despair was so powerful into the bargain. Of course, it could also be that Solft had learned a level of that faithful power for himself, and they had felt the need to undo his faith while they interrogated him. Prentice had no doubt Bluebird would have tortured the poor scholar for every useful detail before he gave him the final mercy of his blade. Staring at the odd space between the fell writing and the severed appendage, Prentice contemplated Solft's final hours and felt a rising shame that he had not saved the man. The stilled hateful chorus began to stir at the fringes of his thoughts, but he shook his head. There would be time for self-pity later. He was about to turn away when he caught sight of something wedged between two of the floorboards in the imprisoning space. He waved the lantern closer again, and in the increased brightness, it looked like a folded piece of parchment or paper. Reflexively he reached for it but managed to stop himself even as Righteous sucked in a horrified breath.

"What are you doing?" she demanded.

"I am...," he began to explain, but his mind was already thinking how to safely fish the paper out of its hiding space. He looked at the floor, the wall, and then around the room. "Come on, let's go outside."

"Right gladly," Righteous muttered vehemently, and she led the way with the lantern. Out on the dockside, the escort was standing by with torches.

"Someone fetch me an axe, or better yet, a stout boathook," Prentice told the line first, and although the man seemed surprised by the request, he moved immediately to obey.

"What you about now, husband?" Righteous asked him quietly.

"There is a piece of something stuck in the floorboards in there, and I want it," he told her, and she responded by giving him a look that made it clear she thought he had taken leave of his senses. Nonetheless, she held the lantern for him once a hook had been brought and he crouched down to get to the smokehouse's side from under the upper jetty. Alternately hammering with the butt end and levering the hook into the gaps, he tore at the boards he was sure backed onto the magickal space. If he could not risk crossing the sigils, he would simply come from the other side. It took a while, and he was sweating by the time he finally tore away one of the boards near the floor just enough for him to reach a hand through.

"Put the lantern down there," he told his wife, pointing to a spot that would let its light shine into the opening. He lay down on the filthy, rotting part of the dock that would never see the sun, hidden as it was by the boards of the walkway above. The stink of the river slime mixed with the waft of old smoke and salt from the cracked boards. Thinking he had a good sense of where he wanted to reach, he carefully threaded his hand through the gap.

Never forgetting the potential danger of reaching too far in and touching the sorcerous symbols, he felt about carefully until his fingers brushed the folded note. Pinching and flicking, hoping for a grip on the barely protruding edge of the paper, his hand and fingers were aching long before he managed to pull it forth. He was beginning to think he would have to tear out more of the wall when the note finally began to slip free. He extracted his hand and rolled over onto his back, holding the paper up triumphantly in the lantern light.

"Oh aye," his wife said to him, her lips twisting in a sceptical frown. "And what if it's just more o' them killin' words?"

He looked at her and blinked a moment. "I had not thought of that."

CHAPTER 59

"A sacrifice on unhallowed ground?"

Amelia read the words aloud from the torn scrap of paper Righteous had presented to her. She looked to the baroness Lace Fang standing by the side of her bed.

"And Prentice thinks this is from Master Solft?"

"He does, Your Grace," Righteous said with a confident nod.

"Hard to believe," Amelia said, looking back at the poorly formed letters, like a child's first attempts at writing. No scrivener of Solft's skill would ever have produced such poor script by choice. If Prentice and Righteous's other deductions were correct, however, then nothing about it had been scribed by choice.

Written with his off-hand, using a splinter dipped in the blood of his severed right hand? she wondered, horrified at the prospect. Even as her mind conjured the image, it was almost beyond her to think of the pale and timid scholar enduring such brutal suffering all for the sake of conveying this one, cryptic message.

What does it mean?

"Does Prentice understand it?" she asked Righteous as she handed the scrap to Farringdon standing on the other side of the bed. Now that Amelia had taken to her seclusion until the birth, she was expected to receive only female company. She did not want for women and girls for the role, servants and ladies-in-waiting, but even so, she absolutely refused to exclude Farringdon from her presence. It was a maddening enough prospect to be confined to her bed for most of the day; to forgo his loving support into the bargain was unthinkable. However, even with *that* flouting of tradition, to admit Prentice or any other man into her presence felt like a step too far, and so any word or report from her knight commander would have to be presented through Prentice's wife for now. It was not something Amelia liked doing, not with the tension already between them both and the hard words of their last conversation.

"I wonder what he tore this scrap from," Farringdon mused, turning the piece over. "He's written on the back of something partially illuminated, that's for certain."

The opposite side of the page from Solft's final blood-scratched note had part of a patterned border, as well as what looked like a section of a bat's wing and the paw of a lion or bear perhaps. The claws of the paw were tearing at the wing.

"In all likelihood, it was one of the books of his research, stolen by the false neophyte after he was kidnapped," Amelia said with a scowl, inwardly cursing the frustration of finding only these fractions of clues. In Dweltford, Prentice and Turley had been like the most cunning of ferrets, and no secrets had seemed safe from them. Here in Bridgetown, they were like blind mice, only coming upon crumbs after the meal was long stolen away by cannier vermin. For herself, Amelia had tried to turn her confinement to some use, reading some of the transcribed verses of the Steeple Aviary, but whenever she did her head ached and her mind wandered—another pleasant gift of late pregnancy, apparently.

"Where are my rats?" she mused and then looked up at Righteous, hopeful the baroness did not take the surly comment amiss. If she did, Righteous's expression revealed nothing. Farringdon was still turning the page over in his hands.

"If this is a bear's paw, that might be a dragon's wing," he offered. "And a sacrifice on unhallowed ground?"

"We have already seen that," Lady Spindle said from the end of the bed. It was rare for her to be in the Paramour's Chambers these days, although Amelia was pleased that the other senior Lace Fang brought news that her husband, Caius Welburne, seemed to be doing well. "We all watched that bloody fool put that sacrist down on the steps of the cathedral. He un-hallowed-dized that ground for certain."

Amelia hid a smirk at her lady-in-waiting's odd turn of phrase, nodding at the truth of it, though. This strange note that had taken so much effort to discover only seemed to reference an act they already understood. What use was that to them now?

Solft knew all of that, she thought, her brow furrowing in concentration. *Why would he drive himself in his last moments or hours to secretly pen this? Was he merely driven mad by his pain, or is there a further secret we need to uncover?*

She contemplated the pieces. A paw and a wing? A dragon and a lion? Or a bear? All those symbols were at play here in Bridgetown's siege. And the wing was torn—a clear heraldic demonstration of defeat. The dragon, if it was a dragon, was being beaten by the paw.

"So, what worth the sacrifice?" she wondered out loud, not really caring if her attendants understood. A part of her chuckled at how she must sound like the ever-pensive Prentice at this moment, so often talking from thoughts many paces ahead of those around him in the discussion. How odd that in this moment when he and she were so distant, he should be present in the habits he had helped her cultivate. It made her think that, short of open rebellion, he would never be fully out of her favor. She would not permit it. He was owed too much.

"I think we might make one or two messages out of what we know, at least, my love," Farringdon said, showing that perhaps Amelia was not quite as far ahead as she imagined. "Either that is a bear's paw or a lion's."

"Prentice says it could be a leopard's as well, or any heraldic cat. From its shape, he says the only pawed things it can't be is a dog or a wolf," Righteous chimed in, and Farringdon acknowledged the wisdom of her statement with a polite nod, taking no umbrage at the interruption. Amelia nodded as well, smiling not at the interaction but at the contribution from Baron Ash. Even in his absence, Prentice was still ahead of them.

"Quite so, My Lady," Farringdon said. "If it be a bear, I think we see the cause for the sacrifice upon the steps."

He paused, clearly to let them question his statement. When it was equally clear that they were happy for him to explain himself, he nodded again.

"The cathedral is part of the earldom and the spiritual side of Baroness-elect Penelope's noble seat. She inherits the obligation to protect the cathedral and its role in her domain's spiritual life. Defiling it had ugly political consequences, but it surely had spiritual implications as well, and not just from the perspective of demolishing the refuge from sorcery it might've provided. Perhaps it removes a further blessing of heaven on the entire domain—curses the town, as it were. With these symbols taken together, and Master Solft's words, I would say this one scrap of paper tells us that the Bear of Bridgetown had the strength to oppose the Dragons of Denay, but the murder of the sacrist on the cathedral steps has undone that strength in a spiritual fashion, somehow."

"You mean the town's cursed, doomed to fall?" Spindle asked, her lips twisting in a frown. "I don't like that news."

"Ay, My Lady, and not something we should want to spread about, either," Farringdon agreed.

Hearing him, Amelia looked to the curtains around her bed "room," knowing that every member of her chambers beyond had heard the words already and that they were now bound to trust to the neophyte's discretion. *If any but Dalflitch had trained them, I might have cause to worry,* she told herself. Her lady seneschal was not present at this moment, being still about the final planning of Sir Turley's return journey and hunt for the stolen transport boat. Even so, her influence was embodied in every one of the chamber ladies and their mores and manners.

"What about her cloth-headedness?" Righteous asked, and Amelia immediately perked up. It was an excellent notion.

"The sacrifice on unhallowed ground might be responsible for the souring of Penelope's mind?" she asked, more rhetorically than anything else. The possibility that they had located the source of the baroness-elect's destabilized mental state was encouraging indeed, even if they had no idea yet how to reverse the sorcery involved.

"That could have motivated Master Solft to desperate measures to inform us," Farringdon said, nodding in agreement. "Tricking one of Penelope's retainers into murdering the sacrist on the cathedral steps might have been the catalyst for some sorcery upon her thoughts, although we should remember that she was already not sweet upon us before that day."

"Some of us aren't like to ever forget, My Lord," Righteous said archly, and Amelia reached out to give her lady-in-waiting's hand a reassuring touch. Whatever damage Righteous had done, it was clear now that the Bluebird had already been hard at work preparing the ground of hostility in Penelope's heart and mind. Silent Hand magicks or not, the girl was also already prideful and foolish long before any army came to seize Bridgetown from her dying father's hands.

"So, what if it's a lion's paw?" Spindle asked suddenly, knocking the conversation on to the second possible interpretation Farringdon had foreseen.

The marquis chewed his lip thoughtfully for a moment, then tilted his head with a frown. "If it is a lion's paw, I would say this predicts the White Lions opposing and defeating the Dragons of Denay, and the sacrifice was purposed to overthrow that outcome. The dead sacrist might be to curse *our* defense of Bridgetown."

Farringdon's face darkened considerably as he said that, and Amelia was sure she understood why. Try as he might, he had yet to devise a successful stratagem for dealing with Daven Marcus's brutal cannons. Although two of the ancient beasts had already been destroyed, that limited achievement had come at the cost of four of the Lions' own guns. Such odds could not be sustained, and even this very morning, more of the Dragon's impossibly large stones had been falling on Loncastel. The keep was said to have taken significant damage, and most of the island's north shore was nothing but rubble now. Like a child who broke his own toys rather than share, it seemed almost as if the Usurper had decided that if Bridgetown was not his, it would be nobody's.

"So, the message is that either the poor fool was stabbed on the steps to make the baroness-elect mad or to make it so we can't beat off the Usurper's big guns," Spindle summarized for them grimly.

"That is not acceptable," Amelia said reflexively, and she looked to each attendant in turn, stopping at her husband. "If we take this word as unavoidable, we might as well simply withdraw our troops now and return to Dweltford. Do any of you want to abandon the town to Daven Marcus' mercies at this stage?"

All shook their heads.

"Penelope would be happy if we did," Righteous said quietly, and though it was true, Amelia found it an unhelpful observation.

"She might be," the archduchess conceded, "right up until the little monster started slaughtering her people and forcing her into a wedding that ill-suited her. Can you imagine Penelope holding her tongue for the sake of a political marriage?"

It was clear from their expressions that none of them could, and they all knew that if Lady Penelope came fully under Daven Marcus's control, he would force her into a marriage advantageous for himself. If the baroness-elect objected, she would likely learn just how cruel the Usurper king could truly be; no one doubted that.

"Bridgetown may not be my people, but I am not yet ready to abandon them to Daven Marcus on the word of obscure prophecy or possible curses," Amelia declared, settling the matter. "Knowing that, what else do we do now?"

"If it's a bear, Your Grace, then there ain't much different we need to do, wouldn't you say?" Righteous offered. "The filly's already as silly and stabled as she can be. No more damage for her to do. She can kick at the stall much as she likes, but it's nothin' to us."

Grim for her but not wrong for us, Amelia agreed inwardly. "Knowing that, what if it is a lion?"

"If we are covered by that curse, assuming it is a curse of some sort, I would say we should set Master Solft to search out the meaning and parameters of the magick," Farringdon said, and his frown turned so twisted that it looked like he had swallowed something impossibly sour. He scratched at his beard as he went on. "But since it cost us the scholar's life simply to find the sorcery out, I don't see we have any other choice but to set Brother Whilte to the mystery."

"How much more do we heap upon the poor man's shoulders?" Amelia asked. Whilte already seemed to be nearly broken with exhaustion. It felt cruel to lay this at his feet as well.

"My Prentice is already speakin' with him 'bout it," Righteous told them.

Amelia nodded and suddenly felt quite weary herself. All this effort to think and it only brought her to the end of the horse race to find Prentice already dismounted and accepting the prize.

Not a prize, she told herself, *just the next stage of the race—a race that has no end, it seems.*

CHAPTER 60

"That is well and good, My Lady," said the archduchess, forcing herself to sound more satisfied than she felt. "Please tell your husband the next time you see him that I am encouraged by his progress."

"I'll be sure to, Your Grace, but I can't say for certain when that will be," Righteous told her. "He's of a will for that training he's doing. Not like to be back to see me in a hurry."

"Building some new, elite company?" Amelia asked, her hidden fear of Prentice's obsessive activities showing itself for a moment. No matter how much she felt she owed him her trust, a part of the archduchess could not stop worrying about another noble rebellion.

"Building *himself* to something, that's all I'd say for sure," Righteous scoffed, clearly confused or annoyed by her husband's actions as well.

"What mean you, My Lady?" Farringdon asked.

"Well, word is he's called on you more'n once to send him training partners, not just fellows from the Gryphon Banner," Righteous explained. "What's they said to you 'bout it?"

Amelia looked to her husband, and he rubbed at the back of his head sheepishly, as if embarrassed to talk about his fellow company commander behind his back. It was exactly the kind of loyalty the archduchess expected from her husband, and from Prentice, mostly. Perhaps Bluebird's sacrifice on unhallowed ground was affecting the White Lions and her trust in their leader. It was not a prospect Amelia enjoyed.

"The few men who've said aught to me about the knight commander's training sessions have...uh...have made it clear he is not teaching them anything, especially," Farringdon explained. "I mean, they say they learn much just by watching, but in the main it's more like being asked to a prizefighter's ring on a harvest day. He challenges them to come at him, and either he beats them off or they beat him down."

"Last time I spoke with Whilte, he's in to heal my Prentice every night. He says if it keeps up like this, there's a chance of some permanent wound." Righteous's tone was full of more concern than she normally ever showed for her husband, but still it was tinged with annoyance as well.

"It troubles you?" Amelia asked, glad at least to hear that there were no rumors of a rebel cadre being built in the midst of her militia.

That would be Bluebird's tactic, not Prentice's, she told herself, finding it hard to believe even as she was sure it was true.

"Troubles, Your Grace? Bloody puts me in my place, is what it does," Righteous said, shaking her head. "He was always fast and strong. Now he's like some hound—half hunting breed, half fighting—and better than either. So flamin' fast I couldn't lay an edge on him, even when I thought to make him earn it."

"You are annoyed...because he is...better...than you?" Amelia asked slowly, caught out by the notion.

"Better than bloody ever!" the baroness insisted. The archduchess looked at Farringdon and he shrugged.

"It's what they say," he confirmed.

"To what end?" Amelia asked, looking at them all again in turn. Farringdon only shrugged once more.

"If Lady Righteous cannot persuade him to reveal his purposes, I doubt I would find him out, my love."

Amelia shook her head and felt her pregnant weariness again, heavily. All these years growing closer to Prentice, coming to understand and trust him more fully, and now he was a closed book even to his devoted wife. Just what had that sacrifice on hallowed ground done to her White Lions, and how were they going to reverse the effects?

"Until Prentice and Whilte give us better word, perhaps we should keep on as we are, Your Grace," Spindle said, showing a welcome practicality. No wonder she and the shrewd Caius suited each other as spouses. The abstract notions of the world were not of much interest to either of them.

"No point surrendering to despair over maybes and could be's," Righteous agreed, nodding.

"Alright, then what do we do in the spirit of keeping on as we are?" Amelia asked.

"For a start, my love, you should keep here, resting and caring for yourself and our child to come," Farringdon told her in a loving command. He rarely expressed any sense of husbandly authority over her in front of others—or indeed, at all—but Amelia could understand why he might at this moment. She probably looked as weary as she felt.

"Yes, husband," she said with a wry frown and a slightly teasing tone that lifted tiny smirks from the Lace Fangs. "Other than that?"

Farringdon nodded seriously. "Other than that, I have been thinking about the Dragon problem," he said. "Prentice's fey man says that each shelter has its own powder supplies and that each is under guard. Daven Marcus has a garrison of knights camped a short distance behind them, and the patrols are well armed and continuous in the night. My hope to send a secret force across to light their powder would be all but impossible to accomplish, although Dahyoor assures me that a proper company of fey riders could sweep the whole Bronze Dragon battery in less than an hour and destroy the lot."

"A proper company?" Amelia asked, wondering what constituted "proper" in fey terms.

"That's my interpretation," Farringdon said. "In truth, I am not nearly so familiar with their speech as the knight commander. The word his squire used was *kesh...kesh*-something. I take it to mean a company of significant size. He promised us that such a company of riders was on its way and due to arrive around the start of spring."

Along with my child, Amelia thought. It would be a significant new year indeed.

"His exact words were 'the Lioness Mother will have her *kesh*...thing-company when the rains cease and the flowers begin their dance in the sun,'" Farringdon went on.

"Poetry-like," Spindle said sourly.

"But at least not as hard to interpret as our scrap o' paper there," Righteous added, nodding at Solft's last missive, now laying on Amelia's blanket.

Lady Spindle acknowledged the truth of the observation with a shrug of her own.

"It seems we are forced to wait for spring while Daven Marcus's bronze toys make a wasteland of Loncastel?" Amelia muttered, feeling as sour as Spindle's expression.

"That's not my plan, Your Grace," Farringdon told her, switching back to her noble term of address now that they were speaking of strategy. "We cannot easily use stealth, but now that the Usurper has moved his army camp close to us, there is the possibility of raiding in force once more."

"He was ready for that last time," Amelia said, and Farringdon nodded glumly a moment.

"He was, indeed, but this time things are different."

"How so?"

"This time, he is all in sight. We can scout the immediate ground and pick out his ranger mercenaries with their stealth, if they are lurking somewhere. We know where all the Dragons are, and we know where his knights and levies are arrayed. And we have the downriver approach for his boats covered by cannons. There is simply so much less treachery to fear this time."

That all sounded very positive to Amelia, but she forced herself to wonder what was being missed. At another time she might have told herself to wonder what Prentice would see that they had not, and when she realized that, it made her even more troubled at their current estrangement, however mild it might be.

"Why would Daven Marcus take such a risk?" she asked.

"Because we have no bridge to sally with," Farringdon said confidently. "We cannot march an army at him, so he uses the security of the uncrossable river to his own advantage, as we use it to ours."

"That don't explain how you think to make this raid you're speakin' of, My Lord," Righteous pointed out.

Farringdon gave her a look of cunning that surprised his wife. "I mean to take a page out of the Redlanders' codex," he said, and then, as if realizing what such a comment might imply, quickly followed up. "Not their sorcery, obviously, but their art for crossing water."

"You want to make a floating bridge?" Amelia asked.

"Something of the sort," he agreed. "I've been speaking to some boat builders. At least one fellow who's lost his business on Loncastel is quite eager to aid us against the Usurper. He says that any length of boats will likely flex on their cables against the river flow. He says anything long enough to cross even the channel from Loncastel to the north bank could be twisted on itself right quickly, meaning that any bridge across might turn into a trap for the men crossing over. That was why the Red Sky held the Murrflow still that night."

"What is to be done then?"

"The gaps in the north bridge," the marquis declared with a lightly triumphant tone. He was speaking on engineering matters now, and his simple pleasure in the task was evident. "Only two spans were actually destroyed, and the pylons in between are stout enough still to tie off floating pieces of bridge."

"And these'll work because...?" Spindle asked.

"Because the lengths of cable or chain will be short and the anchors in the middle will be fixed. We cannot stop the flow of the Murr as the Redlanders did, and if we merely strung boats together, they would need much reinforcement or else the boats and cables would simply act like links in a chain, flexing in the current."

"They couldn't be secured?" Amelia asked.

"They could, but it would take much too long to achieve—days most likely. The enemy would turn the Dragons loose and we'd lose the bridge before we ever got to use it. But our boatwright is building me two special barges, converted from craft already here in Bridgetown and languishing in the war. They'll have raised decks, so close to the height of the existing bridge that it'll be no more than a step down for anyone crossing on it. We'll be able to float them down the north Loncastel channel with the flow, aim each one into one of the two gaps and tie them in place tightly—all in one hour of the candle."

"Truly?" Amelia asked, feeling like this almost sounded too easy.

"My boatwright assures me that pole crews accustomed to steering their way through the tangle of the inner channel bridges and jetties would think nothing of such a straightforward maneuver," Farringdon said with his own confidence.

"So that finishes the bridge back up, but the Dragons still are going to breathe their fire and shot all over it," Righteous protested.

"Hence the raid," Farringdon declared. "We ship the bridge pieces down in the hour before dawn, get them tied off and the whole of Lion Banner crosses in force with the day's first light, aiming straight for the cannons again. Only this time with less than a league to reach the cannons and nothing but open ground between them."

"You make it sound so simple," Amelia said, enjoying his enthusiasm, but remembering that he had felt this confident the previous time the Lions had attempted such a stratagem. It seemed Farringdon was aware of the danger as well.

"We will have Dahyoor ahead of us this time, Your Grace," he said simply. "Many nights' worth of scouting, if I get my way. Only when I am certain that our surprise will be sure will I give the command."

"And we will not have to await the spring for this stratagem?"

"In fact, for the height of the river, it will be better if we do it sooner."

"This is all encouraging news," Amelia said, and she laid her head back against her pillows, closing her eyes. For all their slow progress against their enemies, she was comforted that it was at least some kind of progress. It was enough for her to sleep upon for now, and not until she awakened from her nap later in the day did she realize she had forgotten to dismiss them. When she realized, she chuckled with a touch of embarrassment, which brought her neophytes through the curtains to her bedside. She might have gone into "seclusion," but she was far from alone.

CHAPTER 61

"We will need lamps or torches soon," Whilte said as he clomped along behind Prentice, taking a moment to look up to the sky and the dismal afternoon light.

"Like the last time we were here," Prentice muttered, eyes on the ground and not the sky.

"Yes, I suppose so," the chaplain agreed.

The two men walked eastward along the processional way that led between houses from Great Bridge Road to the cathedral square on Oldbridge Island. Sometimes glimpsed between the houses, Earlsbastion castle loomed on its hill to their left and ahead. The mighty edifice of the Bridgetown cathedral became more and more apparent, as if it was the carved far wall of a hidden valley that they were now approaching through a narrow ravine. For a moment it reminded Prentice of the Gryphons' night journey through secret stone passages in the far west.

When Solft had been with us, he thought and now he did look at the cloud-banked sky, darkly crowding over the town like a somber canopy. It looked like it might begin to rain again at any moment, and that notion turned Prentice back to the ground, keeping his eyes on the slick stones so he did not slip. At the point where their road emptied into the cathedral plaza, a yeoman woman turned the corner ahead of them, carrying a heavy basket on her back. She made no effort to reach her forelock under her bonnet, but she nodded her head as she hurried past them, likely eager to get wherever she was going during the momentary stop in the rain.

Prentice led the way out of the road and over the flagstones, heading straight at the cathedral door across the square, while behind him Whilte's wooden leg gave thumps that echoed off the houses on either side.

"Winter's done its washing of the stains," the chaplain observed as they passed the section of the square where the main of Inxyphos's bear-man slaughter had been done. That day the location had been a fen of blood and bodies, smelling like a charnel pit, but now the pale stone of the flags had been cleansed by the winter downpours, and there was barely a shadow in the color to mark the place. Within a year even that would be gone.

That was where we smelt the salt and smoke, Prentice thought, barely giving the spot more than a glance. Months later and all it had done was to lead him to Master Solft's severed hand. *And his warning, if that is what it is.*

He turned his eyes on the cathedral itself. The pale sandstone of the edifice looked grey in the dismal light, its enormous arched window above the door dark and foreboding with no lights from within. Prentice took a moment to survey it as he approached. It occurred to him that he had not been to a church service in the entire time he had been in Bridgetown, although he let Whilte pray with him and other officers from time to time.

Another thing you fail at, his father's inner voice sneered, but he felt his own inward self sneer back.

For ten years as a convict, no one, not even the least sacrist, gave a damn whether I took a moment to pray, he thought. *Now that I am respectable again, I am supposed to care about such things?*

The Almighty does, his father pushed, and it annoyed Prentice to imagine the hateful old man might think to call God's judgement upon him. God and religion had only ever been a means to an end for his father—a pathway for his son to gain a noble title for the family. Even so, Prentice thought it would likely be a good idea for him to go into the cathedral to pray.

For his own faith, he subscribed to the belief that all creation was God's temple, and a prayer could be made in any place, from the top of the tallest tower to the bottom of the deepest pit, like the shaggy-maned prophet from his dream. Even so, there was something about holy places. His own experiences with *brakkis effar* and sanctified buildings seemed to confirm that.

"In the southern style," Whilte said beside him, and Prentice gave the chaplain a quizzical glance. He nodded toward the cathedral. "No saints in alabaster, nor much in the way of filigree, and surely nothing chased in gold. Just the belltower, the stained glass, and that one frieze of the Lord with the disciples on his Ascension Day. It's the style of the southern faiths rather than the Denay theology."

Prentice studied the features of the cathedral architecture as Whilte pointed them out, noting especially the frieze he described, which occupied a long stretch of stones over the mighty doors, seeming like a beam that held the upper part of the building upon itself. He wondered at the earnest skill expressed in the alabaster carving set into the sandstone. He understood the purpose of the artistry from a Church perspective. Congregants who could neither read nor write came to the cathedral and saw manifest the figures and teachings from sermons. These were the heraldry of theology, carved rather than painted, because the truths they embodied were eternal, or at least should be. Of course, in the midst of this supposedly holy purpose, mortals inserted their own pride and self-importance all too often. Many a high sacrist or other senior patron would finance a statue or stained glass and have their own faces put in the holiest place. All across the Grand Kingdom there were parables embodied, scenes from the gospel or some other religious work, and the face of the Lord was modeled on the man who paid for it. It was the kind of prideful self-aggrandizement that had caused a breakaway faction of the Church to side with the Vec princes in their rebellion. Now it was centuries later, and those men's descendants had their own edifices, proud of the starkness of their buildings, certain that their lack of gold and statues was all they needed to make themselves the holier. And yet princes like Everard of Sunbury still committed the same murderous excesses that stained crimson the hands of the Grand Kingdom peerage.

And Bridgetown stands in the middle, a compromise of the two forms, Prentice thought. *Religiously and politically, it seems.* In that light, Bluebird's sacrifice of the sacrist on the steps made even more sense—the Inquisition punishing a theologically compromised church for its disloyalty, perhaps? At every turn, the Silent Hand seemed to have more than one purpose to its actions. It would not surprise Prentice to discover this was so. Whomever the Mother Church sent to reconsecrate the ground of the cathedral, whenever that might be, could renew a mystical claim over Bridgetown on behalf of the ecclesiarches, bind it afresh with prayers or even ancient magicks.

We live in the shadow of lost powers, half-truths used to cover great truths, he thought as he started walking toward the cathedral again, aiming for the space in front of its steps where the bear Inxyphos had been slain. *Powers that were ancient and forgotten before the first stone of this house to God was even laid.*

Prentice knew that the Almighty kept secrets from men, and in truth, he did not care one way or another about that. If the Creator of all things did not want to reveal something, there was nothing to be done about it. Like the mountain that did not care if men raved at it, what could mortals do when the Creator said no? But if the Almighty willed that a truth should be revealed to mortals, what right did any have to seal it up? Secrets like that rotted the soul—not just the souls of folk but of whole nations, it seemed. Secrets like whomever was giving the Golden Heron their marching orders, so they paid to set a prince like Sunbury to the same vile actions that made Daven Marcus a tyrant. The southern faith eschewed the gold and the statues, but the secrets still rotted their soul.

But is that my responsibility? Prentice wondered. He knew so little of the Vec, really. He was a Grand Kingdom man. Most of what he was told had been colored by the hatred between thrones—temporal and spiritual. And his visions set him to tear down the ancient and false temple in Denay. What right did he have to judge Sunbury and his ilk in the Grey Hill Compact of Princes?

The right of bloodshed? Men are dying at the foot of Sougate. Is that not enough justification to do something?

Suddenly, a detail of his vision of the pit came back to him. The pillar in the pit had to be felled first, before the eagle could be toppled in Denay. That pit had been south of the city in his vision—of Denay—but how far south? Almost without thinking, Prentice turned to face the southern horizon. Could the pit be farther south than he had imagined? His mind balked at the notion, but so many of the pieces seemed to fit. To the south of Bridgetown, the army of the Golden Heron was assaulting the town, and by it, the gateway to the Grand Kingdom. If Daven Marcus was to be safely defeated on the north bank, surely the south would have to be secured. Were the ravens in his vision, in fact, herons? Her grace had seen the Inquisition figured as a flock of different breeds of birds, and of course, Bluebird was first amongst them.

"Could they be hiding in the Vec?" Prentice mused quietly as his feet stepped onto the exact space where the felled bear *brakkis effar* had lain. He could tell, because unlike the stain of the slaughtered yeomanry, the stones here had been etched by the corrosive blood. The flags would have to be replaced or else the memory of the dead beast man would linger forever.

"Who?" Whilte asked him.

"The Silent Hand."

The notion that the Inquisition might be based in the Vec clearly surprised the chaplain, and he rubbed at the stubbled bald spot of his tonsure thoughtfully.

"Is that likely?"

"I have no idea," Prentice said, his own brows furrowing as he looked down at the etched stones. These were why he and

Whilte had returned to the square, to see if there was a missed clue that Solft's note might be pointing towards. At this moment, the location of the Inquisition's headquarters dominated his thoughts, however. Even the hateful chorus was stilled a moment in the power of the question. In trying to interpret his dream, had Prentice failed to look far enough south?

"Why would they lair amongst the rebels they so despise?" Whilte asked. It was the obvious question.

"They move amidst the churchmen and nobles they despise," Prentice retorted, almost without thinking. In his mind, he was seeing again the naked, blood-soaked figure at the bottom of the pit—a man who used blood as ink to purge even the parts of holy writ that he did not want, the keeper of secrets who regarded all men as his inferior. That man would not hesitate to foster a conflict that split the Grand Kingdom apart and left it in constant war across the ancient river that flowed from a divine spring a thousand leagues away. He would likely even consider it good business, keeping all the Grand Kingdom at a state of holy readiness, hoping for a renewed crusade. Once the fey were driven into hiding and the blood sects were banished over the mountain and the salt sea, what stick of fear was left to beat the common folk into submission?

"Is this the clue we have come to find?" Prentice asked. "Could Solft have received a revelation of his own? Could it be that he died to send us farther south, into the Vec?"

"You think your pit to play Samson in is in Town Sobridge? Or somewhere farther still?" Whilte asked him, tipping his head quizzically to one side.

"Play?" Prentice demanded, whirling on the brother. "You think I mean to play? Like a child with a ball or a Young Hopeful with the lives of our militiamen?"

At one level it astonished Prentice how much Whilte's words stung him, and he would later wonder that his pride was now so fragile, if it was his pride. He had shared the details of his dream with the chaplain already, and Whilte knew that Prentice had had more than one such divine insight in the past, yet still he suggested that it might all be a game? Did the cleric truly believe Prentice to be like Cyprian, Cassian, and their ilk? Was he no more than a Wilforn in the eyes of those around him, *playing* at his duties?

"Her grace has stripped me of Sougate and almost every other purpose and meaning I had in her service," he ground out through gritted teeth. "I know that, and I know that everyone else knows it as well, but do you truly think I care nothing for what happens around me? White Lions die under the breath of Dragons on Loncastel, and Sunbury's pressed levies bleed and scald body and soul in front of Sougate. Do you think I have forgotten any of that? Every moment I fail to find the accursed Bluebird and whatever agents he commands, men bleed and die! I am at my limit, sacrist! If you know any obvious clue I have missed, feed it to me like an infant. I swear I will not spit it out!"

Prentice felt himself losing control of his tongue, and he clenched his teeth more tightly in fury, fearful of saying something worse than he already had. Was there anything more pathetic than a man who pitied himself because life was difficult? Life was always difficult. He stared down at the etched stones, as if to will Solft's meaning into his mind by meditating on the spot. He had so little else to go on.

"I am sorry, Prentice," Whilte said quietly after a moment. "I spoke poorly. I did not mean to insult you."

"I am not insulted, Brother," Prentice lied, embarrassed by his show of weakness. "Think no more of it. Our duty is to find Bluebird. Let us focus on that."

The hateful chorus laughed at him. He turned from the etched stone to the steps where the poor sacrist had died under Cassian's blade. More sheltered as it was from the weather, the top of the step had not been as washed by the storms, and no one had been set to clean the man's blood away. The gloomy afternoon revealed an ugly, dark blot.

"They took the corpse but did not think to wash the stain," Whilte muttered grimly as he mounted the step with awkward wooden footfalls. Prentice was sure he meant the word "stain" in more than one sense.

"Why bother with the blood if the building is still defiled?" the knight commander mused, and Whilte nodded with a frown. Prentice felt much the same as the chaplain seemed to. This excursion was yielding no fruit, so far serving only to reinforce their frustration.

"We should pray," Whilte said suddenly. When Prentice looked at him, he shrugged as if his meaning should surely be obvious. "If we want Our Lord to reveal the truth of things to us, if we need his insight to understand his revelation, surely we should ask him, at the very least."

Prentice nodded, accepting the simple wisdom that was strangely difficult to come to. He turned and took the final steps to the cathedral doors, but when his hand touched the latch, the portal resisted. He traced the mighty brass lock with one fingertip.

"You do not happen to have the key?" he asked with a wry smile, which Whilte returned.

"I fear I am not that well regarded in the Bridgetown clergy," he joked, and the two of them looked at the door and then down either side of the portico. There would surely be a side door somewhere, but the rain was starting to fall again. Prentice was reluctant to go tromping through the drops seeking an entrance to a defiled holy place.

"Well, we've prayed on a land parched by ancient curses and been shown the way then," Whilte said. "I don't see why bloodied steps should be much different. We can pray here."

"*You* prayed in the far west and received the vision, Brother," Prentice told him, not meaning to sound resistant but feeling more like his convict self—resentful and dejected.

"Did you never pray?" Whilte asked him, sounding genuinely surprised.

"I prayed that I might deliver her grace's judgement on the Serpent Witch," Prentice admitted. "I prayed to make my family safe and to do my duty."

"So, much the same as today?" Whilte said with a knowing smile, and despite himself, Prentice smiled in return. It was a fair assessment. He nodded to Whilte to begin and bowed his head.

You call on God, Brother, he thought. *I am too bitter to trust for answers from on high today.*

After all your fabled visions and dreams? some part of himself asked, and in this moment, Prentice could not tell if it was his father, his instructors, his own pride, or even the voice of God himself. He shook his head and clamped his mouth closed against his own tongue while he waited for the chaplain to begin to pray. When it came, the prayer was simple, direct, and exactly from scripture.

"Open our eyes, Lord, that we may see."

Prentice recognized the words as a prayer from an ancient prophet whose servant was suffering a lack of faith. He wondered momentarily if this was another sly rebuke, like the "playing at Samson" comment. But he also remembered that the prophet's prayer had revealed an angelic army with chariots of fire, all about the prophet and his servant. Prentice lifted his head, hopeful despite himself of some similar vision.

Around him the square was darker than it had been, as if night had suddenly fallen, though the town had set no new lights. The portico and the cathedral seemed as deeply washed with shadow, if not more so. Then Whilte's staff began to glow with its light, as it so often did in miraculous moments. It drove back the shadows like a dam pushing back floodwaters until the two men, the small part of the portico and steps they occupied, and the doors of the cathedral were encircled with it. The light blazed bright and golden, like summer sunshine, and Prentice looked in all directions, hoping for an angelic sign—a lion or even a chariot. He gazed up and down the portico, trying to see if the panels of the door revealed any words or images, and scoured the darkened square with his eyes, wondering if a hound or an eagle, a raven or a dragon, or even the six-headed serpent of the Redlanders might appear.

There was nothing. Gradually, the light faded away.

"I did not see," Whilte said as the natural gloom of an overcast winter's afternoon reasserted itself over the square, heavier raindrops starting to fall. "Was some clue revealed?"

"No," was all Prentice said in response.

"Nothing?" the chaplain pressed. "Nothing at all?"

"Just your light. At least the Almighty still sees fit to do little miracles upon request," Prentice answered bitterly, and he stepped out into the rain, thinking to return to the camp and the few duties he was still considered worthy to perform.

"That was petty, Prentice," Whilte called after him, falling behind a moment on his wooden leg as he negotiated the steps and pulled the hood of his cassock up over his head.

Prentice did not bother to answer him. The chaplain was not wrong.

CHAPTER 62

For the next weeks of winter, the siege continued very much as it had. Foul weather beat upon Bridgetown, the river rose yet more, and the Dragons continued to duel with the Lions' cannons, their might and numbers a grinding advantage that must soon win outright. The thunder of the guns was so ubiquitous that it seemed no one in the town even noticed it any longer, at least those who were not from Loncastel Island. Loyal militiamen were heartened by the news that their liege was healthy in the last stage of her pregnancy and now in safe seclusion. Banner Sergeant Porth's program of improvements about Runners Field continued, and that seemed to help the men-at-arms crowded into tents to keep their morale high, or at least higher than a winter campaign typically allowed. The open meadow that had once been a nobleman's park to allow knights to joust and ride was becoming transformed into a military district of the town, with semi-paved roads, effective drainage, and numerous other small improvements. Come springtime, Runners Field would likely never be a field again.

Prentice watched the camp's growth daily and found it cheered him some against the miseries of the siege. Of course, his inward father only used the success as another example of why Prentice was becoming even more redundant to the military companies he had founded. Never able to fully silence the criticisms, he sought continually for harsher training and refused to rest each day until his limbs threatened to give out. He had a new, undyed arming doublet and matching trews fitted to go under his armor harness and took to wearing the entire panoply every day. The extra weight was to be an additional challenge to his body, but Soort-Almin had done a finer job of forging the armor than Prentice could have imagined. It fit so well and had so little excess weight that within days, the burden seemed too light to count as training. The joints also fitted so well that there was no need for mail pieces to be worn in the armpits and elbows. Everything was protected by the articulated steel. Even before the first week of wearing it was finished, Prentice had taken to beginning his morning by running a circuit of the camp in armor just to make bearing the steel harness some kind of challenge.

In the training shed he practiced rolling and tumbling in armor and had a hanging pell set to drill his longsword technique against with a heavy wooden copy of his champion blade. There were no longswordsmen amongst the Lions to fence with, except for Knight Captain Farringdon, and Prentice could not justify taking the marquis away from the crucial duty of commanding Loncastel's defenses. The hanging pell was a pole the thickness of a sturdy fencepost, and it dangled by a cable from the roof of the shed like a pendulum, creaking as it did. Prentice then drew a circle on the ground around it and, using his practice longsword, attacked the pole at either end in turn. Once set in motion by the first attack, it would swing wildly, and if he did a poor job of controlling the heavy length of wood with his cuts, thrusts, parries and ripostes, it would crash into his armor and drive him from the circle. Its weight forced him to use correct technique and full strength continuously, and its random nature meant that he was constantly attacking and defending from unpredictable angles. It was the most demanding individual training he had ever faced, remembering it from Ashfield. Even the Seven Rings Cross had not used such a training tool, but that was because they favored training against live opponents. Once he had it in place, using the pell supplanted the other drilling. and Prentice released the militiamen training partners to their duties. They seemed relieved to Prentice's mind, though Solomon still came by some evenings and sat watching whatever training Prentice was about, setting not only longsword against the pell but all the other weapons of the White Lions as well, except the wheellock. Prentice did practice with the firearm, too, but the hanging post was no use for that. In all, Prentice found himself cheered by Solomon's visits, and he let the youth ask him any questions he wished. The lad's eyes searched for every detail of any technique he was watching.

"I can tell you what each attack or parry is *supposed* to be," Prentice told him one evening, breathing heavily after the pell had driven him back out of the ring yet again, having cracked him in the side so that his backplate had rung like a dull gong. "But you must watch me for my errors. Like then. I thought I had control of the enemy, but he swung wild and caught me out because my defense was not live to his motion. A passive defense is often worse than no defense because it is weak but gives you a false sense of security."

Solomon nodded, absorbing every word.

"My Lord, the hundreds come after ninety-nine, do they not?" he asked just before Prentice returned to the circle for the next round.

"In numbers they do. Why do you ask?"

Solomon shrugged. "When she was teaching me my numbers and mathematics, Lady Dalflitch told me to practice the counting with everyday things," he explained. "I do that when I have nothing else to think on, but not much goes as high as a hundred or more. I have less chance to practice that count and forget the knack sometimes."

"Understandable," Prentice told him with a quick smile through. He approved of the young man's diligence at learning. It would no doubt serve him well in coming years. "What have you found to count into the hundreds?"

"Your techniques against the pole, between pausings," Solomon answered easily, as if it was obvious.

The answer caught Prentice by surprise. Even counting attacks and defenses together, it seemed unlikely that he would have a hundred continuous techniques against the hanging pell between each instance of being knocked from the ring. He hoped Solomon's grasp of numbers was not so poor as to get the count wrong. That made so little sense, though. The youth was far from stupid and too diligent to go astray for long. Prentice looked down at the circle on the floor. Obviously, it must be too large, making the training too easy. He would have to redraw it smaller.

"Is that a prayer, My Lord?" Solomon asked, and Prentice started with surprise.

"Why would you think I am praying, lad?" he asked.

"I mean that piece of paper you keep in your belt pouch and read so often."

"In my belt pouch...?" Prentice asked, wondering if Solomon had taken leave of his senses. He looked down and realized the fingers of his free hand were, in fact, half in his belt pouch, and there was a piece of paper he was pushing into it. Suddenly the inner voices were clamoring so loudly that it made his head hurt, the pulse beating in his temples. Even so, he forced himself to pull out the folded note and held it up in the poor lantern light.

"This?" he asked Solomon, as if he expected his young charge to know what the paper was better than he did.

"Ay, My Lord," Solomon answered. "I see you reading it so much, I thought it might be important. I asked Brother Whilte, and he said he has seen you read it as well but didn't know what it was. He guessed it was a prayer, perhaps a word of scripture. He says that you and he have been searching out battle words from the holy writ to use against Redlander magick."

Solomon had the youthful enthusiasm that he brought to every lesson and always had. Prentice looked at the unknown, folded square in his fingers. It was stained, and its edges were feathered and wrinkled. It had been folded and unfolded many times, exactly as if it *had* been read very often. He blinked at it and looked at Solomon. If he had not had it in his hand at the moment he was asked, Prentice would have scoffed at the youth's question. He never read any piece of paper regularly, certainly not with a devotion that might be mistaken for prayer. Not relinquishing his grip on his sword handle, he unfolded the note one-handed and peered at it in the poor light.

"It...uh...it is no prayer," he said simply as he puzzled over the writing inside. "It is...my...uh...my brother's last note to me."

Prentice felt his brows furrow as he looked at the note. It was indeed Xavoer's invitation to Vespers Remembered, the one he had been handed the night after their retreat on the north bank, the night he had dismissed Denholm for cowardice and insubordination. Prentice was sure he had thrown this note away weeks ago. He had no idea how it could have been in his belt pouch, let alone why he would be reading it now, or often.

"It is...a keepsake," he lied to Solomon, his head hammering and desperate to put the whole matter aside. "Think nothing of it."

He shoved the little note into his pouch, crumpling it rather than taking even the time to fold it. Once it was there, the pain in his head began to recede. He took up his blade in both hands and faced the hanging pell as if it were a tireless rival, an enemy that would never be fully defeated.

"Alright, Solomon," he said. "Start your count afresh, but mark only the telling blows. I will do the same, and when we compare our numbers, we will see if your eye is sharp or if you are counting too many failed techniques."

"Yes, My Lord," Solomon said earnestly and saluted.

Good, Prentice thought. *He will learn nothing by watching if everything he sees is colored by pointless hero worship.*

As if the boy would worship you, he thought the hateful chorus would say, though they were strangely quiet for once. Perhaps they did not need to rise from his memories to speak their curses if he could supply their words for them. The thought made him lash at the pell all the harder, as if his wooden practice blade could cut the thick post into pieces, and the pendulum began its crazed swings.

CHAPTER 63

"The damned thing is gone in the night, as if snatched away. Just about ready to put into place and now vanished," Farringdon cursed as he explained the recent blow to his plans for the next raid on the northern bank of the river. One of the two barges that had been being converted to replace the broken bridge spans had been stolen.

"Do you suspect Bluebird's sabotage," Amelia asked her husband while, behind her, a neophyte worked to place extra pillows. Most of the archduchess's time was now spent in bed, and even that did little to salve the aches in her back. She marveled that Righteous had carried twins and trained women at knife fighting all at once.

I must be carrying a whole cohort within me, she often thought. *Or else I am only a frail noblewoman, good for nothing but being married and looking elegant.*

She did not enjoy either notion.

"I wish I could say, my love," Farringdon told her as she settled back into the new mound of bedding behind her. From his expression, it was clear he felt for her discomfort, as his angry frown over the theft of the boat turned to a plaintive look of concern. "If I had to guess, though, I would think it was not. Bluebird has no need for boats that we know of, and if he plotted only sabotage, he surely could have put both to the torch at once, and the boatyard with them. Whoever took our barge only took the one."

"Thieves," Dalflitch said confidently, clearly looking to confirm Farringdon's analysis. "Likely skips, and with crew enough only to snatch the one. The Conclave says there is such a rash of theft that their bailiffs are no use. They are asking us for yet more protection."

They'll be lucky, Amelia thought, knowing even as she did so that she would not actually abandon the guildsmen to be preyed upon by criminals, even though they had treated her so poorly. Bad enough that Bluebird threatened the Conclave's persons. To have these opportunists now snatching at boats threatened trade and the good of the town as a whole.

"I had hoped that with our own loyal skips, we would end smuggling and piracy on the rivers for good," she said sadly. "Not so, it seems."

"The Dwelt is all but sewn up, Your Grace," Dalflitch said in a positive tone. "The Murr River not so. We have some of our spies amongst the riverfolk, as you know, but many of the crews are family and clan based. There is no way for strangers to quickly get inside their activities. And since they owe no loyalty to any side in the civil war, they no doubt are taking advantage of the chaos to feather their own nests, as it were."

"Stealing boats?" Amelia asked rhetorically, but the lady seneschal treated it as a genuine question.

"The largest single expense that any crew can face on the water, Your Grace," she said, and Amelia raised a weary hand to still any further explanation. She understood the problem and already had the relevant details. Including Sir Turley's lost barge, at least five large freight craft had been taken by thieves in just the last few weeks. Amelia shook her head, and though her new position relieved some of her back pain, her heavy belly seemed to press on her chest, making it hard to draw air into her lungs. She paused to catch her breath before speaking again.

Breathless from lying in bed, she thought sourly. Midwives assured her this was not abnormal, but she did not have to like it, either. As much as she wanted her child to come into the world, she found she was beginning to resent its long journey into the light, at least at moments like this.

"And has Baron Prentice still not found our Inquisition friends?" she forced out, despite the lack of air in her lungs.

"No new word, Your Grace," Dalflitch said. "But our eyes see him everywhere."

"Everywhere?" Amelia asked.

"As if he is a one-man patrol of the entire town," Dalflitch explained. "Neophytes and Lace Fangs in mufti regularly return with reports of him being seen on one island or another. Sometimes he walks distracted through the crowd; other times he is marching at full pace. He is always armed and armored, and yet I doubt there is a single street or dock or bridge he has not walked in recent days. Just a lone figure in the crowd."

"By himself?" Amelia noted. "Wasn't there a command that White Lions not be about the town alone?"

"That was after the Young Hopefuls crimes, my love," Farringdon explained. "Although the order is not rescinded, it is not as important as it was. And I suspect it is being flouted deliberately in this case."

"Deliberately?" Amelia asked in shock. "Why?"

Farringdon looked across the bed at Dalflitch. It was clear the pair had already discussed this question.

"Bait, Your Grace," Dalflitch said, her face a frown.

"Bait?" For a moment the word made no sense to Amelia. Then, she realized what was being implied. "Surely he is not being so accursedly foolish! Walking alone, even in armor, down back streets and old docks into the bargain? What happens when a skin thief ambushes him in a back alley and my knight commander is replaced?"

"Prentice knows what he is doing, Your Grace," Farringdon said defensively, switching to her noble term of address as he did so.

A formal protest? Amelia thought, wondering at the implication.

"Do you agree, My Lady?" she asked Dalflitch, but the lady-in-waiting demurred.

"I make it a point not to comment too freely on military matters, Your Grace," she said quietly. "If you wish another opinion, you might ask the baroness. Lady Righteous says he still makes an effort to meet with her each day or second day at the least. He checks on the children and takes a short moment with her. She sees him as he ever was to her."

"No surprise there," Amelia said, not meaning to be critical of her Lace Fang but failing all the same. "He'll be dead in his grave, and she will declare him still ready for the next battle."

"Her loyalty has never been a failing before," Farringdon said, his head down and his voice full of tension. "And if I may say, if your trust in the baron has fallen so low, what would it matter if he were to be replaced by a skin thief? He has so little influence or authority left to exploit."

Amelia looked at her husband in horror. Was that truly what he thought she felt? Prentice had not fallen in her regard. She only meant to use him to his best effect, or so she thought. It was not her fault that the task was beyond him. Almost as soon as that notion was formed in her mind, Amelia felt how unjust it was. None of them had located any solid leads as to Bluebird's whereabouts on the islands, despite so many efforts. Dalflitch had spies everywhere, and yet their lack of discovery never entered Amelia's mind as a failing for a moment. Why was she so disappointed in Prentice's performance? By all accounts he was driving himself day and night in her service. She had removed command of Sougate from his hand but only because his plans for the gatehouse's defense were so superior that it all but ran itself. Why was all that not enough? She sighed heavily.

"Husband, I must ask your forgiveness," she said. "I am going to have to violate my seclusion—likely twice."

"Twice?" Farringdon asked.

"I needs speak with Brother Whilte, and then after, depending on what he says, with Baron Ash."

Farringdon showed no discomfort at the proposed violation of tradition. "I will take word to the chaplain immediately." He bowed and took his leave.

"In the meantime, My Lady," Amelia told Dalflitch, "tell the Conclave that we will send more patrols to the docksides but that we will need bailiffs who can be trusted to give guidance. I don't want White Lions setting upon riverfolk who are simply taking their own boats about because of a misunderstanding."

"A wise thought, Your Grace. I will compose a missive to that effect for the Conclave now."

Come swiftly, Brother Whilte, Amelia thought, finding her mind becoming troubled anew and her recent regret for her treatment of Prentice hardening again to a mistrust of his actions and motives equally.

Something was not right.

CHAPTER 64

An hour later, Farringdon returned with Brother Whilte, escorting him past the neophytes at the door and the rest of the chamber, then waiting with him inside the curtain as he and Amelia spoke. Though it would have been both insulting and nonsensical to suggest that she plotted anything untoward with the chaplain, for decorum's sake her husband chaperoned the private meeting, and Amelia was glad for his presence—she was feeling a growing mistrust of her own feelings.

"I would not doubt his fidelity for even a breath, I urge you, Your Grace," Whilte said of Prentice.

"I do not, or I do not mean to," Amelia told him, forcing herself to be honest. In truth, she had no clear idea how she felt about Prentice right at this moment. "It was not for a testimonial that I called you here. What I wanted to know was if there was anything you could share with me about him at this time—anything that would not violate his trust, at least."

In fact, Amelia would not give a fig if Whilte unfolded Prentice's every secret if that would at least lead to some resolution of their estrangement.

"What would you have me say, Your Grace?" the chaplain asked warily, giving Farringdon a troubled glance that seemed full of concealed meaning.

"How has his recovery from the duel gone, for example? Is there any lingering sign of the poison?" This notion had occurred to Amelia as she had awaited Whilte's coming. Cassian's poison had come from a supernatural source and had nearly killed Prentice. Perhaps it had done some other, lasting damage. She was becoming sure that there must be some secret of Bluebird at work, something no one had imagined yet.

"The poison?" Whilte repeated, eyes wide in surprise. "The poison and the duel are long forgotten, I would say, Your Grace. I treat him almost daily and have seen no sign of the poison's effects or his dueling injuries since well before midwinter."

"If the duel's effects are passed, then why are you treating him, and so often? Have you not enough to care for with the wounded in your infirmary?"

Even as she looked, Amelia could see the continued effects of exhaustion on the devoted cleric—dark circles under his eyes, pallor, and thinness to his flesh. The idea that Prentice might be adding to Whilte's burden unnecessarily offended her, but again she forced the disquiet downward.

"Actually, Your Grace, the infirmary now contains only those who will not ever recover," the chaplain healer reassured her. "All others are returned to their service. My skills are much less needed there now, and I spend as much of my time as I may prayerfully contemplating your other need—the power of scripture. And supporting the knight commander as well, of course."

"But why does Prentice even need your blessings?" she pressed.

"Because his training is so brutal, Your Grace," the chaplain explained, a little shamefacedly, as if he felt somehow culpable for something. "Dislocations, minor broken bones, and Lord alone knows how many cuts and bruises."

"I had no idea. Why so harsh?"

"You would have to ask him, Your Grace," Whilte said earnestly, but he shared another troubled glance with Farringdon, just as Dalflitch had.

What do they know and not want to tell me? she wondered, and a new serpentine paranoia tried to wend its way into her thoughts. Were they plotting against her? Was there a sophisticated conspiracy, a web of lies with Prentice in the middle, pulling all the threads? The venomous thought came strongly, and it reminded her of the spell that had been cast upon her at Aubrey. If it had not been for that previous incident, she could only have imagined how she might have responded to these notions but having that past experience to draw upon helped her to see the thoughts for what they were—a lie meant to undermine her, a hellish falsehood that came from somewhere else. Just as she might stamp a booted foot upon an actual adder when it hissed its way out of the grass and into the light, she crushed the thought in her mind with a contemptuous guffaw, slapping her hand on her mattress and causing both the chaplain and her husband to start with surprise.

"My love?" Farringdon asked.

"Fetch Master Solft's scrap note, if you would, husband," she said, her thoughts moving swiftly now that she was sure she had recognized the threat. Farringdon blinked once, then bowed his head and moved to obey her instructions. His hand had only just reached the curtain when she realized her mistake and bade him hold a moment. Whatever was happening between her and Prentice had begun before the note was discovered. It could not be the source, at least not by itself.

"Wait, husband," she called. "It cannot be that note that is enspelled."

Farringdon looked back to her and cocked his head. Whilte, likewise, seemed surprised by their liege's words.

"You think Prentice under a curse of Inquisition magicks, Your Grace?" the chaplain asked.

Amelia nodded slowly. "Yes, Brother. Prentice...or..." She paused as she baulked at admitting the other possibility, then nodded more vigorously, acknowledging the undeniable truth. "Prentice or myself, or even our relationship specifically."

"How would such a spell have been cast?" Farringdon asked, and he looked to Whilte. The chaplain was staring at the floor, and it seemed his lips were moving in unspoken prayer. "When was anything read to you both?"

Amelia took the question in and quickly sought to sift her memories, trying to recall a document, a writ, any single page of anything that had been read aloud to them or in their joint presence. On one level, it was an almost pointless question. She dealt with documents every day and had since her arrival in Bridgetown. If she did not read them for herself, they were read to her by Dalflitch. Several of those had been in Prentice's hands as well, she knew. Even knowing the Silent Hand had this power at their disposal, neither she nor her advisors had yet divined anything of its limits or parameters. Could a spell be written on a page to work if anyone read it aloud or even simply read it for themselves? If that was the case, any of dozens of documents in the room could be a threat. Or did it require someone specific—a worker of spells—to give the magick function?

"The note he reads," Whilte said quietly, and it was clear he was even uncomfortable to speak of it.

"Who? And what note?" Amelia asked more sharply than she intended. She was becoming more energized as the conversation continued, and it was prompting her to move more than was comfortable for her burdened body.

"The knight commander has a note that he keeps upon his person and looks at often, in the days and the nights," Whilte explained. "I supposed it was a prayer of some kind, seeking a sword of faith, but when Solomon asked of it, he was told it was a note from Baron Ash's brother. A keepsake."

"I know that note," Farringdon said, raising a finger as he shared a memory of his own. "I was there when Prentice received it. It came from his brother, Xavoer, saying that his father was deathly ill and that he should visit soon. Remember, my love? He had it on the table here some days later. He was reading it when Lady Dalflitch enquired after his visit to Bell's Hummock."

"Was that the day he went seeking stoves for the infirmary and returned with none?" Whilte asked.

Farringdon nodded. "I believe so."

Amelia listened to their words and tried to recall the day in question. Had it been the day the Prince of Sunbury had made his first assault on Sougate? That had been a bitter day, and Prentice had seemed so distracted in his anger. In her recall, Amelia could see him sitting there that afternoon, scowling at the tabletop, deep in troubled thought. Lady Dalflitch had been scanning that part of the table too, just before she asked after his trip to the westernmost island. Then, in Amelia's memory, another image showed itself, as if the table was revealed to be a shadow play, and now she looked again. Suddenly, she remembered a note, unfolded open on the table. Prentice had been staring at it. His lips had been moving. It was him.

"He is hexing me!" she almost shouted, pushing herself up painfully from her bed. Spittle flew from her lips as she cursed her treacherous retainer. She could see him clearly in her memory now, laying down the Inquisition's spell upon her, muttering it like a witch in her hut. "It is his doing! Go now, husband, and seize the traitor. Bring him here in chains and I will judge him. He will hang before sundown."

In her fear and fury, Amelia hardly noticed the look between Farringdon and Whilte, but as her husband leaned down to take her by the arms, his face was filled with concern. For his part, the chaplain seemed to stand taller somehow and raised an open hand over her head. His voice was deep and resonant as he spoke over her.

"People who are wicked and deceitful have opened their mouths against you," he intoned. "With lying tongues and words of hatred they have surrounded you and given you accusations for your friendships. They have loved to pronounce a curse. May it come back upon them."

The words seemed to wash through Amelia, and in the main room behind the curtains she heard several of the neophytes cry out in alarm. Then everything was quiet, and the archduchess felt a sudden release, as if a cramping muscle had just relaxed. Sadly, though, it was not a muscle in her aching back.

"What...what just happened?" she asked as she felt her husband lower her gently back to the bed.

"The sword of the word cut the spell from around you, Your Grace," Whilte said, bowing his head with a humble expression, as if embarrassed by having loosed the power of heaven against yet another curse.

Suddenly, Lady Agatha slipped through the curtains. "Is all well, Your Grace?" she asked earnestly. "We heard you cry out, and then the chaplain's staff started to glow a moment."

Amelia looked to Whilte and realized he had left his staff by the door. When he prayed, it must have glowed with its holy light and that was what had alarmed the neophytes. She smiled benignly at her Lace Fang.

"We are well, Agatha," she said. "Something unexpected has happened." Realizing that, of course, all the women of her chamber were waiting for word of her coming labor, she laid a hand on her belly. "Not that, though."

Agatha bobbed a polite curtsey and waited to be dismissed. Amelia waved her away and then took a deep breath. She looked to the two men beside her bed once more.

"He read that note that day, I remember," she told them. "But I cannot believe it was out of treachery."

"Nor I, my love," Farringdon agreed, seeming relieved by her sudden reversal of emotion. "If the spell can be placed so that any reader might bring it to fruition, surely it can be ensorcelled to cause the reader to read it again in another's hearing."

"Or even their presence," Amelia agreed. Even as she looked into her memories again it made sense to her what had happened. Having fallen victim to the spell, whatever else it had done to his thoughts or perceptions, it had also compelled Prentice to read it at the table that day, and the magick had erased its presence from her vision. Others had seen it and noticed its strangeness, but neither she nor Prentice had.

And he still reads it, day and night? she wondered. What power must it have in his thoughts now? What was it causing him to do or not do? Was he unable to find Bluebird because of this curse? The curse that had been placed on her at Aubrey only seemed to dull her mind and make her fear her husband. Whom did Prentice fear? And what could he not see?

"Brother, could you read that paper safely?" she asked Whilte, who looked at her as if she had asked him to spend a night in a cage with a wolf or a lion. He shook his head.

"I have no idea, Your Grace," he said, but his fearful expression changed slowly to one of resolve. "But I have faith to pray and try, if you command it."

"We would be better served destroying it and doing whatever we must to free Prentice's mind from the magick," Farringdon said with unusual firmness. Amelia looked at him and then smiled.

"That would surely be the wisest course, husband," she said. "I will send to Prentice and have him come here so we may pray the incantation over his mind."

"No, Your Grace," Whilte said sternly. "It is no incantation. What I do is by the benevolence of the Almighty. I speak no magick formulae and urge you not to think otherwise. What prayer might work for your mind might also be utterly ill-suited to the knight commander's."

"Very well, Chaplain," Amelia said, accepting his word on the matter. "But should I not summon him regardless?"

"I think that is exactly the right thing to do, Your Grace, and I pledge that I will give my whole will to breaking whatever evil the Silent Hand has laid about Baron Ash's mind."

At that, Whilte left them, and a moment later there was a knock at the main chamber door. Lady Agatha returned with Lady Dalflitch at her side. In the seneschal's hands was an arrow, fletched with the feathers of a fey archer. Also with the shaft was another note. Amelia looked at the simple piece of vellum with some alarm and noted a similar wariness in her husband's expressions.

"Your Grace, I have a message for Knight Captain Farringdon from my husband," Dalflitch explained, and then she noted their faces. "What? Have I interrupted something too marital?"

CHAPTER 65

"Word was sent to the knight captain, but they took a long while findin' him," Knight Sergeant Gennet explained to Prentice.

The straightforward officer looked uncomfortable even telling the knight commander his story, and Prentice was suspicious as to why that was. "How did *that* happen?" he asked.

"Only one runner was sent, and he went to Loncastel first, since the guns were firing and that's where the marquis usually is of a day," Gennet continued. "Course, as luck would, this was one of the rare days that Knight Captain Farringdon was away from the cannons, meeting with her grace. The messenger was sent to the Paramour's Chambers, but by then, the knight captain had been called away by another message and had left for Loncastel after all. Seems the runner tried takin' a back street and they missed each other on the journey."

Prentice was not surprised to learn that White Lions messengers were developing their own short cuts through the town. Despite the seemingly slow pace of the siege through the winter, a delayed message always had the potential to be a disaster.

"Was there a problem on Loncastel?" Prentice asked. He and Gennet were standing on the battlements of Sougate, looking southward at the Veckander army. It seemed as if the entire of the Prince of Sunbury's force was in the field again, massing for another assault.

"No word of problems on the north island, My Lord," Porth told him. "What we heard is that there's come a message from your fey man, scoutin' the north bank of the Murr."

Dahyoor is back? Prentice wondered, surprised to find out in this fashion. He felt the hateful chorus sneering at him, wanting him to believe that even his fey squire no longer trusted in him, going instead straight to Farringdon, Prentice's replacement. Their contempt felt strong, but they had picked a foolish line of attack this time. As dejected as he had begun to feel from day-to-day, he was not fool enough to fall for this. The fey of the Wind Rising saw *his* role in their society as a challenge they were forced to accept as it was. If they thought to withdraw their loyalty from him, there was no reasonable way it would transfer to the marquis-consort.

"What was that message?"

"Don't rightly know, My Lord," Gennet told him honestly. "All I do know for sure is that by the time our messenger got word to Knight Captain Farringdon, Guillam had become too impatient for waitin' and sent to me as next down the line. And I thought we'd need you for this."

Next down the line because he would never think to move up, Prentice heard himself think, and he had no idea whose voice it was in his mind. He managed to ignore it, however, because of the imminence of the enemy attack. Even at this distance, he could make out fresh scaling ladders being brought up amongst the levies on foot in the middle of the Vec army. He remembered the healers and their dire commentary on the state of those levies. In the face of that suffering, his personal discomforts were too petty to even consider.

Even so, the hateful chorus remained, hardly ever retreating to the fringes of his mind anymore. Lately he had come to feel like a wounded buck deer, circled continuously by the wolfpack of disdainful words that never fully let him be. Like a deer with its antlers, he was able to hold the thoughts at bay for now, but he knew his soul was tiring, and soon they would pounce.

He wondered what that would mean, and so he never stopped training, hoping that when the final battle came, he would be strong enough to fight back. A quiet, inner part of his mind—the part that could laugh at the notion of Dahyoor giving allegiance to Farringdon—told him that it was equally ridiculous to fear becoming too tired to fight off wolves only to work himself to exhaustion. Was weariness his enemy or his training tool? That rational element of his thoughts lost fractionally more of its ground each day, however. It was a part of his "antlers," and as he tired, so it faltered. He looked to Sergeant Gennet, who had cocked his head with an odd expression, as if Prentice had said something that confused him.

"Me and Guillam kenned that Sunbury's figurin' to make this break in the weather serve him," Gennet said at last, after Prentice had gone back to studying the enemy array. Beside them, the strong afternoon breeze made the fire under the siege cauldron snap and leap like a loose sail on a ship's mast. That morning, a freshening wind had sprung up from the northeast and it had only grown stronger, breaking the cloud cover apart and driving it away to the south. Bridgetown was receiving its first glimpse of naked sky in months, and it seemed likely that it would be a long glimpse, as the blue vault looked clear all the way to all horizons now. Sergeant Guillam returned to the main battlements with Sootface Kate at his side. The pair had just completed a circuit of the defenders, confirming that everything was in order for when the attack came.

"They brought their crossbows out to us at last, My Lord," Guillam said once he and Kate had saluted Prentice and their senior sergeant. "Bet they're lookin' forward to throwin' some iron back for once."

Prentice nodded without comment. The mercenary crossbow companies were easy to see, forming up on the enemy's eastern flank, with their heavy weapons in hand and leather boxes of ammunition slung over their shoulders. From what he could observe, there were none of the hired missile troops elsewhere on any other part of the Vec lines.

"Does the prince know something about our left flank that we do not?" he asked his officers as he studied the odd choice of formation. For the first time since the winter siege had begun in the south, the Golden Heron's hired mercenaries were in the front ranks, at least on that one side of the battlefield. Of course, the break in the rain was what made the crossbows a viable tactic, but Prentice wanted to know why they were being concentrated.

"I don't know, My Lord," Gennet said, and he turned to the other two.

"I got the same balance of Roar on both sides, My Lord," Kate reported readily.

"And there's just the one cauldron on that wing, but that's the same as the west side," Guillam added. "And there's hoardings all the way along. Long as our lads are careful, not a one of 'em should even notice the crossbow bolts fallin'."

Prentice thought his Claw sergeant was being overly optimistic, but the point was well taken. The defenses on every part of Sougate's battlements were as strong as any castle in the Grand Kingdom had ever had. Yet Prentice knew not to be complacent. While they were making all defenses secure against every foreseeable thing, the enemy was devising something fresh that had never before been imagined. The circling hate inside him whispered continually that Everard of Sunbury and the Golden Heron had already outwitted him, that the men around him were doomed and it would be his fault when the unanticipated blade fell upon their necks. He felt himself chewing the inside of his cheek and clenching his fists as he searched the Vec force for the thing he had not imagined, the thing that would get Gryphons killed.

The enemy wing began to advance, and from behind the crossbowmen came a stream of levies, apparently carrying no weapons but holding a motley collection of tools and other strange objects. Beside the streaming column, like drovers riding on the fringes of a herd of cattle, knights ahorse in flashing steel directed the flow of yeomen toward Sougate's left wing. Around Prentice, the disciplined and practiced Roar gunners tended to their long-matches, blowing on the glowing ends to make sure they were hot and ready to fire. Bucket men hauled water up so that as soon as a cauldron was used, they could refill it. Along the battlements there were empty gaps where the cannons had once been. All the open-air guns had been transferred to the north for the duel with the Dragons. Even now, an occasional shot sounded from Loncastel. In the barracks room below the crenelations, Sougate's last two cannons were already given orders to shoot at will, and the vibration rose through the stones and into Prentice's feet as they spat their first bellowing shots of the day. The cannonballs were black streaks through the air, so swift and difficult to see that a man might imagine them a trick of the light if he did not know what he was looking at. Both bit channels in the mud at the far end of their range and off to the side of the advancing yeomen. The crossbows behind them were not even close to being in danger. Prentice saw it and smirked. Now he understood more, at least.

"That is as far as our two cannons can shoot to the east, I take it," he said.

"'Fraid so, Knight Commander," Sergeant Kate agreed, somewhat shamefaced. "Now that our only ones are the insiders, they really only can aim to the front, mostly. Even hackin' away at the archers' loops only gives them a bit more width of..." Her voice trailed away as she looked back down at the advancing enemy on the flank. "Oh, bugger!"

Guillam spat on the stones and Gennet nodded his head with them.

"Our cannons can't do nothin' to them out on the side like that. They'll get right up close easy as fallin' over."

"And you'll still have 'em eatin' Roar-shot, Sootface, no worry 'bout that," Guillam declared confidently, encouraging his replacement freely in a way that encouraged Prentice as well.

For a sour and difficult man, Sergeant Guillam had become almost transformed in his service to the Gryphon Banner, like the not-quite-crippled Porth, the ever-steady Gennet, and now Sootface Kate. Prentice's militia company was held together with a strong glue.

So, they don't need you anymore, the inward enemy mocked, but Prentice told them to shut up. Men, and likely too many women, were about to start dying.

The crossbowmen stopped their advance while the levies continued until they were clearly within the longest range of a Roar matchlock. No one on the battlements opened fire, however. They were waiting for the command. This was all old hat to them now and there was no nervous shooting. For all that Sougate was a funeral pyre for the Veckanders, that same flame had tempered the Gryphons and refined their discipline to a honed edge. The levies on the ground seemed to mill about a moment, their knightly outriders still urging them forward, and then they were rearranged, with a cadre of especially large-looking fellows at the front, each one carrying a wood and boiled leather pavis, the reasonably lightweight piece of mobile cover that a crossbowman would hide behind while he was reloading. Close up, the hardened hide would not stop a straight shaft of an arrow or a crossbow, let alone a Roarsman's shot, but at a distance it was a lucky shaft that would punch through. Prentice doubted the leather would stop a matchlock ball, even at that distance, but it would at least make it impossible to target the man hiding behind it, keeping him from sight. The burly men with the pavises lined up in the front and began to march forward in a row while behind them came others with digging tools in hand and large baskets of an open wicker on their backs. Seeing all this, the enemy's strategy became clear.

"They will hide behind the pavises as close as they dare," Prentice said, wondering if his officers even needed him to explain this much. "Then they will put the baskets out and shovel them full of as much earth as they will hold. They will have an instant bastion of sorts in less than an hour."

The others watched the advancing forces thoughtfully, as officers should.

"Those baskets ain't goin' to be tall enough to hide much behind," Sootface said professionally. "Not with us able to fire down on them from above."

"They'll fill the first layer, then hoist them leather shields on top," Guillam declared with confidence, reaching into his belt pouch and pulling out two fingers worth of chew that he stuck noisily into his mouth. "And I'll wager silver to straw that once they do that, they'll do another layer o' baskets. Who wants to bet they've been back there all these weeks weaving those things 'til their fingers bled?"

No one took the sergeant up on his offer. Already, the pavis-bearers had reached whatever point they had decided was close enough, and behind them the other levies were beginning to place their baskets and shovel at the mud, filling up the wicker. Like poor serfs rushing to build a wattle and daub hut before the winter, they hacked at the earth in a frenzy, constantly bent-backed, trying to keep hidden behind the enormous, boiled leather shields while they worked.

"They should've been at this for months now," Guillam said, plainly contemptuous of their urgency.

"They couldn't do it in the rain," Gennet observed. "Every shovel full of mud would have run out like a wet slurry through the wicker."

"They could've made baskets with a tighter weave," was Guillam's answer to that.

Prentice looked up at the sky and wondered how long the rain would hold off. There was not a single cloud to see. It would be a bitterly cold night, and if the wind dropped, it could be days before the cloud cover returned. Finally, Sunbury and the Golden Heron had adopted a reasonable tactic. What remained to be seen was how many more sensible decisions the prince had made.

"As soon as those the start to fill, those crossbows will cross the last space and we will have their shots falling on us," he told them.

"And they have chosen the east side because of the wind. When it misdirects their shots, which it will to many, it will only blow them farther along the battlements. Aim at the east tower and the wind will just send it into someone on their left. I would say Prince Everard means to make a good go of this assault, and this is but the very first step in the dance."

The three officers were nodding soberly. They understood what the rest of the afternoon promised and were ready and resolved. Prentice was sure the militiamen around him were listening in and understood the grimness of the approaching hours. Against the hateful whispers of his thoughts, he resolved to show them as much confidence as he could muster, no matter how much of a sham it felt to him.

"You all know what you are doing," he said to the three sergeants, though he spoke loudly enough that for paces in either direction everyone would hear. "Your preparation is thorough and excellent. We can expect them to focus almost their whole strength on the east side for today, and they will be trying to scour us off like clamshells off the jetties in town. Sergeant Kate, the Roar on the left will be doing the main of the firing. Make certain they have powder and shot up to them the whole time, and have the cohorts on the right ready to swap them over after an hour or so. Give your fellows time to rest and fetch a drink."

"Ay, My Lord," Kate said with a salute that slapped against her buffcoat and barrel chest.

"Speaking of water," Prentice said to Gennet. "If they can, they are going to hit us with fire arrows—well, bolts—trying to burn our hoardings out. The wood's likely too damp still, but just in case, have your cauldron bearers ready to do double duty dowsing any fires. A stray flame can still light someone's powder store, and you know what that looks like."

During the cursed summer drought in the Reach, a Roarsman's powder ammunition had caught alight in an ambush, and the resulting flames and explosion had been a vile way for anyone to die. Here on the battlements, with gunners cheek to jowl, one such burning could set off dozens and take a cohort apart almost as easily as the Jerwahl Ranger's grenades.

Gennet saluted as well.

"Anythin' for me, Knight Commander?" Guillam asked, chewing loudly and looking for all the world like the cocksure convict he had once been, eyes alight with mocking confidence.

"You know your duty, Guillam," Prentice told him. "Make sure any ladders get pushed off the walls and any courageous twits who manage to make the climb before you do go with them."

"We can do that, My Lord," the sergeant said with a smile.

Prentice looked down at the slowly growing earthwork, fearful broken men driven by arrogant men-at-arms shoveling dirt like frenzied lunatics. Amongst Grand Kingdom serfs, and convicts especially, the Vec was seen as a near utopia, a land where folk were free to make their own way in the world. Many were the dreams of running away, going wayward and crossing the Murr to the promised land. Looking down, Prentice thought what a myth that was. Had it always been, or were the princes slowly returning to the tyrannies they disavowed when they broke away from Denay? Prentice sighed and shook his head. In a very real sense, it did not matter. Either way, the levies below were going to suffer again. But at least such thoughts distracted him from the inner voices for a time. Perhaps the sounds of Roarshot and the screams of the dying would drown them out completely for a while. It was a vile thing to imagine, and Prentice despised himself for hoping it would be so.

"The longer they go building that earthwork, the easier a job those crossbows will have," he said wearily. It was time to act. "Let your Roarsmen off the leash, Seargeant Kate. Rip those pavises and the men behind them into ribbons. Our day has begun in earnest."

Sootface Kate saluted again and moved immediately to obey. Prentice looked to Guillam a last time.

"Your fellows will have awhile yet at my guess," he said. "Send a runner to Loncastel—no send three, separately—and make sure Knight Captain Farringdon knows what is happening here."

"Ay, My Lord," Guillam answered readily. "And just sayin', Knight Commander, it's good to have you back in charge."

He turned away and Prentice nodded, looking back to the coming battle. He wanted to tell Guillam that he was not back in charge, but he knew it would be a lie. From the moment he stepped onto the Sougate battlements, he had been in command whether he had meant to be or not. He wondered what the archduchess would think of that.

CHAPTER 66

It was nearing sundown when Brother Whilte was heard clomping up the stairs to the top of Sougate. He emerged into the acrid smells of powder smoke, sweat, and some filth. Even confident warriors were known to wet themselves when battle was finally joined, and only novices were ashamed of such realities. Better urine than blood down the front of your trews. The noises of battle were like another noxious cloud all their own, encircling the garrison as the fight went on. For all the growing disgust at the renewed death at the foot of Sougate, Prentice had been enjoying the fell peace that all this horror created in his mind, suppressing the inner tumult. Like a man with an agonizing disease made to forget the pain it was causing because of a sudden burn or broken bone, the knight commander found it a perverse relief. And, of course, he wondered what that said about what kind of man he truly was.

Even so, the chaplain's wooden footstep sounded clearly in his hearing through the chaos, like a lone drumbeat heard through the smoke of the battlefield, distant but distinct. He turned to see the humble man laboring through the crowded ramparts, jostled by bucket carriers and barefoot drummer boys hauling fresh bags of powder to the Roar.

"Welcome to the rock upon which men beat themselves to death," Prentice greeted Whilte, not meaning to speak so bitterly but finding himself unable to stop. Where was the control of his tongue he had lived by for so long? The buck deer was weakening even while the baying wolves were quieted.

"How many require my skills?" the chaplain asked earnestly, eyes casting about at the many militiamen already carrying minor wounds. There was a rattle, as of a handful of pebbles tossed on a roof, when a volley of crossbow quarrels hammered the hoardings. Men ducked and Prentice reflexively tugged Whilte by the arm under a piece of the shelter. None of the shots landed near the two of them, however.

"We are doing quite well, Chaplain, as you can see," he told the clergyman. "Almost none are badly wounded, and despite the disorder, we have had both space and time to take those rare sufferers back to Runners Field. You would be better service to the Lions there this day."

Whilte nodded and looked over the defenses again. "You seem less than happy about the fact, Knight Commander."

Prentice cocked his head at that comment. He waved Whilte forward a short distance to a covered spot next to one of the large cauldrons where river water bubbled at the ready boil. The space beside it where they stood was once a cannon position, now empty. It allowed them to get right up against the crenelations with a shelter over their heads and no risk of getting in the defenders' way. He pointed to the gap in the wall where the cauldron would tip.

"Look and tell me what you see," Prentice commanded Whilte. The chaplain leaned out, one hand on his staff, the other holding onto the corner post of the shelter. Prentice knew what the healer would see—more dead and dying Veckander levies groaning in agony at the foot of the wall, more broken siege ladders, and more churned earth full of death. By focusing on the left wing, the Veckanders were avoiding the remaining cannons, but they were still having to cross the open ground under Roarshot. The simplified earthwork had risen swiftly enough over the last three hours to give a reasonable number of crossbowmen a safe haven to shoot from, but even they were losing their fight against the more numerous and much safer Roar.

"Here they come again," someone shouted from farther down the wall.

Looking out, Prentice saw another scaling ladder being sent forth, carried by thirty or forty men. This was the fourth that had come so far, or was it the fifth? Had he lost count? The Roar fired their volleys, but the Veckanders had learned another new lesson, making sure their ladders were carried by many more men than they actually needed, so that any who fell did not delay the charge. In all too short order, the ladder reached the poorly maintained ditch at the foot of the wall, a mud-swamped trench that no longer served as a useful moat. The desperate crowd pressed as close to the wall as they could, out of sight of the Roar, who could not fire straight down without leaning out over the battlements, and heaved the long wooden construct upward. The safety of their position was only relative, however, since they were now under the projections of the hoardings from where Guillam's militia threw heavy rocks down on their heads. They were also within the splash range of the cauldron Prentice and Whilte were standing beside. The men working the simple and brutal weapon strained to lever it forward in its frame, using long poles to protect themselves from the blistering hot metal. The water steamed as it fell in a scalding cascade, and men below screamed at the horror of it, although it mostly fell beside them rather than on the crowd as a whole. Slowly, the ladder rose while the numbers lifting it were whittled away, but even as it drew close to vertical, long pikes were pushed out from the battlement, tipping the heavy scaling tool backward. The team on the ground did their best to hold it aloft, but it overpowered them and fell. They tried to reset themselves to raise it again, but by the time they put their hands to it, they were barely a third of their original number and the hail of assaults on their heads was too much. They broke and ran, abandoning their ladder, though some helped wounded fellows to limp away.

"A guilder to the stone chucker who can break that!" a corporal in one of the hoardings shouted, meaning the fallen ladder. If it could be destroyed before a new team came up, that would be the best outcome. Bigger stones were dropped now, and the cauldron began to hiss on its fire as its empty belly was slowly refilled by the bucket team.

"You see, Chaplain," Prentice said with an arch tone that embarrassed him but which he could not moderate. "We are winning again, and likely will for months yet. At this rate, Everard will have run out of men to send to the slaughter before the end of summer. We despised the previous prince of Town Sobridge for his bloodthirsty haste. It seems the new one is no better. We are the archduchess' finely dressed slaughterers, and we are no more challenged by these than we would be by any other flock of sheep."

Whilte stared at Prentice, and it was clear that the chaplain did not like what he was seeing.

"It is at her grace's instructions that I come to fetch you," he said after a wary moment. "She has sent messengers around Bridgetown, seeking you out, Knight Commander."

"I have been here since noon," Prentice told him, thinking he understood the chaplain's hesitation now. Her grace had found out that he was here, commanding the bastion in defiance of her orders. Gentle Whilte was a goodly choice to send to bring him to heel. Chasing aggressively after a runaway horse was an excellent way to keep it panicked. The battle fell to a grumbling lull, men moving about the business of preparing for the next round of killing. In the quiet, the hateful chorus seemed to burst out of the shadows, as if the wolfpack saw a chance.

She means to strip you of it all now! they hissed at him. *You have defied her, and he is sent to bring you to heel. It is over. You are useless and finished.*

"In truth, Prentice, her grace has asked me to bring you because of that," Whilte said quietly, as if he could read Prentice's thoughts. The knight commander looked at him in a panic at the impossible notion and realized the chaplain was pointing at something. He looked down and saw that he had his brother's note in his hands. When had he pulled it out of his pouch, and why? And in the midst of battle? He stared at it, bewildered, finding that he could hardly form his thoughts to any order at all. Was this it? Was the buck deer finally exhausted?

"She asks that you bring her that piece of paper, Prentice," the chaplain went on, his voice all but a whisper but somehow easily heard in the endless commotion around them.

"Why?" was all Prentice could think to say.

"Does it matter what her reasons are?" Whilte pressed. "It is her command." He spoke quietly and firmly but slowly also, like a man walking on a frozen river, testing each step with his foot before putting his weight onto it.

"I cannot," Prentice heard himself say, though it felt like someone else's voice. "I *will* not."

Whilte's eyebrows rose in disquieted astonishment, but at that very moment there was a loud cracking noise from the base of the wall and men shouted huzzahs. A stone had damaged the fallen scaling ladder, it seemed. Prentice looked over the ramparts and hoardings, counting the whole thing a welcome distraction. Battle made sense to his weary mind, as disgusting as it was to long for conflict just to quiet his own inner guilt and unworthiness. The odd paper in his hands did not make sense, but it, too, reminded him of his failings and rebellions. It was a note from his brother, an estranged relative he hardly knew. It had led him to the bitterest conversation of all his life, being blamed for every one of his own sufferings by his dying father. What did he care if the archduchess demanded the note from him, and why was it so often in his hands without his knowledge? He tried to make himself give it to Whilte, but his hand would not obey him. Looking the chaplain in the eye, Prentice felt almost plaintive in his need to hand over the meaningless scrap, but he could not do it. In the end, it did not matter as Whilte suddenly snatched it from his fingers, and spinning on his wooden leg like a wheel on its axle, the chaplain thrust the piece of paper into the cauldron's flames.

"Baptize us Lord with the holy spirit and with fir..." the chaplain called out as if to heaven, but the final words were choked off when Prentice exploded at him. The wolfpack curses bayed in his mind, howling at him for his weakness, cursing every breath he had ever taken. Prentice tried to reach for the burning note, but even as he shoved Whilte aside, the paper was blackening to ashes. It was gone. The rage within him, the self-hate that told him he deserved only to be rejected and loathed suddenly seized his limbs, and he took the earnest religious man by the throat, shoving him against the wooden post.

"Damnable fool!" he shouted. "Wretched mongrel. Not enough that you condemned me with your lies, now you take this away too!"

Near incoherent curses flew from Prentice's lips while Whilte's face turned red. Sins between them long repented and forgiven were mixed with Prentice's hatred for himself and his own failings. His father's voice drove him to destroy Whilte, as if that would change his past, delivering him from his conviction as a heretic. His teachers and instructors cursed him as too weak to avenge himself, demanding that he throttle the man for his insolence.

"You damned me, you and your friends!" Prentice shouted. "Your lying testimony took everything from me. Now my father's last words to me as well? I should end you as you ended me! Throw you down amongst the dying at the foot of the wall."

If Prentice's mind had been even partly well, he would have seen the pointlessness of his threat. Whilte's eyes were bulging and his face darkening swiftly. At this rate, the chaplain would be dead in moments. Whoever was around, whoever of the Gryphon Banner understood what was happening amidst the other chaos of battle, none of them moved to intervene.

Kill him! Kill the false friend, false holy man! the wolfpack bayed, and Prentice very nearly did. Again, it seemed only battle saved him from their driving howls. Trumpets sounded from the Vec army, and their ringing tones pierced the hateful haze in Prentice's mind. There were more important things in this day than his personal pains or petty vengeances. As if Whilte's throat were suddenly as hot as the fire beside them, Prentice sprung his fingers apart and pushed the one-legged man aside, causing him to stumble against the stones of the defensive wall. He kept upright only by catching the lip of one of the merlons, choking on gasping breaths.

Prentice turned from Whilte to the rampart's edge once more and looked out over the enemy, all but forgetting the chaplain he had been thinking to murder a moment before. The entire Vec army had divided itself now and there was a clear path through their middle, as if the road south to Town Sobridge was being made open amidst an honor guard. Levies out the front of both sides were carrying more ladders, but the crossbows remained only on the eastern side.

You want to draw some of us away from your main assault, do you? Prentice wondered as he watched.

The Vec force was now divided, with two thirds to the east and one third of their number on the west. It was an arrangement that begged for a sally. If the main of the Gryphon Banner were to march out quickly now, they could encircle that one third and destroy it easily while resisting the two thirds on the other side. Then they could turn on that other side and break them as well. A few hours of battle would spell the end of Everard's army and the Golden Heron's coalition against Bridgetown. But they were forbidden by the archduchess to march out, and even if they did, it would be the Veckander levies who were driven to the slaughter. All the assaults on Sougate added together would not equal the death that would fall on them in that instance. Trumpets sounded again, and both wings came on at the gatehouse bastion at once. Prentice did not move and did not need to give a single command. As he stood still, watching professionals drive broken levies to their death, he heard Sergeant Kate giving her Roarsmen sensible commands, ensuring the gunners were now better distributed along the battlements. Guillam was calling a reserve up from below, shouting for extra pikes to defend the west tower and wall.

The Gryphons' defense was well ready for this late shift in tactics. To either side of him the desperate, pointless assault continued, and in the midst, Prentice stood watching, all but frozen under the cloak of noise that he clung to simply to blot out the self-hatred within.

"I kenned 'em wanting to stop come sundown, but now I ain't so certain," Knight Sergeant Gennet said from behind Prentice's shoulder, and when the words penetrated his mind, the knight commander looked to the sky. The sun was going down, lighting the sky a glorious wash of golds and pinks that would soon shift to reds and thence to night. The first stars were appearing, and the Rampart was beginning to glow more distinctly in its arc across the heavens. And still Prince Everard was driving his army on. For the first time this winter, men in full armor were taking the risks at the foot of the walls. Their steel gave them real chances to survive a glancing or long-ranged Roarshot, along with the advantage of knowing where to avoid the cannons. Even so, no armor was proof against boiling water or a long fall when a siege ladder was pushed off. It might have been a satisfying turn in the battle to see the professionals begin to pay some of the blood price for their leaders' poor strategy, but Prentice felt no such gratification. Perhaps Everard wanted one last throw of the dice before the sun fled fully, or perhaps he meant to assault through the night when the darkness would only lay one more burden on his troops' heads.

They are never going to stop, Prentice thought, and the wolfpack bayed afresh at that thought.

Until you are dead. Until you are dead.

But the enemy inside misunderstood his meaning and he shook his head. Everard and the Golden Heron were not here for him, at least no more than they had come for any one of his militiamen individually. Whatever ill-conceived purpose had brought Prince Everard here, it was clear that he either would not or could not give it up, and all that really meant was death—death of men Prentice was realizing could be saved. If he had not fallen so far in his liege's esteem, he would have been able to convince her to accept the healers' plan, he was sure. White Lions and Gryphons were safe, but he could make the Veckanders safe too, as surely as his plan had given those first convicts a chance to leave the chain behind. Except for the actual links of steel, those levies below were on the chain as truly as the men he had worked beside for a decade in exile over the mountains. He grabbed Gennet by the shoulder and pulled him close.

"Find me Brother Whilte," he said as quietly as he could, and Gennet started in surprise. The knight sergeant pointed to a spot not two paces behind them where the chaplain was stood by, meekly watching Prentice from that short distance. There was a ring of dark bruises growing around his throat, and he had the hunted look of a prey animal watching a predator. Prentice thought to wave the chaplain closer but suspected Whilte would refuse, so he grabbed Gennet's shoulder again and directed him to the watching clergyman. When the gap was closed, Prentice looked at Whilte and felt an overwhelming shame for his actions—another to add to all the others. He bowed his head apologetically a moment and then looked the chaplain in the eyes.

"You...deserve...better," he forced himself to say, though as if each word was a bird released from his hand, the wolfpack curses tried to silence him, biting at the paltry apology, trying to drive Prentice back to his worthless fury at a man who had long ago confessed and repented the sins between them.

For his part, Whilte did not seem much comforted by the words but did not look to flee, and Prentice respected him for that. "I am still bid to take you to her grace," the chaplain said. Prentice nodded and hoped Whilte could see the respect he felt for him, even in spite of what he was about to do.

"No, Brother," Prentice told him. "I will not be going with you."

Whilte looked a little surprised by the flat refusal, but that was much less than the clear astonishment on Gennet's face. Prentice could hardly blame them. He would never have imagined he would be insubordinate to Archduchess Amelia, let alone outright defiant. At least this disloyalty was not born of rebellion.

"Knight Sergeant, I want you to put an escort with Brother Whilte and they are to keep him from returning to the Paramour's Chambers," and despite his growing expression of confusion and disquiet, Gennet managed to salute. Prentice continued his instructions. "They are commanded to ensure the chaplain's complete safety. If the assault continues through the night, then come the dawn, he is to be released."

"Baron Ash...?" Whilte croaked, but Prentice held his hand up for silence. He looked back to the man he had so nearly murdered with his bare hands.

"If the battle goes on, there will be no possibility of a signal being seen," he told the chaplain. "But if Everard retains enough sense to at least let his force rest through the deep watches, you will go with your guards to the east end of Greenmarsh and give your healers the signal."

Now Whilte's expression of disbelief exceeded Gennet's.

"But her grace forbids..."

"Her grace is wrong!" Prentice declared flatly. "Too many have already died, and unless we take the battle up to Everard and the Heron, they will just continue to die. I suspect the fool Vec prince thinks to exhaust our powder stores, as if we cannot bring more from Dweltford. Perhaps it is loyal boat crews of *his* who are stealing the riverboats to prevent us resupplying. If so, it is a strategy as doomed to fail as all his previous strategies, and I do not trust this buffoon to realize *that* before he sacrifices yet more lives on the altar of his idiocy. Come what may, the Gryphons will march out of Sougate on the morrow and put an end to the threat of Town Sobridge. By this time tomorrow, the Archduchy of the Western Reach will include a second Veckander princedom. If you may signal the healers, then perhaps no more levies will need to suffer needlessly. Regardless, once we march forth, you will be free to return to the archduchess and tell her that I will bend my knee in surrender, foreswear my barony, and submit myself to the axe for this offense once victory is won. I trust that my wife's favor with her grace will not suffer and that out of love for her, she will allow my wife's son to inherit my title."

Gennet and Whilte only stared at him for a long while as men shouted, boiling water was cast down, and guns fired. In another quarter of the candle, it would be full night.

"Go to, Knight Sergeant," Prentice insisted after a long moment, and Gennet saluted hesitantly, plainly confused. The knight commander did not blame him. His leader, the man he had trusted to guide him all the way to the headwaters of the Murr, farther west than any living Kingdom men had marched, was now commanding him to outright insubordination to their liege. It was unthinkable, but Prentice hoped that his officer would believe his pledge to take full responsibility and submit himself to execution for this act. He would also understand if Genet refused and would not resent him for it. Prentice was fairly certain that if he had to march out of Sougate alone, he would do it come the dawn all the same. He could not live and let this carnage continue.

"I want to go with you," Whilte said, so softly that Prentice had to read the man's lips to be sure.

"Someone must return to her grace and report my actions," Prentice objected, but Whilte shook his head.

"Send a messenger!"

"Insubordination?" Prentice asked, cocking an eyebrow.

"Seems to be going around, My Lord," Gennet said, and he and Whilte both grinned like madmen for a moment, fear and confusion mixed in full with their jest.

"Alright," Prentice told them. "But otherwise, my orders stand."

Gennet saluted and Whilte nodded. The knight sergeant called for two Fangs to act as escorts for the chaplain and then they were both gone. Once again, Prentice felt alone amidst the mayhem, and the wolfpack was slavering and growling, heard now even over the battle sounds. He did not care. One way or another, tomorrow he would be dead and so many of the poor fellows in front of

Sougate would not be. Whatever else the hateful chorus wanted for him or from him, they had best seize it soon.

CHAPTER 67

Perhaps an hour after sundown, the Veckander army finally gave the day's assaults away at last. The strong wind also dropped, leaving the evening quiet, although an occasional volley of crossbow bolts rattled on the stones of the battlement and the wooden roofs of the hoardings. Sentries began to listen for the thrum of the bowstrings, calling for silence in the meantime, which only meant that the moans of the dying at the foot of the wall were so much easier to hear as well. Near to midnight, a bright light, like a lantern that contained a piece of the sun, was seen on the river to the east of the bastion, shining across the water. It flashed bright and clear for a long while and then was gone. Men muttered about ghosts, and those who knew the story told the tale of the Angel of the Brook, who had saved the Grand Kingdom forces in their first ever battle against the Redlander beast-men.

For the rest of the night, the Sougate bastion became a hive of activity, as quietly as could be achieved, but most of it happened below the battlements and on the bridge behind. The knight commander, who had been seen all through the previous day's defense, had left around the time of the mysterious light, and there was a rumor that he had gone to report to the archduchess in the town proper. Some said that he had come to blows with the Moses of the Gryphons over some unknown quarrel between them, but that was usually scoffed to scorn. Everyone knew how valued the chaplain was and how greatly the knight commander respected the peg-legged clergyman. Baron Ash was back at Sougate two hours later, however, on his horse at the head of the rest of the Gryphon Banner Company and wearing a full panoply of steel plate that seemed to encase his upper body. Orders were given but were few enough that there was plenty of space for rumors. There was talk of men fighting on Loncastel, that Daven Marcus had finally crossed the river, that the knight commander had gone mad, or that Bridgetown was lost completely, to be abandoned. Some said the archduchess had died in childbirth and that Baron Ash was leading them into exile, thinking to make himself the next Prince of Town Sobridge. Each imagining piled on the previous, as well as the mystery of the witchlight or angel glow, so that no possibility seemed quite beyond belief. Thus, it was with a sense of growing anticipation that as the sky began to lighten, the doors of Sougate were thrown open, and two cohorts were sent out to clear the wreckage so that the entire Gryphon Banner Company could march forth and array against the Vec on an open field for the second time in a year.

By the time the sun was cresting the horizon proper, the drums were beating, and massed columns were taking up their formations—squares of three hundred and eighty men with one hundred and twenty Roar gunners positioned in their own smaller squares at the corners, ready to shoot their enemies and then to retreat into the spiked hedge protection of their comrades when the hand-to-hand fighting came. Each combined formation of five hundred stood their own portion of the line with gaps between to allow them to maneuver around each other, and at the front of the whole force, seated on his white-socked horse, Knight Commander Baron Prentice Ash rode alone until the Gryphons' Banner was brought forth by Banner Sergeant Porth and his chosen close guard of Claws.

"How is your arm, Banner Sergeant?" Prentice asked Porth loudly as the senior man marched up with the newly made leather harness for the standard pole slung over his shoulder. The Gryphon Banner, rampant silver heraldic beast on its field of Reach blue, waved on its pole as the one-armed sergeant bore it forth, head high and helmet polished until it flashed in the dawn light like a beacon of its own.

"Hurts like the devil, if I'm honest, My Lord," Porth declared, grimacing with discomfort, holding himself upright and proud, nonetheless. "But if you were going to be here, then I wasn't to miss out, I was damned sure o' that."

"Good man!" Prentice congratulated him, and that raised a smile from his escort. Knowing how busy Porth had kept himself for virtually the whole of winter, it was important that he and his guard cadre knew how respected their efforts and risks were. "Remember that we have no men ahorse and precious few enough drummers, so your fellows will need to be ready to keep you safe and take messages as well."

"We're all full ready to do our runnin' and keepin' the standard safe, My Lord."

Between the state of the ruined farmland and the narrow gate ramp, it took nearly an hour for the Gryphons to march out and array as Prentice had ordered them. During the night, some of the crossbow mercenaries had camped themselves at their little earthwork, and when the Reachermen first started to emerge, those optimistic missile shooters had tried to give them some hell. It had taken the first two cohorts out the doors mere heartbeats, it seemed, to drive them away, however, but that small action had still delayed the arraying some as well. By the time Prentice was ready to give the command to march southward, the sun was rising into the sky and the Veckander force had left their camp and lined up to face them. Almost of equal size to the Gryphon Banner Company, the Prince of Sunbury and Town Sobridge's army was more than a third levies. The enemy force arrayed much as a Grand Kingdom army would, with the pressed peasants in the middle, flanked by men-at-arms afoot in their armor, with a company of knights ahorse on the eastern side of them and then clusters of crossbows on each wing beyond.

Prentice knew it would have been a more effective tactic for him to march the Gryphons straight at the enemy camp earlier in the morn, catching them unawares in the predawn and giving them less chance to marshal their own strength like this. But Whilte's signal had been given, and that meant Prentice needed to allow the healer's plan a chance to work. An attack in the dark before dawn would not have allowed the Reachermen to pick between the levies and the rest of the enemy. Not killing those who had no choice but to be here was one of Prentice's main strategic priorities this day, as mad as such a hope was in the chaos of battle. Also, a night assault would probably have given Everard and his cronies from the Heron a better chance to escape the battle, and that was something Prentice would not allow.

At least that is the plan, the knight commander told himself, knowing that the hateful chorus was already mocking him and readying to laugh at his failure. How could he face an enemy while trying to preserve their lives? What a fool thing to do. Surely his own followers would pay the price for his misguided compassion. It was like a soft-hearted girl caring about the wolf cubs if they lost their mother, not realizing that every night the she-wolf was let to live, more sheep died, and more peasants went hungry or even starved.

The hypocrisy of the wolfpack using such a metaphor was not lost on Prentice, but that did nothing to silence their hunting calls in his mind. They had been at his heels throughout the night, especially when he had gone alone to the training shed to fetch his full armor and weapons, including the two wheellock pistols that he now had with him, along with his champion sword, one gun on his saddle like a lancer, and the other in a sheath at his back. He had kept his ear out all night for word of another summons to Paramour's or the announcement of Knight Captain Farringdon come to arrest him personally. If any other provost had been sent for him, Prentice would have resisted them outright. If the marquis-consort came in person, though, he did not know if he would have the will to oppose him to his face. Such an act might shatter everything the White Lions had been forged to be.

But Everard must be stopped, he told himself as the drumbeat began and battle was at last to be joined. *Better I be broken here, on this field, taking this tyrant into death with me, than we cower another day, serving as his priests of the sacrificial altar.*

Shouts echoed across the field as sergeants and corporals bellowed to their own drummers, and the command to advance echoed over the line in voice and rhythm. The smell of long-match smoke and fear-sweat mingled with the rot of the dead lost to the mud and the metallic tang of armor polished to its finest sheen. Over four thousand booted feet tromped through the churned field. Bare months ago, this was a harvested farmland, and likely come the next planting season it would be fertilized by blood and flesh, tilled by slaughter to make a bountiful harvest, if the sun smiled upon it. For now, it was cold, wet, and bitter, regardless of the rare bright morning. Veckander trumpets disputed with the Gryphons' drums, and the Prince of Sunbury ordered his own forces forward. Now, it began in earnest.

The first strike was the crossbowmen's, their weapons having the longest range. Their bolts flew into the air, a volley of a hundred at least, arcing up to fall on the Gryphons' advancing front. As they did, Prentice leaned forward over his mount's neck. Boots was no destrier. Even if there had been time to fit the gelding with his own plate armor, the poor beast lacked the spirit or strength to bear such a weight. To protect Boots as best he could, Prentice used his own plate-covered body, knowing that he was only truly covering half his horse's exposed area. Nonetheless, it was a technique he had been taught in Ashfield, and though he never mastered it, now was the time to apply the lesson. None of the bolts struck Prentice or Boots, though two rang loudly off the armor of the standard bearer's guards, one of the halberdiers loudly cursing the glancing strike on his helmet. All along the line, Fangs held aloft their round shields over their own heads and their comrades', hoping to deflect the falling iron.

"That's the first one!" Prentice shouted to them as he struggled to bring himself upright in the saddle again. The beat had not wavered, and the steady forward march continued. The White Lions were always to be true to their name, exactly as Prentice had imagined, stalking their enemies like the pride on a hunt. No wild charges, just steady advance until the final, lethal spring. After the long moment while the mercenary missile men ratcheted back their heavy strings and fitted their next shots, another volley fell and some militiamen went down, including one of the standard bearer cadre, but Prentice remained upright on Boots.

Dahyoor should be here, ready to bring Dusty up, if I should lose this fellow, Prentice thought, realizing something that a true knight would already have organized with his squire.

For the third volley, the crossbows were redirected to the Gryphons' flanks, and that was because the levies in the middle were being driven forward. Even the heartless Everard would not hail iron on his own troops' heads, at least not at the start of the battle. Men-at-arms ahorse, as well as the footmen on either side of the peasant fighters, drove the pressed force onward as a mass, the armored professionals dropping back as the men with simple spears did their best to charge forward. The gap between the two enemies was barely a hundred paces now, if that. They were moments apart, and Prentice watched, his teeth gritted while the hateful chorus exalted at his coming doom—a man alone out front and surely no knight on a destrier who might fight his way clear.

Soon, you will be dragged from the saddle to die as you deserve.

Then the levies began to drift to Prentice's right, to the west side of the field. Soon the drift became a stream, and in moments the shuffling peasants began to sprint across the battlefield away from both the Gryphons and their own army. Whenever an army fought with pressed levies there was a risk they might rout, and the tactics and formations of such armies were set to compensate for that. The men-at-arms on the flanks of the peasant mass prevented retreat until the enemy was close enough that they would do the job for them. Once they were this close to the foe, the levies had no choice but to fight or else they would be slain, so the men-at-arms had hung back from their shepherding role, waiting for the levies to take the brunt of the attack. Just as with the assaults on Sougate, the professionals would wait while the lesser men took the greatest risk and then they would aim themselves at the key places on the line to attack to best effect.

Except that the Lions' Roar did not ring out. Not a single shot was fired, and the entire mass of pressed peasants simply moved westward and off the battlefield while the dumbfounded Veckander army shouted orders in confusion, rushed-sounding trumpet blasts trying to reassert command. Prentice and his militia watched as the Golden Heron lost a third of its coalition in a breath. His orders to Gennet, Guillam, and Sootface had been precise. If the levies came on to engage the line, the Gryphons were to feed. But if the Vec peasantry turned aside, they were to be allowed to go. The company would hunt other prey. Even so, watching them stream away, Prentice was not comforted.

If this is a double bluff by Everard, we will soon know, he thought. If the healers had been agents working for the Prince of Sunbury and Town Sobridge, they now had a third of their force on Prentice's flank, ready to turn and assault him from a second side. Regardless of the risk, the Gryphons had their orders, and the drumbeat for advance did not falter. Those Roar on the eastern wing who now had no levies between them and the enemy began their shooting, like the crackling of a forest fire, and iron shot began to pelt the Veckander army, especially aiming for their hated foes, the crossbows. Everard's knights ahorse were clustered on the eastern side as well, doubtless waiting for their chance for glorious charges. As the Roarshot flew amidst them, doing little damage initially but sowing confusion all the same, Prentice made out a particularly splendid cadre of men in gilded and fluted plate, with proud plumes sprouting from their helmets and fine pennants flying on lances. The red sun on green and white of Sunbury was plainly visible amongst the nearby banners. Individual riders were being dispatched to all points of the field, it seemed, and Prentice thought he might be able to make out one man ahorse in the middle, waving his arms about in a panicked fashion.

"Now, princes and bankers of the Vec, discover the purpose for which the White Lions were forged," Prentice muttered, though he was speaking as much to the hateful chorus within as to the distant Prince of Sunbury. He drew his champion sword, the weapon the fey in the distant west called a "death thing"—as if not every weapon were—and he lifted it high. That was the signal for which every drummer was waiting, and the command beat shifted. As the last of the levies escaped to the right, turning back southward many hundreds of paces away, the Gryphon Banner Company began to close up to form a continuous front across the field. Some of the Vec riders were already trying to chase down the escaping levies, but they were just more lost from Everard's diminishing strength. The battle was joined now, and the Roar were hammering at the foe as the Claws and Fangs marched down upon them in a single, inexorable mass. It was time for the Vec to learn the lesson that Prentice had taught the knights of the Reach, the warriors of the fey, and the blood-soaked fighters and beast-men from the red lands.

Now, the Gryphons were on the hunt.

CHAPTER 68

Despite her fatigue, Amelia barely slept all through the night. Dalflitch's message from the fey man Dahyoor—or more truly, from Turley via the fey man's bowshot—had told a grim tale. Chasing his stolen barge, Sir Turley had come upon a skips' cove in a hidden fen on the north bank of the Murr River somewhere between Bridgetown and Aubrey. Dahyoor had sniffed it out from landward and pointed the way for Turley's crew. Upon investigation, they had discovered not merely one missing barge, but likely all of the rivercraft stolen in recent days. The boats were moored together and attended not only by skips who had pirated the craft, but also by what Sir Turley estimated was the whole of the mercenary raiders who had tried coming ashore during the Usurper's first attack on Bridgetown. The hired crews must have snuck west on foot and were now preparing a fresh assault in stolen boats, coming from upriver this time. Unfortunately, Sir Turley and his crew had been spotted, and pirates rowed out to intercept him. He had been forced to retreat upriver himself, away from Bridgetown. As he fled, Sir Turley had given the message to Dahyoor and told the fey scout to ride east. With no other way to cross the water on horseback, the fey archer had launched the written message on an arrow, which had apparently struck a cannon's wheel literally in front of the weapon's main gunner. It had been shot from the north bank, from several hundred paces away at least. No one had actually seen the fey rider himself.

"A cunning ploy," had been Farringdon's assessment of the enemy plan. "They already failed when they attacked the town from downriver, and we've reinforced those approaches since then. In the meantime, we've been treating the upriver side of the islands as safe ground—safe water, I suppose. Now they mean to sail down disguised as local Bridgetowner boats and land their raiders afresh where we have no preparations against them."

"To capture the town?" Lady Dalflitch had asked with a sceptical expression.

"More likely to strike at Loncastel first and take the rest of our cannons to give Daven Marcus a springboard for the other islands. With your permission, Your Grace, I will go there now and prepare our defenses. This note is more than a day old. The enemy boats could already be on their way."

Amelia had given her permission and sent another message to Prentice.

"Bring him to me as soon as you locate him," she had told the messenger. "He must be reinstated as the full commander of the south side of town and given warning of the coming treachery. Assuming, of course, that we can dispel the curse upon his mind."

"Keep faith, Your Grace," Dalflitch had counseled her with an earnest smile. "The word of God is quick and powerful...a discerner of thoughts and hearts."

"My Lady?" Amelia had asked with raised brows and a puzzled smile. "Have you turned religious?"

The notion of the once infamous bedswerver now quoting holy scripture was a striking one, even in a day of many difficult surprises. The usually poised courtier had shrugged and given an uncharacteristic shy smile.

"I trust to Brother Whilte and Baron Prentice, Your Grace," she had said softly, in the manner of a young girl admitting a misdemeanor. "Well, at least when his mind is not accursed by wicked men. But I can read as well, and why should I not turn my spare moments to this sword of the word. Even if I only tread ground already tramped down by wiser minds, surely it hurts me not to add to my education."

"Indeed, My Lady," Amelia had agreed, comforted.

By mid-evening Whilte had not returned and no word had come from him. A messenger sent by Farringdon from Loncastel said that boats had been seen coming in suspicious numbers from the west and that the knight captain was preparing a hot welcome for them if they proved to serve the enemy. Amelia sent more messengers to Runners Field from her own guard cohort garrisoned in the front yard of Paramour's, along with a Lace Fang, Lady Elizabeth. They were told that the knight commander was not in the camp but somewhere abroad in the town. Lady Elizabeth reported that she had thought the sentry with whom she spoke seemed evasive, as if concealing something.

"Do you think him a skin thief?" had been Dalflitch's obvious question, but Beth had only shrugged.

"I've no way to know," she had said honestly.

The lady seneschal had then proposed sending some of the neophytes and Lace Fangs in mufti into the town to track Prentice down.

"We've not had too much trouble locating him before, Your Grace. In the meantime, you could ask Lady Righteous her thoughts as well. Between us we will find the errant knight commander and set what is wrong to right."

Amelia appreciated Dalflitch's encouragement, and the lady-in-waiting's spies were dispatched once again into the dangerous streets.

"Send a message to Earlsbastion," the archduchess commanded. "Inform Lady Penelope of the new threat and our planned response. Invite her to be involved in any way she might wish."

Dalflitch had raised an eyebrow at that.

"She is yet the liege of Bridgetown," Amelia insisted.

"Do we still care about that, Your Grace?" the lady-in-waiting asked in complete seriousness.

"I told her I had come to defend her lands, not take them from her, and I meant it."

Dalflitch accepted the instruction at last, and while she set about the new tasks, Baroness Righteous was summoned to her grace's side. She arrived in the main chamber with her children's nursemaid in tow. Both of the twins were fractious and refusing to be left alone. Only continued nursing and attention would keep them settled, it seemed. Far from annoyed, Amelia found the two infants' presence oddly calming, and she supposed that the spirit of motherhood was readying her for her own child's imminent arrival.

"I swear he would ne'er turn on you, Your Grace," Righteous insisted when she was told of Amelia's concerns, chin thrust out in challenge to the whole world and completely at odds with the gentle rocking she was giving the little girl in her arms.

"I have no doubt either, My Lady," Amelia told her. "It is sorcery, I am convinced."

"Yea, well I find that no comfort neither, if you'll forgive me, Your Grace," Righteous answered her, and Amelia had to concede her that point.

She asked the baroness to remain with her if that was possible, and Righteous took herself and Emma, the wetnurse, to the stuffed chairs by the fire to sit comfortably while the archduchess tried to get some rest. Through the dog watches, Amelia tossed and turned on her mattress, sleeping almost none at all, and when a fresh messenger arrived in the predawn, she was awake before Lady Daisy brought her the note. The Lace Fang handed Amelia the paper while a neophyte held a lit taper to see by.

"From the marquis knight captain," Daisy told her, but as Amelia took it in her fingers, the archduchess shook her head.

"Not like this," she said, and she pushed herself to her feet, the cold of the boards bitter on her swollen soles. Shrugging a warm overrobe onto her shoulders, she led the way into the main chamber to find Dalflitch asleep in the third soft chair, next to Emma and Righteous near the fireplace, while only two other ladies-in-waiting were awake to attend to the chamber's duties. The rest were either abroad or taking their chance to snatch some sleep.

"Fetch candles so that it may be read in good light," Amelia instructed as she took herself to the table. "I will read it while you all watch me closely for any sign of magicks. Then, if you see none, Lady Dalflitch will read it. For all that we have been wary up until now, it has not been enough. Our enemy is canny beyond cunning."

Lady Dalflitch had been stirred, and once the situation was explained, she was joined by every other woman in the Chamber, save for Emma, who fed little Gant since the infant had been roused by the busyness around them. Every face stared intently over the candelabra while Amelia hesitantly unfolded the paper and read its simple contents. It was in her husband's hand and was no more than an update of the situation on Loncastel.

"I read that some of the purloined boats have indeed landed raiders this very night," she told her attendants. "Pirates with axes and knives have made for the cannon emplacements, but Sir Turley's warning has seen them met with stern resistance. Lord Farringdon thinks to throw them back to the river by dawn."

Amelia handed the note to Dalflitch, letting every eye consider her in a most impertinent manner. The days of noble superiority were finished now, for the Western Reach, at least.

"Is that what you read there, My Lady?" she asked. "There are no secret extra words to see?"

Dalflitch confirmed the truth and safety of the note, and after a long moment the room seemed to breathe its own sigh of relief.

"What news of Baron Ash?" Amelia asked.

"None, I fear," was the seneschal's report. "Wherever he is about the town, none can locate him. It could be that he has been ambushed by Bluebird's hired men. He could already be in their grip or even at the bottom of the river, sorry to say."

"Not bloody likely," was Lady Righteous's assessment, and even with Bluebird's spells on Prentice's thoughts, Amelia was inclined to agree. By all accounts, the one thing the Inquisition's magicks had not done was to diminish his fighting ability.

"I understand your confidence, My Lady," Dalflitch conceded, "but your husband has not been seen about the camp or anywhere in the town. If he were on Loncastel, he might have been lost amidst the conflict for a time but surely not all night."

"What about Sougate?" Amelia asked. "And what of Brother Whilte? I sent him yesterday to find the knight commander, and now the chaplain is missing as well. Marquis Farringdon's note said that not all the taken boats had been seen on Loncastel yet. Could others have landed more secretive crews of raiders?"

Amelia had a sudden vision of savage raider crews ranging about Bridgetown in the night, just as the Young Hopefuls had done earlier in the year but now guided by Bluebird more directly and assassinating her retainers. She had a sudden urge to summon back all of the ladies out in mufti. A moment of near overwhelming paranoia shrunk her sense of safety to no more than this room. She immediately looked to her close attendants.

"Do I appear any different?" she demanded and explained the rush of emotion.

"Sounds to me like natural fear," Lady Righteous said with almost casual calm. "We're in the midst of another play for the town, fire and steel, shadows and shadow-play. Seems like a moment's fear is warranted. How's your young'un inside?"

Amelia put her hand on her belly and contemplated her pregnancy. Now would be the worst and yet most typical time for her to experience another moment of false labor, but it seemed her unborn was at peace. That was something comforting, at least. She smiled at Righteous, who was rocking Amy again, dancing back and forth as she so often did.

"We need to find your husband, My Lady," she said earnestly.

"Amen to that, Your Grace."

CHAPTER 69

The neophyte named Joan returned to the Paramour's Chambers just before dawn, accompanied by a messenger in Gryphon Banner Company armor. The messenger had another note, and as the refreshingly bright light of a clear-skied dawn started to filter through the chamber's windows, the wary process of reading the next uncertain message was undertaken with the entire chamber. Before she could be reassured of the paper's non-magickal nature, Amelia was horrified by what she read.

"What is it, Your Grace?" Beth asked earnestly, while Daisy and Righteous peered at her, seeking signs of sorcery. Amelia could only shake her head, and she passed the note to Lady Dalflitch.

"It is from the knight commander," the lady seneschal explained, and she then put her hand to her mouth in shock. "He...he has raised the Gryphon banner in front of Sougate. He has marched out against the Veckander army...against her grace's express command. He is in rebellion."

"Like hell he is!" Righteous spat, eyes aflame. "It's a lie. A Bluebird lie!"

"I don't think so, My Lady," Dalflitch insisted gently. "I know his hand well enough to recognize it, and his words are very specific. Unless we seem both enspelled to you all, I think we must trust the truth of this note."

Righteous looked to the other ladies-in-waiting, as if hopeful that they would declare their mistress and senior peer under the influence of sorcery. Everyone was convinced the two were as sound in their minds as ever, and they all shook their heads. Faced with the inevitable, Righteous all but turned on the silent archduchess, her slipping accent revealing her disquiet.

"He's not 'imself, Your Grace, I swear! He'd ne'er turn on you. It's the scripture-sworn truth. He loves you like a sister. More e'en. There are nights I'm jealous o' ye—that's how much he loves and is loyal..."

"Oh tush, Lady Righteous," Amelia said suddenly, waving the baroness to silence. "Of course he is not himself. I can see that. And if you truly are jealous at times, then let me suggest that you stop it. Every woman here wishes we had the kind of love that you have from your husband, even those of us who are well satisfied with our own marriages."

Righteous made as if to scoff, but as her gaze met Dalflitch's she stopped short and then looked back to Amelia, who gave her the same expression.

"You're in earnest?" she asked, and both liege and senior lady-in-waiting nodded soberly. Amelia would never want any other but Farringdon, and Dalflitch was as besotted with Turley now as she had been the day he saved her from certain death, yet both of them acknowledged in quiet moments that Prentice's devotion to his wife and family was a thing of almost frightening power sometimes. A man so like a weapon, his love was like the naked steel of a drawn sword—clean, pure, and deadly to its enemies.

"Well, that's come dealt from the bottom o' the deck and no mistake," Lady Righteous said, using a tavern gambler's expression for something that should have been impossible but somehow had happened. In other contexts, it would have implied a lie, but Amelia was sure the baroness did not mean it that way. She looked over her gathered courtiers.

"It seems the mystery of where the baron knight commander is has been solved for us," she told them. "The question that comes now is what consequences are we to bear for his actions? Are we even equipped to know them fully?"

"He's like to win, ain't he, Your Grace?" the neophyte named Lilly asked nervously, and all eyes turned on her in affront, either at her speaking out of turn or at her implicit lack of confidence in the Gryphon Banner. Lilly ducked her head in embarrassment. "I'm sorry, but everyone seems so ill-fated 'bout the day. It's put the willies up me, and I didn't know..."

"Your poorly formed fears are for you to face on your bed in the night watches, Lilly," Dalflitch chastised the girl, but Amelia only smiled.

"We don't doubt Baron Ash or the might of his men-at-arms," she said gently. "But we have all surely seen too much to be foolish about what battle can mean for the militia, for the town, and for you and me, Lilly. I think the baron would tell you that even the best cardplayers can be defeated by a bad hand."

Lilly nodded sheepishly, accepting the wisdom being taught. When she looked up, Lady Righteous caught her eye.

"You know I love my lord, and he's the equal of any hundred Veckander knights," she said slyly. "But what if he meets a hundred and *one* of 'em out there on the battlefield? It could happen."

Several of the ladies-in-waiting chuckled at the nonsensical boast, and the tension created by the unexpected news cracked a little.

"So, you won't be executing him for his rebellion like his note says, Your Grace?" Lady Beth asked, the Lace Fang having been permitted to read the note after Dalflitch. The archduchess had not realized that any of her other ladies were so lettered. It was a useful thing to know.

"Expect some austere words to be said, My Lady," Amelia told them with another shake of her head. "But if Baron Ash returns in victory, it will seem more than a little churlish to punish him."

"And what if he doesn't win?"

Amelia gave Righteous a serious glance before answering Beth's last question.

"If he is not victorious, Lady Elizabeth, I expect he will either be dead or so wounded that any punishment I think to devise will be of little burden to him."

That resolute pronouncement knocked the good humor back out of the chamber, and after a moment of sober reflection, Lady Dalflitch clapped her hands like a tutor with an unruly class.

"Come ladies, let us not tarry like a gaggle of breathless maids, gossiping about our fancies for the coming harvest-fest dancing," she said sternly. "Her grace must be helped to her ablutions and her breakfast made. We all have our duties."

Amelia was grateful for the assistance, but before she went back to wash and dress for her day, she wanted to make sure that she put the things she did know and control in order for what was sure to be a harrowing time.

"My Lady, I will send my next notes before I eat, thank you," she told Dalflitch. "Call down to the garrison in the yard for runners. I am no longer willing to have neophytes or even Lace Fangs abroad without escort."

Dalflitch bowed her head.

"How many messengers, Your Grace?"

Amelia ticked them off in her thoughts. "Four, at least. Two for each message. While I suspect it was sworn man's loyalty that made it 'impossible' for our militiamen to find Baron Ash in the night, I think the time has come for us to be more certain of our communication. If a note must get to its source, more than one will be needed for each."

She turned to Lady Elizabeth.

"Your letters have come a long distance. How good is your hand, Beth? Do you think you can take some of the scribing duties from Lady Dalflitch?"

The Lace Fang's eyes went wide behind her butterfly-shaped mask. She bowed her head earnestly, clearly awed by the honor she felt she was being shown.

"My hand is nowhere near My Lady's in beauty or speed, Your Grace, but I will not shame you with less than my best."

Amelia was pleased with the answer, but her smile was disrupted by a kick in her abdomen that both fired off the ache in her back and set her wanting for her chamber pot.

"Very well, ladies," she said as she levered herself out of her chair to head to her "bedchamber." "See that what we know is now shared between our two commanders. Lord Farringdon must be told of the Gryphons' deployment to battle, and Lord Ash must learn of the conflict on Loncastel and the threat of smuggled raiders coming on Bridgetown boats. I don't think he would have stripped the garrisons from the bridges even for a decisive strike against the Golden Heron's army, but he has left them without reserves if Daven Marcus has a heavy plan for this day. Let us not be slow in sending those messages, and even so, Lord willing, let them both find their respective commanders already victorious and securing their conquests."

CHAPTER 70

"It wasn't a bad plan, but it ain't working, My Lord."

Prentice had to agree with Gennet's assessment. He was still watching the conflict from the saddle, but he was now behind the line of battle on the left wing and in front of the cohorts he had kept in reserve. The knight sergeant was at his stirrup, having come up to report the conditions on the right wing. He was talking now about another new tactic Prince Everard had just attempted in the battle. Men-at-arms afoot in full suits of plate had worked to cover their comrades' advance against the Roar by marching in a locked line behind large heater shields. Doubtless like the pavises for the crossbowmen, the hope was that heaters would absorb the massed fire or obscure the bearers long enough for them to close for the charge. It was not a poor notion, only insufficient. The boiled leather archers' shields had not been enough to stop Roarshot from the battlements of Sougate, and these heaters, while made of stouter stuff, were not enough to stop the iron and fire at mere paces. Even with plate armor, the locked wall of shields failed to keep gaps from being punched in their formation. By the time they were close enough to charge, the watchful Roar were already retreating into their own formation's safety, and the shield-bearers found themselves falling on pike and halberds, the shorter and lighter swords they were carrying nowhere near enough to fight their way through the hedge of steel. The attack had been beaten back, as had two charges by knights ahorse on the opposite flank. Everard had been in the lead of both of those, and Prentice still caught glimpses of the red sun banner through the smoke and flying mud now and then. The knight commander looked up to the sky a moment. There was a smattering of small clouds scudding by, but no indication of the rain returning any time soon.

"I make it midmorning, Knight Sergeant," he said to Gennet.

"We could be done by noon at this rate," the officer responded, and as much as he feared to be too optimistic or to be caught out by something for which he was not prepared, Prentice had to agree.

The crossbows on his wing had been annihilated by the Roar with their higher rate of fire, and on the right, Gennet reported them driven off, following after the retreating levies who were streaming back toward their hometown. The two squares of five hundred directly in front Prentice now were in the thick of the fighting, with few Roar safe to emerge to shoot. It was a dense press of bodies, steel ringing on steel, as loyal militia went toe-to-toe, rank-to-rank against professionals who had no more fodder to throw into danger ahead of themselves. If his militiamen felt as he did, Prentice imagined they were venting no small amount of fury for having been forced to spend the winter as executioners.

"Is the prince looking to come around our flank?" Prentice asked, noticing the ruler's banners at the back of the infantry fighting on this wing. Of course, there was no point asking Gennet. On foot he could see so much less than Prentice from this vantage. Nevertheless, a move by Everard now was what the knight commander expected. If he were in the Prince of Sunbury and Town Sobridge's position, that was what he would do. He would take his knights in a single mass back from the line of battle and sweep as far east as he could to return and charge into the Gryphon's left side with lances and all the force they could muster. If it worked, it was a sure tactic that would collapse the Gryphon's formation from the east. If it worked well, it would set off a complete rout.

"We need that square up on the left," he said to Gennet, pointing to one of the two reserve five hundreds. If Everard did swing around on the east, a fresh five cohorts in formation would be able to intercept him. Before Gennet could pass the word to the nearest drummer, a cheer went up from their right. Prentice looked and saw the western half of the battle line collapse as Veckander men-at-arms broke formation and began to run. Already, a small gap was opening between the right and left sides of the battle as the victorious Gryphons started to charge after the fleeing enemy, regular discipline momentarily forgotten in the flush of triumph.

"There!" Prentice shouted at his knight sergeant, pointing at the right wing. "Get in there and reestablish order. Get them back in ranks and then on the march. By the Roar, harry the mongrels all the way back to Sobridge's walls. Understand me?"

Gennet saluted while Prentice turned to the reserves, steering Boots towards their corporals in command.

"You, follow Sergeant Gennet," he shouted at the far square, standing up in his saddle and pointing with large, obvious gestures. Almost immediately the drummers for those cohorts set the marching beat and Gennet moved across to take command of the square. Prentice wheeled to the other five hundred. "You are with me, corporal. We will march into that gap and swing around their backsides to slap them down."

He pointed to the enemy still holding the battle on the left wing. Soon, the Gryphons would have them encircled and there would be nothing Everard's too-small company of knights ahorse could do. The battle was about to be won.

◆○◆

"We've heard some sounds of fightin', Your Grace, but none near to us."

The corporal in command of Amelia's guard garrison was standing with one of his line firsts at the foot of the table while Amelia sat her great chair, receiving her sworn man as a high peer of the realm should. Around the chamber every neophyte had her veil in place and all the Fangs wore their masks. Emma the wetnurse and Lady Dalflitch were the only women present, beside Amelia, who did not have their faces covered.

"That is good news," the archduchess said benignly, hoping she looked more dignified than her pain made her feel. She was almost certain that her time must be coming, but having been through the false labor already, and given the seriousness of the day, she refused to assume and simply pack herself back to her bed.

"What word of the messengers to Loncastel or the battle south of the river?"

"None from either yet, I'm sorry, Your Grace."

Amelia nodded, but her brows furrowed. "Why, then, are you here?"

"Well, a corporal o' the Gryphons is come to ask us go reinforce him on one o' the great bridges," the corporal explained. "Things is getting' fair hairy out there in places, he says."

"If things are becoming so dangerous, then surely her grace's protection should not be reduced," Dalflitch insisted. Her pale face was thunderous, dark eyes staring down her nose in disgust.

"Well, I don't know as it's right dangerous, least not like anyone's gonna fight past our boys," the corporal said apologetically. "But a small lot on a bridge point, if some o' them ranger fellows is chuckin' their pots about, well they could find 'emselves overwhelmed easy enough. I was thinking to take two or three lines worth and just help to drive 'em off. I would leave the main o' your garrison here, Your Grace."

"Like seven lines worth," the line first with him said. "That's seventy men, with the two wagons to use as well. The roof door those Bridgetowner mongrels used to get in 'as been nailed up tight and we 'ave two Roar on the roof watchin'—best shots in the whole company, I swear."

The corporal clicked his tongue at his junior's forwardness, but he cocked his head at Amelia and frowned reluctantly, as if to say that his man's words were true for all that they had been spoken out of turn.

"Very well, Corporal," she told the man. "Go to, for the safety of fellow White Lions. But if you will be more than half an hour of the candle, send word here and to Lord Farringdon so the weakness of the Paramour's defenses is known to those who must know."

The corporal saluted, and a fraction later, the line first followed his example. Before the two men turned to leave, the corporal added his own impertinent encouragement.

"There's word that Bridgetown militia uniforms've been seen about on the street again, Your Grace," he said. "Seems you've been able to finally stir the lady in the castle to light a fire under the buggers and get them about the defense o' their own town. They ain't worth much when they ain't killin' prisoners, but at least they might help us some."

"That is enough of that, Corporal," Dalflitch said dismissively, and the man tugged his forelock to her. Lady Dalflitch might be of some rank, wife of a knight as she was, but she was by no means worthy of a salute. A moment later, he and his subordinate were gone and there were shouts from the yard as he led a fraction of his command away to help the beset White Lions elsewhere in the town.

"That was welcome news about Lady Penelope and the Bridgetown militia, wouldn't you say?" Amelia asked her seneschal.

"Spring flowers that have hidden all winter and now bloomed with a too-early burst of sun?" Dalflitch responded, using the weather as a useful metaphor. "Come the next storms, they will wither again, overwhelmed by the unexpected cold."

Amelia wanted to counsel her lady to be more optimistic, but the assessment was not an unjust one. She pondered the rest of what she knew of the town's evolving military situation and wondered if the time was coming that she and her ladies should be ready to evacuate the Paramour's if something truly untoward happened. Of course, she had no idea whether such a thing was likely to occur, or where they would be well served to go. Loncastel and the Dog's Leg tavern were the best she could think in the immediate turn, but she also hoped that if such a desperate move became necessary, her escort would have plans in place.

"Odd that a Gryphon corporal came to summon Lion Banner blokes for help," Lady Righteous said thoughtfully.

"The confusions of a battle," Lady Dalflitch intoned readily, sounding relaxed, but Amelia was sure she saw some nervousness in the beauty's eyes. In all likelihood, the lady seneschal was remembering their flight from Daven Marcus's failed crusade years ago in the west.

That had been because of the confusion of battle, Amelia thought, recalling the day herself and the chaos that had ensued because Daven Marcus had not made his lines of communication and his chain of command clear to those under him, just like it seemed Prentice's strangled authority had done to her own men-at-arms' leadership structure. *Lord protect us all if I have made the same mistakes as that fool brat.*

CHAPTER 71

The drumbeat echoed over the sweeping fields as the marching Gryphons inexorably pursued the fleeing Veckander forces. The surrounded eastern wing of the enemy battle line had collapsed in less than a quarter of the candle, mercenaries choosing surrender before suicide. Professionals went down on their knees and turned their weapon points to the earth in the universal sign of submission. Whatever ire was raised in the Gryphon Bannermen's blood, they had witnessed the horror of the Bridgetowner militia massacre in the autumn, and they swiftly brought themselves to heel. The rage of battle transformed to the disciplines of victory and conquest.

Prince Everard and as many of his knights ahorse as managed to stay free of the encirclement immediately turned their mounts about and headed for Town Sobridge. Leaving Sergeant Porth with a thousand militiamen to police the field, secure the abandoned tents and supplies, and begin accepting formal surrenders, Prentice called Guillam to him. Knight commander and sergeant rallied their wearied fighters and set them on a forced march south down Great Bridge Road toward the fortified walls of the Vec town. Ahead of them, Sergeant Gennet's other half of the Gryphon Banner was still driving the collapsed enemy west wing in front of themselves, the sting of Roarshot enough to prevent the routing foe from reforming and fighting back. Even as the advance continued, clutches of men-at-arms too exhausted or too wounded to continue fleeing simply went to one knee and put their weapons point down, or else cast them away completely.

"How far we takin' this little stroll, My Lord?" Guillam shouted as they passed by a tiny farming village, two dozen thatched huts astride the road with no headman's house or even an inn or tavern. Whoever inhabited the sparse settlement had fled the battlefield already, that was for certain, and Prentice looked the simple dwellings over, wondering how many of their menfolk were dead at the foot of Sougate or if the two women he had seen at the bastion's postern gate the night they had captured it had been from here.

"We will march all the way to Sobridge, Guillam," Prentice told his Sergeant of the Claws. "We are going to take the place away from the princes for good."

"What if them gates are shut to us?"

"Then we will bring our two cannons down and smash our way through—tonight if the rain holds off," the knight commander declared with a tone of unyielding will. Having come this far and broken the Golden Heron coalition in the field, Prentice was determined to finish the task completely. If he was forced to pause now, he would not be able to begin again. Between the hateful chorus and the submission he owed to his archduchess, he would have no chance to recommence this fight.

Rains are the enemy now, he thought, looking up at the sky once more. The bright but frail sun shone from the middle vault. It was noon, or near enough. Plenty of time to complete the conquest. As he realized that, he also recognized that he had not yet decided if he would honor the desire of the rebel peasants and allow them to form a republic out of Town Sobridge, ruled by whatever assembly they thought to appoint for themselves. Prentice nearly laughed out loud. In fact, the question would never be his to answer. His life would be forfeit as soon as this battle was complete, and any decisions for the future would belong to others. One less burden for his soul was a surprising relief. Though the cursing wolfpack tried to deride him as meaningless, Prentice found himself enjoying once again one of the few existential pleasures he had ever known as a convict—the complete freedom to not care what happened tomorrow. Where he would go or what he would do was never a convict's problem. Someone else had the responsibility to answer that.

As if fear for the future had been some kind of noose, choking off his breath until he realized it was not his to do anything with any longer, Prentice felt fresh air rush into his mind, clearing much of the fog that hid the circling wolves and opening the space around his thoughts for a moment. It was not an empty gap however, for into the space, like a flood released from a dam, memories of his prophetic dream fountained upward. The knight commander especially remembered the pit somewhere south of Denay and the injunction to learn the lesson of Samson.

Still have no idea what that is, he thought, and he wondered what he should look for here in the south as a sign of the Silent Hand's headquarters. They would be hidden, that was certain, but would they be simply unknown or dressed in some institutional disguise?

A place like the Ditch, he told himself. That would be the first thing to look for—something like Aubrey's infamous dungeon. Despite the fact that so much of his visions were figurative, he somehow felt that the pit in his dream was a literal pit of some sort, an actual location underground. The prophet in his dream had said that Prentice himself had survived a pit like the one he was looking for and that meant the cells the Inquisition had tortured him in at Ashfield. Of that much, he was sure.

"Not long now, My Lord," Guillam shouted over the hammer of the drums and the beat of marching feet on firmer ground that had not been churned to mire with pointless attacks. The sergeant was right. The Great Bridge Road curved away gently through a neighborhood outside the walls of Town Sobridge. Livestock traders' yards intermingled with the humble dwellings of unskilled laborers too poor to afford homes inside the town's defensive walls. If there had been any fear of Reachermen coming this far south to besiege the town, these buildings would have been destroyed—likely simply burned away—to deny the militiamen any cover from archers. The fact that everything still stood as normal showed how completely this reversal of fortune had caught Prince Everard unprepared. Through the gaps between houses, Prentice saw glimpses of the retreated enemy massed at the gate, and he wondered what the prince's strategy was now. Perhaps he had an ambush prepared amongst the huts and sheds and fences. He bade Guillam to call a halt and send runners to his other sergeants commanding this far south. A short while later, Sootface Kate, her visage smeared black from battle in accord with her nickname, came from the western flank. It took Gennet longer, the Sergeant of the Fangs apparently having managed to completely swing around the settlement on the outside of the walls and find himself a little berm that had given him a good view of the gates directly.

"The retreating levies have shut the gates behind them, My Lord," the knight sergeant reported with some satisfaction. "From what I could see, I'd say that the Veckander prince is trying to bully or plead his way inside. All his pennants are clustered 'round the barbican.'"

"Oh ho!" Guillam chuckled and clapped his gauntleted hands, leaning his own halberd on his shoulder as he did.

"We saw a gang of fellows in plate who came out of a tight road with the look of blokes about to break and run from the fight," Gennet went on, pointing to the ground in front of the town's west corner, "just past a big sheepfold 'bout two streets that way. They clapped eyes on us and stopped like guilty young'uns, then turned around and went back the way they come."

That was good news, indeed, and the Gryphon officers now smiled predatory smiles.

"Let us get this finished then," Prentice told them. "Kate, take your ten cohorts and sweep around that odd shed on the east side. It looks like Knight Sergeant Gennet's berm runs along the wall and comes someway out behind those farms and whatnot over there. See if there's a spot you can get some height to hold, but even if not, block any chance of the rats deserting the sinking boat that way. Gennet, return to your flank and hold them off on that side. We will give you a short while to get set, then you will hear the advance beat. When you do, start marching cohorts into those streets you saw and flush them all toward the closed gates."

"Are we to advance as well, My Lord, or do we only hold whatever ridgeline we can find?" Sootface asked, and it was clear from her expression she did not want her command to miss out on any final stage of the battle.

"If the roads open out on your side as on the west, then yes, Sergeant, send your own cohorts in to press on all sides. Everyone's main purpose is to make sure none of these mongrels gets to flee, but no one has to miss out either. Watch for ambuscade amongst those huts and sheds, and we will all meet in half an hour out the front of the town gates."

With that, all three saluted and rushed back to their respective sections of the Gryphon's now-divided line of battle. Prentice allowed them what he felt was enough time to be ready and then gave the order for the advance. The drummers began the beat, and it echoed off the town's walls, then was redoubled and redoubled again as it was taken up by the cohorts on the west and east flanks. Three thousand Reach militiamen began the slow march into the last piece of ground between them and the princedom of Town Sobridge. Every man-at-arms was resolute and watchful. The nearly empty peasant settlement was like a thicket in which any number of dangerous foes might hide, waiting to ambush the Gryphons as they came too close. Under the beat of the drums there was the jingle of armor and tack and the tromp of feet—the myriad ubiquitous sounds that accompanied any force on the march—yet somehow it was all subdued. The sense of threat even suppressed the hateful chorus in Prentice's soul and the question of Samson, and the southern pit faded in importance. Doing his best not to think of how his skin crawled with uncertainty, Prentice sat himself fully upright and held Boots to a walk, even though he longed to charge in and find what was happening in front of the gates to the town.

At last, he and Guillam led their cohorts around a final corner in the road, and the way opened out to a market square of sorts, likely kept outside the town's main walls as a way to distinguish between local conclave traders and foreign merchants, the travelers from farther afield not permitted to access the inner mercantile community—a form of protectionism for a settlement that sat astride the most significant road of many nations. Crowded into this marketplace were the remains of Prince Everard's army, pressing back toward the gatehouse as if thinking to simply force their way in by pushing alone. They milled about, knights ahorse trying to keep their temperamental destriers calm while men-at-arms shoved against them, long pennants and banners with no wind draping across the massed men like fallen tents. The encroaching drums hammered on the walls, and as Prentice's command began to fill the north side of the square, Gennet's militiamen began to appear from the west, filtering in smaller groups through the tangle of lesser streets. A short moment later, lines from Sootface Kate's flank appeared on a ridge just under the walls of the town's east. Apparently, the path through that side had proved the more complicated, and they had found it easier to sweep all the way around. Being so close to the walls, they were vulnerable to any attack the town's defenders might think to throw from the ramparts, but looking up, all Prentice could see was a nervous audience of townsfolk. The desperate and defeated Veckander force stopped their anxious movements and turned to face the Gryphon Banner Company, expressions full of dread for whatever was to come next. Prentice gave the signal for the beat to cease, and swiftly, the marching command died away. For a long moment there was near silence, so heavy that it was possible to hear the creak of his saddle beneath him and the fizz of the smoldering long-matches.

"Yield," Prentice shouted, lifting his visor to make sure his words were clear. "In the name of her grace, Amelia Archduchess

of the Western Reach and Aubrey, yield and live else die here
now!"

CHAPTER 72

The broken remnant of the Golden Heron army was a mob, no longer a military formation, and like a fearful crowd, its edges shrank back from their enemy, the men closest looking behind them to where their failed leaders still sat on their horses. Some of the professional men-at-arms afoot were ready to surrender, lowering their shields and even beginning the awkward act of turning their blades about to lower the points, but in the main, they waited for the word from their employer, professionals to the last. Gradually, a channel cleared through the press of men and the gloriously attired Everard of Sunbury and Town Sobridge led his closest cadre of retainers forward on their mounts. The watery, late-winter sunlight flashed on the gold-edged fluting of their armor. The prince's helmet had a fine gold coronet worked into the brow ridge and above that a magnificent fan plume of crimson dyed cockerel's feathers—a recreation of the red sun of his own heraldry, no doubt. His horse snorted and tossed its head. It looked as if the mount had once had a similar plume as its rider's, but only a single red feather remained now, the rest having been knocked away in the battle and retreat. There were comparable minor signs of defeat on each of the prince's bodyguard, about ten knights ahorse in all. With his visor raised, it was clear the defeated prince was muttering something to the rider closest to him, and that quiet message was being passed through them all.

Do not be a fool, little prince, Prentice thought as he watched. A man too proud to bow his knee in defeat could still turn an embarrassing morning's failure into a tragedy to be remembered through history.

They ready their final trap, the hateful chorus whispered. *Do not let them spring it. Slay him now. Slay them all, man and beast, or you will have failed your precious archduchess, and she will have more cause to hate you!*

Prentice almost sneered openly at the worthless paranoia. The moment he had ridden out of Sougate he had accepted that execution was the prescribed fate for his actions. The Gryphon Banner and the Golden Heron's levies had both needed someone to take that burden for them. There was no point fearing his liege's contempt now. He had already rebelled.

But only the once, he told himself and the enemy within. Now that he had them beaten and broken, he would treat with this foe in exactly the way his liege would want. In his heart he was still her man, rebel or no. Since the sun had come up this day Prentice had felt the wolfpack hatred shrinking away somewhat, diminished in its barks and no longer fearsome when it bared its teeth. It was like the relief of battle he had felt the previous day, but stronger and more freeing still. The hateful chorus had not faded from his mind, by no means, but now it felt more like an enemy he could wrestle with rather than a conqueror that had so much power over him. Now as it continued to howl for blood, pushing him on to make a fresh slaughter south of Bridgetown, he was able to hold it back. But the more he watched, the more he could see a final defiance growing in Everard's expression, and the chorus within struggled to rise in response to it. Prentice could feel his hands start to tremble at the renewed effort of controlling his emotions.

"Tell him again. Let them yield and be spared," he whispered to himself through gritted teeth, trying to will himself to make the offer once more. It was harder than he expected, and suddenly his own convict-hearted resentments and longing for justice also sprang into the inward debate. Everard had sent men to die out of pure convenience. The blood of levies at the foot of Sougate cried for justice. This prince of the south could not be permitted to ride away unmolested just because chivalry allowed it and would prevent a fresh massacre. He must be made to answer. Too many notions all demanded time in Prentice's thoughts, and he could feel the sweat trickling down his back—not from the unseasonable sunshine, which hardly warmed the winter air, even so close to noon. No, it was the tension of trying to control so many errant thoughts and bring about a worthy conclusion that he could offer his liege without burdening his conscience further when he stepped into the grave.

"Yield, Prince," he forced himself to shout again, even though the distance between them was half now what it was. "Tell your hired men to lay down their arms and we will accept their pledges of parole. They will be permitted to take their leave of Town Sobridge in peace if they swear their year-and-a-day to her grace."

Surrender and a pledge not to make war again for one year and one day—the typical requirement of a sworn man's surrender, though to Prentice it seemed far too little to exact from them. They should be made to pay what they put Sobridge's peasantry through. Someone would have to pay the debt of justice.

"Have your knights surrender and submit to her grace's judgement," he persisted. "She is merciful, and if no charges of abuse are brought against them or if the charges are not too egregious, she may allow them to offer weregelds."

Where had that come from? The archduchess hated the notion of nobility buying themselves out from under judgement. It had been one of the main points of contention that had driven her and Earl Sebastian apart. Prentice found himself reaching for his belt pouch. He only stopped once his gauntleted fingers brushed over it and he realized his brother's note was no longer within. What had this to do with his family?

"The witch lover wants to loot the last coppers of my treasury," Everard shouted, piercing Prentice's confusion. "He will be disappointed. There's nothing left to take back to his bloodthirsty whore!"

"Damned fool!" Prentice retorted loudly, his control slipping farther and farther from his grasp, feeling the cry for blood rising. "Yield and submit. Put not your men to death yet more!"

"Death rather than northern slavery," Everard bellowed and lifted a sword aloft, as if issuing a heroic rallying cry. Prentice recognized the slogan as one the Vec earls had used centuries before when they had risen in rebellion against the Denay throne originally and named themselves princes in a united compact—a union that had not lasted even a decade after the initial rebellion. The sword in the Prince of Sunbury's hand was comically too large for use on horseback, and Prentice guessed by its golden hilt that it must be the Sunbury honor sword, fellow to the Sobridge longsword that was now wielded by Lady Penelope. It was clearly a footman's weapon, however, designed for use with two hands. Honor could be the only reason for it to be drawn now, and it seemed Everard imagined his sloganeering and honor blade would inspire some kind of impossible snatch of victory from the fire of defeat as he kicked his horse forward to a charge, lowering the too-heavy sword and couching it to use as an awkward lance. His bodyguard also lowered their pennanted lances and spurred forward, inarticulately shouting their own battle cries.

Always suspecting this moment was coming, Prentice did not hesitate. He snatched the saddle pistol from its sheath and raised it, pointing straight at Everard's chest. It was the first time he had used a weapon in actual combat all morning. He pulled the trigger, and a fraction of a moment after the hammer snapped down, the little metal beast coughed in his hand and his shot burst out in fire and smoke. It was not alone. All around the square, Roar gunners waiting ready in the front rank also fired their weapons, while beside them Claws set pikes and halberds outward to fend away this final suicidal charge. Dozens upon dozens of Roarshot hammered into the riders, easily punching through steel at such a close distance, though surely one or two were deflected. Others missed, and while the knights ahorse were torn down, behind them some of the reluctant mercenaries also fell wounded.

That was the extent of their involvement, however. Whatever misbegotten glory Everard hoped to inspire his followers to, the hired men felt no share of it. Even most of the remaining knights ahorse held their ground. Only his most loyal friends fell at his side, and of them, only two survived long enough to engage the pike points that rushed to protect Prentice and Boots. It was over in a moment and the unnatural hush came again, smoke drifting up into the bright sky. Gradually, with the shuffle of feet and the creak and clank of leather and steel, interspersed with the moans of the wounded and dying, the remaining crowd began to turn their weapons to the ground and go down upon their knees, surrendering to the conquering Reachermen.

Prentice dismounted Boots and moved to where Everard lay beside his horse, man and mount both mortally wounded. He leaned down and lifted the prince's visor, revealing an agonized face, drenched in sweat. Prentice understood what that was like.

"There's nothing left for her to loot," the dying man whispered and tried to spit at Prentice in contempt, but he was too weak even for that. "The Heron is bankrupt at their command. There is nothing for her..."

"She would have paid your debts and more," Prentice told him, feeling a cold pity for this fool who clearly had been led around by the nose by the Heron and whatever Silent Hand agents had been whispering in his ears. Was there a Bluebird lurking at the fringes of the Sunbury court as there had been in Dweltford and Bridgetown? "For the lives of the men you fed to Sougate, she would have given you more silver than you could have counted."

Everard had no more words in this world, but his contemptuous expression said everything he thought of Prentice's claim. For a short moment Prentice wondered at them himself. Hadn't the archduchess refused him this option? Hadn't she insisted on letting Everard's pointless assaults continue rather than risk her own retainers? How was Prentice asserting her self-sacrificial mercy now? The battle was over, and his militiamen had been victorious, but that only meant his mind had more space for the even more confused melee of his thoughts, it seemed. The wolfpack might be diminished, but they were not scattered yet.

Beneath him, Everard breathed out a last rattling sigh that was obscured in the quiet by the echo of the town gates being unbarred. A moment later, a crowd of wary yeomen and what Prentice supposed must be local conclave members shuffled forward, pushing three men in fine black robes with bound hands ahead of them. Prentice recognized by description the chisel-cut goatee of Jerrod Froster, the Golden Heron bank's representative for all matters against the Western Reach and the financier of the coalition against her grace. The shaved-headed man stood tall and proud even as his captors shoved him, but eventually the townsmen forced the banker and his two fellows to their knees right there in the dust outside the gate. The submission of Town Sobridge was complete, and for the second time in almost as many years, the Archduchess of the Western Reach had brought a rebel Vec princedom back under Grand Kingdom authority, which only meant there were now any number of new problems to be negotiated, but at least the graveyard of Sougate's footings could cease from taking in new members.

CHAPTER 73

T he morning passed anxiously despite Amelia's every effort to project confidence amongst her ladies. Girls who worked at needle and thread stuck themselves all too often, and twice something was noisily spilt on the floorboards, once with a shattering of porcelain that caused everyone in the kitchen end of the chamber to jump and gasp. Because they had anticipated more moments with outside messengers arriving, Lady Dalflitch had insisted that all neophytes remain veiled the entire time. As noon approached, however, there had been only one further message—a note from Lady Spindle explaining what was happening with her husband's strongroom, which still acted as Amelia's treasury. Caius Welburne, master merchant and Spindle's husband, had turned out his entire hired-guard contingent and now had them sleeping in shifts in his trading house to prevent any looting or pillaging as the situation on the streets of Bridgetown turned chaotic once again, like the first night of the Usurper's siege. Raiders were reported to be attacking parts of Salthatch and Piers, though strangely, there was no word from Bell's Hummock. There was no fresh report from Loncastel either, other than that there were still running battles through the ruins of the docks there, and the sound of the Dragons could be heard roaring again even through the closed windows of Paramour's. Soon after Spindle's note, Amelia told Dalflitch to let the neophytes breathe, and the command to remain veiled was rescinded.

Far too tense herself to rest, Amelia took to a chair near the fire, having a pillow and blanket brought to keep herself comfortable and warm while Lady Elizabeth supervised two neophytes in packing a spare set of clothes into a small chest, more easily carried if they were forced to relocate urgently. Having been made to flee with nothing but the dress she was wearing more than once in her time as ruler of the Reach, Amelia was determined to have at least one change of clothing ready. Even so, the wooden chest would be heavy enough that it would require at least one stout fellow to carry it if they had to move swiftly.

"Perhaps Lady Spindle would forgive me if I put them in a bag," Amelia had said when Beth led the two neophytes out from the curtains, hefting the chest between them. Smaller did not mean light, by any means.

"Perhaps that would be a good idea for us all, Your Grace," Lady Mathilda ventured to offer, and Amelia agreed.

One at a time, neophytes and Lace Fangs were given leave to go to their own sleeping quarters, there to wrap sheets and blankets into travel bundles, each with one change of underdress and whatever other small clothes they felt to need, the governing rule being that the final bundle must be able to be wrapped around them and hung over a shoulder like a bandoleer. Lady Righteous had been quite insistent on that point.

"Whatever happens in the next hours, you all need be ready for a fight," the senior Lace Fang told them. "Stickers to hand, hands free for the battle."

Her words were accepted with all diligence.

"What of you, My Lady?" Amelia asked, nodding to the babe in Righteous's arms and then to Emma the wetnurse.

"I'll be ready, Your Grace," Righteous responded with firm resolution. "I can wrap me babe up good and swift, don't you fear. And Emma, you can go get yourself ready now too. I'll be needin' you to bring the other twin with us 'cause there ain't no way I'm picking 'tween 'em."

"And once Emma is prepared, you will stay beside her to protect you both and both your children," Amelia told the baroness, and Righteous gave her a surprised look.

"My place is protectin' you, Your Gr...," she began to reply, but Amelia cut her off.

"Your place is protecting your heirs, dear Lady. Do not think for an instant to put me above them. If something happened to them, I would never forgive myself. I couldn't do that...I couldn't do that to him."

From her expression, Amelia could tell that Righteous knew she meant Prentice. The baroness nodded as she accepted the command and then dispatched Emma to their rooms so she could ready herself as all the other women were. Seeing the grimness of the air around them, Lady Dalflitch put on a perfectly graceful smile.

"Let us recall that the Lion and Gryphon Banner Companies have successfully fended away all assaults on the town up until now, and for all that matters are now tense, we have little to fear," she counseled them all. "We are safely ensconced behind guards and defenses. We should keep our hearts light and our minds on our right duties."

The young women seemed to accept the instruction, but a moment later, Lady Daisy coughed politely.

"With respect, My Lady, I must disagree with you," she said, drawing an ireful expression from Dalflitch. The newer Lace Fang went on, regardless. "At this very moment, our right duties are not frivolous or light-hearted. Perhaps we are as safe now as we have ever been, but I doubt Verony would call it much safe. And even if that is as it has been all winter, we have the heirs to the Barony of Fallenhill and the future heir the Western Reach as a whole in our charge. Our duty now is to plan our next actions with care and watchfulness."

Whether it was mention of the lost Verony, the duty of care to the future, or something else altogether, Lady Dalflitch blinked only once before she smiled ever so slightly and bowed her head in deference to Lady Daisy's suggestion. With that acknowledgement, Amelia also gave a nod, and the Lace Fangs proceeded to conduct a serious discussion of the likeliest safe locations around the town and the most trustworthy paths from Paramour's to each, pooling their combined knowledge from their days in disguise, spying out her grace's enemies. Amelia marveled at the depth and breadth of their knowledge. Having been frustrated by Bluebird's virtual invisibility, it had been easy to think that nothing had been being achieved all winter.

"If we can trust the south side of Oldbridge, we should be able to make it to Runners Field," Beth offered, the wisest choice as the ladies worked from the assumption that their escort might be overwhelmed in transit. No matter the situation on the rest of the islands, there would still be hundreds of militiamen in the camp.

"True 'nough," a neophyte called Victoria agreed, then offered an objection. "But won't these raider louts have that in mind? They sure'n have some word on the state o' the town from Bluebird, or even just from that first raid. They'll want to split Oldbridge in half and lock that end off, if'n they can."

"Surely," Beth agreed, and Daisy nodded with her.

"Loncastel then? 'Cept that'll put us on main roads, and twice as sure as Runners, they'll be sending blokes to capture the great bridges. To get to Loncastel, we'll be walking straight into more of 'em, I give you the quiet word!"

"Pity Agatha's still out there," another neophyte said. "She knows all them back ways on the north of Oldbridge."

"She's told me a few," Lady Mathilda insisted earnestly, "enough to find our own way if pressed. And if it's Loncastel that we want, there's that boatman's walk hanging under it, the one that lets the fishers come and go under the bridge without the garrison above knowin' nothin' about it."

"What's this?" Amelia asked. She had not tracked every specific piece of news that their spies had brought in throughout their time here, but she was surprised she had not been told of a secret pathway under the bridge from Loncastel to Oldbridge. How was her garrison maintaining control if such a way was left open to smugglers and whatever other ill-intentioned folk might want it? Could Bluebird have been hiding down there the whole time, for instance?

"It's an ancient skips' jetty, Your Grace," Dalflitch explained confidently. "The girls found it some weeks ago and we have been watching it carefully. I had hoped it might be a way that Bluebird was traveling back and forth, perhaps even hopping onto friendly boats we might suborn. Unfortunately, the only birds we have seen nesting under the antique stone are genuine waterfowl—grebes and gulls, far from the ocean and perching on rotting piers."

"But if needs be, we can use it to get safely across to Loncastel?" Amelia asked.

"Well, we might have to cope with the Tollybludgers," Daisy conceded.

"The what?"

"Tollybludgers, Your Grace," Mathilda explained. "Three brothers who dream of 'emselves as a skips' crew. Truth to tell, they're more trolls under a bridge than aught else, but they're hefty beggars and they don't mind swingin' their belayin' pins about to get their toll."

"Tollybludgers, humph!" Beth snorted dismissively. "I almost hope we do have to go underbridge just for a chance to face 'em, and I sure hope they try to toll us. The river ghosts're thirsty for the mongrels' blood, and I'll be glad to do the throat slittin'."

A little surprised at the Lace Fang's violent assertions, Amelia looked about, and Daisy explained.

"The 'bludgers take liberties with tavern girls and doxies up and down the docks, Your Grace. That don't sit well with Beth."

"Nor with me, My Lady," Amelia concurred, and the discussion of possible escapes and hiding places continued for some while. Amelia was starting to wonder if there was any place left in Bridgetown her ladies did not know, as well as marveling that Bluebird was still not located, when a neophyte hammered up the stairs and into the chamber.

"Somethin's happenin' in the yard, Your Grace," she declared without even bothering to curtsy. "An escort, it looks like. Fresh Lions come to move us away."

"Excellent news," Dalflitch said, and there was a brightening to the tense mood amongst the ladies.

To move us away, Amelia noticed her doorkeeper had said, *not "come to save us."* Her Lace Fangs saw the value of extra support but did not count themselves in need of rescue.

"The corporal's returned and he's gettin' the rest of 'em ready to march off," the neophyte continued. "To Loncastel, so they say."

"Then we have our destination," Amelia declared, and she worked to stand up, her back aching with the effort even of that small action. "Lady Dalflitch, go and ask them how they want us arranged and what path we will be taking."

"Will it matter now?" Dalflitch asked, her relieved expression colored with confusion for a moment.

"We yet have ladies abroad in mufti," Amelia explained. "Lady Agatha and the others. We will not be abandoning them. I request one of you ladies to volunteer to remain behind here and warn them where we have gone if they return—one of you skilled in stealth and cunning. It is a dreadful task, and I beg your forgiveness for asking, but we all know that Agatha or one of the others would wait here for you if your places were exchanged."

The ladies of the chamber shared only a momentary set of glances before the girl Victoria stepped forward.

"I can do it, Your Grace. If raiders or some such arrive, I can hide in that secret stairs," she declared confidently. "There's no way out on top no more, but it's a sure bolthole once it's closed up, so I reckon I'll be right. If I don't hear word one way or another by sundown, I can make for the dockside on Piers. I got cousins down there'll take me in and pack me off back up to Dweltford in a skiff if everything else goes to pot."

"I like your plan, My Lady," Amelia said and realized that as a neophyte, Victoria had no right to the title. Looking about, it seemed as if some of the others might have noticed the slip as well. The archduchess smiled and nodded to them. "Yes, ladies, I think the time is come. Official words and special rituals can be attended to later, but each of you, and those abroad, all end this day as Lace Fangs. Our first company of neophytes have ended their training now."

The expression of trust and approval seemed to bathe them in a fresh, warming light, and the already resolute women stood taller, it appeared.

That's good, Amelia thought, *because with my sore back, I certainly can't stand straight for much at a time.* The notion made her smirk until she remembered the unpleasant and likely dangerous journey through the streets they would soon be facing.

CHAPTER 74

"This *is* the only dungeon, My Lord," the healer Halleon Lyle told him as Prentice looked over the tiny space in one basement corner of the foundations of Town Sobridge's small palace—four cells with walls of hardwood bars as thick as a man's arm, two to each side of a short corridor. Inside each were chains on the walls, but none of them were occupied.

"Hardly anyone is ever here," Lyle continued to explain. "In the last year, the prince did have a pamphleteer here, a firebrand who preached overthrow. After the battle in the north, before Everard had come from Sunbury to seize the town, other assemblists bribed the guards to let the fellow out. If Everard even knew he had been here, he showed no concern that he was gone. Last we heard, he's sailed all the way down river to Cragburne."

Reference to battle in the north caught Prentice by surprise until he realized that the healer was referring to the first battle outside Sougate—the one where the previous prince of Town Sobridge had died. The old "previous prince." Everard was the previous prince now. And that battle, the massacre south of Bridgetown, would obviously have been in the north for these folk. It was a tiny clue as to the strange gulf between the two ancient enemy nations that were ostensibly only separated by a single river's worth of water. At another time, Prentice might have mused on the significance, but for now he felt he had a short wick left in the candle of his life. He had already sent a messenger to the Paramour's Chambers reporting their victory and inviting her grace's judgement an hour ago. Even on foot, that message had surely been delivered by now. All that was left was this virtually impossible chance to find some trace of the Inquisition's pit in the south before his neck was offered the noose or the axe.

"The only other prison we have is the cages in market square where they keep folks until the magistrate sees them. It's a bit like pillories to be honest—just being made to wait in there a few days means to get yourself pelted with slops some. Unless someone's a true ruffian, that usually does for justice, especial if it's just some fellows who got drunk in a tavern and took things a shade too far."

The healer shrugged as if that were the worst to which criminality ever descended in Vec society. Prentice doubted that was the whole of their system of law and order, but he was not looking for the civic institutions.

"What of something kept private but where some folk might come and go regularly," he said, realizing how vague he sounded. Surely just about every merchant's warehouse in the town might qualify for that description. Halleon Lyle shook his head, more in bewilderment than rejection.

"I don't really know anything like that. I can ask about for you, but..."

"Never mind," Prentice told the man wearily, and he bowed his head, scratching at his scalp. "Show me the way back out."

Halleon Lyle led him through the captured palace, now occupied by a contingent of the Gryphon Banner to prevent looting and to assert Archduchess Amelia's authority, at least in the immediate term. Whole cohorts were taking control of the town's various strongpoints and other important structures, including the Conclave House, as well as a large grain store that apparently serviced most of the community and a pair of wind-driven mills built on a ridge to the south beyond the town's walls. Although the Vec was a land of rivers, Town Sobridge was unusual in that it was one of the few princedoms not to be built upon a watercourse but rather between two—the Murr on its north border and the Golburn tributaries in the south and west of the province. Lacking a large, easy water source of its own, Town Sobridge harnessed the wind to mill its grain. Returning to the palace's main floor, Prentice was quickly caught by Gennet, bringing his initial report.

"It's early days, Knight Commander, but everything's exactly as they've told us, near as I can tell," he said after saluting. "The mercenaries weren't even much in their tents, seems like. They were taking liberties with all the inns and taverns, the drink and the girls. Like as not there won't be one yeoman here who's sad to see the back of the hired mongrels. I've got some Fangs over at the Conclave House searching through their strongroom, and it looks like Everard kept his own coin here in two big chests, each one larger than the bed I slept in growing up, 'cept they're both almost empty. Just some bags of hacksilver and a few handfuls of copper. I don't know what he's left for his heirs elsewhere, but sure as spitting we didn't loot much of the children's inheritance here."

Poor and hungry from the prince on down, Prentice mused. *Well, poor, at least.* He doubted Everard and his closest retainers had actually ever gone hungry.

"What pillage do you plan on taking, My Lord?" Halleon Lyle asked, drawing himself upright and politely but firmly inserting himself into this conversation between what amounted to conquerors he had assisted in their conquest. By dint of their special status in society, healers were known to be confident and even somewhat haughty in their dealings with the powers that be, but even so, Prentice could see the man Lyle had an appreciation of his and the town's vulnerability at this moment.

"From the town? None," Prentice answered the healer's question. "Her grace's men are paid rightly for their service and under command to take no plunder from the common folk. Her grace may yet levy a toll against the town as a whole for the cost of the battle, but that will be something the conclave and whatever folk your assemblists think to put forward will be permitted to speak to. In the meantime, the knight sergeant here already has provost patrols about, and the command is given. Any militiamen caught thieving from or molesting the local populace will be tried and punished as bandits. If you have any reports of such actions, bring them directly to Knight Sergeant Gennet. You have my pledge that all such will be heard and investigated. We will seize what we wish from Everard's army, but White Lions do not plunder."

Halleon Lyle took a step back from Prentice as if the knight commander had just performed a magick trick, producing something from a puff of smoke or the like.

"That...that is good to hear, My Lord," he said, and he tugged his forelock. "On behalf of the folk of Sobridge, I thank you."

"The credit is to her grace," Prentice told him, "But if you would show your thanks, stir your fellow healers as you promised and begin to honor your part of the arrangement. The day was not too bloody, but there are men wounded and suffering out on the fields who need the work of your talents."

Lyle nodded. "Many are there already, and we will honor our agreement and serve you in your war against your tyrant. Can you tell me, what is your liege's full plan for your war? Will she see him overturned and take his throne for herself?"

Prentice was sure he knew the answer, but he simply shook his head. That was a matter for others, not him.

"Her grace's plans are her own," he said as he turned away to seek the palace doors. Across a hall and portico tiled with a mosaic of blue and green stones that reminded him of the one time he had ever seen the Tassassim Ocean, Prentice marched out of Sobridge's princely residence. The sunlight had not dimmed, and for a moment it stung his eyes as he emerged from the inner shade. A voice called for him across the garden that surrounded the palace like a verdant moat, with fine lawns green from the winter rains and well-tended flowering hedges. It was all very civilized for the command center of a town that had ostensibly been at war with its neighbor for the past several centuries. Blinking against the brightness, he looked for the caller and found a militia line first holding Boots by the bridle, waiting for him, while a short distance behind was Dahyoor sitting his own mount, though not either of Prentice's children's two horses, which he typically rode.

"He says he's got a message for you, Knight Commander," the line first reported, nodding to Dahyoor. "Come from Bridgetown."

Prentice nodded, taking his horse's reins from the militiaman and then looking to his squire.

"Speak your message," he said.

"The archduchess calls for you," Dahyoor told him with typical directness.

She sent you? Prentice thought, and then he immediately realized why she would. Having spent the previous day and night playing hide and seek with her grace's messengers, not to mention putting Whilte under guard, the archduchess would have made sure to finally pick a courier who would get through to him. The hateful chorus tried to mock him, but he only sneered back inwardly, although his lip did curl for just a moment. He quickly schooled his expression to neutrality once more. It was over now. No amount of mocking would make what was coming any worse, and like the day he had chosen to take multiple floggings rather than submit to Liam's abusive authority, Prentice resolved to fear no coming punishment. In truth, he knew that his liege would probably seek to be lenient. Somehow, the imminent execution he had anticipated at dawn this morning now seemed less than a foregone conclusion. Amelia of Dweltford was a compassionate woman in the main. All the same, there was no way she could simply allow his rebellion to stand unpunished. Regardless of how it played out, what was coming would be unpleasant to say the least, and Prentice resolved to face it without shying away. He put his foot into the stirrup and mounted Boots. It gave him a moment's pleasure when he was strong and practiced enough to make his saddle in one go despite the weight of his armor.

Small joys, he told himself and had a sudden memory of Turley seated in the shade outside the walls of Fallenhill on a summer's day, filthy with the wretched soot of the burned town but drinking water and making jokes with fellow convicts. Simple pleasures, indeed. He turned a genuine smile to Dahyoor, but the fey squire was as impassive as usual. Smirking, oddly freed from all his concerns except honoring the next few commands of his liege lady, Prentice turned Boots towards the road that led to the gates. He looked down at the line first still standing, waiting.

"Tell Knight Sergeant Gennet that I am gone to speak with her grace," Prentice commanded the attendant fellow. "Until word comes otherwise, he is in possession of the town. He is to secure it and enforce her grace's peace. Tell him I say to especially keep watch for other princes. Everard's fall will not have been spread abroad just yet, but it will happen sooner than we would wish. Longshepherds, at least, is close enough to try for a swift claim. Any local drovers or boundary riders he can set to scouting duties should be offered silver from my purse to watch in the west and the south. I might not be back this evening, so Gennet is to take whatever steps he sees fit and to command the banner in my absence."

The line first saluted like a man who had been given the honor of his life just to take a message from the knight commander to a senior sergeant.

He has heard your last command to any Gryphon, Prentice reminded himself. *In future he might not count it an honor, but history could well give this low-ranked man an oddly prestigious place.*

It was his father's voice rather than the chorus as a whole that scorned him thinking history would remember him rather than cast his name into obscurity like he deserved, but Prentice hardly listened to the old man. He had led the conquest of a Vec town and trained the original White Lions. The glory would belong to the archduchess, but some diligent historian would likely spare him a footnote, at least; that he did not doubt. Unless, of course, the Inquisition managed to continue its brutal torching of history. Perhaps someone like Master Solft would find a way to subvert even the Silent Hand's conflagratory editing of the collective memory. If he had lived, there was no doubt in Prentice's mind that the renegade scribe would have done it. Remembering Solft also brought back the scholar's final cryptic note, and Prentice thought of how he had seen the deaths of the Vec levies like a pagan sacrifice, Sougate as the altar, the Gryphons forced into the role of "priest" butchers.

A sacrifice on unhallowed ground, Prentice remembered. They had assumed it was a reference to the death of the sacrist on the cathedral steps, but Prince Everard's merciless waste of his own levies' lives also could fit the simple sentence. After the massacre in autumn, surely the fields outside Sougate would count as unhallowed, so vilely bloodied as they had been. Perhaps the message fit both events in their own way. It was not impossible for prophecy to work in such a fashion. Surely the Almighty had the power to give more than one meaning to a statement over time. It was said amongst some scholars that history oft would repeat itself. Prentice imagined the spiritual defilement that might have been brought against Lady Penelope and her family line for the crime of one sacrist slain on cathedral steps. How much worse might the curse on her grace's line, or even his own family, have been for such actions as Everard had forced them to.

If her grace does demand my life, then this was a worthy reason to give it, he told himself. The hateful chorus mocked him, and he had to admit that it was all conjecture. Like all the other fencing with shadows that Bluebird had forced upon them, this could be mere folly, and Solft's last missive might have nothing to do with any of it. He would have to ask the Lord of all Creation when he awoke on the Judgement. An explanation did not seem too great a mercy to hope for from the Almighty.

CHAPTER 75

Amelia felt ever more like a waddling goose as she leaned on the wall to steady herself down the stairs. Ahead and behind her, her ladies-in-waiting lined up the steps, filing out into the false spring brightness that still left the air from outside chilled like a winter's day. When she reached the doorway, Amelia found herself asked to pause. She was flanked by Righteous and Lady Beth, while to one side the garrison line first left behind by the corporal earlier stood with a half line of Fangs, apparently ready to be an additional close escort to her person.

"Just havin' your horses fetched, Your Grace," the line first explained with dutiful politeness as they all watched the full escort arranging itself for the journey. "Corporal Renton didn't want to wait for your mounts, but Sir Turley's lady wife was right insistent. She says that neither you nor she will be walking through the streets."

"Did your corporal have a reason for his reluctance?" the archduchess asked, astonished at how breathless even the short journey down the stairs had made her. If the officer had a worthy reason to forsake her horse, Amelia supposed Dalflitch should respect the man's expertise in war and danger, but she would much rather ride even the otherwise short distance from here to Loncastel. After a prolonged moment's wait, Silvermane and Dalflitch's horse Petal were led into the yard from their nearby stabling by a militiaman with a broad-brimmed kettle helm, his head down so low that his face was hidden.

"Only as to say that we should hurry," the line first answered suddenly, shaking his head. "The lady said horses would make everything faster, and the corporal accepted her word at the last. I think she has the right of it, but I can see why he might want to rush. This has the makings of a dog's breakfast, this does."

"How is that, militiaman?" Amelia pressed, troubled by the pessimistic comment. It seemed the line first was embarrassed by his words, as he forgot to salute her and instead ducked his head and reached up to the brim of his helmet to knuckle his brow where his forelock was hidden.

"All my apologies, Your Grace," he said earnestly, "but this lot Renton's been forced to bring back with him, they're rough as guts. Slovenly, slow to take orders, even in the short time they've been here. We keep hearing in the Lion Banner how the knight commander demands nothing but perfection from the Gryphon and how his sergeants are terrors one and all, even the new woman one. But these lot are embarrassing. Sergeant Franken up in Fallenhill would have 'em marchin' to midnight if they were like this on parade, just as recruits."

Around Amelia a flutter of fingertip conversation was exchanged between her ladies. She caught barely any of the motion and wondered how they were understanding each other at all when Seskia reached forward and touched Lady Righteous's shoulder. The Baroness turned and saw the neophyte's hand signals while she made it seem she was rocking the baby, now swaddled in the bundle over her shoulder.

"Here, militiaman," the senior Lace Fang asked the line first. "Your Corporal Renton? I never knew him for a cannon-taker."

"A what? He never was," the line first answered with a puzzled frown. He looked the short distance across the yard to his superior officer, and Amelia followed his gaze. Sure enough, as the corporal turned slightly, the bronze disc of a cannon-taker was visible, embossed to his left shoulder pauldron. The medallions were awarded only to a very few men, a sign of a singular act of supreme bravery, and each man who possessed one was known for it.

"How'd he get that?" the line first asked, so surprised by what he was seeing that he did not even sound shocked by the shame of stolen honor the little emblem's presence implied.

"And why's the one playing squire carrying a longsword? He's even dressed as a Claw to boot," Lady Beth observed rhetorically, pointing surreptitiously to the fellow holding the two mounts' reins. Amelia looked there as well. Whoever he was, the man still had his head down, but as she watched, he lifted his brow, and she gasped as she recognized the hateful expression under the steel rim of the helmet.

"Cyprian," she whispered. She looked to where Dalflitch stood with Daisy and a neophyte, so close and yet terrifyingly exposed.

"Back inside, Your Grace," Righteous muttered. "This is 'bout to get bloody. We're going to do like Daisy suggested, barricading the doors and hope for true lads to come to our aid."

Amelia gave no resistance as firm hands started to tug her back through the door. The line first turned to look, following a signal from his "officer" and clearly wondering why their charge was now retreating inside.

"Has something been forgotten?" he asked, and Righteous stepped into the gap between the militiaman and the door.

"You a loyal man?" she hissed, and the line first started back as if slapped.

"Since the Red Sky!" he declared, seeming as offended as he was surprised.

"You heard o' skin thieves?" Righteous followed up without hesitation.

The man gave a puzzled nod and then turned his head in horror, shaking it vehemently. "You can't think I..."

Righteous cut him off. "Not you!"

Amelia knew the line first was probably not as slow of thought as he seemed, but watching him unwinding the knotted situation in his mind felt like seeing honey pouring in the winter's cold.

"The time has come to go, Your Grace," Lady Dalflitch called, and as Righteous nodded in the direction of the little conference, the junior officer's face fell with a crushing, horror-filled disappointment. Now he knew what was coming as well, and the inevitable brutality of it was as clear in his eyes as it was in Amelia's mind. It felt like a whole season was crawling past, but it truly must have been bare breaths of time. Amelia could feel the hands pulling her inside, see the predatory smile on Cyprian's hate-filled face, and her lady seneschal waving her forward, puzzled by the delay.

"A moment, My Lady," Righteous called into the yard. "It seems our escort has a tell and is somewhat hopeful about it."

Beside the baroness, Amelia saw the other ladies giving hands signals, now openly and with large gestures, so that they could be made out at the distance. Dalflitch turned for a moment to look at the skin thief corporal, and that was her undoing. "Renton" suddenly lashed out and seized the lady seneschal by her wrist. Dalflitch cried out, and her defiant scream almost swallowed Cyprian's shouted order.

"Now!" the last Young Hopeful commanded, and at the back of the "dog's breakfast" formation, ten men dressed as Roar and carrying matchlocks with lit fuses raised their guns and fired, not at Amelia or her entourage, but at the rooftop. The two marksmen stationed there cried out and one toppled into the yard, smashing against the cobbles with a vile wet thud. Then, as if the honey was warming in the unseasonable sunlight, time began to run faster, and the chaos of hell itself was unleashed. Dalfitch tried to flee, but the skin thief corporal threw her backward at his own men with unhuman power. It was his last act as Daisy and her neophyte companion fell on him, blades flashing at face and neck. Whatever else a skin thief was, their blood was as crimson as any mortal man's.

"Treachery!" the line first bellowed, and two groups of uniformed men-at-arms who should have been able to trust one another as brothers fell to the most savage of possible fighting.

Then Amelia was inside, being forced up the stairs once more. Righteous was at her side, sword drawn as if it were the most natural thing in the world for a mother with a young infant to be carrying in her free hand. In its bundle, the little baby boy Gant began to cry at the harsh jostling he was receiving. The entourage tumbled into the main chamber of Paramour's, and the rising chaos set both Emma and her charge Amy to tears as well. Despite this, however, the rest of Amelia's ladies-in-waiting, now Lace Fangs one and all, set about preparing what could well be their last defense.

We watched all winter and still they outwitted me, Amelia cursed herself, though she could recognize the self-critique was not fully justified. It had taken a second all-out assault on Bridgetown, spells on her and Prentice's mind, not to mention Lady Penelope's, to bring them to this pass, and still, the shape-changers had not yet succeeded. Would there be time to shinny anyone down the outside wall?

The yard outside was a battlefield—Amelia could hear that—while beside her Righteous and Emma were trying to comfort their disrupted charges.

"They must not die this day," she told the two women while she heard furniture being moved to barricade the doors.

CHAPTER 76

Prentice led Dahyoor up the ramp and through Sougate at a trot. They emerged onto the south bridge amongst a cluster of Masnians hefting barrels of powder out and stacking them as if ready to transport. It made Prentice wonder what was happening, and he reined Boots in to call a sentry over. The man was one of a sparse few left behind to garrison the gate while the rest of the Gryphon Banner marched on Town Sobridge, but if he was disappointed with the duty, it did not show in his expression.

"They're sent by the knight captain and the Masnian cannoneer leader," the sentry reported. "Now that we put the Veckanders down out there and there's still fighting on Loncastel, they sent for as much powder as we have. I asked if they were going to take the cannons, too, but that weren't my business, they said."

Nor mine any longer, Prentice thought.

The Masnian gunners all kept their heads down as they worked, and as the knight commander watched them for a moment, he wondered if they realized that much of the powder they were moving looked to be the leached muck from the basement store. Perhaps these men were "drudges," as Benlow Sent-Fane might describe them. It could be that very few of the Masnian cannon crews were even trusted to know the full secrets of black powder alchemy. If so, that was Master Sent-Fane's responsibility. Looking up from the workers stacking barrels and sacks, Prentice could see the pall of smoke hanging over the town to the north, and there was the tolling of Dragon shots.

Perhaps Farringdon has devised a use for the leached powder, he mused, remembering the knight captain's wisdom with modern weapons. He spurred his horse forward once more. They crossed the bridge and then up Great Bridge Road to the crossing from Greenmarsh to Oldbridge. The garrison there saluted as he passed and appeared unmolested by any of the conflict raging to the north. That was a good sign. Since the night of the first raid, Prentice had always been concerned that the Usurper might find a new way to conquer the ancient bridges and cut the islands off from each other to defeat their defenders piecemeal. A short distance into Oldbridge, Dahyoor trotted up beside him and pointed to an unexpected side street.

"This way," he said flatly.

"Why?" Prentice asked, knowing that that way led nowhere near the Paramour's Chambers.

"The archduchess was forced to retreat. She hides now in the cathedral. It has been made safe."

Safe? Hiding in the cathedral? Prentice stared a long moment at his squire, trying to imagine a military situation that would bring Archduchess Amelia to the cathedral in defense while leaving the garrison on the great bridge just passed calmly in place. He was about to insist on a further explanation when a runner's footsteps echoed over the cobbles. A man in a White Lions' buffcoat rushed up and saluted, his kettle helm falling slightly askew as he did so.

"Thank God you're here, knight commander," the man said breathlessly. "There's something happening in the cathedral. You've got to hurry."

Without hesitation, Prentice put his heels to Boots's flanks and clattered down the narrow laneway toward the cathedral square. He knew there were a number of lanes and alleys leading to the paved ground in front of the great church, but only one of those was of a major size, so the area made a certain sense as a defensive location, but there was also no exit on the east side of the square, surrounded as it was in that direction by an ancient retaining wall and the hill of Earlsbastion. If the square was occupied by the enemy, there would be nowhere to retreat to. Boots burst out into the plaza to find it empty, and that relieved Prentice as he rode straight for the cathedral doors.

"In the cathedral" the messenger had said. The last time Prentice had been there, the main doors had been locked. He slipped from the saddle and sprinted up the few steps. Behind him he heard Dahyoor dismount as well. Prentice put a hand to the latch and found it moved for him. He was just about to open the door when a sudden thought stopped him. Like the unexpected sunlight that had cleared away the winter's clouds, lighting the sandstone-paved square behind him with an unseasonable summery glow, this thought was like his old mind, almost forgotten in the dark of the bitter winter past.

"The archduchess?" he muttered, thinking something else. *Not the Lioness Mother?*

"Yes, she is within for you," Dahyoor said behind him.

Prentice carefully switched hands on the latch, moving his right to his weapon hilt, ready to draw his sword.

"You said the archduchess," Prentice repeated with a tight smile and small shake of his head. He could feel the fey man's presence behind him, except it wasn't the fey man. There had been several little tells, now that he thought about it, but the clearest indication that the figure behind Prentice was a skin thief was the fact that he was standing behind him at all. Dahyoor would never have voluntarily dismounted, not just to enter a *kreff* building. Prentice's turn was poised on the balls of his feet, sword coming free from its scabbard with the spinning motion, but he was interrupted as the skin thief barreled into him, bodily forcing him into the now-open door. The shape-changer's physical might was surprising, but Prentice felt he had a good chance to keep his feet even as he staggered through the portal.

Except as soon as Prentice crossed the threshold, something crashed into his mind like the kick of a mule, and he felt himself fall to one knee. Any hope he had of controlling his descent was instantly squashed as he lost all command of his limbs. He wondered what or who must have struck him, thinking that an ambush had been set beyond the door, when his eyes caught the side of the cathedral portal, barely visible as the bright light from outside shone into his eyes, making it hard to see the shadowed interior. But there on the doorpost were sigils, daubed in blood just as he had seen in so many places since taking the fight to the Redlanders and their Blood Sects. The darkness of the cathedral started to crowd out the light, and Prentice wondered if this was how it had felt for others that he had seen slain by the dread lines of mystical script. From the outside, the deaths had all seemed instantaneous. This felt too slow. Nevertheless, the shadows crept in from the edges of his vision, and with them, the wolfpack curses howled afresh, triumphant at last. The silhouetted figure of the skin thief stood in the doorway a moment, then entered, plainly immune to the vile magick.

Of course, Prentice thought bitterly, thinking to smile at the cruel irony the way he had smiled at all the cold brutalities of convict life. After all, in the face of overwhelming evil, what else was there but to laugh and endure? Except there was no more enduring to be done now. He remembered the dark, enclosing feeling of the water in the west and the similar sensation of Cassian's poison during his duel in Earlsbastion. This was like that, but now there would be no swimmer to lift him from the depths and no Whilte to pray away the poison. The last thing he noticed was the skin thief leaning over him and prying his sword from his numb fingers. The blade flashed free for a moment in his vision.

"No more magick for you," the creature hissed in a voice that could have been any one of a hundred, utterly devoid of precise identity.

Then, the darkness closed in completely and there was nothing to hear but the crowing of the hateful chorus, the wolfpack's baleful cries as they sprang upon him at last.

CHAPTER 77

Prentice sensed himself being moved about before he tried to open his eyes. He felt the familiar cold of iron being locked around his wrists and his body being hefted in an odd way until he realized he was being set on his knees. By the motions, he suspected he was being posed in a very specific manner, and as he felt his head being turned about by a rough hand on his chin, imagined he was being made to face something quite specific. It all reminded him of the way he had been treated by the inquisitor who had tortured him under Ashfield all those years ago, and he had the frightening thought that perhaps this was what hell was—endless torment at the hands of supernaturally skilled torturer devils, the earthly ones only shadows of the infernal experts. His knowledge of theology told him that was superstitious nonsense, a false understanding of the Judgement used to terrorize downtrodden folk who did not know how to read the truth for themselves. The manipulating hands continued their unseen tasks, and then, as if from afar, a rumble sounded. At first, Prentice thought it was cannon fire, like the blast of the Bronze Dragons, but it grew in power and shuddered in his numb chest until he recognized it as the growl of the angel lion. Feeling a different, holier kind of terror suddenly grip him, his eyes snapped open, and he was dazzled by color so that he wondered if his sight was damaged. Slowly, the prismatic brightness resolved into clearer images and a darkly silhouetted figure moved about within them, like the shadows of Redlanders or Inxyphos's command of knights as they had used the dragonfly's power to travel across impossible distances. Prentice felt a harsh coldness around his throat, and he realized that the indistinct figure had just fitted him with an iron collar. He heard it click and waited for the sound of the locking bolt, but it did not come. The figure turned away and Prentice's vision began to clear, revealing his condition more completely.

He was on his knees on flagstones, and around him the ground was marked with more symbols in crimson—a series of circles, one inside the next. He wondered if there were seven of them, like the loops of the Seven Rings Cross. If there were, they were not in the correct formation for his fighting school's emblem. Beyond the circles was a large table where his heavy-set jailer was now hunched over, fetching or preparing something else. Past the table were wooden pews, pushed aside and piled upon one another. That told him where he was—on the floor in the middle of the cathedral nave. His wrists were chained, and those chains were connected across to two mighty stone pillars on opposite sides of the of enormous vault, somewhat ahead of where he was. It did not seem like his arms were pulled forward, however, and he suspected each wrist had two chains—one going to the side ahead of him and one to other pillars behind him. Unable to move his head and barely able to force his eyes to look about, all he could do was see the two chains ahead.

Chained between four pillars and too far from any to push them down, he thought. So much for the lesson of Samson, who had put his hands on pillars and toppled the temple of the Philistines in a last suicidal push.

Suddenly, Prentice recalled the four anchor points in the cloister of Vespers Remembered. Whatever had happened there, the blood and torture was about to happen to him here. Unable to take in any more sights at ground level, Prentice looked up and found the source of the multihued light. Far from any magick, ancient or fresh, it was simply the sunlight streaming through the colors of the cathedral's main stained glass. A vast arched window, dozens of feet from base to top, it was like so many such works of art around the world, a myriad of holy stories vibrantly portrayed. In the center was the most significant of all—the Christ nailed in place on crossed beams of dark wood. The artists had captured the agony upon his face, and ruby-like shards of glass portrayed the blood that dripped from his scourging wounds, as well as his pinned hands and feet. The realistic portrayal was given a supernatural cast by a spray of golden shards, representing holy light of some sort that flew out in all directions from the cross, touching on different stories portrayed around the window. Each was a tale of miraculous divine intervention, and the theological imputation was obvious—from the sacrifice of the cross flowed all the divine power of deliverance across all of history. Prentice might have appreciated the beauty of it, both as a work of art and a work of spirituality, were he not so incensed by being here. He could not hear any of the cursing voices in his mind, but that did not matter any longer. He did not need the hateful chorus to explain his failure to him. It was there in the iron on his wrists and about his throat. He lowered his eyes again, and as his gaze traced its way down the magnificent glass, he saw the very tale he had failed to understand. There was Samson, broken manacles on his wrists, shoving the temple pillars aside in his last act of supernatural strength. His hair was shorn to the scalp and his blinded eyes were shown wrapped in a dirty bandage. Prentice thought it a fitting metaphor for his own blindness. He had searched and searched and now would die having not seen for an instant that this was where he should have been looking. This was not the first defiled church his enemies had found a dire use for.

"Not long now and the trumpet will sound," the lion angel's mighty voice rumbled, seeming to fill the entire cathedral with its thunder, though the figure at its torturer's worktable did not appear to hear it. Prentice could well imagine what sort of tools it was readying for the next phase of its plans for him. He had seen them all before. And then the trumpet would sound—to call him to the Judgement?

"Soon, the race will begin," the angel continued, and Prentice realized it was hearkening back to his last dream and not to his coming death.

"I fear I will be running with something of a handicap in that case," he muttered, not so much bitter as merely resigned to his fate now. He could barely move his lips against the paralyzing magick that robbed him of control, but he expected that this creature that had witnessed the formation of the heavens and the earth would likely be able to puzzle out his incoherent grumbling. "Chains are not conducive to footraces, I have found."

"It is not iron that holds you back but ignorance," the angel told him sternly.

"I have sought the answers I was set to find," he ground out through his rebellious lips. "Do I require a divine messenger now to inform me of my inadequacy to the task?"

He had meant the bitter comment as a rebuke of sorts to the condemnation he felt, both in the angel's words and his own heart, but the angel seemed to be neither surprised nor offended by the sharp question.

"It seems you do, else I would not be sent to you."

Prentice chuckled at that, and his eyes flicked to what he was now sure was the skin thief preparing his final sufferings. How long would he be able to speak like this before the enemy noticed him making sounds. During the cursed drought, the Serpent Witch had not heard him have his conversation with the angel. Perhaps he would have another long break to plead his case with the heavenlies, and as he thought that, Prentice felt a flare of hope in himself, a spark to banish the dark shadows that had empowered the hateful chorus and the wolfpack curses through the winter. After all, why would the Almighty give him this pause if not for mercy, if not to complete whatever was left undone. His eyes fixed upon the Samson in the colored glass.

"Was his strength in his hair?" the angel asked.

"Of course, it wa..." Prentice began to answer, but he realized he was wrong. From his theological lessons, remembered haphazardly from his time as a pupil knight, he knew that the point of Samson's story was that the hair was *not* the source of his strength. God had promised the ancient judge of his people prodigious, superhuman might if the man would only never cut his hair, but it was not the hair that had given him strength—that came from God himself. Samson's final act was the sign of that. With his head shorn, and blinded into the bargain, he had nonetheless achieved one last impossible feat of strength, greater than all his previous.

If I prayed now for such strength, would the Almighty let me pull this defiled temple down on my own head? he wondered, and he heard a short snuffling, as of a lion snorting with amusement.

"You have a race ahead of you yet," the angel told him, as if it had read his mind. "And you still have not learned the lesson."

"Well, what is it then?" he muttered, and again the angel sounded amused with him.

"You are educated and wise, admired for your swift mind by all who know you," it said. "Look again and tell me what you see."

Prentice studied the Samson in the glass, the rendered figure's straining musculature casting impossibly mighty stones aside while other masonry tumbled down to take his life. Amidst the falling blocks, Prentice noticed the golden shards of light extending from the crucifixion portrayed above. The final strength had come to Samson from that central act of eternal power, but why had the Almighty let that power kill Samson as well instead of healing him as, say, Brother Whilte's miraculous ability might?

"Because that was what Samson asked for," he told himself and he heard an approving grumble from his angelic instructor. Until the end, Samson had not learned the true lesson of his strength. He did not need his hair. In fact, he did not need to be strong or even to smash the pillars at all. If Samson had understood the truth of his Creator, he would have known he could have asked for more than he needed, whatever it was—his enemies destroyed, his hands set free of chains, even his eyesight restored.

Feeling himself blink and thankful for the renewing control over his own body as if it was water in the desert, Prentice searched the other stories shown in the glass, seeing the truth he was discovering repeated again and again. The shards of gold touched the shepherd boy felling the giant, and Prentice knew it was no magickal sling or stone that had made the impossible shot. He saw the favored apostle walking on water and then sinking into the waves, only to be rescued despite his failing faith. The power that lifted him from the maelstrom had required no perfection or holiness, only a readiness to cry for aid. In the way of revelation, the truth unfolded itself whole in Prentice's mind like the wings of a magnificent bird unfurled in glory—no, not a bird. The wings of a gryphon, prepared for this moment.

"I have been a fool," he muttered, and the angel did not disagree with him.

"As all are at some time or another," it said, but its tone was not the leastwise cruel or condescending. Foolishness was a fact of the mortal condition, as needful and unavoidable as pain or joy. Prentice wanted to laugh at the relief of it, even as the numbness in his arms began to fade into the ache of limbs held too long in an awkward position.

The lesson of Samson, he thought, realizing that he had been making exactly the same mistake. Faced with lost strength, he had tried to go backward to the outward markers of might, thinking to reclaim his past somehow. Samson had asked only for the return of his strength in order to defeat God's enemies, as if the victory was a burden he had to carry by himself. Prentice realized in the same way that he had gone back to his training, the harshness of his childhood, to meet the demands of God's command as delivered in his dream. But that had only surrendered him back into the spirit of conviction, rejection, and condemnation—exactly as the same practices had done to him the first time around in his life. He had been living like a convict because he was walking the same path that had led him to conviction. His father's curses had bound him into his past and he had all but embraced them rather than learning the new way. After all, when he had been a convict the first time, he had not earned his freedom. No, first his chains had been loosed, and then he had done the deeds that completed his liberation.

"I am so sorry," he muttered, thinking that he had learned the lesson too late, now that he was about to be slain by the skin thief agent only paces ahead of him, and then he chuckled. Having just learned the lesson, he proceeded to make the mistake all over again instantly. The lion angel laughed with him.

"The trumpet is about to sound," it told him. "The race is about to begin."

"Let me be ready," Prentice prayed.

"You will be, for it is you who will sound the blast."

"Then let me run as far and fast as I am able."

"It will be much farther than that," the angel said, and Prentice chuckled one last time. This one sounded more like a strangled choke to his ears, but it was loud enough that, at last, the skin thief noticed, lifting its head and turning to look on him.

Any moment now, he thought, and if he could have made his lips to smile, he thought he probably would have been grinning.

Chapter 78

For a being that could apparently appear however it wished, the skin thief seemed oddly misshapen to Prentice's eyes as it turned from its table of torture implements and stalked towards him. Its eyes seemed dark, its pupils wide, and its eyelids strangely thin. The figure's mouth was thin as well, and nearly lipless. Its nose seemed flat and poorly defined. It had only thin wisps of hair on its scalp that were nonetheless dark and coarse, like the stunted grasses of ocean dunes. Cheek bones, brow, and chin all seemed lumpen and ill-formed. The sight made Prentice wonder if years of feigning others' faces and identities had caused the skin thief to forget its own true self, and when it was not being a fraud, it could not remember enough of who it truly was to form a proper visage of its own. Even its slender limbs, which seemed too long for its torso, had oddly swollen-seeming joints. The skin thief came across the crimson circles on the floor in a kind of capering step and smirked at him when it drew close.

"By heaven and hell, you *are* a strong one," it said, peering into Prentice's eyes and speaking with its voice that seemed to be many voices at once, making Prentice think of the hateful chorus again. His inward tormentors had been quiet since he awoke, and he imagined the lion angel's presence had had something to do with that. Even now, as the skin thief spoke with a similar voice, the chorus did not awaken. The skin thief leaned down and took Prentice by the chin, as if he was an unruly child not paying attention to a chastising parent.

"We wanted to laugh at Bluebird and Inxyphos when they told us of the threat you posed. The fool knight spoke as if you were a devil of hell, sent to undermine our divine work." The skin thief snorted derisively. "As if a devil could escape when we hold the keys to the gates of heaven and hell. Yet you have been the hardest of prey to run down. The number of shots you took and still led the hounds through the woods? And the Horned Man thought he had the spirit of the mighty stags."

The creature-man shook his head pityingly, and Prentice tried to speak. He wanted to demand answers of this contemptuous half-person. How did it know of the Horned Man, and if it knew as much as it seemed to, why had the Inquisition never done anything to truly stop the Redlander threat? Why make secret and treacherous deals with the fey? Try as he might, though, he could not force his lips to form the words. The skin thief noticed his efforts, and it cocked its head to one side, lips twisting into a sneering smile.

"What shots?" it asked, guessing at Prentice's unspoken questions and getting it wrong.

Prentice was at least a fraction comforted to realize that for all its powers, the shapeshifter could not read his thoughts. It was constrained to detect by expressions and gestures, just as all the rest of folk. As he watched, though, the misshapen face flowed about like the rippling of a fine racehorse's muscles under the skin, and in a moment, it resembled someone familiar, though Prentice could not place the name to go with the adopted face. The newly formed man stepped back a moment and held out a single hand, like an orator delivering a speech to a theater audience.

"Fire and iron, shackled and condemned to hell!" the skin thief pronounced dramatically, its voice ringing off the cathedral walls. "Following a witch and her servitor! Better we all drown now than suffer what is to come."

Suddenly Prentice remembered the words and the face—it was the militiaman who had thrown himself to his death in the Murr the night of Daven Marcus's arrival back at the end of autumn.

The skin thief dropped forward, mimicking the suicidal dive into the icy water before converting the motion to a bow and coming up with a smirk, as if expecting applause.

"You can feel the spell afresh, can't you?" the shapeshifter mocked. "That was the first net we threw at your legs, a spell from a feigned retainer, and it should have brought you down to your knees right there. Many lesser men would have broken from that sorcery alone and thrown themselves back into the river, but not you."

You cast a spell on me that night? Prentice wondered. Looking back, he did remember a feeling of bitterness infecting his soul at that time. He had mistaken it simply for fatigue after his convalescence and the long night of fighting. Strangely though, despite the Inquisition mystic's assertion, he did not feel any resurgence of the same bitterness in his soul now. Had the creature cast the spell again just this instant, or did it expect the mere reminder to reinforce the magick? There was so much he did not understand.

"That was when we started to listen to Bluebird's opinion more readily," the skin thief went on, leaning close again. The liquid darkness in its gaze seemed to flash with poison and hate. "So much artifice has been turned upon you. Do you even appreciate the attention we have lavished?"

Prentice had more questions he could not form. What artifice? And why? Were these the secrets in the Songs of the Spire Aviary? It was not pure curiosity that drove him, either. As long as the creature had not yet killed him, there was a possibility that he might be rescued. It was a forlorn hope he would have spurned even an hour ago, if it were only an hour ago he had been knocked unconscious. But he was learning the lesson of Samson now. The Almighty did not point him at the raging water and bid him to swim for his life or drown. The one who created the heavens and the earth by word alone bade him to trust and, if needs be, to walk upon the surface of the waters. Prentice realized now that was how Whilte did it. The chaplain did not wait to understand everything. He let himself be thrust into the fire and trusted not to be burnt. It seemed impossible that Prentice would escape from this moment, but what was impossible for men was possible for the Almighty. In that light, Prentice decided right at this moment to live as if he would win free and thus to learn everything he could from this bizarre, one-sided conversation. The skin thief continued its monologue, reading Prentice's side of the discussion from his paralyzed expression and continuing to get the lines so very wrong.

"After that, we knew we would need the strongest cables to tie you down. Your brother told us of your father's failed petty ambitions. It was from him that we learned the wretched old merchant's final thoughts about you, his greatest disappointment."

The skin thief cocked a sparsely haired eyebrow as its face shed the anonymous militiaman's image but did not transform into Prentice's dying father's face. Nonetheless, its voice momentarily took on the old man's deathbed croak.

"The note was deeply crafted, layers upon layers to make you believe all that we told you, and still it took you days to seek the old goat out. I spoke the spell, but the voice and the hatreds were his. Did you know he resented you so much?"

The skin thief smiled with jeering contempt, as if it hoped to see Prentice's pain in his eyes and looked to enjoy the sight.

Of course I knew, you twit, Prentice thought scornfully. *Of all the things our father did, hiding his disappointment with his children was never one of them.*

"Even then you resisted," the skin thief declared, and it slapped Prentice across the cheek, its smile dissolving into an annoyed frown. The strike was not too powerful, but Prentice felt it all the same, and that was reassuring. Perhaps complete sensation would return to him against the power of the magick around the door.

"The hired thugs in the park were told to seek a man who looked like a drunkard—easy pickings—but when you stalked out of the ancient cloister looking to do battle with the world and that enchanted sword at the ready? They balked. Time and again you have made a mockery of our power."

The skin thief turned away and lifted its hands and eyes upward, as if it, too, were prayerfully considering the stained glass, but it twirled back and the myriad colors seemed to accentuate its unclear identity, as if it were a grey-skinned shadow hidden behind the beautiful glow.

"That was when we realized your true potential," it declared, and again its voice echoed from the vault. "Bluebird had plotted to slay you, to remove you from our path, so we may end the little heretic bitch and her damnable war on our plans. You cannot imagine how frustrating it is to watch her and your fumbling attempts at cunning obstruct our righteous path. Your toy nuns? Your wife and her lace-faced sisters? Playing like children at arts we have practiced as masters since the beginning!"

And yet it all worked against you, didn't it? Prentice thought, and he desperately hoped his lips were smiling as he wanted them to. Perhaps the Bluebird and these liar spies had kept him and the archduchess dancing to their tune all winter, but at least the Reach had made it difficult for them. That thought pleased him no end. The skin thief squatted in front of him, coming face to face once again.

"Are you wondering yet why I have you here?" it asked. "Even dulled with so many spells and the constant hounding of that letter we sent you, you must have enough wit left to question why you haven't simply felt a knife twixt your ribs."

If Prentice could have shrugged, he would have.

"There's so much more at play than you realize," the skin thief went on, and Prentice was reminded of things the archduchess had told him of her encounter with Bluebird—how the minstrel had felt the need to explain his plots to her just for the sense of relief it provided to someone who lived all their days in hiding and deception.

Write yourself a journal then, he thought derisively but then remembered the Inquisition's ruthlessness when it came to written records. He could only imagine the brutal fate that would befall any agent of the Silent Hand who made the mistake of putting his private thoughts down on paper. He recalled other comments made during encounters with those skilled in magicks over the years. Despair had a power in the casting of spells. Weakness, fatigue, and sadness seemed to help curses take root. It was a phenomenon Prentice and others in her grace's service had witnessed for themselves. Perhaps it was a key tactic of the Inquisition to mock, to show its victims the extent of its secret plans just at the end, to empower its own magicks against them—a suicidal militiaman, his dying father, division from the liege he loved and the family he adored. All these things had built powerful despair in him and driven him back to the cold chains of his youth and convicthood. Why bring him here now, though?

"Sac...sacrifice..." Prentice heard his voice rasp out, trying to say *sacrifice on defiled ground.* This was the secret Solft had wanted to bring to them. But still Prentice could not really understand what it meant.

The skin thief started a moment, clearly astonished to hear Prentice speak, though it showed no sense of fear or concern.

"That is enough of that, heretic," it said.

With those words, Prentice gained a sense that it must have been trying to use an enspelling word, though again it felt to have no power upon him. Perhaps it was like the magick of the Serpent Witch that had failed to work against the power of the angel lion in the riverside village in the Reach. Prentice wished he could turn his head about and see if the lion was still somewhere nearby in the shadows of the cathedral, perhaps. If it was, it was obvious the skin thief could not see it. Prentice could feel the ache in his shoulders now, and the bite of iron on his wrists was more noticeable, but still he could not move his head.

"You are even more unruly than that fool Inxyphos," the skin thief went on, apparently satisfied its powers had trapped Prentice in his unseen prison once more, like an insect under glass or encased in amber. "Nevertheless, we made use of Inxyphos, and we will make use of you. Yes, there will be sacrifice, but not you, silly play-knight. You are to be redeemed, brought to serve the Unseen Hand as none before you. Bluebird would still have you killed. Idiot!"

The skin thief stood again and turned back to the table, taking up a metal object that seemed dark in the prismatic light. Turning it over in arthritic-looking fingers, it took a moment for Prentice to recognize the object in the hateful enemy's grip. Then he saw it for what it was—a bronze medallion, similar to a cannon-taker's medal, though about three or four times as large. At this distance, Prentice could not make out the design on the disc, but he was sure it would be a dragon.

"We learned so much from Inxyphos about how the magick works," the creature explained. "Connection, commitment, devotion, and loyalty—these are the powers that underly the sacrifice. You saw some of that in the west, didn't you? Inxyphos told us as much. And with what we learned from your brother, well, you are a resource too useful to let go to waste."

Prentice remembered the way the mantis man and serpent witch *imzuss* coven had made sacrifices of the fey in pairs to empower their magick over the headwaters of the Murr River—pairs of relatives or friends. One had to give up the other to the ritual. Prentice wondered who would have been so bound to Inxyphos as to empower the ritual that had made a bear *brakkis effar* out of him. Then his eyes went to the bronze disc in the skin thief's hand again and he felt a renewed fear, deeper and sharper now.

A sacrifice on defiled ground. But he was to be redeemed?

"Now you begin to see it, don't you?" the skin thief taunted. "There is power in words, power in names, power in the blood and in the places where the blood has fallen. Sacrifice to bind, to change, to embody. Bridgetown's bear has been turned from rebel to servant, and that line has but one last dangling thread in any case. But you? Oh, you? You have shed so much blood, and it has taken the full power of dragons to bring you to heel. The islands have suffered, and your silly jumped-up noblewoman has finally been pinned to them by the Dragons of Denay. So, her blood will bind your devotion, and you will be the one with no one to stop you. Daven Marcus will have his crusade south and the heretic *princes* will be finally laid low."

The skin thief's multifarious voice dripped with contempt on the word "princes" as it danced forward, waving the dragon medallion in Prentice's sight.

"You will be the first true dragon to serve the Silent Hand. We will offer you to the king in Denay, of course, but you will always be ours. Golden thrones are for children. We rule in blood."

From holes in the ground, Prentice thought.

"Hear now how it will be," the mystical agent continued. "The witch Amelia will be brought here and stood right there in front of you. Bluebird insisted we split you from her, and we did a fair job of that, but even then you were devoted. That's how useful you are! Never mind the loyalty of a sworn man or even a family member. She stripped you of almost everything at our urging, our spell working again and again whenever you read the paper. Oh, yes, we watched you reading it as you stalked about the town. She cut you away and still you clung like a barnacle. She disdained you and you tormented yourself for it, like a flagellant. We thought you might even just work yourself to death at one point, but alas for Bluebird's plans, it was not to be."

Prentice felt the familiar icy fury rising from within, the hard and unyielding will that emerged when he faced death on the battlefield. He wanted to shake his head, to at least sneer at this monstrous abomination of a man. He almost believed he could, and as the cold calm settled into his mind, all his fears became still like a morning frost, but his limbs were not so anymore, and he noticed something the skin thief had not. He held himself immobile, no longer trying to move his head lest he give himself away. There was just one more thing he had to discover, and he wasn't sure yet what it was. He only felt the certainty that it was here, and in a moment it would be revealed.

"Alas for Bluebird, but rejoicing for us," the skin thief went on.

For a moment, Prentice realized how precious this insight into the Inquisition's workings would be if he could just live to share it. They were not the monolith they appeared—one body with one mind under Sanguine's will. It seemed the Silent Hand suffered as much from factions and inner ambitions as any other human endeavor.

That alone should tell them they are not so special in the eyes of the Almighty, Prentice thought, and that gave him another thread of the weave. He almost had the whole tapestry now. Soon.

"The Bluebird has bid us take your mistress now, and so we have, but we will not give her to him to use as a mere hazard in the game for Bridgetown. Pah! His vision is so small. We will play for the whole table, and when they bring her here, I will gut her in front of you. Your devoted heart will break, and her blood will bind you to this power. I will lay my commands on you, and you will take the dragon upon you for us, here in the bloodied house on the rocks in the stream that have been pounded and bloodied further by the Dragons of Denay."

Prentice had a sudden thought of all the reports of raiders coming to Bridgetown, the confusion of some battles on some islands but peace in others. It was all to draw the garrisons to odd places, including luring the archduchess's guard cohort away, he had no doubt. If Bluebird had given the final order for the archduchess to be seized, it could only mean that the minstrel agent felt confident to make the play. He had the cards in his hand already. That would mean a fight, because the Lace Fangs would never go quietly, and as this vile mystic had already said, the masked and veiled women of the archduchess's chamber had done excellently well at interfering up until now.

Righteous and the children, he thought, knowing that his wife would go down fighting at their liege's side. If Amelia, Archduchess of Dweltford, was brought here, it would mean Prentice's wife was already dead. And if that was the case, their children would be as well. He had suffered many pains in his life, so many, but this one clenched his heart like a fist in cold steel, the chilled blood it pumped around his veins burning with its frost. A single tear welled in his eye, and he felt it scour its way down his cheek. The skin thief saw it, and it clapped its hands like a delighted child that had finally made its toy top spin properly.

"Yes! I knew we could break you, stiff-necked heretic mongrel!" it called out gleefully. "Prepare yourself. Soon you will be a better servant to Mother Church than your venal father ever imagined. Better than your brother who never rebelled."

Pallas, Prentice thought, the brother who had served these hateful men, or their false front, at least, and had become something as hateful in consequence. A merciless preacher of mercy, as the Wind Rising fey would call them. He pitied his fallen brother who had tried to shoulder the burden that had all but broken Prentice's own back.

The fool burden you went back and tried to carry a second time, he told himself, though without anger. There was no point chastising himself for that now. The archduchess was not yet here, so perhaps there was still time. Prentice looked up at the glass one last moment, seeing that crucified man in the center, a crown of mockery and pain on his brow. A man of sorrows who called himself the rock of salvation—a rock in the midst of the storm and rising waters. The man whom death itself could not defeat, and who would return with a sword in his mouth, who would speak once and defeat all his enemies, finally. All winter they had hoped Solft would uncover the sword of the word for them, or that Whilte would divine his own secrets to it. But each of them had to learn it for themselves; Prentice could see that now. And so, from his remembered studies in Ashfield came the only sword he had needed, and feeling it in his mind the way a longsword rested in his hand, he smiled despite himself.

"What? Is your mind completely broken?" the skin thief demanded, his glee turning to uncertainty and concern. "Can you not hold out but a few moments more? Drive yourself on as you have and let us produce our greatest success."

It seemed the creature thought Prentice's resistance would somehow form a better path for the blood magick—utter despair and an unyielding fight against it in the same heart. Perhaps that was some secret alchemy to great power.

Too bad for you that you will never see it work, Prentice thought, and his smile deepened. As the skin thief leaned in close to puzzle out its prisoner's seemingly miraculous recovery of heart, Prentice reached his freed left hand out and seized the creature by the wrist. Trying to recoil in shock at the impossible freedom, the skin thief's face shifted and changed, its limbs contorting as it reflexively sought strength to fight back. As repulsive as the sensation was in his grip, Prentice was not disgusted or afraid. He had seen this power before. It was the same with the chains. He had never had to escape his manacles as a convict; he had simply obeyed the Lord's call upon his life and the chains had fallen away. It was the same again now. This was the lesson Samson had failed to learn. If the Almighty chooses, the Almighty will empower. Ever the battle belongs to the Lord, and now Prentice knew the sword he had been given for the fight.

"Blessed be the Lord, My Rock," he whispered to the skin thief, who was still wrestling to get its arm free. It stopped a moment, and its greyish skin blanched in terror, as if all its boasts of heavenly power were being unmasked as lies by the simple recitation of believed scripture. The sword that can cut the spells from the air. "*He* trains my hands for war."

In that momentary pause in the struggle, Prentice brought his other arm around his body, drawn wheellock in hand. He put the muzzle under the skin thief's chin and squeezed the trigger in one smooth motion. The detonation echoed thunderously from the roof and walls, and the creature fell dead in a spray of fire and smoke, iron and blood.

Chapter 79

Escaping the despoiled cathedral presented a unique set of challenges, beginning with the arcane circles Prentice had been placed within. They had been six in number, and while they reminded him of the Seven Rings Cross motif that had haunted his winter's training, there appeared no actual connection between the two sets of symbology. Realizing that the eldritch script might have the power to send him back into unconsciousness or to slay him outright, Prentice had been hesitant even to move for a moment until his searching eyes noticed that there were a set of precise gaps in the rings to his left, making him think that completing the circles must be a part of the ritual of the magicks themselves. Gambling that incomplete meant unempowered, he risked steps across the first circle and then the next, and from there he seized his courage and walked out of the half-finished arcane prison safely. Beside the table of torture implements he recovered his helmet and gauntlets, leaving the unsecured iron collar behind in exchange as he refitted his plate bevor over his chin and throat. As with his firearm, the skin thief had not bothered to take Prentice's dagger away, either, but of his sword there was no sign, just the empty scabbard at his belt. It made him wonder how long he had been unconscious, thinking that it must have been time enough at least for the blade to have been disposed of or passed off to another servitor of the Silent Hand.

"Cyprian?" Prentice wondered in a flash of insight. If the Young Hopeful had been serving the Inquisition as suspected, helping them into his liege lady's presence, he could easily have demanded Prentice's sword as reward for his role in Bluebird's plots. It made a perverse kind of sense, Cyprian claiming the sword that was a marker of his brother's lost honor and lost life. To replace the missing blade, the knight commander found a Lions Claw halberd as part of several suits of militiamen's equipment, along with all manner of other clothing suitable to every level of Bridgetown society—disguises kept at the ready to facilitate infiltration. The collection strewn over the displaced pews seemed almost like the costumery maintained by the largest and most successful player companies. The skin thieves could change their faces and bodies at will but needed the garb to complete the character of the people they took on. Prentice realized that he had assumed the shapeshifters simply stole the garments of the folk they mimicked, but as he pulled the halberd out of the midst of the macabre wardrobe, he realized that, of course, keeping the sets of clothes meant they could return to previous stolen identities at need. The skin thief had not been lying when it boasted that their tradition of deceit was ancient and expert.

A swift scout of the doors into the nave showed they all had lines of spelled writing that he was unwilling to risk, even the inner portal to the sacristy, but Prentice managed to find several windows not too far above ground level. After dragging a pew across to stand on, he smashed the diamond panes out of one of them and, dropping the halberd out ahead of him, managed to make the awkward climb through the narrow frame to escape the despoiled holy place. The whole process raised such a din that there was no chance it could be called stealthy. Thankfully, Prentice found himself tumbling out into a small yard on the southeast corner at the rear of the mighty building, a part of the grounds he had never seen before. He was confronted with the rear retaining wall that rose sheer, upward to the castle's hilltop, but to his right a narrow porch curved around the cathedral's southern side and looked to lead back to the main square. Following it at a trot, Prentice rounded a final corner back to the front of the building to find that the plaza was no longer empty. His horse Boots and the pony the skin thief had used to pose as Dahyoor were both there, but they were now accompanied by a cadre of twenty or so men. The two lines worth wore White Lions uniforms, but no Reacherman would mistake them for members of her grace's militia. For a start, they had mail over their buffcoats, something Lions never wore, and they all had tall bearskin hats, which revealed their true identities. These were Jerwahl mercenaries, showing their predisposition for stealth and deception in a new fashion. Disguised, though, they plainly lacked the sense of subtlety a skin thief would possess. Only foreigners could be fooled by the slapdash masquerade. There was, however, one of their number who resembled a true White Lion—their leader it seemed—and when his eyes locked on that man's, Prentice shook his head in bitter recognition.

"Denholm," the knight commander called almost involuntarily as he crossed into the portico through an arch in one of the façade's pillars. A moment later, Prentice was standing at the top of the steps looking down on the failed corporal, now clearly an enemy and the traitor's new mercenary command.

"What ho? Thought I heard a ruckus," Denholm declared with a jaunty sense of surprise. "The lump face said you'd be trapped for good and all time, but the minstrel, he assured us you'd be out, and here you are. Those fellows should learn to believe each other more."

It is not the Inquisition's task to believe but to be sure, Prentice thought, remembering he had once said something similar to the archduchess years ago. How little he had truly understood it then.

"Why are you here, Denholm?" Prentice demanded. "Did you turn traitor, or were you always working against her grace?"

"*Turn* traitor? Turn? Traitor?" the ex-corporal demanded furiously, his mocking smile transforming to a hateful sneer. "It was you betrayed me, you worthless convict turd! You thought to strip me of all I had achieved, everything I deserved. I could see the truth of your lying heroism, and that scared you."

What on earth? Prentice wondered, letting his eyes scan across Denholm's escort as he did. Six of them had long-barreled Masnian wheellocks to hand, while the others were wielding their bardiche axes, another thing no true Reacherman would mistake as belonging to the Lions.

"You've got yourself a nice rear claw there, *knight commander,*" Denholm continued, holding up his own halberd and pointing to Prentice's salvaged armament, sarcastic malice dripping from every word. Denholm's was the only true Lions' weapon amongst the entire fraudulent company. "What happened to your magickal sword?"

The traitor chuckled at that, and the Jerwahl mercenaries joined him, their voices distinctly throaty. Some made small comments to each other in their own tongue.

"You've lost it now, and so you are unmasked," Denholm continued, pointing the polearm in his hand like a rod of authority, making an advocate's accusation in a trial. "That's your secret, isn't it? You're no baron, no knight. You're not even any kind of man-at-arms. Just a fool convict who found a magick sword and thinks that makes him a hero. And you had the audacity to call me a coward. All my life I have been held down by scum like you, stealing my glory. I've forgotten more about battle than you will ever know."

What Prentice knew was that he needed to find a way to escape this crew, some plan that would let him dash for the other side of the plaza. If he could make it to one of the alleys or even the main processional, he might have a strong chance of losing them and making his way to the Paramour's Chambers. Given the confusion that seemed to be infecting Bridgetown's streets, he might be able to link up with some militia bridge garrison and bring them to the fight. Either way, this was the first leg of the race that had been foretold, and he felt his feet twitching in his boots to start the running. Even so, Denholm's boastful allegations brought Prentice up short inwardly. They were so like the condemnations his father—his false father and all the hateful chorus—had made against his soul all winter. But in the early spring sunshine, Denholm's use of such accusations only slid off Prentice like a feeble dagger thrust against his breastplate. Compared to the demonically empowered howls and curses that had almost drowned him in sorrow and rejection, the ex-corporal only sounded like a whining brat to his ears. He shook his head pityingly.

"Relent, Denholm," he told the boastful man. "You have been led astray by liars telling you tales."

"You're the liar! You and all the fools closest to you, telling *their* tales! Hiding away to try to acquire the skills of a man-at-arms, never letting any of them see your ineptitude for too long."

Prentice blinked, marveling at the twisted interpretation of facts Denholm was concocting for himself—no, not for himself. Almost certainly the proud man had had this story provided to him, perhaps word-for-word by Bluebird. In a flash, Prentice could see it in his mind's eye—an embittered former officer, salving his wounded pride in the back of a taphouse, drinking away his last few coppers, a sympathetic ear sitting by him, plying him with some free booze for his tale and then telling him this nonsense. Denholm would have been the perfect recruit for the Silent Hand. It made Prentice wonder how much and what specifically the ex-Gryphon had revealed to their enemies, but those were questions for a quieter day. For now, the clamor of war summoned the knight commander to the race.

There was an odd, bellowing boom somewhere to the south and Prentice turned to see a gust of black smoke rising over the rooftops. The ambushing squad chuckled to themselves again, and Denholm joined them.

"No hope for you now," he declared. "We have destroyed the southern bridge, cutting your precious Gryphons off on the other side. Once your archduchess is given to the king, he will force her husband to surrender his last few men on the north island and it will all be over."

Destroyed the bridge? With the leached powder? Prentice wondered, realizing that the men he had mistaken for cannoneers' "drudges" must have been Jerwahl men in disguise. Surely, they should have known the difference between ruined powder and good? Regardless, Prentice was certain the bridge would still be standing, and that gave him another possibility. He could ride for Town Sobridge and summon the Gryphon Banner, truly tip the scale back in the Reach's favor. He looked at Boots and wondered what kind of chance he would have to snatch his horse from their grasp and make the ride swiftly out of the square. Even if he could do it smoothly, like a fey rider, and get the gelding up to its galloping pace almost instantly, he would have to weather one volley of shots, at least. At close range, Prentice thought that even his fine armor was unlikely to stop a wheellock ball, and Boots surely had no protection of his own. It would be a flight of forlorn hope, but if a shepherd boy trusted that the God of Heaven could guide a slingstone under a giant's helmet brow to slay the monster, Prentice could trust the same God to deflect six gunshots.

Time to lay some money on this faith card, he told himself. So much of theology was thought and word, but the time always came to put coins on the table. As Prentice was forming a swift plan, Denholm must have caught sight of the direction of his gaze, for the traitor moved across to the mercenary holding the two mounts by their bridles. He rubbed his leather-clad hand down Boots's nose possessively.

"Admiring my new horses, convict baron?" he asked mockingly.

"*Your* horses?" Prentice repeated, taking a moment to absorb Denholm's meaning. That seemed to delight the former corporal no end.

"Oh yes, I'm to have everything you denied me and more," he said, still showing Boots a rider's affection. "When your witch is in chains before the Denay throne, I will be given a baronetcy, only one step from a hereditary peerage, and it won't take me long to mount that last step. There'll still be the reconquest of the west to achieve, of course. I can arrange another display of loyalty and heroism for the true king in Denay. It's not that hard."

Prentice wondered how many "arranged" displays of heroism had secured Denholm's promotions in the White Lions while he watched for an opportunity to take back his mount. If he saw the moment, it would have to be a headlong dash. He was certain that the instant he took a step down from the portico, the Rangers would be at him, and as casual as they appeared, there were more than enough to keep him from Boots once they were given half a chance. Even overconfident, twenty to one was insane odds by any measure. Prentice was reminded of Samson again and another of his tales from scripture. The mighty man had faced hundreds of enemy warriors, it was said, wielding no more than the infamous jawbone of an ass. Of course, as far as Prentice knew, the Philistines of scripture had no firearms, but even so, twenty was happily enough to turn his bowels to water. If he had ever finished his Seven Rings Cross training, Prentice would have had to face seven enemies at one time. This was almost three times that number.

"The boy knight wanted your sword, though if you ask me, the minstrel has his own plans for it. Expect to see its magick in the hands of the Denay king when you look up from hell, convict," Denholm went on.

Minstrel? Boy knight? Denay king? Do you never bother to learn anyone's names, Denholm? Prentice wondered.

"I never wanted anything but this chance, and here you've given it to me," the corporal continued to explain, apparently enjoying the sound of his own voice in the open plaza. "Did you know that was the command I was under? If you remained trapped in the daft magick, I could have the horses. If you escaped, and you have, then I could have what I truly wanted—the chance to show *you* what a real warrior can do. No magick sword to help you kill an aged champion now. Just halberd to halberd, and I will have your legend. Denholm who killed the heretic from the west. They'll sing songs about me."

No sooner had the ex-corporal made his declaration than Boots at his side gave a sudden aggressive nip at his hand, the bite likely felt even through the leather of the gauntlet. He recoiled and slapped at the gelding's muzzle.

"Seems you might have trouble winning his loyalty," Prentice mocked. "He knows you for what you are, just as all the men you betrayed will as well."

Denholm's face shifted to rage once more, and he pointed at Boots.

"Shoot the ungrateful beast!" he shouted. "Kill them!"

Prentice had no idea whether Denholm had realized what he was saying when he said, "kill them," but nonetheless, the six gun-armed mercenaries followed his command to the letter, shooting both Boots and the pony. Prentice's horse went down instantly from a shot that pierced the poor beast's chest, but the pony reared wildly, its bridle loosed by the attendant who had stepped back to avoid the gunshots. The mount took at least one shot, visible on its rear flank, and it bolted across the plaza in limping panic. Reflexively, Prentice stepped down halfway to the flagstones at the shooting but held himself back for one last moment. Turning from the butchered horse, Denholm looked to Prentice with a sneer.

"Does that loss trouble you, false captain of war?" he mocked, and he hefted his polearm into a fighting guard, point forward as Lions used the weapon. "I will find other horses. Better horses. In the meantime, face me and I will get back the honor you stole from me. Or flee as the coward you are. These fellows are excellent hunters. They will run you down and butcher you for me. Either way, your legend ends as just a chapter in my saga's rise. Come, duel me or flee, wretch."

"You will regret that," Prentice said, saddened at the death of his loyal mount but also seeing Denholm's mistake. Six shots had felled one horse and wounded the other so that it would have to be put down, but they were also six shots that turned wheellocks into unloaded lumps of wood. Twenty to one was still the insane odds it was always going to be, but Prentice also knew he did not have to defeat twenty. He only had to win free. Once he had broken their circle, he would sprint for his allies and let the enemy face the Lions proper. That had always been the strategy. The White Lions hunted the battlefield as a pride, all together. Duels were only for fighting when there were no other options.

I have been such an ass, missing the true lesson for so long, Prentice thought as he stepped carefully down to the ground level, feigning the caution of a single combatant sizing up a new opponent. He raised his halberd into a high guard. *But I am happy now to have a claw in my hand and call it a jawbone. Come be a Philistine for me, Denholm. The Lord has trained my hands for war.*

He pulled down his helmet's visor and advanced to the fight.

CHAPTER 80

The Jerwahl Rangers shuffled back as Prentice's feet touched the flagstones, clearly instructed to make space for the exigencies of Denholm's longed-for duel. For himself, Prentice doubted the ex-corporal plotted anything like a fair contest, for all his boasting. If the matter turned against him, Denholm would likely signal one of the men with their foreign axes and Prentice would find himself cut from an unseen angle, except that Prentice also planned nothing like a fair duel.

As soon as they were on the same level, Denholm began to circle slowly to his right in the manner of a watchful opponent assessing his foe at the beginning of single combat. It meant nothing to Prentice, who simply maintained his pace out onto the flagstones. He suddenly remembered his combat at the end of the drought against the half-ram men of the fallen Sir Haravind, the first time he had fought at the door of a church. And then there had been Inxyphos the bear man, here on this very ground. In comparison to those instances, Denholm was no more frightening than a three-legged cur with only one tooth left.

Likely expecting the wariness of two foes who respected or feared each other, Denholm was caught wrong-footed as Prentice simply advanced confidently at him. The ex-corporal thrust at the oncoming assailant, but the halberd's point only screeched against Prentice's breastplate. The knight commander barely felt the strike, absorbing the force with his full mass. Denholm drew his weapon back to strike again, circling it in a way that would allow him to deflect Prentice's likely overhand chopping attack, but that was a complete miscalculation. Instead of swinging with power, Prentice thrust the steel-capped butt end of his weapon into Denholm's face. Wearing only a White Lions' Claw kettle helm in accordance with his disguise, the ex-corporal's visage was bare, and the heavy-ended blow struck him like a cudgel hit, making him stagger away like a drunkard. If Prentice had actually wanted to duel the man, the fight was already one half-step from finished. The knight commander had no interest in the traitor, however. He had put his feet to the race, and his course led out through the opposite side of the cathedral square. That meant he had to go through the Jerwahl axes.

Clearly surprised by the speed at which the "duel" had turned, the Rangers nonetheless moved creditably to intercept Prentice as he aimed himself straight past the bloodied Denholm. Two raised their axes, coming at him from either side, while he heard others moving to surround him from behind. It would take only fractions of breaths before he would be fully encircled. Yet for all the danger he was in, Prentice felt again the icy rage that he had not known through the whole of his winter training. Instead of the paralyzing cold that sapped his will and made him wait for the wolfpack to spring, this was the slap in the face of a mountain stream that stung the skin and focused the mind. He almost wanted to exalt, to laugh. Finally, after so many dark months, he was at war in the light once more.

Striking high and low at once, the two axmen sought to put him in an impossible position, aiming for head and knee from opposite sides. Using his halberd, Prentice checked the head-high swing, but at the same time he stepped away from it toward the low sweep, shortening the distance between himself and that second ranger. The high attack was guided away while the low one impacted in the wrong place, not with the heavy steel blade but the wood of the haft. It was precisely the kind of defense that hours with the hanging pell had drilled into his limbs. The foreshortened blow rang on the faulds, the interlocked plate skirt of Prentice's armor, force utterly absorbed. Perhaps if the ranger had wanted to use it to push Prentice out of position, the strike might have been more consequential, but the man had been swinging for his tripping low strike. Once the attack was intercepted, his hands and arms were out of position. Prentice kept going, barging into him and knocking the mercenary backward while trying to hook the other man's axe out of his hands completely with the halberd's back spike. He never got the hooking locked, however, and the axman snatched his weapon's haft away, retreating a step or two in the process. The whole pass should have left Prentice enough of a gap to dash through, but he was sure the Rangers he heard closing behind him would be on him if he tried to make a foot race of it now. Thinking he had no choice but to further widen his space from his enemies, he reversed his path back toward the cathedral and readied for the next set of axe strikes that were already seeking his armored back and head.

And so it went for what might have been mere moments and could have been an hour. Two or three came at him at a time and Prentice defended against them, using the halberd's blade and haft equally, weapon whirling continually, attacking in return whenever he could create an opening and absorbing with his armor whatever he could not parry or escape. There were moments when his steel protection rang so that he might have thought he was trapped in a tolling bell, and other points where he thought for sure that he had made his gap, only to have more mercenaries step in to block his path. If they had fought like the White Lions, they could have trapped him with a hedge of points in short order, so many coordinated weapons overwhelming him eventually, no matter how savagely he attacked them. Or else the Claws would hold him back long enough for the Roar to reload. The Rangers were not used to fighting in such a fashion, however, accustomed instead to using their bombs and wheellocks to disrupt enemy formations and then getting amongst them with swinging axes—a loose configuration for maximizing carnage. In tight against one man, they were forced to fight almost as individuals, with no clamshell explosives thrown and no time to reload their guns. Prentice made especially sure of that last fact, keeping his eyes out for any ranger who stepped back from the melee and looked to be seeking out his firearm. That man Prentice always charged for, and several of them fell straight from the fight. The Rangers had their coats of mail, and their impressive hats were actually built upon solid steel salets that protected their scalps, but as gunners they left their faces bare for better shooting, and mail could be pierced or hacked by sufficiently stern blows. A halberd was capable of both such strikes, and Prentice put his to efficient use. Under his plate steel, his flesh was bruised more than once by a punishing blow, but the weapon of the White Lions' Claws sank deep into enemy mail, and the knight commander counted it fair exchange.

After a time, he found himself in the western half of the square. There were bodies behind him, and while the moans of the wounded told him not all were dead, he was certain none of those would rise again to threaten him this day. The remaining dangerous enemies were now in front of him, covering the opening of the main processional that led from the square to Great Bridge Road. Prentice stared at them through the narrow slits of his visor, taking a pause to plan his next moves. His breathing was heavy under the steel but more from exhilaration than fatigue. In recent weeks he had fought almost to this intensity for hours at a time. The battle so far had not brought him anywhere near his limits.

Knowing that he had whittled the enemies' numbers down at least somewhat, Prentice was surprised by the crowd that still confronted him. Others must have come from somewhere in the meantime to reinforce their comrades. That would mean that even more might arrive soon, possibly through the other alleys of the plaza. If he tried to make a dash now, he could find himself running headlong into a completely fresh bunch, looking to encircle him. His best path was straight through the crowd that was at least partially weakened. With Boots's death, he had given up any hope of reaching the Gryphon Banner Company. He would have to trust that someone else would take word to Gennet and the other sergeants. Surely the smoke from the bridge should draw some attention in the south. He suspected Denholm, or perhaps a disguised skin thief, had likely dispatched the limited detachment left to hold Sougate itself simply from a strategy of pure pragmatism, but there would be other militiamen between the south gate bastion and the captured Veckander town. In the meantime, his efforts would be best focused on reaching the archduchess and coordinating whatever defense could be brought to her. From down the laneway, more Jerwahl men could be seen approaching, several of them holding their wheellocks high, obviously loaded and ready to fire.

Best they not get the chance to use them, Prentice told himself, and with no battlecry, no defiant scream, just silent resolve, he marched forward alone toward the growing company of enemies. There was no doubt that they had numbers enough to fell one man-at-arms, but the ones closest to Prentice, the ones who had thought themselves his invincible captors only a short while ago, had watched him carve his impossible path across the square over the open plaza where he had once faced the bear Inxyphos and slain it. Magick sword or no, this convict nobleman from the west was not the inept coward they had been told to expect. From the fear in their expressions, Prentice imagined they doubted he was anything less than an impossible hero, like a Samson or a David. The knight commander scoffed inwardly, knowing he was just a man, however skilled or bold, and like any man, death had its appointment with him somewhere. But if these enemies were terrified at this moment, he had no desire to let them change their minds.

Driving them ahead of him, Prentice's silent advance pushed the panicked front ranks into the calmer reinforcements behind, spreading the infection of fear. Some cowered against the houses at the side of the lane as Prentice forced the crowd back into the tighter confines of the processional road, and his forward motion meant he had overrun them, even though his advance was more inexorable than swift now. He could not leave them there for all they seemed broken, however, since any man he left hale behind him could easily attack his back when he was not looking. He felled one such cowering axman, his own halberd blade slashing the enemy's face open and then catching upon and almost severing the man's hand with the follow-through of the strike. The ranger collapsed with a scream, and at that moment two of his reinforcing comrades pushed through the unnerved crowd, wheellocks to their shoulders. Their shots were rushed however, jostled by the others around them. The first missed entirely, biting the whitewashed wall behind Prentice. The second was better, but the angle of its path was just oblique enough that the strong steel curve of Prentice's helmet deflected the ball. He felt his head jerk to one side, the metal ringing in his ears. It hurt, but no more than a slap to a bare head might. His new armor was fine indeed. Prentice turned to look at the gunners and both men's eyes went wide with terror, as did those in the faces of the others around them, as if their enemy had just proved himself bullet-proof on top of being fearless and ruthless.

Let them believe whatever they want, Prentice told himself, and he threw himself at the two gunners, one of whom all but clawed at his fellows to try to escape while the other one tried to use his gun like a club to defend himself. He went down, and those around him fell back yet more.

And so it went on, some of the mercenaries summoning up the courage to do what they were hired to, no doubt thinking that surely one man could not be too difficult to defeat. Yet with every failed attempt, Prentice drove them back a step farther and they became a fraction less resolved still, their fear infecting whatever reinforcements came to aid them. One man could not drive a hundred before him. That was a work of legend, not of modern warfare. Yet still, the lone, silent Reacherman in helm and plate came on at them. They made few if any telling cuts, and each ranger who did so paid for the achievement with his life. Down one road and then the next Prentice marched, and they sought to block his path, fruitless at every step. Long and bitter had been the winter that led Prentice to this day of false spring, and all that bitterness left a cold steel that would not yield—not until he reached his liege, his wife, and the reasons he had to draw his every breath.

At last, he attained the corner that would turn onto Paramour's laneway and suddenly the Rangers seemed to be evaporating in front of him, like mist in the spring morning or as the winter clouds had these last two days. Prentice heard the drumbeat of Lions on the attack, and the garrison from the ancient bridge that connected Oldbridge and Loncastel marched into his view, hacking his unnerved enemies apart from the opposite direction. They took the intersection in moments, and many of the panicked Rangers looked glad to throw down their arms and surrender. Prentice found himself alone in an open space, facing his own militiamen, who regarded him with suspicious expressions. Realizing that few of the Lion banner would have seen him yet in this new armor, he laughed and pushed back his visor to show them his face.

"Have you forgotten your knight commander already, Reachermen?" he cried. "I know I have been at other duties through the dark of winter, but it is not that long, surely?"

"My Lord!" one of the Fangs cried out, lifting his sword over his head, and Prentice smiled to recognize his adopted son Solomon. He realized that what he was facing was a mixed cohort—Lions and Gryphons together. He wondered at the day's battles on Loncastel that had pressed them to this situation. It had never been the plan for the two banners to combine in this fashion, though he was glad to think they had.

"Quiet in the ranks!" the commanding corporal bellowed reflexively, and that pleased Prentice as well. He loved Solomon, and the fact that the lad lived was a reward in itself, but the banner companies survived on coordination and discipline.

Uncoordinated action led to the kind of destruction that had just befallen the Jerwahl Rangers. Once disrupted, the mercenaries had lacked the regulation to reform themselves under pressure.

The mixed cohort's commander presented himself with a salute. "What word, knight commander? Is the Gryphon on the return? Knight Captain Farringdon has bid us wait for you. He is sore pressed, though, holding onto Loncastel."

"The Gryphon is yet in the south," Prentice told the man. "Send word that lancers be dispatched to bring the second banner company back to Bridgetown, if they can be spared. Tell them to be wary crossing at Sougate. The Usurper's raiders have tried to destroy it with powder. It should still stand, but it likely burns yet."

Prentice looked over his shoulder to point almost directly southward at the rising column of smoke from the southern bridge. The corporal followed Prentice's indication and then nodded with a confused expression, looking back to his overarching commander.

"If the Gryphon is south of the bridge, then...?"

"I was taken prisoner by deception," Prentice cut off the man's confused question, not wanting to waste time with long explanations. He had to ensure that Paramour's was secure as soon as possible. "I managed to escape and must immediately see to the archduchess' safety. I am certain similar deceit has been directed at her."

"You escaped?" the corporal asked, still staring southward.

"They were holding me in the cathedral," Prentice explained, thinking the fellow was confused by the assertion that he had been captured and the seemingly contradictory notion that the southern bridge had been sabotaged into the bargain.

"The cathedral?" the man repeated, and Prentice was about to cuff him to get his mind back to his duties, when he realized the corporal was not staring at the smoke column as Prentice thought. The man was looking straight down Great Bridge Road. Scattered on the cobbles as far back as they could see before the road curved slightly around various houses and buildings, were the bodies of the slain or wounded whom Prentice had fought through. Most wore Jerwahl coats over their mail, either having shirked their disguises sometime during their invasion or else not having enough for them all to play at fakery. During his long fight, Prentice had not even realized the change in his enemies' clothing. He looked back to the broken and defeated prisoners now kneeling, their hands interlaced behind their heads. Not one of them was in White Lions colors. None of those had been with Denholm at the cathedral. A rough count of the prisoners and visible corpses looked to be at least thirty. Prentice snorted and smiled wryly as he turned back to his astonished officer.

"Send a line to the next bridge garrison and look to getting Great Bridge Road and the cathedral square secured. No one goes in the church itself; it has been cursed with Redlander magick. That is to be left for Brother Whilte. In the meantime, gather up every one of these Masnian mongrels that still lives and put them in chains. Some will be dressed in our uniforms, and if those still breathe, do not waste chains on them. No one who poses as a Lion or Gryphon to our faces survives their attempted deception. Do you understand?"

"My Lord?" the corporal asked distractedly, still staring down the road. Then he seemed to realize who it was he was talking to, and he turned back, saluting. "At once, Knight Commander."

"Good man," Prentice encouraged him. "Now give me half of one of your cohorts. I am headed to Paramour's."

Soon enough, Prentice was double marching toward his liege's apartments with fifty militiamen at his back. His fury had dimmed some, and now he was feeling the ache of tired muscles. No doubt there were injuries in amongst the general discomfort that he did not recognize, but clearly none of them was such a danger that they needed immediate treatment, which was good because Whilte was still south of Bridgetown, and Prentice had just ordered that the chaplain be directed first toward the cathedral upon his return.

CHAPTER 81

The yard of Paramour's was a field of slaughter, dead Lions and enemies scattered about, left where they had fallen. It was hard to see which was who amongst the slain, since almost all the bodies wore some version of Reacher militia uniforms, but a quick glance made it clear that the loyal men-at-arms had given an excellent account of themselves and not one body was outside the gate, which made Prentice think that none of his had tried to run. The ache in his limbs was flushed away as sudden fury washed through his veins like ice water.

"Secure those wagons and police the dead," he shouted over his shoulder as he rushed to the Chambers' open door. He found his first neophyte there, her broken body bent over one of the chairs from the main chamber. It had clearly been being used to block the entrance but was not up to the task. Axe blow bites out of the door showed how determined the attackers had been to gain entry. The girl, dressed as a nun, must have been felled almost as soon as they had broken through. Prentice did not recognize her to know her name, but her brutal fate only deepened the furious chill within him, and every breath in his lungs felt like the winds that blew down from the mountaintops of the Azures—the crying breath of the Gryphon.

Mounting the steps three at a time, Prentice clattered upward, casting his halberd away for a hindrance. With the rage in his heart, he feared no lurking ambush.

"Righteous!" he shouted as he went, lifting his visor. "Sweet beloved, be alive!"

It was a nonsense thing to say, and yet he meant every word. He was here for his liege and his duty to her, but what he cared for most was his wife and children. He burst into the chamber through the open door to face a charnel house. Dead men in armor were strewn amidst the wreckage of the archduchess's chamber, and ladies-in-waiting who should be about the gentle matters of the nobility instead lying slain with blades in their hands. The calm eye of Prentice's inner storm made a swift count of bodies as he stalked about the chamber, crying out for his family. Though the room was a butcher's block, he was reasonably certain this was not the whole of Archduchess Amelia's household. Some of the women were obviously not here. Those who were had sold their lives dearly indeed from the look of it.

Prentice shoved a fallen chair aside, thinking to go to the bedchamber end of the room when an agonized groan drew his attention. Vaulting the enormous table in the middle of the room, now pushed askew, he found Lady Daisy half-hidden under it, pressed up against the heavy wooden legs. The young woman's waning moon lace mask was knocked askew and her face beneath was a ruin. She had one eye swollen shut and myriad small cuts amidst her pale freckles. Streaks of blood were sprayed in her hair, in her eyebrows, and down across her ears. Her cheeks were dark, while her throat was a mass of bruises under the grip of a dead man-at-arm's gauntlet. From the wheezing sounds of her shallow breaths, the death grip had crushed her windpipe, and without a healer she would surely die in moments. Prentice turned the armored body on top of her over, thinking to give her a few breaths more by removing the heavy weight from her chest, and he found himself looking into the empty eyes of Cyprian, last of the Young Hopefuls, slain, with no more hope left to him. It was all Prentice could do to not spit into the sneering rictus, but the youth was a corpse, and any contempt shown his body now would not make his eternal fate any worse. Still, Prentice felt the longing.

"Knight Commander? You came for us," Daisy whispered, blood and spittle gurgling out of her damaged throat, making the words slur.

"I came," he told her, reflexively reaching for her hand and finding it wrapped, white-knuckled, around a stiletto that was embedded to the hilt in the dead Cyprian's body.

"Daft idjit seemed to think he could put me down with a handful o' smacks from his gauntlet. Din't e'en give me the respect o' his sword," the girl said as Prentice unwound her fingers and took them in his own. "Took a couple goes, but I managed to get me sticker up under his backplate—gap there in the faulds, small but findable for a stiletto. Got me his kidney well and good. Should've seen his eyes change when he realized I done for him. He tried to throttle me, but it was so sweet to feel him fade."

She sighed and her one good eye closed.

"You did well, My Lady," Prentice told her earnestly. He wanted to rant, to smash the arrogant squire's body beside her for what he had done, but instead he forced himself to comfort the dying woman. She had but few breaths left now, and he could see it. He also had an urgent duty to pursue, and petty vengefulness would serve that not at all. "I will see her grace hears of your bravery, and your family. But where is she, Lady Daisy? Where is the archduchess?"

"They wanted...to...take..." the Lace Fang struggled to say, but it was clear that each word was a burden too great for her wounded flesh. She was spending the last of her life, and before she could say anymore, her final breath rattled from her chest. Behind him, Prentice heard movement, and he knew he would have to give his men orders to search for the archduchess, but where to begin?

The cathedral? That had been the skin thief's plan, the archduchess dragged to the defiled church for a blood sacrifice. Prentice shook his head. That plan had been knocked askew as soon as he escaped, and according to Denholm's foolish boast, it had never been Bluebird's preferred option in any case. What had the self-deluded traitor said? That Archduchess Amelia would be presented to Daven Marcus and used as a hostage to force the Loncastel garrison to surrender? That needed a boat to transport her across the river, and a boat meant a dock, somewhere.

The whole damnable town is docks, Prentice cursed inwardly and then locked that emotional thought away as pointless. The mountain was not conquered by cursing at it but by climbing, one step at a time.

"We must send news of this to Loncastel at once," he said and was about to stand up again when someone moved close behind him. Before he knew what was coming, the point of a dagger was less than a knuckle's length from his eye and another hand was wrapped around him from the opposite side, gripping at the lip of his bevor. The solid plate was too fully interlocked with the rest of the armor to be pulled aside, but that was not the assailant's intent. Prentice knew that immediately. His throat and chin protection was being used as a handle to let his attacker hold on more completely if he started to struggle against the dagger thrust.

"You have his voice and his armor," a feminine voice hissed beside his helmet. "I'll bet if I let you get turned about, you'll even have his face. But I seen bad fellows with borrowed faces enough today, so you got but one chance to sway me to thinkin' you are who you look like, or we go at it 'til there ain't no blood in my veins. Cause if you ain't him, then I owe his memory at least that much."

"My darling wife," Prentice answered, not moving a muscle and feeling happier than he ever imagined he could be when faced with a fatal dagger thrust, "I owe you an apology. I know you once demanded that no one but you help me to put my armor on, but I ken that since you said such about my old panoply, which is gone now, and this is a new suit, it was alright for me to get a militiaman to play squire."

Her grip on him loosed a fraction, no doubt recognizing the secret truth of his comment, marking him as no skin thief. Prentice took the moment to seize her wrist while he stood up and flipped his wife around his body, using a wrestler's throw to bring her lighter weight into his grip fully so that she gave a minor gasp. If he wanted, he could have pinned her, but instead he only turned her dagger aside and hugged her against himself.

"Heavens above, you twit," she gasped. "You'll crush the life from me."

Prentice loosened his grip and allowed Righteous to get her feet under her once more.

"You trust it is me?" he asked, staring into her eyes behind her lace half mask.

"I know it's you now," she responded, and when he leaned in to kiss her, she returned it. Then he pulled her closer again and hugged her while he kissed her face and then the top of her head.

"I love you," he breathed. "Now tell me our children are not here."

In his arms, Righteous began to shudder, and he heard her begin to weep. Pushing her back to arm's length in alarm, Prentice searched her eyes once more as they brimmed to overflowing with hot tears.

"She wouldn't let me, husband," Righteous protested between sobs. "I know we're sworn and are nobles of her lands and all such, but she wouldn't let me do my duty to her."

"What are you saying?" Prentice demanded, a sudden rising panic shoving away his pleasure at their reunion.

"She made me. I was ready to be at her side. I could've put a dozen o' those mongrels down. I could hear 'em, all in armor with heavy blades, and they still struggled with our girls. Oh, how they did me and Spindle proud, but I wasn't permitted..."

Prentice took her by the chin and forced his overwrought wife to look him in the eye.

"Wild Rose, where are Gant and Amy?" he insisted, and with a forlorn nod, Righteous pointed over her shoulder at the secret stairwell's open door.

"Back there with Emma, swaddled and fed," she mumbled. "Amy's asleep, if you can believe it."

With a renewed sense of relief, Prentice's mind swiftly put together what had happened, and he realized the archduchess must have insisted that Righteous protect her twins before even their liege. His wife's emotion was not grief over the loss of her children but shame that she had not stood by Archduchess Amelia in the moment of greatest need. Such was a mother's burden, though. Almost no purpose would ever take precedence over her children, no matter the cost to loyalty or duty.

"I was ready, in case they came searching for our little niche, but it was Dalflitch and her grace they wanted—only them—and once they cleared a path, they retreated."

"They only took those two?" Prentice asked, knowing that not all the Lace Fangs or neophytes were dead in Chambers. Where were the others?

"Maybe they took others," Righteous offered. "I only know what we could hear through the wood. Just as soon as they had their mitts on her grace and Lady Dalflitch, that was when one of 'em called to make their way back out. There was mutterin's of that bitch Penelope, and a few other things didn't make a lot o' sense."

"Could some of the maids of the chamber have followed them if they simply turned to flee with two hostages?" Prentice pressed. Now that he knew his family was safe, he had his other duties to fix upon. If any neophytes or Lace Fangs had survived, he expected they would have tried to follow at a safe distance if they could. They were all proven loyal, and despite the skin thief in the cathedral's contempt, more than adept at arts of stealth and cunning.

"Not all of 'em were here, husband," Righteous explained as militiamen finally began to filter into the room, their expressions showing the same mix of fury and horror that Prentice was feeling. "We had girl's afield, searchin' you out and tryin' to get a sense o' the nonsense on the streets. The archduchess sent Lady Beth out the window as well, just as the mongrels were beatin' down the door, and Agatha is about somewhere, too."

Before Prentice could ask his next question, a line first stepped over the bodies and presented himself urgently, saluting with a slapping fist to his chest.

"There's a fair-haired little maid out in the yard, insists to see you, My Lord," he reported. "Looks like a fishwife to me and ain't much o' one by the skin and bones of 'er, but she's right ferocious 'bout comin' in. Shall I bring her up or pack 'er off?"

Prentice looked to his wife.

"Agatha," Righteous whispered, identifying the woman outside by her description. Prentice gave the militiaman a nod, and a moment later the tiny Lace Fang was standing in the doorway. Her eyes swept the room, and a stifled sigh of heartbreak expressed her grief more eloquently than words.

"What passes, My Lady?" Righteous demanded with a surprisingly stern tone, and Agatha snapped taut, like a puppet with a drawn string. A moment later, an unspoken conversation was flowing by signals between the two Lace Fangs, and when it concluded, Righteous gestured to Prentice.

"Tell My Lord, Knight Commander," she told the girl in the doorway.

Lady Agatha bowed to Baron Ash. "I know where they've taken her, Knight Commander," she said.

CHAPTER 82

It was called No Prince's Pier, and it was a private jetty for the earls of Bridgetown on the north shore of Oldbridge. The dock butted against the steep slope of Earlsbastion Hill so it could be reached by a switchback stair that let down from a postern gate in the castle's back walls. The pier itself was on exceptionally tall pylons and reached out into the water far above the height of the other docks and jetties around it.

"I first learned of it just 'fore midwinter," Agatha explained as she guided Prentice and the militiamen through backstreets around the eastern foot of Earlsbastion Hill. It was a shorter distance around the castle mount from Paramour's than to go to the western side, but there were also no major roads through this poorer neighborhood, so their twisting path only increased Prentice's impatience even as they rushed. His grip twisted on the haft of his recovered halberd, and the tack of the men jogging behind him rattled and jingled off the locked houses. No one in this part of town was poking their heads out now.

"And it's the baroness-elect's personal dock?" Prentice asked, prying as much information from Dalflitch's skilled spy as he could before they arrived.

"Folks say it still is but seems neither Lady Penelope nor her papa or grandpap ever kept their own boats there," Agatha explained. "It's called No Princes cause it's for the earl's household to escape by if the Vec invades rather than bow their knees in surrender. Seems it's another old tradition that's gone by the wayside, but houseguards still keep watch over it. Every so often a bold skip boasts that he's bought the fellows off to let them use it to bring untaxed goods in, but all the docksiders say that's bollocks, cause the moment word like that gets to the Conclave, they have the bailiffs out to roust the whole northside. Seems the local patricians are very particular 'bout liberties with their liege or her private dock."

Prentice shook his head. Senior folk of society who would resent the liberties taken by the peerage still worked to defend those privileges from flouting by the lower orders. So it was, all the way down society—sullen acceptance of the senior and proud condescension to the inferior. Only the king at the top need not begrudge anyone above him, and only the convicts at the bottom had no one below them to despise. Except, of course, that nothing was ever so simple.

"This raised dock, how do boats let onto it and how do we get down to it?" Prentice asked, raising his voice so that everyone around him could hear. He wanted his diminished command to understand what was waiting for them. Of the fifty odd he had seconded from the bridge garrison, he had just over thirty now. Six had been sent as pairs of messengers to points about to rally the banners. He wanted the main of the Gryphon Company returned to Bridgetown before sundown. Another full line of militiamen he had set to maintain guard at Paramour's. Now that her grace and Lady Dalflitch had been snatched away, he suspected the invaders would show little interest in the location, but his wife and children were still there, and other ladies of the chamber could be returning there soon.

"I can't just let them come back to this wasteland, husband," Righteous had protested when he tried to send her to Loncastel where the main of the Lions' strength would ironically provide safety, despite the Dragons' continued fire that still boomed in the sky every now and then. "If they see this room like jetsam and no archduchess, they won't know what's afoot."

"Very well," Prentice had allowed her. "Wait here until sundown and then make your way to Loncastel directly. And not when the sun's fully down first. The moment the west starts to glow orange, I want you out that door and fleet of foot on Great Bridge Road, a hedge of steel around you and our babes."

"Yes, husband," Righteous had agreed readily, but Prentice wanted her to recognize that he was resolute about this.

"Mark me, Wild Rose. Do not play slipshod with the timing. I will tell the line first the same thing and give him orders to take you out of here by force if you delay."

"Like to see him try," Righteous had scoffed, but Prentice grabbed hold of her shoulder.

"No play in this. Obey me, wife! When the sky begins to orange—Not. One. Breath. Later."

Righteous had then looked straight at him and swallowed, though he doubted she was truly intimidated by his manner. She was too cable-taut and strong-willed to be so easily set aback. Even so, she had suddenly bobbed downward with a precise curtsey that would have done any noblewoman proud for its civility.

"Exactly as you command, my husband," she said, and he believed her. It was an important conviction. What might come next would likely be complex and difficult enough without having to worry about his family's safety all over again.

"There's a second platform at the water level," Agatha outlined, describing No Prince's Pier in as much detail as she could while she kept up with the rushing militiamen. "It floats on the surface like, but it's tight locked to the posts by chains. Any boat will be sure to be tied up there. It's out from the dockside, so the only way to it will be by the higher jetty."

No more than a quarter of the candle later and the cadre of militiamen were at the back of a two-storied warehouse that was built almost flush with the steep eastern side of Earlsbastion's hill. The second floor of the storehouse could be reached by a rough, muddy staircase that had been improvised against the hill's slope. As much trail as steps, it was clearly an access that led to a hatch-like door in the upper story.

"No Prince's Pier is right on the other side of that house," Agatha explained. "It's a tripping step from the roof to the footings. Right as rain."

Prentice nodded and led the way, the militia following single file behind him. Hoisting himself up by the warehouse's gable, he poked his head over to find a flat, slate roof that looked to be sturdy, though he wondered if thirty odd men in armor might push it past its limit. Exactly as Agatha had explained, however, it was no more than five paces from where he was to the stone edge of the private pier of Bridgetown's rulers. Prentice could see part of the switchback staircase and a locked gate that was being guarded by two men in orange and gold livery, arming swords at their sides. They were watching the river with troubled expressions, it seemed to Prentice, and he ducked down before he was spotted.

"This is the word," he whispered to those closest to him, trusting them to pass his instructions back. He explained about the guards and the distance across the roof. "The minute we broach the rooftop, they will have us seen and raised the alarm, so no hesitation. Each man boost the one ahead of you. I want us to pop up like a fisherman's float and then over that slate like whippets."

He assigned the closest men to tackle the two guards at the steps and hold the gate for as long as they could against any reinforcements that might come from the castle. The rest he told to follow him closely. He had not had a chance to see the exact situation on the water end of the pier, but he intended to give them no delay.

"Whatever boats are there, if God is kind, one of them will hold the archduchess, not yet snatched away."

Even as he told them that, he knew the extreme hope he was investing in their timing. It had to have been at least half an hour since the archduchess and Lady Dalflitch had been taken hostage. If he had been Bluebird, he would already have had them on a craft across the river, even if all he had to hand was a coracle with a broken oar. The north channel was a short row. Or else they could just cast off and let the river take them east, since all downriver was in the Usurper's control already.

"Whether it is one craft or fifty tied up on that dock, none of them leave the pier, understand?" he told his men. "We want our liege and lady peers back safely, so Roar, look to your shots. Nothing wild. Be marksmen with the eyes of hunting hawks."

The six gunners down the line nodded when the quiet word reached them, their hands too busy with their long-matches to waste on salutes. The smell of smoke was already filling the air behind the warehouse. All down the line, militiamen showed resolute expressions. Each one was ready to die before their liege lady was snatched out of their grip once more. Prentice had only one more instruction.

"My Lady," he said, addressing Agatha personally, "what comes next is likely to be the hardest of steel work..."

"Don't try to order me to remain behind, Baron!" Agatha cut him off, the small-boned woman reminding Prentice of an angry forest creature defending its nest against a predator. "I won't do it, I just won't."

Prentice held up his hand to quiet her.

"Let me speak. This is steel work, and odds are that Bluebird has raiders, plus whatever Bridgetowners Penelope has to lend him. We will fight our way through them, but you are not to waste your time trying to take on any enemy men-at-arms."

Agatha made to object again, but Prentice put a gauntleted finger to her lips.

"Your duty is to the archduchess and your seneschal mistress," he insisted. "However swift or slow it is for us to fight through, I want you looking for a canny path to wherever you think the prisoners are being kept. Cut them free and then help them straight into the water. That will keep them safe while we put the enemy down. You can swim, can you not?"

Agatha tilted her head and gave him a derisive look.

"Only since I could walk. I'm a riverfolk lass, you know."

Prentice smiled. There was no more time to waste, but he had just one command left for all of them.

"This is going to be a melee from the get go. No formations, no neat lines. Just every one of us after the prizes. Do not stop because I certainly will not." He put his hand up to the gable again and felt someone step behind to boost him upward. A glance over his shoulder showed it was Solomon, and that made Prentice smile.

"Oh, and one last thing," he told them as he tensed for the upward surge. "If you see an elderly fellow in blue or motley, take care with him. If the warbler opens his mouth to sing a note or even mutter a word, put him down. Blade, bullet, or even your bloody fists. He doesn't survive another meeting with a Reacherman."

With that, he turned to face the warehouse, eyes on the gable and roof edge above him. "The Lord trains my hands for war."

Then, he gave Solomon the nod and vaulted upward.

CHAPTER 83

Prentice's feet touched the slate, and he was in motion immediately, aiming diagonally across the corner of the roof. He felt one of the tiles crack under his weight, but it did not slow him. A half dozen paces and he was at the opposite side, leaping the narrow gap to the stones of the pier's landward end. The two heights were almost exact, and it was ridiculous to imagine that this building had not been so constructed to give skips or other low fellows access to this supposedly private jetty. They could have built a gangway across the gap from slate to flagstones and it would not have been any more obvious. He landed the simple leap with a clatter and was turning towards the river before the guards at the staircase gate even raised any alarm. Soon enough, they were shouting, but their voices only mixed in with the clatter of White Lions coming one after the other, thumping over the warehouse and making the simple crossing. In moments there was the sound of combat behind him, but Prentice had eyes only for what was ahead.

The stone footings ended before the jetty even reached the water's edge, the wooden walkway projecting out over a dockside road below, high enough for a man to stand upright beneath. Prentice's boots drummed on the planks, drawing the attention of a motley collection of armed men at the pier's outward end. Bearskin hats mixed amongst buff-coated marigold militia and pirate raiders, marked by their lack of armor, bare feet, and boarding pikes with curved-hook heads. There was even a small handful of men-at-arms in full plate in their midst, which made Prentice think these were lesser knights or squires sent by Daven Marcus to risk themselves for this bold action—the Young Hopefuls of the Denay court, as it were.

May they suffer similar fates, he thought, not slowing for a moment. Out over the water, on the right-hand side of the walkway, was the lower platform Agatha had described, and there was only one boat tied there—a simple barge with a canvass canopy along its length and an open space at the rear. Eyes switching back and forth between enemy fighters and the boat, Prentice could not make out the two women he had come to save, but there looked to be a grey-haired head in the pilot's end of the barge.

"Bluebird!" Prentice shouted as loudly as he could manage, flipping up his visor to be heard. "Yield your prisoners."

The minstrel spy poked his head fully out of the barge, and sighting Prentice, sighed in disgust, the gesture so exaggerated that it was easily visible over the many paces distance.

"Oh, heaven's damnation take you, wretched heretic," Bluebird shouted at him and then looked back into the boat. Quickly, two individuals leaped out from within—one obviously a riverman while the other seemed like a religious figure, wearing a clean white cassock with the hood up over his head. That one moved straight to the ladder that linked the upper and lower pier, obviously climbing to join the battle. His presence put Prentice in mind of a healer, someone like Whilte, but serving either Daven Marcus or the Inquisition directly. Before Prentice could puzzle the man out, another voice on the upper deck drew his attention.

"Where is Cyprian?" demanded Lady Penelope, pushing through the mixed guards around her. Her brilliantly polished armor flashed in the sunlight, and she was as glorious as the day of her failed accession. She had the Sobridge prince's longsword in hand and a visored salet on her head. For once, though, she had foregone the skirt she typically wore. Now she was in steel from head to toe.

"Your last cousin has gone the way of all male cousins in Bridgetown," Prentice told her coldly, unconcerned for her loss in the face of this treachery. The girl supposedly loved honor but now sold herself to secret actions—stealth and hostage-taking.

"You've killed my whole family, you convict bastard!" the noblewoman screamed, and the men around her growled. "I'll hang you from my gates by your balls. Face me without your magick sword and finally feel my wrath."

"Me first," Solomon shouted from beside Prentice, and soon enough the whole of the Lions who had come for the rescue were formed up beside their knight commander. The mixed enemies assembled as well, and Prentice saw Jerwahl mercenaries amongst them level their guns, while at least one hefted a clamshell bomb in his hands. For a moment, the two small forces faced each other, and despite Prentice's warning of a confused melee, it was clear that the coming combat would be a formation battle in microcosm—a narrow but open space, with two forces facing one another at weapon point. How matched were their skills and might? Would the stratagems Prentice had devised for his militiamen work in such a small number? It did not matter. The Lions had no choice but to win. Prentice gave a sidelong glance down to the lower platform and caught a glimpse of Agatha, flying sure-footed on the wet timbers, tackling the boatman just as he loosed the barge's bowline. A single trail of blood sprayed from the back of the man's leg as she ducked low, passing him and kicking out the injured limb so that he tumbled into the river. Then she was heading on, and Prentice knew that meant she would be forced to face Bluebird by herself. That was not a fight he would wish on anyone. He turned back to the men ahead of him, thinking to force his way through and down to the barge by the ladder the religious enemy had just used to come up.

"Lay on!" he shouted and flipped down his visor, lifting his halberd. Apparently thinking he was accepting her challenge, Penelope did the same and started forward at a run, catching those behind her a fraction unready. The White Lions, however, were one pride, and they advanced reflexively at their knight commander's order. Lady Penelope aimed herself at Prentice, only to be confronted by the Claws in a hedge. Even as she tried to hack her way through the polearm points, Solomon stepped in between, as he had no doubt been planning to from the beginning. He put his round shield in her path, and absorbing the blows of her sword, turned her to one side so Lions could push past while he drove her into a nearly single combat at the jetty's far side.

Gunfire ripped up and down the jetty as the two forces closed in an instant—the Lions utterly resolved, their enemies with nowhere to flee. A grenade was thrown, but it must have bounced badly for it was halfway to the river on the left side before it detonated. Even so, the force shook the boards and knocked many off their feet. One man fell to the water with a cry, and Prentice had no way to know if it was friend or foe. The press was tight, but it was nothing like the one-sided affair of his battle from the cathedral. With militiamen at his back, he felt free to simply exploit openings, fighting his way through and leaving enemies behind for others to deal with. Trusting to his allies, it seemed like only moments before he burst through to the far end of the jetty, finding it empty except for the lone religious figure in his robe.

"Stand aside, brother," Prentice told the man. "I will not harm you if I do not have to."

"Well do you call me *brother*," the figure declared in an unexpectedly recognizable voice, throwing back his hood to reveal a head of close-cropped pale blonde hair. "But you will not harm me. I am your doom heretic."

Prentice gasped in horror, lifting his visor to discover if somehow what he was seeing was not really there.

"Pallas?" he asked unthinkingly. The religious figure seemed thinner than he remembered his brother—cheeks drawn, dark circles around the eyes—but it was clearly Prentice's youngest sibling. As if it had been a child's puzzle, thrown into the air and impossibly landing in exactly the right places to reveal the picture, Prentice suddenly realized what the clues he had never understood had actually pointed to all winter. Bluebird's skin thieves had dangled images of his father and his older brother Xavoer in front of him as misdirection while they prepared Pallas. What had the shapeshifter said in the cathedral? They had learned so much from Inxyphos and from Prentice's brother. The knight commander had assumed it had meant Xavoer, revealing whatever family secrets had been necessary to empower their written spells. But now he connected those words to the chains they had put upon him and to the similar chains in the Bell's Hummock abbey—fresh chains that had been so wrenched at that one had been torn from the bricks, no doubt by a mighty force, while ghostly groans were heard in the night and rituals of blood were conducted in front of a golden bear.

"Brother, no, your soul," Prentice whispered, feeling a moment's compassion for young Pallas as the Inquisitorial devotee stripped off his cassock and stood naked on the boards in the late afternoon sun. Then, the sound that had made the rich islanders fear ghosts in their building arose from Pallas's throat—a roar that no human mouth should ever have been able to utter. In short order, his limbs began to stretch and amber fur broke out thick on his skin as his flesh acquired muscle upon muscle. In moments, the last and truest *brakkis effar* bear of Bridgetown had risen to such height and mass that he towered over Prentice, and he roared again through a snout full of murderous fangs. In that moment, the Knight Commander of the Western Reach, founder of the Lions and the Gryphons, resolved to burn the Inquisition in every hole it hid. He would not rest until every last vile finger of the Silent Hand was cut off. No one, no family, no land should have to suffer again as his had. But first, Prentice had to survive the next few breaths.

And me without my "magick" sword, he thought, wondering if Samson had ever thought the jawbone of an ass too weak a weapon to fight impossible odds.

CHAPTER 84

Prentice gave his brother several quick strikes, aiming for the muzzle, the belly, a paw, and never the same location twice. He hoped to keep the *brakkis effar* off balance. None of the blows seemed to do much good, though, and it felt as if Pallas was toying with him. There was less madness in this bear man's eyes, Prentice thought, and the transformation was so much more natural and complete seeming. When Inxyphos had taken his beast form, the former Inquisition knight had been misshapen, as if the rough drawing that had inspired his animalism had imposed an equally rough appearance. Perhaps it had only taken the beautiful golden bear on the wall of Vespers Remembered to inspire this more complete embodiment of a dire animal.

More than that, Prentice told himself as he stepped back out of the swing of one mighty paw. It was not as swift as it should have been, so either his brother was taking his time, or perhaps this was the first moment Pallas had been fully free in this new shape, and he might simply have been experimenting with the limits. He was clearly less wild than Inxyphos, and Bluebird had had him chained during the ritual, likely to give him a longer time to accustom himself to the power.

The ritual?

That thought revealed more threads of the tapestry, and Prentice's heart clenched a little tighter. *Brakkis effar* were made with the blood of the devoted and loyal, built on commitments of love and hate. The skin thief had wanted to use the archduchess's blood and Prentice's devotion to her to bind him as a dragon man. What loyal or loving blood had been shed to empower Pallas's ritual? Wilforn was the obvious first answer, but suddenly Prentice knew exactly how his father, and perhaps even his older brother as well, had perished.

Another swipe of the brutal paw drew Prentice's mind fully into the combat once more, and he deflected it with a sweep of his halberd. He would have reversed the defensive maneuver to strike his brother's face, but it was impossible. The force of the animal blow was too great, and rather than Prentice pushing the limb out of the way, he was himself knocked backward, the impact shuddering through his hands such that he was almost certain the wooden pole was cracked. It might be sound for one more hit, but he did not like its chances. In the back of his mind, he knew that every moment this fraternal battle went on was another where Lady Agatha was forced to face Bluebird alone. Nonetheless, he was pushed into retreat as Pallas followed up with claw after claw, and once he even snapped with those mighty jaws, fangs scraping over Prentice's spaulder-protected shoulder. The weight of it drove him to one knee, but the steel held, and he managed to lay his halberd's axe blade against Pallas's hairy side as he staggered back even farther, barely regaining his feet in time. The weapon's edge seemed to do little more than trim the fur, though the impact jarred Prentice's hands again, as if he had planted the axe into the wood of the jetty pylons.

Behind the two brothers' combat, the rest of No Prince's Pier was finding its own battle winding swiftly down. Later, they would learn from prisoners that Bluebird had not warned even one of them that Pallas might become what he had, so when the roaring transformation occurred it unnerved the Usurper's forces. White Lions were completely familiar with fighting beast-men, however, and that, coupled with the fact that their opponents in this fight were such a mongrel mix of factions, meant that their discipline and strategy quickly decided the conflict. Thus, as they began to take full control of the pier, several of the Roar found themselves free to aid their leader. Two Roarsmen shot Pallas directly, hitting the mighty mass and successfully drawing blood. The bear man reared once again and bellowed back at them. Prentice could hear the jetty's boards groaning under the weight. He thrust hard, hoping to make enough of a gap to slip by his brother. His first aim was still to reach the archduchess in the boat and stop Bluebird casting off. His thrust was only partially effective, however, and Pallas drove him back with another snap of his jaws.

And I thought Inxyphos had been strong, Prentice jested inwardly, remembering the blow he had taken from the previous bear man, strong enough to ruin his brigandine and almost crush his chest beneath. So far, his new plate was proving superior to his previous armor. *I must congratulate Turley's armor smith on the quality of his work.*

But first, he had to survive this fight.

Pallas came on again, and all sense of restraint was gone now. Prentice took a storm of hammering blows, barely able to hold himself on his feet as the paws struck steel and the claws scraped over it. While gunshots popped and bullets bit at the beast, Prentice would later learn that the thing that had saved him from the punishing, overwhelming assault was the last Jerwahl mercenary on the pier, the grenadier. Dropping his final lit bomb as he was run through by one of the Fangs, the weapon detonated beside the man's body, ending the melee and splitting the jetty's boards apart. Prentice was thrown backwards into the water, his now fully enraged brother reaching for him with both forepaws, fearless of his own safety. They tumbled for a seemingly endless instant and then struck the river with a splash. Clad in steel, Prentice plunged downward as if the water was not even there. He remembered his fall into the river in the far west, clutching the mystically inscribed iron. That had weighed far less than his plate armor overall, but holding onto it had been awkward and took away a hand for swimming. The steel he was now wearing had its weight distributed over his limbs and body, and he had both arms free. Also, he was far from the weakened man who had been blown into the river the night of the invasion, needing to be fetched up from the depths by rescuing hands. He immediately worked to right himself under the water and look for the surface, knowing he had moments before he ran out of breath. How deep was the river here?

As he clawed toward the light above, wishing he could easily remove his helmet but knowing it would take too much of his precious time, he could hear dark sounds through the water in his ears, like the thunder of rapids but pulsing and confused. It might have been the crash of the surf if they had not been hundreds of leagues from any ocean. Then he realized what it must be. Pallas was thrashing at the water, possibly still seeking him out, and while Prentice was no woodsman, he knew enough to know that bears were good swimmers. That spurred Prentice on, and a moment later his head broke through the water. Turning about clumsily in his helmet and armor while he fought with his whole strength to tread water, he looked for the nearest thing he might cling to for support. In his youth at Ashfield, he had been taught how to swim in armor, and while the final test had been a river crossing without aid, his instructors had always been insistent that the first thing to do was find a boat, a log, anything with buoyancy to aid in keeping afloat. Prentice had been adept in the skill and exertion, but that was close to twenty years ago now. He was sure he had only moments before he went under again when he turned about and his hand fell on stable, floating wood. At first, he thought it must be a boat, perhaps even the edge of Bluebird's barge, but a breath later he realized it was the lower deck of the pier, dislodged by the explosion and now swinging free in the current by the one landward end chain. With a groaning effort, he hauled himself out of the water, rolling over the boards and turning in the direction of his brother's furious bellows, wary of the danger.

He soon found he was safer than expected, however. Whether Pallas's bear form inherited its namesake's talent for swimming or not, continuous stinging fire from the Roar on the jetty and, unexpectedly, the general dockside, was keeping the bear man from taking to the water with any peace. The final clamshell bomb must surely have slain most, if not all, of the Roar who had come from Paramour's, but it looked as if others had arrived from some other direction—reinforcements from Loncastel. At least two other militiamen were spluttering and beating at the water, having been knocked from the pier in the explosion but not yet dead. Prentice wanted to help them, but he had another duty, and with one eye still watchful in case his brother became a threat again, he scanned the water for the barge. It took a moment with the bounce of the floating deck on the choppy surface, but eventually he sighted the craft, fifty paces off and gaining way, a grey-haired figure poling the vessel forward with the skill of a born riverman.

"Damn them!" Prentice spat, and he pushed himself up uncomfortably to his hands and knees, muscles now certainly aching from the day's exertions. Oddly mundane amidst so many other events and sensations, his stomach grumbled for its emptiness, as well. Was it only this morning that he had ridden out to assault Town Sobridge? His predawn breakfast seemed so long ago.

"Might I crave your assistance, My Lord?" a quiet feminine voice asked him, and Prentice turned to see Agatha clinging to the side of the deck. He moved over to her on hands and knees, not confident enough yet to stand on the rocking timbers.

"Are you injured?" he asked as he reached out a hand.

"Some," she explained, accepting his aid, "but the main problem's my skirt. I thought to get it off when I tumbled, but my dagger got caught before I could cut the dashed thing away, and now it's wrapped round my feet. It'd be draggin' me down if not for this deck."

Prentice hauled the Lace Fang from the water, who emerged all but naked from the waist down, with only her clout to cover her dignity, and her skirt exactly as she described, twisted about her ankles. Once she was safe on the boards, he turned away from her while she hacked the soaked and damaged garment finally free. It was a naively chivalrous gesture since there were dozens of men-at-arms now crowded on the riverside who would be seeing what he chose to hide his eyes from, but he did it all the same.

"You can look now, My Lord," she said, and he turned back to discover that she had wrapped the skirt's remains around her waist like a towel, leaving her lower legs bare but at least going some small distance towards modesty. "Thank you."

Prentice nodded once, but he turned his eyes downriver toward his brother, who was now floating away, it seemed, neither fighting the flow nor seeking to rejoin Bluebird. The minstrel's barge was already drawing even with Loncastel's eastern headland, and he was clearly steering for the middle of the channel in case any Roar on the north island might take a snapshot. Breathing heavily, Prentice felt his shoulders sag. There was no hope of stopping the barge now.

"Damn, he cut me but good," Agatha said, and now that she was out of the river, watery blood was flowing out of a slash in the side of her bodice. Prentice finally removed his helmet and placed it on the deck, then looked to her injury.

"May I?"

She nodded, and he examined the wound through the damaged piece of clothing. It was clear it pained her, but it did not look too deep. Best the young woman be given to a healer's care swiftly or the filthy water of the riverside would be sure to give her an infection. It occurred to Prentice that he almost certainly had his share of risky cuts as well.

"It is not bad," he reassured her as he sat back on his ankles. "The water makes the blood flow more readily. It looks worse than it is."

"Mongrel wanted my kidney, I'll wager," the girl said, and her face contorted in pain as she felt the injury for herself. "Baroness Righteous and Lady Spindle always said the old fellow was uncanny fast, but I could hardly believe it. I was sure I had him, and he just made a dance of it. Even with that limp."

The limp was the result of his wife and Lady Spindle's previous encounter with Bluebird, and Prentice smirked to think it was becoming a permanent feature of the vile man's life.

"If he wanted a thrust to your side like you say, you did well to restrict him to just that cut," he observed. "Did you manage to lay an edge on him for yourself?"

"Don't think so, My Lord," Agatha said remorsefully. "It was fast as anything I ever done with a blade, and I was in the river almost straight after he tagged me. I know he had the stern line free before I even got to him, so I figure he went easy on me, fixing on getting away more than having a fight."

"Did you see her grace or Lady Dalflitch?" Prentice asked, her but she shook her head, even more downcast.

"Sorry, but no, My Lord. But sure, he must have had them, the way he rabbited like that."

"I fear so, My Lady."

Prentice let out another heavy breath and then sat down to rest his arms on his knees. Shouts came from the shoreline, and a short while later the lone restraining chain creaked as a team of militiamen hauled the deck in to shore. Prentice helped Agatha up into helpful hands first and then followed on himself, accepting aid to bring him onto the jetty after passing off his helmet for someone to take. Relieved faces greeted him, but he had no time for congratulations or post-battle celebrations.

"How many are lost?" he asked first, and while the number was more than he would ever have liked, it was not so dire as he feared. He tried not to be especially relieved, but he was when he learned that Solomon had been one of the survivors.

"Had the baroness-lady down to grappling, My Lord," the young Fang reported when Prentice sought him out. The baroness-elect was being carried away on a stretcher improvised from two halberds and a cloak, injured but alive, and under guard by Prentice's order. "We were wrestling on the deck, and my shield was becoming a mongrel to handle, when that bomb went off and the thing blessed us both. It was sitting right against the deck so the fragments that might have torn our heads off bit into the shield."

Solomon hefted up the protective disc and there were two or three obvious pieces of shattered iron embedded in the steel. Prentice thought the youth's assessment was likely correct. Any of those shards might have been fatal if they had hit a face or throat.

"I come off fine, My Lord, save for the ringing in my ears," Solomon continued, "but the Bridgetown lady, she got a big whack of something in her foot or ankle. Whatever it was, thing tore the back off her vambrace and broke her foot. That took the fight right out of her and then I had her prisoner. I kenned you'd want her captured for trial."

"Excellent work, militiaman," Prentice told his adoptive son and clapped him affectionately on the shoulder. Solomon responded by saluting. That gave Prentice another small reason to smile in the midst of this long and terrible day full of victories and defeats.

"Get you back to your cohort," he told Solomon. "And be ready because our day is not over yet. I am heading to Loncastel, as will almost all the White Lions. They have our liege, and that only means that the next part is going to be devilish complicated."

"We can handle devilish, My Lord."

Prentice smiled again as Solomon accepted his dismissal and left. The knight commander allowed himself one last look downriver at where his brother was now out of sight. Perhaps he had died by Roarshot and his transformed flesh was sinking to the riverbed or being washed to the distant ocean. The White Lions could indeed handle devilish.

But just how much more devilish can they make it for us? he wondered.

CHAPTER 85

"Knight captain's down the east o' the island, My Lord, lookin' to the gun spot that's shootin' downriver. It'll take him a little while to make it back here," Knight Banner Sergeant Markas of the Lion Company reported to Prentice as they stood looking out a rear window on the upper floor of the Dog's Leg Tavern. At one time, the wood-shuttered portals had existed to allow cool air or some daylight into the taphouse's private upper room. The only thing for the windows to show then had been the rear wall of a warehouse and a tiny muddy yard. The warehouse was gone now, consumed by Dragon shots and fire, as were the buildings that had flanked it for hundreds of paces in either direction. After the long winter of the Bronze Dragons' hammering Loncastel Island, it was now possible to stand at this window and see all the way to the island's western end and almost all the way east to the remains of the bridge to Norgate. From the docklands back, the stone balls of the Usurper's cannons had hammered one side of the island to rubble. Standing looking through the glassless windows, panes long since shattered by flying debris, Prentice watched the Dragons continue their destruction, emplacements belching smoke and fire with each booming shot. Given the range and extent of their power, the place where he and Markas were standing would not be safe once those gunners decided to aim for the tavern, even so far back from the north side. Daven Marcus was finally getting the chance to play with his favorite toys the way he had always wanted, smashing an enemy to dust. It was clear his gunners were also enjoying the unseasonable sunshine, exploiting the opportunity to aim clearly and move powder freely, despite the fact that they still had friendly raiders fighting in some of the locations they were targeting.

"How many cannons do we still have in the fight?" Prentice asked the standard bearer.

"Three, if we include the one the knight captain fetched up from Sougate this morn," said Markas. "He wanted to get it in place on top o' the keep, but it were intercepted by some o' them pirate fellows and he took a pair o' cohorts to the rescue. Then word come of a raid on the last gun facin' east, and after throwin' 'em back, he had to reset the whole thing for shootin' again. He's been at this fight since afore dawn. Could be this is the last o' what we do to hold this island, My Lord."

Prentice looked askance at Markas. The man was no coward and not given to defeatism, which only made his pessimistic assessment the more telling. It was there in his exhausted face, with dark smudges under his eyes and days' worth of dirt caking his cheeks. Just as the battle for Loncastel had ground the docklands to rubble, so it was wearing away the Lion Banner Company as well.

"The knight captain is to be commended that he has lost as few of our lives as he has," Prentice said, looking back out the window at the island of ruin. It seemed to him as if it could take a century or more for Loncastel to recover from this siege, if it ever did. Any superstitious folk would surely wonder how many hordes of ghosts were lingering in this graveyard.

"I will take that as a compliment, Knight Commander, but I will have the heart to accept it only if the news I have been given is false," Farringdon said from the door, and Prentice glanced to see that the marquis had arrived. Prentice turned back to the window, not wanting to look the young nobleman in the face. He had to have this conversation, but in the short time it had taken to summon Farringdon from the battlefront, he had not been able to formulate the words for it.

"The news is true, My Lord," he said simply. All words would be inadequate, so he opted for less over more.

"My wife...?" Farringdon asked, his voice weakening a little with the fear he was clearly working to hold in check.

"Taken, along with Lady Dalflitch," Prentice explained. The days might have turned sunny, but the spring was not yet quite upon them, and sundown would be soon. He had no time for anything other than directness. "The Lace Fangs sold themselves dearly, but they were overwhelmed."

Farringdon nodded.

"And your children?" he asked.

Prentice turned upon him in shock. Seeing the threatening despair in the marquis-consort's eyes, Prentice felt tears suddenly well in his own. The man's wife and unborn child were in the clutches of a mad tyrant, and he took this moment to enquire after the well-being of Prentice's family? It touched Prentice to his core.

"They live, hidden, by our liege lady's command," he said, feeling a lump form in his throat before he could resettle his emotions. He swallowed hard.

"That is some good news at least, My Lord," Farringdon said, and while Prentice was certain he had to force himself to it, there was no doubt the man was sincere. Prentice reached out and took Farringdon by the upper arm as a man might with his younger brother, looking him directly in the eye.

"She lives," he told Farringdon earnestly. "The plot is to use her as a hostage to force our surrender."

"I assumed as much," the knight captain answered. He turned his head to the window. "Daven Marcus can hammer Loncastel down to the waterline, but he still has no way to bring a significant force across the river, not now that we've thrown his boats back a second time. We captured over a dozen big craft on the west just this morning, including my two bridge barges."

"That is good news," Prentice said, but before he could explain why, Farringdon's nerve finally cracked, and he whirled at his superior officer.

"Is it, Prentice? Is that good news? Good enough to overcome the fact that my dearest loves are in the hands of that monster? I know how hostage-taking works. Do you think the Usurper of the Denay throne, regicide and patricide, will treat my wife and child with honor, even if he means to barter them for our capitulation? He could offer her back to me and only deliver after he's taken her eyes, her hands, her feet and the babe from her womb. Do you doubt he plots exactly that or some similar monstrosity? I lost my father to unspeakable flames. I...I..."

Prentice let the rage come out of his friend.

"She lives," Prentice said to him quietly once more, "and has been across the river no more than an hour of the candle. Whatever else he plots, Daven Marcus will cherish the opportunity to gloat. His cruelty is limitless, but it is not without patience. Likely he is mistreating her, but nothing the Lioness Mother has not endured before. Do not let fear or despair claim you yet."

Farringdon's expression was bewildered, but Prentice had to admit he was impressed at how quickly the young former prince was regaining his self-possession.

"What hope do I have to hold despair at bay?" he asked, with a tone that said he was desperate to be persuaded back from the brink before he tumbled into the black abyss that was opening before him.

"I have called the Gryphon back from Town Sobridge," Prentice explained. "They will be here within the hour—the entire banner, less a detachment I have left with Sergeant Porth to fulfill our obligations to the town's yeomen."

"You took the princedom in a day?" Farringdon asked, his misery tinged with a shade of wonderment.

"Aided by Everard's murderous ineptitude," Prentice said with a nod. "Our enemies also plotted to shut us across the river by blowing up the Sougate bridge, but they made a hash of it."

"A right dog's breakfast, by the word, My Lord," Markas added enthusiastically. "Scorched the boards and that's all. Thing's still as sound as bedrock."

The knight banner sergeant grinned. News of the utterly failed plot to destroy the bridge had spread rapidly through the Lion Banner reserves gathered in the streets around the Dog's Leg and had become a source of rare mirth. Farringdon nodded, accepting these pieces of news, and Prentice could see him weaving the threads in his thoughts.

"So, you mean to march out to face them?" Farringdon asked and cast another glance at the ruins, the river, and the colossal cannon emplacements beyond.

Another stone flew through the air and struck hard somewhere east. Agonized cries arose, accompanied by shouts for aid and summoning healers. That, at least, they would soon have. The promised healers were marching with the Gryphon. Prentice had sent an insistent word that they must be dispatched when he summoned back his banner company. The healers would accompany them, or he would loot the town and abandon it to whatever Veckander lord thought himself strong enough to hold it. It was a harsh word, but the Reach's need was too acute.

"You want to leave her in his grip overnight?" Farringdon asked, his despair clearly turning towards anger.

"I want to bring those barges down and have them in place within the next half hour," Prentice contradicted him. "As soon as they are there, the Lion Banner will march out to commence the fight, and the Gryphon will march straight through the town, right up Great Bridge Road, and out behind us to reinforce. I mean to interrupt Daven Marcus' gloating before his scribes even put ink to parchment to pen his demand for our surrender."

Prentice intended every word, and it was clear Farringdon believed him, but the candle flame of hope it lit in his eyes was swiftly overwhelmed by his awareness of the realities of the strategic situation.

"We cannot bring the barges in the light, Prentice," he said. "The Dragons will destroy them. Look at the clear air. They will sight them easily and likely make matchwood before we even reach the bridge. Or do you mean to sweep them around one of the southern channels? Surely, we can't do that by sundown."

Now that the Heron army was dismissed and Daven Marcus's river fleet had wasted more strength in a second set of raids, it would have been feasible to bring Farringdon's makeshift bridge pieces the long way round, safely out of sight of the Bronze Dragons almost the whole way. But the knight captain was correct; it could not be done swiftly enough to outrace the coming evening. It had been one of the myriad factors Prentice had been contemplating as he rushed from No Prince's Pier to Loncastel, but he had arrived to find an utterly unexpected solution. He took a rolled piece of parchment from his belt pouch and handed it to Farringdon.

"A second and better bit of good news, My Lord," he said as the knight captain looked warily at the note. He could understand Farringdon's reluctance. It was only this time yesterday that Whilte had destroyed the enspelled letter that had been the cause of so many of their maladies and burdens through the winter. "It is not that one, knight captain."

"It come by arrow 'round noon, My Lord," Markas said earnestly. "I got it a bit later, and it was what I sent to you for original like. Only the knight commander got here first."

"And I made certain to have friends watch me closely when I read it," Prentice added reassuringly. Farringdon nodded, not seeming fully mollified in his concerns but choosing to take the risk. He opened the tiny letter and read its contents swiftly. As he did, his eyes widened in astonishment.

"This is true?"

"I have no reason to doubt," Prentice told him. "The fletching on the arrow was Dahyoor's, and no one on this side of the river saw anyone shooting—all the marks of a fey message."

"Around noon? That means Sir Turley is only hours away by now."

"That is my estimate," Prentice agreed.

Farringdon nodded again, his thoughts visibly faster in his eager eyes now that he had more hope.

"It will be an all-or-nothing risk," the knight captain said at last, his face settling into grim resolve. He looked up at the sky through the window, shaking his head. "An hour at most until sunset and then a short winter's twilight."

"Our liege and lady are amidst the thorns, My Lord," Prentice said. "We have no choice but to grasp the nettle and pull them free. I have already sent word to Runners Field. Every last militiaman is on the march, and the lancers are prepared to lead the way the moment those barges are in place. I am explaining my commands to you, Knight Captain, not asking your opinion or permission."

"Grasp the nettle," Farringdon repeated, and then he slowly saluted.

Prentice knew he had no need to further explain the knight captain's role in the coming battle, and he trusted the man to hold his nerve while his wife was in such peril.

A moment later Farringdon was heading for the door but paused for one last instant, looking back over his shoulder. "Are you truly returned to us, My Lord?"

Prentice smiled and nodded. "Whilte burnt the spell paper yestereve," he explained gently. "That went a long way to clearing my head. Then..." Prentice paused a breath. How much did he want to try to explain about the skin thief and everything else that had happened since the cathedral? It could take hours when even moments would be a waste. "Then I had a sudden theological insight that shone a light on my other errors and misperceptions," he finished, knowing what a ridiculous characterization it was but amusing himself all the same. "Once our Lioness, your lady wife, is safe and well amidst her Lions and Gryphons, I will happily unfold the tale for you."

"I will hold you to that, Knight Commander Baron Ash," Farringdon told him, and a moment later he was through the door.

Another booming Dragon shot drew Prentice's attention to the window and a stone ball fell no more than twenty paces short of the Dog's Leg, the shattering stone throwing a gout of dust and fine pebbles that blew in through the open gallery.

"They've kenned somethin' leadership-like is happenin' here, I'd say, My Lord," Markas said, staring out beside Prentice through the cloud. "Mayhap they've got spotters hidden in the river's edge can make you out just."

The bannerman's symbolic noose lanyard was no longer pristine white, but as the dust in the air settled on it, its previous dirt was covered so that it was the color of powdered mortar. Markas's face was the same hue, and Prentice imagined his own visage was similar.

"We will be gone before they get their line on us, Knight Sergeant," he said. "Come what may, I intend us to be quit of the Dog's Leg for good by sundown. I am sure the taverner will be glad to see us gone."

Between having a body nailed to his taphouse's façade and now waiting for it to be demolished like the rest of the island, Prentice imagined the tavern's owner cursed the day the White Lions had come to Bridgetown. He did not blame the man, but Markas's next comment surprised him.

"I reckon I'm gonna regret that some, My Lord," he said, following after Prentice as they headed for the door themselves. "I've learned some fondness for the place and its gin."

Prentice cocked an eyebrow and Markas smirked.

"I mean it tastes like bilgewater," he told his leader, "But it kind of grows on a fellow."

"So does the pox," Prentice joked, and Markas coughed out a dusty laugh.

"Aye, that it does."

CHAPTER 86

The western sky was tinging golden toward orange and the Rampart ribbon was beginning to show more clearly in the firmament when two flat-decked square barges began poling their way down the north channel of the river, the ruined island on their right, the Usurper's mighty army on their left. Not one of the rivermen guiding the craft wanted to be there, and they would likely have cringed at every push of their poles, making the whole process slower except that it had been made clear to them how important their mission truly was. There was not a living soul on Loncastel that was not about to risk their lives just as flagrantly as these rivermen were being asked to, so the polers channeled their fear into frenetic activity and the craft moved as fast as they could make them. Though the journey itself was not too long a distance, they had to aim for tight and specific gaps between the wrecked pylons of Norgate bridge. There would be no safe chances for second bites of the apple. Everything must be perfect, and that only made the journey all the more tense.

By the time the first barge was almost in place, it was clear that the crews of the Bronze Dragons had sighted the unusual activity, and once that initial makeshift span began to slot inward to be tied off, they understood the barges' purpose. Watchers on Loncastel could just make out the crews rushing to the laborious task of recalibrating their guns for the fresh targets. The second barge was heading towards its place when it struck an unseen piece of bridge wreckage below the waterline on its front starboard corner.

It spun out of alignment, and while that was no great danger for its experienced crewmen, it was a significant delay. The rivermen shouted and cursed as they struggled to regain their approach against the flow of the river, the pressure to hurry only making the task that much more difficult. Once they had fought the awkward craft back to its destination and were ready to begin tying it off, the first redeployed Dragon was firing upon them. An awesome stone shot clipped another of the bridge's pylons farther back from the north shore, tearing off masonry before plunging into the water. That was all but no damage as far as the bridge was concerned, but as a first shot it was so close to the correct range and elevation that the cannon's crew would certainly be throwing telling attacks in short order. The makeshift bridge had perhaps less than another quarter of the candle to live. It would not see nightfall, that was certain.

Or it would have been.

Lined across the meadows from west to east, each Bronze Dragon had spent the winter ensconced in firing positions that had grown more and more secure, indentured laborers building better shelter and continually adding to the defensive earthworks. The White Lions had managed to destroy only three enemy guns across the whole siege, and now the duel of cannons was utterly one-sided. The Bronze Dragons were so secure that they may as well have been hidden behind the legendary iron-scaled sides of their namesake creatures. As such, it came as an unspeakable shock when the firing position farthest west in their line erupted in an explosion that lit the dimming sky with a column of flame. All other gunner teams hesitated, knowing that the worst possible fate had befallen their comrades. Somehow, a loose flame had lit the firing bastion's powder store. They had seen the smoke from the less effective blast on Sougate bridge earlier in the day and felt smug at their enemies' misfortune. This eruption was so much worse, and every Denay gunner paused in appreciation of the loss of brethren cannoneers. They turned their attention to exacting revenge on the already brutalized island in front of them and the over-optimistic bridge that was forming across the channel.

Then, the next Bronze Dragon's powder stores exploded, and that sent flaming wreckage trailing smoke over the blasted meadows. Gunners and their pressed yeoman work crews ran to smother any flames that came nearby while others farther to the east looked at each other in growing alarm. They had maintained perfect powder safety for the entire siege, and now in mere moments, two separate crews had fallen victim to the same misfortune. Sabotage was the most likely explanation, though each man in his royal red surcoats and gilded coat of plates was too disciplined to simply bandy the notion about, not so soon. Cannoneers handled one of the world's most dangerous substances every day. They were men of nerve and self-control. Crew captains directed their commands to look for enemies, to search the ammunition stores swiftly for any hidden flames—secretly placed wicks or fuses, or anything out of place at all. The sky was turning to purple, and the smoke plumes were already blocking out the last of the setting sun. Twilight was almost upon them. Whatever stealthy infiltrators the Reachermen had smuggled over the river had to be located.

It was then that they heard two beats, one obscuring the other as they both mingled amidst the smoke and failing light. The recognizable one echoed from Bridgetown—the beat of White Lions' drums—the Reachermen on the march. From under Loncastel Keep, the Lion Banner Company emerged in force, hundreds of lancers leading the way with their horses in twin columns.

It was horses that gave shape to the second rhythm, the drum of hoofbeats over the ground. Those of the Bronze Dragon gun crews who recognized the sound swiftly realized that the hoofs they heard were not beating out of the besieged town, however. They were echoing through the smoke from the west, and moments after that was understood, it was confirmed as wave upon wave of riders burst from the haze, and horse archers with lit fire arrows that trailed bright streaks under the darkening sky emerged from the dense cloud. A broad swathe of the meadows behind the cannons had been left open and empty to make it easier to bring ammunition resupplies and to keep the rest of the Denay army camp safe from exactly the kinds of explosions that were now befalling the Dragons. As if charging down a broad, militarized avenue, members of three *keshiyaas* of the Wind Rising fey, over four hundred riders in all, pelted westward over the open fields, flanked on one side by the cannons and on the other by the original ridge and finally the enemy tents. Fire arrows fell amongst powder stores, on the still-damp roofs of the cannons' firing shelters, and into the tents. Two days of pale sun had not been enough to dry much of their targets, but tent cloth made ready fuel, and any powder barrel or sack kept safe from the winter rain was an eager detonator.

By the time the fey assault had made their first ride along the meadow "road" behind the Bronze Dragons, five separate powder storage areas had thrown gouts of flame into the sky like erupting volcanoes. The force of the explosions shook the ground even through the vibration of hundreds of galloping ponies, but the earthworks that had protected cannons and ammunition from enemy fire now also protected the surrounding areas from the detonations. Embankments of dirt and rock absorbed much of the danger or simply threw the fire upward. After the fey reached the eastern end of the row, they ran into the emerging Lion Company Lancers, but like two schools of fish who had no interest in hunting one another, the Wind Rising simply circled around their more heavily armored allies and then turned to gallop back the way they had come. With no more lit arrows to hand, they nonetheless had quivers full enough and eyes sharp enough to hunt Denay men-at-arms individually in the twilight. They rode on the west side of the enemy camp for the rest of the battle, shooting any that tried to flee in that direction but keeping otherwise out of the way to not target Reachermen in the confusion.

"Looks like we will need no torches for the next hour at least," Prentice said to himself from the saddle as he watched the fires light up the Usurper's camp.

Dusty had been fetched for him from Runners Field, and the lancers who performed that task were incensed when they learned of Boots's fate. Not one man-at-arms would have shirked their duty to end a wounded mount's suffering, but the blunt slaughter of a loyal beast was tantamount to murder in their eyes.

Prentice was alone at the north end of the bridge for a moment while the Lion Company formed up to confront whatever defense the Denay trumpets were summoning. After the fey had opened the assault and then ridden away, it was determined that the Bronze Dragon farthest to the east had not been disabled or much troubled by fire, evidenced by the fact that the disciplined crew had attempted to keep up their targeting of the bridge. Farringdon had led the lancers away to finish that last monster personally. A short while later, a fresh drumbeat resounded from Loncastel, and behind the knight commander the bridge boards began to thump under hundreds and then thousands of footfalls.

"Not too late for the dance are we, My Lord?" Sergeant Guillam shouted as he drew near, leading the Gryphon Banner's first cohorts to join the battle.

"Your second dance of the day, Sergeant," Prentice called back. "And long walks in between. I think we can forgive a little tardiness."

"Too kind, My Lord. What's yer orders?"

"Have you sergeants split the remainders by thirds?" Prentice asked him, wanting to confirm that the commands he had sent by runner to summon his company had been obeyed before he started to deploy them. His orders had been for each sergeant to take ten cohorts under their individual command, one thousand militiamen each. Porth was to be left a thousand to secure Town Sobridge against any kind of swift capture by someone like the Earl of Longshepherds. The remaining three or so thousand were thus split in thirds between Guillam, Knight Sergeant Gennet, and Sergeant Kate.

"Did you order us to, or didn't you?" Guillam retorted, as if the notion of disobedience or any other failure to obey orders was unthinkable.

"More than officers present, Sergeant! Mind your tongue!" Prentice rebuked him. Guillam saluted, but his cheeky smile did not dim for an instant. Prentice had more pressing concerns. He pointed north toward the battle's front. "Get your ten in behind Sedgewick's lot on the other side of those gun bastions and be ready to put them wherever he tells you. After that, look to the lay of the land and kill or capture any Denay man you find, armed or not."

"That we can do, My Lord," Guillam shouted and continued to march with his contingent into the flame-lit evening. "Isn't that right, lads and maids?"

That raised a cheer from the nearest column, and the shouts progressed backwards over the bridge. Prentice idly wondered a moment how many of Guillam's thousand might actually be women. Sootface Kate was perfect evidence that in all likelihood some others were quietly in amongst the ranks, making no noise of their unusual role, but it was surely not too many. All the same, that was a contemplation for another time, and he watched the arriving Gryphons march to the fight with resolute steps. It pleased him to see their courage and strength, even at the end of such a demanding day. When Gennet arrived with his thousand, Prentice directed him to the east to secure the battle's right flank behind Farringdon's lancers and to intercept any enemies that might still be aboard the Usurper's fleet downriver, thinking to come ashore.

"If the ground is clear and you can keep touch with the rest of us, look to seize Lazy Farmers," he told the knight sergeant, "but take care in the dark. Do not risk leaving yourself open to being encircled."

Gennet accepted his orders, and when his ten cohorts had marched past, Sergeant Sootface tromped up, matchlock on her shoulder and firing pole in her other hand like a walking staff.

"Different duty for your cohorts, Kate," Prentice told her. "We need enemy powder secured, guns too if they have survived our fey friends' ambush. Steer you safely clear of any spots that are burning, but whatever powder is unscathed is ours now. Set Roarsmen to the plunder. They know the risks. Your Fangs and Claws are to be your sentries and to take any prisoners they find. Keep weather eyes out, especially if any of those bearskin helmet fellows from Jerwahl are lurking. The kingslayer will set them to trouble us if he has any more of them left in his hire."

"I hope he does, My Lord," she shouted at him over the rising din of battle and the roar of the flames. "I got a bone to pick with them 'fellows.'"

"Cannons and powder for tonight, Sergeant Sootface," Prentice emphasized with a warning tone. "And keep everyone back from the west end of the field. The fey are down that way, and even their eyes will struggle to pick Reacher from Denay in this morass."

Dahyoor's note had said that the moment the banners were ready to attack, day or night, the *keshiyaas* would ride and do what they had done and then secure the left wing of the field. More than that the tiny piece of paper had not contained. Perhaps Prentice's caution was unwarranted, but with no more than that to plan by, this was his decision. As Sergeant Kate's thousand moved to their duties, her impressive voice shouting instructions and warnings about the dangers of black powder, Prentice spurred Dusty up the trampled Great North Road to join the battle and be ready to respond as the chaotic situation continued to unfold. Somewhere in this hellish insanity of death, fire, and steel were Archduchess Amelia and Lady Dalflitch. Every moment the clash continued was another in which they could be wounded or killed.

Fast action and decisive, Prentice thought, knowing that nothing less would suffice now.

CHAPTER 87

"Fled again?" Farringdon exclaimed bitterly. His voice was hoarse from hours of shouting commands. He tipped a wineskin up and swallowed heavily. Having removed his helmet, his face showed itself to be filthy with blood and dirt. In the firelight, he looked halfway from mortal to monster, even for men-at-arms who had faced *brakkis effar* in their time. Prentice looked from the marquis-consort to the prisoner who was being held upright by two Claws. Dressed in the tabard of a royal steward, the deep red and gold cloth torn and soot-stained, the captured man also sported a swollen wrist that was surely broken. Prentice had ordered the militiamen who had taken the steward prisoner to be gentle with the wound but had not yet allowed him the mercy of a healer's attention. One would be called, but only after Farringdon had learned the situation. Standing now in one of the captured enemy tents, the knight commander bid the enemy servant to repeat his story.

"An odd fellow, he was," the steward began, clearly working to seem earnest and cooperative, but wincing and hissing with pain between sentences. "Come right up from the stone pier in the east and told me to fetch him to the king. Just like that. I nearly cuffed the doddery fool for a cur, but somehow I found I had to do what he said."

Prentice had already heard this tale, but he still snorted a taut laugh at Bluebird being described as "doddery." Even with his limp there were few men half the minstrel's age who would be as adroit or sharp-minded. Whatever else the Bluebird's flaws, doddering was not one of them.

"So where is he? And the women who were with him?"

"The women, yes…" the steward trailed away, his head hanging so that his pudding-bowl hair fell over his eyes. It looked as if his pain had overwhelmed him and he was sinking into unconsciousness, but Prentice had already seen this the first time through the tale and knew what it was now.

"A spell from Bluebird," he told Farringdon, who looked ready to draw his sword and kill the prisoner in his impatience. "He cannot remember her grace or Lady Dalflitch. The very thought puts him into a slumber."

"Then how do we find out what happened to them?" Farringdon demanded. After long hours of night battle, the desperate husband's nerves were plainly too frayed to concern himself with niceties like polite speech.

Prentice begrudged him none of it. "We find out the same way we tried to track the lost learning. If we cannot find the trees, we can find the parts of the forest they set burning to hide them."

Prentice stepped to the prisoner, standing head down with his wounded arm still cupped defensively in the other hand. "Where did Daven Marcus go?" he asked softly, leaning close to the man's ear. Even so, the steward started awake as if by a trumpet's blast, and that was followed immediately by an agonized groan. He hugged his wounded hand to his chest and whimpered in pain. "You want that seen to?" Prentice asked him sternly. "Finish your tale."

"The king, he left, almost as soon as the old fellow met with him. There was some acrimony to it, I thought. Bold of some dotard to show such affront to his majesty like that, but the king was…er…merciful. He…he always is, of course."

That last insistence made Prentice think that the steward was in the habit of protecting Daven Marcus's reputation. Knowing the tyrant's predilections from too many sources, he imagined that most of the kingslayer's household staff had to maintain a kind of two-minded opinion of their master or else be the next to suffer his attentions. How many other servants had this steward seen tortured or abused by the Usurper of Denay?

"Left to go where?" Farringdon demanded.

"North, My Lord. I was told aught else."

"North? What help is that to us? The entire of the Grand Kingdom is north of here."

"He did not go back downriver by boat," Prentice reassured his second-in-command, "and by the rest of this fellow's report you will find that Bluebird did not expect the sudden flight. Daven Marcus had no horse for *him*. I think our friend from the Inquisition expected the Usurper to use his hostages the way we imagined and was caught wrong-footed to learn Daven Marcus had another plan."

He turned to the prisoner again. "Tell him when they left."

"His majesty was in his saddle just as the first plume of fire went up in the west. He rode with his chosen hundred and a carriage, giving orders for the rest of the army to stay and throw any rebels back into the river." The timid servant quailed a little, as if realizing his captors might take offense. "His words, my lords. Rebels was his majesty's words."

Farringdon clenched the wineskin in his grip, and for a moment Prentice expected him to hit the prisoner with it. Then the marquis-consort released a long sighing breath.

"Is that all?" he demanded.

Prentice nodded slowly, and the steward did the same with far greater rapidity. Tears were now glistening on the man's cheeks, and a moment later, Farringdon sneered at him in disgust.

"Oh, get him to a healer, for God's sake," he commanded the two militiamen holding the prisoner, and Prentice gave them a nod to confirm the order. A moment later he and Farringdon were alone in the tent.

"He was in the camp at the start of the battle, and he has taken them by carriage," Prentice said quietly. "That's why the rest of his army have spent the last hours fighting that withdrawal up the

North Road. They are buying their liege time to make his retreat, and damn them for their courage, they have done a fine job of it."

Although the early surprise had rendered the Bronze Dragons insignificant to the battle, the rest of the fight had been a long, slow grind, with Daven Marcus's army making a creditable fighting retreat for hours. Once the full night's darkness had come upon them, there had been no space for complicated maneuvers that might have made the battle swift or decisive.

"Where has he taken her then? Denay?" Farringdon asked, shaking his head against the fears that must surely have been dominating his thoughts. Prentice knew what that felt like—had known it for the whole of winter—but he had had enough of listening to the wolfpack's howls crying despair in the night. His feet were set to the race now. Somewhere ahead was the finish line, where Daven Marcus and the monster Sanguine in his pit waited to be put down like the hounds they were.

"Denay seems most likely," Prentice agreed, though he had some other suspicions.

"Why? To put her on trial?"

Again, that seemed a true possibility to Prentice. He and Farringdon were thinking alike, and that made him hope that he would be able to persuade the Marquis-consort to agree to his plan when he broached it. In this matter, he did not want to have to give the knight captain a direct command. He would if he was forced, but he would prefer not.

"He might want a trial, right in the midst of the Denay court, like rebels of old," Prentice conceded. "Or he might simply wish for time and safety in which to torment them. I know that is not what you want to hear, but it seems likely, and in truth, the two would easily overlap."

Farringdon growled and then took another rough swig from the wineskin. Prentice let him take the moment. When the skin was drained, the knight captain tossed it aside.

"I assume you have a plan, Prentice?" he said at last, his jaw clenched. He stared at the knight commander through lidded eyes, like an enraged beast. This vile war brought such emotions out of even the gentlest man, it seemed.

Prentice nodded solemnly. "Wherever he is going, I have no intention of allowing him to get there. Before dawn, I will ride with the Wind Rising and we will run him down."

"I will bring the lancers with you," Farringdon insisted, but Prentice shook his head.

"The lancers are needed here and are nowhere near as swift or as enduring as the fey in any case, My Lord. You know this. The Denay army is still a barricade across the path, protecting their escaping king. Someone must command the army here, keeping up the pressure so they cannot easily rally. I will have to ride with the fey westerly around them, through woods and farm villages. No straight road to catch up by."

"So, give the fey to me and I will lead the hunt while you command the battle. You're the better leader by far, in any case."

"No," Prentice said flatly, and Farringdon started towards him as if to hit his commander, but before anything happened, the Baron of Fallenhill made the incontrovertible objection. "The fey will not follow you."

"They'll follow me if you tell them to..." Farringdon snapped, but his eyes showed that he could see the truth of Prentice's point. Finally, fury melted and tears gently welled forth. His tone became one of heartbreak and pleading. "You cannot ask this of me, Prentice. She is my wife, my beloved. I *have* to ride for her. What would you do if it was Righteous? Or Gant, or Amy?"

"I would do what was best to see them saved, not simply throw myself at the nearest road in blind hopes I picked the right one," Prentice counseled his knight captain. He wasn't sure it wasn't a lie. Nonetheless, this was why armies needed discipline and professionalism, so that fool decisions were set aside for successful tactics. "Do you think I will spend one breath less or shed one less drop of my blood for her than you?"

"She is not your wife, Prentice!" Farringdon shouted.

"No, she is not. She is my liege lady, and my life is sworn to her, along with my honor and the service of my entire family line. I have never held any of it back from her, not even when the mongrels laid spells and snares around my very thoughts." Prentice let his own fury show through in his expression, the unyielding emotion that would let him fight through any number of enemies to victory, to triumph, or to death.

The two men stared at one another through the dim torchlight, and Prentice could feel the pact forming unspoken between them. His feet were to the race but not his alone, not any longer. The White Lions, the entire of the Western Reach were committed now, and woe betide the Grand Kingdom if it clung to its kingslayer king.

"You will leave directly?" Farringdon asked.

"Shortly, and surely by dawn," Prentice told him. "I need to gather some supplies and attend to a handful of other brief things. An hour will not tell in this race, not once we have the Wind Rising in the saddle."

"I thought the fey were always in the saddle," Farringdon jested weakly, and Prentice acknowledged the truth of that with a shrug.

"Regardless, set yourself to arranging the army. Let the cohorts rest some now and gather supplies. If you are on the road by noon tomorrow, that will be good time for an early spring march. Sack Bridgetown for the victuals if you must."

"After everything we have done to save the place?"

"We have saved it—saved it from the Usurper and from its own failed nobility. It belongs to our liege lady now, and it can show its fealty by rendering the aid we need to rescue her and defeat her enemies."

Farringdon accepted Prentice's word and then the pair left the tent. Around them, the captured enemy camp was the typical mix of weary celebration and securing supplies that followed almost every battle. Personal plundering was forbidden and drinking was to be kept to a minimum, but there would be more than a few sore heads ruing their surreptitious tippling when the White Lions marched again come the new day.

"You know this ends in Denay, don't you, My Lord?" Farringdon asked, as if seeking a pledge from Prentice that they would take this army all the way north and sack the capital.

"Not if we can finish it sooner, Knight Captain," Prentice told him. "Our liege wants her throne secure and the Usurper punished. Beyond that, I have no purposes."

And that is another lie, he thought, but he felt no guilt for it. Visions and theological discussions were not for this night. The pit in the south where Sanguine lurked had not shown itself in Town Sobridge, and now that his thoughts were clear he was convinced it was not south of the Murr at all. Wherever it was actually located, it was somewhere south of Denay, but only that much had been clear from his dream. He had learned the lesson of Samson now and had the sword of the word in his hand, at least enough for what was coming next. The entire Grand Kingdom might be north of the Murr River, but that also included everywhere in the Kingdom that was south of Denay. Somewhere between where he stood and the capital far away was a deep pit, and in the bottom of it squatted the blood-drenched toad who called himself Sanguine. Come what may, Prentice had every intention of finding him in his hole and burning him out like the vermin he was.

EPILOGUE

Every bump and thud of the Great North Road shuddered up through the carriage's wheels as it rolled away from the Murr as swiftly as its horse team could be driven. The crack of the coachman's long whip echoed and the hoofbeats of the escorting knights ahorse never waned as they continued through into the night, all of which barely registered for Archduchess Amelia seated on one of the carriage's two bench seats, doing her very best to brace herself against the bone-numbing vibrations. It would have been uncomfortable for anyone—surely it was for her one fellow passenger—but for the noble mother-to-be, it was only the background to a far more intense experience.

"I must apologize, My Lady," she said as the pain in her belly receded and she felt able to unclench her teeth once more. "I confess I did not ever think we would again find ourselves traveling in such a manner."

Lady Dalflitch looked at Amelia with a concerned expression. The cut upon the lady-in-waiting's brow had ceased to flow, but the trickle of blood that it left had run into one eyebrow and then down the beautiful seneschal's left cheek. With only one candle lantern between them, it was hard to see anything of each other's faces clearly, but that much was unmistakable.

"I am certain, Your Grace, that you also never intended to be in labor in the back of a wagon," Dalflitch replied, and she offered a sympathetic smile. "It is no false one this time, is it?"

"I fear not, My Lady," Amelia said. She was unsure when during their abduction the first cramps had come upon her, but no matter which way she moved her body, these were not fading away as the clenches of false labor had in recent weeks. They had been there in her belly already when she had been forced into the carriage, she knew that, and that made her think she must have been experiencing them while she and Dalflitch were dragged by their captors up from the stone pier on the north bank of the river. But before that, her memory was hazy, as if seen through the warping panes of a thick glass window, the images refusing to come into focus.

"Bluebird," she murmured in disgust and spat bile into the wing of her sleeve. Although the exact memories of her journey refused to show their true forms, all through them she could feel the lilt of the minstrel's singing voice. He must have ensorcelled them during the journey to keep them docile.

Where is your sword, oh God? she wondered, wishing she had had some prayer to hand with which to fight the magick off. Could Whilte have done it if he had been with them?

"I have been trying to mark the times you mention them, Your Grace," Dalflitch said earnestly, referring to Amelia's contractions. "But I fear I've lost the count more than once. Would that Lady Daisy was with us."

"With respect, My Lady, I would not that anyone else was here with us," Amelia joked. "Indeed, I *would* that we were also not here."

Dalflitch nodded, sparing her liege a wan shadow of a polite smile. Then she looked away at the window, as if to stare out through the shutters at the passing night.

"As dour as our position is, I would still prefer this for her than where she lies at the moment," she said quietly.

Amelia nodded, understanding the sentiment. The power of Bluebird's song over her memories commenced around the time she and Dalflitch had been dragged into the afternoon light in the Paramour's yard. Of the moments before that she had better recall, though she wished she did not. A confused whirlwind of images and sounds, her memories were nonetheless vivid. She had thrust Righteous and the wetnurse into the secret stairwell herself, closing the door behind them just before the axes started to split the apartments' outer door. Lace Fangs and neophytes had thrown furniture at the inner door, and some tried to move the monolithic main table, but it was too heavy by far, and in the confusion the attempt only served to keep them separated from each other. Then the men in steel were breaking through, smashing furniture and women with equal abandon. Some White Lions tried to rush to their defense but too little, too late. Amelia had seen several of her closest retainers felled, cut down like animals at the slaughterer's blade, though each and every one sold her life with a fury. That was how she saw Lady Daisy, the freckled, moonfaced girl midwife who could fight with such resolve, go to her doom, driven to the floorboards by that hateful wretch Cyprian, punching her face again and again with his gauntleted fists.

As if that were somehow more manly or more merciful than his sword, Amelia thought, and she felt incensed tears streak down her cheeks. The young woman had not deserved to die like that. None of her ladies had. The next contraction began, and her memories were shoved roughly aside. A low groan grew in her throat until she felt she was wailing, huffing just to keep her breath. Seeing her liege lady's pain, Lady Dalflitch turned to look up at the carriage's ceiling and began to beat upon the boards with the palm of her hand.

"You there!" she shouted, her words barely discernible over Amelia' anguished cries. "We need aid! Now, you louts! Her grace needs help."

All through the contraction, Dalflitch banged and shouted, and Amelia's belly was just beginning to relax once more when the carriage came to a sudden halt. A moment later, the outside latch was drawn back and one of the door's flung open. Morning light streamed in, and Amelia flinched from its sudden brightness.

We've driven all through the night, she thought, astonished by how long the journey had been without them realizing it. A sneering man-at-arms looked inside, eyes narrowed.

"Shut your damned wailing, you witches, or I'll..."

"Her grace is giving birth, twit!" Dalflitch cut across the man's rebuke. "Send for a midwife and healer, or she will lose the child."

The man seemed ready to take insult at being so spoken to, but a swift moment later he looked at Amelia more closely. She was in less pain, in between contractions, but she imagined she appeared a red-faced mess all the same. After impertinently examining her, the man-at-arms snorted contemptuously and pulled back out of the doorway, closing and locking it behind him.

"I fear he might not care about my child's safety," Amelia said, knowing that Daven Marcus likely would be overjoyed to see the heir to the Western Reach stillborn on the carriage floor. She realized suddenly that they had not seen the Usurper king yet. Was he even with them, or had he sent her somewhere else? Perhaps he was remaining behind to conquer Bridgetown and kill the rest of her people. It could be that as she was giving birth, her entire legacy was being burned to the waterline behind her. The notion brought fresh tears that she struggled to restrain. She was so tired.

A short while later the door opened again and a nun leaned in, a severe-looking woman with dark eyes that were, if anything, colder than the man-at-arms' had been. The woman seemed familiar somehow, but either her own condition or the nun's tight-fitted wimple made it hard for Amelia to be sure. The religious figure climbed in and placed an ungentle hand on Amelia's belly, examining her like a piece of livestock. A moment later she reached behind herself to some attendant waiting outside and brought back a leather cup containing a sour-smelling liquid. She tried to put the cup to Amelia's lips, but the archduchess shied from the drink.

"Swallow this or lose your bastard whelp," the nun commanded, her manner making it clear that she felt no personal preference for either outcome. Somewhat fearfully, Amelia accepted the cup and drank. The liquid was thick and tasted of something that reminded her of burned herbs.

"What is it?" Amelia asked once the cup was withdrawn.

"A physick," the nun told them as she stepped back outside. "We are to present you whole at the end of this journey. The child is preferred but not necessary." Her words made Amelia shiver.

"What does it do?" Dalflitch asked as the stern nun put a hand to the door. "It is not healthy for a woman to be sedated in birthing."

"Hark at the whore's wisdom," the nun retorted. She seemed about to simply close the door without answering but then relented. Her expression showed nothing that might be called compassion, but it did soften a shade, Amelia thought. "The draught will delay the labor. The clutching in your belly will be less frequent but not cease. There is nothing that will stop it now, but by our ministrations you may yet be days about your birthing. If the pain is too much for you, pray we are not delayed in reaching our destination." She started to close the door, but just before it sealed out the daylight once again, she added, "Assuming you slattern witches even know how to pray. Best learn fast, I'd say."

Then she was gone, and they had only their little candle lamp to see each other by, and the wax in that surely had not too much longer to last either. How much more was their journey to be?

"I half expected to see the kingslayer himself leaning in," she told Lady Dalflitch, trying to sound braver than she felt.

"I was anticipating Duke Robant myself, Your Grace," the lady seneschal told her. "The fact that neither goblin showed themselves to gloat is a good sign, I would say."

"How is that, My Lady?" Amelia asked, wondering what positive notion Dalflitch had found in their dire circumstances.

"Knowing Daven Marcus as we do, Your Grace, the only thing I can imagine keeping him away from these two toys he is longing to torment would be a battle," Dalflitch explained, and she leaned forward, taking Amelia by the hands. "Keep faith, Your Grace. You saw the light outside. The storms have not returned.

That wasn't thunder we heard as they bundled us away. It was explosions. The White Lions are fighting to free us right this moment, I would swear to it. That is why they are spiriting us away as fast and as far as they can."

"Away and out of reach," Amelia whispered, wanting to be encouraged but afraid all the same.

"They could fly us over the sea to Aucks. Lord Farringdon would sprout wings and follow, do not doubt."

Amelia smirked at the ridiculous notion.

"And as for Knight Commander Ash?" Dalflitch added. "He will fight to the gates of hell before he lets them snatch you away. You know it is so."

Amelia nodded. The two most important men in her life, leaders of her Lion Banner Company and her Gryphon Banner Company, were unwavering in their loyalty. They would be giving everything they had to come to the two ladies' rescue.

"But the Inquisition has hamstrung Prentice," she whispered, tears flowing freely now, despite her longing to hope. "They have laid chains on his mind."

"Then pity them, Your Grace. No man has ever made a pet of a lion or laid a taming leash on a mythical gryphon. The creatures they have thought to chain will turn and devour them. Just watch."

GLOSSARY

The Grand Kingdom's social structure is broken into three basic levels which are then subdivided into separate ranks: the nobility, the free folk, and the low born.

The Nobility

King/Queen – There is one King, and one Queen, his wife. The king is always the head of the royal family and rules from the Denay Court, in the capital city of Denay.

Prince/Princess – Any direct children of the king and queen.

Prince of Rhales – This title signifies the prince who is next in line of succession. This prince maintains a separate, secondary court of lesser nobles in the western capital or Rhales.

Duke/Duchess – Hereditary nobles with close ties by blood or marriage to the royal family, either Denay or Rhales.

Earl; Count/Countess; Viscount; Baron/Baroness – These are the other hereditary ranks of the two courts, in order of rank. One is born into this rank, as son or daughter of an existing noble of the same rank, or else created a noble by the king.

Baronet – This is the lowest of the hereditary ranks and does not require a landed domain to be attached.

Knight/Lady – The lowest rank of the nobility and almost always attached to military service to the Grand Kingdom as a man-at-arms. Ladies obtain their title through marriage. Knights are signified by their right to carry the longsword, as a signature weapon.

Squire – This is, for all intents and purposes, an apprentice knight. He must be the son of another knight (or higher noble) who is currently training, or a student of the academy.

The Free Folk

Patrician – A man or woman who has a family name and owns property inside a major town or city. Patricians always fill the ranks of any administration of the town in which they live, such as aldermen, guild conclave members, militia captains etc.

Guildsmen/townsfolk – Those who dwell in large towns as free craftsmen and women tend to be members of guilds who act to protect their members' livelihoods and also to run much of the city, day to day.

Yeoman – The yeomanry are free farmers that possess their own farms.

The Low Born

Peasants – These are serfs who owe feudal duty to their liege lord. They do not own the land they farm and must obtain permission to move home or leave their land.

Convicts – Criminals who are found guilty of crimes not deserving of the death penalty.

Military Order

Knight Captain, Knight Commander & Knight Marshall – Every peer (King, Prince or Duke) has a right to raise an army and command his lesser nobles to provide men-at-arms. They then appoint a second-in-command, often the most experienced or skilled soldier under them. A duke his Knight Captain; a prince his Knight Commander; and the King his Knight Marshal.

Knights – These are the professional soldiers of the Grand Kingdom. All nobles are expected to join these ranks when their lands are at war, and they universally fight from horseback.

Men-at-Arms –A catch all term for any man with professional training who has some right or reason to be in this group, including squires and second and third sons of nobles.

Bannermen – This is a special form of man-at-arms. These are soldiers who are sworn directly to a ranking noble.

Free Militia – The free towns of the Grand Kingdom have an obligation to raise free militias in defence of the realm.

Rogues Foot – A rogue is a low born or criminal man and so when convicts are pressed into military service, they are the rogues afoot (or "on foot") which is shortened to rogues foot.

Other Titles and Terms

Apothecary – A trader and manufacturer of herbs, medical treatments and potions of various sorts.

Chirurgeon – A medical practitioner, akin to a doctor or surgeon, especially related to injuries (as opposed to sickness, which is handled by an apothecary).

Ecclesiarchs – ruling members of the Church. Their ranks correspond (very roughly) to noble ranks. The ecclesiarchy refers to the power of the Church where it rules with its own power, like a nation within the nation. Monasteries, churches, cathedrals and the Academy in Ashfield are all part of the Church lands, where religious law overrides King's Law.

Estate – A person's estate can be their actual lands, but can also include their social position, their current condition (physical, social or financial), or any combination of these things.

Fiefed – A noble who is fiefed possesses a parcel of land over which they have total legal authority, the right to levy taxes and draft rogues or militia.

Frater – brother (from the Latin word)

Hoi Polio – the common folk

King's Law – This is the overarching, national law, set for the Grand Kingdom by the king, but does not always apply in the Western Reach.

Magistrate – Civil legal matters of the Free Folk and Peasantry are typically handled by magistrates, who render judgements according to the local laws.

Marshals/Wardens – Appointed men who manage the movement of large groups, especially of nobles and noble courts when in motion. They appoint the order of the march and resolve disputes.

Physick – A term for a person trained in the treatment of medical conditions, but without strict definition.

Proselytize – Attempt to convert someone from one religion, belief, or opinion to another.

Pugilist - A professional boxer.

Provost – (short for provost marshal) junior officers assigned to sentries or patrol for the purpose of military discipline. In the case of the White Lions militia, the typical rank of a provost is a Line First. Roughly equivalent to military police duty.

Republicanists – Rare political radicals, outlawed in the Grand Kingdom and the Vec who seek to create elected forms of government, curtailing or overturning monarchical rule.

Seneschal – The administrative head of any large household or organisation, especially a noble house of a baron or higher.

Surcoat – The outer garment worn by a man-at-arms over their armor. Typically dyed in the knight's colours (or their liege lord's colours in the case of a bannerman) and embroidered with their heraldry.

Te tree – A tree, known for its medicinal properties.

The Rampart – A celestial phenomenon that glows in the night across the sky from east to west in the northern half of the sky.

About Matt Barron

Matt Barron grew up loving to read and to watch movies. He always knew he enjoyed science fiction and fantasy, but in 1979 his uncle took him to see a new movie called *Star Wars* and he was hooked for life. Then *Dungeons and Dragons* came along and there was no looking back. He went to university hoping to find a girlfriend. Instead, the Lord found him, and he spent most of his time from then on in the coffee shop, witnessing and serving his God. Along the way, he managed to acquire a Doctorate in History and met the love of his life, Rachel. Now married to Rachel for more than twenty years, Matt has two adult children and a burning desire to combine the genre he loves with the faith that saved him.

Learn more at:

mattbarronauthor.com

ALSO BY MATT BARRON

Rage of Lions

Prentice Ash

Rats of Dweltford

Lions of the Reach

Eagles of the Grand Kingdom

Serpents of Summer

The Mantis and the Mirrored Sky

Bears of Bridgetown

Dragons of Denay

Ravens of the Pit

More from Publisher

Be sure to check out our other great science fiction and fantasy stories at:

bladeoftruthpublishing.com/books